P9-AGR-370

HAROLD ROBBINS

The Carpetbaggers

A TOM DOHERTY ASSOCIATES BOOK
NEW YORK

This is a work of fiction. All the characters, organizations, and events portrayed in this novel are either products of the author's imagination or are used fictitiously.

THE CARPETBAGGERS

Copyright © 1961 by Harold Robbins

Originally published in 1961 by Trident Press, a division of Simon & Schuster Inc.

A Forge Book
Published by Tom Doherty Associates, LLC
175 Fifth Avenue
New York, NY 10010

www.tor-forge.com

Forge® is a registered trademark of Tom Doherty Associates, LLC.

ISBN-13: 978-0-765-35146-3
ISBN-10: 0-765-35146-3

First Tor Edition: May 2007

Printed in the United States of America

0 9 8 7 6 5 4 3 2 1

For
BILLY TARWATER

A profile in courage.
An inspiration to all.

ACKNOWLEDGMENT

To Herbert Alexander
In Memoriam

Harold's friend and editor, Herb Alexander,
created the country's first hardback/paperback
book line in order to publish this novel.

To Tom Doherty
Who carries on the good work.

CONTENTS

PREFACE

...And behind the Northern Armies came another army of men. They came by the hundreds, yet each traveled alone. They came on foot, by mule, on horseback, on creaking wagons or riding in handsome chaises. They were of all shapes and sizes and descended from many nationalities. They wore dark suits, usually covered with the gray dust of travel, and dark, broad-brimmed hats to shield their white faces from the hot, unfamiliar sun. And on their back, or across their saddle, or on top of their wagon was the inevitable faded multicolored bag made of worn and ragged remnants of carpet into which they had crammed all their worldly possessions. It was from these bags that they got their name. The Carpetbaggers.

...And they strode the dusty roads and streets of the exhausted Southlands, their mouths tightening greedily, their eyes everywhere, searching, calculating, appraising the values that were left behind in the holocaust of war.

...Yet not all of them were bad, just as not all men are bad. Some of them even learned to love the land they came to plunder and stayed and became respected citizens.

JONAS—1925

Book One

1

THE SUN WAS BEGINNING TO FALL FROM THE SKY into the white Nevada desert as Reno came up beneath me. I banked the Waco slowly and headed due east. I could hear the wind pinging the biplane's struts and I grinned to myself. The old man would really hit the roof when he saw this plane. But he wouldn't have anything to complain about. It didn't cost him anything. I won it in a crap game.

I moved the stick forward and came down slowly to fifteen hundred feet. I was over Route 32 now and the desert on either side of the road was a rushing blur of sand. I put her nose on the horizon and looked over the side. There it was, about eight miles in front of me. Like a squat, ugly toad in the desert. The factory.

CORD EXPLOSIVES

I eased the stick forward again and by the time I shot past, I was only about a hundred feet over it. I went into an Immelmann and looked back.

They were at the windows already. The dark Mexican and Indian girls in their brightly colored dresses and the men in their faded blue work clothes. I could almost see the whites of their frightened eyes looking after me. I grinned again. Their life was dull enough. Let them have a real thrill.

I pulled out at the top of the Immelmann and went on to twenty-five hundred feet. Then I hit the stick and dove right for the tar-pitched roof.

The roar from the big Pratt & Whitney engine crescendoed and deafened my ears and the wind tore at my eyes and face. I narrowed my lids and drew my lips back across my teeth. I could feel the blood racing in my veins, my heart pounding and the juices of life starting up in my gut.

Power, power, power! Up here where the world was like a toy beneath me. Where I held the stick like my cock in my hands and there was no one, not even my father, to say me no!

The black roof of the plant lay on the white sand like a girl on the white sheets of a bed, the dark pubic patch of her whispering its invitation into the dimness of the night. My breath caught in my throat. Mother. I didn't want to turn away. I wanted to go home.

Ping! One of the thin wire struts snapped clean. I blinked my eyes and licked my lips. The salty taste of the tears touched my tongue. I could see the faint gray pebbles in the black tar of the roof now. I eased back on the stick and began to come out of the dive. At eight hundred feet, I leveled off and went into a wide turn that would take me to the field behind the factory. I headed into the wind and made a perfect three-point landing. Suddenly I was tired. It had been a long flight up from Los Angeles.

Nevada Smith was walking across the field toward me as the plane rolled to a stop. I cut the switches and the engine died, coughing the last drop of fuel out of its carburetor lungs. I looked out at him.

Nevada never changed. From the time I was five years old and I first saw him walking up to the front porch, he hadn't changed. The tight, rolling, bowlegged walk, as if he'd never got used to being off a horse, the tiny white weather crinkles in the leathery skin at the corner of his eyes. That was sixteen years ago. It was 1909.

I was playing around the corner of the porch and my father was reading the weekly Reno paper on the big rocker near the front door. It was about eight o'clock in the morning and the sun was already high in the sky. I heard the clip-clop of a horse and came around to the front to see.

A man was getting off his horse. He moved with a deceptively slow grace. He threw the reins over the hitching post and walked toward the house. At the foot of the steps, he stopped and looked up.

My father put the paper down and got to his feet. He was a big man. Six two. Beefy. Ruddy face that burned to a crisp in the sun. He looked down.

Nevada squinted up at him. "Jonas Cord?"

My father nodded. "Yes."

The man pushed his broad-brimmed cowboy hat back on his head, revealing the crow-black hair. "I hear tell you might be looking for a hand."

My father never said yes or no to anything. "What can you do?" he asked.

The man's smile remained expressionless. He glanced slowly across the front of the house and out on the desert. He looked back at my father. "I could ride herd but you ain't got no cattle. I can mend fence, but you ain't got none of them, either."

My father was silent for a moment. "You any good with that?" he asked.

For the first time, I noticed the gun on the man's thigh. He wore it real low and tied down. The handle was black and worn and the hammer and metal shone dully with oil.

"I'm alive," he answered.

"What's your name?"

"Nevada."

"Nevada what?"

The answer came without hesitation. "Smith. Nevada Smith."

My father was silent again. This time the man didn't wait for him to speak.

He gestured toward me. "That your young'un?"

My father nodded.

"Where's his mammy?"

My father looked at him, then picked me up. I fit real good in the crook of his arm. His voice was emotionless. "She died a few months back."

The man stared up at us. "That's what I heard."

My father stared back at him for a moment. I could feel the muscles in his arm tighten under my behind. Then before I could catch my breath, I was flying through the air over the porch rail.

The man caught me with one arm and rolled me in close to him as he went down on one knee to absorb the impact. The breath whooshed out of me and before I could begin to cry, my father spoke again.

A faint smile crossed his lips. "Teach him how to ride," he said. He picked up his paper and went into the house without a backward glance.

Still holding me with one hand, the man called Nevada began to rise again. I looked down. The gun in his other hand was like a live black snake, pointed at my father. While I was looking, the gun disappeared back in the holster. I looked up into Nevada's face.

His face broke into a warm, gentle smile. He set me down on the ground carefully. "Well, Junior," he said. "You heard your pappy. Come on."

I looked up at the house but my father had already gone inside. I didn't know it then but that was the last time my father ever held me in his arms. From that time on, it was almost as if I were Nevada's boy.

I had one foot over the side of the cockpit by the time Nevada came up. He squinted up at me. "You been pretty busy."

I dropped to the ground beside him and looked down at him. Somehow I never could get used to that. Me being six two like my father and Nevada still the same five nine. "Pretty busy," I admitted.

Nevada stretched and looked into the rear cockpit. "Neat," he said. "How d'ja get it?"

I smiled. "I won it in a crap game."

He looked at me questioningly.

"Don't worry," I added quickly. "I let him win five hundred dollars afterward."

He nodded, satisfied. That, too, was one of the things Nevada taught me. Never walk away from the table after you win a man's horse without letting him win back at least one stake for tomorrow. It didn't diminish your winnings by much and at least the sucker walked away feeling he'd won something.

I reached into the rear cockpit and pulled out some chocks. I tossed one to Nevada and walked around and set mine under a wheel. Nevada did the same on the other side.

"Your pappy ain't gonna like it. You messed up production for the day."

I straightened up. "I don't guess it will matter much." I walked around the prop toward him. "How'd he hear about it so soon?"

Nevada's lips broke into the familiar mirthless smile. "You took the girl to the hospital. They sent for her folks. She told them before she died."

"How much do they want?"

"Twenty thousand."

"You can buy 'em for five."

He didn't answer. Instead, he looked down at my feet. "Get your shoes on and come on," he said. "Your father's waiting."

He started back across the field and I looked down at my feet. The warm earth felt good against my naked toes. I wriggled them in the sand for a moment, then went back to the cockpit and pulled out a pair of Mexican huarachos. I slipped into them and started out across the field after Nevada.

I hate shoes. They don't let you breathe.

2

I KEPT RAISING SMALL CLOUDS OF SAND WITH THE huarachos as I walked toward the factory. The faint clinical smell of the sulphur they used in making gunpowder came to my nose. It was the same kind of smell that was in the hospital the night I took her there. It wasn't at all the kind of smell there was the night we made the baby.

It was cool and clean that night. And there was the smell of the ocean and the surf that came in through the open windows of the small cottage I kept out at Malibu. But in the room there was nothing but the exciting scent of the girl and her wanting.

We had gone into the bedroom and stripped with the fierce urgency in our vitals. She was quicker than I and now she was on the bed, looking up at me as I opened the dresser drawer and took out a package of rubbers.

Her voice was a whisper in the night. "Don't, Joney. Not this time."

I looked at her. The bright Pacific moon threw its light in the window. Only her face was in shadows. Somehow, what she said brought the fever up.

The bitch must have sensed it. She reached for me and kissed me. "I hate those damn things, Joney. I want to feel you inside me."

I hesitated a moment. She pulled me down on top of her. Her voice whispered in my ear. "Nothing will happen, Joney. I'll be careful."

Then I couldn't wait any longer and her whisper changed into a sudden cry of pain. I couldn't breathe and she kept crying in my ear, "I love you, Joney. I love you, Joney."

She loved me all right. She loved me so good that five weeks later she tells me we got to get married. We were sitting in the front seat of my car this time, driving back from the football game.

I looked over at her. "What for?"

She looked up at me. She wasn't frightened, not then. She was too sure of herself. Her voice was almost flippant. "The usual reason. What other reason does a fellow and a girl get married for?"

My voice turned bitter. I knew when I'd been taken. "Sometimes it's because they want to get married."

"Well, I want to get married." She moved closer to me.

I pushed her back on the seat. "Well, I don't."

She began to cry then. "But you said you loved me."

I didn't look at her. "A man says a lot of things when he's humping." I pulled the car over against the curb and parked. I turned to her. "I thought you said you'd be careful."

She was wiping at her tears with a small, ineffectual handkerchief. "I love you, Joney. I wanted to have your baby."

For the first time since she told me, I began to feel better. That was one of the troubles with being Jonas Cord, Jr. Too many girls, and their mothers, too, thought that spelled money. Big money. Ever since the war, when my father built an empire on gunpowder.

I looked down at her. "Then it's simple. Have it."

Her expression changed. She moved toward me. "You mean—you mean—we'll get married?"

The faint look of triumph in her eyes faded quickly when I shook my head. "Uh-uh. I meant have the baby if you want it that bad."

She pulled away again. Suddenly, her face was set and cold. Her voice was calm and practical. "I don't want it that bad. Not without a ring on my finger. I'll have to get rid of it."

I grinned and offered her a cigarette. "Now you're talking, little girl."

She took the cigarette and I lit it for her. "But it's going to be expensive," she said.

"How much?" I asked.

She drew in a mouthful of smoke. "There's a doctor in Mexican Town. The girls say he's very good." She looked at me questioningly. "Two hundred?"

"O.K., you got it," I said quickly. It was a bargain. The last one cost me three fifty. I flipped my cigarette over the side of the car and started the motor. I pulled the car out into traffic and headed toward Malibu.

"Hey, where you going?" she asked.

I looked over at her. "To the beach house," I answered. "We might as well make the most of the situation."

She began to laugh and drew closer to me. She looked up into my face. "I wonder what Mother would say if she knew just how far I went to get you. She told me not to miss a trick."

I laughed. "You didn't."

She shook her head. "Poor Mother. She had the wedding all planned."

Poor Mother. Maybe if the old bitch had kept her mouth shut, her daughter might have been alive today.

It was the night after that, about eleven thirty, that my telephone began to ring. I had just about fogged off and I cursed, reaching for the phone.

Her voice came through in a scared whisper. "Joney, I'm bleeding."

The sleep shot out of my head like a bullet. "What's the matter?"

"I went down to Mexican Town this afternoon and now something's wrong. I haven't stopped bleeding and I'm frightened."

I sat up in bed. "Where are you?"

"I checked into the Westwood Hotel this afternoon. Room nine-o-one."

"Get back into bed. I'll be right down."

"Please hurry, Joney. Please."

The Westwood is a commercial hotel in downtown L.A. Nobody even looked twice when I went up in the elevator without announcing myself at the desk. I stopped in front of Room 901 and tried the door. It was unlocked. I went in.

I never saw so much blood in my life. It was all over the cheap carpeting on the floor, the chair in which she had sat when she called me, the white sheets on the bed.

She was lying on the bed and her face was as white as the pillow under her head. Her eyes had been closed but they flickered open when I came over. Her lips moved but no sound came out.

I bent over her. "Don't try to talk, baby. I'll get a doctor. You're gonna be all right."

She closed her eyes and I went over to the phone. There was no use in just calling a doctor. My father wasn't going to be happy if I got our name into the papers again. I called McAllister. He was the attorney who handled the firm's business in California.

His butler called him to the phone. I tried to keep my voice calm. "I need a doctor and an ambulance quick."

In less than a moment, I understood why my father used Mac. He didn't waste any time on useless questions. Just where, when and who. No why. His voice was precise. "A doctor and an ambulance will be there in ten minutes. I advise you to leave now. There's no point in your getting any more involved than you are."

I thanked him and put down the phone. I glanced over at the bed. Her eyes were closed and she appeared to be sleeping. I started for the door and her eyes opened.

"Don't go, Joney. I'm afraid."

I went back to the bed and sat down beside it. I took her hand and she closed her eyes again. The ambulance was there in ten minutes. And she didn't let go of my hand until we'd reached the hospital.

3

I WALKED INTO THE FACTORY AND THE NOISE AND. the smell closed in on me like a cocoon. I could feel the momentary stoppage of work as I walked by and I could hear the subdued murmur of voices following me.

"El hijo."

The son. That was how they knew me. They spoke of me with a fondness and a pride, as their ancestors had of the children of their *patrones*. It gave them a sense of identity and belonging that helped make up for the meager way in which they had to live.

I walked past the mixing vats, the presses and the molds and reached the back stairway to my father's office. I started up the steps and looked back at them. A hundred faces smiled up at me. I waved my hand and smiled back at them in the same way I had always done, ever since I first climbed those steps when I was a kid.

I went through the door at the top of the stairway and the noise was gone as soon as the door closed behind me. I walked down the short corridor and into my father's outer office.

Denby was sitting at his desk, scribbling a note in his usual fluttery fashion. A girl sat at a desk across from him, beating hell out of a typewriter. Two other persons were seated on the visitor's couch. A man and a woman.

The woman was dressed in black and she was twisting a small white handkerchief in her hands. She looked up at me as I stood in the doorway. I didn't have to be told who she was. The girl looked enough like her mother. I met her eyes and she turned her head away.

Denby got up nervously. "Your father's waiting."

I didn't answer. He opened the door to my father's office and I walked through. He closed the door behind me. I looked around the office.

Nevada was leaning against the left wall bookcase, his eyes half closed in that deceptive manner of alertness peculiar to him. McAllister was seated in a chair across from my father. He turned his head to look at me. My father sat behind the immense old oak desk and glared. Outside of that, the office was just as I remembered it.

The dark oak-paneled walls, the heavy leather chairs. The green velvet drapes on the windows and the picture of my father and President Wilson on the wall behind the desk. At my father's side was the telephone table with the three telephones and right next to it was the table with the ever present carafe of water, bottle of bourbon whisky and two glasses. The whisky bottle was about one-third filled. That made it about three o'clock. I checked my watch. It was ten after three. My father was a bottle-a-day man.

I crossed the office and stopped in front of him. I looked down and met his angry glare. "Hello, Father."

His ruddy face grew even redder. The cords on his neck stood out as he shouted, "Is that all you got to say after ruining a day's production and scaring the shit out of half the help with your crazy stunts?"

"Your message was to get down here in a hurry. I got here as quickly as I could, sir."

But there was no stopping him now. He was raging. My father had that kind of a temper. One moment he would be still and quiet, and the next, higher than a kite.

"Why the hell didn't you get out of that hotel room when McAllister told you? What did you go to the hospital for? Do you know what you've done? Left yourself wide open for criminal charges as an accomplice abetting an abortion."

I was angry now. I had every bit as much of a temper as my father. "What was I supposed to do? The girl was bleeding to death and afraid. Was I supposed to just walk out of there and leave her to die alone?"

"Yes. If you had any brains at all, that's just what you'd have done. The girl died, anyway, and your staying there didn't make any difference. Now those goddam bastards outside want twenty thousand dollars or they'll call for the police! You think I've got twenty thousand dollars for every bitch you plug? This is the third girl in a year you got caught with!"

It didn't make any difference to him that the girl had died. It was the twenty grand. But then I realized it wasn't the money, either. It went far deeper than that.

The bitterness that had crept into his voice was the tip-off. I looked at him with a sudden understanding. My father was getting old and it was eating out his gut. Rina must have been at him again. More than a year had passed since the big wedding in Reno and nothing had happened.

I turned and started for the door without speaking. Father yelled after me. "Where do you think you're going?"

I looked back at him. "Back to L.A. You don't need me to make up your mind. You're either going to pay them off or you're not. It doesn't make any difference to me. Besides, I got a date."

He came around the desk after me. "What for?" he shouted. "To knock up another girl?"

I faced him squarely. I had enough of his crap. "Stop complaining, old man. You ought to be glad that someone in your family still has balls. Otherwise, Rina might think there was something wrong with all of us!"

His face twisted with rage. He lifted both hands as if to strike me. His lips drew back tightly across his teeth in a snarl, the veins in his forehead stood out in red, angry welts. Then, suddenly, as an electric switch cuts off the light, all expression on his face vanished. He staggered and pitched forward against me.

By reflex, my arms came out and I caught him. For a brief moment, his eyes were clear, looking into mine. His lips moved. "Jonas—my son."

Then his eyes clouded and his full weight came on me and he slid to the floor. I looked down at him. I knew he was dead even before Nevada rolled him over and tore open his shirt.

Nevada was kneeling on the floor beside my father's body, McAllister was on the telephone calling for a doctor and I was picking up the bottle of Jack Daniel's when Denby came in through the door.

He shrank back against the door, the papers in his hand trembling. "My God, Junior," he said in a horrified voice. His eyes lifted from the floor to me. "Who's going to sign the German contracts?"

I glanced over at McAllister. He nodded imperceptibly. "I am," I answered.

Down on the floor, Nevada was closing my father's eyes. I put down the bottle of whisky unopened and looked back at Denby.

"And stop calling me Junior," I said.

4

BY THE TIME THE DOCTOR CAME, WE HAD LIFTED my father's body to the couch and covered it with a blanket. The doctor was a thin, sturdy man, bald, with thick glasses. He lifted the blanket and looked. He dropped the blanket. "He's dead, all right."

I didn't speak. It was McAllister who asked the question while I swung to and fro in my father's chair. "Why?"

The doctor came toward the desk. "Encephalic embolism. Stroke. Blood clot hit the brain, from the looks of him." He looked at me. "You can be thankful it was quick. He didn't suffer."

It was certainly quick. One minute my father was alive, the next moment he was nothing, without even the power to brush off the curious fly that was crawling over the edge of the blanket onto his covered face. I didn't speak.

The doctor sat down heavily in the chair opposite me. He took out a pen and a sheet of paper. He laid the paper on the desk. Upside down, I could read the heading across the top in bold type. Death Certificate. The pen began to scratch across the paper. After a moment, he looked up. "O.K. if I put down embolism as the cause of death or do you want an autopsy?"

I shook my head. "Embolism's O.K. An autopsy wouldn't make any difference now."

The doctor wrote again. A moment later, he had finished and he pushed the certificate over to me. "Check it over and see if I got everything right."

I picked it up. He had everything right. Pretty good for a doctor who had never seen any of us before today. But everybody in Nevada knew everything about the Cords. Age 67.

Survivors: Wife, Rina Marlowe Cord; Son, Jonas Cord, Jr. I slid it back across the desk to him. "It's all right."

He picked it up and got to his feet. "I'll file it and have my girl send you copies." He stood there hesitantly, as if trying to make up his mind as to whether he should offer some expression of sympathy. Evidently, he decided against it, for he went out the door without another word.

Then Denby came in again. "What about those people outside? Shall I send them away?"

I shook my head. They'd only come back again. "Send them in."

They came in the door, the girl's father and mother, their faces wearing a fixed expression that was a strange mixture of grief and sympathy.

Her father looked at me. "I'm sorry we couldn't meet under happier circumstances, Mr. Cord."

I looked at him. The man's face was honest. I believe he really meant it. "I am, too," I said.

His wife immediately broke into sobs. "It's terrible, terrible," she wailed, looking at my father's covered body on the couch.

I looked at her. Her daughter had resembled her but the resemblance stopped at the surface. The kid had had a refreshing honesty about her; this woman was a born harpy.

"What are you crying about?" I asked. "You never even knew him before today. And only then to ask him for money."

She stared at me in shock. Her voice grew shrill. "How can you say such a thing? Your own father lying there on the couch and after what you did to my daughter."

I got to my feet. The one thing I can't stand is a phony. "After what I did to your daughter?" I shouted. "I didn't do anything to your daughter that she didn't want me to. Maybe if you hadn't told her to stop at nothing to catch me, she'd be alive today. But no, you told her to get Jonas Cord, Jr., at any cost. She told me you were already planning the wedding!"

Her husband turned to her. His voice was trembling. "You mean to tell me you knew she was pregnant?"

She looked at him, frightened. "No, Henry, no. I didn't know. I only said to her it would be nice if she could marry him, that's all I said."

His lips tightened, and for a second I thought he was about to strike her. But he didn't. Instead, he turned back to me. "I'm sorry, Mr. Cord. We won't trouble you any more."

He started proudly for the door. His wife hurried after him. "But, Henry," she cried. "Henry."

"Shut up!" he snapped, opening the door and almost pushing her through it in front of him. "Haven't you said enough already?"

The door closed behind them and I turned to McAllister. "I'm not in the clear yet, am I?"

He shook his head.

I thought for a moment. "Better go down to see him tomorrow at his place of business. I think he'll give you a release now. He seems like an honest man."

McAllister smiled slowly. "And that's how you figure an honest man will act?"

"That's one thing I learned from my father." Involuntarily I glanced at the couch. "He used to say every man has his price. For some it's money, for some it's women, for others glory. But the honest man you don't have to buy—he winds up costing you nothing."

"Your father was a practical man," McAllister said.

I stared at the lawyer. "My father was a selfish, greedy son of a bitch who wanted to grab everything in the world," I said. "I only hope I'm man enough to fill his shoes."

McAllister rubbed his chin thoughtfully. "You'll do all right."

I gestured toward the couch. "I won't always have him there to help me."

McAllister didn't speak. I glanced over at Nevada. He had been leaning against the wall silently all the time. His eyes flickered under the veiled lids. He took out a pack of makin's and began to roll a cigarette. I turned back to McAllister.

"I'm going to need a lot of help," I said.

McAllister showed his interest with his eyes. He didn't speak.

"I'll need an adviser, a consultant and a lawyer," I continued. "Are you available?"

He spoke slowly. "I don't know whether I can find the time, Jonas," he said. "I've got a pretty heavy practice."

"How heavy?"

"I gross about sixty thousand a year."

"Would a hundred thousand move you to Nevada?"

His answer came quick. "If you let me draw the contract."

I took out a pack of cigarettes and offered him one. He took it and I stuck one in my mouth. I struck a match and held it for him. "O.K.," I said.

He stopped in the middle of the light. He looked at me quizzically. "How do you know you can afford to pay me that kind of money?"

I lit my own cigarette and smiled. "I didn't know until you took the job. Then I was sure."

A returning smile flashed across his face and vanished. Then he was all business. "The first thing we have to do is call a meeting of the board of directors and have you officially elected president of the company. Do you think there might be any trouble on that score?"

I shook my head. "I don't think so. My father didn't believe in sharing. He kept ninety per cent of the stock in his own name and according to his will, it comes to me on his death."

"Do you have a copy of the will?"

"No," I answered. "But Denby must. He has a record of everything my father ever did."

I hit the buzzer and Denby came in.

"Get me a copy of my father's will," I ordered.

A moment later, it was on the desk—all official, with a blue lawyer's binding. I pushed it over to McAllister. He flipped through it quickly.

"It's in order," he said. "The stock is yours all right. We better get it probated right away."

I turned to Denby questioningly. Denby couldn't wait to answer. The words came tumbling out. "Judge Haskell in Reno has it on file."

"Call him and tell him to move on it right away," I said. Denby started out. I stopped him. "And when you get through with him, call the directors and tell them I'm having a special meeting of the board at breakfast tomorrow. At my house."

Denby went out and I turned back to McAllister. "Is there anything else I ought to do, Mac?"

He shook his head slowly. "No, not right now. There's only the German contract. I don't know too much about it but I heard your father say it was a great opportunity. It's got something to do with a new kind of product. Plastics, I think he called it."

I ground out my cigarette in the ash tray on the desk. "Have Denby give you the file on it. You look at it tonight and give me a breakdown tomorrow morning before the board meeting. I'll be up at five o'clock."

A strange look began to come over McAllister's face. For a moment, I didn't know what it was, then I recognized it. Respect. "I'll be there at five, Jonas."

He got up and started for the door. I called to him before he reached it. "While you're at it, Mac, have Denby give you a list of the other stockholders in the company. I think I ought to know their names before the meeting."

The look of respect on his face grew deeper. "Yes, Jonas," he said, going out the door.

I swung around to Nevada and looked up at him. "What do you think?" I asked.

He waited a long moment before he answered. Then he spit away a piece of cigarette paper that clung to his lip. "I think your old man is resting real easy."

That reminded me. I had almost forgotten. I got up from the chair and walked around the desk and over to the couch. I picked up the blanket and looked down at him.

His eyes were closed and his mouth was grim. There was a slightly blue stain under the skin of his right temple, going on up into the hairline. That must be the embolism, I thought.

Somehow, deep inside of me, I wanted some tears to come out for him. But there weren't any. He had abandoned me too long ago—that day on the porch when he threw me to Nevada.

I heard the door behind me open and I dropped the blanket back and turned around. Denby was standing in the doorway.

"Jake Platt wants to see you, sir."

Jake was the plant manager. He kept the wheels turning. He also listened to the wind and by now the word must be racing all over the plant.

"Send him in," I said.

He appeared in the doorway beside Denby as soon as the words were out of my mouth. He was a big, heavy man. He even walked heavy. He came into the office, his hand outstretched. "I just heard the sad news." He crossed over to the couch and looked down at my father's body, his face assuming his best Irish-wake air. "It's a sad loss, indeed. Your father was a great man." He shook his head mournfully. "A great man."

I walked back behind the desk. And you're a great actor, Jake Platt, I thought. Aloud I said, "Thank you, Jake."

He turned to me, his face brightening at the thought of his act going over. "And I want you to know if there's anything you want of me, anything at all, just call on me."

"Thank you, Jake," I said again. "It's good to know there are men like you in my corner."

He preened almost visibly at my words. His voice lowered to a confidential tone. "The word's all over the plant now. D'ya think I ought to say something to them? You know them Mexicans and Indians. They're a might touchy and nervous and need a little calming down."

I looked at him. He was probably right. "That's a good idea, Jake. But I think it would seem better if I talk to them myself."

Jake had to agree with me whether he liked it or not. That was his policy. Not to disagree with the boss. "That's true, Jonas," he said, masking his disappointment. "If you feel up to it."

"I feel up to it," I said, starting for the door.

Nevada's voice came after me. "What about him?"

I turned back and followed his glance to the couch. "Call the undertakers and have them take care of him. Tell them we want the best casket in the state."

Nevada nodded.

"Then meet me out in front with the car and we'll go home." I went out the door without waiting for his reply. Jake trotted after me as I turned down the back corridor and went out onto the stairway leading to the plant.

Every eye in the factory turned toward me as I came through that doorway onto the little platform at the top of the staircase. Jake held up his hands and quiet began to fall in the factory. I waited until every machine in the place had come to a stop before I spoke. There was something eerie about it. It was the first time I had ever heard the factory completely silent. I began to speak and my voice echoed crazily through the building.

"*Mi padre ha muerto.*" I spoke in Spanish. My Spanish wasn't very good but it was their language and I continued in it. "But I, his son, am here and hope to continue in his good work. It is indeed too bad that my father is not here to express his appreciation to all you good workers himself for everything you have done to make this company a success. I hope it is enough for you to know that just before he passed away, he authorized a five-per-cent increase in wages for every one of you who work in the plant."

Jake grabbed my arm frantically. I shook his hand off and continued. "It is my earnest wish that I continue to have the same willing support that you gave to my father. I trust you will be patient with me for I have much to learn. Many thanks and may you all go with God."

I started down the steps and Jake came after me. The workers made a path as I walked through. They were silent for the most part; occasionally, one would touch me reassuringly as I passed by. Twice I saw tears in someone's eyes. At least my father didn't go uncried for. Even if they were tears in the eyes of someone who didn't know him.

I came out of the factory into the daylight and blinked my eyes. The sun was still in the sky. I had almost forgotten it was there, it seemed so long ago.

The big Pierce-Arrow was right in front of the door, with Nevada at the wheel. I started across toward it. Jake's hand on my arm stopped me. I turned toward him.

His voice was half whining. "What did you have to go and do that for, Jonas? You don't know them bastards like I do. Give 'em an inch, they'll want your arm. Your father was always after me to keep the pay scale down."

I stared at him coldly. Some people didn't learn fast enough. "Did you hear what I said in there, Jake?"

"I heard what you said, Jonas. That's what I'm talking about. I—"

I cut him off. "I don't think you did, Jake," I said softly. "My first words were *'Mi padre ha muerto.'* My father is dead."

"Yes, but—"

"That means exactly what it says, Jake. He's dead. But I'm not. I'm here and the only thing you better remember is that I'm exactly like him in just one way. I'll take no crap from anyone who works for me, and anyone who doesn't like what I do can get the hell out!"

Jake learned fast. He was at the car door, holding it open for me. "I didn't mean anything, Jonas. I only—"

There was no use explaining to him that if you pay more,

you get more. Ford had proved that when he gave his workers raises the year before. He more than tripled production. I got into the car and looked back at the factory. The black, sticky tar on the roof caught my eye. I remembered it from the plane.

"Jake," I said. "See that roof?"

He turned toward it and peered at it. His voice was puzzled. "Yes, sir?"

Suddenly I was very tired. I leaned back against the cushions and closed my eyes. "Paint it white," I said.

5

I DOZED AS THE BIG PIERCE ATE UP THE TWENTY miles between my father's new house and the factory. Every once in a while, I would open my eyes and catch a glimpse of Nevada watching me in the rear-view mirror, then my eyes would close again as if weighted down by lead.

I hate my father and I hate my mother and if I had had sisters and brothers, I would hate them, too. No, I didn't hate my father. Not any more. He was dead. You don't hate the dead. You only remember them. And I didn't hate my mother. She wasn't my mother, anyway. I had a stepmother. And I didn't hate her. I loved her.

That was why I had brought her home. I wanted to marry her. Only, my father said I was too young. Nineteen was too young, he had said. But he wasn't too young. He married her a week after I had gone back to college.

I met Rina at the country club two weeks before vacation was over. She came from back East, someplace in Massachusetts called Brookline, and she was like no one I had ever met before. All the girls out here are dark and tanned from the sun, they walk like men, talk like men, even ride like men. The only time you can be sure they are something else is in the evenings, when they wear skirts instead of Levi's, for even at the swimming pool, according to the fashion, they look like boys. Flat-chested and slim-hipped.

But Rina was a girl. You couldn't miss that. Especially in a bathing suit, the way she was the first time I saw her. She was

slim, all right, and her shoulders were broad, maybe too broad
for a woman. But her breasts were strong and full, jutting rocks
against the silk-jersey suit that gave the lie to the fashion. You
could not look at them without tasting the milk and honey of
their sweetness in your mouth. They rested easy on a high rib
cage that melted down into a narrow waist that in turn flared
out into slim but rounded hips and buttocks.

Her hair was a pale blond that she wore long, tied back behind her head, again contrary to fashion. Her brow was high,
her eyes wide apart and slightly slanted, the blue of them reflecting a glow beneath their ice. Her nose was straight and not
too thin, reflecting her Finnish ancestry. Perhaps her only flaw
was her mouth. It was wide—not generous-wide, because her
lips were not full enough. It was a controlled mouth that set
firmly on a tapered, determined chin.

She had gone to Swiss finishing schools, was slow to laughter
and reserved in her manner. In two days, she had me swinging
from the chandeliers. Her voice was soft and low and had a
faintly foreign sound that bubbled in your ear.

It was about ten days later, at the Saturday-night dance at the
club, that I first knew how much I wanted her. It was a slow,
tight waltz and the lights were down low and blue. Suddenly
she missed half a step. She looked up at me and smiled that slow
smile.

"You're very strong," she said and pressed herself back
against me.

I could feel the heat from her loins pouring into me as we
began to dance again. At last, I couldn't stand it any more. I
took her arm and started from the dance floor.

She followed me silently out to the car. We climbed into the
big Duesenberg roadster and I threw it into gear and we raced
down the highway. The night air on the desert was warm. I
looked at her out of the corner of my eyes. Her head was back
against the seat, her eyes closed to the wind.

I turned off into a date grove and cut the motor. She was still
leaning back against the seat. I bent over and kissed her mouth.

Her mouth neither gave nor took. It was like a well on an oa-
sis in the desert. It was there for when you needed it. I reached
for her breast. Her hand caught mine and held it.

I lifted my head and looked at her. Her eyes were open and

yet they were guarded. I could not see into them. "I want you," I said.

Her eyes did not change expression. I could hardly hear her voice. "I know."

I moved toward her again. This time, her hand against my chest, stopped me.

"Lend me your handkerchief," she said, taking it from my breast pocket.

It fluttered whitely in the night, then dropped from sight with her hands. She didn't raise her head from the back of the seat, she didn't speak, she just watched me with those guarded eyes.

I felt her searching fingers and I leaned toward her but somehow she kept me from getting any closer to her. Then suddenly, I felt an exquisite pain rushing from the base of my spine and I almost climbed halfway out of the seat.

I took out a cigarette and lit it with trembling fingers as she crumpled the handkerchief into a small ball and threw it over the side of the car. Then she took the cigarette from my mouth and placed it between her lips.

"I still want you," I said.

She gave the cigarette back to me and shook her head.

"Why?" I asked.

She turned her face toward me. It shone palely in the dark. "Because in two days I'm going home. Because in the stock-market crash of twenty-three, my father lost everything. Because I must find and marry a rich husband. I must do nothing to endanger that."

I stared at her for a moment, then started the engine. I backed the car out of the date grove and set it on the road for home. I didn't say anything but I had all the answers for her. I was rich. Or I would be someday.

I left Rina in the parlor and went into my father's study. As usual, he was working at his desk, the single lamp throwing its light down on the papers. He looked up as I came in.

"Yes?" he asked, as if I were someone in his office who had intruded in the midst of a problem.

I hit the wall switch and flooded the room with light. "I want to get married," I said.

He looked at me for a moment as if he was far away. He had been, but he came back fast. "You're crazy," he said unemotionally. He looked down at his desk again. "Go to bed and don't bother me."

I stood there. "I mean it, Dad," I said. It was the first time I had called him that since I was a kid.

He got to his feet slowly. "No," he said. "You're too young."

That was all he said. It would never occur to him to ask who, what, why. No, only I was too young. "All right, Father," I said, turning toward the door. "Remember I asked you."

"Wait a minute," he said. I stopped, my hand on the door-knob. "Where is she?"

"Waiting in the parlor," I answered.

He looked at me shrewdly. "When did you decide?"

"Tonight," I answered. "Just tonight."

"I suppose she's one of those silly little girls who show up at the club dance and she's waiting on pins and needles to meet the old man?" he asked.

I rose to her defense. "She's not like that at all. As a matter of fact, she doesn't even know that I'm in here asking you."

"You mean you haven't even asked her yet?"

"I don't have to," I answered, with the supreme confidence of my years. "I know her answer."

My father shook his head. "Just for the record, don't you think you had better ask her?"

I went out and brought Rina back into the room. "Rina, this is my father; Father, this is Rina Marlowe."

Rina nodded politely. For all you could tell from her manner, it could have been high noon instead of two o'clock in the morning.

Father looked at her thoughtfully. There was a curious expression on his face I had never seen before. He came around his desk and held out his hand to her. "How do you do, Miss Marlowe?" he said in a soft voice. I stared at him. I had never seen him do that with any of my friends before.

She took his hand. "How do you do?"

Still holding her hand, he let his voice fall into a semiamused tone. "My son thinks he wants to marry you, Miss Marlowe, but I think he's too young. Don't you?"

Rina looked at me. For a moment, I could see into her eyes. They were bright and shining, then they were guarded again.

She turned to Father. "This is very embarrassing, Mr. Cord. Would you please take me home?"

Stunned, unable to speak, I watched my father take her arm and walk out of the room with her. A moment later, I heard the roar of the Duesenberg and angrily I looked around for something to vent my spleen on. The only thing available was the lamp on the table. I smashed it against the wall.

Two weeks later, at college, I got a telegram from my father.

RINA AND I WERE MARRIED THIS MORNING. WE ARE AT THE WALDORF–ASTORIA, NEW YORK. LEAVING TOMORROW ON LEVIATHAN FOR EUROPEAN HONEYMOON.

I picked up the telephone and called him.

"There's no fool like an old fool!" I shouted across the three thousand miles of wire between us. "Don't you know the only reason she married you was for your money?"

Father didn't even get angry. He even chuckled. "You're the fool. All she wanted was a man, not a boy. She even insisted that we sign a premarital property agreement before she would marry me."

"Oh, yeah?" I asked. "Who drew the agreement? Her lawyer?"

Father chuckled again. "No. Mine." His voice changed abruptly. It grew heavy and coarse with meaning. "Now get back to your studies, son, and don't meddle in things that don't concern you. It's midnight here and I'm just about to go to bed."

The telephone went dead in my hands. I stared at it for a moment, then slowly put it down. I couldn't sleep that night. Across my mind's eye unreeled pornographic pictures of Rina and my father in wild sexual embrace. Several times, I woke up in a cold sweat.

A hand was shaking me gently. Slowly I opened my eyes. The first thing I saw was Nevada's face. "Wake up, Jonas," he said. "We're home."

I blinked my eyes to clear the sleep from them.

The last piece of sun was going down behind the big house. I shook my head and stepped out of the car. I looked up at the house. Strange house. I don't think I'd spent more than two weeks in it since my father had it built and now it was mine. Like everything else my father had done.

I started for the steps. Rina had thought of everything. Except this. My father was dead. And I was going to tell her.

6

THE FRONT DOOR OPENED AS I CROSSED THE VE-
randa. My father had built a traditional Southern plantation
house, and to run it, he had brought Robair up from New Orleans. Robair was a Creole butler in the full tradition.

He was a giant of a man, towering a full head over me, and as
gentle and efficient as he was big. His father and grandfather
had been butlers before him and even though they had been
slaves, they had instilled in him a pride in his work. He had a
sixth sense for his duties. Somehow, he was always there when
he was wanted.

He stepped aside to let me enter. "Hello, Master Cord." He
greeted me in his soft Creole English.

"Hello, Robair," I said, turning to him as he closed the door.
"Come with me."

He followed me silently into my father's study. His face impassive, he closed the door behind him. "Yes, Mr. Cord?"

It was the first time he had called me Mister, instead of Master. I looked at him. "My father is dead," I said.

"I know," he said. "Mr. Denby called."

"Do the others know?" I asked.

He shook his head. "I told Mr. Denby that Mrs. Cord was
out and I haven't said anything to the other servants."

There was a faint sound outside the closed door. Robair
continued speaking as he moved swiftly toward it. "I figured
you would want to break the sad news yourself." He threw the
door open.

There was no one there. He stepped quickly out the door. I
followed him. A figure was hurrying up the long staircase that
curved around the entrance hall to the upper floor.

Robair's voice was low but held the whip of authority.
"Louise!"

The figure stopped. It was Rina's personal maid.

"Come down here," he commanded.

Louise came down the steps hesitantly. I could see the terrified look on her face as she approached. "Yes, Mr. Robair?" Her voice was frightened, too.

For the first time, Robair let me see how he kept the servants in line. He moved almost lazily but his hand met her face with the impact of a pistol shot. His voice was filled with contempt. "How many times do I tell you not to listen at doors?"

She stood holding her hand to her face. The tears began to run down her cheeks.

"Now you get back to the kitchen. I'll deal with you later."

She ran toward the kitchen, still holding her face. Robair turned back to me. "I apologize for her, Mr. Cord," he said, his voice once more deep and soft. "Ordinarily, my servants don't do such a thing, but that one is pretty hard to keep in her place."

I took out a cigarette and almost before I had it in my mouth, Robair struck a match and held it for me. I dragged deep. "That's all right, Robair. I don't think she'll be with us much longer."

Robair put out the match and carefully deposited it in an ash tray. "Yes, sir."

I looked at the staircase speculatively. Oddly enough, I hesitated.

Robair's voice came over my shoulder. "Mrs. Cord is in her room."

I looked at him. His face was an impenetrable butler's mask. "Thank you, Robair. I'll go up and tell her."

I started up the staircase. His voice held me. "Mr. Cord?" I turned and looked down at him.

His black face gleamed. "What time shall I serve dinner, sir?"

I thought for a moment. "About eight o'clock," I answered.

"Thank you, sir," he said and started for the kitchen.

I knocked softly at Rina's door. There was no answer. I opened it and walked in. Her voice came from the bathroom.

"Louise, bring me a bath towel."

I walked into the bathroom and took a large towel from the stack on the shelf over her dressing table. I started for the enclosed bathtub just as she slid back the glass door.

She was gold and white and gleaming with the water running down her body. She stood there for a moment surprised.

Most women would have tried to cover themselves. But not Rina. She held out a hand for the towel.

She wrapped it around her expertly and stepped from the tub. "Where's Louise?" she asked, sitting down at the dressing table.

"Downstairs," I answered.

She began to dry her face with another towel. "Your father wouldn't like this."

"He'll never know," I answered.

"How do you know I won't tell him?"

"You won't," I said definitely.

It was then that she began to sense something was wrong. She looked up at me in the mirror. Her face was suddenly serious. "Did something happen between you and your father, Jonas?"

She watched me for a moment; there was still a puzzled look in her eyes. She gave me a small towel. "Be a good boy, will you, Jonas, and dry my back? I can't reach it." She smiled up into the mirror. "You see, I really do need Louise."

I took the towel and moved closer to her. She let the big bath towel slide down from her shoulders. I patted the beads of moisture from her flawless skin. The scent of her perfume came up to me, pungent from her bath warmth.

I pressed my lips to her neck. She turned toward me in surprise. "Stop that, Jonas! Your father said this morning you were a sex maniac but you don't have to try to prove it!"

I stared into her eyes. There was no fear in them. She was very sure of herself. I smiled slowly. "Maybe he was right," I said. "Or maybe he just forgot what it was like to be young."

I pulled her off the seat toward me. The towel fell still further until it hung only by the press of our bodies. I covered her mouth with mine and reached for her breast. It was hard and firm and strong and I could feel her heart beating wildly beneath it.

Maybe I was wrong but for a moment, I thought I could feel the fires in her reaching toward me. Then, angrily, she tore herself from me. The towel lay unheeded on the floor now. "Have you gone crazy?" she spit at me, her breast heaving. "You know at any minute now he could come walking through that door."

I stood very still for a second, then let the built-up pressure in my lungs escape in a slow sigh. "He'll never come through that door again," I said.

The color began to drain from her face slowly. "What—what do you mean?" she stammered.

My eyes went right into hers. For the first time, I could see into them. She was afraid. Just like everyone else that had to look into an unknown future. "Mrs. Cord," I said slowly, "your husband is dead."

Her pupils dilated wildly for a moment and she sank slowly back onto the seat. By reflex, she picked up the towel and placed it around her again. "I can't believe it," she said dully.

"What is it that you can't believe, Rina?" I asked cruelly. "That he's dead or that you were wrong when you married him instead of me?"

I don't think she even heard me. She looked up at me, her eyes dry, but there was a gentle sorrow in them—a compassion I never knew she was capable of. "Was there any pain?" she asked.

"No," I answered. "It was quick. A stroke. One minute he was as big as life and roaring like a lion, and the next—" I snapped my fingers. "It was like that."

Her eyes were still on mine. "I'm glad for his sake," she said softly. "I wouldn't have wanted him to suffer."

She got to her feet slowly. The veil came down over her eyes again. "I think you'd better go now," she said.

This was the familiar Rina, the one I wanted to take apart. The distant one, the unattainable one, the calculating one. "No," I said. "I haven't finished yet."

She started past me. "What is there to finish?"

I seized her arm and pulled her back toward me. "We're not finished," I said into her upturned face. "You and me. I brought you home one night because I wanted you. But you chose my father because he represented a quicker return for you. I think I've waited long enough!"

She stared back at me. She wasn't afraid now. This was the ground she was used to fighting on. "You wouldn't dare!"

For an answer, I pulled the towel from her. She turned to run from the room but I caught her arm and pulled her back to me. With my other hand, I caught her hair and pulled her head back so that her face turned up to mine. "No?"

"I'll scream," she gasped hoarsely. "The servants will come running!"

I grinned. "No, they won't. They'll only think it a cry of grief. Robair's got them in the kitchen and not one will come up unless I send for her."

"Wait!" she begged. "Please wait. For your father's sake?"

"Why should I?" I asked. "He didn't wait for me." I picked her up and carried her into the bedroom. Her fists and hands scratched at my face and beat against my chest.

I threw her on the bed, the white satin cover still on it. She tried to roll off on the other side. I grabbed her shoulder and spun her back. She bit my hand and tried to scramble away when I pulled it back. I placed my knee across her thighs and slapped viciously at her face. The blow knocked her back on the pillow. I could see the white marks left by my fingers.

She closed her eyes for a moment and when she opened them, they were clouded and there was a wildness in them that I had never seen before. She smiled and her arms went up around my neck, pulling me down to her. Her mouth fastened against mine. I could feel her body begin to move under me.

"Do it to me, Jonas!" she breathed into my mouth. "Now! I can't wait any more. I've waited so long." Her searching fingers ran down my hip and found my core. She turned her face into the pillow, her movements becoming more frenetic. I could hardly hear her fierce, urgent whisper. "Hurry, Jonas. Hurry!"

I started to get up but she couldn't wait for me to get my clothing off. She pulled me down again and took me inside her. She was like a burning bed of coals. She drew my head down to her neck.

"Make me pregnant, Jonas," she whispered into my ear. "Make me pregnant like you did to those three girls in Los Angeles. Put your life into me!"

I looked into her face. Her eyes were clear and there was a taunting triumph in them. They reflected none of the passion of the body beneath me. Her arms and legs tightened around me.

She smiled, her eyes looking into mine. "Make me pregnant, Jonas," she whispered. "Like your father never would. He was afraid someone would take something away from you!"

"What—what?" I tried to get up but she was like a bottom-less well that I couldn't get out of.

"Yes, Jonas," she said, still smiling, her body devouring me.

"Your father never took any chances. That's why he made me sign that agreement before we got married. He wanted everything for his precious son!"

I tried to get up but she had moved her legs in some mysterious manner. Laughing, triumphant, she said, "But you'll make me pregnant, won't you, Jonas? Who will know but us? You will share your fortune with your child even if the whole world believes it to be your father's."

She rose beneath me, seeking and demanding my life force. In a sudden frenzy, I tore myself from her, just as my strength drained from me. I fell across the bed near her feet.

The agony passed and I opened my eyes. Her head was turned into the pillow and she was crying. Silently I got to my feet and left the room.

All the way down the hall to my room, I kept thinking, my father cared, he really cared. Even if I didn't see it, he loved me.

He loved me. But never enough to show it.

By the time I got to my room, the tears were rolling down my cheeks.

7

I WAS ON THE TINY INDIAN PINTO THAT I HAD when I was ten years old, galloping insanely across the dunes. The panic of flight rose within me but I didn't know what I was running from. I looked back over my shoulder.

My father was following me on the big strawberry roan. His jacket was open and blowing in the wind and I could see the heavy watch chain stretched tight across his chest. I heard his voice, weird and eerie in the wind. "Come back here, Jonas. Damn you, come back!"

I turned and urged the pinto to even greater speed. I used my bat unmercifully and there were tiny red welts on the horse's side from where I had hit him. Gradually, I began to pull away.

Suddenly, as if from nowhere, Nevada was beside me, riding easily on his big black horse. He looked across at me calmly. His voice was low. "Go back, Jonas. It's your father calling you. What kind of a son are you, anyway?"

I didn't answer, just kept urging my horse on. I looked back again over my shoulder.

My father was pulling his horse to a stop. His face was very sad. "Look after him, Nevada." I could hear him only faintly, for there was a great distance between us. "Look after him, for I haven't the time." He turned the strawberry roan around and began to gallop away.

I stopped my pony and turned to look after him. He was already growing smaller in the distance. Even his outline was fading in the sudden tears that leapt to my eyes. I wanted to cry out after him, "Don't go, Father." But the words stuck in my throat.

I sat up in bed, my skin wet with perspiration. I shook my head to get the echo of the dream out of it. Through the open window I could hear the sound of horses coming from the corral in back of the house.

I went over to the window and looked out. The sun was at five o'clock and casting a long morning shadow. Down in the corral, several of the hands were leaning against the fence, watching a rider trying to break a wiry bay colt. I squinted my eyes against the sun.

I turned from the window quickly. That was the kind of medicine I needed. Something that would jar the empty feeling out of me, that would clean the bitter taste from my mouth. I pulled on a pair of Levi's and an old blue shirt and started from the room.

I headed down the corridor to the back stairs. I met Robair just as I came to them. He was carrying a tray with a glass of orange juice and a pot of steaming coffee. He looked at me without surprise.

"Good morning, Mr. Jonas."

"Good morning, Robair," I replied.

"Mr. McAllister is here to see you. I showed him into the study."

I hesitated a moment. The corral would have to wait. There were more important things I had to do. "Thank you, Robair," I said, turning for the front staircase.

"Mr. Jonas," he called after me.

I stopped and looked back at him.

"If you're goin' to talk business, Mr. Jonas, I find you always talk better if you got something in your stomach."

I looked at him; then at the tray. I nodded and sat down on the top step. Robair set the tray down beside me. I picked up the glass of orange juice and drained it. Robair poured the coffee and lifted the cover from the toast. I sipped at the coffee. Robair was right. The empty feeling was in my stomach. It was going away now. I picked up a slice of toast.

If McAllister noticed the way I was dressed, he made no comment about it. He came directly to the point. "The ten per cent of minority stock is divided as follows," he said, spreading some papers on the desk. "Two and one half per cent each, Rina Cord and Nevada Smith; two per cent each, Judge Samuel Haskell and Peter Commack, president of the Industrial Bank of Reno; and one per cent to Eugene Denby."

I looked at him. "What's the stock worth?"

"On what basis?" he asked. "Earnings or net worth?"

"Both," I answered.

He looked down at his papers again. "On the basis of average earnings the past five years, the minority stock is worth forty-five thousand dollars; on the basis of net worth maybe sixty thousand dollars." He lit a cigarette. "The earning potential of the corporation has been declining since the war."

"What does that mean?"

"There just isn't the demand for our product in peacetime that there is in war," he answered.

I took out a cigarette and lit it. I began to have doubts about the hundred thousand a year I was paying him. "Tell me something I don't know," I said.

He looked down at the papers again, then up at me. "Commack's bank turned down the two-hundred-thousand-dollar loan your father wanted to finance the German contract you signed yesterday."

I put the cigarette out slowly in the ash tray. "I guess that leaves me a little short, doesn't it?"

McAllister nodded. "Yes."

My next question took him by surprise. "Well, what did you do about it?"

He stared at me as if I were psychic. "What makes you think that I did?"

"You were in my father's office when I got there and I know he wouldn't call you just to settle with that girl's parents. He could have done that himself. And you took the job. That meant you were sure of getting your money."

He began to smile. "I arranged another loan at the Pioneer National Trust Company in Los Angeles. I made it for three hundred thousand, just to be on the safe side."

"Good," I said. "That will give me the money I need to buy out the minority stockholders."

He was still staring at me with that look of surprise in his eyes when I dropped into the chair beside him. "Now," I said, "tell me everything you've been able to find out about this new thing my father was so hot about. What was it you called it? Plastics?"

8

ROBAIR SERVED A RANCH-STYLE BREAKFAST: steak and eggs, hot biscuits. I looked around the table. The last plate had been cleared away and now Robair discreetly withdrew, closing the big doors behind him. I drained my coffee cup and got to my feet.

"Gentlemen," I said, "I know I don't have to tell you what a shock it was yesterday to find myself suddenly with the responsibility of a big company like Cord Explosives. That's why I asked you gentlemen here this morning to help me decide what's best for the company."

Commack's thin voice reached across the table. "You can count on us to do what's right, son."

"Thank you, Mr. Commack," I said. "It seems to me that the first thing we have to do is elect a new president. Someone who will devote himself to the company the same way my father did."

I looked around the table. Denby sat at the end, scribbling notes in a pad. Nevada was rolling a cigarette. He glanced up at me, his eyes smiling. McAllister sat quietly next to him. Haskell and Commack were silent. I waited for the silence to grow heavy. It did. I didn't have to be told who were my friends.

"Do you have any suggestions, gentlemen?" I asked.

Commack looked up at me. "Do you?"

"I thought so yesterday," I said. "But I slept on it and this morning I came to the conclusion that it's a pretty big nut to crack for someone with my experience."

For the first time that morning. Haskell, Commack and Denby brightened. They exchanged quick looks. Commack spoke up. "That's pretty sensible of you, son," he said. "What about Judge Haskell here? He's retired from the bench but I think he might take the job on to help you out."

I turned to the Judge. "Would you, Judge?"

The Judge smiled slowly. "Only to help you out, boy," he said. "Only to help you out."

I looked over at Nevada. He was smiling broadly now. I smiled back at him, then turned to the others. "Shall we vote on it, gentlemen?"

For the first time, Denby spoke up. "According to the charter of this company, a president can only be elected by a meeting of the stockholders. And then only by a majority of the stock outstanding."

"Let's have a stockholder's meeting, then," Commack said. "The majority of stock is represented here."

"That's a good idea," I said. I turned to the Judge, smiling. "That is if I can vote my stock," I added.

"You sure can, boy," the Judge boomed, taking a paper from his pocket and handing it to me. "It's there in your father's will. I had it admitted to probate this morning. It's all legally yours now."

I took the will and continued. "All right, then, the director's meeting is adjourned and the stockholder's meeting is called to order. The first item on the agenda is to elect a president and treasurer of the company to replace the late Jonas Cord."

Commack smiled. "I nominate Judge Samuel Haskell."

Denby spoke quickly. Too quickly. "Second the nomination."

I nodded. "The nomination of Judge Haskell is noted. Any further nominations before the slate is closed?"

Nevada got to his feet. "I nominate Jonas Cord, Junior," he drawled.

I smiled at him. "Thank you." I turned to the Judge and my voice went hard and flat. "Do I hear the nomination seconded?"

The Judge's face was flushed. He glanced at Commack, then at Denby. Denby's face was white.

"Do I hear the nomination seconded?" I repeated coldly.

He knew I had them. "Second the nomination," the Judge said weakly.

"Thank you, Judge," I said.

It was easy after that. I bought their stock for twenty-five thousand dollars and the first thing I did was fire Denby.

If I was going to have a secretary, I didn't want a prissy little sneak like him. I wanted one with tits.

Robair came into the study, where McAllister and I were working. I looked up. "Yes, Robair?"

He bowed his head respectfully. "Miss Rina would like to see you in her room, suh."

I got to my feet and stretched. This sitting at a desk for half a day was worse than anything I'd ever done. "O.K., I'll go right up."

McAllister looked at me questioningly.

"Wait for me," I said. "I won't be long."

Robair held the door for me and I went up the stairs to Rina's room. I knocked on the door.

"Come in," she called.

She was sitting at her table in front of a mirror. Louise was brushing her hair with a big white brush. Rina's eyes looked up at me in the mirror.

"You wanted to see me?" I asked.

"Yes," she answered. She turned to Louise. "That's all for now," she said. "Leave us."

The girl nodded silently and started for the door. Rina's voice reached after her. "And wait downstairs. I'll call when I want you."

Rina looked at me and smiled. "She has a habit of listening at keyholes."

"I know," I said, closing the door behind me. "What is it you wanted to see me about?"

Rina got to her feet. Her black negligee swirled around her. Through it I could see she was wearing black undergarments, also. Her eyes caught mine. She smiled again. "What do you think of my widow's weeds?"

"Very merry-widowish," I answered. "But that isn't what you asked me up for."

She took a cigarette and lit it. "I want to get out of here right after the funeral."

"What for?" I asked. "It's your house. He left it to you."

Her eyes met mine through a cloud of smoke she blew out. "I want you to buy the house from me."

"What'll I use for money?"

"You'll get it," she said flatly. "Your father always got it for the things he wanted."

I studied her. She seemed to know exactly what she was doing. "How much do you want?" I asked cautiously.

"One hundred thousand dollars," she said calmly.

"What?" I exclaimed. "It isn't worth more than fifty-five."

"I know," she said. "But I'm throwing in something else— my stock in the Cord Explosives Company."

"The stock isn't worth the difference!" I exploded. "I just bought twice as much this morning for twenty-five thousand!"

She got to her feet and walked over to me. Her eyes stared coldly up at me. "Look, Jonas," she said coldly, "I'm being nice about it. Under the Nevada law, I'm entitled to one-third your father's estate, will or no will. I could break the probate of the will just like that if I wanted to. And even if I couldn't, I could tie you up in court for five years. What would happen to all your plans then?"

I stared at her silently.

"If you don't believe me, why don't you ask your lawyer friend downstairs?" she added.

"You already checked?" I guessed.

"Damn right I did!" she snapped. "Judge Haskell called me as soon as he got back to his office!"

I drew in my breath. I should have known the old bastard wouldn't let go that easy. "I haven't got that kind of money," I said. "Neither has the company."

"I know that," she said. "But I'm willing to be reasonable about it. I'll take fifty thousand the day after the funeral and your note endorsed by the company for ten thousand a year for the next five years."

I didn't need a lawyer to tell me she'd had good advice. "O.K.," I said, starting for the door. "Come on downstairs I'll have McAllister prepare the papers."

She smiled again. "I couldn't do that."

"Why not?" I demanded.

"I'm in mourning," she said. "How would it look for the widow of Jonas Cord to come downstairs to transact business?" She went back to her vanity table and sat down. "When the papers are ready, send them up."

9

IT WAS FIVE O'CLOCK WHEN WE GOT OUT OF THE taxi in front of the bank building in downtown Los Angeles. We went through the door and walked back to the executive offices in the rear of the bank. McAllister led me through another door marked PRIVATE. It was a reception room.

A secretary looked up. "Mr. McAllister." She smiled. "We thought you were in Nevada."

"I was," he replied. "Is Mr. Moroni in?"

"Let me check," she said. "Sometimes he has a habit of leaving the office without telling me." She disappeared through another door.

I looked at McAllister. "That's the kind of secretary I want. She's got brains and a nice pair of boobs to go with them."

He smiled. "A girl like that gets seventy-five, eighty dollars a week. They don't come cheap."

"Yuh gotta pay for anything that's good," I said.

The secretary appeared in the doorway, smiling at us. "Mr. Moroni will see you now, Mr. McAllister."

I followed him into the inner office. It was large, with dark, wood-paneled walls. There was a big desk spang in the middle of it and a small man with iron-gray hair and shrewd dark eyes sitting behind it. He got up as we came into the room.

"Mr. Moroni," McAllister said, "this is Jonas Cord."

Moroni put out his hand. I took it. It wasn't the usual soft banker's hand. This one was hard and callused and the grip was strong. There were many years of labor contained in that hand and most of them had not been behind a desk. "It's good to meet you, Mr. Cord," he said with a faint trace of an Italian accent.

"My pleasure, sir," I said respectfully.

He waved us to the chairs in front of his desk and we sat down. McAllister came right to the point. When he had finished, Moroni leaned forward across his desk and looked at me. "I'm sorry to hear about your loss," he said. "From everything I've heard, he was a very unusual man."

I nodded. "He was, sir."

"You realize, of course, this makes quite a difference?"

I looked at him. "Without trying to stand on a technicality, Mr. Moroni, I thought the loan was being made to the Cord Explosives Company, not to either my father or me."

Moroni smiled. "A good banker makes loans to companies but he always looks at the man behind the company."

"My experience is limited, sir, but I thought the first objective of a good banker was to achieve adequate collateralization for a loan. I believe that was inherent in the loan agreement that Mr. McAllister made with you."

Moroni smiled. He leaned back in his chair and took out a cigar. He lit it and looked at me through a cloud of smoke. "Mr. Cord, tell me what you believe the primary responsibility of the borrower is."

I looked at him. "To make a profit on his loan."

"I said the borrower, Mr. Cord, not the lender."

"I know you did, Mr. Moroni," I said. "But if I didn't feel I would make a profit on the money you're going to lend me, there'd be no point in my taking it."

"Just how do you expect to make that profit?" he asked. "How well do you know your business, Mr. Cord?"

"Not as well as I should, Mr. Moroni. Certainly not as well as I will next week, next month, next year. But this much I do know. Tomorrow is coming and a whole new world with it. There'll be opportunities to make money that never existed in my father's time. And I'll take advantage of them."

"I presume you're referring to this new product you're acquiring by the German contract?"

"That's part of it," I said, even if I hadn't thought of it until he mentioned it.

"Just how much do you know about plastics?" he asked.

"Very little," I admitted.

"Then what makes you so sure it's worth anything?"

"Du Pont and Eastman's interest in the American rights. Anything they're interested in has to be worth something. And, your agreement to lend us the money to acquire those rights. As soon as I clear up a few things here, I intend to spend two or three months in Germany learning everything there is to know about plastics."

"Who will run the company while you're away?" Moroni asked. "A great deal can happen in three months."

"Mr. McAllister, sir," I said. "He's already agreed to join the company."

A kind of respect came into the banker's face. "I know my directors may not agree with me, Mr. Cord, but I've decided to give you your loan. It has certain elements of speculation that may not conform to what they consider sound banking practices, but the Pioneer National Trust Company was built on loans like this. We were the first bank to lend money to the producers of motion pictures and there's nothing quite as speculative as that."

"Thank you, Mr. Moroni," I said.

He picked up the telephone on his desk. "Bring in the Cord loan agreement and the check."

"You will note," he said, "that although the loan is for three hundred thousand dollars, we have extended your credit under this agreement to a maximum of five hundred thousand dollars." He smiled at me. "One of my principles of banking, Mr. Cord. I don't believe in budgeting my clients too closely. Sometimes a few dollars more make the difference between success and failure."

Suddenly I liked this man. It takes one crap-shooter to recognize another. And this man had it. I smiled at him. "Thanks, Mr. Moroni. Let's hope I make a lot of money for both of us." I leaned over and signed the loan application.

"I'm sure you will," Moroni said and pushed the check across the desk at me.

I picked it up and gave it to McAllister without looking at it. I got to my feet. "Thank you again, Mr. Moroni. I'm sorry I have to run but we have to get back to Nevada tonight."

"Tonight? But there aren't any trains until morning."

"I have my own plane, Mr. Moroni. That's how we came up. We'll be home by nine o'clock."

Moroni came around his desk. There was a look of concern on his face. "Better fly low, Mr. Cord," he said. "After all, we just gave you a lot of money."

I laughed aloud. "Don't worry, Mr. Moroni. It's as safe as an automobile. Besides, if anything happens to us on the way down, just stop payment on the check."

They both laughed. I could see the look of nervousness cross McAllister's face, but to his credit, he didn't say anything.

We shook hands and Moroni walked us to the door. "Good luck," he said as we walked out into the reception room.

A man was sitting on the couch. He got to his feet slowly. I recognized Buzz Dalton, the pilot whose plane I had won in a crap game. "Hey, Buzz," I called. "Don't you say hello to your friends?"

A smile broke over his face. "Jonas!" he exclaimed. "What the hell are you doin' here?"

"Diggin' for a little scratch," I said, taking his hand. "You?"

"The same," he answered, a dejected look coming over his face again. "But no luck so far."

"Why?" I asked.

Buzz shrugged. "I got a mail contract. L.A. to Frisco. Twelve months guaranteed at ten thousand a month. But I guess I'll have to pass it up. I can't get the dough to buy the three planes I need. Banks think it's too risky."

"How much do you have to borrow?"

"About twenty-five grand," he said. "Twenty for the planes and five to keep them flying until the first check comes in."

"Yuh got the contract?"

"In my pocket," he said, taking it out.

I looked at it. "It sounds like a good deal to me."

"It is," he answered. "I got it all worked out. I can net five grand a month after expenses and amortization. Here's the paper I worked out on that."

The figures seemed right to me. I had a good idea what it cost to run a plane. I turned around and looked at Moroni. "You meant what you said in there? About my additional credit? There's no strings on it?"

He smiled. "No strings at all."

I turned back to Buzz. "You got your money on two conditions," I said. "I get fifty per cent of the stock in your company and chattel mortgage on your planes amortized over twelve months, both payable to the Cord Explosives Company."

Buzz's face broke into a grin. "Man, you got yourself a deal!"

"O.K.," I said. I turned to Mr. Moroni. "Would you be kind enough to arrange the details for me? I have to be back tonight."

"I'll be glad to, Mr. Cord." He smiled.

"Make the loan for thirty thousand dollars," I said.

"Hey, wait a minute," Buzz interrupted. "I only asked for twenty-five."

"I know," I said, turning back to him with a smile. "But I learned something today."

"What's that?" Buzz asked.

"It's bad business to lend a guy just enough money to give him the shorts. That's takin' a chance and you both can lose. If you really want him to make it, lend him enough to make sure he can do the job."

My father had the biggest funeral ever held in this part of the state. Even the Governor came down. I had closed the plant and the little church was packed to the rafters, with the overflow spilling out into the street.

Rina and I stood alone in the small pew down in front. She stood straight and tall in her black dress, her blond hair and her face hidden by the black veil. I looked down at the new black shoes on my feet. They were my father's shoes and they hurt. At the last minute, I'd discovered I didn't have anything in the house except huarachos. Robair had brought the shoes down from my father's closet. He had never worn them. I promised myself I would never wear them again, either.

I heard a sigh run through the congregation and looked up. They were closing my father's coffin. I had a last quick glimpse of his face, then it was gone and there was a curious kind of blankness in my mind and for a moment I couldn't even remember what he looked like.

Then the sound of weeping came to my ears and I looked around out of the corners of my eyes. The Mex women from the plant were crying. I heard a snuffle behind me. I half turned. It was Jake Platt, tears in his whisky eyes.

I looked at Rina standing next to me. I could see her eyes through the dark veil. They were clear and calm. From the congregation behind us came the sound of many people weeping for my father.

But Rina, his wife, didn't weep. And neither did I, his son.

10

IT WAS A WARM NIGHT, EVEN WITH THE BREEZE THAT came in through the open windows from across the desert. I tossed restlessly on the bed and pushed the sheets down from me. It had been a long day, starting with the funeral and then going over plans with McAllister until it was time for him to leave. I was tired but I couldn't sleep. Too many thoughts were racing through my mind. I wondered if that was the reason I used to hear my father pacing up and down in his room long after the rest of the house had gone to bed.

There was a sound at the door. I sat up in bed. My voice jarred the stillness. "Who is it?"

The door opened farther and I could see her face; the rest of her dissolved into the darkness along with the black negligee. Her voice was very low as she closed the door behind her. "I thought you might be awake, Jonas. I couldn't sleep, either."

"Worried about your money?" I asked sarcastically. "The check's over there on the dresser along with the notes. Just sign the release and it's yours."

"It isn't the money," she said, coming still further into the room.

"What is it, then?" I asked coldly. "You came to say you're sorry? To express your sympathy? Is this a condolence call?"

She was standing next to the bed now and looked down at me. "You don't have to say things like that, Jonas," she said simply. "Even if he was your father, I was his wife. Yes, I came to say I'm sorry."

But I wasn't satisfied with that. "Sorry about what?" I flung at her. "Sorry he didn't give you more than he did? Sorry that you didn't marry me instead of him?" I laughed bitterly. "You didn't love him."

"No, I didn't love him," she said tightly. "But I respected him. He was more a man than anyone I ever met."

I didn't speak.

Suddenly she was crying. She sat down on the edge of the bed and hid her face in her hands.

"Cut it out," I said roughly. "It's too late for tears."

She put her hands down and stared at me. In the darkness, I could see the wet silver sparkle rolling down her cheeks. "What do you know it's too late for?" she cried. "Too late to love him? It isn't that I didn't try. It's just that I'm not capable of love. I don't know why. It's the way I am, that's all. Your father knew that and understood it. That's why I married him. Not for his money. He knew that, too. And he was content with what I gave him."

"If that's the truth," I said, "then what are you crying for?"

"Because I'm frightened," she said.

"Frightened?" I laughed. It just didn't fit her. "What are you afraid of?"

She took a cigarette from somewhere in her negligee and put it in her mouth unlit. Her eyes shone at me like a panther's eyes must in a desert campfire at night. "Men," she said shortly.

"Men?" I repeated. "You—afraid of men? Why, you're the original teasing—"

"That's right, you stupid fool!" she said angrily. "I'm afraid of men, listening to their demands, putting up with their lecherous hands and one-track minds. And hearing them disguise their desire with the words of love when all they want is just one thing. To get inside me!"

"You're crazy!" I said angrily. "That's not the only thing we think of!"

"No?" she asked. I heard the rasp of a match and the flame broke the darkness. She looked down at me. "Then look at yourself, Jonas. Look at yourself lusting for your father's wife!"

I didn't have to look to know she was right. I knocked the match angrily from her hand.

Then, all at once, she was clinging to me, her lips placing tiny kisses on my face and chin, her body trembling with her fears. "Jonas, Jonas. Please let me stay with you. Just for tonight," she cried. "I'm afraid to be alone!"

I raised my hands to push her away. She was naked beneath the black negligee. Her flesh was cool and soft as the summer desert breeze and her thrusting nipples rasped across the palms of my rising hands.

I froze, staring at her in the darkness. There was only her face before me, then the taste of her salty tears on her lips and mine. The anger inside me washed away in the cascading torrent of desire. And with only my devil to guide us, together we plunged into the fiery pleasures of our own particular hell.

I awoke and glanced at the window. The first flicker of dawn was spilling into the room. I turned to look at Rina. She was lying on my pillow, her arm flung across her eyes. I touched her shoulder lightly.

She took away her arm. Her eyes were open; they were clear and calm.

She got out of bed in a smooth, fluid motion. Her body shone with a young, golden translucence. She picked up her black negligee from the foot of the bed and slipped into it. I sat there watching her as she walked over to the dresser.

"There's a pen in the top right drawer," I said.

She took out the pen and signed the release.

"Aren't you going to read it?" I asked.

She shook her head. "What for? You can't get any more than I agreed to give you."

She was right. She had forgone all rights to any further claims in the estate. Picking up the check and the notes, she walked to the door. She turned there and looked back at me.

"I won't be here when you get back from the plant."

I looked at her for a moment. "You don't have to go," I said.

Her eyes met mine. I thought I caught a hint of sadness in them. "No, Jonas," she said softly. "It wouldn't work out."

"Maybe," I said.

"No, Jonas," she said. "It's time you got out from under the shadow of your father. He was a great man but so will you be. In your own way."

I reached for a cigarette on the bedside table and lit it without speaking. The smoke burned into my lungs.

"Good-by, Jonas," she said. "Good luck."

I stared at her for a moment, then I spoke. My voice was husky from the cigarette. "Thank you," I said. "Good-by, Rina."

The door opened and shut quickly and she was gone. I got out of bed and walked over to the window. The first morning red of the sun was on the horizon. It was going to be a scorcher.

I heard the door open behind me and my heart leaped inside my breast. She had come back. I turned around.

Robair came into the room carrying a tray. His white teeth flashed in a gentle smile. "I thought you might do with a cup of coffee."

When I got down to the plant, Jake Platt had a gang of men up on the roof, painting it white. I grinned to myself and went inside.

That first day was hectic. It seemed that nothing went right. The detonator caps we had sent to Endicott Mines were faulted and we had to rush-ship replacements. For the third time that year, Du Pont underbid us on a government contract for pressed cordite.

I spent half the day going over the figures and it finally boiled down to our policy on percentage of profit. When I suggested that we'd better re-examine our policy if it was going to cost us business, Jake Platt protested. My father, he said, claimed it didn't pay them to operate on a basis of less than twelve per cent. I blew up and told Jake Platt that I was running the factory now and what my father had done was his own business. On the next bid, I'd damn sure make certain we underbid Du Pont by at least three cents a pound.

By that time, it was five o'clock and the production foreman came in with the production figures. I'd just started to go over them when Nevada interrupted me.

"Jonas," he said.

I looked up. He had been there in the office all day but he was quiet and sat in a corner and I had even forgotten that he was there. "Yes?" I answered.

"Is it all right if I leave a little early?" he asked. "I got some things to do."

"Sure," I said, looking down at the production sheets again. "Take the Duesenberg. I'll get Jake to drive me home."

"I won't need it," he said. "I left my own car in the lot."

"Nevada," I called after him. "Tell Robair I'll be home for dinner at eight o'clock."

There was a moment's hesitation, then I heard his reply. "Sure thing, Jonas. I'll tell him."

I was through earlier than I had expected and pulled the

Duesenberg up in front of the house at seven thirty, just as Nevada came down the steps with a valise in each hand.

He stared at me in a kind of surprise. "You're home early."

"Yeah," I answered. "I finished sooner than I thought."

"Oh," he said and continued down the steps to his car. He put the valises in the back.

I followed him down and I could see the back of his car was filled with luggage. "Where you going with all that stuff, Nevada?"

"It's mine," he said gruffly.

"I didn't say it wasn't," I said. "I just asked where you were going."

"I'm leavin'."

"On a hunting trip?" I asked. This was the time of the year Nevada and I always used to go up into the mountains when I was a kid.

"Nope," he said. "Fer good."

"Wait a minute," I said. "You just can't walk out like that."

His dark eyes bore into mine. "Who says I can't?"

"I do," I said. "How'm I going to get along without you?"

He smiled slowly. "Real good, I reckon. You don't need me to wet-nurse you no more. I been watchin' you the last few days."

"But—but," I protested.

Nevada smiled slowly. "All jobs got to end sometime, Jonas. I put about sixteen years into this one and now there's nothing left for me to do. I don't like the idea of drawing a salary with no real way to earn it."

I stared at him for a moment. He was right. There was too much man in him to hang around being a flunky. "You got enough money?"

He nodded. "I never spent a cent of my own in sixteen years. Your pappy wouldn't let me."

"What are you going to do?"

"Join up with a couple of old buddies. We're takin' a Wild-West show up the coast to California. Expect to have a real big time."

We stood around awkwardly for a moment, then Nevada put out his hand. "So long, Jonas."

I held onto his hand. I could feel the tears hovering just beneath my eyelids. "So long, Nevada."

He walked around the car and got in behind the wheel. Starting the motor he shifted into gear. He raised his hand in farewell just as he began to roll.

"Keep in touch, Nevada," I yelled after him, and watched until he was out of sight.

I walked back into the house and went into the dining room. I sat down at the empty table.

Robair came in with an envelope in his hand. "Mr. Nevada left this for you," he said.

Numbly I opened it and took out a note written laboriously in pencil:

DEAR SON,
   I ain't much of a man for good-bys, so this is it. There ain't nothing any more for me to do around here so I figure it's time I went. All my life I wanted to give you something for your birthday but your pappy always beat me to it. Your pappy gave you everything. So until now there was nothing you ever wanted that I could give you. In this envelope you will find something you really want. You don't have to worry about it. I went to a lawyer in Reno and signed it all over good and proper.
   Happy birthday.

                                        Your friend,
                                        Nevada Smith

I looked at the other papers in the envelope. They were Cord Explosives Company stock certificates endorsed over to my name.

I put them down on the table and a lump began to come up in my throat. Suddenly, the house was empty. Everybody was gone. My father, Rina, Nevada. Everybody. The house began to echo with memories.

I remembered what Rina had said, about getting out from under the shadow of my father. She was right. I couldn't live in this house. It wasn't mine. It was his. For me, it would always be his house.

My mind was made up. I'd find an apartment in Reno. There wouldn't be any memories in an apartment. I'd turn the house over to McAllister. He had a family and it would save him the trouble of looking for one.

I looked down at Nevada's note again. The last line hit me. Happy birthday. A pain began to tie up my gut. I had forgotten and Nevada had been the only one left to remember.

Today was my birthday.

I was twenty-one.

The Story of
NEVADA SMITH

———————————

Book Two

1

IT WAS AFTER NINE O'CLOCK WHEN NEVADA PULLED
the car off the highway onto the dirt road that led to the ranch.
He stopped the car in front of the main house and got out. He
stood there listening to the sounds of laughter coming from the
casino.

A man came out on the porch and looked down at him.
"Hello, Nevada."

Nevada answered without turning around. "Hello, Charlie. It
sounds like the divorcées are having themselves a high ol' time."

Charlie smiled. "Why shouldn't they? Divorcin' is a pretty
good piece of business for most of 'em."

Nevada turned and looked up at him. "I guess it is. Only, I
can't get used to the idea of ranchin' women instead of cattle."

"Now, mebbe, you'll get used to it," Charlie said. "After all,
you own fifty per cent of this spread. Time you settled down
and got to work on it."

"I don't know," Nevada said. "I kinda got me the travelin' itch. I figger I been in one place long enough."

"Where you goin' to travel?" Charlie asked. "There ain't no place left. The country's all used up with roads going to every place. You're thirty years late."

Nevada nodded silently. Charlie was right but the strange thing was he didn't feel thirty years late. He felt the same as he always did. Right for now.

"I put the woman in your cabin," Charlie said. "Martha and I been waitin' supper for you."

Nevada got back into the car. "Then I better go an' get her. We'll be back as soon as I git washed up."

Charlie nodded and went back inside as the car started off. At the door, he turned and looked after it as it wound its way up the small hill toward the back of the ranch. He shook his head and went inside.

Martha was waiting for him. "How is he?" she asked anxiously.

"I don't know," he answered, shaking his head again. "He seems kinda mixed up an' lost to me. I just don't know."

The cabin was dark when Nevada went in. He reached for the oil lamp beside the door and put it on a table. He struck a match and held it to the wick. The wick sputtered a moment then burst into flame. He put the chimney back on and replaced the lamp on the shelf.

Rina's voice came from behind him. "Why didn't you turn on the electricity, Nevada?"

"I like lamp light," he said simply. "Electric light ain't natural. It's wearin' on the eyes."

She was sitting in a chair facing the door, her face pale and luminous. She was wearing a heavy sweater that came down over the faded blue jeans covering her legs.

"You cold?" he asked. "I'll start a fire."

She shook her head. "I'm not cold."

He stood there silent for a moment, then spoke. "I'll bring in my things an' wash up. Charlie and Martha waited supper for us."

"I'll help you bring them in."

"O.K."

They came out into the night. The stars were deep in the

black velvet and the sound of music and laughter came faintly to them from down the hill.

She looked down toward the casino. "I'm glad I'm not one of them."

He handed her a suitcase. "You never could be. You ain't the type."

"I thought of divorcing him," she said. "But something inside me kept me from it even though I knew it was wrong from the beginning."

"A deal's a deal," he said shortly as he turned back into the cabin, his arms full.

"I guess that's it."

They made two more trips silently and then she sat down on the edge of the bed as he stripped off his shirt and turned to the washbasin in the corner of the small bedroom.

The muscles rippled under his startlingly white skin. The hair covering his chest was like a soft black down as it fell toward his flat, hard stomach. He covered his face and neck with soap and then splashed water over it. He reached for a towel blindly.

She gave it to him and he rubbed vigorously. He put down the towel and reached for a clean shirt. He slipped into it and began to button it.

"Wait a minute," she said suddenly. "Let me do that for you."

Her fingers were quick and light. He felt their touch against his skin like a whisper of air. She looked up into his face, her eyes wondering. "How old are you, Nevada? Your skin is like a young boy's."

He smiled suddenly.

"How old?" she persisted.

"I was born in eighty-two, according to my reckoning," he said. "My mother was a Kiowa and they didn't keep such good track of birthdays. That makes me forty-three." He finished tucking the shirt into his trousers.

"You don't look more than thirty."

He laughed, pleased despite himself. "Let's go and git some grub."

She took his arm. "Let's," she said. "Suddenly, I'm starving."

It was after midnight when they got back to the cabin. He opened the door and let her enter before him. He crossed to the fireplace and set a match to the kindling. She came up behind him and he looked up.

"You go on to bed," he said.

Silently she walked into the bedroom and he fanned the kindling. The wood caught and leaped into flame. He put a few logs over it and got up and crossed the room to a cupboard. He took down a bottle of bourbon and a glass and sat down in front of the fire.

He poured a drink and looked at the whisky in the glass. The fire behind it gave it a glowing heat. He drank the whisky slowly.

When he had finished, he put the empty glass down and began to strip off his boots. He left them beside the chair and walked over to the couch and stretched out. He had just lighted a cigarette when her voice came from the bedroom door.

"Nevada?"

He sat up and turned toward her. "Yeah?"

"Did Jonas say anything about me?"

"No."

"He gave me a hundred thousand dollars for the stock and the house."

"I know," he replied.

She hesitated a moment, then came farther into the room. "I don't need all that money. If you need any—"

He laughed soundlessly. "I'm O.K. Thanks, anyway."

"Sure?"

He chuckled again, wondering what she would say if she knew about the six-thousand-acre ranch he had in Texas, about the half interest in the Wild-West show. He, too, had learned a great deal from the old man. Money was only good when it was working for you.

"Sure," he said. He got to his feet and walked toward her. "Now go to bed, Rina. You're out on your feet."

He followed her into the bedroom and took a blanket from the closet as she got into bed. She caught his hands as he walked by the bed. "Talk to me while I fall asleep."

He sat down on the side of the bed. "What about?" he asked.

She still held onto his hand. "About yourself. Where you were born, where you came from—anything."

He smiled into the dark. "Ain't very much to tell," he said.

"As far as I know, I was born in West Texas. My father was a buffalo-hunter named John Smith and my mother was a Kiowa princess named—"

"Don't tell me," she interrupted sleepily. "I know her name. Pocahontas."

He laughed softly. "Somebody told you," he said in mock reproach. "Pocahontas. That was her name."

"Nobody told me," she whispered faintly. "I read it someplace."

Her hand slipped slowly from his and he looked down. Her eyes were closed and she was fast asleep.

Quietly he got up and straightened the blanket around her, then turned and walked into the other room. He spread a blanket on the couch and undressed quickly. He stretched out and wrapped the blanket around him.

John Smith and Pocahontas. He wondered how many times he had mockingly told that story. But the truth was stranger still. And probably, no one would believe it.

It was so long ago that there were times he didn't believe it himself any more. His name wasn't Nevada Smith then, it was Max Sand.

And he was wanted for armed robbery and murder in three different states.

2

IT WAS IN MAY OF 1882 THAT SAMUEL SAND CAME into the small cabin that he called home and sat down heavily on a box that served him for a chair. Silently his squaw woman heated some coffee and placed it before him. She moved heavily, being swollen with child.

He sat there for a long time, his coffee growing cold before him. Occasionally, he would look out the door toward the prairie, with its faint remnant patches of snow still hidden in the corners of rises.

The squaw began to cook the evening meal. Beans and salt buffalo meat. It was still early in the day to cook the meal, because the sun had not yet reached the noon, but she felt vaguely disturbed and had to do something. Now and then, she would glance at Sam out of the corners of her eyes but he was lost in a troubled world that women were not allowed to enter. So she kept stirring the beans and meat in the pot and waited for his mood and the day to pass.

Kaneha was sixteen that spring and it was only the summer before that the buffalo-hunter had come to the tepees of her tribe to purchase a wife. He had come on a black horse, leading a mule that was burdened heavily with pack.

The chief and the council of braves came out to greet him. They sat down in a circle of peace around the fire with the pot of stew cooking over it. The chief took out the pipe and Sam took out a bottle of whisky. Silently the chief held the pipe to the glowing coals and then, when it was lit, held it to his mouth and puffed deeply. He passed it to Sam, who puffed and in turn passed it to the brave seated next to him in the circle.

When the pipe came back to the chief, Sam opened the bottle of whisky. He wiped the rim of it carefully and tilted it to his lips, then offered it to the chief. The chief did the same and took a large swallow of the whisky. It burned his throat and his eyes watered and he wanted to cough, but he choked back the cough and passed the bottle to the brave seated next to him.

When the bottle came back to Sam, he placed it on the ground in front of the chief. He leaned forward and took a piece of meat out of the pot. He chewed elaborately on the fatty morsel with much smacking of his lips and then swallowed it.

He looked at the chief. "Good dog."

The chief nodded. "We cut out its tongue and kept it tied to a stake that it would be properly fat."

They were silent for a moment and the chief reached again for the bottle of whisky. Sam knew it was then time for him to speak.

"I am a mighty hunter," he boasted. "My gun has slain thousands of buffalo. My prowess is known all across the plains. There is no brave who can feed as many as I."

The chief nodded solemnly. "The deeds of Red Beard are known to us. It is an honor to welcome him to our tribe."

"I have come to my brothers for the maiden known as Kaneha," Sam said. "I want her for my squaw."

The chief sighed slowly in relief. Kaneha was the youngest of his daughters and the least favored. For she was tall for a maiden, almost as tall as the tallest brave, and thin, her waist so thin that two hands could span it. There was not enough room inside her for a child to grow, and her face and features were straight and flat, not round and fat, as a maiden's should be. The chief sighed again in relief. Kaneha would be no problem now.

"It is a wise choice," he said aloud. "The maiden Kaneha is ripe for child-bearing. Already her blood floods thickly to the ground when the moon is high."

Sam got to his feet and walked over to the mule. He opened one of the packs and took out six bottles of whisky and a small wooden box. He carried them back to the circle and placed them on the ground before him. He sat down again.

"I have brought gifts to my brothers, the Kiowa," he said. "In appreciation of the honor they show me when they allow me to sit in their council."

He placed the whisky bottles in front of the chief and opened the little box. It was filled with gaily colored beads and trinkets. He held the box so that all could see and then placed it, too, before the chief.

The chief nodded again. "The Kiowa is grateful for the gifts of Red Beard. But the loss of the maiden Kaneha will be a difficult one for her tribe to bear. Already she has won her place among us by her skills in her womanly crafts. Her cooking and sewing, her artistry in leather-making."

"I am aware of the high regard in which the Kiowa hold their daughter Kaneha," Sam said formally. "And I came prepared to compensate them for their loss."

He got to his feet again. "For the loss of her aid in feeding the tribe, I pledge the meat of two buffalo," he said, looking down at them. "For the loss of her labor, I give to my brothers this mule which I have brought with me. And to compensate them for the loss of her beauty, I bring them—"

He paused dramatically and walked back to his mule. Silently he untied the heavy rolled pack on its back. He carried the pack back to the seated council and laid it on the ground before them. Slowly he unrolled it.

A sigh of awe came unbidden from the circle. The chief's eyes glittered.

". . . the hide of the sacred white buffalo," Sam said. He looked around the circle. Their eyes were fixed on the beautiful white skin that shone before them like snow on the ground.

The albino buffalo was a rarity. The chief that could be laid to rest on such a sacred hide was assured that his spirit would enter the happy hunting grounds. To the skin-traders, it might be worth almost as much as ten ordinary hides. But Sam knew what he wanted.

He wanted a woman. For five years, he had lived on these plains and had been able only to share the services of a whore once a year at trading time in the small room back of the skin-trader's post. It was time he had a woman of his own.

The chief, so impressed with the munificence of Sam's offer that he forgot to bargain further, looked up. "It is with honor that we give the mighty hunter Red Beard the woman Kaneha to be his squaw."

He rose to his feet as a sign that the council was over.

"Prepare my daughter Kaneha for her husband," he said. He turned and walked toward his tent and Sam followed him.

In another tent, Kaneha sat waiting. Somehow, she had known that Red Beard had come for her. In keeping with maidenly modesty, she had gone into the waiting tent so that she might not hear the bargaining. She sat there calmly, for she was not afraid of Red Beard. She had looked into his face many times when he had come to visit her father.

Now there was the sound of babbling women coming toward the tent. She looked toward the flap. The bargaining was over. She only hoped that Red Beard had at least offered one buffalo for her. The women burst into the tent. They were all talking at once. No bride had ever brought greater gifts. The mule. Beads. Whisky. The hide of a sacred white buffalo. Two buffalo for meat.

Kaneha smiled proudly to herself. In that moment, she knew that Red Beard loved her. From outside the tent came the sound of the drums beginning to beat out the song of marriage. The women gathered in a circle around her, their feet stamping in time to the drums.

She dropped her shift to the ground and the women came close. One on each side of her began to unplait the long braid that hung past her shoulders. Two others began to cover her body with grease from the bear, which was to make her fertile. At last, all was done and they stepped back.

She stood there naked in the center of the tent, facing the flap. Her body shone with the grease and she was straight and tall, her breasts high and her stomach flat, her legs straight and long.

The flap opened and the medicine man entered. In one hand he carried the devil wand, in the other the marriage stick. He shook the devil wand in the four corners of the tent and sprang twice into the air to make sure there were no devils hovering over them, then he advanced toward her. He held the marriage stick over her head.

She looked up at it. It was made of highly polished wood, carved into the shape of an erect phallus and testes. Slowly he lowered it until it rested on her forehead. She closed her eyes because it was not seemly for a maiden to look so deeply into the source of a warrior's strength.

The medicine man began to dance around her, springing high into the air and mumbling incantations over her. He pressed the stick to her breasts, to her stomach, to her back and buttocks, to her cheeks and to her eyes, until now it was covered with the bear grease from her body. Finally, he leaped into the air with a horrible shriek and when his feet touched the earth again, everything was silent, even the drums.

As in a trance, she took the marriage stick from the medicine man. Silently she held it to her face, then her breasts, then her stomach.

The drums began again, beating slowly. In time with their rhythm, she lowered the stick between her legs. Her feet began to move in time to the drums, slowly at first, then faster as the drums picked up tempo. Her long black hair, which hung to her buttocks, began to flare out wildly as she began to move around the circle of women, holding out the marriage stick for their blessing and cries of envy.

The circle completed, she once more stood alone in its center, her feet moving in time with the drums. Holding the marriage stick between her legs, she began to crouch slightly, lowering herself onto it.

"Ai-ee," the women sighed as they swayed to the tempo of the drums.

"Ai-ee," they sighed again in approbation as she lifted herself from the stick. It was not seemly for a maiden to be too eager to swallow up her husband.

Now they held their breath as once more the stick began to enter her. Each was reminded of her own marriage, when she, too, had looked up at the circle of women, her eyes pleading for help. But none dared move forward. This the bride must do for herself.

Through Kaneha's pain, the drums began to throb. Her lips grew tight together. This was her husband, Red Beard, the mighty hunter. She must not disgrace him here in the tent of women. When he himself came into her, instead of his spirit, the way for him must be easy and quick.

She closed her eyes and made a sudden convulsive movement. The hymen ruptured and she staggered as a wave of pain washed over her. The drums were wilder now. Slowly she straightened up and removed the marriage stick. She held it out proudly toward the medicine man.

He took it and quickly left the tent. Silently the women formed a circle around her. Naked, in its center so she would be shielded from other eyes, she walked to the tent of the chief.

The women stood aside as she entered. In the dim light, the chief and Sam looked up at her. She stood there proudly, her head raised, her eyes respectfully looking over their heads. Her breasts heaved and her legs trembled slightly. She prayed that Red Beard would be pleased with what he saw.

The chief spoke first, as was the custom. "See how profusely she bleeds," he said. "She will bear you many sons."

"Aye, she will bear me many sons," Sam said, his eyes on her face. "And because I am pleased with her, I pledge my brothers the meat of an additional buffalo."

Kaneha smiled quickly and left the tent to go down to the river to bathe. Her prayers had been answered. Red Beard was pleased with her.

Now she moved heavily, swollen with his child, as he sat at the table wondering why the buffalo didn't come. Something inside him told him they would never come again. Too many had been slain in the last few years.

At last, he looked up from the table. "Git the gear together," he said. "We're moving out of here."

Kaneha nodded and obediently began to gather up the household things while he went out and hitched the mules to the cart. Finished, he came back to the cabin.

Kaneha picked up the first bundle and started for the door when the pain seized her. The bundle fell from her hands and she doubled over. She looked up at him, her eyes filled with meaning.

"You mean now?" Sam asked, almost incredulously.

She nodded.

"Here, let me help you."

She straightened up, the seizure leaving her. "No," she said firmly in Kiowa. "This is for a woman, not for a brave."

Sam nodded. He walked to the door. "I'll be outside."

It was two o'clock in the morning when he first heard the cry of a baby from inside the cabin. He had been half dozing and the sound brought him awake into a night filled with stars. He sat there tensely, listening.

About twenty minutes passed, then the door of the cabin opened and Kaneha stood there. He struggled to his feet and went into the cabin.

In the corner on a blanket in front of the fire lay the naked baby. Sam stood there, looking down.

"A son," Kaneha said proudly.

"Well, I'll be damned." Sam touched it and the baby squalled, opening its eyes. "A son," Sam said. "How about that?" He bent over, looking closely.

His beard tickled the baby and it screamed again. Its skin was white and the eyes were blue like the father's, but the hair was black and heavy on his little head.

The next morning they left the cabin.

3

THEY SETTLED DOWN ABOUT TWENTY MILES OUT-side of Dodge City and Sam started to haul freight for the stage lines. Being the only man in the area with mules, he found himself in a fairly successful business.

They lived in a small cabin and it was there Max began to

grow up. Kaneha was very happy with her son. Occasionally, she would wonder why the spirits had not given her more children but she did not worry about it. Because she was Indian, they kept to themselves.

Sam liked it that way, too. Basically, he was a very shy man and his years alone on the plains had not helped cure his shyness. He developed a reputation in the town for being taciturn and stingy. There were rumors floating around that actually he had a hoard of gold cached out on his place from the years he was a buffalo-hunter.

By the time Max was eleven years old, he was as lithe and quick on his feet as his Indian forebears. He could ride any horse he chose without a saddle and could shoot the eye out of a prairie gopher at a hundred yards with his .22. His black hair hung straight and long, Indian fashion, and his eyes were dark blue, almost black in his tanned face.

They were seated at the table one night, eating supper, when Sam looked over at his son. "They're startin' up a school in Dodge," he said.

Max looked up at his father as Kaneha came to the table from the stove. He didn't know whether he was supposed to speak or not. He kept eating silently.

"I signed you up for it," Sam said. "I paid ten dollars."

Now Max felt it was time for him to speak. "What fer?"

"To have them learn you to read an' write," his father answered.

"What do I have to know that fer?" Max asked.

"A man should know them things," Sam said.

"You don't," Max said with the peculiar logic of children. "And it don't bother you none."

"Times is different now," Sam said. "When I was a boy, there warn't no need for such things. Now ever'thing is readin' or writin'."

"I don't want to go."

"You're goin'," Sam said, roaring suddenly. "I already made arrangements. You can sleep in the back of Olsen's Livery Stable durin' the week."

Kaneha wasn't quite sure she understood what her husband was saying. "What is this?" she asked in Kiowa.

Sam answered in the same language. "A source of big knowledge. Without it, our son can never be a great chief among the White Eyes."

This was enough reason for Kaneha. "He will go," she said simply. Big knowledge meant big medicine. She went back to her stove.

The next Monday, Sam brought Max over to the school. The teacher, an impoverished Southern lady, came to the door and smiled at Sam.

"Good morning, Mr. Sand," she said.

"Good mornin', ma'am. I brought my son to school."

The teacher looked at him, then at Max, then around the yard in front of the school cabin. "Where is he?" she asked in a puzzled voice.

Sam pushed Max forward. Max stumbled slightly and looked up at the teacher. "Say howdy to yer teacher," Sam said.

Max, uncomfortable in his clean buckskin shirt and leggings, dug his bare feet into the dirt and spoke shyly. "Howdy, ma'am."

The teacher looked down at him in stunned surprise. Her nose wrinkled up in disgust. "Why, he's an Indian!" she cried. "We don't take Indians in this school."

Sam stared at her. "He's my son, ma'am."

The teacher curled her lip cuttingly. "We don't take half-breeds in this school, either. This school is for white children only." She began to turn her back.

Sam's voice stopped her. It was icy cold as he made probably the longest speech he ever made in his life. "I don't know nothin' about your religion, ma'am, nor do I mind how you believe. All I do know is you're two thousand miles from Virginia an' you took my ten dollars to teach my boy the same as you took the money from ever'body else at the meetin' in the general store. If you're not goin' to learn him the way you agreed, you better take the next stage back East."

The teacher stared at him indignantly. "Mr. Sand, how dare you talk to me like that? Do you think the parents of the other children would want them to attend school with your son?"

"They were all at that meetin'," Sam said. "I didn't hear none of them say no."

The teacher looked at him. Sam could see the fight go out of her. "I'll never understand you Westerners," she said helplessly.

She looked down at Max disapprovingly. "At any rate, we can't have him in school in those clothes. He'll have to wear proper clothes like the other children."

"Yes, ma'am," Sam said. He turned to Max. "Come on," he said. "We're goin' to the store to get you regular clothes."

"While you're at it," she said, "get him a haircut. That way, he won't seem any different from the others."

Sam nodded. He knew what she meant. "I will, ma'am," he said. "Thank you, ma'am."

Max trotted along beside him as they strode down toward the general store. He looked up at his father. It was the first time he had thought about it. "Am I different than the others, Pa?"

Sam looked down at him. It was the first time he'd thought about it, too. A sudden sadness came into him. He knelt down in the dust of the street beside his son. He spoke with the sudden knowledge that came from living off the earth.

"Of course you're different," he said, looking into Max's eyes. "Everybody in this world is different, like there are no two buffalo alike or no two mules. Everybody is alike an' yet everybody is different."

By the end of Max's first year in school, the teacher was very proud of him. Much to her surprise, he had turned out to be her best pupil. His mind was quick and bright and he learned easily. When the term ended, she made sure to get Sam's promise that his son would return in the fall.

When the school closed down for the summer, Max brought his clothing back from Olsens' and settled down. During that first week, he was kept busy repairing all the damage done to the cabin by the winter.

One evening, after Max had gone to bed, Kaneha turned to her husband. "Sam," she said in English.

Sam almost dropped the leather harness on which he had been working. It was the first time in all their years together that she had called him by name.

Kaneha felt the blood rush into her face. She wondered at her temerity. Squaws never spoke to their husband except in reply. She looked down at the floor in front of her. "It is true that our son has done well in the school of the White Eyes?"

She could feel his gaze boring into her. "It's true," she heard his voice reply.

"I am proud of our son," she said, lapsing into Kiowa. "And

I am grateful to his father, who is a mighty hunter and great provider."

"Yes?" Sam asked, still watching.

"While it is true that our son learns many things in the school of the White Eyes that make mighty medicine, there are things also that he learns that disturb him greatly."

"Such as?" Sam asked gently.

She looked up into his face proudly. "There are some among the White Eyes who say to our son that he is less than they, that his blood does not run red like theirs."

Sam's lips tightened. He wondered how she would know this. She never came into town, she never left the place. He felt a vague guilt stir inside him. "They are stupid children," he said.

"I know," she said simply.

He reached out his hand and touched her cheek gratefully. She caught his hand and held it to her cheek. "I think it is time we send our son to the tents of the mighty chief, his grandfather, so that he may learn the true strength of his blood."

Sam looked into her face. In many ways, it was a wise suggestion. In one summer with the Kiowa, Max would learn all the things he needed to survive in this land. He would also learn that he came from a family that could trace its blood further back than any of the jackals who tormented him. He nodded. "I will take our son to the tents of my brothers, the Kiowa," he said.

He looked at her again. He was now fifty-two and she was little more than half his age. She was still straight and slim and strong; she had never run to fat the way Indian women usually did. He felt his heart begin to swell inside him.

He let the harness drop from his hand and he drew her head down to his chest. His hand stroked her hair gently. Suddenly he knew what he had felt deep inside him all these years. He turned her face up to him. "I love you, Kaneha," he said.

Her eyes were dark and filled with tears. "I love you, my husband."

And for the first time, he kissed her on the mouth.

4

IT WAS ABOUT TWO O'CLOCK ON A SATURDAY AF-
ternoon three summers later when Max stood on a wagon in
the yard back of Olsen's Livery Stable, pitching hay up into the
open loft over his head. He was naked above his buckskin
breeches and his body was burnt a coppery black by the blazing
sun that hung overhead. The muscles rippled easily in his back
as he forked the hay up from the wagon.

The three men came riding into the yard and pulled their
horses up near the wagon. They did not dismount but sat there,
looking at him.

Max did not interrupt his work and after a moment, one of
them spoke. "Hey, Injun," he said. "Where is the Sand boy?"

Max threw another forkful into the loft. Then he sank the
pitchfork into the hay and looked down at them. "I'm Max
Sand," he said easily, resting on the fork handle.

The men exchanged meaningful looks. "We're lookin' fer
yer pappy," the man who had spoken before said.

Max stared at them without answering. His blue eyes were
dark and unreadable.

"We were over at the stage line but the place was closed.
There was a sign there that said your pappy hauled freight."

"That's right," Max said. "But this is Saturday afternoon an'
he's gone home."

One of the others pushed forward. "We got a wagonload of
freight we got to get over to Virginia City," he said. "We're in a
hurry. We'd like to talk to him."

Max picked up the pitchfork again. He tossed another forkful of hay into the loft. "I'll tell him when I get home tonight."

"We cain't wait that long," the first man said. "We want to
make the deal and get on out of here tonight. How do we find
your place?"

Max looked at them curiously. They didn't look like settlers
or miners or the usual run of people that had freight for his father to haul. They looked more like gunmen or drifters, the

way they sat there with their guns tied low on their legs, their hats shading their faces.

"I'll be th'ough here in a couple of hours," Max said. "I'll take you out there."

"I said we was in a hurry, boy. Your pappy won't like it none if he hears we gave our load to somebody else."

Max shrugged his shoulders. "Follow the north road out about twenty miles."

Without another word the three turned their horses around and began to ride out of the yard. Their voices floated back on the lazy breeze.

"Yuh'd think with all the dough ol' Sand's got buried, he'd do better than bein' a squaw man," one of them said.

Max heard the others laugh as he angrily pitched hay up into the loft.

It was Kaneha who heard them first. Her ears were turned to the road every Saturday afternoon for it was then that Max came home from school. She went to the door and opened it. "Three men come," she said, looking out.

Sam got up from the table and walked behind her and looked out. "Yeah," he said, "I wonder what they want."

Kaneha had a premonition of danger. "Bolt the door and do not let them enter," she said. "They ride silently like Apache on the warpath, not open like honest men."

Sam laughed. "You're just not used to seein' people," he said. "They're probably jus' lookin' for the way to town."

"They come from the direction of town," Kaneha said. But it was too late. He was already outside the door.

"Howdy," he called as they pulled their horses up in front of the cabin.

"You Sam Sand?" the one in the lead asked.

Sam nodded. "That's me. Whut kin I do for you gents?"

"We got a load we want hauled up to Virginia City," the man said. He took off his hat and wiped his face on his sleeve. "It's pow'ful hot today."

"It shore is," Sam nodded. "Come on inside and cool off a bit while we talk about it."

The men dismounted and Sam walked into the cabin.

"Fetch a bottle of whisky," he said to Kaneha. He turned back to the men. "Set yourself down. What kind'a freight yuh got?"

"Gold."

"Gold?" Sam asked. "They ain't enough gold out heah to haul in a wagon."

"That ain't what we hear," one of the men said. Suddenly there were guns in their hands. "We hear you got enough gold buried out heah to fill up a wagon."

Sam stared at them for a moment, then he laughed. "Put your guns away, gents," he said. "Yuh don' believe that crazy yarn, do yuh?"

The first man came slowly toward him. His arm flashed and the gun whipped across Sam's face. Sam fell backward against the wall. He stared up at the man incredulously.

"Yuh'll tell us where it is befo' we through," the man said tightly.

The air in the cabin was almost unbearably hot. The three men had drawn off into a corner and were whispering among themselves. Occasionally they would glance across the room at their captives.

Sam hung limply, tied to the support post in the center of the cabin. His head sagged down on his naked chest and the blood dropped down his face, matting on the graying red hair of his beard and chest. His eyes were swollen and almost closed, his nose broken and squashed against his cheek.

Kaneha was tied in a chair. Her eyes were fixed unblinkingly on her husband. She strained to turn her head to hear what the men were saying behind her but she could not move, she was bound too tightly.

"Mebbe he ain't really got the gold," one of the men whispered.

"He's got it all right," the first one said. "He's jus' tough. Yuh don' know them ol' buffalo hunters like I do."

"Well, you ain't never goin' to make him talk the way yuh're goin'," the short man said. "He's gonna die first."

"He'll talk," the first man answered. He went to the stove and took a burning coal from it with a pair of fire tongs. He walked back to Sam and pulled his head back against the post by his hair. He held the tongs in front of Sam's face. "Wheah's the gold?"

Sam's eyes were open. His voice was a husky croak. "They ain't none. For God's sake wouldn't I tell yuh if they was?"

The man pressed the burning coal against Sam's neck and shoulder. Sam screamed in pain. "They ain't no gold!" His head fell sideways. The man withdrew the burning coal and the blood welled up beneath the scorched flesh and ran down his chest and arm.

The man picked up a bottle of whisky from the table and took a swig from it. "Th'ow some water on him," he said. "If'n he won't talk for hisself, mebbe he'll talk for his squaw."

The youngest man picked up a pail and threw water over Sam. Sam shook his head and opened his eyes. He stared at them.

The oldest man put the bottle down and walked over to Kaneha. He took a hunting knife from his belt. The other men's eyes followed him. He cut the rope that bound her to the chair. "On yer feet," he said harshly.

Silently Kaneha rose. The man's knife moved quickly behind her and her shift fell to the floor. She stood there naked before them. The youngest man licked his lips. He reached for the whisky and took a drink, his eyes never leaving her.

Holding Kaneha by the hair, his knife to her back, the oldest man pushed her over toward Sam. They stopped in front of him.

"It's been fifteen years since I skinned an Injun, squaw man," he said. "But I ain't fergot how." He moved swiftly around in front of her, his knife moving lightly up and down her skin.

A faint thin line of blood appeared where the knife had traced from under her chin down her throat through the valley between her breasts across her stomach and coming to a stop in the foliage of her pubis.

Sam began to cry, his own pain forgotten, his body wracked with bitter sobs. "Leave her be," he pleaded. "Please leave her be. They ain't no gold."

Kaneha reached out her hand. She touched her husband's face gently. "I am not afraid, my husband," she said in Kiowa. "The spirits will return evil to those who bring it."

Sam's face fell forward, the tears running down from his eyes across his bearded and bleeding cheeks. "I am sorry, my dear one," he said in Kiowa.

"Tie her hands to the legs of that table," the older man commanded.

It was done quickly and he knelt over her, his knife poised at her throat. He looked back up toward Sam. "The gold?" he asked.

Sam shook his head. He could not speak any more.

"My God," the youngest man said in a wondering voice. "I'm gittin' a hard on."

"That's an idee," the man with the knife said. He looked up at Sam. "I'm shoah the man wouldn' min' if'n we used his squaw a little bit before we skinned her. Injuns are downright hospitable that way."

He got to his feet. He put the knife on the table and unbuckled his gun belt.

Kaneha drew back her legs and kicked at him.

He swore softly. "Hold her laigs," he said. "I'll go first."

It was almost seven o'clock when Max rode up to the cabin on the bay horse that Olsen lent him. The cabin was still and there was no smoke coming from the chimney. That was strange. Usually, his mother would be cooking when he got home.

He swung down off the horse and started for the cabin. He stopped suddenly, staring at it. The door was open and moved lazily in the thin breeze. An inexplicable fear came into him and he broke into a run.

He burst through the door and came to a stop in surprised shock, his eyes widening in horror. His father hung tied to the center post, his mouth and eyes open in death, the back of his head blown away by the .45 that had been placed in his mouth and fired.

Slowly Max's eyes went down to the floor. There was a shapeless mass lying in a pool of blood, which bore the outline of what once had been his mother.

The paralysis left him at the same moment he started to scream, but the vomit that rose in his throat choked off the sound. Again and again he gagged until there was no more inside him. He clung weakly to the side of the door, the sour stench from his stomach all around.

He turned and staggered blindly out of the cabin. He sank to the ground outside and began to cry. After a while, his tears were gone. He rose to his feet wearily and walked around to the back of the house to the watering trough.

He plunged his head in and washed the vomit from his face and clothing. Then, still dripping, he straightened up and looked around.

His father's horse was gone but the six mules were browsing unconcernedly in the corral and the wagon was still under the lean-to in back of the cabin. The four sheep and the chickens of which his mother had been so proud were still in the pen.

He wiped his arms across his eyes. He had to do something, he thought vaguely. But he couldn't bring himself to bury what was in the cabin. They weren't his mother and father; his parents could never look like that. There was only one thing to do.

He walked over to the stack of firewood and gathered up an armful. Then he walked back into the house and put it down on the floor. It took him almost a half hour until firewood lay covering the floor like a blanket, three layers thick. He looked at it thoughtfully for a moment then turned and went outside again.

He took the harness down from the lean-to wall and hitched the mules up to the wagon. He picked up a crate and went through the pen, throwing all the chickens into it. He placed the crate in the wagon. Then one by one, he lifted the sheep into the wagon and tied them to the floor rings.

He led the team of mules and the wagon around to the front of the cabin and tied the bay horse's lead to the back of the wagon. Then he walked them all to the road about two hundred yards from the house and tethered the team to a small scrub tree and went back to the house.

He picked up the pitch bucket and went inside. Slowly he smeared the pitch over the firewood that lay on the floor. He kept his eyes down and away from the bodies of his parents. He stopped at the door and smeared the last of the pitch on that.

He hesitated a moment, then remembering something, he went back into the cabin. He reached up on the shelf where his father had kept his rifle and pistol but they were not there. He pushed his hand farther along the shelf and felt something soft. He took it down.

It was a new buckskin shirt and breeches his mother had made for him. It was bright and soft and clean-chamois colored. Again his eyes filled with sudden tears. He rolled it up under his arm and went back to the door.

He held a match to the pitch stick until it was blazing brightly. After holding it for a second more to make sure, he threw it into the cabin and stepped back from the open door.

He looked up at the sky in sudden surprise. The sun had just gone down and night had fallen in quick anger. The stars stared balefully down on him.

A cloud of heavy, billowing smoke poured out of the doorway. Suddenly, there was a crack like thunder and a flame leaped through the doorway as the tinder-dry wood caught fire.

He walked down to the road and got up on the wagon and began to drive to town. He did not look back until three miles later, when he reached the top of a small rise.

There was a bright-orange flame reaching high into the sky where his home had been.

5

HE DROVE THE WAGON INTO THE YARD BEHIND Olsen's Livery Stable. Then he got down and walked across to the house that stood next to it. He climbed up the back steps and knocked at the door.

"Mister Olsen," he called out.

A shadow darkened the light of the window. The door opened and Olsen stood there. "Max!" he said. "What you doin' back here?"

Max stared up into Olsen's face. "They killed my ma and pa," he said.

"Killed?" Olsen exclaimed in surprise. "Who killed?"

Attracted by the sound of her husband's voice, Mrs. Olsen appeared in the doorway behind him.

"The three men," Max said. "They asked me an' I gave them the directions to my house. An' they killed 'em." He hesitated a moment and his voice almost broke. "An' they stole Pa's hoss an' took his rifle an' pistol, too."

Mrs. Olsen saw into the shock that lay behind the boy's façade of calm. She pushed her husband out of the way and reached out to Max. "You come inside an' let me fix you somethin' hot to drink," she said.

He looked into her eyes. "They ain't time, ma'am," he said. "I got to be gettin' after them." He turned to Olsen. "I got the mules an' the wagon an' four sheep an' sixteen chickens outside in the yard. Would you give me a hundred dollars an' the pinto for 'em?"

Olsen nodded. "Why, sure, boy," he said. The mules and the wagon alone were worth three times that. "I'll even give you the big bay if you want. He's a better hoss. An' I'll throw in a saddle, too."

Max shook his head. "No, thank you, Mr. Olsen. I want a pony I can ride without a saddle an' one that's used to the plains. He won't have as much to tote an' I'll move faster that way."

"All right, if that's the way you want it."

"Can I have the money now?" Max asked.

"Sure, boy," Olsen answered. He turned back into the room.

Mrs. Olsen's voice stopped him. "Oh, no, you're not," she said. She drew Max into the house firmly. "First, he's goin' to eat something. Then he's goin' to sleep. Time enough in the morning for him to start."

"But they'll be further away by then," Max protested.

"No they won't," she said with woman's logic. "They got to stop to sleep, too. They won't be any further ahead of you then than they are right now."

She closed the door behind him and led him over to the table. She pushed him into a chair and placed a plate of soup in front of him. Automatically he began to eat.

"I'll go outside an' unhitch the team," Mr. Olsen said.

When he came back into the house, Max was sleeping, his head resting in his crossed arms on the table.

Mrs. Olsen gestured her husband to silence. "You just can't let him go after those men by himself," she whispered.

"I got to go, ma'am." Max's voice came over her shoulder.

She turned around and looked at him. "You can't," she cried out. "They're grown men an' they'll hurt you. Why, you're just a boy!"

He looked up into her face and she was aware for the first time of the pride that glowed deep in those dark-blue eyes. "They hurt me all they're goin' to, ma'am," he said. "I'm 'bout sixteen, an' with my mother's people, a boy ain't a boy no more once he's sixteen. He's a man."

On his second day out of Dodge, he slowed his pinto to a walk and studied the side of the road carefully. After a few minutes, he stopped and dismounted. He looked along the edge of the road carefully.

The four horses had stopped here. They had milled around for a little while and then two of them had gone back onto the road toward Virginia City. The other two had gone eastward across the plains.

He remounted and rode along the plains, his eyes searching out the trail until he found what he was looking for. One of the horses had been his father's. He recognized the shoe marking in the soft earth. It was lighter than the other marking, which meant he was not being ridden, but led. It also meant that the man up ahead must have been the leader, otherwise they wouldn't have let him take the horse, which was the most valuable thing they had stolen.

A few miles farther along the trail, he saw some horse droppings. He stopped his horse and jumped down. He kicked at the dung with his foot. It was not more than seven hours old. They had wasted more time along the trail than he'd thought they would. He got back on the pinto and pushed on.

He rode most of that night, following the trail in the bright moonlight. By the evening of the next day, he was less than an hour behind his quarry.

He looked up at the sky. It was about seven o'clock and would be dark soon. The man would be stopping to make camp if he hadn't already. Max got off his horse and waited for night to fall.

While he sat there, he cut a forked branch from a scrub tree and fitted a round stone onto it. Then he bound the stone to the crotch with thin strips of leather, winding them down the branch to make a handle. When he was finished, he had a war club as good as any he'd learned to make the summer he spent with the Kiowa.

It was dark then and he got to his feet, fastening the club to his belt. He took the horse by the halter and started forward cautiously on foot.

He walked slowly, his ears alert for any strange sound, his nostrils sniffing at the breeze for the scent of a campfire.

He was in luck, for he caught the scent of the campfire from about a quarter mile away. He tied the pinto to a bush and pulled the rifle from the pack on the horse's back. Silently he moved forward.

The whinny of a horse came to his ears and he dropped to the ground and peered forward. He figured the horses were tied about three hundred yards ahead of him. He looked for the campfire but couldn't find it.

Cautiously he made his way downwind from the horses in a wide circle. The smell of the campfire was strong in his nostrils now. He raised his head from the tall plain grass. The campfire was about two hundred yards in front of him. He could see the man, sitting hunched over it, eating from a frying pan. The man was no fool. He had picked a camp site between two rocks. That way, he could be approached only from in front.

Max sank back into the grass. He would have to wait until the man was asleep. He stretched out and looked up at the sky. When the moon was up, a few hours from now, it would be time for him to move. Until then, it would do no harm for him to rest. He closed his eyes. In a moment, he was sleeping soundly.

His eyes opened suddenly and he stared straight up at the moon. It hung white and high in the sky over him. He sat up slowly and peered over the grass.

The campfire was glowing faintly now, dying slowly. He could see the shadow of the man lying near the rocks. He started to inch forward. The man snored lightly and turned in his sleep. Max froze for a moment, then the figure was still again and Max inched forward a little farther. He could see the man's outstretched hand, a gun at the tip of the fingers.

He crawled around behind and picked up a small pebble from the ground beside him. Silently he took the war club from his belt and got up into a half crouch. Holding his breath in tightly, he threw the stone near the man's feet.

With a muttered curse, he sat up, looking forward, his gun in his hand. He never knew what hit him as Max brought the war club down on his head from behind.

Max came back with the pinto about the time that dawn was breaking in the east. He tied his horse to the scrub near the others and walked back to look at the man.

His eyes were still closed. He was breathing evenly though there was a smear of blood along his cheek and ear where the club had caught him. He lay naked on his back on the ground, his arms and legs outstretched tautly, staked to the ground.

Max sat down on the rock and began to whet his knife along its smooth surface. When the sun came up, the man opened his eyes. They were dull at first, then gradually they began to clear. He tried to sit up and became aware that he was tied down. He twisted his head and looked at Max.

"What's the idee?" he asked.

Max stared at him. He didn't stop whetting his knife. "I'm Max Sand," he said. "Remember me?"

Max walked over to him. He stood there looking down, the knife held loosely in his hand. There was a sick feeling inside him as he looked at the man and pictured what must have happened in the cabin. The image chased the feeling from him. When he spoke, his voice was calm and emotionless. "Why did you kill my folks?"

"I didn't do nothing to them," the man said, his eyes watching the knife.

"You got my pa's hoss out there."

"He sol' it to me," the man replied.

"Pa wouldn' sell the on'y hoss he had," Max said.

"Let me up outa here," the man screamed suddenly.

Max held the knife to the man's throat. "You want to tell me what happened?"

"The others did it!" the man screamed. "I had nothin' to do with it. They wanted the gold!" His eyes bugged out hysterically. In his fear, he began to urinate, the water trickling down his bare legs. "Le' me go, you crazy Injun bastard!" he screamed.

Max moved swiftly now. All the hesitation that he had felt was gone. He was the son of Red Beard and Kaneha and inside him was the terrible vengeance of the Indian. His knife flashed bright in the morning sun and when he straightened up the man was silent.

Max looked down impassively. The man had only fainted, even though his eyes stared upward, open and unseeing. His eyelids had been slit so they could never again be closed and the flesh hung like strips of ribbon down his body from his shoulders to his thighs.

Max turned and walked until he found an anthill. He scooped the top of it up in his hands and went back to the man. Carefully he set it down on the man's pubis. In a moment, the tiny red ants were everywhere on the man. They ran into all the blood-sweetened crevices of his body, up across his eyes and into his open mouth and nostrils.

The man began to cough and moan. His body stirred. Silently Max watched him. This was the Indian punishment for a thief, rapist and murderer.

It took the man three days to die. Three days of the blazing sun burning into his open eyes and blistering his torn flesh while the ants industriously foraged his body. Three days of screaming for water and three nights of agony as insects and mosquitoes, drawn by the scent of blood, came to feast upon him.

At the end, he was out of his mind, and on the fourth morning, when Max came down to look at him, he was dead. Max stared at him for a moment, then took out his knife and lifted his scalp.

He went back to the horses and mounted his pinto. Leading the other two animals, he turned and rode north toward the land of the Kiowa.

The old chief, his grandfather, came out of his tepee to watch him as he dismounted. He waited silently until Max came up to him.

Max looked into the eyes of the old man. "I come in sadness to the tents of my people," he said in Kiowa.

The chief did not speak.

"My father and mother are dead," he continued.

The chief still did not speak.

Max reached to his belt and took off the scalp that hung there. He threw it down in front of the chief. "I have taken the scalp of one of the murderers," he said. "And I come to the tent of my grandfather, the mighty chief, to spend the time of my sorrow."

The chief looked down at the scalp, then up at Max. "We are no longer free to roam the plains," he said. "We live on the land that the White Eyes allow us. Have any of them seen you as you approached?"

"None saw me," Max answered. "I came from the hills behind them."

The chief looked down at the scalp again. It had been a long time since the scalp of an enemy hung from the post before his tepee. His heart swelled with pride. He looked at Max. The White Eyes could imprison the bodies but they could not imprison the spirit. He picked up the scalp and hung it from the post then turned back to Max.

"A tree has many branches," he said slowly. "And when some branches fall or are cut down, other branches must be grown to take their place so their spirits may find where to live."

He took a feather from his headdress and held it toward Max. "There is a maiden whose brave was killed in a fall from his horse two suns ago. She had already taken the marriage stick and now must live alone in a tent by the river until his spirit is replaced in her. Go now and take her."

Max stared at him. "Now?" he asked.

The chief thrust the feather into his hand. "Now," he said, with the knowledge of all his years. "It is the best time, while the spirit of war and vengeance still rages like a torrent in your blood. It is the best time to take a woman."

Max turned and picked up the lead and walked down through the camp with the horses. The Indians watched him silently as he passed by. He walked slowly with his head held high. He reached the bank of the small river and followed it around a bend.

A single tent stood there, out of sight of the rest of the camp. Max walked toward it. He tied the horses to some shrubs and lifted the flap of the tent and walked in.

The tent was empty. He lifted the flap again and looked out. There was no one in sight. He let the flap down. He walked to the back of the tent and sat down on a bed of skins stretched out on the floor.

A moment later the girl came in. Her hair and body were wet from the river and her dress clung to her. Her eyes went wide as she saw him. She stood there poised for flight.

She wasn't much more than a child, Max saw. Fourteen, maybe fifteen at the most. Suddenly he knew why the chief had sent him down here. He picked up the feather and held it toward her. "Don't be afraid," he said gently. "The mighty chief has put us together so that we may drive the devils from each other."

6

ASTRIDE THE WIRY PINTO, MAX CAME DOWN THE ramp from the railroad car behind the last of the cattle. He waited a moment until the last steer had entered the stockyard and then dropped the gate behind it. He took off his hat and wiped the sweat from his forehead on his sleeve and looked up at the sun.

It hung almost overhead, white hot, baking into the late spring dust of the yards. The cattle lowed softly as if somehow they, too, knew they had come to the end of the road. The long road that led up from Texas, to a railroad that took them to Kansas City, and their impending doom.

Max put the hat back on his head and squinted down the fence to where the boss sat with the cattle-buyers. He rode down toward them.

Farrar turned as he stopped his horse beside them. "They all in?"

"They all in, Mr. Farrar," Max answered.

"Good," Farrar said. He turned to one of the cattle-buyers. "The count O.K.? Eleven hundred and ten head I make it."

"I make it the same," the buyer said.

Farrar got down from the fence. "I'll come over to your office this afternoon to pick up the check."

The buyer nodded. "It'll be ready."

Farrar got up on his horse. "C'mon, kid," he said over his shoulder. "Let's get over to the hotel and wash some of this steer-shit stink off'n us."

"Man," Farrar said, after a bath. "I feel twenty pounds lighter."

Max straightened up from putting on his boots and turned around. "Yeah," he said. "Me, too."

Farrar's eyes widened and he whistled. Max had on an almost white buckskin shirt and breeches. His high-heeled cowboy boots were polished to a mirror-like sheen and the kerchief around his throat was like a sparkle of yellow gold against his dark, sun-stained skin. His hair, almost blue black, hung long to his shoulders.

Farrar whistled again. "Man, where'd you get them clothes?"

Max smiled. "It was the last set my ma made for me."

Farrar laughed. "Well, you shore enough look Injun with them on."

Max smiled with him. "I am Indian," he said quietly.

Farrar's laughter disappeared quickly. "Half Indian, kid," he said. "Your pappy was white and he was a good man. I hunted with Sam Sand too many years to hear you not proud of him."

"I am proud of him, Mr. Farrar," Max said. "But I still remember it was white men killed him an' Ma."

He picked his gun belt up from the chair and strapped it on. Farrar watched him bend over to tie the holster to his thigh. "You still ain't give up lookin' for them?" he asked.

Max looked up. "No, sir, I ain't."

"Kansas City's a big place," Farrar said. "How you know you'll find him here?"

"If he's here, I'll find him," Max answered. "This is where he's supposed to be. Then I'll go down into West Texas an' get the other one."

Farrar was silent for a moment. "Well, dressed like that, you better look out he don't recognize you and find you first."

"I'm hopin' he does," Max said quietly. "I want him to know what he's dyin' for."

Farrar turned away from the bleak look in the boy's eyes and picked up a shirt. Max waited quietly for him to finish dressing. "I'll pick up my time now, Mr. Farrar," he said when the man had pulled on his trousers.

Farrar walked over to the dresser and picked up his poke. "There you are," he said. "Four months' pay—eighty dollars—an' the sixty dollars you won at poker."

Max put the money in a back pocket without counting it. "Thanks, Mr. Farrar."

"Sure I can't talk you into comin' back with me?" Farrar asked.

"No, thank you, Mr. Farrar."

"You can't keep all that hate in your soul, boy," the older man said. "It ain't healthy. You'll only wind up harmin' yourself."

"I can't help that, Mr. Farrar," Max said slowly. His eyes were empty and cold. "I can't ferget it's the same breast that fed me that bastard's usin' to keep his tobacco in."

The door closed behind him and Farrar stood there staring at it.

Mary Grady smiled at the boy. "Finish your whisky," she said, "while I get my dress off."

The boy watched her for a moment, then drank the whisky quickly. He coughed as he went over to the edge of the bed and sat down.

Mary looked over at him as she slipped the dress up over her head. "How are you feelin'?"

The boy looked at her. She could see the vagueness already in his eyes. "All ri', I guess," he answered. "I ain' used to drinkin' so much."

She came over and stood looking down at him, her dress over her arm. "Stretch out and shut your eyes. You'll be all right in a few minutes."

He looked up at her dumbly, without response.

She put out her hand and pushed his shoulder. A hint of awareness sparked in his eyes. He tried to get to his feet, his hand locked around the butt of his gun, but the effort was too much. He collapsed, falling sideways across the bed.

Expertly Mary bent over him and lifted his eyelid. The boy was out cold. She smiled to herself and crossing to the window, looked out into the street.

Her pimp was standing across the street in front of a saloon. She raised and lowered the shade twice in the agreed signal and he started toward the hotel.

She was dressed by the time he got up to the room. "You took long enough gettin' him up here," he said surlily.

"What could I do?" she said. "He wouldn't drink. He's just a kid."

"How much did he have on him?" the pimp asked.

"I don't know," Mary answered. "The money's in his back pocket. Get it an' let's get out of here. This hotel always gives me the creeps."

The pimp crossed to the bed and pulled the money out of the boy's back pocket. He counted it swiftly. "A hundred and thirty dollars," he said.

Mary went over to him and put her arms around him. "A

hundred and thirty dollars. Maybe we can take the night off now," she said, kissing his chin. "We could go over to my place and have a whole night together."

The pimp looked down at her. "What? Are you crazy?" he rasped. "It's only eleven o'clock. You can turn three more tricks tonight."

He turned to look down at the boy while she picked up her pocketbook. "Don't forget the bottle of whisky," he said over his shoulder.

"I won't," she answered.

"He don't look like no cowboy," he said. "He looks more like an Indian to me."

"He is," she said. "He was looking for some guy who had a tobacco pouch made from an Indian woman's skin." She laughed. "I don't think he even wanted to get laid. I got him up here by lettin' him think I knew who he was lookin' for."

The pimp looked down thoughtfully. "He's carryin' a gun, too. It should be worth somethin' to the guy he's lookin' for to know about him."

"You know who he's lookin' for?"

"Maybe," the pimp said. "C'mon."

It was almost two o'clock in the morning before the pimp found the man he was looking for. He was playing cards in the back of the Golden Eagle.

The pimp touched him on the shoulder cautiously. "Mr. Dort," he whispered.

"What the hell do you want?"

The pimp licked his lips nervously. "I'm sorry, Mr. Dort," he apologized quickly. "I got some information that I think you ought to have."

The pimp looked around the table nervously. The other men stared at him. "Maybe it's better private like, Mr. Dort," he said. "It's about that tobacco pouch."

He pointed to the table where it lay.

Dort laughed. "My Injun-tit tobacco pouch? Somebody's allus tryin' to buy it. It ain't for sale."

"It's not that, Mr. Dort," the pimp whispered.

Dort turned his back to him. "What the hell are you tryin' to tell me?"

"I figger it's worth somethin'—"

Dort rose swiftly. He grabbed the pimp's jacket and slammed him tightly against the wall. "What should I know?" he asked.

"It should be worth something, Mr. Dort," the pimp said, his eyes wide in fright. Dort was one of the worst killers in town.

"It'll be worth something," Dort said menacingly. "If you don't talk real quick—"

"There's an Indian kid in town lookin' for you," the pimp said in terror. "He's packin' a gun."

"An Injun kid?" Dort questioned. Slowly his grip relaxed. "What did he look like?"

Quickly the pimp described Max.

"His eyes, was they blue?" Dort asked harshly.

The pimp nodded. "Yeah. I saw them when he picked one of my girls up in the saloon. That's how come I didn't know he was Indian at first. You know him?"

Dort nodded without thinking. "I know him," he said. "That was his mother's."

All their eyes were on the tobacco pouch now. Dort picked it up and put it in his pocket.

"What're you goin' to do?" the pimp asked.

"Do?" Dort repeated dully. He looked at the pimp, then at the table of men around him. He couldn't run away now. If he did, everything would be gone. His reputation, his position in this oblique society.

"Do?" he said again, this time with growing strength and conviction. "I aim to do what I shoulda done a year ago. Kill him." He turned back to the pimp. "Where is he?"

"I'll take you to him," the pimp said eagerly.

The others at the table looked at each other for a moment, then silently got to their feet. "Wait for us, Tom," one of them called. "This oughta be some fun."

When they got to the hotel, Max had already left. But the hotel clerk told them where they could find him tomorrow. At the stockyards at two o'clock. The clerk was supposed to meet him there and collect a dollar for the room.

Dort threw a silver dollar on the counter. "There's your dollar," he said. "I'll collect it for you."

* * *

Farrar leaned against the fence, watching Max cut the prime steers into the feed pen. A man was leaning on the fence next to him. "That boy's got a sixth sense with a horse," Farrar said, without looking at him.

The man's voice was noncommittal. "Yeah." He finished rolling a cigarette and stuck it in his mouth. "Got a match?"

"Why, sure," Farrar said, reaching into his pocket. He struck a match and held it toward the man. His hand froze as he saw the tobacco pouch in his hand.

The man followed his gaze. "What you lookin' at?"

"That tobacco pouch," Farrar said. "I ain't seen nothin' like it."

The man laughed. "Ain't nothin' but an ol' squaw tit," he said. "They the best things for keepin' tobacco moist an' fresh. They ain't much for wear, though. This one's gettin' awful thin."

Suddenly, Farrar turned from the fence to signal Max. "I wouldn't do that if I were you," the man said.

There was a rustle of movement behind him and Farrar became aware of the other men. He watched helplessly as Max dropped the gate on the last of the steers and rode over to them.

Max got off his horse and tied it to a post. "All finished, Mr. Farrar," he said with a smile.

"That was good ridin', boy," the man said. He threw the tobacco pouch to Max. "Here, have yourself a smoke."

Max caught it easily. "Thanks, mister," he said. He looked down at the pouch to open it. He looked up at the man, then down at the pouch again, his face going pale.

The pouch fell from his fingers and the tobacco spilled onto the ground. He stared up at the man. "I never would've known you, you hadn't done that," he said softly.

Dort laughed harshly. "It's the beard, I reckon."

Max started to back away slowly. "You're one of them, all right. Now I recognize you."

"I'm one of them," Dort said, his hand hovering over his gun. "What're you goin' to do about it?"

Unconsciously Farrar and the others moved to the side. "Don't do anything, Max," Farrar called hoarsely. "That's Tom Dort. You got no idea how fast he is."

Max didn't take his eyes from Dort's face. "It don't make no difference how fast he is, Mr. Farrar," he said. "I'm goin' to kill him."

"Go for your gun, Injun," Dort said heavily.

"I'll wait," Max said softly. "I want you to die slow, like my ma."

Dort's face was turning red and flushed in the hot sun. "Draw," he said hoarsely. "Draw, you goddam half-breed son of a two-bit Injun whore. Draw, damn you!"

"I ain' in no hurry to kill you," Max answered softly. "I ain' even goin' for your head or heart. I'm goin' to shoot you in the balls first, then a couple of times in the belly. I wanna watch you die."

Dort began to feel fear growing in him. Out of the corner of his eye, he saw the watching men. He stared at Max. The boy's face shone with hatred; his lips were drawn back tightly across his teeth.

Now, Dort thought, now. I might just as well get it over with. His hand moved suddenly toward his gun.

Farrar saw the movement but fast as he shifted his eyes, it wasn't quick enough to see Max's gun leap into his hand. It roared almost before Dort's gun had cleared its holster.

The gun fell from Dort's hand and he sank to his knees in the dirt, his hands grabbing at his crotch.

Max started walking toward him slowly.

Dort kneeled there for a moment in almost a praying position, then lifted his hand and looked at it. The blood ran down from his fingers. He stared up at Max. "You son of a bitch!" he screamed and grabbed for the gun in the dirt beside him.

Max waited until Dort lifted the muzzle toward him, then he fired twice again.

The bullets threw Dort over backward and he lay on the ground, his body twitching slightly. Max walked closer and stood over him, looking down, the smoking gun still in his hand.

Two days later, Max was given his choice of joining the Army or standing trial. There was a lot of talk about a war with Cuba and the judge was very patriotic. The chances were Max could have got off on self-defense, but he didn't dare take the chance even with witnesses.

He had a date he had to keep, with a man whose name he didn't even know.

7

NEVADA STIRRED RESTLESSLY, WITH THE VAGUE feeling that someone else was in the room with him. Automatically he reached for a cigarette, and when his hand hit empty air and fell downward against the side of the couch, he came awake.

It was a moment before he remembered where he was, then he swung his legs off the couch and reached for his pants. The cigarettes were in the right-hand pocket. He put one in his mouth and struck a match.

The flame flared in the darkness and he saw Rina sitting in the deep chair, looking at him. He drew deeply on the cigarette and blew out the match. "Why ain't you sleeping?" he asked.

She took a deep breath. "I couldn't sleep," she said. "I'm afraid."

He looked at her quizzically. "Afraid, Rina? Afraid of what?"

She didn't move in the chair. "I'm afraid of what will happen to me."

He laughed quietly, reassuringly. "You're all set and you're young. You got your whole life in front of you."

Her face was a luminous shadow in the darkness. "I know," she whispered. "That's what I tell myself. But the trouble is I can't make myself believe it."

Suddenly, she was on her knees on the floor in front of him. "You've got to help me, Nevada!"

He reached out and stroked her hair. "Things take time, Rina," he said.

Her hands caught at his. "You don't understand, Nevada," she said harshly. "I've always felt like this. Before I married Cord, before I ever came out here. Even when I was a little girl."

"I reckon, sometime or other, everyone's afraid, Rina."

Her voice was still hoarse with terror. "But not like me! I'm different. I'm going to die young of some horrible disease. I know that, Nevada. I feel it inside."

Nevada sat there quietly, his hand absently stroking her head as she cried. "Things'll be different once you get back East," he said softly. "There'll be young men there an—"

She raised her hand and looked up at him. The first faint flicker of morning light illuminated her features. Her eyes were wide and shining with her tears. "Young men, Nevada?" she asked and her voice seemed to fill with scorn. "They're one of the things I'm afraid of. Don't you think if I weren't, I'd have married Jonas instead of his father?"

He didn't answer.

"Young men are all alike," she continued. "They only want one thing from me." Her lips drew back across her white teeth and she spat the words out at him. "To fuck! To do nothing but fuck, fuck, fuck!"

He stared at her, a kind of shock running through him at hearing her clear and venomously ladylike articulation of the so familiar word. Then it was gone and he smiled.

"What do you expect, Rina?" he asked. "Why are you tellin' me all this?"

Her eyes looked into his face. "Because I want you to know me," she said. "I want you to understand what I'm like. No man ever has."

The cigarette scorched his lips. He put it out quickly. "Why me?"

"Because you're not a boy." The answer came quickly. "You're a grown man."

"An' you, Rina?" he asked.

Her eyes became almost defiant but her voice betrayed her unsureness. "I think I'm a Lesbian."

He laughed.

"Don't laugh!" she said quickly. "It's not so crazy. I've been with girls and I've been with men. And I've never made it with a man, not with any man like I have with a girl." She laughed bitterly. "Men are such fools. It's so easy to make them believe what they want to. And I know all the tricks."

His male vanity was aroused. "Maybe that's because you ain't never come up against a real man."

A challenging note came into her voice. "Oh, no?" He felt her fingers lightly search his thighs beneath the blanket and find his phallus. Quickly she threw the blanket aside and pressed her head into his lap. He felt the movement of her lips, and suddenly he was angry.

He pulled her head back by the hair. "What're you tryin' to prove?" he asked harshly.

Her breath came hard and uneven. "That you're the man," she whispered. "The one man that can make me feel."

He stared at her, not answering.

"You are the one, Nevada," she whispered. "I know it. I can feel it down inside me. You can make me whole again. I'll never be afraid any more."

She turned her head again but his hand held her firm. Her eyes were wide and desperate. "Please, Nevada, please. Let me prove how I can love you!" She began to cry again.

Suddenly, he got to his feet and went over to the fireplace. He stirred the coals alive, fed them kindling and another log. A moment later, a crackling heat came sparkling into the room. He turned to look at her. She was still sitting on the floor in front of the couch, watching him.

Slowly he walked back toward her. "When I asked you up here, Rina, I thought I was doin' the right thing." He sat down and reached for a cigarette.

Before he could light it, she held a match for him. "Yes, Nevada?" she questioned softly.

The flame glowed in his eyes and died as the match went out. "I ain't the man you're lookin' for, Rina."

Her fingers touched lightly on his cheek. "No, Nevada," she said quickly. "That's not true."

"Mebbe not," he said and a slow smile came over his lips. "But I figger I'm too young. You see, all I want to do with you is—fuck, fuck, fuck!"

She stared at him for a moment and then she began to smile. She got up quickly and took the cigarette from his mouth. Her lips brushed fleetingly against his for a moment, then she walked to the fire and turned to face him. She put the cigarette between her lips and inhaled deeply.

Then she made a slight movement and the robe fell to the floor. The leaping fire turned her naked body into red gold. Swiftly she threw the cigarette into the fireplace behind her and started back toward him.

"Maybe it's better this way," she said, coming down into his outstretched arms. "Now we can be friends."

8

"THE SHOW'S IN TROUBLE," THE CASHIER SAID.

Nevada glanced at Rina. She was looking out the window of the ticket wagon, watching the last act of the Wild-West show going on in the arena. The faint sounds of the whooping and yelling drifted back to them on the still, warm air.

"How much trouble?" Nevada asked, his eyes coming back from her.

"Enough," the cashier said flatly. "We're booked in a week behind Buffalo Bill Cody's show for the whole summer. If these two weeks are any indication, we'll drop forty thousand this season."

A bugle sounding a charge hung in the air. Nevada shifted in his uncomfortable wooden chair and began to roll a cigarette. The performance was almost over now. The cavalry was coming to the rescue of the beleaguered pioneers. He stuck the cigarette in his mouth.

"How'd you let a stupid thing like that happen?" he asked, the cigarette dangling unlit from his lips.

"Wasn't my fault, Nevada," the cashier answered quickly. "I think the agent sold us out."

Nevada didn't answer. He lit the cigarette.

"What you going to do?" the cashier asked worriedly.

Nevada filled his lungs with smoke. "Play out the season."

"For forty grand?" The cashier's voice was shocked. "We can't afford to lose that much money!"

Nevada studied him. The cashier's face was flushed and embarrassed. He wondered why the man seemed so upset. It wasn't his money that was going to be lost.

"We can't afford not to," Nevada said. "We fold up, we lose all our top hands. They won't sign with us for next year if we dump 'em now."

Nevada got to his feet, walked over to the window and looked out. The Indians were riding out of the arena with the whooping cavalry hot after them. He turned back to the cashier. "I'm takin' Mrs. Cord down to the railroad station. I'll drop in at the agent's office after that. You wait for me here. I'll be back."

"O.K., Nevada," the cashier answered.

Nevada took Rina's arm as they went down the wagon steps. They cut across the field to his car. All around them hustled performers, hurrying their horses to the corral, racing to their wagons to change clothes, yelling to each other about their plans for the evening.

Rina turned to him as they reached the car. "Let me stay with you, Nevada, please."

He smiled slowly. "I thought we had that settled."

"But, Nevada." Her eyes grew serious. "There's nothing for me back East. Really. Here, at least, I can feel alive, excitement—"

"Stop actin' like a kid," he said. "You're a grown woman now. This ain't no life for you. You'd be sick of it in a week."

"I'll buy half your losses this season if you let me stay," she said quickly.

He looked at her sharply. He thought she hadn't even heard the conversation back in the wagon, she had seemed so engrossed in the show. "You can't afford it," he said.

"And you can?" she countered.

"Better'n you," he said quickly. "I got more'n just the one thing goin' for me."

She stared at him for a moment, then got into the car. She didn't speak until they were at the station and she was ready to board the train.

"You'll write me, Nevada?" she asked.

"I ain't much for writin'," he said.

"But you'll keep in touch?" she persisted. "You'll answer if I write you?"

He nodded.

"You'll let me come and visit you sometimes?" she asked. "If I'm lonely and frightened?"

"That's what friends're for," he said.

A hint of moisture came into her eyes. "You've been a good friend, Nevada," she said seriously.

She kissed him on the cheek and climbed up the steps of the Pullman car. At the door, she turned and waved brightly, then disappeared inside. He saw her face appear in the window for a moment as the train began to move. Then she was gone and he turned and walked out of the station.

He walked up a rickety flight of stairs that led into a dust-ridden corridor. The paint on the door was scratched and worn, the lettering simple and faded.

DANIEL PIERCE—BOOKING AGENT

The office lived up to the reputation of the corridor outside. A girl looked up at him from a littered desk. Her hair bore traces of its last henna rinse, the gum cracked in her mouth as she asked, almost hostilely, "What d'ya want?"

"Dan Pierce in?" he asked.

She studied Nevada for a moment, her eyes taking in his worn leather jacket, the faded Levi's, the wide-brimmed cowboy hat. "If you're lookin' for a job," she said, "there ain't any."

"I'm not lookin' for a job," he said quickly. "I'm lookin' for Mr. Pierce."

"You got an appointment?"

Nevada shook his head. "No."

"He don't see nobody without an appointment," she said brusquely.

"I'm from the Wild-West show," Nevada said. "He'll see me."

A spark of interest appeared on her face. "The Buffalo Bill show?"

Nevada shook his head. "No. The Great Southwest Rodeo."

"Oh." The interest vanished from her face. "The other one."

Nevada nodded. "Yeah, the other one."

"Well, he ain't here," she said.

"Where can I find him?" he asked.

"I don't know. He went out to a meeting."

Nevada's voice was insistent. "Where?"

Something in his eyes made her answer. "He went over to Norman Pictures. He's on the back lot trying to sell them some client for a Western."

"How do I get there?"

"It's out on Lankershim Boulevard, past Universal, past Warner's."

"Thanks," he said and walked out.

★ ★ ★

He saw the big billboard in front of Universal as soon as he turned onto Lankershim.

UNIVERSAL PICTURES
THE HOME OF TOM MIX AND TONY
SEE
RIDERS OF THE PURPLE SAGE
A UNIVERSAL PICTURE

A few minutes later, he passed another sign in front of Warner Bros.

WARNER BROS. PRESENT
MILTON SILLS
IN
THE SEA HAWK
A VITAGRAPH PICTURE

The Norman studio was about five miles farther down the road. The usual billboard was out in front.

BERNARD B. NORMAN PRODUCTIONS
PRESENT
THE SHERIFF OF PEACEFUL VILLAGE
WITH AN ALL-STAR CAST

He turned in at the big gate where a gateman stopped him.

"Is Dan Pierce here?" Nevada asked.

"Just a moment, I'll see." The guard went back into his booth and checked a sheet of paper. "You must be the man he's expecting," he said. "He's on the back lot. Follow the road there right out. You can't miss it."

Nevada thanked him and put the car into gear. He drove slowly, for the road was filled with people. Some were actors in varying costumes but most seemed ordinary working men, wearing overalls and work clothes. He rolled past some very large buildings and after a few minutes was out in the clear. Here there was nothing but scrub grass and hills.

He came to another sign as he reached the foot of the first hill.

PEACEFUL SET
PARK CARS HERE

He followed the arrow. Just off the side of the road were a number of cars and trucks. He pulled in next to one of them and got out.

"Dan Pierce up there?" Nevada asked a man sitting in one of the trucks.

"Is he with the *Peaceful* crew?" the driver asked.

"I reckon," Nevada said.

"They're just over the hill."

At the crest of the hill, Nevada paused and looked down. A little below was a knot of people.

"Roll 'em, they're coming!" a heavy voice shouted.

Suddenly a stagecoach came roaring along the dirt road below him. Just as it took the curve, Nevada saw the driver jump off and roll to the side of the road. A moment later, the horses broke free of their traces and the coach tilted off the side of the road and went tumbling down the hill.

The dust had scarcely subsided when a voice shouted, "Cut! Cut! God damn it, Russell. You jumped too soon. The stage didn't go over the hill for a full forty frames after you!"

The driver got up from the side of the road and walked slowly toward the group of men, dusting his jeans with his hat.

Nevada started down the hill. He searched the crowd for Pierce, but didn't see him anywhere.

A man walked past, carrying a can of film. "Is Dan Pierce around?" Nevada asked.

The man shrugged his shoulders. "I dunno. Ask him," he said, pointing at a young man wearing knickers.

"Is Dan Pierce around?"

The young man looked up. "He had to go up to the front office for a phone call."

"Thanks," Nevada said. "I'll wait for him." He began to roll a cigarette.

The stentorian voice was shouting again. "Is Pierce back with that goddam stunt man yet?"

"He went to phone him," the young man said. A startled look came to his face as he looked at Nevada again. "Wait a minute, sir," he yelled and started toward Nevada. "You the guy Pierce was expecting?"

"I guess so."

"Come with me," the young man said.

Nevada followed him into the group of men clustered around a tall man next to the camera.

The young man stopped in front of him. "This is the man Pierce was expecting, sir."

The man turned and looked at Nevada, then pointed at a cliff on the next hill. Below the cliff flowed a wide stream of water. "Could you jump a horse off that cliff into the water?"

Nevada followed the pointing finger. It was about a sixty-foot drop and the horse would have to leap out at least fifteen feet to land in the water.

"We have the stream dug twenty-five feet deep right there," the director said.

Nevada nodded. That was deep enough. "I reckon it can be done," he said.

The director broke into a smile. "Well, I'll be goddamned!" he roared. "We finally found us a man with balls." He clapped Nevada on the back. "You go over there and the wrangler will give you the horse. We'll be ready just as soon as we get this shot here."

He turned back to the cameraman. Nevada tapped him on the shoulder. "I said I reckon it can be done," he said. "I didn't say I'd do it."

The director stared at him curiously. "We're paying triple the stunt rate; isn't ninety dollars enough for you? O.K., I'll make it a hundred."

Nevada smiled. "You got me wrong. I came out here lookin' for Dan Pierce. I ain't no stunt-rider."

The director's mouth twisted contemptuously. "You cowboys are all alike. All talk and no guts."

Nevada stared at him for a minute. He felt the hard knot of anger tightening inside him. He was tired of this, of the runaround he'd been getting ever since Pierce's office. His voice went cold. "It'll cost you five hundred dollars for me to take a horse off that cliff."

The director stared at him, then broke into a smile. "You must've heard that every man in Hollywood turned that jump down."

Nevada didn't answer.

"O.K. Five hundred it is," the director said casually and turned back to the cameraman.

Nevada stood near the horse's head, feeding him an occasional lump of sugar. The horse nuzzled his hand. He patted the horse's neck. It was a good horse. The animal responded quickly and there wasn't a frightened bone in his body.

"We're about ready," the director said. "I've got cameras covering you from every angle, so you don't have to worry which way to look. You go when I give the signal."

Nevada nodded and mounted the horse. The director stood limned against the edge of the cliff, his hand raised in the air. Suddenly, his hand dropped and Nevada dug his spurs into the horse. The animal leaped forward in almost a full gallop. Nevada gave him his head and led him into the jump.

Nevada took him high and the horse started down, his legs stiff, braced for a short fall. Nevada felt the great beast's heart suddenly pound between his legs as his hoofs didn't meet the expected ground.

The animal writhed in sudden panic as it began to tumble forward. Quickly Nevada kicked free of the stirrups and threw himself over the horse's side. He saw the water rushing up toward him and hoped he had jumped far enough so that the horse didn't land on top of him.

He hit the water in a clean dive and let the momentum carry him deep. He felt an explosion in the water near him. That would be the horse. His lungs were burning but he stayed down as long as he could.

At last, he had to come up. It seemed like forever till he broke the surface, gasping. He turned his head and saw the horse floating on its side, its head twisted in a peculiar manner. There was a look of great agony in its eyes.

He turned and swam quickly toward the bank. Angrily he strode toward the director.

The director was smiling. "That was great. The greatest shot ever made!"

"That hoss's back is probably broke!" Nevada said. He turned and looked out at the horse again. The animal was struggling to keep its head above water. "Why don't somebody shoot the poor son of a bitch?" Nevada demanded.

"We already sent for the wrangler to bring a rifle. He's back on the other hill."

"That hoss'll be drowned before he gets here," Nevada snapped. "Hasn't anybody got a gun?"

"Sure, but nobody could hit him. A revolver's no good at that distance."

Nevada stared at the director. "Give me a gun."

Nevada took the gun and hefted it in his hand. He spun the cylinder. "These are blanks," he said. Someone gave him bullets. He reloaded the gun quickly and walked over to the side of the stream. He fired at a piece of wood in the water. The gun dragged a little to the left. He waited a moment until the horse raised its head again, then shot the animal between the eyes.

Nevada walked back and gave the director the gun. Silently the big man took it and held out a pack of cigarettes. Nevada took one and the director held the match for him. Nevada let the smoke fill his lungs.

A man came running up, gasping and short of breath. "I'm sorry, Mr. Von Elster," he said hoarsely. "I just can't locate that stunt man anywhere. But I'll get you another one tomorrow."

"Didn't anybody tell you? He showed up already, Pierce. We just made the shot."

Pierce stared at him. "How could he? I just left him back at—"

The director stepped to one side, revealing Nevada. "Here he is. See for yourself."

Pierce looked at Nevada, then at the director. "That's not the one. That's Nevada Smith. He owns the Great Southwest Rodeo and Wild-West Show." He turned back to Nevada and stuck his hand out. "Good to see you, Nevada." He smiled. "What brings you out here?"

Nevada glared at him. The anger bubbled up again inside him. He lashed out quickly and Pierce hit the ground in shocked surprise. He stared up at Nevada. "What's got into you, Nevada?"

"What I want to know is how much the Cody show got into you!"

Von Elster stepped between them. "I've been looking for someone like you a long time, Smith," he said. "Sell your show and come to work for us. I'll pay you two fifty a week to start."

Pierce's voice came up from the ground. "Oh, no you don't, Von Elster. A thousand a week or nothing!"

Nevada started to speak. "You shut up!" Dan Pierce told him authoritatively. "I'm your agent and don't you forget it!" He turned back to Von Elster. "This stunt will be all over Hollywood in an hour," he said. "I could take him down the line to Universal or Warner's. They'd snap him up like that."

Von Elster stared at the agent. "Five hundred," he snapped. "And that's my last offer."

Pierce grabbed Nevada's arm. "Come on, Nevada. We'll go over to Warner's. Every studio's looking for somebody to give Tom Mix a little competition."

"Seven fifty," Von Elster said.

"For six months, then a thousand a week and corresponding increases semiannually thereafter."

"It's a deal," Von Elster said. He shook hands with Pierce and then turned to Nevada. He smiled and held out his hand. "What did you say your name was?"

"Smith, Nevada Smith."

They shook hands. "And how old are you, young fellow?"

Pierce answered before Nevada could speak. "He's thirty, Mr. Von Elster."

Nevada started to open his mouth in protest but the pressure of Pierce's hand on his arm kept him silent.

"We'll make that twenty-nine for publicity." Von Elster smiled. "Now, you two come on with me down to the front office. I want to tell Norman we finally found the Sheriff of Peaceful Village!"

Nevada turned away to hide a smile. He wondered what the men down on the prison farm so many years ago would have said had they known he'd finally turned up wearing a badge. Even if it was only in the movies.

9

"MY GOD!" THE WARDEN HAD SAID WHEN THEY brought Max into his office. "What do they think they're doin' down there? This is a prison, not a reform school!"

"Don't let his looks fool you none, Warden," the tobacco-chewing deputy said, throwing the papers on the desk for the warden to sign. "He's a mean one, all right. He killed a man down in New Orleans."

The warden picked up the papers. "What's he up for? Murder?"

"Nope," the deputy replied. "Unlawful use of a weapon. He beat the murder rap—self-defense." He let go a wad into the spittoon. "This guy caught him in some fancy lady's bedroom."

"I was the lady's bodyguard, Warden," Max said.

The warden looked up at him shrewdly. "That didn't give you the right to kill a man."

"I had to, Warden," Max said. "He was comin' at me with a knife an' I had to defend myself. I had no clothes on."

"That's right, Warden." The deputy cackled lewdly. "Naked as a jaybird he was."

"Sounds like a genuine case of self-defense to me," the warden said. "How come they hang a bum one like this on him?"

"It was a cousin of the Darcys he croaked," the deputy said quickly.

"Oh," the warden said. That explained everything. The Darcys were pretty important people in New Orleans. "In that case, you're lucky you didn't get the book." He signed the papers and pushed them across the desk. "Here y'are, Deputy."

The deputy picked up the papers and unlocked Max's handcuffs. "So long, rooster."

The warden got to his feet heavily. "How old are you, boy?"

"'Bout nineteen, I reckon," Max answered.

"That's kinda young to be bodyguardin' one of them fancy women down in New Orleans," the warden said. "How'd you come to that?"

"I needed a job when I got out of the Army," Max answered. "An' she wanted someone who was fast with a gun. I was fast enough, I reckon."

"Too fast," the warden said. He walked around the desk. "I'm a fair man but I don't hold with no trouble-makers. You-all just get up every mornin', do your work like you're tol' an' you'll have no trouble with me."

"I understand, Warden," Max said.

The warden walked to the door of his office. "Mike!" he roared.

A giant Negro trusty stuck his head in the door. "Yassuh, Warden."

"Take this new man out and give him ten lashes."

The surprise showed on Max's face.

"There's nothin' personal in it," the warden said quickly. "An ounce of prevention, I always say. It kinda sticks in your mind if you ever think about makin' any trouble." He walked back around his desk.

"C'mon, boy," the Negro said.

The door closed behind them and they started down the corridor. The trusty's voice was warm and comforting. "Don' you worry none about them lashes, boy," he said. "I knocks you out with the first one an' you never feels the other nine!"

Max had reached New Orleans about Mardi Gras time early that year. The streets were filled with laughing, shoving people and somehow he absorbed the warmth of their mood. Something about the whole town got inside him and he decided to stay over a day or two before riding on to West Texas.

He put his horse in a livery stable, checked into a small hotel and went down into the Latin Quarter, looking for excitement.

Six hours later, he threw down a pair of tens to three sevens and that was that. He had lost his money, his horse, everything but the clothes on his back. He pushed his chair back and got to his feet.

"That cleans me, gents," he said. "I'll go roun' to the stable an' fetch my hoss."

One of the gamblers looked up at him. "May I be so bold as to inquire, suh, what you intend to do after that?" he asked in his soft Southern accent.

Max shrugged and grinned. "I dunno. Get a job, I reckon."

"What kind of job?"

"Any kind. I'm pretty good with hosses. Punch cattle. Anything."

The gambler gestured at Max's gun. "Any good with that?"

"Some."

The gambler got to his feet casually. "Lady Luck wasn't very kind to you tonight."

"You didn' help her much," Max said.

The gambler's hand streaked toward his coat. He froze, staring into the muzzle of Max's gun. It had come out so fast that he hadn't even sensed the motion.

"A man can get killed doin' foolish things like that," Max said softly.

The gambler's face relaxed into a smile. "You are good," he said respectfully.

Max slipped his gun back into the holster. "I think I've got a job for you," the gambler said. "That is if you don't mind working for a lady."

"A job's a job," Max said. "This ain't no time to be gettin' choosy."

The next morning, Max and the gambler sat in the parlor of the fanciest house in New Orleans. A Creole maid came into the room. "Miss Pluvier will see you now." She curtsied. "If you will please follow me."

They followed her up a long, gracious staircase. The maid opened a door and curtsied as they walked through, then closed the door after them. Max took two steps into the room and stopped in his tracks, gawking.

He had never seen a room like this. Everything was white. The silk-covered walls, the drapes at the windows, the wood-work, the furniture, the canopy of shimmering silk over the bed. Even the carpet that spread lushly over the floor was white.

"Is this the young man?" a soft voice asked.

Max turned in the direction of the voice. The woman surprised him even more than the room. She was tall, almost as tall as he was, and her face was young, very young; but her hair was what did it more than anything else. It was long, almost to her waist, and white, blue-white like strands of glistening satin.

The gambler spoke in a respectful voice. "Miss Pluvier, may I present Max Sand."

Miss Pluvier studied Max for a moment. "How do you do?" Max nodded his head. "Ma'am."

Miss Pluvier walked around him, looking at him from all angles. "He seems rather young," she said doubtfully.

"He's extremely capable, I assure you," the gambler said. "He's a veteran of the recent war with Spain."

She raised her hand carelessly, interrupting his speech. "I'm sure his qualifications are satisfactory if you recommend him," she said. "But he does seem rather dirty."

"I just rode in from Florida, ma'am," Max said, finding his voice.

"His figure is rather good, though." She continued as if he hadn't spoken. She walked around him again. "Very broad shoulders, almost no hips at all. He should wear clothes well. I think he'll do."

She walked back to the dressing table where she had been standing. She turned to face them. "Young man," she asked, "do you know what you're supposed to do?"

Max shook his head. "No, ma'am."

"You're to be my bodyguard," she said matter-of-factly. "I have a rather large establishment here. Downstairs, we have several gaming rooms for gentlemen. Of course, we provide other discreet entertainments. Our house enjoys the highest reputation in the South and as a result, many people are envious of us. Sometimes, these people go to extremes in their desire to cause trouble. My friends have persuaded me to seek protection."

"I see, ma'am," Max said.

Her voice became more businesslike. "My hours will be your hours," she said, "and you will live here with us. Your wages will be a hundred dollars a month. Twenty dollars a month will be deducted for room and board. And under no circumstances are you to have anything to do with any of the young ladies who reside here."

Max nodded. "Yes, ma'am."

Miss Pluvier smiled. She turned to the gambler. "Now, if you will be kind enough to take him to your tailor and have six suits made for him—three white and three black—I think everything will be in order."

The gambler smiled. "I'll attend to it right away."

Max followed him. At the door, he stopped and looked back. She was seated at the dressing table in front of the mirror, brushing her hair. Her eyes glanced up and caught his. "Thank you, ma'am," he said.

"Please call me Miss Pluvier," she said coldly.

It was after three o'clock one morning when Max came into the foyer from the gaming rooms on his nightly tour of inspection. Already, the cleaning women were busy in the downstairs rooms. He paused at the front door.

"Everythin' locked up, Jacob?" he asked the tall Negro doorman.

"Tighter'n a drum, Mistuh Sand."

"Good," Max smiled as he started for the staircase, then stopped and looked back. "Did Mr. Darcy leave?"

"No, suh," the Negro replied. "He spendin' the night with Miss Eleanor. You don' have to worry, though. I move 'em to the gol' room."

Max nodded and started up the staircase. Darcy had been his only problem the last few months. The young man was determined not to be satisfied until he had spent a night with the mistress of the house. And tonight he had been rather unpleasant about it.

Max stopped at the top of the stairway. He knocked at a door and went in. His employer was seated at her dressing table, a maid brushing her hair. Her eyes met his in the mirror.

"Everythin's locked up, Miss Pluvier," he said.

Her eyebrows raised questioningly. "Darcy?"

"In the gold room with Eleanor at the other end of the house."

"*Bon.*" She nodded.

Max stood there looking at her, his face troubled. She saw his expression in the mirror and waved the maid from the room. "You are disturbed, *chéri?*"

He nodded. "It's Darcy," he admitted. "I don't like the way he's actin'. I think we ought to bar him."

"La." She laughed. "We can't do that. The family is too important."

She laughed again happily and came toward him. She placed her arms around his neck and kissed him. "My young *Indien* is jealous." She smiled. "Do not worry about him. He will forget about it soon. All young men do. I have seen it happen before."

A little while later, he lay beside her on the big white bed, his eyes delighting in the wonder of her lovely body. He felt her fingers stroking him gently, reawakening the fires inside him. He closed his eyes.

He felt her soft lips brushing his flesh; her whispering voice seemed to float upward to him. *"Mon coeur, mon indien, mon chéri."* He heard the soft sounds of her pleasure as she raised her lips from him. Through his almost closed lids he could see the blurred sensuality of her face.

"The weapon you carry has turned into a cannon," she murmured, her fingers still stroking him gently.

His hand reached out and stroked her hair. An expression of

almost frightened ecstasy came into her face and he closed his eyes. He could feel the trembling begin deep inside him. How could a woman know so much? From what deep spring could such a fountain of pleasure come? He caught his breath. It was almost unbearable, this strange delight. It was like nothing he had ever known.

There was a soft sound at the door. He turned his head slightly, wondering what it could be. Suddenly, the door burst open and Darcy was there in the room.

He felt her roll away from him as he sat up; then her voice from the foot of the bed: "Get out of here, you damned idiot!"

Darcy stared at her stupidly. He weaved slightly, his eyes bewildered. His hand came out of his pocket and a shower of bills fell to the floor. "See, I brought a thousand dollars with me," he said drunkenly.

She got out of the bed. She stormed toward him regally, unaware of her nudity. She raised a hand, pointing to the door. "Get out, I said!"

Darcy just stood there staring at her. "My God," he mumbled huskily. "I want you."

Max finally found his voice. "You heard Miss Pluvier," he said. "Get out."

For the first time, Darcy became aware of him. His face began to flush with anger. "You," he said thickly. "You! All the time I was begging, pleading, it was you. You were laughing at me all the time!"

A knife appeared in his hand suddenly. He thrust quickly and Max rolled off the bed to the floor as the knife stabbed the satin sheets. Max snatched a pillow from the bed and held it in front of him as he backed toward the chair from which his gun hung.

Darcy's eyes were glazed with rage. "You were laughing all the time," he mumbled. "Every time you did it you were laughing at me."

"You better get out of here before you get hurt," Max said.

Darcy shook his head. "And have you laugh at me some more? Oh, no. This time I'm going to do the laughing."

He lunged with the knife again. This time it caught in the pillow and he fell against Max, who was shoved against the wall. The gun went off, and a look of surprise came over Darcy's face as he slumped to his knees, then sprawled out on the floor. The naked woman stared at Max. Quickly she knelt beside Darcy.

She reached for his pulse, then dropped his hand. "You didn't have to kill him, you fool!" she said angrily.

Max looked at her. Her breasts heaved excitedly and there was a fine moisture in the valley between them. He had never seen her look so beautiful. "What was I supposed to do?" he asked. "He was comin' at me with a knife!"

"You could have knocked him out!" she snapped.

"What was I supposed to hit him with?" he snapped back, feeling the anger rise in him. "My cannon?"

She stood very still for a moment, staring at him. Then she turned and walked to the door. She looked out into the hallway. The house was quiet. The shot had been muffled by the pillow. Slowly she closed the door and came back toward him.

He stood there watching the blurred, sensual look come back into her face. She sank to her knees before him, and he felt her lips press against his thighs. "Do not be angry with Anne-Louise, my stalwart, wild stallion," she whispered. "Make love to me."

He reached down to lift her to the bed. But she held his arms. "No," she said, pulling him down to the floor beside her. "Here."

They made love for the last time on the floor, lying next to a dead man. In the morning, Anne-Louise Pluvier calmly turned him over to the police.

10

THE EAST, WEST AND SOUTH OF THE PRISON WAS bounded by a swamp, along which the cypresses rose high and spilled their leaves onto the murky surface of the water. The only way out was to the north, across the rice paddies tended by Cajun tenant farmers. There was a small village eighteen miles north of the prison and it was here that most prisoners trying to escape were caught and brought back to the prison by the Cajuns for the ten-dollar bounty offered by the state. Those who were not caught were presumed dead in the swamp. There had been only two such cases reported in the prison's twenty years of operation.

One morning in May, after Max had been there a few

months, the guard checking out his hut reported to one of the trusties the absence of a prisoner named Jim Reeves.

The trusty looked around. "He ain't here?"

"He ain't out in the latrines, neither," the guard said. "I looked."

"He's gone, then," the trusty said. "I reckon he went over the wall in the night."

"That Jim Reeves sure is a fool," the guard said softly. He turned on his heel. "I better go tell the warden."

They were lined up in front of the kitchen, getting their coffee and grits, when Max saw one of the guards ride out of the prison and start up the road toward the village.

He sat down against the wall of one of the huts and watched the guard disappear up the road while he ate. Mike, the giant Negro trusty who had given him ten lashes the day he arrived, came over and sat down beside him.

Max looked over at the trusty. "That all the fuss they make over a man gettin' out?"

Mike nodded, his mouth filled with grits. "What you expec' them to do?" he asked. "They'll git him back. You wait and see."

He was right. The next morning, while they were at breakfast again, Jim Reeves came back. He was sitting in a wagon between two Cajuns, who carried their long rifles in the crooks of their arms. The prisoners looked up at him silently as he rode by.

When they came back from their work in the evening, Jim Reeves was tied naked to the whipping post. Silently the trusties led the prisoners to the compound, so that they could view the punishment before they had their meal.

The warden stood there until all the prisoners were in line. "You men know the penalty for attempted escape—ten lashes and fifteen days in the cage for each day out." He turned to Mike, standing next to him. "I don't want him knocked out. He must be conscious so he can rue the folly of his action."

Mike nodded stolidly and stepped forward. The muscles along his back rippled and the long snake wrapped itself lightly around the prisoner. It seemed to caress him almost gently, but when Mike lifted it from the victim's back, a long red welt of blood bubbled and rose to the surface.

A moment later, the prisoner screamed. The snake rippled around him again. This time, his scream was pure agony. The prisoner fainted three times before the lashing was completed. Each time, the warden stepped forward and had a pail of water thrown into his face to revive him, then ordered the lashing continued.

At the end, Jim Reeves hung there from the post, unconscious. Blood dripped down his back from his shoulders, across his buttocks and the top of his thighs.

"Cut him down and put him in the cage," the warden said.

Silently the men broke ranks and formed a food line. Max looked at the cage as he got on the line. The cage was exactly that—steel bars forming a four-foot cubicle. There was room to neither walk, stand or even stretch out full length. There was only space enough to sit or crouch on all fours like an animal. There was no shelter from the sun or the elements.

For the next thirty days, Jim Reeves would live there like an animal—without clothing, without medical attention, with only bread and water for his food. He would live there in the midst of his pain and his excrement and there was no one who would speak to him or dare give him aid, under penalty of the same punishment.

Max took his plate of meat and beans around to the side of the hut, where he would not have to look at the cage. He sank to the ground and began to eat slowly.

Mike sat down next to him. The big Negro's face was sweating. He began to eat silently. Max looked at him and couldn't eat any more. He pushed his plate away from him, rolled a cigarette and lit it.

"You ain't hungry, man?" Mike asked. "I'll eat that there food."

Max stared at him for a moment, then silently turned the plate over, spilling the contents on the ground.

Mike stared at him in surprise. "What for you do that, man?" he asked.

"Now I know why you stay here as a trusty instead of leavin' like you should," Max said. "You're evenin' up with the whole world when you swing that snake."

A look of understanding came into the trusty's eyes. "So that's what you' thinkin'," he said softly.

"That's what I'm thinkin'," Max said coldly.

The Negro looked into Max's eyes. "You don' know nothin'," he said slowly. "Years ago, when I first got here, I seen a man git a beatin' like that. When they cut him down, he was all tore up, front an' back. He died less'n two days after. Ain't a man died since I took the rope. Tha's more'n twelve years now. An' if you looked close, you would have seen they ain't a mark on the front of him, nor one lash laid over the other. I know they's lots of things wrong about my job, but somebody's gotta do it. An' it mought as well be me, because I don' like hurtin' folks. Not even pricks like Jim Reeves."

Max stared down at the ground, thinking about what he had just heard. A glimmer of understanding began to lighten the sourness in his stomach. Silently he pushed his sack of makings toward the trusty. Without speaking, Mike took it and rolled himself a cigarette. Quietly the two men leaned their heads back against the hut, smoking.

Jim Reeves came into the hut. It was a month since he had been carried out of the cage, encrusted in his own filth, bent over, his eyes wild like an animal's. Now his eyes searched the dark, then he came over to the bunk where Max lay stretched out and tapped him on the shoulder. Max sat up.

"I got to get outa here," he said.

Max stared at him in the dark. "Don't we all?"

"Don't joke with me, Injun," Reeves said harshly. "I mean it."

"I mean it, too," Max said. "But ain't nobody made it yet."

"I got a way figured out," Reeves said. "But it takes two men to do it. That's why I come to you."

"Why me?" Max asked. "Why not one of the men on a long stretch?"

"Because most of them are city men," Reeves said, "and we wouldn' last two days in the swamp."

Max swung into a sitting position. "Now I know you're crazy," he said. "Nobody can get th'ough that swamp. It's forty miles of quicksand, alligators, moccasins an' razorbacks. The only way is north, past the village."

A bitter smile crossed Reeves's face. "That's what I thought," he said. "It was easy, over the fence and up the road. Easy, I thought. They didn' even call out the dogs. They didn' have to. Every damn Cajun in the neighborhood was out lookin' for me."

He knelt by the side of Max's bunk. "The swamp," he said. "That's the only way. I got it figured out. We get a boat an'—"

"A boat!" Max said. "Where in hell we goin' to get a boat?"

"It'll take time," Reeves said cautiously. "But ricin' time is comin' up. Warden leases us out to the big planters then. Prison labor is cheap an' the warden pockets the money. Them rice paddies is half filled with water. There's always boats around."

"I don't know," Max said doubtfully.

Reeves's eyes were glowing like an animal's. "You want to lose two whole years of your life in this prison, boy? You got that much time just to throw away?"

"Let me think about it," Max said hesitantly. "I'll let you know."

Reeves slipped away in the dark as Mike came into the hut. The trusty made his way directly to Max's bunk. "He been at you to go th'ough the swamp with him?" he asked.

The surprise showed in Max's voice. "How'd you know?"

"He's been at ev'ybody in the place an' they all turned him down. I figgered he'd be gettin' to you soon."

"Oh," Max said.

"Don' do it, boy," the giant trusty said softly. "No matter how good it looks, don' do it. Reeves is so full of hate, he don' care who gets hurt so long as he gets out."

Max stretched out on the bunk. His eyes stared up into the dark. The only thing that made sense in what Reeves had said was the two years. Max didn't have two years to throw away. Why, in two years, he'd be twenty-one.

11

"MAN, THIS IS REAL FOOD," MIKE SAID ENTHUSIAS-tically as he sat down beside Max, his plate piled high with fat back, chitterlings, collard greens and potatoes.

Max looked over at him wearily. Stolidly he pushed the food into his mouth. It was better than the prison food, all right. They didn't see as much meat in a week as they had on their plates right now. But he wasn't hungry. He was tired, bent-over tired from pulling at the rice all day. He didn't think he'd ever straighten out.

Reeves and another prisoner sat down on the other side of

him. Reeves looked over his plate at him, his mouth working over the fat meat. "Picked yourself a gal yet, boy?"

Max shook his head. They were there all right. Cajun girls, young and strong, with their short skirts and muscular thighs and legs. Plenty of them, all over the fields, working side by side with the men, their hair flying and their teeth flashing and the female smell of them always in your nostrils. It didn't seem to matter to them that the men were prisoners. Only that they were men and for once there were enough of them to go around.

"I'm too tired," Max said. He put his plate down and rubbed his ankle. It was sore from the leg iron and walking in the water all day.

"I'm not," the prisoner next to Reeves said. "I been savin' up my hump a whole year for this week. I'm gonna git me enough to last me till nex' yeah."

"Better not pass it up, Injun," Reeves said. "There ain't nothin' in this world like Cajun girls."

"Man, that's the truth," the other prisoner said excitedly.

"You got one picked out?" Reeves asked across Max to Mike. His eyes were cold and baleful.

Mike didn't answer. He just kept eating.

Reeves's face darkened. "I seen you out there on the field. Walkin' up an' down with that rifle in your hands. Showin' the girls what you got in them tight pants."

Mike still didn't reply. He began to wipe up the gravy in his plate with pieces of bread.

Reeves's laugh was nasty. "There's always some half-wit girl lookin' for a big buck nigger with a cock as long as my arm. An' I bet you just can't wait to stick it into some white girl. That's all you niggers think of, stickin' it in white women."

Mike stuck the last piece of bread into his mouth and swallowed it. Regretfully he looked down at the empty plate and got to his feet. "Man, that was sho' good."

"I'm talkin' to you, nigger," Reeves said.

For the first time, Mike looked down at him. Almost lazily he bent over Max and with one hand picked Reeves up by the throat. He held him writhing in the air at the level of his head. "You talkin' to me, jailbird?"

Reeves quaked, his voice choking in his throat.

Mike began to shake Reeves gently. "Remember one thing,

jailbird," he said. "I'm a trusty an' you' jus' a prisoner. You likes stayin' healthy, you better learn to shut you' mouth."

Reeves's arms flailed helplessly in the air. His face was almost purple. Mike shook him a few more times, then casually flung him at the wall of the bunkhouse, about five feet away.

Reeves crashed against the wall and slid down it to the floor. His eyes glared at Mike. His lips moved but no sound escaped them.

Mike smiled at him. "You' learnin', jailbird," he said. "You' learnin'." He picked up his empty plate. "I'm goin' see if I can't scrounge me some more of these eats. I swear if they ain't the best I ever tasted."

Reeves struggled to his feet as the trusty walked away. "I'll kill him!" he swore tightly. "Honest to God, someday before I get out of here, I'll kill that nigger!"

There was an air of expectancy in the bunkhouse that night. Max was stretched out on his bunk and the feeling was contagious. Suddenly, he wasn't tired any more. He couldn't sleep.

The guard had come and checked the leg irons, fastening each man to the bed post. He had gone to the door and stood there for a moment. Then he laughed into the dark and went out.

Almost immediately, Max heard the scratch of a match, then a faint glow spread through the darkness. Max turned toward the light. Somehow one of the men had got a candle. It burned almost gaily at the head of his bed.

There was a subdued sound of laughter in the room. Max heard a voice say, "At leas' this time we can see what they look like."

"I don't care what they look like," another voice answered quickly, "as long as they got big tits."

Still another voice said raucously, "Your pecker won't know what to do, it's so used to yoh lily-white hand."

A soft laughter rippled through the room. About a half hour passed. Max could hear the sounds of restless movements, men twisting anxiously in their bunks.

"You reckon maybe they won't show up?" a voice asked nervously.

"They'll show up, all right," another prisoner replied. "They been waitin' for this as long as we have."

"Sweet Jesus." An anguished voice came from the far end of

the room. "I can't hold it no more. All day long I been thinkin' about them women, about tonight—" His voice trailed off in a hoarse moan.

For a moment, the room filled with the sounds of the men turning restlessly in their bunks. Max felt the sweat come out on his forehead and his heart began to beat heavily. He rolled over on his stomach, feeling the sweet, heavy warmth suddenly spread into his loins. For a moment he writhed, caught in the fire of a wild desire, then angrily he forced himself to turn over. He rolled a cigarette with trembling fingers. He felt shreds of the tobacco fall around him but he finally lit it and dragged the smoke deep into his lungs.

"They ain't comin'," a voice cried, almost on the verge of tears.

"They ain't nothin' but a bunch of cock-teasers!" another voice said angrily. "T' hell with them."

Max lay quietly in his bunk, letting the smoke trickle through his nostrils. The candle sputtered and flickered out and now the bunkhouse was pitch black. Mike's voice came softly from the next bunk. "How you doin', boy?"

"All right."

"Gimme a drag of that there butt."

Their hands touched briefly as Max silently held the cigarette out. The cigarette glowed and cast a faint shine over Mike's face as he dragged on it.

"Don' worry, boy." His voice was soft and reassuring. "They'll show up any moment now the candle's out. What those damn fools can't seem to understan' is them women don' want to see 'em, anymore'n they want theyselves to be seen."

A moment later, the bunkhouse door opened and the women began to come in. They entered silently, their bare feet making the faintest whisper on the floor.

Max turned in his bunk, hoping he could catch a glimpse of the one that would come to him. But all he could see were shadows that entered and then were lost in the dark. A hand touched his face. He started.

"Are you young or old?" a voice whispered.

"Young," he whispered back.

Her hand found his and brought it to her cheek. For a moment, his fingers explored her face gently. Her skin was soft and warm. He felt her lips tremble beneath his fingers. "Do you want me to stay with you?" she whispered.

"Yes."

Swiftly she came into the bunk beside him and he buried his head in the softness of her bosom. A great warmth and gentleness welled up inside him.

As if from a great distance, he heard a man across the room begin to cry softly. "My darling," he said, "my darling wife. You don't know how I've missed you."

Max turned his face up to the woman. As she bent to kiss his lips, he felt the tears rolling down her cheeks and he knew that she also had heard.

He closed his eyes. How could he tell this woman he couldn't even see what he felt? How could he tell her she brought kindness and love into this room?

"Thank you," he whispered gratefully. "Thank you, thank you, thank you."

On the fourth day at the rice fields, Reeves came over to him. "I been wanting to talk to you," he said quickly. "But I had to wait until that damn nigger wasn't around. I got a boat!"

"What?"

"Keep yer voice down," Reeves said harshly. "It's all arranged. It'll be in that big clump of cypresses south of the prison the day after we get back."

"How d'you know?"

"I got it fixed with my girl," Reeves said.

"You sure she ain't jobbin' you?"

"I'm sure," Reeves answered quickly. "These Cajun girls all want the same thing. I told her I'd take her to New Orleans with me if she helped me escape. The boat'll be there. Her place is out in the middle of nowhere. It'll be a perfect place to hide out until they stop lookin' for us."

He glanced up quickly and began to move off.

That evening, Mike sat down next to Max at chow. For a long time, there were only the sounds of eating, the scraping of spoons on plates.

"You goin' with Reeves now that he got his boat?" Mike asked suddenly.

Max stared at him. "You know that already?"

Mike smiled. "Ain' no secrets in a place like this."

"I don' know," Max said.

"Believe me, boy," the Negro said sincerely, "thirty days in the cage is a lot longer than the year an' a half you got to go."

"But maybe we'll make it."

"You won't make it," Mike said sadly. "Fust thing the warden does is get out the dogs. They don' get you, the swamp will."

"How would he know we went by the swamp?" Max asked quickly. "You wouldn' tell him?"

The Negro's eyes had a hurt expression. "You knows better'n that, boy. I may be a trusty, but I ain't no fink. The warden's gonna know all by himself. One man allus goes by the road. Two men allus goes by the swamp. It's like it was the rule."

Max was silent as he dragged on his cigarette.

"Please don' go, boy," Mike said. "Don' do nothin' to make me have to hurt you. I want to be you' friend."

Max looked at him, then smiled slowly. He reached out his hand and rested it on the big man's shoulder. "No matter what," he said seriously, "you're my friend."

"You goin'," Mike said. "You' mind's made up." Mike got to his feet and walked off slowly.

Max looked after him, puzzled. How could Mike know what he himself didn't know? He got to his feet and scraped off his plate.

But it wasn't until he was over the fence the next night and racing madly toward the clump of cypresses with Reeves at his side that he knew how right Mike had been.

Then Reeves was scrambling around at the foot of the cypresses, sunk half to his knees in the murky swamp water, swearing, "The bitch! The no-good lying Cajun whore!"

There was no boat there.

12

THEY PUSHED THEIR WAY THROUGH THE REEDS, sloshing in the water up to their waist, and up onto a hummock. They sank to their haunches, their chests heaving, their lungs gulping in great mouthfuls of air. From a great distance, they could hear the baying of a hound.

Reeves slapped at the insects around his head. "They're gaining on us," he mumbled through swollen lips.

Max looked at his companion. Reeves's face was swollen and distorted from insect bites, his clothing torn. Reeves stared back at him balefully. "How do you know we ain't been goin' in circles? Three days now and we ain't seen nothing."

"That's how I know. If we was goin' in circles, we woulda run into them sure."

"I can't keep this up much longer," Reeves said. "I'm goin' crazy from bug bites. I'm ready to let 'em take me."

"Maybe you are," Max said, "but I ain't. I ain't got this far to go back an' sit in a cage." He got to his feet. "Come on. We rested enough."

Reeves looked over at him. "How come them bugs don't bother you?" he asked resentfully. "It mus' be your Injun blood or somethin'."

"Might be," Max said. "Also might be that I don't scratch at 'em. Come on."

"Can't we stay here for the night?" Reeves complained.

"Uh-uh," Max said. "We got another two hours of daylight. That's another mile. Let's go."

He pushed off into the water. He didn't look back, but a moment later, he heard Reeves splash into the water behind him. It was almost dark when he found another hummock.

Reeves sprawled flat on the ground. Max looked down at him. For a moment, he felt almost sorry for him, then he remembered the fierce hatreds that flamed in Reeves and he wasn't sorry any more. He'd known what he was doing.

Max took out his knife and hacked swiftly at one of the long canes. He sharpened the end to a pointed spear. Then he sloshed out into the water. He stood there motionlessly for almost fifteen minutes, until he saw an indistinct shape swimming under the surface. He held his breath, waiting for it to come closer. It did and he moved swiftly. The spear flashed into the water.

He felt the pull against his arms as he lifted the spear free of the water. A large, squirming catfish was impaled on the tip.

"We got a good one this time," he said, returning to Reeves. He squatted down beside him and began to skin the fish.

Reeves sat up. "Start a fire," he said. "We'll cook this one."

Max was already chewing on a piece. He shook his head. "The smell of a fire carries for miles."

Reeves got to his feet angrily. "I don't give a damn," he snarled, his face flushing. "I ain't no damn Injun like you. I'm cookin' my fish."

He scrambled around, gathering twigs. At last, he had enough to start a small fire. His hand groped in his pocket for matches. He found one and scraped it on a log. It didn't light. Angrily he scraped it again. He stared at the match. "They're still wet," he said.

"Yeah," Max answered, still chewing stolidly on the fish. It was rubbery and oily but he chewed it slowly, swallowing only a little at a time.

"You c'n start a fire," Reeves snapped.

Max looked up at him. "How?"

"Injun style," Reeves said, "rubbin' two sticks together."

Max laughed. "It won't work. The wood's too damp." He picked up a piece of the fish and held it up toward Reeves. "Here, eat it. It ain't so bad if you chew it slow."

Reeves took the fish and squatted down beside Max, then began to chew on it. After a moment, he spat it out. "I can't eat it." He was silent for a moment, his arms wrapped around himself. "It's gettin' damn cold out here," he said, shivering slightly.

Max looked at him. It wasn't that cold. Faint beads of perspiration stood out on Reeves's face and he was beginning to tremble.

"Lay down," Max said. "I'll cover you with grass—that'll keep you warm."

Reeves stretched out and Max bent down and touched his face. It was hot with fever. Max straightened up slowly and went to cut some more grass.

It was a hell of a time for Reeves to come down with malaria. Reluctantly he took one of his matches from its oilskin wrapping and lighted a fire.

Reeves continued to shake spastically beneath the blanket of swamp grass and moan through his chattering teeth. Max glanced up at the sky. The night was almost gone. Unconsciously he sighed. He wondered how long it would take for the warden to catch up with them now.

He dozed, swaying slightly, as he sat. A strange sound hit his subconscious and suddenly he was awake.

He reached for his fishing spear and crouched down. The sound came again. Whatever it was, it was large. He heard the sound again, closer this time. His legs drew up beneath him. He was set to lunge the spear. It wasn't much but it was the only weapon he had.

Then Mike was standing there casually, his rifle crooked in his arm. "You' a damn fool, boy," he said. "Shoulda knowed better'n to light a fire out here."

Max got to his feet. He could feel fatigue spread over him now that it was over. He gestured to the sick man. "He got the fever."

Mike walked over to Reeves. "Sure 'nough," he said, his voice marveling. "That warden, he was right. He figgered Reeves would get it after three days in the swamp."

Mike sat down next to the fire and warmed his hands. "Man but that fire sure do feel good," he said. "You should'n'a waited aroun'."

"What else could I do?"

"He would'n'a waited if it was you."

"But it wasn' me," Max said.

The Negro looked down at the ground. "Maybe you better git goin' now, boy."

Max stared at him. "What do you mean?"

"Git goin'," Mike said harshly.

"But the rest of the posse?"

"They won' catch up fo' a couple of hours," Mike said. "They be satisfied catchin' Reeves."

Max stared at him, then looked off into the swamp. After a moment, he shook his head. "I can't do it," he said.

"You' a bigger fool than I thought, boy," Mike said heavily. "'Twas him, he'd be off in the swamp now."

"We busted out together," Max answered. "It's only fittin' we go back together."

"All right, boy," Mike said in a resigned voice. He got to his feet. "Drown that fire."

Max kicked the fire into the water, where it sputtered and died. He glanced back and saw Mike pick up Reeves as if he were a baby and sling him over his shoulder. Max started back into the swamp toward the prison.

"Where at you goin', boy?" Mike's voice came from behind him.

Max turned around and stared.

Mike pointed in the opposite direction. "The end o' the swamp about twenty-fi' miles that way."

Sudden comprehension came to Max. "You can't do it, Mike. You ain't even officially a prisoner no more."

The big man's head nodded. "You' right, boy. I ain't a prisoner. That means I kin go where I wants an' if I don't want to go back, they can't say nothin' about it."

"But it's different if they catch you helpin' me."

"If they catch us, they catch us," Mike said simply. "Anyway, I don't wanta be the one who lays the snake on you. I can't do it. You see, we's really frien's."

Eight days later, they came out of the swamp. They stretched out on the hard, dry ground, gasping for breath. Max raised his head. Far in the distance, he could see smoke rising on the horizon.

"There's a town there," he said excitedly, scrambling to his feet. "We'll be able to git some decent grub."

"Not so fast," Reeves said, pulling him down. Reeves was still yellow from the fever but it had passed. "If it's a town, there's a general store. We'll hit it tonight. No use takin' any chances. They might be expectin' us."

Max looked over at Mike. The big Negro nodded.

They hit the store at two in the morning. When they came out, they all wore fresh clothing, had guns tucked in their belt and almost eighteen dollars they had found in the till.

Max wanted to steal three horses from the livery stable and ride out. "Ain't that just like an Injun?" Reeves said sarcastically. "They'll trace horses faster'n us. We'll keep off the road two or three days, then we'll worry about horses."

Two days later, they had their horses. Four days later, they knocked off a bank in a small town and came out with eighteen hundred dollars. Ten minutes later, they were on their way to Texas.

13

MAX CAME INTO FORT WORTH TO MEET THE TRAIN that was to bring Jim Reeves's daughter from New Orleans. He sat in the barber chair and stared at himself in the mirror. The face that looked back was no longer the face of a boy. The trim black beard served to disguise the high cheekbones. He no longer looked like an Indian.

Max got out of the chair. "How much do I owe you?"

"Fifty cents for the haircut, two bits for the beard trim."

Max threw him a silver dollar.

Mike came off the side of the building against which he had been leaning and fell into step. "It's about time fer the train to be comin' in," Max said. "I reckon we might as well walk down to the station."

Three and a half years before, they had come into Fort Worth one night with seven thousand dollars in their saddlebags. Behind them they had left two empty banks and two dead men. But they had been lucky. Not one of them had been identified as other than an unknown person.

"This looks like a good town," Max had said enthusiastically. "I counted two banks comin' in."

Reeves had looked up at him from a chair in the cheap hotel room. "We're through with that," he said.

Max stared at him. "Why? They look like setups."

Reeves shook his head. "That's where I made my mistake last time. I didn't know when to quit." He stuck a cigarette in his mouth.

"What we goin' to do, then?" Max asked.

Reeves lit the cigarette. "Look aroun' for a good legitimate business. There's lots of opportunity out here. Land is cheap and Texas is growin'."

Reeves found the business he was looking for in a little town sixty-five miles south of Fort Worth. A saloon and gambling hall. In less than two years, he had become the most important man in town. Then he started a bank in a corner of the gambling house and, a little time later, began to acquire land. There was even talk of electing him mayor.

He bought a small ranch outside of town, fixed up the house and moved out of the rooms over the saloon. A little while after that, he moved the bank out of the saloon, which Max then operated, and ensconced it in a small building on the main street. In less than a year, people began to forget that he had ever owned the saloon and began to think of him as the town banker. He began to grow quietly rich.

He needed but one thing more to complete his guise of respectability. A family. He sent discreet inquiries back to New

Orleans. He learned that his wife was dead and his daughter was living with her mother's relatives. He sent her a telegram and received one in return, saying that she would arrive at Fort Worth on the fifth of March.

Max stood looking down the platform at the disembarking passengers. "You know what she looks like?" Mike asked.

"Just what Jim tol' me and it's been ten years since he saw her."

Little by little, the passengers walked away until the only one left was a young woman, surrounded by several valises and a small trunk. She kept looking up and down the platform. Mike looked at Max questioningly. "You reckon that might be her?"

Max shrugged his shoulders.

They walked down to the young woman. Max took off his Stetson. "Miss Reeves?"

A smile of relief appeared on the young woman's face. "I declare, I'm glad to see you," she said warmly. "I was beginnin' to think Daddy never received my telegram."

Max returned her smile. "I'm Max Sand," he said. "Your father sent me to meet you."

A fleeting shadow crossed the girl's face. "I half expected that," she said. "Daddy's been too busy to come home for ten years."

Max guessed that she didn't know her father had been in prison. "Come," he said gently. "I've got a room for you over at the Palace Hotel. You can clean up and sleep there tonight. We got a two-day trip home, so we won't start till morning."

By the time they reached the hotel, twenty minutes later, Max was in love for the first time in his life.

Max tied his horse to the hitching post in front of the Reeves ranch house. He climbed up the steps and knocked at the door. When Reeves's daughter opened it, her face looked tired and strained, as if she'd been weeping. "Oh, it's you," she said in a low voice. "Come in."

He followed her into the parlor. He reached for her, suddenly concerned. "Betty, what's wrong?"

She slipped away from his hands. "Why didn't you tell me you were an escaped convict?" she asked, not looking at him.

His face settled into cold lines. "Would it have made any diff'rence?"

She met his look honestly. "Yes," she said. "I'd never have let myself get this involved if I'd known."

"Now that you do know," he persisted. "Does it matter?"

"Yes," she said again. "Oh, don't ask me. I'm so confused!"

"What else did your father tell you?"

She looked down at her hands. "He said I couldn't marry you. Not only because of that but because you're—you're half Indian!"

"An' just because of that, you stopped lovin' me?"

She stared down at her twisting hands without answering. "I don't know how I feel," she said finally.

He reached out and pulled her toward him. "Betty, Betty," he said huskily. "Las' night at the dance, you kissed me. You said you loved me. I haven't changed since then."

For a moment, she stood quietly, then pulled herself away from him. "Don't touch me!" she said quickly.

Max stared at her curiously. "You don' have to be afraid of me."

She shrank from his hand. "Don't touch me," she said, and this time the fear in her voice was much too familiar for Max not to recognize it. Without another word, he turned and left the room.

He rode straight into town to the bank and walked into the back room that served Reeves as an office.

Reeves looked up from the big roll-top desk. "What the hell do you mean bustin' in here like this?" he demanded.

Max stared at him. "Don't try to bull-shit me, Reeves. You already done a good job on your daughter."

Reeves leaned back in his chair and laughed. "Is that all?" he asked.

"It's enough," Max said. "Las' night she promised to marry me."

Reeves leaned forward. "I gave you credit for more brains'n that, Max."

"It don't matter now, Reeves. I'm movin' on."

Reeves stared at him for a moment. "You mean that?"

Max nodded. "I mean it."

"You takin' the nigger with you?"

"Yeah," Max said. "When I get our share of the money."

Reeves swung his chair around and took some bills from the safe behind him. He threw them down on the desk in front of Max. "There it is."

Max looked down at it, then at Reeves. He picked up the money and counted it. "There's only five hundred dollars here," he said.

"What did you expect?" Reeves asked.

"We came into Fort Worth with seven thousand. My share of that alone was twenty-three hundred an' we ain't been exactly losin' money in the saloon." Max took a ready-made from Reeves's desk and lit it. "I figger Mike an' me's due at least five thousand."

Reeves shrugged. "I won't argue," he said. "After all, we been through a lot together, you an' me. If that's what you figure, that's what you get."

He counted the money out on the desk. Max picked it up and put it in his pocket. "I didn't think you'd part with it so easy," he said.

He was halfway to the saloon when someone hailed him from the rear. He turned around slowly.

The sheriff and two deputies advanced on him, their guns drawn. Reeves was with them.

"What's up, Sheriff?" Max asked.

"Search him," Reeves said excitedly. "You'll find the money he stole right on him."

"Stole?" Max said. "He's crazy! That money's mine. He owed it to me."

"Keep your hand away from your gun," the sheriff said, moving forward cautiously. He stuck his hand in Max's pocket. It came out with a sheaf of bills.

"See!" Reeves yelled. "What did I tell you?"

"You son of a bitch!" Max exploded. He flung himself toward Reeves. Before he could reach him, the sheriff brought his gun butt down along the side of Max's head. It was just at that moment that Mike looked out the window of the room over the saloon.

Reeves walked over to Max and looked down at him. "I shoulda known better than to trust a half-breed."

"Pick him up, boys, an' tote him over to the jail," the sheriff said.

"Better get over to the saloon and get his nigger friend, too," Reeves said. "He was probably in on it."

Mike saw the sheriff look over at the saloon, then begin to

walk toward it. He didn't wait any longer. He went down the back stairs and got the hell out of town.

Reeves rode along the road to his ranch, half humming to himself. He was feeling good. For the first time, he was secure. Max wouldn't dare talk; it would only make it worse for him. And the nigger was gone. Leave it to a nigger to run when things got rough. He was so wrapped up in his thoughts that he never heard the crack of the snake as it whipped out from behind the trees and dragged him down off his horse.

He scrambled to his feet and reached for his gun but the next crack of the snake tore it from his fingers. Mike walked slowly toward him, the big whip coiling slowly back up his arm.

Reeves screamed in terror.

The big snake cracked again and Reeves spun around and tumbled over backward into the dust. He got to his hands and knees and began to crawl, then scrambled to his feet and tried to run. The snake ran down the road after him and crept between his legs, throwing him to the ground. He turned his head and saw Mike's arm go up into the air, the long black whip rising with it.

He screamed as the snake tore into him again.

Sometime early the next morning, the sheriff and his deputies came across a body lying at the side of the road. During the night, someone had torn the bars from the window of the jail's only cell and Max had escaped.

One of the deputies saw the body first. He wheeled his horse over beside it and looked down.

The sheriff and the other deputy wheeled their horses. For a long while, they stared down at the mutilated body. Then one of them took off his hat and wiped the cold, beaded sweat from his forehead. "That looks like Banker Reeves."

The sheriff turned and looked at him. "That *was* Banker Reeves," he said. He, too, took off his hat and wiped his face. "Funny," he added. "The only thing I know of that can do that to a man is a Louisiana prison snake."

14

THE NAME OF THE VILLAGE IN SPANISH WAS VERY long and difficult for Americans to pronounce, so after a while they gave it their own name. Hideout. It was a place to go when there was nowhere else to turn, when the law was hot on your neck and you were tired of sleeping nights on the cold prairie and eating dry beef and cold beans from a can. It was expensive but it was worth it. Four miles over the border and the law could not reach you.

And it was the only place in Mexico where you could always get American whisky. Even if you had to pay four times the price for it.

The *alcalde* sat at his table in the rear of the cantina and watched the two *americanos* come in. They sat down at the table near the door. The smaller one ordered tequila.

The *alcalde* watched the two with interest. Soon they would be going away. It was always like that. When first they came, they'd have nothing but the best. The finest whisky, the best rooms, the most expensive girls. Then their money would run short and they'd begin to reduce their expenses. First, the room would be changed for a cheaper one; next, the girls would go. Last, the whisky. When they got down to drinking tequila, it meant that before long, they'd be moving on.

He lifted his glass and drank his tequila quickly. That was the way of the world. He looked at the smaller man again. There was something about him that had caught his eye. He sighed, thinking of his youth. Juárez would have liked this one: the Indian blood in the *Jefe* told him instinctively which ones were the warriors. He sighed again. Poor Juárez, he wanted so much for the people and got so little. He wondered if before the *Jefe* died, he had realized that the only reason for his failure was that the people didn't want as much for themselves as he had wanted for them. He stared at the *americanos,* remembering the first time he had seen them. It was almost three years ago.

They had come into the cantina quietly, weary and covered

with the dust of their travels. Then, as now, they had sat at the table near the door.

The bottle and glasses were on the table when the big man at the bar had come over to them. He spoke to the smaller man, ignoring the other. "We don't allow niggers in this here saloon."

The smaller man didn't even look up. He filled his friend's glass first, then his own. He lifted it to his lips.

The glass shattered against the floor and silence abruptly fell across the cantina. "Get your nigger outa here," the big man said. He stared at them for a moment, then turned and strode back to the bar.

The Negro started to rise but the smaller man stopped him with a gesture from his eyes. Slowly the Negro sank back into his chair.

It was only when the smaller man left the table to go to the bar that the *alcalde* realized that he wasn't as small as he had first thought. It was only by comparison to the Negro that he seemed small.

"Who makes the rules here?" he asked the bartender.

The bartender gestured toward the rear. "The *alcalde, señor.*"

The *americano* turned and came toward the table. His eyes surprised the *alcalde;* they were a hard, dark blue. He spoke in Spanish, with a trace of Cuban accent. "Does the swine speak the truth, *señor?*"

"No, *señor,*" the *alcalde* replied. "All are welcome here who have the money to pay their way."

The man nodded and returned to the bar. He stopped in front of the man who had come over to his table. "The *alcalde* tells me my friend can stay," he said.

The man turned to him angrily. "Who the hell cares what that greaser thinks? Just because we're across the border, doesn't mean I have to drink with niggers!"

The smaller man's voice was cold. "My friend eats with me, drinks with me, sleeps with me, and he's not goin'." He turned his back calmly and went back to his table.

He was just seating himself again when the angry *americano* started for him. "If you like niggers so much, nigger-lover, see how you like sleepin' with a dead one!" he shouted, pulling his gun.

The smaller *americano* seemed scarcely to move but the gun was in his hand, smoke rising from its barrel, the echo of a shot fading away in the rafters of the cantina. And the loud-mouthed one lay dead on the floor in front of the bar.

"I apologize for the disturbance we have made against the hospitality of your village," he said in his strange Spanish.

The *alcalde* looked down at the man on the floor, and shrugged. *"De nada,"* he said. "It is nothing. You were right. The swine had no grace."

Now, almost three years later, the *alcalde* sighed, remembering. The little one had grace, much grace—natural like a panther. And the gun. *Caramba!* There had never been anything so fast. It seemed almost to have a life of its own. What a *pistolera* this one would have made. Juárez would have been proud of him.

Several times each year, the two friends would quietly disappear from the village and as quietly reappear—several weeks, sometimes several months later. And each time they came back, they had money to pay for their rooms, their women, their whisky.

But each time, the *alcalde* could sense a deeper solitude in them, a greater aloneness. There were times he felt a strange kind of pity for them. They were not like the others that came to the village. This way of life held no pleasure for them.

And now they were drinking tequila again. How many times before they would go out like this and never return? Not only to this village but to nowhere on this earth.

Max swallowed the tequila and bit into the lime. The tart juice burst into his throat, giving his mouth a clean, fresh feeling. He looked at Mike. "How much we got left?"

Mike thought for a moment. "Maybe three more weeks."

Max rolled a cigarette and lit it. "What we gotta do is make a big hit. Then maybe we could go up into California or Nevada or someplace where they don' know us an' git ourselves straightened out. Money shore don' last long around this place."

The Negro nodded. "It sho' don'," he agreed. "But that ain' the answer. We gotta split up. They lookin' for us together. When they see me, it's like you carryin' a big ol' sign with you' name on it."

Max filled his glass again. "Tryin' to get rid of me?" He smiled, throwing the liquor down his throat and reaching for the lime.

Mike said seriously, "Maybe 'thout me, you could settle down someplace an' make a life fo' yourself. You won' have to run no mor'."

Max spit out a lime seed. "We made us a deal to stick together. We get enough money this time, we'll head for California."

The door opened and a tall, redheaded cowboy came in. He walked over to their table and dropped into an empty chair. "Ol' Charlie Dobbs got here in the nick o' time, I reckon." He laughed. "That there tequila'll eat the linin' off your stomach sure as hell. Bartender, bring us a bottle of whisky."

The bartender put whisky and glasses on the table and walked away. Charlie filled the glasses and they drank.

"What brings you back, Charlie?" Max asked. "I thought you were headin' up Reno way."

"I was. But I run into the biggest thing ever I saw. It was too good to pass up."

"What kinda job?" Max asked, leaning across the table.

Charlie lowered his voice. "A new bank. You remember I tol' you I heard las' year they were minin' for oil up in Texas? I decided to pay them diggin's a visit on my way north." He poured another drink and swallowed it quickly. "Well, they found it all right. It's the craziest thing you ever saw. They sink a well down in the groun' an' instead of water, up comes oil. Then they pipe it off, barrel it an' ship it east. There's oil all over the place an' that bank's just bustin' with money."

"Sounds good to me," Max said. "What's the deal?"

"A local man set up the job but he needs help. He wants two shares, we get one share each."

"Fair enough," Max said. He turned to Mike. "What do you think?"

Mike nodded. "When we pull the job?" he asked.

Charlie looked at him. "Right after the new year. The bank is gettin' in a lot of money then for new diggin'." He refilled all the glasses. "We'll have to start tomorrow. It took me three weeks to ride down here."

15

MAX PUSHED HIS WAY INTO THE SALOON BEHIND Charlie Dobbs. It was crowded with oil-miners and cowboys and the dice table and faro layouts were working full blast. Men were standing three deep around them waiting for a chance at the games.

"What'd I tell you?" Charlie chortled. "This is a real boom town all right." He led the way down the bar to where a man was standing by himself.

The man turned and looked at him. "You took long enough gettin' here," he said in a low voice.

"It's a long ride, Ed," Charlie said.

"Meet me outside," Ed said, throwing a silver dollar on the bar and walking out. He glanced quickly at Max as he passed.

Max caught a glimpse of pale gimlet eyes without expression. The man seemed to be in his late forties, with a long, sandy mustache trailing across his lip. There was something familiar about him but Max couldn't place it. There was only the feeling that he had seen him before.

The man was waiting outside the saloon for them. He walked ahead and they followed him into a dark alley. He turned to face them. "I said we needed four men," he said angrily.

"There's another man, Ed," Charlie said quickly. "He's layin' up just outside of town."

"All right. You got here just in time. Tomorrow night—that's Friday night—the president and the cashier of the bank work late makin' up the riggin' crews' payrolls for Saturday. They usually get through about ten o'clock. We get them as they come out the door an' hustle them back inside. That way, they can open the safe for us; we don't have to blow it."

"All right with me," Charlie said. "What do you think, Max?"

Max looked at Ed. "They carry guns?"

"I reckon. You afraid of gunplay?"

Max shook his head. "No. I jus' like to know what to expect."

"How much you think we'll get?" Charlie interjected.

"Fifty thousand, maybe more."

Charlie whistled. "Fifty thousand!"

"You'll drift over here one at a time. Quiet. I don't want no one to be lookin' at us. We'll meet in back of the bank at nine thirty sharp." Ed looked at them and they nodded again. He started to walk away, then came back. He peered at Max. "Ain't I seen you someplace before?"

Max shrugged his shoulders. "Mebbe. I been aroun'. You look familiar to me, too."

"Maybe it'll come to me tomorrow night." He started to walk down the alley.

Max watched him until he turned into the street. He turned slowly to Charlie. "There's somethin' about that man. I got the feelin' I should know who he is."

Charlie laughed. "Let's go. Mike'll be wonderin' what happened to us."

"Set yourself!" Ed whispered hoarsely. "They're comin'!"

Max pressed tightly against the wall near the door. On the other side of the doorway, Ed and Charlie were waiting. He could hear the sound of two men's voices as they approached the door inside the bank.

They all moved at once as the door opened, pushing it inward with sudden force.

"What the hell's goin'—" a voice said from the darkness inside. It was followed by a thud, then the sound of a body falling.

"You keep your mouth shet, mister, if you want to keep livin'!" There was a frightened gasp, then silence. "Git them into the back room." Ed's voice came harshly.

Max bent swiftly and pulled the fallen man along the floor toward the back. There was the sound of a match behind him and then a lamp cast a tiny glow in the back room. He pulled the man into the room. He slumped and lay still when Max let him go.

"Check the front door!" Ed hissed.

Max ran back to the door and peeped out. The street was quiet and deserted. "No one out there," he said.

"Good," Ed said. "Let's get to work." He turned to the other of the two men. "Open the safe."

The man was in his late fifties. He was staring at the man on the floor with a horror-stricken look. "I—I can't," he said. "Only Mr. Gordon can. He's the president, the only one who knows the combination."

Ed turned to Max. "Wake him up."

Max knelt beside the man. He turned his face. The head looked peculiar, the jaw hung slack. Max looked up at Ed. "Ain't nothin' goin' to wake him up. You caved his head in."

"My God!" the other man said. He seemed almost ready to faint.

Ed stepped around in front of him. "I reckon you're goin' to have to open the safe, after all."

"B—but I can't," the bank clerk said. "I don't know the combination."

Ed hit him viciously across the face. The man fell against a desk. "Well, learn it, then!"

"Honest, mister," he sobbed. "I don't know it. Mr. Gordon was the only one. He was—"

Ed hit him again. "Open that safe!"

"Look, mister," the man begged. "There's over four thousand dollars in that desk there! Take it and don't hit me any more, please. I don't know the combination—"

Ed moved around the desk and opened the center drawer. He took out a package of bills and stuffed it into his jacket. He walked around the desk and stood in front of the kneeling bank clerk. "Now, open the safe!" he said, hitting the man again.

The man sprawled out on the floor. "I don't know, mister, I don't know!"

When Ed drew his foot back to kick him, Max touched his shoulder. "Maybe he's tellin' the truth."

Ed stared at him for a moment, then lowered his foot. "Maybe. I know how we can find out fast." He gestured at Max. "Get back on the door."

Max walked back through the bank to the front door and looked out again. The street was still deserted. He stood there, quietly alert.

Ed's voice came to him from the back room. "Tie the bastard to the chair."

"What are you gonna do?" the bank clerk protested in a weak voice.

Max walked back and looked in the room. Ed was kneeling

in front of the potbellied stove, stirring the poker in the live coals. Charlie straightened up from tying the clerk and looked at Ed curiously. "What're you doin'?"

"He'll talk if this red-hot poker gits close enough to his eyes," Ed said grimly.

"Wait a minute," Charlie protested. "You think the guy is lyin', kill him."

Ed got to his feet and turned on Charlie angrily. "That's the trouble with you young ones nowadays. You got no guts, you're too squeamish. He can't open no safe if he's dead!"

"He can't open it if he don't know the combination, either!"

"You don't like it, scram!" Ed said savagely. "There's fifty thousand bucks in that there safe. I'm goin' to git it!"

Max turned from the door and started back toward the front of the bank. He had taken about two steps when he was stopped by Ed's voice, coming from the back room.

"This'll work, believe me," Ed was saying. "'Bout ten, twelve years back, Rusty Harris, Tom Dort an' me gave the treatment to an ol' buffalo-skinner an' his squaw—"

Max felt his stomach heave and he reached for the wall to keep from falling. He closed his eyes for a moment and the scene in the cabin came back to him—his father hanging lifelessly, his mother crumpled on the floor, the orange glow of the fire against the night sky.

His head began to clear. He shook it. A cold, dead feeling replaced the nausea. He turned toward the back room.

Ed was still kneeling in front of the stove. Charlie stood across the room, his face white and sick. "The ol' miser had gold stashed somewhere aroun' the place. Everybody in Dodge knew it—" Ed looked up and saw Max, who had crossed the room and was standing over him. "What're you doin' here? I tol' you to cover the door!"

Max looked down at him. His voice was hollow. "Did you ever git that gold?"

A puzzled look crossed Ed's face.

"You didn't," Max said, "because there wasn't any to start with."

Ed stared at him. "How do you know?"

"I know," Max said slowly. "I'm Max Sand."

Recognition leaped into Ed's face. He went for his gun, rolling sideways away from Max. Max kicked the gun from his hand and Ed scrambled after it as Max pulled the white-hot poker from the fire. Ed turned, raising the gun toward Max, just as the poker lunged at his eyes.

He screamed in agony as the white metal burned its way through his flesh. The gun went off, the bullet going wild into the ceiling above him, then it fell from his hand.

Max stood there a moment, looking down. The stench of burned flesh reached up to his nostrils. It was over. Twelve years and it was over.

He turned dully as Charlie pulled at his arm. "Let's git outa here!" Charlie shouted. "The whole town'll be down on us in a minute!"

"Yeah," Max said slowly. He let the poker fall from his hand and started for the door. Mike was holding the horses and they leaped into the saddle. They rode out of town in a hail of bullets with a posse less than thirty minutes behind them.

Three days later, they were holed up in a small cave in the foothills. Max came back from the entrance and looked down at his friend. "How you doin', Mike?"

Mike's usually shiny black face was drawn and gray. "Poorly, boy, poorly."

Max bent over and wiped his face. "I'm sorry," he said. "We ain't got no more water."

Mike shook his head. "It don' really matter, boy. I got it good this time. I's th'ough travelin'."

Charlie's voice came from the back of the cave. "It'll be dawn in another hour. We better git movin'."

"You go, Charlie. I'm stayin' here with Mike."

Mike pushed himself to a sitting position, his back against the wall of the cave. "Don' be a fool, boy," he said.

Max shook his head. "I'm stayin' with you."

Mike smiled. His hand reached for Max's and squeezed it gently. "We's friends, boy, ain't we? Real friends?"

Max nodded.

"An' I never steered you bad, did I?" Mike asked. "I'm goin' to die an' they's nothin' you can do about it."

Max rolled a cigarette, lit it and stuck it in Mike's mouth. "Shut up an' rest."

"Open my belt."

Max leaned across his friend and pulled the buckle. Mike

groaned as the belt slid off. "Tha's better," he said. "Now look inside that belt."

Max turned it over. There was a money pouch taped to the inner surface.

Mike smiled. "They's five thousand dollars in that pouch. I been holdin' out for the right time—now. It was for the day we lef' this business."

Max rolled another cigarette and lit it. He watched his friend silently. Mike coughed. "You was born thirty years too late for this business. They ain't no mo' room in this worl' for a gun fighter. We come in at the tail end with nothin' but the leavin's."

Max still sat silently, his eyes on Mike's face. "I'm still not goin'."

Mike looked up at him. "Don' make me feel like I picked the wrong one back there in that prison," he said. "Not now when I'm a dyin' man."

Max's face broke into a sudden smile. "You're full of shit, Mike."

Mike grinned up at him. "I kin hold the posse off all day. By then, you'll be so far no'th, they'll never catch up to you." He started to laugh and suddenly stopped as he began to cough blood. He reached up a hand to Max. "He'p me to my feet, boy."

Max reached out and pulled Mike up. The big man leaned against him as they moved toward the mouth of the cave. They came out into the night and there was a small breeze just picking up at the edge of the cliffs.

For a moment they stood there, savoring the physical closeness of each other, the small things of love that men can share, then slowly Max lowered his friend to the ground.

Mike looked down the ridge. "I can hol' them here forever," he said. "Now, 'member what I said, boy. Go straight. No more thievin'. No more gun fightin'. I got you' word, boy?"

"You got my word, Mike."

"If you breaks it, I sure's hell'll come back an' haunt you!" the big man said. He turned his head away and looked down the ridge. "Now git, boy," he said huskily. "Dawn is breakin'." He reached for the rifle at his side.

Max turned and walked over to his horse. He mounted and sat there for a moment, looking back at Mike. The big colored man never turned to look back. Max dug his spurs into his horse and it leaped away.

It wasn't until an hour later, when the sun was bright and Max was on the next ridge, that he began to wonder about the quiet. By this time, there should have been the sound of gunfire behind him.

He never knew that Mike had died the moment he was out of sight.

He felt naked at first without his beard. Rubbing his fingers over his cleanly shaven face, he walked into the kitchen.

Charlie looked up from the kitchen table. "My God," he exclaimed. "I never would've known you!"

Martha, his wife, turned from the stove. She smiled suddenly. "You're much younger than I thought. And handsomer, too."

Max felt a flush of color run up into his cheeks. Awkwardly he sat down. "I figgered it's time for me to be movin' on."

Charlie and his wife exchanged quick looks.

"Why?" Charlie asked. "You own half this spread. You just can't go off an' leave it."

Max studied him. He rolled a cigarette and lit it. "We been here three months now. Let's stop kiddin' ourselves. This place can't carry the both of us."

They were silent. Max was right. Even though he had advanced the money to buy the ranch, there wasn't enough in it yet for all of them.

"What if somebody recognizes you?" Martha asked. "Your poster's in every sheriff's office in the southwest."

Max smiled and rubbed his chin again. "They won't recognize me. Not without the beard."

"You better think up a new name for yourself," Charlie said.

Max blew out a cloud of smoke. "Yeah. I reckon so. It's time. Everything's gotta change."

But the name hadn't come to him until the day he stood in the hot Nevada sun looking up at old man Cord and young Jonas. Then it came easy. As if it had been his own all his life.

Smith. Nevada Smith.

It was a good name. It told nothing about him.

He looked down at the little boy staring up at him with frightened eyes, then at the cold black gun in his other hand.

He saw the child follow his eyes. He dropped the gun back into his holster. He smiled slowly.

"Well, Junior," he said. "You heard your pappy."

He turned to his horse and led it around to the bunkhouse, the boy trotting obediently behind him. The bunkhouse was empty. The boy's voice piped up behind him. "Are you going to live here with Wong Toy?"

He smiled again. "I reckon so."

He picked out one of the bunks and spread his bedroll on it. Quickly he put his things away. When he turned around, the boy was still watching him with wide eyes.

"You're really goin' to stay?" the child asked.

"Uh-huh."

"Really?" the boy insisted. "Forever?" His voice caught slightly. "You're not goin' to go away like the others? Like Mommy did?"

Something in the child's eyes caught inside him. He knelt beside the boy. "I'll stay jest as long as you want me to."

Suddenly, the boy flung his arms around Nevada's neck and pressed his cheek close to his face. His breath was soft and warm. "I'm glad," he said. "Now you can learn me to ride."

Nevada straightened up, the boy still clinging to his legs. He walked outside and put the boy up on the saddle of his horse. He started to climb up behind him when suddenly the gun was heavy against his thigh.

"I'll be back in a minute," he said, and went back into the bunkhouse. Quickly he pulled the tie strings and unbuckled the gun belt. He hung it on a nail over his bunk and went out again into the white sunlight.

And he never strapped the gun on again.

16

RINA STEPPED DOWN FROM THE TRAIN INTO THE bright, flashing shadows of afternoon sun lacing the platform. A tall uniformed chauffeur stepped forward and touched his hand to his cap. "Miss Marlowe?"

Rina nodded.

"Mr. Smith sends his apologies for not being able to meet

you, ma'am. He's tied up at meetings at the studio. He says he'll see you for cocktails."

"Thank you," Rina said. She turned her face away for a moment to hide her disappointment. Three years was a long time.

The chauffeur picked up her valises. "If you'll follow me to the car, ma'am?"

Rina nodded again. She followed the tall uniform through the station to a shining black Pierce-Arrow limousine. Quickly the chauffeur stowed the bags up front and opened the door for her. The tiny gold insignia emblazoned over the handle shone up at her.

$$\frac{N}{S}$$

She settled back and reached for a cigarette. The chauffeur's voice through the speaker startled her. "You'll find them in the container near your right hand, ma'am."

She caught a glimpse of the man's quick smile in the rearview mirror as he started the big motor. She lit a cigarette and studied the interior of the car. The gold insignia was everywhere, even woven into the upholstery.

She leaned her head back. She didn't know why she should be surprised. She had read enough in the newspapers about him. The forty-acre ranch, and the thirty-room mansion he had built right in the middle of Beverly Hills. But reading about it never made it seem real. She closed her eyes so she could remember how it had become a reality for her.

It had been about five months after she'd come back East. She'd gone down to New York for a week of shopping and a banker friend of her father's had asked her to attend the premiere of a motion picture produced by a company in which he had a substantial interest.

"What's it called?" she had asked.

"The Sheriff of Peaceful Village," the banker had answered. "It's a Norman picture. Bernie Norman says it's the greatest Western ever made."

"Westerns bore me," she'd answered. "I had enough of that when I was out there myself."

"Norman says he has a new star in the man that's playing the lead. Nevada Smith. He says he'll be the biggest—"

"What was that name?" she interrupted. She couldn't have heard right.

"Nevada Smith," the banker repeated. "An odd name but these movie actors always have fancy names."

"I'll go," she had said quickly.

She remembered walking into the theater—the crowds, the bright lights outside, the well-groomed men and bejeweled women. And then that world seemed to vanish with the magic of the image on the screen.

It was near the end of the picture now and alone in a dreary room, the sheriff of Peaceful Village was putting on his gun, the gun he had sworn never to touch again.

The camera moved in close to his face, so close that she could almost see the tiny pores in his skin, feel his warm breath. He raised the gun and looked at it.

She could feel the weariness in him, see the torture of decision tighten his lips, set his square jaw, flatten the high, Indian-like cheekbones into the thin lines that etched their way into his cheeks. But his eyes were what held her.

They were the eyes of a man who had known death. Not once but many times. The eyes of a man who understood its futility, who felt its pain and sorrow.

Slowly the sheriff walked to the door and stepped outside. The bright sunlight came down and hit his face. He pulled his dark hat down over his eyes to shield them from the glare and began to walk down the lonely street. Faces of the townspeople peeked out at him from behind shutters and windows and curtains. He didn't return their glances, just walked forward stolidly, his faded shirt beginning to show the sweat pouring from him in the heat, his patched jeans looking threadbare against his lean, slightly bowed legs. The bright metal of his badge shone on his breast.

Death wore soft, expensive clothing. No dust marred the shine of his boots, the gleaming ivory handle of his gun. There was hatred in his face, the pleasurable lust to kill in his eyes, and his hand hovered like a rattlesnake above his holster.

They looked deep into each other's eyes for a moment. Death's eyes glittered with the joy of combat. The sheriff's were weary with sadness.

Death moved first, his hand speeding to his gun, but with a speed almost too quick for the eye to follow, the sheriff's gun seemed to leap into his hand. Death was flung violently backward to the ground, his gun falling from his hand, his eyes already glazing. His body twitched as two more bullets tore in him, and then he lay still.

The sheriff stood there for a moment, then slowly put his gun back into the holster. He turned his back on the dead man and began to walk down the street.

People began to flock out of the buildings. They watched the sheriff, their faces bright with battle lust. He did not return their glances.

The girl came out onto a porch. The sheriff stopped in front of her.

The girl's eyes were dim with tears.

The sheriff's were wide and unblinking. An expression of contempt suddenly came into his face. Disgust with her demand for blood, disgust for a town full of people who wanted nothing but their own form of sacrifice.

His hand moved up to his shirt and tore off the badge. He flung it into the dirt at her feet and turned away.

The girl looked down at the badge in shock, then up at the sheriff's retreating back. She started to move after him, then stopped.

Far down the street, the sheriff was mounting his horse. He turned it toward the hills. His shoulders slumping and head bowed, wearily he moved out of their lives and into the bright, glaring sunlight, as the screen began to fade.

There was silence as the lights came up in the theater. Rina turned to the banker, who smiled embarrassedly at her and cleared his throat. "That's the first time a movie ever did this to me."

Oddly enough, she felt a lump in her own throat. "Me, too," she said huskily.

He took her arm. "There's Bernie Norman over there. I want to go over and congratulate him."

They pushed their way through a crowd of enthusiastic well-wishers. Norman was a heavy-set man with dark jowls; his eyes were bright and elated. "How about that guy, Nevada Smith?" he asked. "Did you ever see anything like it? Still want me to get Tom Mix for a picture?"

The banker laughed and Rina looked up at him. He didn't laugh very often. "Tom Mix?" He chortled. "Who's he?"

Norman hit the banker on the back. "This picture will net two million," he said happily. "And I got Nevada Smith starting another picture right away!"

The limousine turned into a driveway at the foot of the hill. It passed under an iron gateway over which the now familiar insignia was emblazoned and began to wind its way up the narrow roadway to the top of the hill. Rina looked out the window and saw the huge house, its white roof turning blood orange in the falling sun.

She began to feel strange. What was she doing here? This wasn't the Nevada she knew. Suddenly, frantically, she opened her purse and began to search through it for Nevada's cablegram. Then it was in her hand and she felt calmer as she read it.

She remembered sending him a wire from Switzerland last month. It had been three years since she had heard from him. Three years in which she had kept on running. The first six months she spent in Boston, then boredom set in. New York was next, then London, Paris, Rome, Madrid, Constantinople, Berlin. There were the parties, the hungers, the fierce affairs, the passionate men, the voracious women. And the more she ran, the more frightened and alone she became.

And then came the morning in Zurich when she awoke with the sun shining in her eyes. She lay naked in bed, a white sheet thrown over her. Her mouth was dry and parched; she felt as if she hadn't had a drink of water in months. She reached for the carafe on the night table and when it wasn't there, she first realized she wasn't in her own room.

She sat up in a room that was furnished in expensive European fashion but wasn't familiar at all. She looked around for her robe but there wasn't a single item of her clothing anywhere. Vaguely she wondered where she was. There were cigarettes and matches on the night table and she lit one. The acrid smoke bit into her lungs as the door opened.

An attractive dark-haired woman came into the room. She paused when she saw Rina sitting up in bed. A smile came to her lips. She came over to the bed. "Ah, you are awake, *ma chérie*," she said softly, bending and kissing Rina on the mouth.

Rina stared up at her, her eyes wide. "Who are you?"

"Ah, my love, you do not remember me?"

Rina shook her head.

"Maybe this will refresh your memory, my darling," the woman said, dropping her gown and pressing Rina's head to her naked full bosom. "There now, do you remember how much we loved each other?" Her hand caressed Rina's face. Angrily Rina pushed it away.

The door opened again and a man came in. He held a bottle of champagne in one hand and was completely nude. He smiled at them. "Ah," he said. "We are all awake once again. The party was getting dull."

He crossed the room and held the champagne bottle out to Rina. "Have some wine, darling," he said. "The trouble is— one wakes up with such a terrible thirst, no?"

Rina held her hands to her temples. She felt the throbbing pulse beneath her fingers. It was a nightmare. This wasn't real. It couldn't be.

The man stroked her head solicitously. "A headache, no? I will bring some aspirin."

He turned and left the room. Terrified, Rina looked up at the woman. "Please," she begged. "I think I'm going out of my mind. Where are we?"

"In Zurich, of course, at Philippe's place."

"In Zurich?" Rina questioned. "Philippe?" She looked up at the woman. "Was that Philippe?"

"*Mais non,* of course not. That was Karl, my husband. Don't you remember?"

Rina shook her head. "I don't remember anything."

"We met at the races three weeks ago in Paris," the woman said. "You were alone in the box next to Philippe's. Your friend could not come, remember?"

Rina closed her eyes. She was beginning to remember. She had placed a bet on the beautiful red roan and the man in the adjoining box had leaned over. "A very wise choice," he had said. "That is my horse. I am Le Comte de Chaen."

"The count in the next box!" Rina exclaimed.

The woman nodded. She smiled again. "You remember," she said in a pleased voice. "The party began in Paris but it was too warm there, so we drove here to Philippe's chalet. That was almost two weeks ago."

"Two weeks?"

The woman nodded. "It has been a wonderful party," she said. She sat down on the bed next to Rina. "You're a very beautiful girl."

Rina stared at her, speechless. The door opened again and Karl came in, a bottle of aspirin in one hand, the champagne in the other. A tall blond man wearing a dressing robe followed him. He threw some photographs down on the bed. "How do you like them, Rina?"

She stared down at the pictures. A sick feeling began to come up into her throat. This could not be her. Not like this. Nude. With that woman and those men. She looked up at them helplessly.

The count was smiling. "I should have done better," he said apologetically. "But I think there was something the matter with the timer."

The woman picked them up. "I think you did well enough, Philippe." She laughed. "It was so funny. Making love with that little bulb in your hand so you could take the picture."

Rina was still silent.

Karl bent over her. "Our little *Américaine* is still sick," he said gently. He held out two aspirins to her. "Here, take these. You will feel better."

Rina stared up at the three of them. "I'd like to get dressed, please," she said in a weak voice.

The woman nodded. "But of course," she said. "Your clothes are in the closet." They turned and left the room.

Rina got out of bed and washed her face quickly. She debated over taking a bath but decided against it. She was in too much of a hurry to leave. She dressed and walked out into the other room.

The woman was still in her peignoir, but the men had changed to soft shirts and white flannels. She started to walk out without looking at them. The man named Karl called, "Mrs. Cord, you forgot your purse."

Silently she turned to take it from him, her eyes avoiding his face.

"I put in a set of the photographs as a memento of our party."

She opened the bag. The pictures stared obscenely up at her. "I don't want them," she said, holding them out.

He waved them aside. "Keep them. We can always make more copies from the negatives."

Slowly she lifted her eyes to his face. He was smiling. "Perhaps you would like a cup of coffee while we talk business?" he asked politely.

The negatives cost her ten thousand dollars and she burned them in an ash tray before she left the room. She sent the cable to Nevada from the hotel, as soon as she had checked in.

I'M LONELY AND MORE FRIGHTENED THAN I EVER WAS BEFORE. ARE YOU STILL MY FRIEND?

His reply reached her the next day, with a credit for five thousand dollars and confirmed reservations from Zurich through to California.

She crinkled the cablegram in her fingers as she read it once more while the limousine climbed to the top of the hill. The cable was typical of the Nevada she remembered. But it didn't seem at all like the Nevada she was coming to see.

I AM STILL YOUR FRIEND.

It was signed "Nevada."

17

NEVADA LEANED BACK IN HIS CHAIR AND LOOKED around the large office. An aura of tension had crept into the room. Dan Pierce's face was bland and smiling. "It isn't the money this time, Bernie," he said. "It's just that we feel the time is right. Let's do a picture about the West as it really was and skip the hokum that we've been turning out for years."

Norman looked down at his desk for a moment, his hand toying with the blue-covered script. He assumed an earnest expression. "It isn't the script, believe me, Dan," he said, turning to Von Elster for assurance. "We think it's great, don't we?"

The lanky, bald director nodded. "It's one of the greatest I ever read."

"Then why the balk?" the agent asked.

Norman shook his head. "The time isn't right. The industry is too upset. Warner's has a talking picture coming out soon. *The Lights of New York.* Some people think that when it comes out, silent movies will be finished."

Dan Pierce laughed. "Malarkey! Movies are movies. If you want to hear actors talk, go to the theater, that's where talk belongs."

Norman turned to Nevada, his voice taking on a fatherly tone. "Look, Nevada, have we ever steered you wrong? From the day you first came here, we've treated you right. If it's a question of money, that's no problem. Just name the figure."

Nevada smiled at him. "It isn't the money, Bernie. You know that. Ten thousand a week is enough for any man, even if income taxes have gone up to seven per cent. It's this script. It's the first real story I've ever read out here."

Norman reached for a cigar. Nevada leaned back in his chair. He remembered when he had first heard of the script. It was last year, when he was making *Gunfire at Sundown.*

One of the writers, a young man with glasses and a very pale skin, had come over to him. "Mr. Smith," he asked diffidently. "Can I trouble you for a minute?"

Nevada turned from the make-up man. "Why, sure——" He hesitated.

"Mark Weiss," the writer said quickly.

Nevada smiled. "Sure, Mark, what can I do for you?"

"I've got a script I'd like you to read," Weiss said quickly. "I spent two years researching it. It's about one of the last gun fighters in the Southwest. I think it's different from anything that's ever been made."

"I'd be glad to read it." That was one of the hazards of being a star. Everyone had a script they wanted you to read and each was the greatest ever written. "What's it called?"

"*The Renegade.*" He held out a blue-covered script.

The script felt heavy in his hand. He opened it to the last page and looked at the writer doubtfully. The script was three times standard length. "Pretty long, isn't it?"

Weiss nodded. "It is long but there was no way I could see to cut it. Everything in there is true. I spent the last two years checking old newspaper files through the entire Southwest."

Nevada turned back to the make-up man, the script still in his hand. "What happened to him?" he asked over his shoulder.

"Nobody seems to know. One day he just disappeared and nothing was ever heard about him again. There was a posse after him, and they think he died there in the mountains."

"A new story's always good," Nevada said. "People are getting tired of the same old heroes. What do you call this guy?"

The writer's voice seemed to hang in the air. "Sand," he said. "Max Sand."

The script slipped from Nevada's fingers. He felt the blood rush from his face. "What did you say?" he asked hollowly.

Weiss stared at him. "Max Sand. We can change it but that was his real name."

Nevada shook his head and looked down at the script. It lay there in the dust. Weiss knelt swiftly and picked it up. "Are you all right, Mr. Smith?" he asked in a concerned voice.

Nevada took a deep breath. He felt his self-control returning. He took the script from the outstretched hand and forced a smile.

A look of relief came into Weiss's face. "Thanks, Mr. Smith," he said gratefully. "I really appreciate this. Thanks very much."

For a week, Nevada couldn't bring himself to read it. In some strange way, he felt that if he did, he'd be exposing himself. Then one evening, he came into the library after dinner, where Von Elster was waiting, and found him deeply engrossed in this script.

"How long have you been sitting on this?" the director asked.

Nevada shrugged. "About a week. You know how it is. These writers are always coming up with scripts. Is it any good?"

Von Elster put it down slowly. "It's more than good. It's great. I want to be the director if you do it."

Late that night, the lamp still burning near his bed, Nevada realized what the director meant. Weiss had given depth and purpose to his portrait of a man who lived alone and developed a philosophy born of pain and sadness. There was no glamour in his crimes, only the desperate struggle for survival.

Nevada knew as he read it that the picture would be made. The script was too good to be passed up. For his own self-protection, he had to make the picture. If it escaped into someone else's hands, there was no telling how much further they'd delve into the life of Max Sand.

He bought the script from Weiss the next morning for one thousand dollars.

Nevada returned to the present suddenly. "Let's hold it for a year," Bernie Norman was saying. "By then, we'll know which way to jump."

Dan Pierce looked across at him. Nevada knew the look. It meant that Pierce felt he'd gone as far as he could.

"Chaplin and Pickford had the right idea in forming United Artists," Nevada said. "I guess that's the only way a star can be sure of making the pictures he wants."

Norman's eyes changed subtly. "They haven't had a good year since," he said. "They've dropped a bundle."

"Mebbe," Nevada said. "Only time will tell. It's still a new company."

Norman looked at Pierce for a moment, then back to Nevada. "O.K.," he said. "I'll make a deal with you. We'll put up a half million toward the picture, you guarantee all the negative cost over that."

"That's a million and a half more!" Pierce answered. "Where's Nevada going to get that kind of money?"

Norman smiled. "The same place we do. At the bank. He won't have any trouble. I'll arrange it. You'll own the picture one hundred per cent. All we'll get is distribution fees and our money back. That's a better deal than United Artists can give. That shows you how much we want to go along with you, Nevada. Fair enough?"

Nevada had no illusions. If the picture didn't make it, his name would be on the notes at the bank, not Norman's. He'd lose everything he had and more. He looked down at the blue-covered script. A resolution began to harden inside him.

Jonas' father had said to him once that it wasn't any satisfaction to win or lose if it wasn't your own money, and you'd never make it big playing for table stakes. This picture just couldn't miss. He knew it. He could feel it inside him.

He looked up at Norman again. "O.K., Bernie," he said. "It's a deal."

When they came out into the fading sunlight in front of

Norman's bungalow office, Nevada looked at the agent. Pierce's face was glum. "Maybe you better come down to my office," he muttered. "We got a lot of talking to do."

"It can keep till tomorrow," Nevada said. "I got company from the East waitin' for me at home."

"You just bit off a big nut," the agent said.

They started toward their cars. "I reckon it's about time," Nevada said confidently. "The only way to make real money is to gamble big money."

"You can also lose big that way," Pierce said dourly.

Nevada paused beside his white Stutz Bearcat. He put his hand affectionately on the door, much in the same manner he did with his horses. "We won't lose."

The agent squinted at him. "I hope you know what you're doing. I just don't like it when Norman comes in so fast and promises us all the profits. There's a monkey somewhere."

Nevada smiled. "The trouble with you, Dan, is you're an agent. All agents are suspicious. Bernie came in because he had to. He didn't want to take any chances on losin' me." He opened the door and got into the car. "I'll be down at your office at ten tomorrow morning."

"O.K.," the agent said. He started toward his own car, then stopped and came back. "This talking-picture business bothers me. A couple of other companies have announced they're going to make talkies."

"Let 'em," Nevada said. "It's their headache." He turned the key, pressed the starter and the big motor sprang into life with a roar. "It's a novelty," he shouted to the agent over the noise. "By the time our picture comes out people will have forgotten all about talkies."

The telephone on the small table near the bed rang softly. Rina walked over and picked it up. It was one of those new French telephones, the first she'd seen since she'd returned from Europe. The now familiar insignia was in the center of the dial, where the number usually was printed. "Hello."

Nevada's familiar voice was in her ear. "Howdy, friend. You all settled in?"

"Nevada!" she exclaimed.

"You got other friends?"

She laughed. "I'm unpacked," she said. "And amazed."

"At what?"

"Everything. This place. It's fabulous. I never saw anything like it."

His voice was a quiet whisper in her ear. "It's not very much. Paltry little spread, but I call it home."

"Oh, Nevada," she laughed. "I still can't believe it. Why did you ever build such a fantastic house? It's not like you at all."

"It's part of the act, Rina," he said. "Like the big white hat, the fancy shirts and the colored boots. You're not really a star unless you have the trappings."

"With N Bar S on everything?" she asked.

"With N Bar S on everything," he repeated. "But don't let it throw you. There are crazier things in Hollywood."

"I've got so much to tell you," she said. "What time will you be home?"

"Home?" He laughed. "I am home. I'm down in the bar, waiting for you."

"I'll be down in a minute," she said, then hesitated. "But, Nevada, how will I find the bar? This place is so immense."

"We got Indian guides just for occasions like this," he said. "I'll send one up after you."

She put down the telephone and went over to the mirror. By the time she had finished applying lipstick to her mouth, there was a soft knock at the door.

She crossed the room and opened it.

Nevada stood there, smiling. "Beg pardon, ma'am," he said with mock formality. "I jes' checked the entire joint an' you won't believe it, but I was the only Indian around!"

"Oh, Nevada!" she said softly.

Then suddenly she was in his arms, her face buried against the hard muscles of his chest, her tears staining the soft white front of his fancy shirt.

JONAS—1930
—————————————

Book Three

1

THE LIGHTS OF LOS ANGELES CAME UP UNDER THE
right wing. I looked over at Buzz, sitting next to me in the
cockpit. "We're almost home."

His pug-nosed face crinkled in a smile. He looked at his
watch. "I think we got us a new record, too."

"The hell with the record," I said. "All I want is that mail
contract."

He nodded. "We'll get it now for sure." He reached over and
patted the dashboard. "This baby ensured that for us."

I swung wide over the city, heading for Burbank. If we got
the airmail contract, Chicago to Los Angeles, it wouldn't be
long before Inter-Continental would span the country. From
Chicago east to New York would be the next step.

"I see in the papers that Ford has a tri-motor job on the
boards that will carry thirty-two passengers," Buzz said.

"When will it be ready?"

"Two, maybe three years," he answered. "That's the next step."

"Yeah," I said. "But we can't afford to wait for Ford. It could take five years before something practical came from them. We gotta be ready in two years."

Buzz stared at me. "Two years? How are we gonna do it? It's impossible."

I glanced at him. "How many mail planes are we flying now?"

"About thirty-four," he said.

"And if we get the new mail contract?"

"Double, maybe triple that many," he said. He looked at me shrewdly. "What're you gettin' at?"

"The manufacturers of those planes are making more out of our mail contracts than we are," I said.

"If you're talkin' about buildin' our own planes, you're nuts!" Buzz said. "It would take us two years just to set up a factory."

"Not if we bought one that was already in business," I answered.

He thought for a moment. "Lockheed, Martin, Curtiss-Wright, they're all too busy. They wouldn't sell. The only one who might is Winthrop. They're layin' off since they lost that Army contract."

I smiled at him. "You're thinkin' good, Buzz."

He stared at me in the dim light. "Oh, no. I worked for old man Winthrop. He swore he'd never—"

We were over Burbank airport now. I swung wide to the south end of the field where the Winthrop plant stood. I banked the plane so Buzz could see from his side. "Look down there."

Up through the darkness, illuminated by two searchlights, rose the giant white letters painted on the black tarred roof.

CORD AIRCRAFT, INC.

The reporters clustered around us as soon as we hit the ground. Their flash bulbs kept hitting my eyes and I blinked. "You tired, Mr. Cord?" one of them yelled.

I rubbed my unshaven cheeks and grinned. "Fresh as a daisy," I said. A stone on the field cut into my foot. I turned back to the plane and yelled up to Buzz. "Hey, throw me my shoes, will you?"

He laughed and threw them down and the reporters made a great fuss about taking my picture while I was putting them on.

Buzz climbed down beside me. They took some more pictures and we started to walk toward the hangar. "How does it feel to be home?" another reporter yelled.

"Good."

"Real good," Buzz added.

We meant it. Five days ago, we took off from Le Bourget in Paris. Newfoundland, New York, Chicago, Los Angeles—five days.

A reporter came running up, waving a sheet of paper. "You just broke the Chicago-to-L.A. record!" he said. "That makes five records you broke on this flight!"

"One for each day." I grinned. "That's nothin' to complain about."

"Does that mean you'll get the mail contract?" a reporter asked.

Behind them, at the entrance to the hangar, I could see McAllister waving frantically. "That's the business end," I said. "I leave that to my partner, Buzz. He'll fill you gentlemen in on it."

I cut away from them quickly, leaving them to surround Buzz while I walked over to McAllister. His face wore a harassed expression. "I thought you'd never get here on time."

"I said I'd be in by nine o'clock."

He took my arm. "I've got a car waiting," he said. "We'll go right to the bank from here. I told them I'd bring you down."

"Wait a minute," I said, shaking my arm free. "Told who?"

"The syndication group that agreed to meet your price for the sublicensing of the high-speed injection mold. Even Du Pont's coming in with them now." He took my arm again and began to hurry me to the car.

I pulled free again. "Wait a minute," I said. "I haven't been near a bed for five days and I'm beat. I'll see them tomorrow."

"Tomorrow?" he yelled. "They're waiting down there now!"

"I don't give a damn," I said. "Let 'em wait."

"But they're giving you ten million dollars!"

"They're giving me nothing," I said. "They had the same chance to buy that patent we did. They were all in Europe that year but they were too tight. Now they need it, they can wait until tomorrow."

I got into the car. "The Beverly Hills Hotel."

McAllister climbed in beside me. He looked distraught. "To-morrow?" he said. "They don't want to wait."

The chauffeur started the car. I looked over at McAllister and grinned. I began to feel a little sorry for him. I knew it hadn't been an easy deal to swing.

"Tell you what," I said gently. "Let me get six hours' shut-eye and then we can meet."

"That will be three o'clock in the morning!" Max exclaimed.

I nodded. "Bring them to my suite in the hotel. I'll be ready for them then."

Monica Winthrop was waiting in the suite. She got up from the couch and put out her cigarette as I came in. She ran over and kissed me. "Oh, what a beard!" she exclaimed in mock surprise.

"What're you doin' here?" I asked. "I was looking for you at the airport."

"I would have been there but I was afraid Daddy would show up," she said quickly.

She was right. Amos Winthrop was too much of a heller not to recognize the symptoms. The trouble was he couldn't divide his time properly. He let women interfere with his work and work interfere with his women. But Monica was his only daughter and, like all rakes, he thought of her as something spe-cial. Which she was. But not in the way he thought.

"Mix me a drink," I said, walking past her to the bedroom. "I'm going to slip into a hot tub. I smell so loud I can hear myself."

She picked up a tumbler filled with bourbon and ice and fol-lowed me into the bedroom. "I had your drink ready," she said. "And the tub is full."

I took the drink from her hand. "How'd you know when I got here?"

She smiled again. "I heard it on the radio."

I sipped at the drink as she came over to me. "You don't have to take a bath on my account," she said. "That smell is kind of exciting."

I put the drink down and walked into the bathroom, taking off my shirt. When I turned to close the door, she was right be-hind me. "Don't get into the tub yet," she said. "It's a shame to waste all that musky maleness."

She put her arms around my neck and pressed her body against me. I sought her lips but she turned her face away and buried it in my shoulder. I felt her take a deep, shuddering breath. She moaned softly and the heat came out of her body like steam from an oven.

I turned her face up to me with my hand. Her eyes were almost closed. She moaned again, her body writhing. I tugged at my belt and my trousers fell to the floor. I kicked them aside and backed her toward the vanity table along the wall. Her eyes were still closed as she leaped up on me like a monkey climbing a coconut tree.

"Breathe slow, baby," I said as she began to scream in a tortured half whisper. "I may not smell as good as this for years."

The water was soft and hot, and weariness washed in and out as it rippled against me. I reached behind me, trying to get to my back with the soap. I couldn't make it.

"Let me do that," she said.

I looked up at her as she took the washcloth from my hand and began to rub my back. The slow, circular motion was soothing and I leaned forward and closed my eyes. "Don't stop," I said. "That feels good."

"You're just like a baby. You need someone to take care of you."

I opened my eyes and looked up at her again. "I been thinkin' that, too," I said. "I think I'll get a Jap houseboy."

"A Jap houseboy won't do this," she said. I felt her tap my shoulder. "Lean back. I want to rinse the soap off."

I leaned back in the water, my eyes still closed. She moved the washcloth over my chest and then down. I opened my eyes. She was staring down at me.

"It looks so small and helpless," she whispered.

"That wasn't what you said a little while ago."

"I know," she said, still in that whisper, the foggy look coming back into her eyes.

I knew the look. I reached up and put my arm around her neck and pulled her down on the edge of the tub. I felt her hand go down and cover me with the washcloth as we kissed. "You're growing strong," she whispered, her mouth moving against mine.

I laughed and just then the telephone rang. We turned quickly, startled, and the water spashed up and drenched the front of her dress. Silently she took the phone from the vanity and gave it to me. "Yes?" I growled into it.

It was McAllister. He was down in the lobby.

"I said three o'clock," I snapped.

"It is three o'clock," he answered. "Can we come up? Winthrop's with us, too. He said he has to see you."

I looked over at Monica. That was all I needed. To have her father come up and find her in my room. "No," I said quickly. "I'm still in the tub. Take 'em into the bar and buy 'em a drink."

"The bars are all closed."

"O.K., then, I'll meet you in the lobby," I said.

"The lobby's no place to close this deal. There's no privacy. They won't like it at all. I don't understand why we can't come up."

"Because I got a broad up here."

"So what?" he answered. "They're all broad-minded." He laughed at his pun.

"The girl's Monica Winthrop."

There was silence on the other end of the telephone. Then I heard him sigh wearily. "Christ!" he said. "Your father was right. You just never stop, do you?"

"Time enough for me to stop when I'm your age."

"I don't know," he said wearily. "They won't like the idea of meeting in the lobby."

"If it's privacy they want," I said, "I know just the place."

"Where?"

"The men's room, just off the elevators. I'll meet you there in five minutes. That'll be private enough!"

I put down the phone and got to my feet. I looked at Monica. "Hand me a towel," I said. "I gotta go downstairs and see your father."

2

I CAME INTO THE MEN'S ROOM, RUBBING MY CHEEK. I still had the five-day beard. I hadn't had time to shave. I grinned at the sight of them, all engrossed in their duties, not even looking around as I entered.

"The meeting will come to order, gentlemen," I said.

They looked over their shoulders at me, a startled expression on their faces. I heard one of them mutter a faint damn under his breath and wondered what minor tragedy brought that out.

McAllister came over to me. "I must say, Jonas," he said rather pompously. "You have a rather peculiar choice of meeting place."

I stared at him. I knew he was talking for the benefit of the others, so I didn't really mind. I looked down at his trousers. "Aw, Mac," I said. "Button your fly before you start talking." His face grew red and his hand dropped quickly to his trouser front.

I laughed and turned to the others. "I'm sorry to put you to this inconvenience, gentlemen," I said. "But I have a space problem up in my room. I've got a box up there that takes up almost the whole place."

The only one who got it was Amos Winthrop. I saw a knowing grin appear on his face. I wondered what his expression would be if he knew it was his daughter I was talking about.

By this time, Mac had recovered his aplomb and stepped in to take over. There were introductions all around and then we got down to business. As Mac explained to me, the three big chemical corporations had set up a separate company to sublicense from me. It was this company which would make the first payment and guarantee the royalties.

I had only one question to ask. "Who guarantees the money?"

Mac indicated one of the men. "Sheffield here," he said. "Mr. Sheffield is one of the partners of George Stewart, Inc."

I looked at Sheffield. Stewart, Morgan, Lehman were all good names down on the Street. I couldn't ask for better people financially. There was something about the man's face that seemed familiar. I searched my memory. Then I had it.

F. Martin Sheffield. New York, Boston, Southampton, Palm Beach. Harvard School of Business, summa cum laude, before the war. Major, U.S. Army, 1917–18. Three decorations for bravery under fire. Ten-goal polo-player. Society. Age now—from his appearance, about thirty-five; from the record, forty-two.

I remembered he'd come to visit my father about ten years ago. He'd wanted then to float a public issue for the company. My father had turned him down.

"No matter how good they make it sound, Junior," my father had said, "never let 'em get their hooks into you. Because then they run your business, not you. All they can give you is money when the only thing that counts is power. And that they always keep for themselves."

I stared at Sheffield. "How're you goin' to guarantee the payments?"

His dark, deep-set eyes glittered behind the pince-nez bifocals. "We're on the contract with the others, Mr. Cord," he said.

His voice was surprisingly deep for a slight man. And very sure of itself. It was as if he did not deign to answer my question, as if everybody knew that Stewart's name on a contract was guarantee enough.

Maybe it was, but something about him rankled deep inside me. "You didn't answer my question, Mr. Sheffield," I said politely. "I asked how the money was to be guaranteed. I'm not a banker or a Wall Street man, I'm just a poor boy who had to leave school and go to work because his pappy died. I don't understand these things. I know when I go into a bank and they ask me to guarantee something, I have to put up collateral—like land, mortgages, bonds, something of value—before they give me anything. That's what I mean."

A faintly cold smile came to his thin lips. "Surely, Mr. Cord, you don't mean to imply that all these companies might not be good for the amount promised?"

I kept my voice bland. "I didn't mean anything like that, Mr. Sheffield. It's just that men who have had more experience than I, men who are older and know more, tell me that these are unsettled times. The market's broke and banks are failing all over the country. There's no telling what might happen next. I'd like to know how I'm goin' to be paid, that's all."

"Your money will be guaranteed out of income that the new company will earn," Sheffield said, still patiently explaining.

"I see," I said, nodding my head. "You mean I'll be paid out of money you earn if I grant you the license?"

"That's about it," he said.

I took a cigarette from my pocket and lit it. "I still don't understand. Why can't they pay me all at once?"

"Ten million dollars is a large amount of cash, even for these companies," he said. "They have many demands on their capital. That's why we're in the picture."

"Oh," I said, still playing it dumb. "You mean you're going to advance the money?"

"Oh, no," he said quickly. "That's not it at all. We're simply underwriting the stock, providing the organizational capital to make the new company possible. That alone will come to several million dollars."

"Including your brokerage fees?"

"Of course," he answered. "That's quite customary."

"Of course."

He shot a shrewd look at me. "Mr. Cord, you object to our position?"

I shrugged my shoulders. "Not at all. Why should I? It's not my place to tell other people how to run their business. I have enough trouble with my own."

"But you do seem to have some doubts about our proposition."

"I do," I said. "I was under the impression I was to receive ten million dollars for these rights. Now I find I'm only *guaranteed* ten million dollars. There's a difference between the two. In one case, I'm paid outright, in the other, I'm an accidental participant in your venture, subject to the same risks that you are but with a limitation put upon the extent of my participation."

"Do you object to that kind of deal?"

"Not at all. It's just that I like to know where I stand."

"Good. Then we can get down to signing the papers." Sheffield smiled in relief.

"Not yet," I said and his smile vanished as quickly as it had come. "I'm willing to become a participant in the manner suggested but if I'm to take that risk, I feel I should be guaranteed fifteen million, not ten."

For a moment, there was a shocked silence, then everybody began to talk at once. "But you already agreed to ten!" Sheffield protested.

I stared at him. "No, I didn't. This is the first time we met."

Mac was blowing a gasket. "Wait a minute, Jonas. You led me to believe you'd listen to an offer of ten million dollars!"

"Well, I listened."

For the first time, I saw his lawyer's calm ruffled. "I acted in good faith on your behalf. I won't be a party to this kind of underhanded negotiation. If this deal doesn't go through as agreed, I'm through! I'm resigning!"

I stared at him impassively. "Suit yourself."

Mac raged. "Your trouble is you're getting too big for your breeches! I remember when you were still wet behind the ears—"

I was angry now; my voice went icy cold. "The trouble is you're just the lawyer and it's my property you're dealing with. I'll make the decision as to what I do with it—sell it or give it away, whatever I want to do. It's mine, I own it and you work for me. Remember that!"

Mac's face went white. I could see it all working around in his mind. The hundred thousand a year I was paying him. The bonus participation in profits. The house he lived in. The schools his kids were going to. His position in society. I wondered if at that moment he wasn't regretting the sixty-thousand-a-year practice he'd given up to come to me.

But I couldn't bring myself to feel sorry for him. He knew what he was doing. He even wrote his own contract, on his own terms. He wanted money and he got it. It was too late now for him to start complaining.

I looked at the others. They were staring at us. I knew then, sorry for Mac or not, I had to give him a leg up. "Aw, come off it, Mac," I said, making my voice warm and friendly. "We're too close to let a stupid thing like this come between us. Forget it. There'll be other deals. The important thing to do is to get your new contract signed so that I can be sure none of these other pirates steal you away from me."

I saw the look of relief flood into his face. "Sure, Jonas," he said. He hesitated. "I guess we're both a little bit overtired. Me with the negotiation, you with that record-breaking flight. I guess I just misunderstood what you told me."

He turned to the others. "I'm sorry, gentlemen," he said smoothly, himself once more. "It's my fault. I didn't mean to mislead you but I misunderstood Mr. Cord. My apologies."

An awkward silence fell in the room. For a moment nobody spoke, then I grinned and walked over to the urinal. "This is just so we don't have to write this meeting off as a total loss," I said over my shoulder.

It was Sheffield who made the first break. I heard him whispering hurriedly to the others. When I turned around, he looked at me. "Split it with you," he said. "Twelve five."

They wanted it real bad if they came up that quickly. At first, I shook my head, then I had an idea. "I heard a great deal about you from my father," I said. "He said you were a real sportsman, that you'd gamble on anything."

A smile appeared on his thin lips. "I've been known to wager a bit at times," he admitted.

"For two and a half million dollars, I'll bet you can't pee into that far urinal from where you're standing," I said, pointing to the one about four feet from him. "If you do, the deal is yours for twelve five. If you don't, I get fifteen."

His mouth hung open, his eyes staring behind their glasses. "Mr. Cord!" he sputtered.

"You can call me Jonas," I said. "Remember it's for two and a half million dollars."

He looked at the others. They stared back at him. Then at me. Finally the Mahlon Chemical man spoke up. "It's two and a half million dollars, Martin. I'd take a shot at it for that kind of money!"

Sheffield hesitated a moment. He looked at Mac but Mac wouldn't meet his gaze. Then he turned toward the urinal, his hand going to his fly. He looked at me. I nodded. Nothing happened. Nothing at all. He just stood there, a red flush creeping up his collar into his face. A moment passed, another moment. His face was red now.

I broke the silence. "All right, Mr. Sheffield," I said with a straight face. "I concede. You win the bet. The deal is for twelve five."

He stared at me, trying to read my mind. I kept my expression blank. I held out my hand toward him. He hesitated a moment, then took it.

"May I call you Martin?" I asked.

He nodded, a faint smile appearing on his thin lips. "Please do."

I shook his hand. "Martin," I said solemnly. "Your fly is open!"

3

MCALLISTER MADE THE NECESSARY CHANGES IN the contracts and we signed them right there. It was after four thirty when we came out into the lobby. I started for the elevator when Amos Winthrop tapped me on the shoulder.

I didn't want to talk to him. "Can it keep until morning, Amos?" I asked. "I gotta get some sleep."

His face crinkled in a knowing smile. He hit me on the shoulder jovially. "I know the kind of sleepin' you want to do, boy, but this is important."

"Nothing can be that important."

The elevator door opened and I stepped into it. Amos was right beside me. The operator started to close the doors. "Just a minute," I said.

The doors rolled open again and I stepped out. "All right, Amos," I asked. "What is it?"

We walked over to a couch and sat down. "I need another ten thousand," he said.

I stared at him. No wonder he was always broke. He spent it faster than they could print it. "What happened to all the cash you got for your stock?"

An embarrassed expression crossed his face. "It's gone," he said. "You know how much I owed."

I knew. He owed everybody. By the time he got through with his creditors and his ex-wives, I could see where the fifty grand had gone. I was beginning to feel sorry I'd included him in the deal but I'd thought he'd be able to contribute something to the company. At one time, he was one of the best designers of aircraft in the country.

"Your contract doesn't provide for advances like that," I said.

"I know," he answered. "But this is important. It won't happen again, I promise. It's for Monica."

"Monica?" I looked at him. This was going to be good. "What about her?"

He shook his head. "I want to send her to her mother in England. She's too much for me. I can't control her any more. She's seeing some guy on the sly and I have a feeling if she isn't balling him already, she soon will be."

For a moment, I stared at him. I wondered if this wasn't a gentle form of blackmail. It could be that he already knew and was taking this way of letting me know. "Do you know the guy?"

He shook his head. "If I did, I'd kill him," he said vehemently. "A nice sweet innocent kid like her."

I kept my face impassive. Love is blind but parents are blinder. Even a cheater like Amos, with all his knowledge, was no smarter than Joe Doakes in Pomona. "You talk to her?"

He shook his head again. "I tried but she won't listen. You know how kids are nowadays. They learn everything in school; you can't teach them anything. When she was sixteen, I found a package of Merry Widows in her pocketbook."

He should have stopped her then. He was about three years too late. She was nineteen now and carried her own brass ring. "Guys like you never learn."

"What was I supposed to do?" he asked truculently. "Keep her locked in her room?"

I shook my head. "You could have tried being her father."

"What makes you such an expert?" he snapped. "You won't talk like that after you have kids of your own."

I could have told him. I had a father who was too busy with his own life, too. But I was tired. I got to my feet.

"What about the money?" he asked anxiously.

"I'll give it to you," I said. A feeling of disgust suddenly came up in me. What did I need guys like this around me for? They were like leeches. Once they got into you, they never let go. "As a matter of fact, I'll give you twenty-five thousand."

An expression of surprised relief flooded across his face. "You will, Jonas?"

I nodded. "On one condition."

For the first time, caution came into his eyes. "What do you mean?"

"I want your resignation."

"From Winthrop Aircraft?" His voice was incredulous.

"From Cord Aircraft," I said pointedly.

The color began to drain from his face. "But—but I started the company. I know everything about it. I was just planning a new plane that the Army will sure as hell go for—"

"Take the money, Amos," I said coldly. "You've had it." I started for the elevator. I stepped inside and the boy closed the doors in his face. "Going up, Mr. Cord?" he asked.

I stared at him. That was a stupid question. What other way was there to go?

"All the way," I said wearily.

Monica was lying across the bed in the tops of my pajamas, half asleep. She opened her eyes and looked at me. "Everything go all right?"

I nodded.

She watched me as I threw my shirt across a chair. "What did Daddy want?"

I stepped out of my trousers and caught the pajama bottoms she threw at me. "He just turned in his resignation," I said, kicking off my shorts and getting into the pajamas.

She sat up in bed, her brown eyes widening in surprise. "He did?"

I nodded.

"I wonder why?"

I looked at her. "He said it had something to do with you. That he wanted more time to be your father."

She stared at me for a moment, then began to laugh. "Well, I'll be damned," she said. "All my life I wanted him to pay some kind of attention to me and now, when I don't need him any more, he suddenly wants to play daddy."

"Don't need him any more?"

She nodded. "Not any more. Ever," she said slowly. She came off the bed and laid her head against my chest. Her voice was a childlike whisper of confidence. "Not now that I have you. You're everything to me—father, brother, lover."

I stroked her soft brown hair slowly. Suddenly, a surge of sympathy came up inside me. I knew how alone you could be when you were nineteen.

Her eyes were closed and there were faintly blue weary hollows in the soft white flesh beneath them. I pressed my lips lightly to her forehead. "Come to bed, child," I said gently. "It's almost morning."

She was asleep in a moment, her head resting on my shoulder, her neck in the crook of my arm. For a long time, I couldn't fall asleep. I lay there looking down at her quiet face as the sun came up and light spilled into the room.

Damn Amos Winthrop! Damn Jonas Cord! I cursed all men who were too busy and self-centered to be fathers to their children.

I began to feel weariness seep through me. Half asleep, I felt her move beside me and the warmth of her long, graceful body flowed down along my side. Then sleep came. The dark, starless night of wonderful sleep.

We were married the next evening at the Little Chapel in Reno.

4

I SAW THE GLEAMING PHOSPHORESCENCE MOVING in the water and flicked the fly gaily across the stream just over the trout. The instinct came up in me. I knew I had him. Everything was right. The water, the flickering shadows from the trees lining the bank, the bottle-blue, green and red tail of the fly at the end of my line. Another moment and the bastard would strike. I set myself when I heard Monica's voice from the bank behind me.

"Jonas!"

Her voice shattered the stillness and the trout dived for the bottom of the stream. The fly began to drag and before I turned around, I knew the honeymoon was over.

"What is it?" I growled.

She stood there in a pair of shorts, her knees red and her nose peeling. "There's a telephone call for you. From Los Angeles."

"Who?"

"I don't know," she answered. "It's a woman. She didn't give her name."

I looked back at the stream. There were no lights in the water. The fish were gone. That was the end of it. The fishing was over for the day.

I started toward the bank. "Tell her to hold on," I said. "I'll be up there in a minute."

She nodded and started back to the cabin. I began to reel in the line. I wondered who could be calling me. Not many people knew about the cabin in the hills.

When I was a kid, I used to come up here with Nevada. My father always intended to come along but he never did make it.

I came out of the stream and trudged up the path. It was late in the afternoon and the evening sounds were just beginning. Through the trees I could hear the crickets beginning their song.

I laid the rod alongside the outside wall of the cabin and went inside. Monica was sitting in a chair near the telephone, turning the pages of a magazine. I picked up the phone. "Hello."

"Mr. Cord?"

"Yes."

"Just a moment," the operator sang. "Los Angeles, your party is on the wire."

I heard a click, then a familiar voice. "Jonas?"

"Rina?"

"Yes," she said. "I've been trying to get you for three days. Nobody would tell me where you were, then I thought of the cabin."

"Great," I said, looking over the telephone at Monica. She was looking down at the magazine but I knew she was listening.

"By the way," Rina said in that low, husky voice. "Congratulations. I hope you'll be very happy. Your bride's a very pretty girl."

"You know her?"

"No," Rina answered quickly. "I saw the pictures in the papers."

"Oh," I said. "Thanks. But that isn't why you called."

"No, it's not," she said with her usual directness. "I need your help."

"If it's another ten you need, I can always let you have it."

"It's for more money than that. Much more."

"How much more?"

"Two million dollars."

"What?" I all but yelled. "What the hell do you need that much money for?"

"It's not for myself," she said. Her voice sounded very upset. "It's for Nevada. He's in a bind. He's about to lose everything he's got."

"But I thought he was doing great. The papers say he's making a half million dollars a year."

"He is," Rina said. "But—"

"But what?" I pulled out a cigarette and fished around for a match. I knew Monica saw me but she kept her nose buried in the magazine. "I'm listening," I said, dragging on the cigarette.

"Nevada's hocked everything he has to make a picture. He's been working on it for over a year and now everything's gone wrong and they don't want to release it."

"Why?" I asked. "Is it a stinker?"

"No," she said quickly. "It's not that. It's great. But only talking pictures are going. That's all the theaters will play."

"Why didn't he make a talking picture to start with?" I asked.

"He started it more than a year ago. Nobody expected talkies to come in the way they did," she answered. "Now the bank's calling his loan and Norman won't advance any more money. He claims he's stuck with his own pictures."

"I see," I said.

"You've got to help him, Jonas. His whole life is wrapped up in this picture. If he loses it, he'll never get over it."

"Nevada never cared that much about money," I said.

"It isn't the money," she said quickly. "It's the way he feels about this picture. He believes in it. For once, he had a chance to show what the West was really like."

"Nobody gives a damn what the West was really like."

"Did you ever see one of his pictures?" she asked.

"No."

A shade of disbelief crept into her voice. "Weren't you curious to see what he looked like on the screen?"

"Why should I be?" I asked. "I know what he looks like."

Her voice went flat. "Are you going to help?"

"That's a lot of dough," I said. "Why should I?"

"I remember when you wanted something real bad and he gave it to you."

I knew what she was talking about. Nevada's stock interest in Cord Explosives. "It didn't cost him two million bucks," I said.

"It didn't?" she asked. "What's it worth now?"

That stopped me for a moment. Maybe it wasn't yet, but in five more years it would be.

"If he's in that much of a jam," I said, "why didn't he call me himself?"

"Nevada's a proud man," she said. "You know that."

"How come you're so interested?"

"Because he's my friend," she said quickly. "When I needed help, he didn't ask any questions."

"I'm not promising anything," I said. "But I'll fly down to L.A. tonight. Where can I reach you?"

"I'm staying at Nevada's," she said. "But you better let me meet you someplace. I don't want him to know I called you."

"O.K.," I said. "I'll be at the Beverly Hills Hotel about midnight."

I put down the telephone. "Who was that?" Monica asked.

"My father's widow," I said, walking past her toward the bed-room. "Pack your bags. I'm taking you back to the ranch. I have to go down to L.A. on business tonight."

"But it's only been five days," she said. "You promised we'd have a two-week honeymoon."

"This is an emergency."

She followed me into the bedroom as I sat down on the bed and pulled off my waders. "What will people think if we come back from our honeymoon after only five days?" she said.

I stared up at her. "What the hell do I care what they think?"

She began to cry. "I won't go," she said, stamping her foot.

I got to my feet and started out. "Then stay!" I said angrily. "I'm going down the hill to get the car. If you're not ready when I get back, I'm leaving without you!"

What was it with dames, anyway? You stood in front of some two-bit preacher for five lousy minutes and when you walked away, everything was turned inside out.

Before you were married, it was great. You were the king. She stood there with one hand on your cock to let you know she wanted it, and with the other, tried to light your cigarette, wash your back, feed your face and smooth your pillow all at the same time.

Then come the magic words and you got to beg for it. You got to go by the book. Play with it, warm it up, treat it gentle. You got to rest on your elbows and light her cigarettes and carry her wrap and open doors. You even have to thank her when she lets you have it, the same piece she couldn't stop of-fering you before.

I pulled the car up in front of the cabin and tooted the horn. Monica came out carrying a small bag and stood there waiting for me to open the car door. After a moment, she opened the door and got in with a grieved expression. And she wore the same expression for the two hours it took us to drive back to the ranch.

It was nine o'clock when I pulled up in front of the house. As usual, Robair was at the door. His expression didn't change when I stayed in the car after he took out Monica's valise. His eyes flicked across my face as he turned and bowed to Monica. "Evenin', Miz Cord," he said. "Ah have you' room all tidied up an' ready for you." Robair looked at me again and turned and went back up the steps.

When Monica spoke, her voice was low and taut as a bow-string. "How long will you be gone?"

I shrugged. "As long as it takes for me to finish my business." Then I felt a softening inside me. What the hell, after all we'd only been married for five days. "I'll get back as quick as I can."

"Don't hurry back!" she said and stalked up the steps and into the house without a backward glance.

I swore angrily and threw the car into gear, then started up the road to the plant. I kept the old Waco in the field behind it. I was still angry when I climbed into the cockpit and I didn't begin to feel better until I was twenty-five hundred feet up and heading toward Los Angeles.

5

I LOOKED DOWN AT THE BLUE-COVERED SCRIPT IN my hand, then back up at Rina. Time hadn't taken anything away from her. She was still slim and strong and her breasts jutted like rocks at the canyon edge and I knew they would be just as hard to the touch. The only things that had changed were her eyes. There was a sureness in them that hadn't been there before.

"I'm not much for reading," I said.

"I thought that was what you'd say," she said. "So I arranged with the studio to screen the picture for you. They're waiting down there right now."

"How long you been out here?"

"About a year and a half. Ever since I came back from Europe."

"Staying at Nevada's all this time?"

She nodded.

"You sleeping with him?"

She didn't evade. "Yes. He's very good for me."

"Are you good for him?" I asked.

Her eyes were still on mine. "I hope so," she said quietly. "But that doesn't really matter. You don't give a damn whether I am or I'm not."

"I was just curious," I said, getting to my feet and dropping the script on the chair. "I was just wondering what it takes to keep you."

"It's not what you think," she said quickly.

"What is it, then?" I shot back. "Money?"

"No." She shook her head. "A man. A real man. I never could make it with boys."

That touched home. "Maybe I'll make it in time," I said.

"You just got married five days ago."

I stared at her for a moment. I could feel all the old familiar excitement climbing up in me. "Let's go," I said tersely. "I haven't got all night."

I sat in the darkened projection room with Rina on one side of me and Von Elster, the director, on the other.

Rina hadn't lied. The picture was great, but for only one reason. Nevada. He held the picture together with an innate core of strength that somehow illuminated the screen.

It was the strength I had always felt in him but up there it was larger, more purposeful, and no one could escape it. He started out on that screen as a sixteen-year-old boy and rode off into the hills in the end as a twenty-five-year-old man. Not once during the whole picture was I ever aware of his real age.

I leaned back in my chair with a sigh as the lights came up. I reached for a cigarette, still feeling the excitement of the screen. I lit the cigarette and dragged on it. The surging reached down into my loins. There was still something missing, I felt vaguely. Then I felt the heat in my thighs and I knew what it was.

I looked at Von Elster. "Outside of that small bit about the madam in New Orleans and the convict's daughter in the cow town, there aren't any women in the picture."

Von Elster smiled. "There are some things you don't do in a Western. Women is one of them."

"Why?"

"Because the industry feels that the image of the clean, strong man must be preserved. The hero can be guilty of any crime but fornication."

I laughed and got to my feet. "Forgive the question," I said. "But why can't you just add voices the way you did the music? Why make the whole thing over?"

"I wish we could," Von Elster said. "But the projection speed of silent film is different from sound film. Talking film is projected at the speed of speech, while silent film moves much faster, depending on dialogue cards and broader action to carry the story."

I nodded. Mechanically, what he said made sense. Like everything else in this world, there was a technology to this business and it was beginning to interest me. Without mechanics, the whole thing would be impossible.

"Come back to the hotel with me. I'd like to talk some more about this."

I saw a sudden look of caution come into Rina's eyes. She glanced at Von Elster, then turned to me. "It's almost four o'clock," she said quickly. "And I think we've gone about as far as we can without Nevada."

"O.K.," I said easily. "You bring him up to the hotel in the morning. Eight o'clock, all right?"

"Eight o'clock will be fine."

"I can drop you off at your hotel, Mr. Cord," Von Elster said eagerly.

I glanced at Rina. She shook her head imperceptibly. "Thanks," I said. "Rina can drop me on her way home."

Rina didn't speak until the car pulled to a stop in front of the hotel. "Von Elster is on the make," she said. "He's worried. He's never made a talking picture before and he wants to do this one. It's a big picture and if it comes off, he'll be in solid again."

"You mean he's shaky?" I asked.

"Everybody in Hollywood is. From Garbo and Gilbert on down. No one is sure just what talking pictures are going to do to their career. I hear John Gilbert's voice is so bad that MGM won't even pencil him in for another picture."

"What about Nevada's voice?"

"It's good," she said. "Very good. We made a sound test the other day."

"Well, that's one less thing to worry about."

"Are you going to do it?" she asked.

"What's in it for me if I do?" I countered.

"You could make a lot of money," she said.

"I don't need it," I said. "I'll make a lot of money, anyway."

Her eyes turned to me, her voice was cold. "You haven't changed, have you?"

I shook my head. "No. Why should I? Does anybody? Did

you?" I reached for her hand. It was cold as ice. "Just how much are you willing to give to bail Nevada out?"

Her eyes were steady on mine. "I'd give everything I've got if it would help."

I felt a kind of sadness creeping into me. I wondered how many people would say that for me. Right then, I couldn't think of one. I let go of her hand and got out of the car.

She leaned toward me. "Well, Jonas, have you made up your mind?"

"Not yet," I said slowly. "There's a lot more I have to know about."

"Oh." She leaned back disappointedly.

"But don't you worry," I said. "If I do it, you'll be the first one I come to for payment."

She signaled the chauffeur. He put the car into gear. "Knowing you," she said quietly, "I never expected anything else."

The limousine rolled away and I turned and walked into the hotel. I went up to my room and opened up the script. It took about an hour and a half to go through it. It was almost six o'clock before I closed my eyes.

6

THE TELEPHONE KEPT BANGING AWAY AT MY HEAD. I shook my head to clear it and looked at my watch. It was a few minutes past seven. I picked up the phone.

"Mr. Cord? Von Elster here. I'm sorry to bother you so early, but I'm down in the lobby with Mr. Norman. It's very important we see you before you meet with Nevada."

"Who's Norman?" I asked, still trying to clear my head.

"Bernard B. Norman of Norman Pictures. That's the company releasing the picture. Mr. Norman feels he can be of help to you in making the right kind of deal with Nevada."

"Why should I need any help?" I asked. "I've known Nevada all my life."

His voice grew confidential. "Nevada's all right, Mr. Cord. But his agent, Dan Pierce, is a very sharp man. Mr. Norman just wants to give you a few pointers before you tangle with him."

I reached for a cigarette. Von Elster hadn't lost any time. He'd run right back to his boss the minute he smelled my money. I didn't know what they wanted but I was damn sure it boded no good for Nevada.

"Wait down there until I can get dressed. I'll call you."

I put down the phone and finished lighting the cigarette. The blue cover of the script caught my eye. I picked up the telephone again. I gave the operator Tony Moroni's home number out in the valley.

"Sorry to wake you up, Tony," I said. "This is Jonas."

His soft voice chuckled over the phone. "That's all right, Jonas. I get up early, anyway. By the way, congratulations on your marriage."

"Thanks," I said automatically, suddenly remembering I hadn't even thought about Monica since I came to town. "Did you bank Nevada Smith's new picture?"

"*The Renegade?*"

"Yeah."

"Yes, we did," he answered.

"What's the story on it?" I asked.

"It's a good picture," he said. "It would have a better chance if it were a talkie, but it's a good picture."

"If you think it's good, why are you calling your loan?"

"Let me ask a question first, Jonas," he said. "Exactly what is your interest?"

"I don't know yet," I said frankly. "Nevada's my friend. I want to find out what's happening. Why are you calling the loan?"

"You know how we work," he explained. "We made the loan to Smith on his collateral plus the guarantee of the Norman Pictures Company. Now Bernie Norman needs credit to remake some of his own pictures, so he's withdrawing his guarantee. Automatically, that means we have to call in the loan."

No wonder Von Elster and Bernie Norman were down in the lobby waiting to see me. They didn't want anybody to interfere with their fingering Nevada.

"Exactly what happens to Nevada?" I asked.

"If he can't pay the loan, we foreclose on the picture, then all his collateral goes into an escrow account. Then we liquidate until we recover."

"What do you do with the picture then?" I asked. "Junk it?"

"Oh, no." He laughed softly. "Then we turn it over to Norman to release. That gives Bernie a chance to get his money out. He has about four hundred thousand in it. After he recovers, the overage is paid to us. When our loan is paid off, we turn over what's left to Smith."

The whole thing was beginning to make sense. By the time any money got to Nevada, he'd have had it. "What's the chances on any overage?" I asked.

"Not very good," Tony answered. "Under the present deal, the distribution fees are very low and Nevada Smith's money comes out first. When we take over, the fees will triple and his share will come out last."

"Who gets the fees—the bank?"

He laughed again. "Of course not. Bernie does. He's the distributor."

Now I had it. The boys downstairs were going to make it real big. Screw Nevada. That way, they could grab themselves off a big one for practically nothing. I wondered just how smart Nevada's agent could be if he let him stick his head into a trap like that.

"One more question, Tony," I said, "and I'll stop bothering you. How much more money should it take to make *The Renegade* over as a talkie?"

He was silent for a moment. "Let's see," he said. "The sets are still standing, they have all the costumes. That's about half the cost. Maybe another million; less, if they're lucky."

"Is it worth it?"

He hesitated. "I usually don't venture opinions on pictures. Too many things can happen."

"This time, venture," I said. "I need an opinion from somebody who hasn't any ax to grind."

"From every report I've had, it could be a very good gamble."

"Thanks," I said. "Now do me a favor. Hold off any action on the loan until I talk to you later in the day. Maybe I'll come in on the guarantee in place of Norman."

"You'll still need another million after that."

"I know," I answered. "But my writing hand's still good. I can always sign another note."

Moroni laughed pleasantly as we said our good-bys. He wasn't worried. He knew I could cover the money easily out of the advance I got from the syndicate that leased the patents on my plastic mold. Bankers always were ready to lend you as much money as you wanted, so long as you could put up collateral.

I looked down at my watch as I put down the phone. It was almost seven thirty and I felt fuzzy. I started to pick up the phone, then changed my mind. The hell with them. Let them wait if they wanted to see me. I turned and went into the bathroom to take a shower.

The telephone rang three different times while I was under the shower. I stood there letting the hot water soak into my skin and wash away the weariness. It was almost eight o'clock when I came out of the bathroom and the telephone began ringing again.

It was Von Elster again. His voice was low and conspiratorial. "Nevada, his agent and Rina are on their way up," he whispered. "They didn't see us."

"Good," I said.

"But how are we going to meet?"

"I guess it's too late now," I said easily. "I'll just have to take my chances with Nevada's agent, I guess. Tell your Mr. Norman I appreciate his offer, though. If there's anything I need, I'll call him."

I heard his gasp of shock as I hung up. I laughed and wondered how he was going to explain that to his boss. I climbed into my trousers and was reaching for a shirt when a knock came at the door.

"Come in," I yelled from the bedroom. I heard the door open and finished buttoning up my shirt. I looked for my shoes but they were over on the other side of the bed. It wasn't worth walking over to get them so I came out in my bare feet.

Rina was already seated on the big couch. Nevada and another man were standing in the middle of the room. A slow smile came over Nevada's face. He held out his hand. "Jonas," he said warmly.

I took his hand awkwardly. It seemed funny to shake hands with him as one would with a stranger. "Nevada."

There were faint lines of strain in the corners of his eyes, but for a moment they disappeared as he looked up into my face. "You're lookin' more like your pappy every day, son."

"You're lookin' pretty good yourself. Where'd you get them duds?"

A faint tinge of sheepishness came into his face. "That's part of the act," he said. "I got to wear 'em. The kids expect it." He fished in his pocket with that familiar gesture and came up with a package of makin's. He began to roll a cigarette. "I been readin' a lot about you in the papers. Flyin' from Paris to Los Angeles, gettin' married an' all. Your wife with you?"

I shook my head.

He glanced at me shrewdly. In that moment, I knew he knew how it was with Monica and me. He could read me like a book. I could never hide anything from him. "Too bad," he said. "I'd like to have met her."

I looked at the other man to change the subject. Nevada caught himself quickly. "Oh, this is Dan Pierce, my agent."

We shook hands and I came right to the point. "I saw your picture last night," I said. "I liked it. Too bad you have to make it over."

"I thought talking pictures wouldn't last," Nevada said.

"That's not the whole story, Nevada," Pierce broke in angrily. He turned to me. "Nevada wanted the picture silent, sure, but by the time we'd started shooting, he saw he was wrong. We tried then to turn it into a talkie but we couldn't."

"Why?"

"Norman wouldn't let us," Pierce said. "He only had one sound stage at that time and he was using it for one of his own pictures. He insisted we start shooting right away or he'd withdraw his guarantee."

The picture was clear now. The whole thing had been a sucker play from the start. I looked at Nevada. I didn't understand it. He was a better poker player than that.

Nevada read me again. "I know what you're thinkin', boy," he said quickly. "But I wanted to make this picture. It said something that none of the other phonies I'd been in even came close to."

"What about Norman?" I asked. "How come they won't advance you the money to shoot it over?"

"They've run out of credit," Nevada said. "That's why the bank is calling the loan."

"That's a lot of crap!" Pierce exploded again. "We're caught in a squeeze play. Bernie Norman makes the bank call our loan and the bank turns the picture back to him. He gets it for peanuts—about a third what it would have cost him to make it."

"How much would it take to make the picture over?" I asked.

Nevada looked at me. "About a million bucks."

"Plus the loan the bank is calling," Pierce added quickly.

I turned to him. "Would you still have Norman release the picture?"

He nodded. "Sure. They've got ten thousand contracts on it an' if it's a talkie, not a theater will cancel out."

"If it's silent?"

"We'll be lucky to get fifteen hundred," he said. "They all want talkies."

"What do you think I should do?"

Nevada hesitated a moment, then his eyes came squarely on mine. "I wouldn't do it if I was you," he said frankly. "You could blow the whole bundle."

I saw the look that Pierce threw him. It was filled with anger but also with a peculiar sort of respect. To Pierce I was just another sucker. But to his credit, he recognized that I was something more to Nevada.

I stared at him for a moment, then turned and looked down at Rina, sitting on the couch. Her face was impassive. Only her eyes were pleading.

I turned back to Nevada. "I'll take the shot," I said. "But only on one condition. I'll buy you out and it will be my picture. And when we make it again, we'll make it the way I want it. There'll be no arguments; everybody will do as they're told. You included. If I'm going to lose the hand, at least I want to deal the cards."

Nevada nodded. He'd heard my father say the same words often enough. And he'd been the one who taught me always to reach for the deal when the stakes were high.

"But what do you know about making pictures?" Pierce asked.

"Nothing," I said. "But how many people do you know who have made a talking picture?"

That stopped him. I could see the comprehension come into his eyes. What I had said was true. It was a new business. There were no veterans any more. I turned back to Nevada. "Well?"

"I don't know," he said slowly. "I'm lettin' you take the whole risk. I can't lose anything."

"You're wrong!" Pierce said quickly. "If it's a stinker, your career is shot!"

Nevada smiled at him. "I got along pretty good before," he said. "I'm a little old to worry about anything I fell into by accident."

"Well, Nevada?"

He stuck out his hand and the worry lines around his eyes lifted suddenly and he was young again. "It's a deal, Junior."

I took his hand and then went over to the telephone. I called Moroni at the bank. "Make arrangements to transfer the loan to Cord Explosives," I said.

"Good luck, Jonas," he said with a chuckle. "I had the feeling you were going to do it."

"Then you knew more than I did."

"That's what makes a good banker," he said.

I hung up and turned back to the others. "Now, the first thing I do is fire Von Elster."

Nevada's face was shocked. "But Von is one of the best in the business," he protested. "He's directed every picture I ever made. He discovered me."

"He's a lousy little shit," I said. "The minute he thought you were in trouble, he tried to sell you out. He had Bernie Norman up here at seven o'clock this morning. They wanted to give me some free advice. I didn't talk to them."

"Now maybe you'll believe me when I say Bernie was behind the squeeze," Pierce said.

"Like it or not, Nevada," I said, "we made a deal. It's my picture and what I say goes."

He nodded silently.

"The next thing I want is for Pierce to arrange for me to see as many of the talkies as possible in the next three days. Then, next weekend, I'll fly you all to New York. We're goin' to spend three or four days goin' to the theater. We might even pick up a stage director while we're there. We'll see." I paused to light a cigarette and saw a sudden look come over Nevada's face. "What are you smiling at?"

"Like I said, you're gettin' more like your pappy every day."

I grinned back at him. Just then, the waiter came in with breakfast. Nevada and Pierce went into the bathroom to wash up and Rina and I were left alone.

There was a gentle look on her face. "If you'd only let yourself go, Jonas," she said softly, "I think you might become a human being."

I looked into her eyes. "Don't try to con me," I said. "We both know why I did it. You and I made our deal last night."

The gentle look faded from her face. "Do you want me to blow you right now?" she asked.

I knew I had hit her from the way she spoke. I smiled. "I can wait."

"So can I," she replied. "Forever, if I have to."

Just then the telephone rang. "Get it," I said.

Rina picked it up and I heard a voice crackle for a moment, then she handed the phone to me. "Your wife."

"Hello, Monica."

Her voice was filled with anger. "Business!" she shrieked. "And when I call you up, some cheap whore answers. I suppose you're going to tell me it's your stepmother!"

"That's right!"

There was an angry click and the phone went dead in my hands. I looked down at it for a moment, then began to laugh. Everything was so right.

And so wrong.

7

I LOOKED OUT THE WINDOW AT THE FIELD. THERE were several planes warming up on the line, the red, white and blue ICA gleaming in the circle along their sides and under their wings. I looked down at the planning board, then up at the designer.

Morrissey was young, even younger than I. He had graduated from M.I.T., where he'd majored in aeronautical engineering and design. He wasn't a flier; he was of a new generation that walked on the sky. What he proposed was radical. A single-wing, two-motor plane that would outlift anything in the air.

He set his glasses lower on his nose. "The way I see it, Mr. Cord," he said in his precise manner, "is that by deepening the wings, we get all the lift we need and also increase our fuel capacity. Plus which, we have the added advantage of keeping our pilot in direct visual control."

"What I'm interested in is the payload and speed," I said.

"If my calculations are correct," Morrissey said, "we should be able to carry twenty passengers in addition to the pilot and copilot at a cruising speed of about two fifty. It should fly for about six hours before refueling."

"You mean we could fly from here to New York with only one stopover in Chicago?" Buzz asked skeptically. "I don't believe it!"

"That's what my calculations show, Mr. Dalton," Morrissey said politely.

Buzz looked at me. "You can throw away your money on fool schemes like this," he said, "but not me. I've been through too many of these pipe dreams."

"About how much would it take to build the first one?" I asked Morrissey.

"Four hundred, maybe five hundred thousand. After we get rid of the bugs, we can produce them for about a quarter of a million."

Dalton laughed raucously. "A half million bucks for one airplane? That's crazy. We'll never get our money out."

First-class passage coast to coast by train was over four hundred dollars. It took almost four full days. Plus meals, it came to more than five hundred bucks per passenger. A plane like this would have a payload of seven grand a trip, plus the mail franchise, which would bring it up to about eighty-five hundred dollars. Flying five trips a week, in less than twenty weeks we could get all our costs back, plus operating expenses. From there on in, it would be gravy. Why, we could even afford to throw in free meals on the flight.

I looked down at my watch. It was almost nine o'clock. I got to my feet. "I have to get down to the studio. They're shooting the first scene today."

Dalton's face turned red with anger. "Come off it, Jonas. Get down to business. For the past month and a half, all you been doin' is spending time at that goddam studio. While you're jerkin' off with that lousy picture, we got to find ourselves a plane to build. If we don't, the whole industry will get ahead of us."

I stared at him, unsmiling. "As far as I'm concerned," I said, "we have one."

"You're not—" he said incredulously, "you don't mean

you're goin' to take a chance with this?"

I nodded, then turned to Morrissey. "You can start building the plane right away."

"Wait a minute," Dalton snapped. "If you think ICA is going to foot the bill, you're crazy. Don't forget I own half of the stock."

"And Cord Explosives owns the other half," I said. "Cord Explosives also holds over half a million dollars of mortgages on ICA planes, most of which are past due right now. If I fore-closed on them, I'd wind up owning all of Inter-Continental Airlines."

He stared at me angrily for a moment, then his face relaxed into a grin. "I shoulda known better, Jonas. I shoulda learned my lesson when I lost that Waco to you in the poker game."

I smiled back. "You're a great flier, Buzz. You stick to flying and leave the business end to me. I'll make a rich man out of you yet."

He reached for a cigarette. "O.K.," he said easily. "But I still think you're nuts to build this plane. We could lose our shirt on it."

I didn't answer as we walked out to my car. There was no use explaining to Buzz the simple rules of credit. ICA would order twenty of these planes from Cord Aircraft. The two companies would then give chattel mortgages on them to Cord Explosives. And Cord Explosives would discount those mortgages at the banks, even before the planes were built. The worst that could happen, if the plane was no good, was that Cord Explosives would end up with a whopping tax deduction.

I got into the car. "Good luck with the picture!" Buzz yelled after me as I pulled away.

I turned into the main gate at the Norman studios. The guard looked out and waved me on. "Good morning, Mr. Cord," he called. "Good luck, sir."

I smiled and drove toward the parking lot. There was a small marker with my name on it. MR. CORD. They didn't miss a trick when it came to sucking ass. There was a reserved table with my name on it in the executive dining room. I also had a private bungalow with a suite of offices and two secretaries, a liquor cabinet stocked to the brim, an electric refrigerator, a private can and shower, a dressing room, a conference room and two secretarial offices in addition to my own.

I went through the back door of my bungalow and directly into my office. I wasn't at the desk more than a moment when one of the secretaries came in. She stood in front of the desk, looking very efficient with her notebook and pencil. "Good morning, Mr. Cord," she said brightly. "Any dictation?"

I shook my head. You'd think by this time she'd know better. For the past five weeks, this had been going on every morning. I never write anything—messages, memos, instructions. If I want anything written, I call McAllister. That's what lawyers are for.

The telephone on my desk buzzed. She picked it up. "Mr. Cord's office." She listened a moment, then turned to me. "They've completed rehearsal on Stage Nine. And they're ready for their first take. They want to know if you'd like to come down."

I got up. "Tell them I'm on my way."

Stage Nine was at the far end of the lot. We built the New Orleans set there because we figured it was quieter and there wouldn't be any interfering sounds coming across from the other stages. I began to hurry along the brick paths, cursing the distance, until I saw a messenger's bicycle leaning against one of the executive bungalows. A moment later, I was pedaling like mad down the path. I heard the messenger start yelling behind me.

I pulled around in front of Stage Nine and almost crashed into a man opening the door. He stood there and looked at me in shocked surprise. It was Bernie Norman. "Why, Mr. Cord," he said. "You didn't have to do that. You could have called for a car to bring you down here."

I leaned the bike against the wall. "I didn't have time, Mr. Norman," I said. "They said they were ready to start. It's my money and my time they're spending in there."

They were ready to play the first scene, the one where Max, as a young man, is having his first interview with the madam of the fancy house. That wasn't the opening of the picture, but that's the way they shoot them. They make all the interior scenes first, then the exteriors. When it's all finished, an editor splices it together in its proper sequence.

The actress playing the madam was Cynthia Randall, Norman's biggest female star. She was supposed to be the sexiest thing in the movies. Personally, she didn't do a thing for me. I like my women with tits. Two make-up men and a hairdresser were hovering over her as she sat in front of the dressing table that was part of the set.

Nevada was standing over in the other corner, his back to me, talking to Rina. He turned around as I came up and a chill ran through me as memory dragged up a picture of him from my childhood. He looked even younger than he did when I first saw him. I don't know how he did it; even his eyes were the eyes of a young man.

He smiled slowly. "Well, Junior. Here we go."

I nodded, still staring at him. "Yeah," I said. "Here we go."

Somebody yelled, "Places, everybody!"

"I guess that means me," Nevada said.

Rina's face was turned toward the set, a rapt expression in her eyes. A man pushed past carrying a cable. I turned away from him and almost bumped into another man. I decided to get out of the way before I did any damage.

I wound up near the sound booth. From there I could see and hear everything. Now I knew why pictures cost so much money. We were on our eleventh take of that same scene when I noticed the sound man in the booth. He was bent over the control board, his earphones tight to his head, twisting the dials crazily. Every other moment, I could see his lips move in silent curses, then he would spin the dials again.

"Something wrong with the machine?" I asked.

He looked up at me. I could tell from his look he didn't know who I was. "There's nothing wrong with the machine," he said.

"Something's bothering you?"

"Look, buddy," he said. "We both need our jobs, right?"

I nodded.

"When the boss tells yuh to make somebody look good, yuh do what he says—yuh don't ask no questions. Right?"

"Right," I said.

"Well, I'm doin' my best. But I ain't God. I can't change the sound of voices."

I stared at him, a kind of dismay creeping over me. I had only Rina's word that Nevada's voice test had been O.K. "You mean Nevada Smith?"

He shook his head. "Naah," he said contemptuously. "He's O.K. It's the dame. She comes over so nasal it sounds like her voice is coming out of her eyeballs."

The sound man turned back to his machine. I reached over and snatched the earphones off his head. He turned angrily. "What the hell's the idea?"

But I had them on by then and there was nothing he could do but stand there. Nevada was speaking. His voice came through fine—there was a good sound to it. Then Cynthia Randall began to speak and I didn't know whether to believe my eyes or my ears.

Her voice had all the irritating qualities of a cat wailing on the back fence, with none of the sexual implications. It shivered its way down my spine. A voice like that could put an end to sex, even in the fanciest house in New Orleans. I ripped the earphones from my head and thrust them into the sound man's astonished hands. I started out on the set. A man grabbed at me but I angrily pushed him aside.

A voice yelled, "Cut!" and a sudden silence fell over the set. Everyone was staring at me with strangely startled expressions.

I was seething. All I knew was that someone had played me for a patsy and I didn't like it. I think the girl knew why I was there. A look of caution appeared in her eyes, even as she tried to bring a smile to her lips.

Bernie Norman hurried onto the set. A flicker of relief showed in her face and I knew the whole story. She reached for Bernie's arm as he turned toward me. "Mr. Cord," he asked, "is anything wrong?"

"Yeah," I said grimly. "Her. Get her off the set. She's fired!"

"You just can't do that, Mr. Cord!" he exclaimed. "She has a contract for this picture!"

"Maybe she has," I admitted, "but not with me. It wasn't my pen she squeezed the last drop of ink out of."

Bernie stared at me, the pale coming up underneath his tan. He knew what I was talking about. "This is highly irregular," he protested. "Miss Randall is a very important star."

"I don't care if she's the Mother of God," I interrupted. I held out my wrist and looked down at the watch and then back up at him. "You've got exactly five minutes to get her off this set or I'll close down this picture and hit you with the biggest lawsuit you ever had!"

* * *

I sat down on the canvas chair with my name on it and looked around the now deserted set. Only a few people hovered about, moving like disembodied ghosts at a banquet. I looked over at the sound man hunched over his control board, his ear-phones still glued to his head. I closed my eyes wearily. It was after ten o'clock at night.

I heard footsteps approaching and opened my eyes. It was Dan Pierce. He'd been on the phone trying to borrow a star from one of the other studios. "Well?" I asked.

He shook his head negatively. "No dice. MGM wouldn't lend us Garbo. They're planning a talking picture for her themselves."

"What about Marion Davies?"

"I just hung up on her. She loves the part but it isn't the kind of thing she feels she can do. Maybe we should've stuck with Cynthia Randall. It's costing you thirty grand a day to sit around like this."

I lit the cigarette and stared up at him. "I'd rather drop it now than be laughed out of the theater and lose it all later."

"Maybe we could bring an actress in from New York?"

"We haven't the time," I said. "Ten days, three hundred grand."

Just then, Rina came up with some sandwiches. "I thought you'd be hungry," she said, "so I sent out for these."

I took one and bit into it somberly. She turned and gave one to the second man. "Thanks, Miss Marlowe."

"You're welcome," she said and walked back to where she'd been sitting with Nevada.

"Too bad you can't find one that sounds like her," the sound man mumbled through a mouthful of sandwich.

I looked at him. "What do you mean?"

"She's got somethin' in her voice that gets yuh," he said. "If it came through on the sound track like that, you'd have them falling out of the balconies."

I stared at him now. "You mean Rina?"

He nodded and swallowed his mouthful. "Yeah." A slow, meaningful grin came to his lips. "An' if I ain't crazy, she'd photograph like a roll in the hay, too. She's all woman."

I turned to Dan. "What do you think?"

"It's possible," he admitted cautiously.

"Then, let's go," I said, getting to my feet. "Thirty grand a day is a lot of money."

Rina took it as a big joke when I asked her to speak a few of the lines into the microphone. She still didn't think I meant it when I called the crew back for a full-scale screen test. I don't think she took me seriously at all until we sat in the screening room at two that morning and watched her and Nevada play one scene.

I'd never seen anything like her on the screen before. Whatever it was she had, it was twice as strong up there on the screen. She just plain made your mouth water.

I turned to her. "Go home and go to bed. I want you in wardrobe at six o'clock tomorrow morning. We start shooting at nine."

She shook her head. "Uh-uh, Jonas. The joke's gone far enough. I won't have any part of it."

"You be on that set ready to shoot at nine!" I said grimly. "You're the one who called, not me, remember?"

I looked at Nevada. There was a puzzled expression on his face. And something about the clear innocence in his eyes hit me wrong. "And you better see to it that she shows up!" I said angrily.

I turned and stormed out of the projection room, leaving them staring after me with shocked faces.

8

I OPENED ONE EYE SLOWLY AND PEERED AT MY wrist watch. Two o'clock! I sat up quickly and the pain almost split my skull. I groaned out loud and the door opened.

It was Dan, already dressed in cream-colored slacks and a loud sports shirt. He held a glass of what looked like tomato juice. "Here," he said. "Drink it down, pal. It'll wash the fuzz away."

I lifted the glass to my lips. It tasted awful going down but he was right. A moment later, my head began to clear. I looked around the bedroom. It was a shambles. "Where are the girls?" I asked.

"I paid them off an' sent them home."

"Good." I got to my feet woozily. "I gotta get down to the studio. They were going to start shooting at nine."

Dan smiled. "I called and told them you were tied up but would get down there this afternoon. I figured it was better if you got some sleep. That was a hectic night."

I grinned at him. It sure was.

Dan and I had really tied one on the night before. I'd met him coming off the set and offered to give him a lift downtown. But on the way we'd decided to stop and eat. I was wound up tighter than a dollar watch and he'd offered to help me unwind. Steaks at a spot he knew, which ought to have been closed but wasn't, along with bourbon and later the works. The works came out of his little black book, which all agents seem to carry. I'd unwound all right but now I wondered if they'd ever be able to wind me up again.

His Jap houseboy had shirred eggs and sausages ready when I came out of the shower. I was starved. I ate six eggs and about a dozen of the little bangers. When I put down my fourth cup of coffee Dan smiled and asked, "How are yuh feeling now?"

I grinned back at him. "I never felt better in my life." It was true. For once I felt relaxed and loose. There wasn't the usual tightening in my gut as I thought about the day. "You said something about getting down to business?"

We'd talked the night before, more than I usually did with a stranger. But Dan Pierce was different. He was a type I hadn't encountered before and he fascinated me. He was tough, shrewd and knew what he wanted. I was in over my head and I knew it. I wouldn't be for long, but until I got the hang of it I could use someone like Dan Pierce.

"I sold my agency this morning to MCA."

"What for?"

"Because I'm coming in with you."

"Aren't you jumping the gun a little?" I asked. "I'm only in for this one picture. What'll you do after that?"

Dan smiled. "That's what you say. It even might be what you really believe, right now. But I know different. You got a feel for this business—a natural feel for it that not many people have. And there's a challenge that you can't resist. You just found another gambling game. You'll stick."

I sipped at the coffee. It was strong and black, just the way I liked it. "And just how do you figure you can help?" I asked.

"Because I know all the angles in this business, all the dirty tricks it would take you a long time to find out about. You're a busy man and time's the most valuable thing you've got. I wouldn't be worth half as much if motion pictures were your only business. But it's not. And it never will be. It's just another game of craps."

I stared at him. "Give me a free sample."

"For one thing," he said quickly, "I wouldn't have started the picture until I'd had a sound test on everyone."

"That's something I already learned. I want a sample of what I don't know."

He reached around behind him for a blue-covered script. "If Rina comes off on the screen like that test indicates, we can make a few changes in this and save ourselves four hundred thousand dollars."

"How?"

"By building up her story and confining more of the picture to the New Orleans episode. It'll save five weeks of exteriors and nobody knows yet how good those microphones work outside."

I reached for a cigarette. "If we did that," I said slowly, "what happens to Nevada? His part would be cut way down."

Dan's eyes met mine steadily. "Nevada's not my problem any more, he's MCA's. I'm workin' for you now an' I figure you already used up all the sentiment you're entitled to on this picture. This is just like any other kind of business. The big thing is to make money."

I dragged on the butt and sipped at the coffee. For the first time since Rina called, I was back to normal. For a while, she'd had me spinning like a top. I didn't know whether I was coming or going. I felt different now. "What kind of deal do you have in mind?"

"No salary. Just a ten-per-cent piece of the action and an expense account."

I laughed. "I thought you said you sold your agency."

"That's the only way I can figure my compensation without adding to your overhead."

"Don't kid me," I said. "You'd be living off the expense account."

"Sure I will. But even with a salary, I would. How do you expect me to do a job for you if I can't spend money? Money is the only thing in this town nobody talks back to."

"I'll give you a ten-per-cent participation in profits. But no stock interest."

He studied me for a moment. "What about the expense account?"

"That's O.K."

He stuck out his hand. "It's a deal."

It was after three o'clock when we walked onto Stage Nine. The place was jumping, a mumble of buzzing, efficient noise, as they got ready for the next take. Nevada was standing on the edge of the set; Rina wasn't anywhere in sight. I stopped near the sound man. "How's it coming?"

He looked up at me and grinned. "Sounds great," he said, tapping his earphones.

I smiled and walked over to Nevada. He was talking to the director and they both turned as I came up. "How's she doing?"

The new director shrugged. "She was a little nervous at first but she's settling down. She'll be O.K."

"She'll be great," Nevada said warmly. "I never figured all the times she cued me on the script that it would come in handy for her too."

One of the assistant directors hurried up. "We're ready now, Mr. Carrol."

The director nodded and the assistant turned around and yelled, "Places, everybody!"

The director walked over to the camera as Nevada moved out on the set. I turned and saw Rina entering from the side. I stared, unable to believe my eyes. Her long, white-blond hair was tied up on top of her head and they'd bound her breasts so tight she looked like a boy. Her mouth was painted in a tiny Cupid's bow and her eyebrows were penciled to a thin, unnatural line. She was no longer a woman—she was a caricature of every ad in *Vanity Fair*.

Dan's face was impassive. He stared at me, his eyes unrevealing. "They did a good job," he said. "She's right in the image."

"She don't look like a woman."

"That's what they go for."

"I don't give a damn what they go for! I don't like it. Broads that look like that are a dime a dozen in this town."

A faint smile came into Dan's eyes. "You don't like it, change it," he said. "You're the boss. It's your picture."

I stared at him for a moment. I felt like walking out onto the set and blowing a fuse. But instinct held me back. I knew one more display like yesterday's would demoralize the whole crew. "Tell Carrol I want to see him," I said to Dan.

He nodded approvingly. "Smart," he said. "That's the right way to do it. You may need me even less than I thought!" He walked over to the director.

A moment later, the director called a ten-minute break. He came over to me and I could see he was nervous. "What seems to be the trouble, Mr. Cord?"

"Who O.K.'d that make-up and costume?"

The director looked at me, then over his shoulder at Rina. "I'm sure it was approved by wardrobe and make-up," he said. "Nevada told them to give her the full treatment."

"Nevada?"

He nodded. I looked at Dan. "I want everybody concerned in my office in ten minutes," I said.

"Right, Jonas."

I turned and walked out of the building.

9

I LOOKED AROUND THE OFFICE. I GUESS THE STUdio knew what they were doing after all. It was just large enough to hold all of us.

Dan sat in an easy chair to the left of my desk, Carrol, the new director, beside him. Rina and Nevada were on the couch, and across the room from them was the cameraman. On the other side of the room were the make-up man and the head of the wardrobe department, a slim woman of indeterminate age, with a young face and prematurely-gray hair, wearing a simple tailored dress. Finally, my secretary was on my right, with the inevitable pencil poised over her pad.

I lit a cigarette. "All of you saw that test last night," I said. "It was great. How come that girl wasn't on the set this afternoon?"

Nobody answered. "Rina, stand up." Silently she got to her feet and stood there looking at me. I glanced around the room again. "What's her name?"

The director coughed and laughed nervously. "Mr. Cord, everybody knows her name."

"Yeah? What is it?"

"Rina Marlowe."

"Then why don't she look like Rina Marlowe instead of an ass-end combination of Clara Bow, Marion Davies and Cynthia Randall? She sure as hell doesn't look like Rina Marlowe!"

"I'm afraid you don't understand, Mr. Cord."

I looked around. "What's your name?"

She stared right back at me. "I'm Ilene Gaillard," she said. "I'm the costume designer."

"All right, Miss Gaillard. Suppose you tell me what I don't understand."

"Miss Marlowe has to be dressed in the very forefront of fashion," she said calmly. "You see, Mr. Cord, though we make certain concessions to the period in which the picture takes place, the fundamental design must carry forward the latest in high fashion. That's what most women go to the movies to see. Motion pictures set the style."

I squinted at her. "Style or no style, Miss Gaillard, it doesn't make sense that a girl should have to look like a boy to be in fashion. No man in his right mind could be interested in a figure like that."

"Don't blame Miss Gaillard, Jonas. I told her to do it."

I turned to Nevada. "You told her?"

He nodded.

Sooner or later, it was bound to happen. I let my voice grow cold. "It's my money that's on the line now and the deal was that I'm the boss. So from now on, you worry about your acting. Everything else is my headache."

Nevada's lips tightened and deep in his eyes I could see the hurt. I turned away so that I wouldn't have to see it. Rina was watching with a curious kind of detachment.

"Rina!" She turned to me, an impassive mask dropping quickly over her eyes. "Go into the bathroom and wash all that muck off your face. Put on your usual make-up."

Rina left the room silently and I went back behind my desk and sat down. Nobody said a word until she came back into the room, her mouth wide again, her lips full and her eyebrows flowing into the natural curve of her brow. Her hair spilled like white shimmering gold down to her shoulders. But there was still something wrong. Underneath the negligee, her body was still a straight line.

"Go back in there and get out of that harness you're wearing."

Still silent, she did as I told her. And this time when she came out, she moved. Nobody could miss the fact that there was a woman underneath that negligee.

"That's more like it," I said. "We'll shoot those scenes again now."

Rina nodded and turned away. Miss Gaillard's voice stopped her. "We can't photograph her like that."

I looked at the designer. "What did you say?"

Miss Gaillard stood up. "We can't shoot her like that. Her bust bounces."

I laughed. "What's the matter with that? Tits should bounce."

"Of course," the designer said quickly. "But on the screen everything is exaggerated." She looked at the cameraman. "Isn't that right, Lee?"

The cameraman nodded. "That's right, Mr. Cord. They won't look natural at all."

"We'll have to put some kind of brassière on her," Miss Gaillard said.

"O.K. Go see what you can do."

A moment later, Rina and the designer came out of the bathroom. They walked toward me. It was better than the original harness but they didn't look as good as they did without restraint. It just didn't look right to me.

I got up from the desk and walked over to Rina. "Let me see."

Rina looked at me, her eyes deliberately distant. Impassively she dropped the negligee from her shoulders, holding it to her by the crook of her elbows. "Turn right," I said. "Now left."

I stepped back and looked at Rina. I knew what it was now. Whenever she turned, the brassière pulled and flattened, which was what gave her breasts that unnatural look. I looked at the designer. "Maybe if we took off the shoulder straps?"

Ilene Gaillard shrugged. "We can try." She reached over and pushed down the straps.

Rina stood there, her eyes fixed on some distant point over my shoulder. "Now turn." The brassière still cut into her breasts. "Unhh–unhh," I said. "I still don't like it."

"There's one other thing I can try."

"O.K.," I said.

A few minutes later, they came out again. Rina wore a wire-ribbed contraption almost like a small corset, except it didn't come down over her hips. And when she moved, her breasts didn't. You could see them all right, but they looked as if they had been molded out of plaster of Paris.

I looked at the designer. "Isn't there some way we can cut out some of those wires?"

"I think that looks fine, Mr. Cord. Anyway, I don't see why you're so worried about her bustline. Her legs are good and you'll see plenty of them."

"Miss Gaillard, since you're not a man, I don't expect you to understand what I'm getting at. I can see all the legs I want to see just walking down the street. Just answer my question, please."

"No, we can't cut the wires, Mr. Cord," she replied, equally polite. "If we do, she might as well be wearing nothing. There wouldn't be enough rigidity to support her."

"Maybe if I show you what I want, you can do it. Take it off, Rina," I said, walking over to her.

Impassively Rina turned aside for a moment. When she turned around again, the contraption was in one hand and with the other she held the top of the negligee closed.

I took it and tossed in onto my desk. I put my hands to the top of Rina's negligee and pushed it down until it formed a square across her breast just above the nipples. Her breasts rose like twin white moons against my dark, clenched fists. I looked back at the designer. "See what I mean?"

Maybe she didn't but there wasn't a man in the room whose eyes weren't popping out of his head.

"What you want is impossible, Mr. Cord. Rina's a big girl. Thirty-eight C. There isn't a brassière made that could support her bust like that. I'm a designer, Mr. Cord, not a structural engineer."

I let go of Rina's negligee and turned to Miss Gaillard. "Thank you," I said, going over to the telephone. "That's the first constructive idea I've heard since this meeting started."

Morrissey was there in less than twenty minutes.

"I've got a little problem, Morrissey. I need your help."

His nervousness disappeared slightly and he looked around shyly. "Anything I can do, Mr. Cord."

"Stand up, Rina," I said. Slowly she got to her feet and walked around us. Morrissey's eyes widened behind his glasses. I was glad to see that other things could occupy his mind besides airplanes.

"There isn't a brassière made that can keep them from jiggling," I said. "And still look natural. I want you to design one that will."

He turned back to me, an expression of shock on his face. "You're joking, Mr. Cord!"

"I was never more serious in my life."

"But—but I don't know anything about brassières. I'm an aeronautical engineer," he stammered, blushing a bright pink.

"That's why I called you," I said calmly. "I figured if you can design planes that have to withstand thousands of pounds of stress you ought to be able to come up with something that would hold up a little thing like a pair of tits." I turned to the costume designer. "Fill him in on what he needs to know."

Miss Gaillard looked at me, then at Morrissey. "Perhaps it would be better if we worked in my office in Wardrobe. I have everything there you might need."

Morrissey had been staring at Rina's breasts while the designer spoke. For a moment, I thought he was paralyzed, then he turned around. "I think I might be able to do something."

"I knew you could," I said, smiling.

"I'm not promising anything, of course. But it's a very intriguing problem."

I kept a straight face. "Very," I said solemnly.

Morrissey turned to the designer. "Do you happen to have a pair of calipers?"

"Calipers? What do we need calipers for?"

Morrissey looked at her in amazement. "How else would we be able to measure the depth and the circumference?"

She stared at him blankly for a moment, then, taking his arm, began to walk him toward the door. "I'm sure we can get a pair from Engineering. You'd better come with us, Rina."

Morrissey was back in a little over an hour. He came in waving a sheet of paper. "I think we've got it! It was really very simple once we found the point of stress. The weight of each breast pulls to either side. That means the origin of stress falls between them, right in the center of the cleavage."

I stared at him. His language was a curious mixture of engineering and wardrobe design. But he was too wrapped up in his explanation to pay attention to my look. "The whole thing then became a problem of compensation. We had to find a way to utilize the stress to hold the breasts steady. I inserted a V-shaped wire in the cleavage using the suspension principle. Understand?"

I shook my head. "You went way past me."

"You know the principle used in a suspension bridge?"

"Vaguely," I said.

"Under that principle, the more pressure the mass exerts against itself, the more pressure is created to hold it in place."

I nodded. I still didn't understand it completely. But I had all I needed for now. What I wanted to know was would it work?

I didn't have long to wait for the answer. Rina came into the office shortly after that with Ilene Gaillard. Deliberately she let the wrap fall to the floor and stood there in the repaired negligee.

"Walk toward Mr. Cord," the designer said.

Slowly Rina walked toward me. I couldn't take my eyes from her. The sweetest pair of knockers a man ever put his head down on. She stopped in front of my desk and looked down at me. For the first time that afternoon, she spoke. "Well?"

I was conscious of the effort it took to raise my eyes and look up into her face. Her eyes were cold and calculating. The bitch was always exactly aware of the effect she had on me. She started to turn away. "One more thing, Miss Gaillard," I said. "Tomorrow when we start shooting, I want her in a black negligee, instead of that white one. I want everybody to know she's a whore, not a virgin bride."

"Yes, Mr. Cord." Ilene came up to my desk, her eyes shining. "I really think we're going to set a new style with Miss Marlowe. Unless I'm completely mistaken, women all over the world will be trying for her style once this picture comes out."

I grinned at her. "We didn't set the fashion, Miss Gaillard," I said. "Women looked like women long before either of us was born."

She nodded and started out. I looked around the room. The meeting was over and everybody was getting stiffly to his feet. Nevada was the last one out and I called him back.

He came back to my desk. I turned and looked at my secretary. She was still sitting there, her book filled with shorthand notes. "What've you got there?" I asked.

"The minutes of the meeting."

"What for?"

"It's a company rule," she said. "Minutes of all executive meetings are recorded and copies circulated."

"Give me that book." I held it over the wastebasket and set a match to it. When the flame caught, I dropped it into the basket and looked up at her.

She was staring at me with an expression of horror.

"Now trot your fat little ass out of here," I said. "And if I ever hear of any minutes of meetings in this office ever showing up outside these walls, you'll be looking for another job."

Nevada was smiling as I turned back to him. "I'm sorry I had to speak the way I did, Nevada."

"That's all right, Junior. I shouldn't have shot my mouth off."

"There's a lot of people in this town think I'm a sucker and that I got conned into a bum deal. You and I know that's not true but I have to stop that kind of talk. I can't afford it."

"I understand, Junior. Your pappy was the same way. There was only one boss when he was around."

Suddenly, I realized how far apart we'd grown. For a moment, I had a wave of nostalgia for my childhood, when I could always reach out to Nevada for assurance. It wasn't that way any more. It was exactly the opposite. Nevada was leaning on me. "Thanks, Nevada," I said, forcing a smile to my lips. "And don't worry. Everything'll turn out all right now."

He turned and I watched him walk out of the office. Shortly after he left Dan Pierce came into the office. I reached for a cigarette and lit it. "About what you said this morning. I think we ought to change the script. You better send for the writers right away."

He grinned knowingly. "I already did."

10

WE COMPLETED THE PICTURE IN FOUR WEEKS. Nevada knew what was happening but he never said a word. Two weeks after that, we held the first sneak preview at a theater out in the valley.

I got there late and the studio publicity man let me in. "There are only a few seats left on the side, Mr. Cord," he apologized.

I looked down at the orchestra. There was a section roped off in the center for studio guests. It was jammed. Everybody at the studio from Norman on down was there. They were all waiting for me to fall on my ass.

I went up into the balcony just as the lights went down and the picture came on. I found my way in the dark to a seat in the middle of a bunch of youngsters and looked up at the screen.

My name looked funny up there.

JONAS CORD PRESENTS—

But the feeling left when the credits were over and the picture began. After ten minutes had passed I started to sense a restlessness in the kids around me. "Aw, shit," I heard one of them whisper. "I thought this was gonna be somethin' different. It's just another friggin' Western."

Then Rina came on screen. Five minutes later, when I looked around me, the kids' faces were staring up at the screen, their mouths partly open, their expressions rapt. There wasn't a sound except their breathing. Next to me sat a boy holding a girl's hand tightly in his lap. When Rina finally pulled Nevada down onto the bed with her, I could feel the kid squirm. He whispered, "Jesus!"

I reached for a cigarette and began to smile. Nobody had to tell me this picture was box office. When I came down into the lobby after it was over, Nevada was standing in the corner surrounded by kids and signing autographs. I looked for Rina.

She was at the other end of the lobby surrounded by reporters. Bernie Norman was hovering over her like a proud father.

Dan was standing in the center of a circle of men. He looked up as I came over. "You were right, Jonas," he cried jubilantly. "She creamed 'em. We'll gross ten million dollars!"

I gestured and he followed me out to my car. "When this is over," I said, "bring Rina to my hotel."

He stared at me. "It's still eating yuh, isn't it?"

"Don't lecture me, just do as I say!"

"What if she won't come?"

"She'll come," I said grimly. "Just tell her it's collection day!"

It was one o'clock in the morning and I was halfway through a bottle of bourbon when the knock came on the door. I went over and opened it.

Rina walked into the room and I closed the door. She turned to face me. "Well?"

I gestured toward the bedroom. She looked at me for a moment, then shrugged her shoulders and nonchalantly started for the bedroom. "I told Nevada I was coming here," she said over her shoulder.

I spun her around violently. "What the hell did you do a damnfool thing like that for?"

Her eyes appraised me calmly. "Nevada and I are going to get married. I told him I wanted to be the first to tell you."

I couldn't believe my ears. "No!" I shouted hoarsely. "You can't. I won't let you. He's an old man, he's through. You'll be the biggest star in the business when this picture comes out."

"I know."

"If you know, then why? You don't need him. You don't need anybody."

"Because when I needed him, he helped me," she said evenly. "Now it's my turn. He needs me."

"He needs you? Why? Because he was too proud to do his own crawling?"

"That's not true and you know it!"

"Making you a star was my idea!"

"I didn't ask you for it," Rina said angrily. "I didn't even want it. Don't think I didn't see what you were doing. Cutting down his part in his own picture, building me up as a monument to your own ego while you were ruining him!"

"I didn't see you trying to stop me," I said. "We both know he's on the way out. There's a new kind of cowboy over at one of the studios. A singing cowboy. He uses a guitar instead of a gun!"

"You know everything, don't you!" Her hand slashed angrily out at my face. I could feel its sting even as she spoke. "That's why he needs me more than ever!"

I exploded and grabbed her by the shoulders, shaking her violently. "What about me? Why do you think I went into this? Not for Nevada. For you! Did you ever stop to think that when I came rushing up here to see you, that maybe I needed you?"

She stared into my eyes angrily.

"You'll never need anybody, Jonas, only yourself. Otherwise, you wouldn't have left your wife down there all by herself. If you had any feelings at all, even pity, you'd have gone down there, or had her come up here."

"You leave my wife out of this!"

She turned to pull away and the front of her dress tore down to her waist. I stared at her. Her breasts rose and fell and I could feel the fever climb up in me. "Rina!" I crushed my mouth down on hers. "Rina, please."

Her mouth moved for a moment as she struggled to get away from me, then she was pressing herself closer and closer, her arms around my neck. That's the way we were when the door behind me opened. "Get outa here!" I said hoarsely, without bothering to turn around.

"Not this time, Jonas!"

I gave Rina a shove toward the bedroom, then turned around slowly to face my father-in-law and another man. Behind them was Monica, standing in the doorway. I stared at her. She had a belly way out to here.

The hollow echo of triumph was in Amos Winthrop's voice as he spoke. "Ten grand was too much to give me to send her away before." He chuckled quietly. "How much do you think it'll cost you to get rid of her now?"

As I stared at Monica, I began to curse myself silently. No wonder Amos Winthrop could laugh. I'd known Monica for less than a month before we got married. Even to my untrained eyes, she was at least five months' pregnant. That meant she was two months gone when she married me.

I cursed myself again. There's no fool like a young fool—my old man always used to say. And, as usual, my father was right.

That wasn't my cake she was baking in her oven.

The Story of
RINA MARLOWE

Book Four

1

CAREFULLY RINA CLOSED THE MAGAZINE, TURN-
ing down the corner of the page that she had been reading, and
let it drop on the white sheet that covered her.

"Did you want something, dear?" Ilene's voice came from
the deep armchair near the bed.

Rina turned to look at her. Ilene's face was thinned by concern. "No," Rina said. "What time is it?"

Ilene looked down at her watch. "Three o'clock."

"Oh," Rina said. "What time did the doctor say he'd come?"

"Four," Ilene answered. "There's nothing I can get for you?"

Rina shook her head. "No, thanks. I'm fine." She picked up
the magazine again, riffled through the pages, then threw it back
on the coverlet. "I wish to hell they'd let me out of here!"

Ilene was out of the chair now. She looked down at Rina
from the side of the bed. "Don't fret," she said quickly. "You'll
be out soon enough. Then you'll wish you were still here. I

heard that the studio's just waiting for you to get out so they can put you to work in *Madame Pompadour*."

Rina sighed. "Not that old chestnut again. Every time they get stuck for a picture, they take that one down off the shelf and dust it off. Then they make a big announcement and as soon as they get all the trade stories and publicity they can, back it goes on the shelf."

"Not this time," Ilene said earnestly. "I spoke to Bernie Norman in New York yesterday. He has a new writer on it and said the script was shaping up great. He says it's got social significance now."

Rina smiled. "Social significance? Who's writing it—Eugene O'Neill?"

Ilene stared at her. "You knew all the time."

Rina shook her head. "No, I didn't. It was just a wild guess. Has Bernie really got O'Neill?"

Ilene nodded. "He expects to have a copy of the script sent over to you as soon as O'Neill is finished."

Despite herself, Rina was impressed. Maybe this time, Bernie really meant it. She felt a surge of excitement flow into her. O'Neill was a writer, not an ordinary Hollywood hack. He could make something of the story. Then the excitement drained out of her, leaving her even more weary than before. Social significance. Everything that was done these days bore the tag. Ever since Roosevelt took office.

"What time is it?"

"Ten after three," Ilene answered.

Rina leaned back against the pillow. "Why don't you go out and get a cup of coffee?"

Ilene smiled. "I'm all right."

"You've been here all day."

"I want to be here," Ilene answered.

"You go." Rina closed her eyes. "I think I'll take a little nap before the doctor comes."

Ilene stood there for a moment, until she heard the soft, shallow breath of rest. Then gently she straightened the covers and looked into Rina's face. The large eyes were closed, the cheeks thin and drawn tightly across the high cheekbones. There was a faintly blue pallor beneath the California tan. She reached down and brushed the white-blond hair back from Rina's forehead, then quickly kissed the tired mouth and left the room.

The nurse seated in the outer room looked up. "I'm going down for a cup of coffee," Ilene said. "She's sleeping."

The nurse smiled with professional assurance. "Don't worry, Miss Gaillard," she said. "Sleep is the best thing for her."

Ilene nodded and went out into the corridor. She felt the tightness in her chest, the mist that constantly had pressed against her eyes these last few weeks. She came out of the elevator and started for the coffee shop.

Still lost in her thoughts, she didn't hear the doctor until her hand was on the door. "Miss Gaillard?" For a moment, she had no voice. She could only nod dumbly. "Mind if I join you?"

"Not at all," she said.

He smiled and held the door open for her. They went inside to a corner table. The doctor waved his hand and two cups of coffee appeared before them. "How about a bun?" he asked. "You look as if you could use a little food." He laughed in his professional manner. "There's no sense in having another patient just now."

"No, thank you," she said. "The coffee will do fine."

The doctor put down his coffee cup. "Good coffee."

She nodded. "Rina is sleeping." She said the first thing that came into her mind.

"Good." The doctor nodded, looking at her. His dark eyes shone brightly through the bifocals. "Does Miss Marlowe have any relatives out here?"

"No," Ilene answered quickly. Then the implication hit her. She stared at him. "You mean . . ." Her voice trailed off.

"I don't mean anything," the doctor said. "It's just that in cases like this, we like to know the names of the next of kin in case something does happen."

"Rina has no relatives that I know of."

The doctor looked at her curiously. "What about her husband?"

"Who?" Ilene's voice was puzzled.

"Isn't she married to Nevada Smith?" the doctor asked.

"She was," Ilene answered. "But they were divorced three years ago. She's been married since then to Claude Dunbar, the director."

"That ended in divorce, too?"

"No," Ilene answered tersely. Her lips tightened. "He committed suicide, after they'd been married a little over a year."

"Oh," the doctor said. "I'm sorry. I guess I haven't had much time these last few years to keep up with things."

"If there's anything special that needs to be done, I guess I'm the one who could do it," she said. "I'm her closest friend. She gave me power of attorney."

The doctor stared at her silently. She could read what was in his mind behind those shining bifocals. She drew her head up proudly. What did it matter what he thought? What did it matter what anyone thought now?

"Did you get the results from the blood tests?"

The doctor nodded.

She tried to keep her voice from shaking. "Is it leukemia?"

"No," he said. He could see the hope spring up in her eyes. Quickly he spoke to avoid the pain of disappointment. "It was what we thought. Encephalitis." He noted her puzzled expression. "Sometimes it's called sleeping sickness."

The hope in Ilene refused to die. "Then she has a chance?"

"A very small one," the doctor said, still watching her carefully. "But if she lives, there's no telling what she'll be like."

"What do you mean?" Ilene asked harshly.

"Encephalitis is a virus that settles in the brain," he explained slowly. "For the next four or five days, as the virus builds up in intensity, she will be subject to extraordinary high fevers. During these fevers, the virus will attack the brain. It is only after the fever breaks that we'll be able to tell how much damage she has sustained."

"You mean her mind will be gone?" Ilene's eyes were large with horror.

"I don't know," the doctor said. "The damage can take many forms. Her mind; perhaps she'll be paralyzed or partly so; she may know her own name, she may not. The residual effects are similar to a stroke. It depends on what part of the brain has been damaged."

The sick fear came up inside her. Quickly she caught her breath against it, her face paling. "Breathe deeply and sip a little water," the doctor said.

She did as he commanded and the color flooded back into her face. "Is there anything we can do? Anything at all?"

"We're doing everything we can. We know so little about the disease; how it's transmitted. In its more common form, in tropical countries, it's supposed to be carried by insects and transmitted by their bite. But many cases, in the United States and elsewhere, just appear, with no apparent causation at all."

"We just got back from Africa three months ago," Ilene said. "We made a picture there."

"I know," the doctor said. "Miss Marlowe told me about it. That was what first made me suspicious."

"But no one else is sick," Ilene said. "And we were all out there for three months, living exactly the same way, in the same places."

The doctor shrugged. "As I said, we aren't really sure what causes it."

Ilene stared at him. A note of bewilderment crept into her voice. "Why couldn't it be me?" she asked. "She has so much to live for."

The doctor reached across the table and patted her hand. With that one warm gesture, she no longer resented him, as she did most men. "How many times in my life have I heard that question? And I'm no closer to the answer now than when I first began to practice."

She looked at him gratefully. "Do you think we should say anything to her?"

His dark eyes grew large behind his glasses. "What purpose would it serve?" he asked. "Let her have her dreams."

Rina heard the dim voices outside the door. She was tired, weary and tired, and everything was a soft, blurred haze. Vaguely she wondered if the dream would come again. The thin edges of it poked at her mind. Good. It was coming.

Softly, comfortably now, she let herself slip down into it. Further and further she felt herself dropping into the dream. She smiled unconsciously and turned her face against the pillow. Now she was surrounded by her dream. The dream of death she had dreamed ever since she was a little girl.

2

IT WAS COOL IN THE YARD BENEATH THE SHADE OF the giant old apple trees. Rina sat in the grass and arranged the dolls around the small wooden plank that served as a table.

"Now, Susie," she said to the little dark-haired doll. "You must not gulp your food."

The black eyes of the doll stared unwinkingly back at her.

"Oh, Susie!" she said in imaginary concern. "You spilled it all over your dress! Now I'll have to change you again."

She picked up the doll and undressed it quickly. She washed the clothes in an imaginary tub, then ironed them. "Now you stay clean," she exclaimed in pretended anger.

She turned to the other doll. "Are you enjoying your breakfast, Mary?" She smiled. "Eat it all up. It'll make you big and strong."

Occasionally, she would glance toward the big house. She was happy to be left alone. It wasn't very often that she was. Usually, one or the other of the servants would be calling her to come back in. Then her mother would scold her and tell her that she was not to play in the yard, that she must stay near the kitchen door at the far side of the house.

But she didn't like it there. It was hot and there was no grass, only dirt. Besides, it was near the stables and the smell of the horses. She didn't understand why her mother always made such a fuss. Mr. and Mrs. Marlowe never said anything when they found her there. Once, Mr. Marlowe even had picked her up and swung her high over his head, tickling her with his mustache until she almost burst with hysterical laughter.

But when she'd come inside, her mother had been angry and had spanked her bottom and made her go up to their room and stay there all afternoon. That was the worst punishment of all. She loved to be in the kitchen while her mother cooked the dinner. Everything smelled so good. Everybody always said her mother was the best cook the Marlowes had ever had.

She heard footsteps and looked up. Ronald Marlowe threw

himself to the ground beside her. She looked down again and finished feeding Susie, then said in a matter-of-fact voice, "Would you like some dinner, Laddie?"

He sniffed disdainfully from the superiority of his lofty eight years. "I don't see anything to eat."

She turned toward him. "You're not looking," she said. She forced a doll's plate into his hand. "Eat it. It's very good for you."

Reluctantly he pretended to eat. After a moment, he was bored and got to his feet. "I'm hungry," he said. "I'm going in and get some real food."

"You won't get any," she said.

"Why not?"

"Because my mommy's still sick and nobody cooked."

"I'll get something," he said confidently.

She watched him walk away and turned back to her dolls. It was turning dusk when Molly, the upstairs maid, came out looking for her. The girl's face was red from crying. "Come, macushla," she said, sweeping Rina up in her arms. "It's your mither that wants to set eyes on ye again."

Peters, the coachman, was there, as was Mary, the downstairs maid, and Annie, the scullery helper. They were standing around her mother's bed and they made way for her as she came over. There was also a man in a black suit, holding a cross in his hand.

She stood very still near the bed, looking at her mother solemnly. Her mother looked beautiful, her face so white and calm, her white-blond hair brushed back softly from her forehead. Rina moved closer to the bed.

Her mother's lips moved but Rina couldn't hear what she was saying. The man in the black suit picked her up. "Kiss your mother, child," he said.

Obediently Rina kissed her mother's cheek. It was cool to her lips. Her mother smiled again and closed her eyes, then suddenly opened them and looked upward unseeingly. Quickly the man shifted Rina to his other arm. He reached down and closed her mother's eyes.

Molly held out her arms and the man gave Rina to her. Rina looked back at her mother. She was sleeping now. She looked beautiful, just as she did in the early mornings when Rina would awaken and stare at her over the edge of the bed.

Rina looked around the room at the others. The girls were

crying, and even Peters, the coachman, had tears in his eyes. She looked up into Molly's face. "Why are you crying?" she asked solemnly. "Is my mommy dead?"

The tears came afresh in the girl's eyes. She hugged Rina closely to her. "Hush, child," she whispered. "We're crying because we love her."

She started out of the room with Rina in her arms. The door closed behind them and Rina looked up into her face. "Will Mommy be up in time to make breakfast tomorrow?"

Molly stared at her in sudden understanding. Then she sank to her knees in the hallway at the top of the back stairs. She rocked back and forth with the child in her arms. "Oh, my poor little child, my poor little orphan child," she cried.

Rina looked up at her and after a moment, the tears became contagious and she, too, began to cry. But she didn't quite know why.

Peters came into the kitchen while the servants were eating supper. Rina looked up at him and smiled. "Look, Mr. Peters." She laughed happily. "I had three desserts!"

Molly looked down at her. "Hush, child," she said quickly, the tears coming again to her eyes. "Finish your ice cream."

Rina stared at her thoughtfully and lifted the spoon again to her mouth. She couldn't understand why the girls began to cry every time they spoke to her. The home-made vanilla ice cream tasted cool and sweet. She took another spoonful.

"I just spoke to the master," Peters said. "He said it would be all right if we laid her out in my room over the stable. And Father Nolan said we could bury her from St. Thomas'."

"But how can we?" Molly cried, "when we don't even know if she was a Catholic? Not once in the three years she's been here did she go to Mass."

"What difference does that make?" Peters asked angrily. "Did she not make her confession to Father Nolan? Did she not receive the last rites from him and take the Holy Sacraments? Father Nolan is satisfied that she was a Catholic."

Mary, the downstairs maid, who was the oldest of the three girls, nodded her head in agreement. "I think Father Nolan is right," she said. "Maybe she'd done something and was afraid to go to Mass, but the important thing was that she came back to the church in the end."

Peters nodded his head emphatically. "It's settled, then," he said, starting for the door. He stopped and looked back at them. "Molly, take the child to sleep with you tonight. I'm goin' down to the saloon and get sivral of the boys to help me move her tonight. Father Nolan said he'd send Mr. Collins over to fix her up. He told me the church would pay for it."

"Oh, the good Father," Mary said.

"Bless him," Annie said, crossing herself.

"Can I have some more ice cream?" Rina asked.

There was a knock at the door and Molly opened it quickly. "Oh, it's you, mum," she exclaimed in a whisper.

"I came to see if the child was all right," Geraldine Marlowe said.

The girl stepped back. "Won't you come in, mum?"

Mrs. Marlowe looked over at the bed. Rina was sleeping soundly, her dolls, Susie and Mary, on either side of her. Her white-blond hair hung in tiny ringlets around her head. "How is she?"

"Fine, mum." The girl bobbed her head. "The poor darlin' was so exhausted with the excitement, she dropped off like that. Mercifully she doesn't understand. She's too young."

Geraldine Marlowe looked at the child again. For a moment, she thought of how it would be if she were the one to go, leaving her Laddie alone and motherless. Though, in a way, that was different, for Laddie would still have his father.

She remembered the day she had hired Rina's mother. Her references were very good although she had not worked for several years. "I have a child, ma'am," she'd said in her peculiarly precise schoolbook English. "A little girl, two years old."

"What about your husband, Mrs. Osterlaag?"

"He went down with his ship. He and the child never saw each other." She'd looked down at the floor for a moment. "We had the child late in life, ma'am. We Finns don't marry young; we wait until we can afford it. I lived on our savings as long as I could. I must go back to work."

Mrs. Marlowe had hesitated. A two-year-old child might turn out to be an annoyance.

"Rina would be no problem, ma'am. She's a good child and very quiet. She can sleep in my room and I'd be willing to have you take out of my wages for her board."

Mrs. Marlowe had always wanted a little girl but after Laddie was born, the doctor had told her there would be no more children. It would be good for Laddie to have someone to play with. He was getting entirely too spoiled.

She'd smiled suddenly. "There will be no deduction from your wages, Mrs. Osterlaag. After all, how much can a little girl eat?"

That had been almost three years ago. And Rina's mother had been right. Rina had been no trouble at all.

"What will happen to the child, mum?" Molly whispered.

Mrs. Marlowe turned to the servant girl. "I don't know," she said, thinking about it for the first time. "Mr. Marlowe is going to inquire in town tomorrow about her relatives."

The servant girl shook her head. "He won't find any, mum," she said positively. "I often heard the mither say there was no family at all." Her eyes began to fill with tears. "Oh, the poor, poor darlin'. Now she'll have to go to the county home."

Mrs. Marlowe felt a lump come up in her throat. She looked down at Rina, sleeping peacefully in the bed. She could feel the tears stirring behind her own eyes. "Stop your crying, Molly," she said sharply. "I'm sure she won't have to go to the county home. Mr. Marlowe will locate her family."

"But what if he doesn't?"

"Then we'll think of something," she said. She crossed the room and stepped quickly out into the narrow hallway. There was a scuffling sound behind her. She turned around.

"Aisy now, boys!" She heard Peters' voice. Then he appeared, backing through the doorway across the hall. She pressed herself back to let them pass.

"Beggin' your pardon, mum," he said, his face flushed with exertion. "A sad, sad thing."

They went past with their shrouded burden, impregnating the still, warm air with a faint but unmistakable odor of beer. She wondered if she had done the right thing when she'd persuaded her husband to allow them to use the apartment over the stables. An Irish wake could well turn into a shambles.

She heard their heavy footsteps on the stairs as they carried Bertha Osterlaag, born in a small fishing village in Finland, down to her eventual funeral in a strange church, and her grave in a strange land.

3

HARRISON MARLOWE COULD SEE HIS WIFE'S HEAD bent over her embroidery from the doorway. He crossed the room quietly, and bending over the back of her chair, quickly kissed her cheek. His wife's voice held the usual delightful shock. "Oh, Harry! What if the servants are watching?"

"Not tonight." He laughed. "They're all thinking about their party. I see Mary's all dressed up."

A tone of reproach came into his wife's voice. "You know it's not a party they're having."

He crossed in front of her, still smiling. "That's not what they call it," he said. "But leave it to the Irish to make a party out of anything." He walked over to the sideboard. "A little sherry before dinner?"

"I think I'd like a Martini tonight, if you don't mind, dear," Geraldine said hesitantly.

He turned in half surprise. When they had been in Europe on their honeymoon a bartender in Paris had introduced them to the new drink and ever since, it had served as a sort of signal between them.

"Of course, my dear," he said. He pulled at the bell rope. Mary appeared in the doorway. "Some cracked ice, please, Mary."

The girl curtseyed and disappeared. He turned back to the sideboard and took down a bottle of gin, the French vermouth and a tiny bottle of orange bitters. Using a measuring jigger, he carefully poured three jiggers of gin into the cocktail shaker and one of vermouth. Then ceremoniously he allowed four drops of bitters to trickle into the shaker. By this time, the ice was already on the sideboard beside him and he filled the shaker to the brim with ice. Carefully he put the top on the shaker and began to shake vigorously.

At last, the drink was cold enough. He unscrewed the cap and carefully poured the contents into glasses. The shaker empty, he dropped a green olive into each glass, then stood back and surveyed them with approval. Each glass was filled to the brim—one more drop and it would overflow, one drop less and it would not be full.

Geraldine Marlowe lifted hers to her lips. She wrinkled her nose in approval. "It's delicious."

"Thank you," he said, lifting his own glass. "Your good health, my dear."

He put his glass down wonderingly and looked at his wife. Perhaps what he had heard was true—that women didn't really bloom until they were older, and then their desire increased. He calculated swiftly. He was thirty-four; that made Geraldine thirty-one. They had been married seven years and with the exception of their honeymoon, their life had assumed a pattern of regularity. But now, twice in less than a week. Perhaps it was true.

If it was, it was all right with him. He loved his wife. That was the only reason he went down to that house on South Street. To spare her the humiliation of having to endure him more than she wanted. He lifted his drink again.

"Did you find out anything about Bertha's family today?" she asked.

Harrison Marlowe shook his head. "There's no family anywhere. Perhaps in Europe, but we don't even know what town she came from."

Geraldine looked down at her drink. Its pale golden color glowed in the glass. "How terrible," she said quietly. "What will happen to the child now?"

Harrison shrugged his shoulders. "I don't know. I suppose I'll have to notify the authorities. She'll probably go to the county orphanage."

"We can't let that happen!" The words burst from Geraldine's lips involuntarily.

Harrison stared at her in surprise. "Why not?" he asked. "I don't see what else we can do."

"Why can't we just keep her?"

"You just can't," he said. "There are certain legalities involved. An orphaned child isn't like a chattel. You can't keep her because she happens to be left at your house."

"You can speak to the authorities," Geraldine said. "I'm sure they would prefer to leave her with us rather than have her become a public charge."

"I don't know," Harrison said. "They might want us to adopt her to make sure that she doesn't become a charge."

"Harry, what a wonderful idea!" Geraldine smiled and got out of her chair, then walked to her husband. "Now, why didn't I think of that?"

"Think of what?"

"Adopting Rina," Geraldine said. "I'm so proud of you. You have such a wonderful mind. You think of everything."

He stared at her speechlessly.

She placed her arms around his neck. "But then you always wanted a little girl around the house, didn't you? And Laddie would be so happy to have a little sister."

He felt the soft press of her body against him and the answering surge of warmth well up inside him.

She kissed him quickly on the lips, then, as quickly, turned her face away from him almost shyly as she felt his immediate response.

"Suddenly, I'm so excited," she whispered meaningfully, her face half hidden against his shoulder. "Do you think it would be all right if we had another Martini?"

Dandy Jim Callahan stood in the middle of his office, looking at them. He rubbed his chin thoughtfully. "I don't know," he said slowly. "It's a difficult thing you ask."

"But, surely, Mr. Mayor," Geraldine Marlowe said quickly, "you can do it."

The mayor shook his head. "It's not so easy as you think, my dear lady. You forget the church has something to say about this, too. After all, the mother was Catholic and you just can't take a Catholic child and turn it over to a Protestant family. At least, not in Boston. They'd never stand for it."

Geraldine turned away, the disappointment showing clearly in her face. It was then for the first time that she saw her husband as something other than the nice young Harvard boy she had married.

He stepped forward and there appeared in his voice a quality of strength that she had never heard before. "The church would like it even less if I were to prove that the mother was never a Catholic. They'd look pretty foolish then, wouldn't they?"

The mayor turned to him. "You have such proof?"

"I have," Marlowe said. He took a sheet of paper out of his pocket. "The mother's passport and the child's birth certificate. Both clearly state they were Protestant."

Dandy Jim took the papers from him and studied them. "If you had these, why didn't you stop them?"

"How could I?" Marlowe asked. "I didn't receive them until today. The servants and Father Nolan made all the arrangements last night. Besides, what difference does it make to the poor woman? She's getting a Christian burial."

Dandy Jim nodded and gave the papers back. "This will be very embarrassing to Father Nolan," he said. "A young priest with his first church making a mistake like that. The Bishop won't like it at all."

"The Bishop need never know," Marlowe said.

Dandy Jim stared at him thoughtfully but didn't speak.

Marlowe pressed. "There's an election coming up next year."

Dandy Jim nodded, "There's always an election."

"That's true," Marlowe said. "There will be other elections and campaigns. A candidate needs contributions almost as much as he needs votes."

Dandy Jim smiled. "Did I ever tell you I met your father?"

Marlowe smiled back. "No, you didn't. But my father often mentioned it. He told me many times how he threw you out of his office."

Dandy Jim nodded. "That's true. Your father has a wild temper. One would almost take him for an Irishman. And all I did was ask him for a small campaign contribution. That was about twenty years ago. I was running for City Council then. Do you know what he said to me then?"

Marlowe shook his head.

"He swore that if ever I was so much as elected to the post of dog-catcher, he'd take his family and move out." Dandy Jim was smiling. "He won't like it when he hears you've contributed to my campaign fund."

Marlowe stood his ground. "My father is my father and I respect him very much," he said, "but what I do with my money and my politics is my concern, not his."

"You have other children?" Dandy Jim asked.

"A boy," Geraldine answered quickly. "Laddie is eight."

Dandy Jim smiled. "I don't know," he said. "Someday women will have the vote and if that little girl is brought up on the hill, that's one vote I may never get."

"I promise you this, Mr. Mayor," Geraldine said quickly. "If that day ever comes, the women of my household will always vote for you!"

Dandy Jim's smile grew broader. He made a courtly bow. "It is a weakness of politicians to always be making deals."

The next day, Timothy Kelly, the mayor's secretary, appeared at Marlowe's office in the bank and picked up a check for five hundred dollars. He suggested that Marlowe talk to a certain judge in the municipal court.

It was there the adoption was made. Quickly, quietly and legally. When Marlowe departed the judge's chambers, he left with the judge a birth certificate for one white female child named Katrina Osterlaag.

In his pocket was a birth certificate in the name of his daughter, Rina Marlowe.

4

UNDERNEATH THE OVERSIZED UMBRELLA PLANTED in the sand, Geraldine Marlowe sat in a canvas chair, her parasol at her side. Slowly she moved her fan back and forth.

"I can't remember a summer as hot as this," she said breathlessly. "It must be over ninety here in the shade."

Her husband grunted from the chair next to hers, his head still immersed in the Boston newspaper, which arrived on the Cape one day late.

"What did you say, Harry?"

He folded his paper and looked at his wife. "That Wilson's a damn fool!"

Geraldine was still looking at the ocean. "What makes you say that, dear?"

He tapped the paper vigorously. "That League of Nations thing. Now he says he's going to Europe and see to it that peace is insured."

Geraldine looked at him. "I think that's a wonderful idea,"

she said mildly. "After all, we were lucky this time. Laddie was too young to go. The next time, it may be different."

He snorted again. "There won't be a next time. Germany is through forever. Besides, what can they do to us? They're on the other side of the ocean. We can just sit back and let them kill each other off if they want to start another war."

Geraldine shrugged her shoulders. "You better move in closer under the umbrella, dear," she said. "You know how red you get in the sun."

Harrison Marlowe got up and moved his chair farther under the umbrella. He settled back in the chair with a sigh and buried himself in the newspaper once more.

Rina appeared suddenly in front of her mother. "It's been an hour since I had lunch, Mother," she said. "Can I go into the water now?"

"May I," Geraldine corrected automatically. She looked at Rina. She had grown up this summer. It was hard to believe she was only thirteen.

She was tall for her age, almost five three, only one inch shorter than Laddie, who was three years older. Her hair was bleached completely white from the sun and her skin was deeply tanned, so dark that her almond-shaped eyes seemed light by comparison. Her legs were long and graceful, her hips just beginning to round a little and her breasts came full and round against her little girl's bathing suit, more like a sixteen-year-old's.

"May I, Mother?" Rina asked.

"You may," Geraldine nodded. "But be careful, dear, don't swim too far out. I don't want you to tire yourself."

But Rina was already gone. Geraldine Marlowe half smiled to herself. Rina was like that; she was like none of the other girls Geraldine knew. Rina didn't play like a girl. She could swim and outrun any of the boys that Laddie played with and they knew it. She didn't pretend to be afraid of the water or hide from the sun. She just didn't care whether her skin was soft and white.

Harrison Marlowe looked up from his paper. "I have to go up to the city tomorrow. We're closing the Standish loan."

"Yes, dear." The faint, shrill voices of the children floated lazily back toward them. "We'll have to do something about Rina," she said thoughtfully.

"Rina?" he questioned. "What about Rina?"

She turned to him. "Haven't you noticed? Our little girl's growing up."

He cleared his throat. "Umm—yes. But she's still a baby."

Geraldine Marlowe smiled. It was true what they said about fathers. They spoke more about their sons but secretly they delighted in their daughters. "She's become a woman in the past year," she said.

His face flushed and he looked down at his paper. In a vague way, he had realized it, but this was the first time they had spoken about it openly. He looked toward the water, trying to find Rina in the screaming, splashing crowd. "Don't you think we ought to call her back? It's dangerous for her to be so far out in the deep water."

Geraldine smiled at him. Poor Harrison. She could read him like a book. It wasn't the water he was afraid of, it was the boys. She shook her head. "No. She's perfectly safe out there. She can swim like a fish."

His embarrassed gaze met her own. "Don't you think you ought to have a little talk with her? Maybe explain some things to her. You know, like I did with Laddie two years ago?"

Geraldine's smile turned mischievous. She loved to see her husband, who was usually so sure of himself, positive about his tiniest conviction, flounder around like this. "Don't be silly, Harry." She laughed. "There's nothing I have to explain to her now. When a thing like that happens, it's just natural to tell her everything she should know."

"Oh," he said in a relieved voice.

She turned thoughtful again. "I think Rina's going to be one of those lucky children who make the transition from adolescence without any of the embarrassing stages," she said. "There's not the slightest trace of gawkiness about her and her skin is as clear as a bell. Not a sign of a blemish or a pimple. Not like Laddie at all."

She turned back toward the ocean. "Just the same, I think we'd better do something about Rina. I'd better get her some brassières."

Marlowe didn't speak.

She turned to him again. "I honestly think her bust is as large as mine already. I do hope it doesn't get too big. She's going to be a very beautiful girl."

He smiled slowly. "Why shouldn't she be?"

She reached for his hand, quietly returning his smile. They both knew what he meant. Neither of them ever thought of Rina as anything but their own natural child.

"Would you mind very much if I came into town with you tonight?" she asked softly. "It would be nice to stay in a hotel for one evening."

He pressed her hand. "I think it would be very nice."

"Molly could look after the children," she said. "And I'd have time to do a little shopping tomorrow before we return."

He looked at her and grinned. "I agree with you," he said in a mock-solemn voice. "The cottage down here is a little crowded. I'll call the hotel and make sure they have a shakerful of Martinis waiting for us the moment we arrive."

She dropped his hand. "You lecher!" she exclaimed, laughing.

Rina swam with easy, purposeful strokes, her eyes fixed on the diving raft out past the rolling surf. Laddie should be out there with his friend Tommy Randall. She came up out of the water almost at their feet. The boys were stretched out on their backs, faces up to the sun, and they sat up as Rina began to climb the ladder.

Laddie's face showed his annoyance at her invasion of their sanctum. "Why don't you stay back there with the girls?"

"I've got as much right out here as you have," she retorted, after catching her breath, straightening the shoulder straps of her too-small bathing suit.

"Aw, go on," Tommy said, looking up. "Let her stay."

Rina glanced at him swiftly from the corners of her eyes and saw his gaze fixed on her partly revealed breasts. It was at that exact moment that she began to turn into a woman.

Now even Laddie was staring at her with a curious look she had never before noticed in his eyes. Instinctively she let her hands fall to her sides. If that was all it took to make them accept her, let them look. She sat down opposite them, still feeling their gaze on her.

A dull ache began to throb in her breasts and she looked down at herself. Her nipples were clearly limned against the black jersey of her bathing suit. She looked up again at the boys. They were staring at her quite openly now.

"What are you looking at?"

The two boys exchanged quick, embarrassed glances and immediately looked away. Tommy fixed his eyes out over the water and Laddie looked down at the raft.

She stared at Laddie. "Well?"

The red flush crept up from Laddie's throat.

"I saw you. You both were looking at my chest!" she said accusingly.

The boys again exchanged quick glances. Laddie got to his feet. "Come on, Tommy," he said. "It's getting too crowded out here!"

He dove from the raft and a moment later, his friend followed. Rina watched them swimming toward the shore for a moment, then stretched back on the raft and stared up into the bright sky. Boys were strange creatures, she thought.

The tight bathing suit cut into her breasts. She shrugged her shoulders and her breasts leaped free of the encumbering suit. She looked down at herself.

They were white against the dark tan of her arms and throat and the nipples were flushed and pink and fuller than she had ever seen them before. Tentatively she touched them with her fingertips. They were hard as tiny pebbles and a warm, pleasant kind of pain flashed through them.

The warmth of the sun began to fill them with a sweet, gentle ache. Slowly she began to massage the ache away and gradually the warmth spilled from her breasts down into her body. She felt herself go hazy with a contentment she had never known before.

5

RINA STOOD IN FRONT OF THE MIRROR AND ADjusted the straps on the brassière. She took a deep breath. She turned to her mother, sitting on the bed behind her.

"There, Mother," she said proudly. "How does it look?"

Geraldine looked at her daughter doubtfully. "Perhaps if you moved it to the last hook," she said hesitantly and delicately.

"I tried, Mother," Rina answered. "But I can't wear it like that. It cuts into me."

Geraldine nodded. Next time, she would get a larger size but who ever would have thought a thirty-four would be so tight on such a slender frame?

Rina turned back to the mirror and looked at herself with satisfaction. Now she was beginning to look outside more like she felt inside. She noticed her mother watching her in the mirror.

"Do you think I could get some new bathing suits too, Mother?" she asked. "The ones I have are too small for me."

"I was just thinking that," her mother answered. "And some new dresses, too. Maybe Daddy will drive us down to Hyannis Port after breakfast."

Rina flashed a happy grin and ran to her mother. She threw her arms around her. "Oh, thank you, Mother!" she cried happily.

Geraldine drew Rina's head down to her breast. She kissed the top of the white-blond head and turned the child's tanned face up to hers. She looked down into Rina's eyes, her fingers lightly stroking her daughter's cheek. "What is happening to my little girl?" she asked almost sadly.

Rina caught her mother's hand and kissed her open palm. "Nothing, Mother," she said with the sureness and confidence that was to become an integral part of her. "Nothing but what you told me. I'm growing up."

Geraldine looked down into her daughter's face. A sudden mist came into her eyes.

"Don't be in too much of a hurry, my baby," she said, pressing Rina's head closely to her bosom. "We have too few years for childhood."

But Rina scarcely heard her. And if she had, it was doubtful that the words would carry any meaning. For they were only words and words were as futile against the strong forces awakening inside her as the waves breaking fruitlessly against the shore outside the window.

Laddie turned and swiftly threw the ball to first base. The runner spun and slid back toward safety, his heels kicking up a fine spray of dust. When the dust cleared, they could hear the umpire call, "Yer out!" and the game was over.

The boys clustered about him, pounding his back happily. "Swell game, Laddie!" "Good pitching!" Then they dispersed and he and Tommy were alone, threading their way back to the beach.

"What yuh doin' this afternoon?" Tommy asked.

Laddie shrugged his shoulders. "Nothin'." He was still thinking about that wild pitch that Mahoney hit for a home run. He should never have let the ball get away from him like that. He had to do better if he wanted to make the varsity team at Barrington the next spring. He made up his mind to spend an hour every afternoon pitching into a barrel. They said that was how Walter Johnson had developed his control.

"The Bijou's got a new Hoot Gibson picture," Tommy said.

"I saw it back in Boston." Laddie looked at his friend. "When's Joan coming down again?"

"My cousin?" Tommy asked.

"Yuh know anyone else by that name?" Laddie asked sarcastically.

"Maybe this weekend," Tommy answered.

"Then maybe we'll take her to the movies," Laddie said.

"Big deal!" Tommy snorted. "It's O.K. for you but what about me? It's no fun sitting next to you and watching you cop feels. Who'm I goin' to take?"

"I don't know," Laddie answered.

Tommy walked along for a moment, then snapped his fingers. "I got it!" he said excitedly.

"Who?"

"Your sister. Rina."

"Rina?" Laddie said. "She's just a kid."

Tommy laughed. "She ain't such a kid. They're really poppin' out on her. They look even bigger lately than when we seen 'em on the raft a couple weeks ago."

"But she's only thirteen," Laddie said.

"My cousin Joan's only fourteen now. She was thirteen last summer when you were nuzzlin' her on the back porch."

Laddie looked at him. Maybe Tommy was right. Rina was growing up. He shrugged his shoulders. "O.K.," he said finally. "You ask her. It won't do any good, though. I don't think my mother will let her go."

"She will if you ask her," Tommy said surely.

"I'm goin' in to shower an' put on my suit," Laddie said. "I'll meet yuh on the beach."

"O.K.," Tommy answered. "See yuh."

The cottage was cool and silent after the heat and noise at the game. Slowly Laddie walked through to the kitchen. "Molly?" he called.

There was no answer and he remembered it was Thursday, Molly's day off. He heard a noise upstairs and walked over to the staircase. "Mother?"

Rina's voice came down to him. "They drove down to Hyannis Port to have dinner with some people."

"Oh," he said. He went back into the kitchen and opened the icebox. He took out a bottle of milk and a piece of chocolate cake and put them on the table. He drank the milk from the bottle and ate the cake with his fingers. It wasn't until after he had finished that he remembered he'd promised himself he wouldn't touch any sweets in hopes that his skin would clear up.

He sat there in a kind of lethargy. He heard the bathroom door slam and footsteps leading back to Rina's room. Idly he wondered what she was doing home at this time of the afternoon. Usually she was down at the beach already with her giggling bunch of silly girl friends.

Maybe Tommy was right. She was growing up. Certainly the way she brazenly sat there on the raft with her boobs half hanging out and letting them goggle at her didn't make her seem like a kid. Tommy was right about one thing, though. They were bigger than his cousin's.

A picture of Rina sitting on the raft flashed through his mind: the way she looked at them while they looked at her; her hair falling wet and straight to her shoulders, her lower lip pouting and kind of heavy.

He felt a familiar heat surge through him. He half groaned aloud. Oh, no, not again. He'd promised himself after the last time, he'd stop. He got to his feet abruptly. He wouldn't do it this time. He picked up the empty plate and put it in the sink, then walked out of the kitchen and started up the stairs. He'd grab a cold shower and then beat it out to the beach.

Rina's room was opposite the head of the staircase and the door was partly open. He was almost halfway up when the light spilling from her room caught his eye. There was a movement inside the room and he stopped on the staircase, his heart pounding. Slowly he sank to his knees so that only his eyes were above the top of the landing.

Rina had just crossed the room and was standing in front of the mirror, her back to the door, clad only in a brassière and a pair of bloomers. While he watched, she reached behind her and unfastened the brassière, then, half turning, stepped out of the bloomers. Holding them in her hand, she crossed the room and came back in a moment, carrying a bathing suit. She paused again in front of the mirror and stepped into the suit. Slowly she pulled it up over her breasts and straightened the shoulder straps.

He felt faint beads of perspiration across his forehead. This was the first time he had ever seen a grown-up girl completely naked. He had never thought they could be so beautiful and exciting.

Walking quietly, he passed her room and went into his own. He closed the door and sank, still trembling, to the bed. For a long moment, he sat there, the pain of the heat surging inside him bending him almost double.

Slowly he reasoned with himself. No. He mustn't. Not again. If he gave in to it now, he would always give in to it. At last, he began to feel better. He wiped his forehead with his arm and got to his feet.

All you needed was a little self-control and determination. He began to feel proud of himself. What he had to do was remove himself from all kinds of temptation. That meant everything. Even the French pictures he had bought from the candy store down in Lobstertown.

Quickly he opened a dresser drawer and burrowing underneath a broken slat, came out with the pictures. He placed them on the dresser drawer face down. He wouldn't even look at them one last time. He'd flush them down the toilet when he went in to take his shower.

He undressed rapidly and put on his bathrobe. He walked back to the dresser and caught a glimpse of his face in the mirror. It was filled with a noble resolve. It was amazing how quickly resolution could reflect itself. He turned and left the room, forgetting the pictures that lay on the dresser.

He was drying himself in front of the mirror when he heard her footsteps turn down the hall to his room. Suddenly, he froze as he remembered. The pictures were still on the dresser. He grabbed for the bathrobe on the door behind him.

It was too late. When he got to his room, she was standing

near the dresser, the pictures in her hand. She looked up at him in surprise. "Laddie, where did you get these pictures?" she asked, a curious excitement in her voice.

"Give them to me!" he demanded, walking toward her.

"I will not!" she retorted, turning her back to him. "I haven't finished looking at them yet."

Lithely she spun away from his outstretched hand, across the room to the far side of the bed. "Let me finish," she said calmly. "Then you can have them back."

"No!" he shouted hoarsely, flinging himself across the bed at her.

She turned to avoid his grasp but his hand caught her shoulder. The pictures flew from her hand as she fell to the bed beside him. She reached for the pictures. His hand caught at her shoulder strap to keep her from getting them, and the strap broke in his hand. He froze suddenly, staring at one white breast that had escaped the bathing suit.

"You broke my strap," she said quietly, making no move to cover herself, her eyes watching his face.

He didn't answer.

She smiled slowly and raised her hand to her breast, rubbing her palm gently across the nipple. "I'm just as pretty as any of the girls in those pictures, aren't I?"

He was fascinated, unable to speak, his eyes following the deliberate movement of her hand. "Aren't I?" she asked again. "You can tell me. I won't tell anyone. Why do you think I let you watch while I was undressing?"

"You knew I was watching?" he asked in surprise.

She laughed. "Of course, stupid. I could see you in the mirror. I almost burst out laughing. I thought your eyes would pop out of your head."

He could feel the tension begin to build up inside him. "I don't think that's funny."

"Look at me," she said. "I like you to look at me. I wish everybody could."

"That's not right," he said.

"Why isn't it?" she demanded. "What's wrong with it? I like to look at you, why shouldn't you look at me?"

"But you never did," he said quickly.

A secret smile came to her lips. "Oh, yes I did."

"You did? When?"

"The other afternoon when you came back from the beach. There was no one home and I watched you through the bathroom window. I saw everything you did."

"Everything?" The word escaped from him in a groan of dismay.

"Everything," she said smugly. "You were exercising your muscle." Her eyes looked into his. "I never knew it could get so big. I always thought it was little and kind of droopy like it was when you were a little boy."

There was a tightness in his throat and he could hardly speak. He began to get up from the bed. "I think you better get out of here," he said hoarsely.

She looked up at him, still smiling. "Would you like to look at me again?"

He didn't answer.

Her hand reached up and took down the other shoulder strap. She wriggled out of her bathing suit. He stared down at her naked body, feeling his legs begin to tremble. He saw her eyes move down over him. His bathrobe hung open. He looked at her again.

"Now take off your bathrobe and let me see all of you," she said.

As if in a daze, he let the bathrobe slip to the floor. With a groan, he sank to his knees beside the bed, holding himself.

Quickly she rolled across the bed and looked down at him. A faint sound of triumph came into her voice. "Now," she said, "you can do it for me."

His hand reached up to touch her breast. She let it rest there for a moment, then suddenly moved away from him. "No!" she said sharply. "Don't touch me!"

He stared at her dumbly, the agony pouring through him in waves.

Her heavy-lidded eyes watched him.

"Do it for me," she said in a husky voice. "And I'll do it for you. But don't touch me!"

6

ALL THROUGH THE MOVIE, LADDIE COULD HEAR them giggling and whispering. He could imagine what they were doing in the darkened theater, even though he couldn't see. His mind flamed with visions.

Now Tommy was offering Rina a gumdrop. He could see him casually holding the bag toward her, the back of his hand seemingly accidentally pressing against her breast. Laddie shifted restlessly in his seat, trying to pierce the dark out of the corner of his eye, but it was a waste of time. He couldn't see anything.

"May I have some candy?" Joan's voice came from the darkness.

"What?" he asked, startled for a moment. "Yeah. Sure." He held the bag toward her.

She turned as she helped herself from the bag and he felt the soft press of her breasts. But it served only to remind him of Rina. He sank back into his seat unhappily.

They stopped in front of Tommy's cottage on the way home. "How about some pop?" Joan asked. "We've got a big bottle in the icebox."

Laddie shook his head. "No, thanks," he said quickly. "It's almost eight o'clock and I promised Mother we'd be home before dark."

Rina didn't say anything.

"Maybe you could come over later?" Joan asked. "After you've taken Rina home?"

Rina looked at him. He flushed. "I don't think so," he answered. "I'm pretty tired. I wanted to get to bed early."

Joan shot a curious look at him, then silently turned and walked into the cottage. There was an awkward moment until Tommy spoke. "Well, good night, then," he said. "See yuh on the beach tomorrow."

They walked the rest of the way home in silence. It was already dark when they climbed up the steps to the porch. He opened the screen door and held it for her.

She started to enter the house, then stopped when she saw he made no move to follow her. "Aren't you coming in?"

He shook his head. "Not right now. I think I'll stay out for a little while."

"I think I will, too," she said quickly, stepping back onto the porch.

He let the screen door swing shut. Its clatter echoed through the house. "Is that you, children?" Geraldine Marlowe called.

"Yes, Mother," Rina answered. She glanced quickly at Laddie. "Can we stay outside for a little while, Mother? It's so hot tonight."

"All right. But only for half an hour, Rina. I want you in bed by eight thirty."

"O.K., Mother."

Laddie crossed the porch and sat down on the large wicker chaise. Rina followed and sat down beside him. "Why did Joan want you to come back?" she asked suddenly.

He didn't look at her. "I dunno."

"Did she want you to do it for her?"

"Of course not!" he said indignantly.

"I don't like Joan," she said suddenly. "She's a—she's a hyp—a hypo—"

"A hypocrite." He supplied the word for her, surprised by the unexpected depth of her perception. "What makes you say that?"

"Tommy wanted me to touch him in the movies, but when I wouldn't, he took Joan's hand and she did."

"No!" The word escaped him involuntarily. Rina was right. The little bitch *was* a hypocrite.

"And she never even looked at him once," Rina continued. "She was always looking at the screen and once she even asked you for some candy."

He stared at her wonderingly.

"I wonder if they're doing it now," she said thoughtfully.

A picture of Joan and Tommy flashed through his mind. He began to get excited.

"I'm not a hypocrite, am I?" she asked. A slow smile came to her lips. She moved and he felt her fingers brush across his thigh. She looked into his face. "Would you like to do it now?" she whispered.

"Now?" he said in a stunned voice. He glanced over his shoulder back to the house.

"They won't come out," she said quietly. "Father is reading his newspaper and Mother is knitting. I saw them through the doorway."

"But—" he stammered. "But—how?"

She smiled again, her fingers taking the handkerchief from his breast pocket.

Geraldine looked up at the mantel clock. It was just eight thirty. She heard the screen door slam and Rina came into the room. Her daughter's eyes were bright and shining and her face wore a happy smile. The smile was infectious and Geraldine smiled back at her.

"Did you have a good time at the movies, dear?"

Rina nodded. "A wonderful time, Mother," she said excitedly. "It was such fun. You don't know how great it is to be able to see a picture without all those brats squalling and running up and down the aisles like they do in the afternoons."

Geraldine laughed. "It was only yesterday that you were one of those brats."

Rina's face suddenly turned serious. "But I'm not any more, am I, Mother?"

Geraldine nodded her head gently. "No, darling. You're quite grown up now."

Rina spun around happily. "That's right, Mother," she said gaily. "I'm quite grown up now."

Geraldine laughed. "Now up to bed with you, young lady. You still need your rest."

"O.K., Mother." Rina bent over her and quickly kissed her cheek. "Good night."

She crossed the room and kissed her father's cheek. "Good night, Father."

She ran out of the room and they could hear her feet running up the stairs. Harrison Marlowe lowered his paper. "She seems quite happy."

"Why shouldn't she be?" Geraldine said. "Her first date. Every girl is excited after her first date."

He put down the paper. "What do you say we go out on the porch for a bit of air?"

They came out into the night. "Laddie?" she called.

"Over here, Mother."

She turned and saw him rising from the chaise. "Did you have a good time?"

"All right," he said shortly.

"Rina wasn't any bother, was she?"

"No."

"You don't sound happy about having to take her with you."

"It was O.K., Mother," he said tensely.

"Sometimes, son," his father said, "we have to do things even if we don't like it. One of them is looking after your sister. That's a brother's job."

"I said it was all right, Father," he snapped.

"Laddie!" his mother exclaimed in surprise.

Laddie looked down at the floor. "I'm sorry, Father," he said in a low voice.

She moved over and looked into his face. "Are you feeling all right, Laddie?" she asked with concern. "You look flushed and warm to me and your face is all perspired. Here, let me wipe it for you." Her hand sought his breast-pocket handkerchief. "Why, Laddie, what happened to your handkerchief? I saw it in your pocket when you left."

For a moment there was something in his eyes that reminded her of a stricken animal, then it was gone. "I—I guess I lost it," he stammered.

She touched his forehead. "Are you sure you haven't a fever?"

"I think you'd better go up to bed, son," his father said.

"Yes, Father." He turned to his mother and kissed her. "Good night," he said and went quickly into the house.

"I wonder what's the matter with him?"

Harrison Marlowe snorted. "I know what's the matter with him."

"You do?"

He nodded. "He's spoiled, that's what. He's so used to having everything the way he wants it, he sulks when he has to do a little thing like chaperon his sister. He's angry because he couldn't sit over in the Randall's yard and spoon with Tommy's cousin Joan."

"Harry, you're being horrid!"

"No I'm not," he said. "Take it from me. I know boys. What he needs is a little discipline." He began to pack his pipe. "And you're doing the same with Rina. Giving her everything she wants. She'll be spoiled soon, too."

"I know what's bothering you," she said. "You just don't like the idea of them growing up. You'd like to keep them children forever."

"No. But you have to admit they are spoiled."

"Maybe they are a little," she admitted.

He smiled. "Well, anyway, it's a good thing they'll be going back to school next month. Barrington's good for Laddie."

"Yes," she agreed. "And I'm glad Rina's been accepted at Jane Vincent's school. They'll make a little lady out of her."

For Laddie, it was a summer of pain and torture, of wild physical sensation and excruciating, conscience-stricken agonies. He couldn't sleep, he couldn't eat, he was afraid to look at her in the mornings and then, when he saw her, he couldn't bear to let her out of his sight. Jealous tortures flamed inside him when he saw her smiling or talking to other boys. Visions born of his knowledge of her would fill his mind and he could see them with her the way he had been. An uneasy, frightened contentment would steal through him when they were together.

And lurking all the while in the deep recesses of his mind was the fear—the fear of discovery, the fear of seeing the hurt and shock and loathing come to the faces of his parents once they knew.

But when she looked at him, smiled at him, touched him, all that was suddenly gone and he would do anything in the world to please her. He abased himself, groveled before her, wept with the agony of his self-flagellation. Then the fear would return. Because there was no escaping the fact. She was his sister. It was wrong.

It was with a feeling of relief that he saw the crazy summer come to an end. It was over, he thought. Away from her, he would be able to find himself again, to control the fevers that she set raging in his blood. When they would come again to the beach next summer, it would be different. He would be different, she would be different.

No more, he would say to her. No more. It's wrong.

That was what he believed when he returned to school at the end of that summer.

7

"I'M PREGNANT," SHE SAID. "I'M GOING TO HAVE A baby."

Laddie felt a dull ache spread over him. Somehow, this was the way he'd always known it would turn out. Ever since that first summer two years ago. He looked up at her, squinting his eyes against the sun. "How do you know?"

She spoke quietly, as if she were just talking about the weather. "I'm late," she said simply. "I've never been late before."

He looked down at his hands. They were sun-darkened against the white sand. "What are you going to do?"

"I don't know," she answered. Her white-blond hair glittered in the sunlight as she turned and looked out at the ocean. "If nothing happens by tomorrow, I guess I'll have to tell Mother."

"Will you—will you tell her about us?"

"No," she said swiftly, in a low voice. She picked the next question from his lips. "I'll tell her it was Tommy, or Bill, or Joe," she answered, still not looking at him.

Despite himself, he felt a twinge of jealousy. "Did you—with all of them?" he asked hesitantly.

Her dark eyes fixed on his own now. "No," she said emphatically. "Of course not. Only with you."

"What if she talks to them? Then she'll know you're lying."

"She won't," Rina said positively. "Especially when I tell her I don't know which one it was."

He stared at her. In so many ways, she was older than he. "What do you think she'll do?"

Rina shrugged her shoulders. "I don't know. There's not very much she can do, I guess."

He watched her walk down the beach to meet some friends, then rolled over in the sand and placed his head on his arms. He groaned aloud. It had happened. Somewhere in the back of his mind he had always known it would. He remembered the night just a few short weeks ago.

They had come down to the beach that summer as they did

every year. But this time, it was going to be different. He had sworn it to himself. And he had told her, too.

"No more," he said. "It's stupid, it's kid stuff. You stick to your friends and I'll stick to mine. We'll only get in trouble if we keep it up."

She had agreed. Even promised. And he had to admit she had kept her word. It was he who had broken his vow. And all because of that damned bottle of orange pop.

It had been a rainy afternoon and they were alone in the cottage. It was hot and humid and the air clung heavily to his body, sheathing it in an invisible choking blanket. His shirt and trousers were wringing with perspiration when he went into the kitchen. He opened the icebox but the usual bottle of orange pop he kept there was gone. He closed the icebox door angrily.

He went upstairs and past her open door before his mind absorbed what his eyes had seen. He walked back and stood in the open doorway. She was naked on the bed, half reclining, the bottle of orange pop in her hand. She was staring at it intently.

He felt the pulse begin to hammer in his head, the perspiration break out anew beneath his clothing. "What are you doing with my orange pop?" he asked. He knew he sounded stupid, even as he spoke.

She moved her head slightly on the pillow and looked at him. Her eyes were heavy-lidded and hazy. "Drinking it," she answered huskily, putting it to her mouth. "What do you think?"

The soda overflowed her mouth and ran in orange driblets down her cheeks, across her breasts to the convex of her belly and onto the white sheet. She smiled at him and held out the bottle. "Want some?"

As if he were someone else, he saw himself cross the room and lift the bottle to his lips. It was warm from her touch. He felt the sweetness of the liquid spill into his mouth. He looked down at her.

She was smiling up at him. "You're excited," she said softly. "And you said you wouldn't be any more. But you are."

Some of the orange soda spilled down across his shirt as he suddenly realized he had betrayed himself. He turned to go but her hand caught him around the thigh. He almost screamed with the sudden inflaming agony of her touch.

"Just this once more," she whispered. "And then never again."

He stood frozen, afraid to move, afraid he would stumble and fall because of the trembling within him. "No," he said hoarsely.

"Please," she whispered, her fingers opening, searching.

He stood there as if paralyzed. An anguished moan came from deep within him. There would be no more of this, no more humiliation, no more groveling before her. This time she would learn to leave him alone.

With one hand, he seized her wrists and bent her back to the bed. Her eyes were still confident, still unafraid as they watched him. Suddenly, he pressed his lips to hers. Her mouth was warm and moist and still tasted of the orange soda. Then he moved his head and his lips were traveling down her body, across her throat, over her breasts.

It was then she began to fight him. "No!" she whispered, writhing away from him. "No! Don't touch me!"

But he didn't even hear her. He could feel the red rage pumping in his temples; there was a congestion in his chest. He felt her hand pull loose and rake his chest, leaving a clean, hot path of pain in its wake. Bewildered, he looked down at himself and saw the bloody traces of her fingernails on his flesh. A terrible anger rose up in him.

"You cock-teaser!" he yelled, swinging his free hand. The blow caught her on the side of her face, knocking her back against the bed. She stared up at him with frightened eyes.

"You bitch!" he said, tearing his belt from his trousers. He raised her arms over her head and lashed her wrists to the iron bedpost. He picked up the half-empty bottle from the bed where it had fallen. "Still thirsty?"

She shook her head.

He tilted the bottle and began to laugh as the orange soda ran down over her. "Drink!" he said. "Drink all you can!"

The bottle flew from his hands as she kicked it away. He caught at her legs and pinned them against the bed with his knees. He laughed wildly. "Now, my darling little sister, there'll be no more games."

"No more games," she gasped, staring up into his eyes. His face came down and his mouth covered hers. She felt herself begin to relax.

Then the fierce, sharp pain penetrated her body. She screamed. His hand came down heavily over her mouth, as again and again the pain ripped through her.

And all that was left was the sound of her voice, screaming silently in the confines of her throat, and the ugliness and horror of his body on her own.

Laddie rolled over on the sand. It was all over now. Tomorrow his mother would know. And it would be his fault. They would blame him and they would be right. No matter what, he shouldn't have let it happen. A shadow fell across him and he looked up.

Rina was standing there. She dropped to the sand beside him. "What are we going to do?"

"I don't know," he said dully.

She reached a hand out to his. "I shouldn't have let you do it," she whispered.

"You couldn't have stopped me," he said. "I must have been crazy." He looked at her. "If we were anybody else, we could run away and get married."

"I know."

His voice turned bitter. "It isn't as if we were really brother and sister. If only they hadn't adopted—"

"But they did," Rina said quickly, and with a sure knowledge. "Besides, we can't blame it on them. It wasn't their fault." She felt the tears come into her eyes. She sat there silently as they rolled down her cheeks.

"Don't cry."

"I—I can't help it," she whispered. "I'm scared."

"I am, too," he said. "But crying won't help."

The tears kept rolling silently down her cheeks. After a moment, she heard his voice. She looked at him. His lips moved awkwardly. "Even if you are my sister, you know that I love you?"

She didn't answer.

"I've always loved you, I guess. I couldn't help it. Somehow, the other girls were nothing when I compared them with you."

"I guess the reason I was so bad was because I was jealous of the girls you went with," she confessed. "I didn't want them to have you. That's why I did what I did. I couldn't let any other boy touch me. I couldn't stand them."

His hand tightened on her fingers. "Maybe it'll turn out all right yet," he said, trying for reassurance.

"Maybe," she said, a dull hopelessness in her voice.

Then they ran out of language and they turned and watched the surf run away with their childhood.

Laddie sat at the helm of his small sailboat and watched his mother in the bow. He felt a gust of wind take the sail and automatically he compensated for the drift while scanning the sky. There were squall clouds coming up ahead. Time to head for the dock. Slowly he began to come about.

"Turning back?" he heard his mother call.

"Yes, Mother," he replied. It seemed strange to have her aboard. But she had wanted to come. It was almost as if she had sensed there was something troubling him.

"You've been pretty quiet this morning," she said.

He didn't meet her gaze. "I have to concentrate on the boat, Mother."

"I don't know what's the matter with you children," she said. "You're both so moody lately."

He didn't answer. He kept his eyes on the squall clouds up ahead. He thought about Rina. Then himself. Then his parents. A sorrow began to well up inside him. He felt his eyes begin to burn and smart.

His mother's voice was shocked. "Why, Laddie, you're crying!"

Then the dam broke and the sobs racked his chest. He felt his mother's hand draw his head down to her breast as she had done so often when he was a baby. "What's the matter, Laddie? What's wrong?" she asked softly.

"Nothing," he gasped, trying to choke back the tears. "Nothing."

She stroked his head gently. "Something is wrong," she said softly. "I know there is. You can tell me, Laddie. Whatever it is, you can tell me. I'll understand and try to help."

"There's nothing you can do," he cried. "Nothing anybody can do now!"

"Try me and see." He didn't speak, his eyes searching her face for something, she didn't know what. A curious dread came into her. "Has it—is it something to do with Rina?"

It was as if the muscles that held his face together all dissolved at once. "Yes, yes!" he cried. "She's going to have a baby! My baby, Mother," he added through tight lips. "I raped her, she's going to have my baby!"

"Oh, no!"

"Yes, Mother," he said, his face suddenly stony.

The tears sprang to her eyes and she covered her face with her hands. This couldn't happen to her children. Not her children. She had wanted everything for them, given them everything. After a moment, she regained control of herself. "I think we'd better turn back," she managed to say quietly.

"We are, Mother," he said. He looked down at his hands on the tiller. The words slipped from him now. "I don't know what got into me, Mother." He stared at her with agonized eyes, his voice strained and tense. "But growing up isn't what it's cracked up to be, it's not what it says in books. Growing up's such a crock of shit!"

He stopped in shock at his own language. "I'm sorry, Mother."

"It's all right, son."

They were silent for a moment and the waves slapped wildly against the hull of the boat. "You mustn't blame Rina, Mother," he said, raising his voice. "She's only a kid. Whatever happened was my fault."

She looked up at her son. A glimmer of intuition pierced the gray veil that seemed to have fallen in front of her eyes. "Rina's a very beautiful girl, Laddie," she said. "I think anyone would find it difficult not to love your sister."

Laddie met his mother's eyes. "I love her, Mother," he said quietly. "And she really isn't my sister."

Geraldine didn't speak.

"Is it terribly wrong to say that, Mother?" he asked. "I don't love her like a sister. I love her"—he searched for a word—"different."

Different, Geraldine thought. It was as good a word as any.

"Is it terribly wrong, Mother?" Laddie asked again.

She looked at her son, feeling a sorrow for him that she could not explain. "No, Laddie," she said quietly. "It's just one of those things that can't be helped."

He took a deep breath, beginning to feel better. At least she understood, she hadn't condemned him. "What are we going to do, Mother?" he asked.

She looked into his eyes. "The first thing we have to do is let Rina know we understand. The poor child must be frightened out of her mind."

He reached forward and took his mother's hand, pressing it to his lips. "You're so good to us, Mother," he whispered, looking gratefully into her eyes.

They were the last words he ever spoke. For just at that moment, the squall came roaring in from the starboard side and capsized the boat.

Rina watched stolidly as the lobstermen brought the pitifully small bodies to the shore and laid them on the beach. She looked down at them. Laddie and Mother. A vague spinning began to roar inside her. A cramp suddenly seized her groin and she doubled over, sinking to her knees in the sand beside the still figures. She closed her eyes, weeping as a terrible moisture began to seep from her.

8

MARGARET BRADLEY LOOKED DOWN WEARILY AT the papers on her desk. They were covered with the hen-tracked hieroglyphics of the girls who trooped through her science classes. Abruptly she pushed them to one side and got to her feet. She walked over to the window and looked out restlessly. She was bored, tired of the never-ending, day-in, day-out routine.

Looking out into the gray dusk of evening, she wondered why Sally's letter hadn't arrived yet. It had been more than two weeks since she'd heard from her and usually letters came regularly twice a week. Could it be that Sally had found someone else? Another friend with whom she could share those *intime* whispered secrets?

There was a hesitant knock at the door and she turned toward it. "Yes?"

"A special-delivery letter for you, Miss Bradley." It was the quavering voice of Thomas, the porter.

Quickly she opened the door and took the letter. "Thank you very much, Thomas," she said, closing the door.

She leaned against it, looking down at the letter in her hand. She began to feel brighter. It was Sally's handwriting. She crossed to her desk and rapidly tore open the envelope.

> Dear Peggy,
> Yesterday I was married. . . .

The knock at the door was so low that at first she did not hear it. It came again, a little louder this time. She raised her head from the desk. "Who is it?" she called in her husky voice.

"Rina Marlowe, Miss Bradley. May I see you for a moment?"

Wearily the teacher got to her feet. "Just a moment," she called.

She walked into the bathroom and looked at herself in the mirror. Her eyes were red-rimmed and swollen, her lipstick slightly smeared. She looked older than her twenty-six years. She turned on the tap and cleaned the make-up from her face with a washcloth. She stared at herself. For ten years, she and Sally had been inseparable. Now it was over.

She replaced the washcloth on the rack and walked out to the door. "Come in," she said, opening it.

Rina looked into the teacher's face. Miss Bradley looked as if she had been crying. "I'm sorry if I disturbed you," she said. "I can come back later if you like."

The teacher shook her head. "No, that's all right," she answered. She crossed to the small desk and sat down behind it. "What is it?"

Rina shut the door behind her slowly. "I was wondering if I could be excused from the dance Saturday night?"

Margaret Bradley stared at her. For a moment, she couldn't believe her ears. Missing the monthly dance was considered the ultimate punishment. The girls would do anything rather than lose that privilege. It was the only time boys were allowed within the confines of the school. "I don't understand," she said.

Rina looked down at the floor. "I just don't want to go, that's all."

It wasn't because the boys didn't like her. The teacher knew it was quite the opposite. The slim, blond sixteen-year-old standing before her was surrounded by boys at every dance. She came from a good family. The Marlowes were well known in Boston. Her father was a banker, a widower.

"That's a rather strange request," she said. "You must have a reason."

Rina still looked down at the floor. She didn't answer.

Margaret Bradley forced a smile to her lips. "Come now," she said in a friendly voice. "You can talk to me. I'm not that much older than you that I wouldn't understand."

Rina looked up at her and she was surprised by the deep revelation of fear in the girl's eyes. Then it was gone and she looked down at the floor again.

The teacher got up and walked around the desk. She took Rina's hand and led her to a seat. "You're afraid of something," she said gently.

"I can't stand them touching me," she whispered.

"Them?" Margaret Bradley asked, her voice puzzled. "Who?"

"Boys. They all want to touch me and my skin creeps." Rina looked up suddenly. "It would be all right if they just wanted to dance or to talk but they're always trying to get you alone someplace."

"What boys?" The teacher's voice was suddenly harsh. "We'll soon put a stop to their coming here."

Rina got up suddenly. "I'd better go," she said nervously. "I didn't think it would work, anyway."

She started for the door. "Wait a minute!" Margaret Bradley's voice was commanding. Rina turned and looked back at her. "Did any of them do more than—than just touch you?"

Rina shook her head.

"How old are you?"

"Sixteen," Rina answered.

"I guess by now you know that boys are always like that."

Rina nodded.

"I felt the same way when I was your age."

"You did?" Rina asked. A note of relief came into her voice. "I thought I was the only one. None of the other girls feel the way I do."

"They're fools!" The teacher's voice was full of a harsh anger, but she checked herself sharply. There was no sense in allowing her bitterness to expose her. "I was just going to make myself a cup of tea," she said. "Would you care to join me?"

Rina hesitated. "If it wouldn't be too much trouble."

"It won't be any trouble at all," Margaret Bradley said.

"Now, you just sit down and make yourself comfortable. I'll have the tea ready in a minute."

She went into the small kitchenette. To her surprise, she found herself humming as she turned on the burner beneath the teakettle.

"I think a summer in Europe between now and the time she goes to Smith in the fall would be of great benefit to her," Margaret Bradley said.

Harrison Marlowe leaned back in his chair and looked at the teacher across the white expanse of the dinner table, then at Rina, seated opposite her. What he saw inspired a kind of confidence in him. A plain, not unattractive young woman in her late twenties, he imagined. She wore simple, tailored clothes, almost mannish in their effect, that seemed to proclaim her profession. She had none of the foolish mannerisms that so many of the young women had today. There was nothing of the flapper about her. She was very serious and businesslike.

"Her mother and I often spoke about Rina going to Europe," he began tentatively.

"No girl is considered quite finished if she hasn't spent some time there," the teacher said assuredly.

Marlowe nodded slowly. It was a great responsibility bringing up a daughter. Somehow he had never realized it until several months ago, when he had come into the parlor and found Rina there.

She was wearing a dark-blue dress that somehow made her seem older than her years. Her white-blond hair shone in the semidimness.

"Hello, Father."

"Rina!" he exclaimed. "What are you doing home?"

"I got to thinking how awful it must be for you to come into this great big empty house and find yourself all alone," she said, "so I thought I'd take a few days off from school."

"But—but what about your studies?" he asked.

"I can make them up easily enough."

"But—"

"Aren't you glad to see me, Father?" she asked, interrupting.

"Of course I am," he said quickly.

"Then why don't you kiss me?" She turned her cheek toward

him. He kissed her cheek. As he straightened up, she held him with her arm. "Now I'll kiss you."

She kissed him on the mouth and her lips were warm. Then she laughed suddenly. "Your mustache tickles!"

He smiled down at her. "You always said that," he said fondly. "Ever since you were a little girl."

"But I'm not a little girl any longer, am I, Father?"

He looked at her, beautiful, almost a woman in her dark-blue dress. "I guess not," he said.

She turned to the sideboard. "I thought you might like a drink before dinner."

The bottles of liquor were all ready for him. He walked over to the sideboard. She even had cracked ice in the bucket. "What's for dinner?" he asked.

"I had Molly make your favorite. Roast chicken, *rissolé* potatoes."

"Good," he said, reaching for a bottle of whisky. Her voice stopped his hand.

"Wouldn't you like a Martini? You haven't had one for a long time."

He hesitated a moment, then reached for the bottle of gin. It wasn't until he turned around that he realized there were two cocktails in his hand. Habit was a strange commander. He turned to put one of them back on the sideboard.

"May I, Father? I'm past sixteen. There are many girls at school whose parents allow them a cocktail at dinner."

He stared at her, then poured half of one drink back into the shaker. He gave her the half-filled glass. He raised his glass in a toast.

She smiled, sipping delicately at her glass. "This is delicious," she said, in exactly the same words and tone of voice he had so often heard his wife use.

He felt the hot, uncontrollable tears leap into his eyes and turned away swiftly so that she would not see. Her hand caught at his sleeve and he turned back to her. Her eyes were deep with sympathy. He let her draw him down slowly to the couch beside her.

And then, for a moment, he wasn't her father. He was just a lonely man weeping against the breast of his mother, his wife, his daughter. He felt her young, strong arms around his shoulders, her fingers lightly brushing his hair. He heard the rumble of her whispered voice within her chest. "Poor Daddy, poor Daddy."

As suddenly as it had come, the moment was gone and he was aware only of the firm, taut breasts against his cheek. Self-consciously he raised his head. "I guess I made a fool of myself," he said awkwardly.

"No, Father," she said quietly. "For the first time in my life, I didn't feel like a child any more. I felt grown up and needed."

He forced a tired smile to his lips. "There's time enough for you to grow up."

Later that night, after dinner, she came over and sat on the arm of his chair. "I'm not going back to school any more," she said. "I'm going to stay home and keep house for you."

He smiled. "You'd get bored with that quickly enough," he said. "You'd miss the excitement of school, of boy friends—"

"Boys!" she said scornfully. "I can do without them. They're a bunch of grubby little animals always mooning after you. I can't stand them."

"You can't, eh?" he said quizzically. "Just what kind of man would please your majesty?"

She looked down at him seriously. "I think an older man," she said. "Someone like you, maybe. Someone who makes me feel safe and secure and needed. Boys are always trying to get something from you, show that they're stronger, more important."

He laughed. "That's only because they're young."

"I know," she answered, still serious. "That's why they frighten me. They're only interested in what they want; they don't care about me." She leaned over and kissed the top of his head. "Your hair is so nice with that touch of gray in it." A note of regret came into her voice. "Too bad I can't marry you. I love you, Father."

"No!" he said sharply, so sharply that he surprised even himself with the inexplicable violence of his reaction.

"No what, Father?" she asked, startled.

He got to his feet and stared down at her. "No, you're not staying home. You're going back to school tomorrow. I'll have Peters drive you up."

She stared up at him and her eyes began to well with tears. Suddenly, she was a little girl again. "Don't you love me, Father?" she cried. "Don't you want me to stay with you?"

He stared at her for a moment, then compassion filled him.

"Of course I love you, darling," he said quietly. "But don't you see, we can't put ourselves in a shell to protect ourselves from the world around us."

"But all I want is to be with you, Daddy!"

"No, child, no," he said patiently. "I know that's the way you feel now but someday, when you're older, and maybe married with children of your own, you'll understand."

She tore herself from his arms and faced him angrily. "No!" she stormed. "I'll never get married! I'll never have children! I'll never let some boy get his dirty hands on me!"

"Rina!" he exclaimed in a shocked voice.

She stared at him dumbly, then her face dissolved into tears again. "Oh, Father!" she cried in a hurt, broken voice. "Can't you see? It's not I, it's you who don't understand!"

"Rina, darling," he said, reaching for her. But she had already fled the room. He heard her running footsteps on the staircase, then her door slammed.

He came back to the present slowly, looking down the long dining table at the teacher, then at Rina. Her eyes were shining, brightly expectant.

"I am sure that if Rina's mother were alive, Miss Bradley," Marlowe said in his oddly formal manner, "she would be as happy as I am to entrust our daughter to your very capable hands."

Margaret Bradley looked quickly down at her soup, so that he could not see the sudden triumph in her eyes. "Thank you, Mr. Marlowe," she said demurely.

9

THEY STAYED ON DECK UNTIL THEY HAD PASSED the Statue of Liberty and Ellis Island, until the water was a bottle green beneath the ship and they could no longer see the shore.

"Excited?" Margaret Bradley asked.

Rina's eyes were sparkling. "It's like a dream."

Margaret smiled. "It will get better and better. Right now we'd best go down to our cabin and rest up a bit before dinner."

"But I'm not the least bit tired," Rina protested.

"You will be," Margaret said firmly but pleasantly. "We'll be aboard the *Leviathan* for six days. You'll have plenty of time to see everything."

She nodded in silent approval as they entered their cabin. Harrison Marlowe wasn't cheap when he did something for his daughter. It was a first-class cabin, with twin beds and private bath. He hadn't hesitated, either, when she'd suggested that Rina would need a new wardrobe. Instead, he'd simply written a check for a thousand dollars and told her that if it wasn't sufficient, she should let him know.

They had got only a few things in New York; the rest they would get in Paris. But without saying anything to Rina, she had ordered several things and had them sent directly to the ship. She couldn't wait to see the expression on Rina's face when she saw them.

The boxes were on the bed but she did not call attention to them. She wanted the moment to be just right. She took off her light spring coat and sank into a deep, comfortable chair. Opening her purse, she took out a package of cigarettes. It wasn't until after she had lit one that she became aware that Rina was staring at her. Then she realized that Rina had never seen her smoke.

She held out the package. "Have one?"

Rina hesitated.

"Go ahead," she urged. "It's all right. You'll find most European women smoke; they're not so provincial as we are."

She watched Rina light a cigarette and laughed as she coughed. "Don't swallow the smoke."

Rina held the smoke in her mouth and let it out slowly. "How's that?"

Margaret smiled. "Fine."

"This is fun, Miss Bradley."

Margaret looked at her. "Now that we're really on our way, I think we can dispense with formalities. From now on, you may call me Peggy." She got to her feet. "Would you like to bathe first, Rina?"

Rina shook her head. "No, Miss Bradley, you can go first if you like."

Margaret shook her head, smiling. "Peggy."

"I mean Peggy."

"That's better," Margaret said.

* * *

She looked up as Rina came out of the bathroom, tying the belt of her robe. Her long blond hair fell to her shoulders, looking even more silvery against her dark tan. There was a low knock at the door. Rina looked at her questioningly.

"I ordered sherry," she explained. "It's good for your appetite the first day at sea. I find it helps prevent *mal de mer.*"

She took the tray from the steward and gave one glass to Rina. "Cheers," she said, smiling and sipping the wine slowly.

"It's nice," Rina said.

"I'm glad you like it."

Rina put the glass down. "Shall I wear my new blue suit tonight?"

Margaret assumed a shocked expression. "First-class dining is formal, Rina."

"I have a few of my party dresses," Rina said. "I can wear one of them."

"Not those horrible dresses they wear at the school dances?"

A hurt expression appeared on Rina's face. "I thought they were very pretty."

Margaret laughed. "For children, perhaps. But not for a young lady going to Europe."

"I don't know what to wear, then," Rina said helplessly.

She had teased Rina enough. "Those boxes on the bed are yours," she said casually. "I think you might find something to wear in one of them."

The expression on Rina's face as she opened the boxes was all that Margaret had hoped for. Rina put on a stark black cocktail gown that clung to her figure, revealing her naked shoulders. As they walked into the dining salon, an hour later, every male eye followed them.

Possessively Margaret reached across the table and patted Rina's hand. "You look lovely, my dear."

Margaret put down the towel and turned to look at herself in the full-length mirror. Pleased with her reflection, she ran her hands down along her sides, then stretched luxuriously. Her small breasts with their tiny nipples were no larger than many men's, and her hips were flat and her legs straight.

She slipped into the silk pajamas, quickly buttoning the fly front of the long, man-tailored trousers, then fastening the tightly fitting bolero jacket. She brushed her dark hair straight back and pinned it. Once more, she glanced at the mirror. At a quick glance, few could tell her from a male.

Pleased, she left the bathroom and entered the stateroom. "You can go in now, Rina."

Rina stared at her in amazement. "Miss Bradley—Peggy, I mean—those pajamas!"

Margaret smiled at her. "Like them?"

Rina nodded.

Margaret was pleased. "They're made of genuine Chinese brocade. A friend sent me the material from San Francisco. I designed them myself." One thing she could always say for Sally— she had good taste. Of all the things she had ever given her, these pajamas were her favorite.

Rina got out of her chair and took a cotton nightgown from the bureau. She started for the bathroom.

"Wait a minute," Margaret said. She went to her bureau and took out a small box. "While I was at it," she said, "I also bought you a few nightgowns."

She watched Rina's face as she opened the box. "They're real silk!"

"I was afraid that all you had were those horrible school shifts."

Rina looked down at the box. "There's a different color for every night in the week," she said. "They're all so beautiful, I don't know which to wear first."

Margaret smiled again. "Why don't you wear the white one tonight?"

"O.K.," Rina said. She picked it up and started again for the bathroom. She stopped at the door. "I don't know how to thank you, Peggy," she said gratefully. "You make everything seem so wonderful."

Margaret laughed happily. "That's just the way I want it to be for you," she said. She looked at Rina as if the idea had just come to her. "What do you say we celebrate tonight? While you're changing, I'll order a bottle of champagne. We'll have a little party all by ourselves."

"That would be fun." Rina smiled. "I always wanted to drink champagne but Father would never let me."

"Well, this will be a secret between us." Margaret laughed, reaching for the telephone. "I promise I won't tell him."

★ ★ ★

Rina put down her glass and began to giggle.

Margaret leaned back in her chair, still holding hers by its fragile stem. "What's funny?"

"My nightgown crinkles and gives off tiny sparks when I move."

"That's static electricity," Margaret said. "Silk is a very good conductor."

"I know," Rina answered quickly. "I remember that from your class." She ran her hand down along the gown. "It gives off tiny blue sparks. Can you see them?"

"No."

Rina leaped to her feet. "I'll turn off the lights," she said. "You'll be able to see them then."

She turned off the lights and stood in front of Margaret. "Watch," she said. She ran her hands down the sides of her gown. There was a faint crackling and tiny sparks appeared at her fingertips. Rina picked up her glass and emptied it. She held the glass toward Margaret. "May I have some more, Peggy?"

"Of course," Margaret answered, refilling her glass.

Rina held it to her lips and sipped. "Champagne is nothing but pop made from wine," she said seriously. "But it tastes better. It's not as sweet."

"It's getting warmer in here, don't you think?"

"It is getting warmer," Rina answered. "Do you want me to turn on the fan?"

"Oh, no," Margaret said quickly. "We'd only catch cold in the draft. I'll just slip off my jacket."

She felt Rina's eyes on her small bosom and she picked up her glass quickly. "Do you mind?"

Rina shook her head. She lifted her glass and took another sip. "Do you hear music?"

Margaret nodded. "It's the orchestra from the ballroom. They're playing a waltz."

Rina got to her feet. She swayed in time to the music. "I love to dance," she said. She glided lightly around the room, the white gown flaring out as she turned, showing her long, tanned legs.

Margaret felt a weakness in the pit of her stomach as she got to her feet. "I love to dance, too," she said, making a mock bow. "May I have this dance, Miss Marlowe?"

Rina looked at her, smiling. "Just this one. All the others are taken, Miss Bradley."

Margaret shook a reproachful finger at Rina. "Mr. Bradley, if you please."

Rina laughed. "Of course. Just this one, Mr. Bradley."

Margaret put her arm around Rina's waist. They both laughed as the tiny blue sparks crackled from Rina's gown. Margaret felt her legs tremble as the warmth from Rina's breasts came through the gown. Holding the young girl firmly, she led her into the dance. They spun furiously in a circle as the music reached a crescendo, then abruptly halted.

Rina looked up into her face. Margaret smiled at her. "We'd better have some more champagne." She poured Rina a glass and picked up her own. "You're a very good dancer, Rina."

"Thank you. You lead better than any of the boys that ever came to the school dances. You do everything so well." Rina swayed slightly. "The dancing made me dizzy."

"Perhaps you'd better lie down on your bed for a moment."

Rina shook her head. "And break up our party?"

"Lie down for a minute. You won't break up the party. I'll come and sit on the bed."

"O.K.," Rina said. She walked over to the bed and put her glass on the night table, then stretched out on the white sheet.

Margaret sat down beside her. "Feel better?"

"The room is still spinning," Rina said.

Margaret bent over her and stroked her forehead lightly. "Close your eyes for a moment."

Obediently Rina closed her eyes. They were silent for a moment while Margaret continued to stroke her forehead. "That's better," Rina said softly. "The spinning has gone."

Margaret didn't answer, but kept stroking her head lightly. Rina opened her eyes and looked at her. Margaret reached for her glass. "A little more champagne?"

Rina nodded. She sipped and handed it back to Margaret, who smiled at her, then put the glass down.

"I'm glad we're going to Europe together," Rina said suddenly. "I've never really had a close girl friend before. The girls at school always seemed such ninnies to me. Always talking about boys."

"They're nothing but silly children, most of them," Margaret said. "That's why I liked you the moment you came into my room that night. I knew you were different, more mature."

"Ever since Laddie died, I couldn't stand boys," Rina said.

"Laddie?"

"My brother," Rina explained. "He and my father are the only two men that I ever really liked."

"He must have been very nice," Margaret said.

"He was." Rina turned her head away. "I think I was in love with him."

"That's nothing," Margaret said quickly. "All girls love their brothers."

"He really wasn't my brother, you know. I was adopted."

"How do you know you loved him?" Margaret asked, faint jealousy stirring within her.

"I know," Rina answered. "And I think he loved me, too."

"You do?" Margaret asked, the jealousy stronger. "Did he— did you?"

Rina looked away. "I never spoke to anyone about it before."

"You can talk to me," Margaret said. "I'm your friend. We have no secrets between us."

"You won't be angry with me?"

"I won't be angry with you," Margaret said almost sharply. "Tell me!"

Rina's voice was muffled by the pillow. "I wouldn't let him touch me because I was afraid of what would happen. Then one day, he came into my room and tied my hands to the bed with his belt and he did it to me. He hurt me so bad!"

"He couldn't have loved you so much if he hurt you."

"But he did!" Rina said wildly. "Don't you see, Peggy? I wanted him to. All the time I kept daring him and when he did, I knew I loved him. But he went out in the boat with Mother and they died." She began to sob. "It was my fault because I wanted him to. Can't you see that I was the one who was supposed to die, not Mother? She took my place in the dream. Now I don't even dream the dream any more."

"You'll dream your dreams again," Margaret said slowly, holding Rina's head against her bosom.

"No, I won't!"

"Yes, you will," Margaret said firmly. "Tell me about it and I'll help you."

Rina stopped sobbing. "Do you think you could?" she asked, her eyes searching Margaret's face.

"Tell me and we'll see."

Rina took a deep breath. "I dreamed that I was dead and everybody was around my bed, crying. I could feel how much they loved me and wanted me because they kept begging me not to die. But I couldn't do anything about it. I was dead."

Margaret felt a cold shiver of excitement tremble through her. Slowly she got to her feet. "Close your eyes, Rina," she said quietly, "and we'll act out your dream. Whom do you want me to be?"

Rina looked up at her shyly. "Will you be Laddie?"

"I'll be Laddie," Margaret answered. "Now you close your eyes."

Margaret looked down at the girl. Suddenly her eyes began to fill with tears. A sudden fear began to tear through her. Rina was dead. Rina was really dead. "Rina!" she cried hoarsely. "Please don't die! Please!"

Rina did not move and Margaret fell to her knees beside the bed. "Please, Rina. I can't live without you." She leaned over the bed and covered Rina's face with kisses.

Rina opened her eyes suddenly, a small, proud smile on her face. "You're really crying," she said, her fingers touching Margaret's cheek. She closed her eyes again contentedly.

Slowly Margaret slipped the nightgown off. "You're beautiful," she whispered. "You're the most beautiful woman in the world. You're much too beautiful to die."

Rina looked up at her. "Do you really think I'm beautiful?"

Margaret nodded. She ripped off her pajama bottoms and let them fall to the floor. "All you have to do is look at me to see how beautiful you really are." She caught Rina's hand and pressed it to her breasts, then down across her stomach to her thighs. "Feel how flat I am, just like a man?"

Slowly she sank down onto the bed beside Rina, gently caressing her breasts, pressing her lips to the soft, cool cheeks.

"I feel so safe with you, so good," Rina whispered. "You're not like the other boys, I don't like them to touch me. I'm afraid of them. But I'm not afraid of you."

With a cry of agony, Margaret rolled, her knees forcing Rina's legs apart. "I love you, Rina! Please don't die!"

She pressed her mouth against Rina's. For a moment, she felt the fire of her tongue and then she heard Rina's voice whispering huskily. "Laddie, fuck me, fuck me! I love you, Laddie!"

10

RINA LOOKED DOWN AT HER WATCH. IT WAS HALF past two. "I really must be going," she said.

"To hurry after such a lunch?" Jacques Deschamps spread his hands. "It is sacrilege. You must have a liqueur before you go."

Rina smiled at the slim, graying *avocat*. "But—I—"

"You have been in Paris for more than a year," Jacques interrupted, "and you still have not learned that one does not hurry after a meal. Whatever it is, it will wait." He hissed at a passing waiter. "Psst!"

The waiter stopped and bowed respectfully. "Monsieur?"

Rina sank back into her chair. Jacques looked at her questioningly. "Pernod. Over ice."

He shuddered. "Over ice," he repeated to the waiter. "You heard mademoiselle."

The waiter looked at her quickly with that glance of appraisal that all Frenchmen seemed to share. "Over ice, monsieur," he said. "The usual for you?"

Jacques nodded and the waiter left. He turned back to Rina. "And how does the painting go?" he asked. "You are making progress?"

Rina laughed. "You know better than that. I'm afraid I'll never be a painter."

"But you are having fun?"

She turned and looked out at the street. The faint smell of May that came only to Paris was in the air. The truck drivers were already in their shirt sleeves and the women had long since begun to abandon their drab gray and black winter coats.

"You do not answer," he said.

She turned back to him as the waiter came with their drinks. "I'm having fun," she said, picking up her drink.

"You are not sure?" he persisted.

She smiled suddenly. "Of course I'm sure."

He lifted his glass. "*À votre santé.*"

"*À votre santé,*" she echoed.

He put his glass down. "And your friend?" he asked. "How is she?"

"Peggy's fine," Rina said automatically. She looked at him steadily. "Peggy is very good to me. I don't know what I'd do without her."

"How do you know?" he said quickly. "You have never tried. You could be many things. You are young, beautiful. You could marry, have children, you could even—"

"Be your mistress?" She smiled, interrupting.

He nodded and smiled. "Even be my mistress. That is not the worst thing that could happen. But you remember my terms."

She looked into his face. "You're a very kind man, Jacques," she said, remembering the afternoon she had first heard them.

She and Peggy had been in Paris a few months and had just found their apartment, after her father had given his permission for her to stay in Paris for a year. Peggy had taken her to a party given by a professor at the University, where she had just begun to work.

Rina felt very alone at the party. Her French was not good enough to let her mix easily and she had retreated to a corner. She was leafing through a magazine when she heard a voice. "Miss *Américaine?*"

She looked up. A slim, dark man with a touch of gray at his temples was standing there. He was smiling gently.

"*Non parle fran—*"

"I speak English," he said quickly.

She smiled.

"And what is a pretty girl like you doing all alone with a magazine?" he asked. "Who is fool enough to bring you to a party like this and then—" He gestured expressively.

"My friend brought me," Rina said, indicating Peggy. "She has just got a job at the University."

Peggy was talking animatedly with one of the professors. She looked very attractive in her slim, tailored suit. "Oh," he said, a strangely quizzical look on his face.

"And whom did you bring?"

"No one." He shrugged. "Actually. I came in the hopes of meeting you."

She glanced at his hands and saw that he wore a wedding ring, as so many Frenchmen did. "You don't expect me to believe that?" she said. "What would your wife say?"

He smiled and laughed with her. "My wife would be very understanding. She could not come with me. She is very, very pregnant." He held his arms out in an exaggerated circle in front of him.

She laughed again and just then, Peggy's voice came over her shoulder. "Having fun, darling?"

Some weeks later, she was alone in the apartment one afternoon when the telephone rang. It was Jacques and she met him for lunch. And several times after that.

Then one afternoon—it had been a day just like this one—they sat dawdling over their liqueurs. "Why are you so afraid of men?" he asked her suddenly.

She felt the red fire creep up into her throat and over her face. "What makes you say that?"

"I have the feeling," he said. "Inside. I know."

She looked down at her drink. She didn't speak.

"Your friend is not the answer," he said.

She looked up at him. "Peggy has nothing to do with it. She's a good friend, no more."

He smiled knowingly. "You are in France, remember? There is nothing wrong, we understand such things. But I do not understand you. You are not the usual kind who lives like that."

She could feel her face flaming now. "I don't think that's very nice of you."

He laughed. "It is not," he admitted frankly. "But I do not like to see you waste yourself."

"You'd like it better if I went to sleep with some clumsy fool who knows nothing and cares less about the way I feel?" she said angrily.

He shook his head. "No. I would not like that at all. I would like you to come to bed with me."

"What makes you think it would be any different with you?"

He looked into her eyes. "Because I am a man, not a boy. Because I would want to please you. Boys are like bulls; they think only of themselves. In this you are right. But because of this, do not think that it is only women who know how to make love. There are men also who are aware of the sensitivities."

"Like yourself?" she asked sarcastically.

"Like myself. Do you think I see you again and again only because I have a purely intellectual interest in you?"

She laughed suddenly. "At least you are honest."

"I am a great believer in the truth."

A few months later, on a rainy afternoon, she went to his apartment and it was just as he said. He was kind and gentle and she did not hurt at all. And all the while, she felt the power in her, the power to bring him to a point of ecstasy from which he would never return, a power that could never turn into terror for her because she could always control it or him.

She watched him buttoning his shirt in front of the mirror. "Jacques."

He turned. "What is it, my sweet?"

She held out her arms to him. "Come here, Jacques."

He came over to the bed. He bent swiftly and kissed her naked breast. "When you make love, my darling," he said, "your nipples are full like bursting purple plums. Now they are like little pink poppies."

"It was like you said it would be, Jacques."

"I am glad."

She took his strong brown hands in her own and looked down at them. His gold wedding ring shone up at her. She looked up into his face. "I think I would like to be your mistress," she said softly.

"*Bon,*" he said. "I had hoped you would say that. That is why I took this little apartment. You can move in tonight."

She was surprised. "Move in here?"

He nodded. "If you do not like this place, I will get another."

"But I can't do that! What about Peggy?"

"What about her?" He shrugged. "It is *fini.*"

"Can't we just go on like this? I'll meet you here whenever you like."

"You mean you will not move in?"

She shook her head. "I can't. What would Peggy do? She needs my help to keep the apartment. Besides, if my father ever found out, he'd kill me."

"But he does not worry about your living with that—that *lesbienne?*" he said bitterly.

"You don't know my father. Back in Boston, they don't ever think about things like that."

"What does he think she is?"

"What she has always been," she answered. "My teacher, my companion."

He laughed shortly. "She has been your teacher, yes."

"Oh, Jacques," she said in a hurt voice. "Don't spoil everything now. Why can't we go on like this?"

He looked at her. "Then you won't move in here?"

"I can't," she said. "Don't you understand, I can't."

He got to his feet, and walked back to the dresser. He finished buttoning his shirt and picked up his tie.

"I don't see what difference it would make. After all, you're married. How much time do you think you could spend here, anyway?"

He studied her. "That is different," he said coldly.

"Different?" she shouted in anger. "Why is it different for you and not for me?"

He stared at her. "A man may be unfaithful to his wife, as she may to him if she is so minded. But a man is never unfaithful to his mistress, nor is a woman unfaithful to her lover."

"But Peggy is not a man!"

"No, she is not," he said grimly. "She is something worse than a man."

Rina looked at him for a moment. She drew her head up proudly. "Those are your terms?" she asked quietly.

She sat there proudly, her back straight, her naked breasts magnificent over her deep chest. He could see the outlines of her ribs against her flesh as they rose and fell with her breath. Never in my life have I known so much beauty, he thought. Aloud he said, "If that's the way you put it, those are my terms."

She didn't answer.

"I just don't understand," she said. She looked up at him. "You had better hand me my dress."

That had been many months ago and oddly enough, they still remained friends. She raised the Pernod to her lips and emptied her glass. "And now I really must go," she said. "I promised Pavan I would be at his studio by three o'clock."

He raised an eyebrow. "Pavan? You have taken up sculpting?"

She shook her head. "No, I'm modeling for him."

Jacques knew how Pavan worked. He used many models for just one statue. He was always trying to create the ideal. He would never succeed.

She felt his quizzical gaze sweep down to her breasts. She laughed. "No, it's not what you think."

"No?" he asked. "Why not?"

"He says they're too large."

"He is mad," Jacques said quickly. "But then, all artists are mad. What is it, then?"

She got to her feet. "My pubis," she said.

For the first time since she had known him, he was speechless. She laughed.

He found his voice. "But why?"

"Because it's the highest mountain any man will ever climb, he says, and more men will die trying to climb it than ever fell from Mount Everest." She smiled and bent over him. "But we won't tell him that you survived the ascent, will we, Jacques?"

She kissed his cheek quickly and turned and walked out onto the sidewalk. He watched her until she was lost in the crowded street, then turned back to the waiter. "Psst!" he said. "I think I will have another drink!"

11

SHE HURRIED PAST THE POLITE GREETING OF THE concierge, up the three narrow flights of the staircase. She'd stayed at the studio later than she thought. There would be just enough time to prepare dinner before Peggy got home.

Rina went through the tiny living room into the kitchen. Swiftly she lit the gas under the hot-water heater for the tub and with the same match, the oven, leaving the flame low. She took the small, browned chicken she'd just purchased, already cooked, at the corner rotisserie and put it into a pan and into the oven to keep warm. Rapidly she sliced bread from a long loaf, arranged it next to a large piece of cheese and began to set the table. In a few minutes, she was finished.

She looked down at her watch. There would even be time enough for a bath if the water was hot enough. She walked over and felt the tank. It was lukewarm. There would be enough if she didn't fill the tub more than half full.

She walked back into the living room on her way to the bathroom, her fingers already busy with the buttons of her blouse. The door opened and she turned toward it. "You're early," she said.

Peggy looked at her coldly and without answering, she closed the door behind her. Rina shrugged her shoulders. Peggy had these moods. One moment, she'd be bright, warm and gay, the next cold, even sullen. It would pass. "There's some wine and cheese on the table if you'd like something before dinner," she said, starting for the bathroom again.

Peggy's hand spun her around. "I thought I told you not to see Deschamps again!"

Rina stared at her. So that was it. Someone must have seen them at the restaurant and told Peggy. Strange that of all the men they knew, Peggy was jealous of none except Jacques. The younger men never upset her, but Jacques, with his curious, confident smile and the bright-gray hair at his temples, always managed to upset her.

"I just ran into him and he invited me to lunch," she said. It wasn't that she was afraid of Peggy's jealous rages but she didn't feel like having a quarrel. "I just couldn't be rude."

"Then where were you all afternoon?" Peggy demanded. "You weren't at art school, you weren't home. I kept calling both places until I became frantic with worry."

"I didn't feel like going to school," she said.

Peggy's eyes squinted at her. "You didn't walk over to his apartment, by any chance?"

Rina stared back at her. "No, I didn't."

"He was seen entering his apartment with a blonde about four o'clock."

Rina raised an eyebrow. Jacques hadn't wasted any time. "I'm not the only blonde in Paris," she said.

"He didn't answer his phone," Peggy said accusingly.

Rina smiled. "I can't say that I blame him, do you?"

Peggy's hand slashed across Rina's face. "You're lying!"

Rina's hand flew to her cheek. She stared at Peggy.

The other side of her face flamed as Peggy slapped her again.

She grabbed Rina's shoulders and began to shake her. "Now I want the truth!"

"I told you the truth!" Rina screamed. She struck out at Peggy wildly.

Peggy fell back in surprise at the sudden onslaught. A hurt expression came over her face. "Why do you do these things to me when you know I love you so much?"

Rina stared at her. For the first time, a feeling of revulsion swept over her. First for Peggy, then for herself.

Almost instantly, Peggy threw herself to her knees, her arms clasped around Rina's thighs. "Please, please, darling, don't look at me like that. Don't be angry with me. I'm sorry. I was crazy jealous."

Rina's face ached where it had been slapped. Suddenly, she was tired. "Don't do that again—ever," she said wearily.

"I won't, I won't," Peggy promised wildly. "It's just that I can't bear to think of that lecher getting his filthy hands on you again."

"He's not a lecher, he's a man," Rina said. She looked down at Peggy. A faint note of contempt came into her voice. "A real man. Not an imitation!"

"I have shown you more than you would learn from all the men in the world."

A sudden knowledge came to Rina—the first faint revelation of self-truth. A cold fright ran through her. She looked down at the dark-brown head pressed against the front of her skirt.

"That's what's wrong. You're so anxious to show me love, to teach me love. But it's all from the outside in. Why can't you teach me to feel love, to give love?" Slowly she pushed Peggy away from her. And then, for the lack of a better place to do it, she dropped to her knees and turned her face into Peggy's bosom and began to cry.

"Cry, lover, cry," Peggy whispered. "Cry it all out. I'll always take care of you. That's what love is for."

It was early when Amru Singh arrived at the party that Pavan was giving to celebrate the unveiling of his master statue. It was about six o'clock when Amru Singh made his obeisance to his host, politely refused a drink and took his usual place against the wall in the empty room.

As was his habit, he took off his shirt and folded it neatly and placed it on the floor. Then he took off his shoes—he wore no socks—and placed them next to the shirt. He took a very deep breath and placing his back against the wall, slid down until he was seated squarely on the shirt with his legs crossed beneath him.

It was thus that he could observe, without turning his head, the actions of every person in the room. It was also from this position that he could most easily fill his mind. He thought about many things, but mostly about the vanities and ambitions of man. Amru Singh was seeking a man whose vanities and ambitions transcended the personal, aspiring only to the glory that had been buried by the centuries deep in the human spirit. That he had not yet found such a man did not discourage him.

He felt his muscles lock in the familiar tension which was at the same time relaxed and comforting; he felt his breathing become slower, shallower. He closed off a corner of his mind for a few minutes, though his eyes remained open and alert. It could be any night, perhaps tonight, that his search would be ended.

But he could already feel the evil spirit of the goddess Kali unleashed in the room. With an inward shrug of his shoulders, he cast from him the feeling of disappointment. There were so many little people in the room.

On the floor, in the corner behind the big sofa, a man and a woman were committing an act of fornication, hidden, or so they thought, from the others. He thought of the positions of obscenity carved high into the walls of the temple of the goddess and felt a distaste seep through him. This ugly copulation, which he could observe through the space between the high Regency legs of the couch, was not justified by even a holy worship of the evil one.

In a niche near the door, with a single light shining down on it from above, stood the draped statue on a pedestal. It stood there very still, like a corpse in a shroud, and did not even stir when the door opened for two newly entered guests. Without moving his eyes, Amru knew them. The blond American girl and her friend, the dark woman. He closed his mind to them as the clock began to toll the hour and Pavan began his speech.

It was nothing but a repetition of what he had been saying all evening, and many times before, but at its finish, he suddenly began to weep. He was very drunk and he almost fell as, with a quick gesture, he tore the covering from the statue.

There was a silence in the room as all looked at the cold marble form of the statue. It was scaled to two-thirds life size and carved from a rose-blush Italian marble that took on a soft hue of warm life from the light in the room. The figure stood poised on tiptoe, the hands held over her upturned face, reaching for her lover, the sun.

Then the silence was broken as all at once began to comment and congratulate the sculptor. That is all except one. He was Leocadia, the art dealer. A small, gray man with the thin, pursed lips of the money-changer.

In the end, no matter what anyone said, his was the final judgment. It was he who determined its value. It did not matter that the price he set might forever prohibit a sale; his evaluation was the recognition of art.

Pavan approached him anxiously. "Well, monsieur?" he asked. "What do you think?"

Leocadia did not look at Pavan. He never looked at anyone while he spoke to him. The artists claimed that he could not meet their gaze because he was a parasite living better from the proceeds of their life's blood than they themselves did. "The market for sculpture is very weak," he said.

"Bah!" Pavan snorted. "I do not ask about the market. I ask about my work!"

"Your work is as always," the dealer said evasively.

Pavan turned and gestured, his arm outflung toward the silent statue. "Look at those breasts. I took them from different girls to achieve the symmetry that nature did not provide. And the face. Flawless! Notice the brow, the eyes, the cheekbones, the nose!" He was suddenly silent, staring up at the statue. "The nose," he said, almost whispering.

He turned toward the models, huddling against the wall. "Bring monsieur a bottle of wine! The nose, monsieur," he said accusingly. "Why did you not tell me about the nose?"

Leocadia was silent. This was no time to tell Pavan he had found nothing at fault with the nose. He had a reputation to maintain.

"My chisel!" Pavan roared. He climbed upon a chair and positioned the chisel delicately. He scraped the stone slightly, then polished the surface with his sleeve. The marble shone once more and he stepped down and looked.

Suddenly he screamed in frustrated agony. "It's wrong!" he cried. "It's all wrong! Why didn't you tell me, monsieur? Why did you let me make a fool of myself?"

Leocadia still did not speak.

Pavan stared dumbly at the dealer, tears coming to his eyes, then he turned and violently swung the mallet at the statue's head. The marble cracked and the head fell into fragments on the floor. Pavan began to swing wildly at the rest of the statue. The arms fell, then a shoulder; a crack appeared across the bust and that, too, shattered. The statue rocked crazily on its pedestal, then crashed forward.

Pavan knelt over the pieces, swinging his mallet like a man possessed. "I loved you!" he screamed, tears streaming down his cheeks. "I loved you and you betrayed me!" At last, he sank exhausted to the floor, amidst the debris.

As suddenly as they had come, the tears stopped and Pavan began searching frantically among the pieces of shattered marble. At last, he found what he sought. He got to his feet. Holding the fragment in his hand, he weaved unsteadily toward the art dealer. Cupping the marble in his hands, he held it out. "I see now where I went wrong, monsieur," he said. "Do you?"

Leocadia looked at the piece of stone. He didn't even know what it was intended to be. But again, this was no time for him to speak. He nodded cautiously.

"Thank God!" Pavan cried. "Thank the good Lord that I did not destroy the sole thing of beauty in the stupidity of my disappointment!"

The crowd pushed forward to see what Pavan held in his hand. It seemed to be only a piece of broken marble. "What is it?" one of them whispered to another.

"You stupid fools! Do you not recognize where you come from? The soul itself of a woman's beauty?" Pavan roared.

He got to his feet and stared at them balefully. "This is fit only for the gods themselves to lie upon!" He looked down at the stone in his hands and a tender look came over his face.

"Now I see my error," he said. "It is around this tiny core that I will carve into stone the perfect Woman!" He looked around at them dramatically.

Leocadia looked at the piece of marble again. So that was

what it was. Almost immediately, he thought of the fat young Egyptian prince who had come into the gallery. This was something he would appreciate. "A thousand francs," he said.

Pavan looked at the dealer, his confidence suddenly restored. "A thousand francs!" he said scornfully.

"Fifteen hundred, then," Leocadia murmured.

Pavan was caught up now in the never-ending struggle between artist and dealer. He turned to his fellow artists. "Only fifteen hundred francs he offers me!"

He whirled back to the dealer. "Not a centime less than twenty-five hundred and a commission to do the sculpture of the woman from whom this was taken!" he shouted.

Leocadia looked down at the floor. "How can I undertake such a commission when I do not know the model?"

Pavan spun around. The models looked at each other curiously, wondering which of them had posed for that particular portion of the statue. But it was none of them. Suddenly, Pavan's arm shot out. "You!" he shouted, pointing. "Come here!"

They turned and followed his pointing finger. Rina stood frozen to the spot. Her face began to flame, then hands pulled her forward, propelling her toward the sculptor.

Pavan seized her hand and turned toward the dealer. For once, Leocadia looked. Almost immediately, he looked away again. "Agreed!" he murmured.

A deep bellow of triumph arose from the sculptor's throat. He lifted Rina into his arms and kissed her excitedly on both cheeks. "You will live forever, my lovely one!" he cried proudly. "I will carve your beauty into the stone for all eternity to worship!"

Rina began to laugh. It was crazy. They were all crazy. Pavan began to sing lustily, dragging her with him in an erratic dance. He lifted her up onto the pedestal where the statue formerly stood. She felt hands tugging at her dress, at her clothing. She reached out her arms to brace herself, to keep from falling. Then she was completely nude on the pedestal. A strange hush fell over the room.

It was Pavan himself who led her down. He threw a cloth around her as she started to walk toward the bathroom. One of the models handed her her torn clothing. Rina took it and closed the door behind her. A moment later, she reappeared.

Peggy was waiting for her. She half led, half dragged Rina toward the door. The door slammed behind them.

Suddenly, one of the curtains in the mind of Amru Singh lifted. Through the thin wooden partition behind his head, he could hear dim voices.

"Are you crazy?"

"It wasn't that important, Peggy."

"What if it gets into the papers? The next thing you know, it will be picked up and spread all over the front pages in Boston!"

Rina's laughter echoed gaily. "I can just see the headline now," she said. "Boston girl chosen as most beautiful cunt in Paris!"

"You sound as if you're proud of it."

"Why shouldn't I be? It's the only thing I've ever done for myself."

"Once it gets around, every man in Paris will be after you. I suppose you'd like that."

"Maybe I would. It's time I began to grow up, stopped taking your word for everything."

There was the sound of a vicious slap, then an angry voice. "You're a whore, a cheap whore, and that's how a whore should be treated!"

There was a moment's silence. "I told you never to do that again!"

He heard the sound of another slap. "Whore, bitch! That's the only language you understand!" There was a pause, then "Rina!" The hidden sound of fear was in the voice. Amru Singh thought it sounded much like the trainer of the tiger who steps into the cage only to find his kitten has become a full-grown cat. "What are you doing? Put down that shoe!"

Then there was a half-pitched scream and the sound of a body falling, tumbling erratically down the long, steep stair well. And for the first time in the memory of anyone there, Amru Singh left a party before the last guest had departed.

Rina was standing at the railing, her face ashen, looking down the stair well. Her sharp-pointed high-heeled shoe was still in her hand. He took the shoe from her fingers and bending down, slipped it on her foot.

"I never even touched her!"

"I know," Amru Singh said quietly.

She collapsed suddenly against him. He could feel the wild, frightened beating of her heart against his chest. "She slipped and fell over the railing!"

"Don't say anything to anyone!" he whispered commandingly. "Leave the talking to me!"

Then the door behind them opened and two departing guests came out into the hall. Amru Singh turned toward them, his hand pressing Rina's face against his chest so that she could scarcely breathe, let alone speak. "There's been an accident," he said calmly. "Call a doctor."

He felt Rina begin to cry against his shoulder. He looked down at the shining blond head. A strange satisfied look came into his dark, deep-set eyes.

His portent had come true. The evil goddess, Kali, had struck. But this time, she was not to receive the innocent as a further sacrifice to her power, no matter how carefully she had contrived to plant the guilt.

12

RINA WAS STANDING ON HER HEAD, THE LENGTH of her body against the wall, when Jacques entered the apartment. He stood there for a moment, looking at her slim body, sheathed in the tight black leotard, her hair shining as it spilled over on the floor.

"What are you doing?" he asked politely.

She smiled an upside-down smile at him. "Standing on my head."

"I can see that," he answered. "But why?"

"Amru Singh says it is very good for the brain. The blood washes the brain and a new perspective is given to the world. He is right, too. You just don't know how different everything looks upside down."

"Did Amru Singh also tell you how one goes about kissing a girl who is standing on her head?" he asked with a smile.

"No," she answered. A mischievous smile came over her face. "I thought of that myself!" She arched her back quickly and moved her legs.

He laughed aloud. There was no mistaking the invitation of the Y she made against the wall. He bent forward quickly, placing his head between her outstretched legs, and kissed her.

She collapsed on the floor in laughter. "It is good to hear you laugh," he said. "You did not laugh much at first."

"I wasn't happy at first."

"And you are happy now?" he asked.

The laughter was still in her eyes as she looked up at him. "Very happy." She was a very different person from the dazed girl he had seen that night several months ago. He remembered the telephone ringing beside his bed.

"Monsieur Deschamps?" a deep, quiet voice had asked.

"*Oui?*" he replied, still half asleep.

"My apologies for disturbing your rest," the voice continued, in French with a peculiar British and yet not quite British accent. "My name is Amru Singh. I am with a friend of yours, Mademoiselle Rina Marlowe. She needs your help."

He was awake now. "Is it serious?"

"Quite serious," Amru Singh replied. "Mademoiselle Bradley had an accident. She was killed in a fall and the police are being very difficult."

"Let me speak with Mademoiselle Marlowe."

"Unfortunately, she is in no position to come to the telephone. She is in a state of complete shock."

"Where are you?"

"At the studio of Monsieur Pavan, the sculptor. You know the place?"

"Yes," Jacques answered quickly. "I will be there in half an hour. In the meanwhile, do not let her talk to anyone."

"I have already seen to that," Amru Singh said. "She will not speak with anyone until you arrive."

Jacques did not quite understand what Amru Singh had meant until he saw Rina's ashen face and the blank look in her eyes. The police had efficiently isolated her in the small dressing room of the studio.

"Your friend seems to be in a very bad state of shock, monsieur," the Inspector said when Jacques introduced himself. "I have sent for a doctor."

Jacques bowed. "You are very kind, Inspector. Perhaps you

can tell me what happened? I just arrived, in response to a telephone call from a mutual friend."

The Inspector gestured broadly. "It is nothing but routine, Monsieur. Mademoiselle Bradley fell down the stairs. We require only a statement from Mademoiselle Marlowe, who was the only person with her at the time."

Jacques nodded. There must be more to it than that, he thought. Or why would Amru Singh have sent for him? "May I go into the dressing room?"

The Inspector bowed. "Of course, monsieur."

Jacques entered the small room. Rina was seated on a small chair, half hidden behind a tall man wearing a turban.

"Monsieur Deschamps?"

Jacques bowed. "At your service, Monsieur Singh." He glanced at Rina. She didn't seem to see him.

When Amru Singh spoke, his voice was soft, as if he were speaking to a child. "Your friend Monsieur Deschamps is here, mademoiselle."

Rina looked up, her eyes blank, unrecognizing.

Jacques looked at Amru Singh questioningly. The man's dark eyes were inscrutable. "I was at the scene of the accident, Monsieur Deschamps. She was very upset and seemed under a compulsion to accept blame for her friend's accident."

"Did she have anything to do with it?" Jacques asked.

"As I already explained to the police," Amru Singh said blandly, "nothing I saw led me to think so."

"What did she say to them?"

"I thought it best that she not speak with them," Amru Singh replied.

"Are you a doctor?"

"I am a student, monsieur," Amru Singh replied.

Jacques looked up at him. "Then how were you able to keep her from speaking to the police?"

Amru Singh's face was impassive. "I told her not to."

"And she obeyed?" Jacques asked.

Amru Singh nodded. "There was little else she could do."

"May I speak to her?"

"If you wish," Amru Singh answered. "But I suggest someplace other than here. They would perhaps misconstrue what she might say."

"But the police have already sent for a doctor," Jacques said. "Will he not—"

Amru Singh smiled. "The doctor will merely confirm that she is in shock."

Which was exactly what the doctor did. Jacques turned to the Inspector. "If you will permit me, Inspector, I shall escort Mademoiselle Marlowe to her home. I will bring her down to your office tomorrow afternoon, after her own physician has attended her, to make a statement."

The Inspector bowed.

In the taxi, Jacques leaned forward and gave the driver Rina's address.

"I think it would be better if Mademoiselle Marlowe were not to go to her own apartment," Amru Singh said quickly. "There is much there to remind her of her late friend."

Jacques thought for a moment, then gave the driver his other address.

Amru Singh walked into the apartment and Rina followed him docilely. Jacques closed the door behind them. Amru Singh led her to a chair. He gestured and she sat down. "I have taken away my shoulder," he said quietly. "I can no longer speak for you. You must speak now for yourself."

Rina raised her head slowly. Her eyes were blinking as if she were awakening from a deep sleep. Then she saw him.

Instantly, the tears rushed to her eyes. She flung herself into his arms. "Jacques! Jacques!" she cried. "I knew you would come!"

She began to sob, her body trembling against him. The words kept tumbling from her lips in wild, disjointed sentences.

"Shh," he whispered soothingly, holding her. "Don't be afraid. Everything will be all right."

He heard the door open and close behind him. He turned his head slightly. Amru Singh was gone.

The following day, they went to the Inspector's office. From there, they went to her flat and moved her things to his apartment. Two nights later, when he had come into the apartment unexpectedly, Amru Singh rose from a chair.

"Amru Singh is my friend," Rina said hesitantly.

Jacques looked at her, then at the Indian. He stepped forward quickly, his hand outstretched. "If he is your friend," he said, "then he is my friend, also."

The Indian's white teeth flashed in a smile as their hands met in a warm clasp. From that time until now, the three of them had dinner together at least once a week.

Jacques turned the key in the door. He stepped aside to let Rina enter, then followed her into the bedroom. As soon as she entered, she kicked off her shoes. She sat down on the edge of the bed, rubbing her feet. "Ah, that feels good."

He knelt in front of her and massaged her foot. He smiled up at her. "You were very beautiful tonight."

She looked at him mischievously. "*Monsieur le Ministre* thought so," she teased. "He said if I should ever consider another liaison, to keep him in mind."

"The old lecher!" Jacques swore. "He must be all of eighty years old—and at the Opera, too!"

She got up from the bed and took her dress off, then seated herself, yoga fashion, on the floor. Her legs were crossed under her, her arms formed a square in front of her chest.

"What are you doing?" he asked in surprise.

"Preparing for meditation," she answered. "Amru Singh says that five minutes' meditation before going to sleep relieves the mind and the body of all its tensions."

He removed the studs from his shirt and placed them on the dresser. He watched her in the mirror. "It would be very easy for me to become jealous of Amru Singh."

"That would make me very unhappy," she said seriously. "For then I would have to stop seeing Amru."

"You would do that for me?"

"Of course," she said. "I love you. He is only my friend, my teacher."

"He is my friend, too," he said, as seriously. "I would be very unhappy if you let a jesting remark disturb that relationship."

She smiled. He smiled back at her and turned back to the dresser. He began to take off his shirt. "And what have you learned from our friend today?"

"There is a good possibility that I may soon be free of the death wish that has governed many of my actions since I was a child," she answered.

"Good," Jacques said. "And how is this to come about?"

"He is teaching me the yoga exercises for childbearing. It will give me control over my entire body."

"I don't see how that will help. The exercises are important only when having a child."

"I know," she said.

Something in her voice made him look at her in the mirror. Her face was impassive as she held the position of meditation. "What brought that subject up?" he asked.

Her eyes flicked up at him. "You," she said. "Doctor Fornay says that you have made me *enceinte*."

Suddenly, he was on the floor beside her, holding her in his arms and kissing her, talking of divorcing his wife so that the child would be born at the family villa in the south of France.

She placed a finger on his lips. It seemed to him as if she had suddenly become older than he. "Come, now," she said gently. "You are acting like an American, with stupid, provincial ideas. We both know that a divorce would ruin your career, so speak no more about it. I will have the child and we will go on as we are."

"But what if your father finds out?"

She smiled. "There is no need for him to know. When I go home for a visit, I will merely say I made an unfortunate marriage and no one will be the wiser."

She laughed and pushed him toward the bathroom. "Now go. Take your bath. You have had enough excitement for one day. Did you get the Boston papers for me?"

"They're in my brief case."

He sank into the tub. The water was warm and relaxing and gradually he could feel the excited tempo of his heart return to something that approximated normal. Slowly and with a feeling of great strength and luxury, he began to lather himself.

He came out of the bathroom, tying his robe. Rina wasn't in the bedroom and he walked through into the living room. Something in the way she was sitting at the table, staring down at the newspaper, sent a frightened chill racing through his body. "Rina!"

She turned toward him. Slowly her eyes lifted. He had never seen such depths of torture in his life. It was as if she had lost all hope of redemption. "I can't have the baby, Jacques," she whispered in an empty voice.

His voice grated in his throat. "What?"

The tears were beginning to well into her eyes. "I must go home," she whispered.

"Why?" he cried, the hurt already beginning.

She gestured to the paper, and he walked over and looked down over her shoulder.

A banner headline streamed across the entire page:

HARRISON MARLOWE INDICTED
FIFTH-GENERATION BOSTON BANKER
CRIMINALLY IMPLICATED IN FAILURE
OF FAMILY BANK

Below was a three-column picture of Harrison Marlowe.

He caught her shoulders. "Oh, my darling!" he said.

He could barely hear her whispered, "And I wanted this baby so."

He knew better than to argue with her. One thing he understood as a Frenchman—filial duty. "We'll have another baby," he said. "When this is over, you'll return to France."

He could feel her move within the circle of his arms. "No," she cried, "Doctor Fornay told me there will never be another child!"

13

THE LARGE OVERHEAD FAN DRONED ON AND THE August heat lay heavy and humid in the Governor's office. The slightly built, nervous male secretary showed Rina to a chair in front of the massive desk.

She sat down and watched the young man, standing nervously next to the Governor, pick up sheet after sheet of paper as the Governor signed each one. At last he was finished and the secretary picked up the last sheet of paper and hurried out, closing the door behind him.

She looked at the Governor as he reached across the desk and took a cigar from a humidor. For a moment, she caught a glimpse of piercing dark eyes, set deep in a handsome face. His voice was slightly husky. "Do you mind if I smoke, Miss Marlowe?"

She shook her head.

He smiled, taking a small knife and carefully trimming the end of the cigar. He placed it in his mouth and struck a match. The flame burned brightly yellow, large and small, with his breath as he drew on the cigar. She was conscious of the faintly pleasant smell of Havana leaf as he dropped the match into an ash tray.

He smiled again. "One of the few pleasures my physician still allows me," he said. He had a simple yet extraordinary clear voice that easily filled the room, though he spoke quietly, like an actor trained to have his whispers heard in the far reaches of the second balcony. He leaned across the desk, his voice lowering to a confidential whisper. "You know, I expect to live to be a hundred and twenty-five and even my physician thinks I might make it if I cut down on my smoking."

She felt the convincing warmth and intensity flow toward her and for the moment, she believed it, too. "I'm sure you will, Governor."

He leaned back in his chair, a faintly pleased look on his face. "Just between us, I don't really care whether I live that long or not," he said. "It's just that when I die, I don't want to leave any enemies, and I figure the only way I'll ever do that is to outlive them all."

He laughed and she joined him, for the moment forgetting her reason for being there. There was something incredibly young and vital about him that belied the already liberal sprinkling of gray in his thick, lustrous black hair.

He looked across the massive desk at her, feeling once again the rushing of time against him. He drew on his cigar and let the smoke out slowly. He liked what he saw. None of this modern nonsense about dieting and boyish bobs for her. Her hair fell long and full to her shoulders.

He looked up and suddenly met her eyes. Almost instantly, he knew that she had been aware that he was studying her. He smiled without embarrassment. "You were a child when I approved your adoption papers."

Her words put him at ease. "My mother and father often told me how kind you were and how you made it possible for them to adopt me."

He nodded slowly. It was smart of them to tell her the truth. Sooner or later, she'd have found out, anyway. "You're eighteen now?"

"Nineteen next month," she said quickly.

"You've grown a little since I saw you." Then his face turned serious as he placed the cigar carefully in the ash tray. "I know why you've come to see me," he said in his resonant voice. "And I'd like to express my sympathy for the predicament your father is in."

"Have you studied the charges that are being made against him?" Rina asked quickly.

"I've looked over the papers," he admitted.

"Do you think he's guilty?"

The Governor looked at her. "Banking is like politics," he said. "There are many things which are morally right and legally wrong. That they may be one and the same thing doesn't matter. Judgment is rendered only on the end result."

"You mean," she said quickly, "the trick is—not to get caught!"

He felt a glow of satisfaction. He liked quick, bright people, he liked the free exchange of ideas that came from them. Too bad that politics attracted so few of that kind. "I wouldn't be cynical," he said quietly. "It isn't as simple as that. The law is not an inflexible thing. It is alive and reflects the hopes and desires of the people. That's why laws are so often changed or amended. In the long run, we trust that eventually the legal and the moral will come together like parallel lines which meet in infinity."

"Infinity is a long time for a man my father's age to wait," she said. "No one has that much time. Not even you if you live to one hundred and twenty-five."

"Unfortunately, decision will always remain the greatest hazard of leadership," he answered. "Your father assumed that hazard when he authorized those loans. He justified it to himself because without them, certain mills might be forced to close, throwing many people out of work, and causing others to lose their investment or principal means of support. So your father was completely right morally in what he did.

"But legally, it's another story. A bank's principal obligation is to its depositors. The law takes this into account and the state has rules governing such loans. Under the law, your father should never have made those loans because they were inadequately collateralized. Of course, if the mills hadn't closed and the loans had been repaid, he'd have been called a public benefactor, a farseeing businessman. But the opposite happened and now these same people who might have praised him are screaming for his head."

"Doesn't it make any difference that he lost his entire fortune trying to save the bank?" Rina asked.

The Governor shook his head. "Unfortunately, no."

"Then, is there nothing you can do for him?" she asked desperately.

"A good politician doesn't go against the tide of public opinion," he said slowly. "And right now the public is yelling for a scapegoat. If your father puts up a defense, he'll lose and get ten to fifteen years. In that case, I'd be long out of office before he was eligible for parole."

He picked up the cigar from the ash tray and rolled it gently between his strong white fingers. "If you could convince your father to plead guilty and waive jury trial, I'll arrange for a judge to give him one to three years. In fifteen months, I'll grant him a pardon."

She stared at him. "But what if something happens to you?"

He smiled. "I'm going to live to be a hundred and twenty-five, remember? But even if I weren't around, your father couldn't lose. He'd still be eligible for parole in twenty months."

Rina got to her feet and held out her hand. "Thank you very much for seeing me," she said, meeting his eyes squarely. "No matter what happens, I hope you live to be a hundred and twenty-five."

From her side of the wire partition, she watched her father walk toward her. His eyes were dull, his hair had gone gray, even his face seemed to have taken on a grayish hue that blended softly into the drab gray prison uniform.

"Hello, Father," she said softly as he slipped into the chair opposite her.

He forced a smile. "Hello, Rina."

"Is it all right, Father?" she asked anxiously. "Are they—"

"They're treating me fine," he said quickly. "I have a job in the library. I'm in charge of setting up a new inventory control. They have been losing too many books."

She glanced at him. Surely he was joking.

An awkward silence came over them. "I received a letter from Stan White," he said finally. "They have an offer of sixty thousand dollars for the house."

Stan White was her father's lawyer. "That's good," she said.

"From what they told me, I didn't think we'd get that much. Big houses are a glut on the market."

"Some Jews want it," he said without rancor. "That's why they'll pay that much."

"It was much too big for us and we wouldn't live there when you come home, anyway."

He looked at her. "There won't be very much left. Perhaps ten thousand after we take care of the creditors and Stan."

"We won't need very much," she said. "We'll manage until you're active again."

This time his voice was bitter. "Who would take a chance on me? I'm not a banker any more, I'm a convict."

"Don't talk like that!" she said sharply. "Everyone knows that what happened wasn't your fault. They know you took nothing for yourself."

"That makes it even worse," he said wryly. "It's one thing to be condemned for a thief, quite another for being a fool."

"I shouldn't have gone to Europe. I should have stayed at home with you. Then perhaps none of this would have happened."

"It was I who failed in my obligation to you."

"You never did that, Father."

"I've had a lot of time to think up here. I lay awake nights wondering what you're going to do now."

"I'll manage, Father," she said. "I'll get a job."

"Doing what?"

"I don't know," she replied quickly. "I'll find something."

"It's not as easy as that. You're not trained for anything." He looked down at his hands. "I've even spoiled your chances for a good marriage."

She laughed. "I wasn't thinking of getting married. All the young men in Boston are just that—young men. They seem like boys to me; I haven't the patience for them. When I get married, it will be to a mature man, like you."

"What you need is a vacation," he said. "You look tired and drawn."

"We'll both take a vacation when you come home," she said. "We'll go to Europe. I know a place on the Riviera where we could live a whole year on less than two thousand dollars."

"That's still a long way off," he said. "You need a vacation now."

"What are you getting at, Father?" she asked.

"I wrote to my cousin Foster," he said. "He and his wife, Betty, want you to come out and stay with them. They say it's beautiful out there and you could stay with them until I could come out to join you."

"But then I wouldn't be able to visit you," she said quickly, reaching for his hands in the narrow space beneath the bars.

He pressed her fingers. "It will be better that way. Both of us will have less painful things to remember."

"But, Father—" she began to protest.

The guard started over and her father got to his feet. "I've already given Stan White instructions," he said. "Now, you do as I say and go out there."

He turned away and she watched him walk off through eyes that were beginning to mist over with tears. She didn't see him again until many months later, when she was on her way to Europe again on her honeymoon. She brought her husband out to the prison.

"Father," she said, almost shyly, "this is Jonas Cord."

What Harrison Marlowe saw was a man his own age, perhaps even older, but with a height and youthful vitality that seemed characteristic of the Westerner.

"Is there anything we can get you, Father?" she asked.

"Anything we can do at all, Mr. Marlowe?" Jonas Cord added.

"No, no, thank you."

Cord looked at him and Harrison Marlowe caught a glimpse of deep-set, penetrating blue eyes. "My business is expanding, Mr. Marlowe," he said. "Before you make any plans after leaving here, I'd appreciate your speaking with me. I need a man with just your experience to help me in refinancing my expansion."

"You're very kind, Mr. Cord."

Jonas Cord turned to Rina. "If you'll excuse me," he said, "I know you want some time alone with your father. I'll be waiting outside."

Rina nodded and the two men said good-by. For a short time, father and daughter looked at each other, then Rina spoke. "What do you think of him, Father?"

"Why, he's as old as I am!"

Rina smiled. "I told you I'd marry a mature man, Father. I never could stand boys."

"But—but—" her father stammered. "You're a young

woman. You have your whole life ahead of you. Why did you marry him?"

Rina smiled gently. "He's an extremely wealthy man, Father," she said softly. "And very lonely."

"You mean you married him for that?" Then suddenly he understood the reason for her husband's offer. "Or so he could take care of me?" he asked.

"No, Father," she said quickly. "That isn't why I married him at all."

"Then why?" he asked. "Why?"

"To take care of me, Father," she said simply.

"But, Rina—" he began to protest.

She cut him off quickly. "After all, Father," she said, "you yourself said there wasn't anything I could do to take care of myself. Wasn't that why you sent me out there?"

He didn't answer. There wasn't anything left for him to say. After a few more awkward moments, they parted. He stretched out on the narrow cot in his cell and stared up at the ceiling. He felt a cold chill creeping through him. He shivered slightly and pulled the thin blanket across his legs. How had he failed her? Where had he gone wrong?

He turned his face into the hard straw pillow and the hot tears began to course down his cheeks. He began to shiver as the chill grew deeper within him. Later that night, they came and took him to the prison hospital, with a fever of a hundred and two. He died of bronchial pneumonia three days later, while Rina and Jonas Cord were still on the high seas.

14

THE PAIN BEGAN TO ECHO IN HER TEMPLES, CUT-ting like a sharp knife into the dream. She felt it begin to slip away from her, and then the terrible loneliness of awakening. She stirred restlessly. Everyone was fading away, everyone except her. She held her breath for a moment, fighting the return to reality. But it was no use. The last warm traces of the dream were gone. She was awake.

She opened her eyes and stared unrecognizingly for a moment around the hospital room, then she remembered where she was. There were new flowers on the dresser opposite the foot of the bed. They must have brought them in while she slept.

She moved her head slowly. Ilene was dozing in the big easy chair near the window. It was night outside. She must have dozed the afternoon away.

"I have a terrible headache," she whispered softly. "May I have some aspirin, please?"

Ilene's head snapped forward. She looked at Rina questioningly.

Rina smiled. "I've slept away the whole afternoon."

"The whole afternoon?" It was the first time in almost a week that Rina had been conscious. "The whole afternoon," Ilene repeated. "Yes."

"I was so tired," Rina said. "And I always get a headache when I nap during the day. I'd like some aspirin."

"I'll call the nurse."

"Never mind, I'll call her," Rina said quickly. She started to raise her hand to the call button over her head. But she couldn't lift her arm.

She looked down at it. It was strapped to the side of the bed. There was a needle inserted into a vein on her forearm, attached to a long tube which led up to an inverted bottle suspended from a stand. "What's that for?"

"The doctor thought it would be better if they didn't disturb your rest to feed you," Ilene said quickly. She leaned across the bed and pressed the buzzer.

The nurse appeared almost instantly in the doorway. She walked quickly to the bed and stood next to Ilene, looking down at Rina. "Are we awake?" she asked with professional brightness.

Rina smiled slowly. "We're awake," she said faintly. "You're a new one, aren't you? I don't remember you."

The nurse flashed a quick look at Ilene. She had been on duty ever since Rina was checked into the hospital. "I'm the night nurse," she answered calmly. "I've just come on."

"I always get a headache when I sleep in the afternoon," Rina said. "I was wondering if I could have some aspirin?"

"I'll call the doctor," the nurse said.

Rina turned her head. "You must be exhausted," she said to Ilene. "Why don't you go home and get some rest? You've been here all day."

"I'm really not tired. I grabbed forty winks myself this afternoon."

The doctor came into the room just then and Rina turned toward the door. He stood there blinking his eyes behind his shining glasses. "Good evening, Miss Marlowe. Did you have a good rest?"

Rina smiled. "Too much, doctor. It's left me with a headache." Her brows knit. "It's a peculiar kind of a headache, though."

He came over to the side of the bed and put his fingers on her wrist, finding her pulse. "Peculiar?" he asked, looking down at his watch. "How do you mean peculiar?"

"It seems to hurt most when I try to remember names. I know you and I know my friend here"—she gestured to Ilene—"but when I try to say your name, the headache comes and I can't remember."

The doctor laughed as he let go of her wrist. "That's not at all unusual. There are some types of migraine headaches which make people forget their own name. Yours isn't that bad, is it?"

"No, it's not," Rina answered.

The doctor took an ophthalmoscope from his pocket and leaned over. "I'm going to look into your eyes with this," he said. "This makes it possible for me to see behind them and we may find out that your headache is due to nothing but simple eyestrain. Don't be frightened."

"I'm not frightened, doctor," Rina answered. "A doctor in Paris once looked at me with one of those. He thought I was in shock. But I wasn't. I was only hypnotized."

He placed his thumb in a corner of her eye and raised the eyelid. He pressed a button on the instrument and a bright light reflected through the pin-point hole. "What's your name?" he asked casually.

"Katrina Osterlaag," she answered quickly. Then she laughed. "See, doctor, I told you my headache wasn't that bad. I still know my name."

"What's your father's name?" he asked, moving the instrument to the other eye.

"Harrison Marlowe. See, I know that, too."

"What's your name?" he asked again, the light making a half circle in the upper corner of her eye.

"Rina Marlowe," she answered. She laughed aloud. "You can't trick me, doctor."

He turned off the light and straightened up. "No, I can't," he said, smiling down at her.

There was a movement at the door and two attendants wheeled in a large, square machine. They pushed it over to the side of the bed next to the doctor.

"This is an electroencephalograph," the doctor explained quietly. "It's used to measure the electrical impulses emanating from the brain. It's very helpful sometimes in locating the source of headaches so we can treat them."

"It looks very complicated," Rina said.

"It's not," he answered. "It's very simple, really. I'll explain it to you as we go along."

"And I thought all you had to do was take a few aspirins for a headache."

He laughed with her. "Well, you know how we doctors are," he said. "How can we ever justify our fees if all we do is recommend a few pills?"

She laughed again and the doctor turned toward Ilene. He nodded silently at her, his eyes gesturing to the door. He had already turned back to Rina by the time she had opened it.

"You'll come back later, won't you?" Rina asked.

Ilene turned around. The attendants were already plugging in the machine and the nurse was helping the doctor prepare Rina. "I'll be back," Ilene promised. She walked out and closed the door gently behind her.

It was almost an hour later when the doctor came out of the room. He dropped into a chair opposite Ilene, his hand fishing in his pocket. It came out with a crumpled package of cigarettes, which he held out to her. She took one and he struck a match, holding it first for her, then for himself.

"Well?" she asked through stiff lips.

"We'll be able to tell more when we study the electroencephalogram," he said, dragging on his cigarette. "But there are already definite signs of deterioration in certain neural areas."

"Please, doctor," she said. "In words that I can understand."

"Of course," he said. He took a deep breath. "The brain already shows signs of damage in certain nerve areas. It is this damage that makes it difficult for her to remember things—simple, everyday things like names, places, time. Everything in her memory is present, there is no past, perhaps no today. It is an unconscious effort to recall these little things that causes the strain and brings on the headache."

"But isn't that a good sign?" she asked hopefully. "This is the first time in almost a week that she seems partly normal."

"I know how concerned you are," he said cautiously. "And I don't want to appear unduly pessimistic, but the human mechanism is a peculiar machine. It is a tribute to her physical stamina that she's holding up as well as she is. She's going through recurrent waves of extremely high fever, a fever that destroys everything in its path. It's almost a miracle that when it abates slightly, even for a moment, as it just has, she can return to a semblance of lucidity."

"You mean she's slipping back into delirium?"

"I mean that her temperature is beginning to climb again," he answered.

Ilene got to her feet quickly and crossed to the door. "Do you think I can speak to her again before she slips back?"

"I'm sorry," he said, shaking his head. He got to his feet. "Her temperature began to rise about twenty minutes after you left the room. I put her in sedation to ease the pain."

She stared at the doctor. "Oh, my God!" she said in a low voice. "How long, doctor? How long must she suffer like this?"

"I don't know," he said slowly. He took her arm. "Why don't you let me drive you home? There's nothing you can do tonight, believe me. She's asleep."

"I'd—I'd like to look in on her just for a moment," she said hesitantly.

"It's all right, but let me warn you. Do not be upset by her appearance. We had to cut off most of her hair to make the electroencephalogram."

Ilene closed the door of her office and crossed to her desk. There were some preliminary sketches of the costumes for a new picture waiting for her approval. She flicked on the light and walked over to the built-in bar.

She took down a bottle of Scotch and filled a glass with ice cubes. Covering the ice with the whisky, she went back to her desk, sat down and picked up the sketches. She sipped at the drink as she studied them.

She pressed a button in the arm of her chair and an overhead spotlight set in the ceiling shone down onto the drawings. She turned her chair toward the pedestal on her left, trying to imagine the dress on the model.

But her eyes kept misting over with tears. The sketches seemed to disappear and all she could see was Rina standing there on the pedestal, the white light shining down on her long blond hair—the white-blond hair that still hung in angry clinging tufts to the pillow under her shorn head.

"Why did you have to do it, God?" she cried aloud angrily at the ceiling. "Why do you always have to destroy the beautiful things? Isn't there enough ugliness in the world?"

The tears kept blurring in her eyes, but through them, she could still see Rina as she stood on the pedestal for the first time, the white silk shimmering down over her body.

It wasn't long ago. Five years. And the white silk was for a wedding gown. It was just before Rina's marriage to Nevada Smith.

15

IT STARTED OUT AS A QUIET WEDDING BUT IT turned into a circus, the biggest publicity stunt ever to come out of Hollywood. And all because David Woolf had finally made it into the bed of the redheaded extra who had a bit-role in *The Renegade*.

Though he was a junior publicist, just one step above the lowest clerk in the department, and made only thirty-five a week, David was a very big man with the girls. This could be explained in one word. Nepotism. Bernie Norman was his uncle.

Not that it did him much good. But the girls didn't know that. How could they know that Norman could scarcely stand the sight of his sister's son and had only given him the job to shut her up? Now, in order to keep his nephew from annoying him, he had given his three secretaries orders to bar David from his office, no matter what the emergency.

This annoyed David, but right now it was far from his mind. He was twenty-three and there were more important considerations at hand. What a difference between the broads out here and those back home. He thought of the usherettes back at the Bijou Theater in New York, the frightened little Italian girls and the big brassy Irish, and the quickies that took place in the deserted second balcony or out on the empty stage in back of the big screen while the picture unfurled itself over their nervous heads. Even back there, Bernie Norman's name had been a help to him. Why else would they take an eighteen-year-old kid off a junk wagon and make him an assistant manager?

The girl was talking. At first David didn't hear her. "What did you say?" he asked.

"I'd like to go to the Nevada Smith wedding."

Her position may have been oblique but her approach wasn't. He recognized it. "It's going to be a small affair," he said.

Her voice was clearer now as she looked up at him. "There'll still be a lot of important people there who'd never see me any other way."

"I'll see what I can do," he said.

It was a little while later, when he was making his third greedy attempt to grab the brass ring, that the idea came to him. "Yeow!" he yelled suddenly as the far-reaching implications unfurled in his mind.

Startled, the girl looked up at him and saw a blindly rapt expression on his face. "Take it easy, honey. You'll wake the neighbors," she whispered softly, thinking he had reached his climax.

And, in a manner of speaking, he had.

Bernie Norman prided himself on being the first executive in the studio each day. Every morning at seven o'clock, his long black chauffeur-driven limousine would swirl through the massive steel gates of the executive entrance and draw to a stop in front of his office building. He liked to get in early, he always said, because it gave him a chance to go through his correspondence, which was at least twice as voluminous as that of anyone else in the studio, before his three secretaries came in. That way, the rest of his day could be left free for anyone who came to his door. His door was always open, he claimed.

Actually, he got there early because he was a born snoop.

Though no one ever spoke about it, everyone in the studio knew what he did the moment the front door closed behind him. He would prowl through the silent offices, executive and secretary alike, looking at the papers lying on desks, peeking into whatever desk drawers happened to be unlocked and examining the contents of every letter and memo. It got so that whenever an executive wanted to be sure that something got to Norman's attention, he would leave a rough draft of his message lying innocently on his desk when he went home.

Norman justified this to himself easily. He was merely keeping his finger on the pulse of things. How could one man control so complicated an organization, otherwise?

He arrived at the door to his own private office that morning about eight o'clock, his inspection having taken a little longer than usual. He sighed heavily and opened his door. Problems, always problems.

He started for his desk, then froze with horror. His nephew David was asleep on his couch, sheaves of papers strewn over the floor around him. Bernie could feel the anger bubbling up inside him.

He crossed the room and pulled David from the couch. "What the hell are you doing sleeping in my office, you bum bastard!" he shouted.

David sat up, startled. He rubbed his eyes. "I didn't mean to fall asleep. I was looking at some papers and I must have dozed off."

"Papers!" Norman yelled. "What papers?" Quickly he picked one up. He turned horror-stricken eyes back to his nephew. "The production contract for *The Renegade!*" he accused. "My own confidential file!"

"I can explain," David said quickly, awake now.

"No explanations!" Norman said dramatically. He pointed to the door. "Out! If you're not out of the studio in five minutes, I'll call the guards and have you thrown out. You're through. Fired! *Fartig!* One thing we don't tolerate in this studio—sneaks and spies. My own sister's son! Go."

"Aw, come off it, Uncle Bernie," David said, getting to his feet.

"Come off it, he tells me!" Norman roared. "Half the night his mama keeps me up with telephone calls." His voice unconsciously mimicked his sister's nasal whine. "'My Duvidele didn't come home yet, all night he didn't come home. Maybe he vass in a accident.' Accident, hah! I should tell her her little Duvidele was fucking all night the redheaded *shiksa* extra from the studio, hah! Get out!"

David stared at his uncle. "How did you know?"

"Know?" his uncle roared. "I know everything that goes on in this studio. You think I built a business like this fucking in furnished rooms all night? No! I worked, I tell you, I worked like a dirty dog. Day and night!"

He walked over to the chair behind his desk and sank into it. He clasped his hand over his heart in an exaggerated gesture. "Aggravation like this, from my own flesh and blood first thing in the morning, I need like another *luch im kopf!*" He unlocked his desk and took out a bottle of pills. Quickly he swallowed two and leaned back in his chair, his eyes closed.

David looked at his uncle. "You all right, Uncle Bernie?"

Slowly Norman opened his eyes. "You still here?" he asked in the voice of a man making a supreme effort to control himself. "Go!" His eyes fell on the papers still on the floor. "First pick up the papers," he added quickly. "Then go!"

"You don't even know why I came here this morning," David said tentatively. "Something very important came up."

His uncle opened his eyes and looked at him. "If it's something important, come to see me like everybody else. You know my door is always open."

"Open?" David laughed sarcastically. "If Christ himself came into this studio, those three harpies wouldn't let him in to see you!"

"Don't bring religion into it!" Norman held up a warning hand. "You know my policy. Everybody's the same as everybody else. Somebody wants to see me, they talk to my number-three girl, she talks to my number-two girl, my number-two girl talks to my number-one girl. My number-one girl thinks it important enough, she talks to me and the next thing you know, you're in my office!" He snapped his fingers. "Like that! But don't come sneaking around in the night, looking at confidential papers! Now go!"

"O.K." David started for the door. He should have known better than to try to do anything for the old bastard. "I'm going," he said bitterly. "But when I walk out this door, you look good—real good, because you're throwing out a million dollars along with me!"

"Wait a minute!" his uncle called after him. "I like to be fair. You said you had something important to tell me? So tell it. I'm listening."

David closed the door. "Next month, before the picture opens, Nevada Smith and Rina Marlowe are getting married," he said.

"You're telling me something?" His uncle glowered. "Who cares? They didn't even invite me to the wedding. Besides, Nevada's finished."

"Maybe," David said. "But the girl isn't. You saw the picture?"

"Of course I saw the picture!" Norman snapped. "We're sneaking it tonight."

"Well, after the sneak, she's going to be the hottest thing in the business."

His uncle looked up at him, a respect dawning in his eyes. "So?"

"From the papers, I see nobody's got her under contract," David said. "You sign her this morning. Then——"

His uncle was already nodding his head.

"Then you tell them you want to give them the wedding. As a present from the studio. We'll make it the biggest thing ever to hit Hollywood. "It'll add five million to the gross."

"So what good does that do us?" Norman asked. "We don't own any of the picture, we don't share in the profits."

"We get a distribution fee, don't we?" David asked, his confidence growing as he saw the intent look on his uncle's face. "Twenty-five per cent of five million is one and a quarter million dollars. Enough to carry half the cost of our whole distribution setup for a whole year. And the beautiful thing about it is we can charge all our expenses for the wedding to publicity and slap the charge right back against the picture. That way, it doesn't cost us one penny. Cord pays everything out of his share of the profit."

Norman got to his feet. There were tears in his eyes. "I knew it! Blood will tell!" he cried dramatically. "From now on you're working for me. You're my assistant! I'll tell the girls to have the office next door made ready for you. More than this I couldn't ask from my own son—if I had a son!"

"There's one more thing."

"There is?" Norman sat down again. "What?"

"I think we should try to make a deal with Cord to do a picture a year for us."

Norman shook his head. "Oh, no! We got enough crazy ones around here without him."

"He's got a feeling for pictures. You can see it in *The Renegade*."

"It was a lucky accident."

"No it wasn't," David insisted. "I was on the set through the whole thing. There wasn't anything in the picture that he didn't have something to do with. If it wasn't for him, Marlowe would never be the star she's going to be. He has the greatest eye for cunt I ever saw in my life."

"He's a *goy*," Norman said deprecatingly. "What do they know about cunt?"

"The *goyim* knew about cunt before Adam led Eve out of the Garden of Eden."

"No," Norman said.

"Why not?"

"That kind of man I don't want around," Norman said. "He won't be satisfied just to make a picture. Pretty soon, he'll want to run the whole thing. He's a *balabuss*, he's not the kind who would work with partners."

He got up and walked around the desk toward his nephew. "No," he said. "Him I won't do business with. But your other ideas I like. This morning we'll go out and get the girl's signature on the contract. Then we'll tell them about the wedding. Nevada won't like it but he'll do it. After all, he's got his own money in the picture and he won't be taking any chances!"

David saw to it that a special print of the newsreel of the wedding was sent on to Cord, who was in Europe at the time. When Jonas walked into the small screening room in London, where he had arranged for it to be run off, the lights immediately went down and a blast of music filled the room. On the screen, lettering was coming out of a turning camera until there was nothing else to be seen.

NORMAN NEWSREEL
THE FIRST WITH
THE FINEST IN
PICTURES!

The dramatically somber voice of the narrator came on under a long shot of a church, around which crowds of people swirled.

All Hollywood, all the world, is agog with excitement over the fairy-tale wedding in Hollywood today of Nevada Smith and Rina Marlowe, stars of the forthcoming Bernard B. Norman release The Renegade.

There was a shot of Nevada riding up to the church resplendently dressed in a dark, tailored cowboy suit, astride a snow-white horse.

Here is the groom, the world-famous cowboy Nevada Smith, arriving at the church with his equally famous horse, Whitey.

Nevada walked up the steps and into the church, with the police holding back mobs of screaming people. Then a black limousine drew up. Bernie Norman got out and turned to assist Rina. She stood for a moment, smiling at the crowd, then taking Norman's proffered arm, began to walk into the church, as the camera moved in for a close-up.

And here is the bride, the lovely Rina Marlowe, star of The Renegade, *on the arm of Bernard B. Norman, noted Hollywood producer, who will give the bride away. Miss Marlowe's wedding gown is ivory Alençon lace, designed especially for her by Ilene Gaillard, famous couturière, who also designed the exciting costumes that you will see Miss Marlowe wear in the Bernard B. Norman picture* The Renegade.

The camera then cut to the exterior of Nevada's Beverly Hills home, where there was a tremendous tent with throngs of people milling about it.

Here on the lawn of the palatial home of Nevada Smith is the tent erected by the Bernard B. Norman studio workmen as their tribute to the famous couple. It is large enough to shelter and feed a thousand guests and is the largest of its kind ever set up anywhere in the world. And now let us say hello to some of the famous guests.

The camera rolled down the lawn as the announcer introduced many famous stars and newspaper columnists, who paused in the midst of their obviously carefully posed groups to smile and bow in the direction of the camera. The camera moved on up the steps to the entrance of the house as Nevada and Rina appeared in the doorway. A moment later, Norman stood between them. Rina held a large bouquet of roses and orchids in her arms.

Here again is the happy bride and groom, together with their friend, the famous producer Bernard B. Norman. The bride is about to throw her bouquet to the eagerly waiting crowd.

There was a shot of Rina throwing her bouquet and a scramble of pretty young girls. The flowers were finally caught by a red-haired, sloe-eyed girl and the camera moved in for a quick close-up of her.

The bouquet was caught by Miss Anne Barry, a close friend of the bride's. Miss Barry, a beautiful redhead, also has an important role in The Renegade *and has just been placed under contract by Norman Pictures for her fine portrayal in that part.*

The camera then moved in for a final close-up. Rina, Norman and Nevada smiled into the theater. Norman was standing between them, one arm placed in fatherly fashion around Nevada's shoulder, the other hidden from view behind the bride. They all laughed happily as the scene faded.

Lights in the screening room came up as Jonas got to his feet and, unsmiling, walked out of the room. There was a cold feeling in the pit of his stomach. If that was the way Rina wanted it, she could have it.

But what Jonas didn't see, and neither could anyone else who had been looking at the screen, was Bernie Norman's left hand, hidden behind Rina's back.

It was comfortably and casually exploring the rounded contours of her buttocks.

16

IT HAD BEEN AFTER EIGHT O'CLOCK WHEN ILENE heard the door to her outer office open. She put down the small palette and wiped the smudges of paint from her hands on her loose gray smock. She turned toward the door just as Rina came in.

"I'm sorry to hold you up, Ilene," Rina apologized. "We went overtime on the set tonight."

Ilene smiled. "It's O.K. I had some work to finish up, anyway." She looked at Rina. "You look tired. Why don't you sit down and rest a few minutes? I heard from the production office that you'd be late so I ordered coffee and sandwiches."

Rina flashed a grateful smile. "Thanks," she said, dropping onto the big couch and kicking off her shoes. "I am tired."

Ilene pushed a coffee table over to the couch. She opened a small refrigerator and took out a tray of sandwiches, which she set down in front of Rina. Opening a large Thermos of black coffee, quickly she poured a cup for Rina.

Rina held the steaming cup to her lips. "This is good," she said over the rim. She sipped again, then leaned her head against the back of the couch. "I'm really so pooped I'm not even hungry."

"You have a right to be," Ilene answered. "You haven't had a week off in the year since you finished *The Renegade*. Three pictures, one right after the other, and next week you're starting another. It's a wonder you haven't collapsed."

Rina looked at her. "I like to work."

"So do I," Ilene replied quickly. "But there's a point where you have to draw the line."

Rina didn't answer. She sipped at her coffee and picked up a copy of *Variety*. Idly she turned the page. She stopped at a headline, read for a moment, then held the paper out to Ilene. "Have you seen this?"

Ilene glanced down at the paper. The headline caught her eye. It was typical Varietese:

THE RENEGADE'S BIGGEST HAUL—BOX OFFICE

In a year filled with cries from moaning exhibitors and anguished producers about the seemingly bottomless pit into which motion-picture grosses are falling, it's encouraging to note one ray of sunshine. It was reliably learned from informed sources that the domestic gross of *The Renegade* passed the five-million-dollar mark last week, a little less than one year after release. Based on these figures, the Rina Marlowe vehicle, with many subsequents still to be played in the U.S. and the rest of the world still to be heard from, can be expected to gross at ten million dollars. *The Renegade*, a Norman release, was produced and bankrolled by Jonas Cord, a rich young Westerner better known for his record-breaking flight from Paris to L.A. last year, and also features Nevada Smith.

Ilene looked up from the paper. "I saw it."

"Does that mean everyone got their money back?"

"I guess it does," Ilene said. "That is, if Bernie didn't steal them blind."

Rina smiled. She felt a surge of relief. At least, Nevada didn't have to worry now. She picked up a sandwich and began to eat ravenously. "Suddenly I'm hungry," she said between mouthfuls.

Silently Ilene refilled her coffee cup, then poured one for herself. Rina ate quickly and in a few minutes, she had finished. She took a cigarette from the small box on the table and lit it.

She leaned back and blew the smoke at the ceiling. A faint touch of color came back into her cheeks. "I feel better now. We can try on those costumes as soon as I finish this cigarette."

"No hurry," Ilene said. "I have time."

Rina got to her feet. "We might as well get started," she said, grinding her cigarette out in an ash tray. "I just remembered, I have a breakfast layout to do for *Screen Stars* magazine at six o'clock in the morning."

Ilene walked over to the closet and slid back the doors. Six pairs of circus-style chemise tights, each in a different color, hung there. Rina took one down and turned to Ilene, holding the brief costume in front of her. "They get smaller and smaller."

Ilene smiled. "Bernie himself gave the orders for those. After all, the name of the picture is *The Girl on the Flying Trapeze*."

She took the costume and held it while Rina began to undress. Rina turned her back as she slipped out of her dress and struggled into the tight-fitting costume. "Whew!" she gasped. "Maybe I shouldn't have eaten those sandwiches!"

Ilene stepped back and studied the costume. "Better step up on the pedestal," she said. "There are a few things I'll have to do."

Quickly she chalked out the alterations. "O.K.," she said. "Let's try the next one."

Rina reached behind her to unfasten the hooks. One of them stuck. "You'll have to help me, Ilene. I can't get out of this thing."

Rina stepped down from the pedestal and turned her back to Ilene. Deftly Ilene freed the hook. The cloth parted quickly and her fingers brushed against Rina's naked back. They tingled with the firm, warm touch of her flesh. Ilene felt the rush of blood to her temples. She stepped back quickly as if she had touched a hot iron. Too many times had she been tempted to let a thing like this get her into trouble. It had taken too many years to get this job.

Rina dropped the top of the costume to her waist and struggled to get the tights over her hips. She looked at Ilene. "I'm afraid you'll have to help me again."

Ilene kept her face a mask. "Step back on the pedestal," she said through stiff lips.

Rina got back on the pedestal and turned toward her. Ilene tugged at the garment, her fingers burning where they touched Rina. At last, the tights gave way and Ilene felt Rina shiver as her hand accidentally brushed the soft silken pubis.

"Are you cold?" Ilene asked, stepping back.

Rina stared at her for a moment, then averted her eyes. "No," she answered in a low voice, stepping out of the tights. She picked them up and held them toward Ilene.

Ilene reached for the costume, touched Rina's hand and suddenly couldn't let it go. She looked up at Rina steadily, her heart choking inside her.

Rina shivered again. "No," she whispered, her eyes still looking away. "Please, don't."

Ilene felt as if she were in a dream. Nothing seemed real. "Look at me," she said.

Slowly Rina turned her head. Their eyes met and Ilene could sense her trembling. She saw Rina's nipples burst forth upon her breasts like awakening red flowers on a white field.

She moved toward her and buried her face in the pale soft flax between her hips. They were very still for a moment, then she felt Rina's hand lightly brushing across her hair. She stepped back and Rina came down into her arms.

Ilene felt the hot tears suddenly push their way into her eyes. "Why?" she cried wildly. "Why did you have to marry him?"

As usual, Nevada awoke at four thirty in the morning, pulled on a pair of worn Levi's and went down to the stables. As usual, on his way out, he closed the connecting door between their rooms to let Rina know he had gone out.

The wrangler was waiting with a steaming mug of bitter black range coffee. Their conversation followed the routine morning pattern as Nevada felt the hot coffee scald its way down to his stomach.

The mug empty, and Nevada in the lead, they walked through the stable, looking into each stall. At the end was Whitey's stall. Nevada came to a stop in front of it. "Mornin', boy," he whispered.

The palomino stuck its head over the gate and looked at Nevada with large, intelligent eyes. It nuzzled against Nevada's hand, searching for the lump of sugar it knew would appear there. It wasn't disappointed.

Nevada opened the gate and went into the stall. He ran his hands over the sleek, glistening sides of the animal. "We're gettin' a little fat, boy," he whispered. "That's because we haven't had much to do lately. I better take you out for a little exercise."

Without speaking, the wrangler handed him the big saddle that lay crosswise on the partition between the stalls. Nevada slung it over the horse's back and cinched it tight. He placed the bit in the mouth and led the animal out of the stable. In front of the white-painted wooden building, he mounted up.

He rode down the riding trail to the small exercise track he had built at the foot of the hill in back of the house. He could see the gray spires of the roof as he rode past. Mechanically he put the horse through its paces.

The item he had read in *Variety* came to his mind. His lip curved at the irony. Here he was with the biggest-grossing picture of the year and not once during that whole period had anyone approached him about beginning another. The day of the big Western movie was over. It was too expensive.

At least he wasn't the only one, he thought. Mix, Maynard, Gibson, Holt—they were all in the same boat. Maynard had tried to fight it. He made a series of quickies for Universal, which took about five days to complete. Nevada had seen one of them. Not for him. The picture was choppy and the sound worse. Half the time, you couldn't even understand what the actors were saying.

Tom Mix had tried something else. He'd taken a Wild-West show to Europe and, if the trade papers were right, he and his horse, Tony, had knocked them dead. Maybe that was worth thinking about. The troop he had on the road was still doing all right. If he went out with it, it would do even better. It was that or take up the guitar.

That was the new Western—a singing cowboy and a guitar. He felt a vague distaste even as he thought about it. That chubby little Gene Autry had made it big. The only problem, he'd heard from one of the wranglers, was to keep him from falling off his horse. Tex Ritter was doing all right at Columbia, too.

Nevada looked up again at the house. That was the biggest stupidity of all—a quarter-million-dollar trap. It took more than twenty servants to keep it running and ate up money like a pack of prairie wolves devouring a stray steer. He quickly reviewed his income.

The cattle ranch in Texas had just started to pay off when the Depression hit and now he was lucky if it broke even. His royalties on the sale of Nevada Smith toys and cowboy suits had dwindled as children shifted their fickle loyalties to other stars. All that was left was his share of the Wild-West show and the Nevada divorce ranch. That brought in at most two thousand a month. The house alone cost him six thousand a month just to keep going.

Rina had offered to share the expenses but he'd refused, feeling it was a man's responsibility to pay the bills. But now, even with the bank loans for *The Renegade* paid off, he knew it wouldn't be possible to keep the house going without dipping further into his capital. The sensible thing was to get rid of it.

He'd have to take a loss. Thalberg over at Metro had offered him a hundred and fifty thousand. That way, at least, he'd save the broker's fee.

He made up his mind. There was no use sitting around, waiting for the telephone to ring. He'd go out on the road with the show and sell the house. He began to feel better. He decided to tell Rina when she got back from the studio that night.

The telephone on the pole against the far rail began to ring loudly. He walked his horse over to it. "Yes?"

"Mr. Smith?"

It was the voice of the butler. "Yes, James," he said.

"Mrs. Smith would like you to join her for breakfast in the Sun Room."

Nevada hesitated. Strange how quickly the servants recognized who was important in the family. James now used the same distant formal manner of speaking to him that he had once used in speaking to Rina.

He heard the butler clear his throat. "Shall I tell Mrs. Smith you will be up, sir?" he asked. "I think she's expecting some photographers from *Screen Stars* magazine."

So that was it. Nevada felt a stirring of resentment inside him. This was the first time in months that Rina had called him for breakfast and it took a publicity layout to do it. Almost immediately, he regretted the way he felt. After all, it wasn't her fault. She'd been working day and night for months.

"Tell her I'll be up as soon as I stable the horse," he said.

"Just one more shot of you pouring coffee for Nevada," the photographer said, "and we're finished."

Nevada picked up his cup and extended it across the table to Rina. She lifted the silver coffeepot and poised it over the cup. Professionally and automatically, the smiles came to their lips.

They'd gone through the whole routine. The picture of Rina frying bacon and eggs while he looked over her shoulder at the stove, the burned-toast bit, the popping of food into each other's mouth. Everything the readers of fan magazines had come to expect from movie stars. This was supposed to give them the homey touch.

There was an awkward silence for a moment after the photographers picked up their gear and left. Nevada spoke first. "I'm glad that's over."

"So am I," Rina said. She hesitated, then looked up at the wall clock. "I'd better get started. I'm due in make-up at seven thirty."

She started to get up but the telephone near her began to ring. She sat down again and picked it up. "Hello."

Nevada could hear a voice crackle through the receiver. Rina shot him a funny look, then spoke into the telephone again.

"Good morning, Louella," she said in a sweet voice. "No, you didn't wake me up. Nevada and I were just having breakfast. . . . Yes, that's right—*The Girl on the Flying Trapeze*. It's a wonderful part. . . . No, Norman decided against borrowing Gable from Metro. He says there's only one man who could do the part justice. . . . Of course. Nevada, it's a natural for him. Wait a minute, I'll put him on and let him tell you himself."

She covered the mouthpiece with her hand. "It's Parsons," she whispered quickly. "Bernie decided yesterday he wanted you to play the part of the stunt-rider. Louella's checking on the story."

"What's the matter?" Nevada asked dryly. "Wouldn't MGM lend him Gable?"

"Don't be silly! Get on the phone."

"Hello, Louella."

The familiar, sticky-sweet voice chewed at his ear. "Congratulations, Nevada! I think it's just wonderful that you're to play opposite your lovely wife again!"

"Wait a minute, Louella." He laughed. "Not so fast. I'm not making the picture."

"You're not?" Another Parsons scoop was in the making. "Why?"

"I've already agreed to go out on the road with my Wild-West show," he said. "And that will keep me tied up for at least six months. While I'm away, Rina will look for another house for us. I think we'll both be more comfortable in a smaller place."

Her voice was businesslike now. "You're selling Hilltop?"

"Yes."

"To Thalberg?" she questioned. "I heard he was interested."

"I don't know," he said. "Several people have expressed interest."

"You'll let me know the moment you decide?"

"Of course."

"There's no trouble between you two?" she asked shrewdly.

"Louella!" He laughed. "You know better than that."

"I'm glad! You're both such nice people," she said. She hesitated a moment. "Keep in touch if there's any news."

"I will, Louella."

"Good luck to both of you!"

Nevada put down the telephone and looked across the table. He hadn't meant for it to come out this way, but there was nothing that could be done about it now.

Rina's face was white with anger. "You could have told me about it before you told the whole world!"

"Who had the chance?" he retorted, angry despite himself. "This is the first time we've talked in months. Besides, you might have told me about the picture."

"Bernie tried to get you all day yesterday but you never came to the phone."

"That's a lot of crap," he said. "I was home all day and he never called. Besides, I wouldn't have his handouts—or yours either, for that matter."

"Maybe if you took your nose out of that damn stable once in a while, you'd find out what was going on."

"I know what's going on," he said angrily. "You don't have to start acting like a movie star."

"Oh, what's the use?" she said bitterly. "What did you ever marry me for?"

"Or you me?" he asked, with equal bitterness.

As they stared at each other, the truth suddenly came to both of them. They had married because they both knew they had lost each other and wanted desperately to hold onto what was already gone. With the knowledge, the anger dissipated as quickly as it had come. "I'm sorry," he said.

She looked down at the coffeepot. "I am, too. I told you I was a spoiler, that I wouldn't be any good for you."

"Don't be silly," he said. "It wasn't your fault. It would have happened, anyway. The business is changing."

"I'm not talking about the business," Rina answered. "I'm talking about you and me. You should have married someone who could have given you a family. I've given you nothing."

"You can't take all the blame. We both tried in our own way but neither of us had what the other really needed. We just made a mistake, that's all."

"I won't be able to file for a divorce until after I finish this next picture," she said in a low voice. "It's all right with me if you want to file before then."

"No, I can wait," he said calmly.

She glanced up at the wall clock. "My God! I'm late!" she exclaimed. "I'll have to hurry."

At the door, she stopped and looked back at him. "Are you still my friend?"

He nodded his head slowly and returned her smile, but his voice was serious. "I'll always be your friend."

She stood there for a moment and he could see the sudden rush of tears to her eyes, then she turned and ran from the room.

He walked over to the window, and lifting the curtain, looked out onto the front drive. He saw her come running from the house, saw the chauffeur close the door. The car disappeared down the hill on its way to the studio. He let the curtain fall back into place.

Rina never came back to the house. She stayed that night at Ilene's apartment. The next day, she moved into a hotel and three months later filed for divorce in Reno. The grounds were incompatibility.

And that, except for the legalities, was the way it ended.

17

DAVID HEARD THE VIOLENT SLAM OF THE DOOR IN his uncle's office. He got to his feet quickly and walked to the connecting door. He opened it and found his uncle Bernie seated in his chair, red faced and angry, gasping for breath. He was trying to shake some pills out of the inverted bottle in his hand.

David quickly filled a glass with water from the carafe on the desk and handed it to Norman. "What happened?"

Norman swallowed the two pills and put down the glass. He looked up at David. "Why didn't I go into the cloak-and-suit business with my brother, your uncle Louie?"

David knew no answer was expected, so he waited patiently until Norman continued. "Fifty, a hundred suits they make a day. Everything is calm, everything is quiet. At night, he goes home. He eats. He sleeps. No worries. No ulcers. No aggravations. That's the way a man should live. Easy. Not like a dog. Not like me."

David asked again, "What happened?"

"As if I haven't got enough troubles," Norman complained, "our stockholders say we're losing too much money. I run to New York to explain. The union threatens to strike the theaters. I sit down and work out a deal that at least they don't close the theaters. Then I get word from Europe that Hitler took over all our German properties, offices, theaters, everything! More than two million dollars the *anti-semiten* stole. Then I get a complaint from the underwriters and bankers, the pictures ain't got no prestige. So I buy the biggest, most artistic hit on Broadway. *Sunspots* the name of it is. It's so artistic, even I don't understand what it's all about.

"Now I'm stuck with an artistic bomb. I talk to all the directors in Hollywood about it. I'm not so dumb altogether that it don't take me long to find out they don't understand it neither, so I hire the director who did the play on the stage, Claude Dunbar, a *faigele* if I ever saw one. But fifty thousand he gets.

"A hundred and fifty I'm in already and no box office. So I call up Louie and say lend me Garbo. He laughs in my face. You ain't got enough money, he says. Besides, we got her in prestige of our own. *Anna Christie* by Eugene O'Neill she's making. Good-by, I says and call up Jack Warner. How about Bette Davis? Wait a minute, he says. I sit on the phone ten minutes.

"The *pisher* thinks I don't know what he's doin'? He's calling his brother Harry in New York, that's what he's doin'. Here I am, sitting on long distance in New York with the charges running up by the minute and he's calling back his brother Harry, who is two blocks away from where I'm sitting. Hang up the phone, I feel like telling him. I can call your brother for only a nickel.

"Finally, Jack gets back on the phone to me ninety-five dollars later. You're lucky, he says. We ain't got her penciled in for nothing until September. You can have her for a hundred and fifty grand. For a hundred and fifty, don't do me no favors, I tell him. The most she's gettin' is thirty, thirty-five a picture, maybe not even that.

"How much you want to pay? he asks. Fifty, I says. Forget it, he says. O.K., then, seventy-five, I says. One and a quarter, he says. One even and it's a deal, I says. It's a deal, he says. I hang up the telephone. A hundred and thirty-five dollars the call costs me to talk two minutes.

"So I go back to Wall Street and tell the underwriters and bankers we now got prestige. This picture is goin' to be so artistic, we'll be lucky if we get anybody into the theater. They're very happy and congratulate me and I get on the train and come back to Hollywood."

Bernie ran out of breath suddenly and picked up the glass of water again and drained it. "Ain't that enough trouble for anyone?"

David nodded.

"So enough troubles I got when I walk into my office this morning, you agree? So who do I find waiting but Rina Marlowe, that *courveh*. 'Rina, darling,' I say to her, 'you look positively gorgeous this morning.' Do I even get a hello? No! She shoves the *Reporter* under my nose and says, 'What's this? Is it true?'

"I look down and see the story about Davis in *Sunspots*. 'What are you getting so excited about, darling?' I say. 'That's not for you, a bomb like that. I got a part for you that will kill the people. *Scheherazade*. Costumes like you never in your life saw before.' And you know what she says to me?" He shook his head sadly.

"What?" David asked.

"After all I done for her, the way she spoke to me!" his uncle said in a hurt voice. "'Take your hand off my tits,' she says, 'and furthermore, if I don't get that part, you can shove *Scheherazade* up your fat ass!' Then she walks out the door. How do you like that?" Norman asked in an aggrieved voice. "All I was trying to do was calm her down a little. Practically everybody in Hollywood she fucks but me she talks to like that!"

David nodded. He'd heard the stories about her, too. In the year since she had broken up with Nevada, she seemed to have gone suddenly wild. The parties out at her new place in Beverly Hills were said to be orgies. There was even talk about her and Ilene Gaillard, the costume designer. But as long as nothing got into print, they'd looked the other way. What she did was her own business as long as it didn't affect them. "What are you going to do about it?"

"What can I do about it?" Bernie asked. "Give her the part. If she walked out on us, we'd lose twice as much as we're losing right now."

He reached for a cigar. "I'll call her this afternoon and tell her." He stopped in the midst of lighting it. "No, I got a better idea. You go out to her place this afternoon and tell her. I'm damned if I'll let her make it look like I'm kissing her ass."

"O.K.," David said. He started back toward his own office.

"Wait a minute," his uncle called after him.

David turned around.

"You know who I ran into in the Waldorf my last night in New York?" Bernie asked. "Your friend."

"My friend?"

"Yes, you know who. The crazy one. The flier. Jonas Cord."

"Oh," David said. He liked the way his uncle put it, reminding him of the earlier conversation they had had about Cord some years ago. He and Cord had never exchanged so much as a word. He even doubted if Cord knew he was alive. "How did he look?"

"The same," his uncle replied. "Like a bum. Wearing sneakers and no tie. I don't know how he gets away with it. Anybody else they would throw out, but him? Shows you there's nothing like *goyishe* money."

"You talk to him?" David asked curiously.

"Sure," Norman answered. "I read in the papers where he's making another picture. Who knows, I says to myself, the *schnorrer* might get lucky again. Besides, with prestige like we're stuck with, we could use him. We could pay a lot of bills with his money.

"It's two o'clock in the morning and he's got two *courvehs* on his arm. I walk over and say, 'Hello, Jonas.' He looks at me like he's never seen me before in his life. 'Remember me,' I says, 'Bernie Norman from Hollywood.' 'Oh, sure,' he says.

"But I can't tell from his face whether he really does or doesn't, he needs a shave so bad. 'These two little girls are actresses,' he says to me, 'but I won't tell you their names. Otherwise, you might sign them up yourself. If I like a girl,' he says, 'I put her under contract to Cord Explosives now. No more do I take any chances and let them get away from me the way you signed that Marlowe dame.' With that, he gives me such a playful shot in the arm that for two hours I can't raise my hand.

"I made myself smile even if I didn't feel like it. 'In our business, you got to move fast,' I says, 'otherwise you get left behind the parade. But that's over and done with. What I want to do is talk to you about this new picture I hear you're makin'. We did a fantastic job for you on your last one and I think we should set up a meetin'.'

" 'What's the matter with right now?' he asks. 'It's O.K. with me,' I says. He turns to the girls. 'Wait right here,' he says to them. He turns back to me an' takes my arm. 'Come on,' he says, draggin' me off. 'Come up to my office.'

"I look at him in surprise. 'You got an office here in the Waldorf,' I ask him. 'I got an office in every hotel in the United States,' he says. We get on an elevator an' he says 'Mezzanine, please.' We get off and walk down the hall to a door. I look at the sign. 'Gentlemen,' it says. I look at him. He grins. 'My office,' he says, opening the door. "We go inside an' it's white and empty. There's a table there and a chair for the attendant. He sits down in the chair and suddenly I see he's very sober, he's not smiling now.

" 'I haven't decided yet where I'm going to release the picture,' he says. 'It all depends on where I can get the best deal.' 'That's smart thinking,' I says, 'but I really can't talk until I know what your picture is about.' 'I'll tell you,' he says. 'It's about the fliers in the World War. I bought up about fifty old planes—Spads, Fokkers, Nieuports, De Havillands—and I figger on havin' a ball flyin' the wings off them.'

" 'Oh, a war picture,' I says. 'That's not so good. War pictures is dead since *All Quiet on the Western Front*. Nobody'll come to see them. But since I got experience with you and we was lucky together, I might go along for the ride. What terms you looking for?' He looks me in the eye. 'Studio overhead, ten per cent,' he says. 'Distribution, fifteen per cent with all expenses deducted from the gross before calculating the distribution fees.' 'That's impossible,' I says. 'My overhead runs minimum twenty-five per cent.'

" 'It doesn't,' he says, 'but I won't quibble about it. I just want to point out some simple arithmetic to you. According to your annual report, your overhead during the past few years averaged twenty-one per cent. During that period, *The Renegade* contributed twenty-five per cent of your gross. Deduct that from your gross and you'll find your overhead's up to almost thirty-six per cent. The same thing applies to the studio,' he says. 'Volume governs the percentages and if I supply the volume, I shouldn't be burdened with ordinary percentages. I want some of the gravy, as you picture people call it.'

" 'I couldn't afford it,' I says. 'The way the picture business is going,' he says, 'you can't afford not to.' 'My board of directors would never approve it,' I says. He gets up, smiling. 'They will,' he says. 'Give 'em a couple of years an' they will. Why don't you take a piss long as you're here,' he says. I'm so surprised I walk over to the urinal. When I turn around, he's already gone. The next morning, before I get on the train, I try to locate him but nobody seems to know where he is. His office don't even know he's in New York. He disappeared completely." Bernie looked down at his desk. "A real *meshuggeneh*, I tell you."

David smiled. "I told you he'd learn fast. His arithmetic is right, you know."

His uncle looked up at him. "Don't you think I know it's right?" he asked. "But is he so poor that I have to give him bread from my own mouth?"

"If you'll follow me, sir," the butler said politely, "Miss Marlowe is in the solarium."

David nodded and followed silently up the staircase and to the back of the house. The butler halted before a door and knocked.

"Mr. Woolf is here, mum."

"Tell him to come in," Rina called through the closed door.

The butler held the door open. David blinked as the bright California sun suddenly spilled down on him. The roof of the room was a clear glass dome and the sides were of glass, too.

There was a tall screen at the far end of the room. Rina's voice came from behind it. "Help yourself to a drink from the bar. I'll be out in a minute."

He looked around and located the bar in the corner. There were casual, canvas-covered chairs scattered all about the room and a large white rug over most of the floor.

Ilene Gaillard came out from behind the screen. She was wearing a white shirt with sleeves rolled to just above her elbows, and black man-tailored slacks that clung tightly to her narrow hips. Her white-streaked hair was brushed back in a severe straight line.

"Hello, David. Let me help you."

"Thanks, Ilene."

"Make another Martini for me," Rina called from behind the screen.

Ilene didn't answer. She looked at David. "What will it be?"

"Scotch and water," he answered. "Just a little ice."

"O.K.," she said, her hands already moving deftly behind the bar. She held the drink toward him. "There, how's that?"

He tasted it. "Great."

"Got my Martini ready?" Rina said from behind him.

He turned. She was just coming from behind the screen, tying a white terry-cloth robe around her. From the glimpse he caught of the tanned thigh beneath the robe as she moved, he guessed she was wearing nothing underneath. "Hello, Rina."

"Hello, David," she answered. She looked at Ilene. "Where's my drink?"

"David's obviously here on business," Ilene said. "Why don't you wait until after you've had your talk?"

"Don't be so bossy!" Rina snapped. "Make the drink!" She turned to David. "My father gave me Martinis when I was a child. I can drink them like water. Ilene doesn't seem to understand that."

"Here." Ilene's voice was clipped.

Rina took the Martini from her. "Cheers, David."

"Cheers," David replied.

She belted down half her Martini, then led him to one of the chairs. "Sit down," she said, dropping into another.

"Lovely house you have," he said politely.

"It is nice," she said. "Ilene and I had a wonderful time furnishing it." She reached up and patted Ilene's cheek. "Ilene has the most wonderful sense of color. You should speak to your uncle about letting her try her hand at art direction. I'm sure he'd find out that she could do a terrific job."

"Rina," Ilene said, a happy note in her voice, "I'm sure David didn't come here to talk about me."

"I'll speak to Uncle Bernie," he said politely. "I'm sure she could, too."

"See?" Rina said. "The trouble with Ilene is that she's too modest. She's one of the most talented people I ever met."

She held up her empty glass toward Ilene. "Refill."

David caught a glimpse of her lush, full breasts. It would take more than massage to keep her weight down if she kept on drinking like that.

Rina cut into his thoughts. "Did the old bastard decide to give me that part in *Sunspots?*"

David looked at her. "You have to understand my uncle's point of view, Rina," he said quickly. "You're the most valuable asset the company has. You can't blame him if he doesn't want to put you in a picture that's almost certain to lay an egg."

Rina took the drink from Ilene. "What it all boils down to," she said belligerently, "is that he thinks I can't act. All I'm good for is walking around as near naked as he can get me."

"He thinks you're a fine actress, Rina. But more important, you're the one in a million who is a star. He's just trying to protect you, that's all."

"I'll protect myself," she snapped angrily. "Do I get the part or don't I?"

"You get it."

"Good," she said, sipping her drink. She got out of her chair and he realized that she was slightly drunk. "Tell your uncle for me that I won't wear a brassière the next time I come to his office."

"I'm sure that will make him very happy." David grinned at her. He put down his drink and got to his feet.

"I think he wants to fuck me," she said, weaving slightly.

He laughed. "Who doesn't?" he asked. "I can name at least sixty million men who've thought about it."

"You don't," she said, her eyes suddenly looking right into his. "Who says?"

"I do," she said seriously. "You never asked me."

"Remind me to get up my nerve sometime."

"What's the matter with right now?" she asked, pulling at the sash of her robe. It fell open, revealing her nude body. He stared, so surprised that he was unable to speak.

"Go downstairs, Ilene," Rina said without taking her eyes off him. "And see to it that dinner is on time."

David caught a glimpse of Ilene's eyes as she hurried past him and out the door. If he lived to be a hundred years old, he would never forget the depth of the pain and anguish he saw there.

18

UNTIL HE MET RINA MARLOWE, CLAUDE DUNBAR had been in love with only three things in his life—his mother, himself and the theater—and in that order. His *Hamlet* in modern dress was the most successful Shakespearean production ever played in a New York theater. But it was his direction of *Sunspots*, an otherwise mediocre play, that lifted him to the pinnacle of his career.

Sunspots was a three-character play dealing with two prospectors, living isolated lives at the edge of a great desert, and a young girl, an amnesiac, who wandered into their camp. It develops into a struggle between the men, the younger trying to protect the girl from the lechery of the older, only, after succeeding, to succumb himself to the lechery in the girl.

It was all talk and very little action, and despite a year's run on Broadway, Dunbar had been so surprised when Norman called and told him he had bought the play and wanted him to direct the motion picture that he had agreed without hesitation. It was only after he got to California, however, that he learned who was to play the lead.

"Rina Marlowe!" he'd said to Norman. "But I thought Davis was going to play it."

The producer had stared at him blandly. "Warner screwed me," he said, lowering his voice to a confidential whisper "So right away I thought of Rina."

"But isn't there anyone else, Mr. Norman?" he'd asked, stammering slightly as he always did when upset. "What about the girl who played it on the stage?"

"No name," Norman said quickly. "This is an important property, this play of yours. We have to protect it with all the box office we can get. Rina never made a picture that didn't make money."

"Maybe," Dunbar admitted. "But can she act?"

"There's no better actress in Hollywood than that girl. You're a director. Go over to her house this afternoon with the script and see for yourself."

"Mr. Norman—"

But Norman had already taken his arm and was leading him to the door. "Be fair, Mr. Dunbar. Give the girl a chance, work with her a little. Then if you still think she can't do it, we'll see."

So efficient had the producer been in getting rid of him that he hadn't been aware of it himself until he stood outside the closed door, with the three secretaries staring at him.

He felt his face flush and to cover his embarrassment, he went over to the girl at the desk nearest the door. "Could you tell me where Miss Marlowe lives?" he asked. "And how to get there?"

The secretary smiled. "I can do better than that, Mr. Dunbar," she said efficiently, picking up the telephone. "I'll arrange for a car to pick you up and take you there."

That afternoon, before he went to Rina's house, Claude Dunbar dropped into a theater that was playing her latest picture. He watched the screen in a kind of fascinated horror. There was no doubt that the girl was beautiful. He could even see that she had a type of animalism that would appeal to a certain type of audience. But she wasn't the kind of girl called for in the play.

The girl in the play was somber, introspective, frightened. As she tried to recapture her memory, she looked as she felt—gaunt, tortured and burned out by the heat of the desert. The fact that she was female caused the desire in the men, not her physical appearance. And it wasn't until the very climax that the play revealed the root of her fears to be her own capacity for lechery.

On the screen, Rina was exciting and bold, aware of her sexuality and continually flaunting it before the audience, but there was no subtlety in her acting. And yet, in all honesty, he felt the surge of vitality flowing from her. When she was on the screen, no matter who else was in the scene, he could not take his eyes off her.

He left the theater and went back to his hotel, where the car was going to pick him up. As was usual whenever he was disturbed, he called his mother. "Do you know who they want to play in the picture, Mother?"

"Who?" his mother asked, with her usual calm.

"Rina Marlowe."

His mother's voice was shocked. "No!"

"Yes, Mother," he said. "Mr. Norman tells me they couldn't get Bette Davis."

"Well, you turn right around and come home," his mother said firmly. "You tell Mr. Norman that you have a reputation to consider, that he promised you Davis and you won't accept that blond creature as a substitute!"

"But I already told Mr. Norman I'd talk to Miss Marlowe. He said if I wasn't satisfied after meeting her, he'd try to get someone else."

"All right," she said. "But remember, your integrity counts far more than anything else. If you're not completely satisfied, you come right home."

"Yes, Mother," he said. "Much love."

"Much love and take care," his mother replied, completing their farewell ritual.

Rina entered the room where he was waiting, wearing a black leotard that covered her body from her feet to her neck.

Her pale-blond hair was pulled back straight and tied in a knot behind her head. She wore no make-up.

"Mr. Dunbar," she said, coming toward him unsmiling, her hand outstretched.

"Miss Marlowe," he answered, taking her hand. He was surprised at the strength in her fingers.

"I've looked forward to meeting you," she said. "I've heard a great deal about you."

He smiled, pleased. "I've heard a great deal about you, too."

She looked up and smiled for the first time. "I'll bet you have," she said without rancor. "That's why you're out here the first day you're in Hollywood. You probably wonder why in hell I should want to play in *Sunspots?*"

He was startled at her frank admission. "Why do you, Miss Marlowe? It seems to me you wouldn't want to rock the boat. You've got a pretty good thing going here."

She dropped into a chair. "Screw the boat," she said casually. "I'm supposed to be an actress. I want to find out just how much of an actress I am. And you're the one director who can make me find out."

He stared at her for a moment. "Have you read the script?"

She nodded.

"Do you remember the first lines the girl speaks when she wanders into the camp?"

"Yes."

"Read them for me," he said, giving her the script.

She took the script but didn't open it. " 'My name is Mary. Yes, that's it, I think my name is Mary.' "

"You're saying the lines, Miss Marlowe," he said, frowning at her, "but you're not thinking about them. You're not feeling the effort that goes into the girl's trying to remember her name.

"Think it through like this. I can't remember my name but if I could, it's a familiar one. It's a name I've been called all my life, and yet it's hard for me to remember it. Even though it's a name that is mentioned often in church and I have even said it in my prayers. It's coming back now. I think I've got it. 'My name is Mary. Yes, that's it. I think my name is Mary.' "

Rina stared back at him silently. Then she got up and walked over to the fireplace. She put her hands up on the mantelpiece, her back toward him. She tugged at the knot in her hair and it fell around her shoulders as she turned to face him.

Her face was suddenly gaunt and strained as she spoke. " 'My name is Mary,' " she whispered hoarsely. " 'Yes, that's it. I think my name is Mary.' "

He felt the tiny shivers of goose flesh rising on his arms as he looked at her. It was the same thing he always felt whenever something great in the theater got down inside him.

Bernie Norman came down to the set on the last day of shooting. He shook his head as he opened the door and walked onto the big shooting stage. He should have known better than ever to hire that *faigele* to direct the picture. Worse yet, he should have had his head examined before he ever let them talk him into buying such a story. Everything about it was crazy.

First, the shooting schedule had to be postponed for a month. The director wanted thirty days to rehearse Rina in the part. Norman had to give in when Rina insisted she wouldn't go on before Dunbar said she was ready. That cost a hundred and fifty thousand in stand-by salaries alone.

Then the director had insisted on doing everything like they had done it on stage. To hell with the budget. Another fifty thousand went there. And on top of everything, Dunbar insisted that the sound in each scene be perfect. No looping, no lip-synching. Every word perfect, as it was spoken on the stage. He didn't care how many takes were necessary. Why should he, the bastard? Norman thought. It wasn't his money.

Three months over the schedule the picture went. A million and a half thrown down the drain. He blinked his eyes as he came onto the brilliantly lighted section of the stage.

Thank God, this was the last scene. It was the one in front of the cabin when the girl opens the door in the morning and finds the two men dead, the younger man having killed the older, then himself, when he realized the depths to which the girl had led him. All she had to do was look at the two men and cry a little, then walk off into the desert. Simple. Nothing could go wrong with that. Ten minutes and it would be over.

"Places!"

The two actors stretched out in front of the cabin door. An assistant director and the script girl quickly checked their positions with photographs of the scene previously made and made a few corrections. The hand of one actor was in the wrong place; a smudge had appeared on the cheek of the other.

Norman saw Dunbar nod. "Roll 'em!" There was silence for a moment as the scene plate was shot, then Dunbar called quietly, "Action."

Norman smiled to himself. This was a cinch. There wasn't even any sound to louse this one up. Slowly the door of the cabin began to open. Rina stepped out and looked down at the two men.

Norman swore to himself. You'd think at least the *shmuck* would have enough sense to rip her dress a little. After all, it was supposed to be out on the desert. But no, the dress went right up to her neck like it was the middle of the winter. The finest pair of tits in the whole business Dunbar had to work with and he kept them hidden.

The big camera began to dolly in for a close-up. Rina raised her head slowly and looked into the camera. A moment passed. Another moment. "Cry, damn you!" Dunbar screamed. "Cry!"

Rina blinked her eyes. Nothing happened.

"Cut!" Dunbar yelled. He walked out on the set, stepping over one of the prostrate men to reach her. He looked at Rina for a moment. "In this scene, you're supposed to cry, remember?" he asked sarcastically.

She nodded silently.

He turned around and went back to his place beside the camera. Rina went back into the cabin, closing the door behind her. Again the assistant director and the script girl checked the positions, then walked off the set.

"Roll 'em!"

"Scene three seventeen, take two!" The plateman called and stepped away from in front of the camera quickly.

"Action!"

Everything happened exactly as before until the moment Rina looked into the camera. She stared into it for a moment. Unwinking. Dry eyes. Then, suddenly, she stepped aside.

"Cut!" Dunbar called. He started out onto the stage again.

"I'm sorry, Claude," Rina said. "I just can't. We'd better use make-up."

"Make-up!" the eager assistant director yelled. "Bring the tears!"

Norman nodded. There was no use wasting money. On

screen, nobody could tell the difference. Besides, the phony tears photographed even better—they rolled down the cheeks like oiled ball bearings.

Dunbar turned. "No make-up!"

"No make-up!" his assistant echoed loudly. "Hold the tears!"

Dunbar looked at Rina. "This is the last scene of the picture," he said. "Two men are dead because of you and all I want is one lousy little tear. Not because you feel sorry for them or for yourself. It's just to let me know that somewhere inside you, you still have a soul. Not much, just enough to show you're a woman, not an animal. Understand?"

Rina nodded.

"O.K., then," he said quietly. "Let's take it from the top." He walked back to his place beside the camera. He bent slightly forward, peering intensely as Rina came out the door. She looked down at the men, then up as the camera began to dolly in close. "Now!" Dunbar's voice was almost a whisper. "Cry!"

Rina stared into the approaching camera. Nothing happened.

"Cut!" Dunbar yelled. He strode angrily into the scene. "What the fuck kind of a woman are you?" he screamed at her.

"Please, Claude," she begged.

He stared at her coldly. "For five months we were making this picture. I've worked day and night, for only one reason. You wanted to prove you were an actress. Well, I've done all I could. I'm not going to destroy the integrity of this picture in the last scene because of your inadequacy. You want to be an actress—well, prove it! Act!"

He turned his back on her and walked away. Norman covered his face with his hands. Ten thousand dollars a day this was costing him. He should have known better.

"Action!"

He opened his fingers and peered through them at the scene. This time, he could hear Dunbar speaking to Rina in a low voice.

"That's right, that's right, now you walk out. You look down and see them. First at Paul, then at Joseph. You see the gun in Joseph's hand and you know what has happened. Now you begin to look up. You're thinking, they're dead. Maybe you didn't love them but you lived with them, you used them. Maybe for a moment one of them brings back a piece of your memory—

the memory you lost and never recovered. But for a fraction of a second, the veil lifts. And it's your father, or your brother, or maybe the child you never had, lying there in the sand at your feet. The tears start up in your eyes."

Slowly Norman's hands slipped away from his face. He held his breath as he moved toward the side away from the camera, which blocked his view. Rina was crying. Real tears.

Dunbar was still whispering. "The tears have come but the veil has dropped again and you can't remember why you are crying. The tears stop and your eyes are dry. Now you turn and look out into the desert. Out there in the lonely sand someone is waiting, someone with your memory. You will find that person out there. Then you'll really know who you are. You begin to walk out into the desert . . . slowly . . . slowly . . . slowly."

Dunbar's voice faded as Rina began to walk away, even the proud, straight shape of her back calling for pity. Norman looked around him. The crew were staring at Rina. They had forgotten everything on the set except her. He felt a moisture in his eyes. The damn scene had even got to him.

"Cut!" Dunbar's voice was a hoarse, triumphant shout. "Print it!" He slumped back into his chair, exhausted.

The stage turned into bedlam, with everybody applauding. Even the hard-bitten veterans of the crew were grinning. Norman ran out onto the stage. He grabbed Rina's hand excitedly. "You were wonderful, baby!" he said. "Magnificent!"

Rina looked at him. For a moment, it seemed as if she were far away, then her eyes cleared. She looked toward Dunbar, seated in his chair, surrounded by the camera crew and his assistants, then back at Norman. "Do you really think so?"

"Would I say it if I didn't mean it, baby?" he replied, smiling. "You know me better than that. Now, you take a good couple of weeks' rest. I got *Scheherazade* all set to go."

She turned away from him and watched Dunbar, who was approaching them slowly, the lines of exhaustion showing clearly on his thin, forty-year-old face. "Thank you," she said, taking Dunbar's hand.

He smiled wearily. "You're a great actress, Miss Marlowe," he said, formal once again, now that their work was over. "It was a privilege working with you."

Rina stared at him for a moment, a new vitality flowing into her. "You're out on your feet," she said, concern in her voice.

"I'll be all right with some rest," he said quickly. "I don't think I've slept a night through since the picture began."

"We'll soon fix that," Rina said confidently. "Ilene."

From somewhere in the crowd, Ilene suddenly appeared. "Call James and have him prepare the guest room for Mr. Dunbar."

"But, Miss Marlowe," the director protested. "I can't put you to all that trouble!"

"Do you think I'd let you go back to that empty hotel room the way you're feeling?" Rina demanded.

"But I promised Mother I'd call her the moment the picture was finished."

"You can call her there." Rina laughed. "We do have telephones, really."

Norman clapped Dunbar on the shoulder. "You do like Rina says, Dunbar. You can use the rest. You still got ten weeks of editing in front of you. But don't worry, you got a great picture here. I wouldn't be surprised if you both get Academy Awards!"

Norman didn't believe it when he said it, but that was exactly the way it turned out.

19

NELIA DUNBAR, SIXTY-THREE YEARS OLD AND strong as the proverbial rock, crossed the room and looked down at her son. "That horrible creature," she said quietly.

She slipped into the seat beside her son and took his head on her shoulder. Absently she stroked his forehead. "I was wondering how long it would take you to see her in her true light," she said. "I told you not to marry her."

Claude didn't answer. There was no need to. There was a familiar safety in his mother's arms. There always had been. Even when he was a child and had come running home from school when the boys ganged up on him. His mother knew him. He didn't have to tell her when he was troubled. Instinctively she had moved out to California after his marriage to Rina.

He had never been very strong, always frail and thin, and the intense nervousness of his creative spurts left him drained and exhausted. At times like that, his mother would see to it that he took to his bed—for weeks on end, sometimes. She would serve him his meals, bring him the newspapers, read to him from the books they both loved.

Often he felt that these were the happiest moments of his life. Here in the gentle pastels of the room his mother had decorated for him, he felt warm and comfortable and at ease. Everything he wanted was at his fingertips. The dirtiness and petty meanness of the world were safely locked away outside the walls of that room.

His father had never been more than a vague nebulous shadow. He could scarcely remember him, for he had died when Claude was only five. His father's death had caused scarcely a noticeable ripple in the course of their lives, for they were left well off. They weren't wealthy but never was there want.

"You go back to the house and get what few things you need," his mother said. "You can spend the night here. In the morning, we'll see about a divorce."

He raised his head from his mother's shoulder and looked at her. "But, Mother, I wouldn't even know what to say to a lawyer."

"Don't worry," his mother said confidently. "I'll take care of everything."

He could feel a great weight lifting from his shoulders. Once again, his mother had spoken the magic words. But when he stood in the street in front of the house and saw Rina's car in the driveway, he was afraid to go in. There would only be another scene and he wasn't up to it. He had no more strength.

He looked at his wrist watch. It was almost eleven o'clock. She would be leaving soon because she had a luncheon date at the studio. He walked back down the hill to the cocktail lounge just off the corner of Sunset. He would have a drink while he waited. He would be able to see her car as it came down the hill.

The cocktail lounge was dark as he entered, the chairs still up on the tables. The bar was open, however, and there was already a customer seated with a glass of beer in front of him. Claude climbed up on a stool near the window, from which he could watch the street.

He shivered slightly. It had begun to drizzle as he came down the hill and was turning into one of those nasty, chilly afternoons peculiarly indigenous to sunny California. He shivered again. He hoped he wasn't catching cold. "Whisky and warm water," he said to the bartender, remembering the drink his mother always gave him at the first sign of a cold.

The bartender looked at him peculiarly. "Warm water?"

Claude nodded. "Yes, please." He looked up and noticed that the lone customer was also staring at him—a young man in a yellow lumber jacket. "And a slice of lemon, if you have it," he called after the bartender.

Claude picked up the small steaming mug. He sipped at it and felt its warmth creep down toward his stomach. He turned and looked out the window. It was really raining now. He picked up the mug again and to his surprise, it was empty. He decided to have another. There was time. He knew exactly what Rina was doing right now. He gestured to the bartender.

Right at this moment, she was seated in front of her dressing table, putting on her make-up, until it was precisely the way she wanted it. Then she would fuss with her hair, teasing it until it hung carelessly, but with every strand in its allotted place.

She had a fetish about not getting anywhere on time. She was always at least an hour late, most of the time even later. It used to drive him crazy having to wait for her, but it never seemed to disturb anyone else. They just took it for granted.

Claude looked down at the mug. It was empty again. He ordered another drink. He was beginning to feel better. Rina would be surprised when she came home and found his things gone. No more would she call him half a man. She'd find out just how much of a man he was when the lawyer served her with divorce papers. She'd know then that she couldn't push him around.

And she'd never look at him again the way she had the first night they were married—with pity and yet contempt, and worst of all, the knowledge in her eyes that she saw into him deeply, laying bare the very secrets of his soul, secrets that he kept even from himself.

He had come into the darkened bedroom, holding in his hand a tray on which stood an iced bottle of champagne and two glasses. "I have come bearing wine for my beloved."

They began to make love. Gently and beautifully, the way he had always known it would be, for he was a virgin. And there was comfort in the womanly curve of her body on the bed, lying there so passive and undemanding. He had even begun to compose a poem to her beauty when he felt her searching hand against his flesh.

For the tiniest fraction of a moment, he froze, startled by her alien fingers. Then he relaxed, for her touch was so light and gentle that he was scarcely aware of it. He felt a tremor shake her body, then another, and a sudden burst of heat seemed to rise from her.

Then a cry came from deep within her and she pulled him down toward her, her hands ripping off the bottom part of his pajamas. No longer was she suppliant and gentle, no longer did she care what he felt or needed, she was caught up in a frenzy of her own. Her fingers hurt him as she tried to guide him, to force him into her.

Suddenly, a wild terror began to run through him. A fear of the demanding sexuality of her body, which had lain dormant, waiting only for this moment to feed upon his manhood and devour him. In a near panic, he tore himself free and stood trembling near the bed.

He tried to pull the torn pajamas around him and heard the sound of her breathing become quieter. There was a rustle of the sheets and he looked down at her.

She had turned over on her side and was staring up at him, the sheet carelessly draped over her hips. Her breasts were heavy, the nipples still swollen with passion. Her eyes seemed to flame their way into him. "Are you the kind of man some people say you are?"

He felt the fire burning its way into his cheeks. He had not been unaware of the snide remarks made behind his back, but ordinary people did not understand his absorption in his work. "No!" he said quickly.

"Then what kind of man are you?"

He fell to his knees beside the bed and looked at her. "Please," he cried. "Please, you've got to understand. I married you because I love you but I'm not like the others. My mother says I'm more nervous and high strung."

She didn't answer and he saw the horrible combination of

pity, contempt and knowledge come fleetingly into her eyes. "Don't look at me like that," he begged. "It will be better the next time. I won't be so nervous. I love you. I love you."

He felt her hand touch his head gently, then slowly stroke his temples. Gradually, his tears subsided and he seized her hands, kissing them gratefully. "It will be better, darling," he promised.

But it was never any better. There was something about the complete femaleness of her body, her terrifying sexuality, that frightened him into complete impotency.

"What did you say?" The words took him from the past into the present. He looked up. The other customer, the young man in the yellow jacket, was speaking to him. "I thought you said something to me. I'm sorry."

Claude felt foolish. There was no doubt that he had spoken. Very often he did while lost in thought. He began to feel embarrassed. "I did," he said, quickly trying to cover his embarrassment. "I said it turned into a rather nasty day, didn't it?"

The young man's eyes went past him to the window, then back. "Yes," he said politely. "It sure did."

Claude looked at him. He seemed like a nice enough young man. Handsome, too, in a rough sort of way. Probably an actor, down on his luck, who'd stopped in to nurse a beer until the rain stopped. He picked up his mug. It was empty again. "Let me buy you a drink," he said.

The boy nodded. "I'd like another beer. Thanks."

"Bartender, a beer for the young gentleman," Claude called. He tapped his mug. "And I'll have another of these."

It wasn't until three drinks later, when he saw Rina's car turn downtown onto Sunset, that he got the idea. After all, there were quite a few things he wanted to take with him and he couldn't carry all of them alone.

After he rang the bell the second time he remembered it was Thursday and all the servants were off. He took out his key. They went right up the staircase to his room. He opened the closet and took out a valise. "You empty those drawers," he said to the boy. "I'll get another suitcase."

He left the room for a moment and when he returned, his companion was holding a picture of Rina that had been standing on the bureau. "Who's this?"

"My wife," Claude answered tersely. Then he giggled. "Will she be surprised when she gets home and finds I'm gone."

"You Rina Marlowe's husband?"

Claude nodded. "But not for long now, thank God!"

The boy looked at him strangely. "What do you want to walk out on a dish like that for?" he asked.

Claude snatched the picture angrily from his hand and threw it against the wall. The glass shattered and fell into tiny bits on the carpet. He turned and walked into the bathroom. He took off his jacket and loosened his tie. He turned on the taps to wash his hands but the sound of the water rushing into the basin reminded him suddenly of the time he had walked into the solarium. He remembered the sound the water had made in the fountain as he became aware of Rina, lying nude on the table, being given a massage by Ilene.

Ilene was nude to the waist, her lower half enclosed in the tight-fitting black trousers she usually wore. He noticed the stringy muscles working along her back as her hands moved gently over Rina's body.

Rina had one arm thrown over her face to shield her eyes from the sun. Her body writhed sensuously under Ilene's touch. When they became aware of his presence, Rina lifted her arm. He felt a vague surprise at the straight flatness of Ilene's chest. "Don't stop, darling," Rina said huskily to Ilene.

Obediently Ilene began to massage again. The sensuous rhythm seemed to return to Rina's body as she lay there, her head turned to the side, watching him. After a moment, she put her arms up and drew Ilene's head down to her hips, "Kiss me, lover," she commanded, her eyes still watching Claude.

He turned suddenly and fled from the room, the sound of her mocking laughter, mixed with the sound of the water from the fountain, echoing in his ears.

Remembering, he lifted his hands to his face. It was bathed in perspiration. His clothing clung to him stickily. His skin began to feel crawly. He decided to take a shower.

The hot needle spray of the shower began to relax him. It seemed to bring the inner warmth of the whisky to the surface of his skin. Luxuriously he lathered himself with the delicately scented soap his mother ordered from London especially for him.

He stepped out of the shower, rubbing himself vigorously.

He looked down with satisfaction at his pink, tingling skin. He liked being clean. He looked for his robe, but it wasn't on its usual hook. "Would you get the blue robe from the closet for me, please," he called automatically, without thinking.

He took the bottle of cologne down from the shelf and sprinkled it lavishly into his hand, then began to rub himself down. Some instinct caused him to look up into the mirror. The boy was standing in the open door, watching him. The robe was thrown over his arm. He had taken off his yellow jacket, revealing a dirty white T shirt.

Claude saw the thick black hair that sprouted wildly from the young man's arms, shoulders and chest. A feeling of distaste ran through him. "You can leave it on the chair," he said, covering himself partly with the towel.

Instead, the boy grinned knowingly at him and came into the bathroom, kicking the door shut behind him with his foot.

Claude turned around angrily. "Get out of here!"

The young man didn't move. His smile grew even broader. "Aw, come off it, old man," he said. "You didn't really bring me up here to help you with your packing, did you?"

"Get out or I'll call for help," Claude said, feeling a strangely exciting fear.

The boy laughed. "Who'll hear?" he asked. "I was wise to you the minute you told me the servants were off."

"You horrible thing!" Claude screamed. He felt a stunning blow on the side of his head and he fell sprawling. He pulled himself to his hands and knees. "Please go," he whispered, his voice breaking.

The young man raised his hand threateningly. Instinctively Claude shrank back but he wasn't quick enough. The open palm cracked smartly across the side of his face, knocking his head sideways against the toilet bowl. He stared up at the boy with frightened eyes.

"You don't really want me to go, do you?" the young man said, his hand tugging at the black leather belt around his waist. "You're the kind that likes to get roughed up a little first."

"I am not!"

"No?" The boy laughed derisively, raising the belt. "Don't crap me, I can see."

For a fraction of a moment, Claude did not know what he meant, then he looked down at himself. A crazy thought went racing through his mind. If Rina could only see him now, she would know he was a man.

The belt cut down across his back, sending a thin shiver of agony down his spine. "That's enough!" he whimpered. "Please don't hit me any more!"

He raised himself wearily from the floor and looked out into the bedroom. The boy was gone, taking with him all the money Claude had had with him. Slowly he got into the shower again and turned on the hot water.

He felt his strength returning as the water soaked into his skin. What a horrible thing to have happen, he thought, remembering all the indignities the young man had subjected him to. A warm feeling of satisfaction came to him. If he had been the stronger, he would have shown him. He felt the excitement begin to beat inside his chest as he thought how he would have torn the belt from the young man's hand and beaten him with it until he bled. He felt the sudden surge of power in his loins.

It was precisely at that moment that the truth came to him. "Oh, no!" He cried aloud in shock at the realization. What everyone had said about him was true. It was only he who had been blind to it until his own body betrayed him.

A dazed kind of anger came over him. Leaving the water running, he stepped from the shower stall. He opened the medicine cabinet and took down the old-fashioned straight razor that he had used ever since he began to shave—the razor that had stood proudly for him as a symbol of his manhood.

A wild, crazy kind of anger rolled blindly over him as he slashed viciously at himself. If he was not to be a man, at least he could turn himself into a woman. Again and again, he slashed at himself. Until at last, his strength gone, he collapsed onto the floor.

"Damn you!" he cried. "Damn you, Mother!"

They were the last words he ever said.

20

DAVID WOOLF STOOD IN THE DOORWAY OF THE bathroom, nausea rising in the pit of his stomach. There was blood everywhere, on the white-and-blue tiles of the floor and walls, along the sides of the white bathtub, sink and toilet bowl.

It was hard to believe that it was only thirty minutes ago that the door of his office had burst open to reveal his uncle, his face flushed and purple, as it always was whenever he was upset. "Get right over to Rina Marlowe's house," Bernie Norman said. "One of the boys in publicity just got a tip from the Beverly Hills police station that Dunbar committed suicide."

David was already on his way to the door.

"Make sure she's protected!" the old man called after him. "Two million dollars in unreleased negatives we got on her!"

He picked up Harry Richards, chief of the studio guards, at the gate on the way out. Richards, a former police sergeant, was in good with all the cops. He took the short cut over the back roads through Coldwater Canyon to Sunset. He was at Rina's house in twenty minutes.

Now the two white-jacketed mortuary attendants were lifting Dunbar's somehow shrunken body into the small, basket-like stretcher and covering it with a white canvas sheet.

The attendants picked up the stretcher and David moved aside to let them pass. He lit a cigarette as they carried the body through the bedroom and out into the corridor. The first acrid taste of smoke settled his stomach. A faint screaming came from the downstairs foyer and he started hurriedly for the door, wondering if somehow Rina had got away from the doctor. But when he got to the head of the staircase, he saw that it wasn't Rina at all. It was Dunbar's mother.

She was struggling to free herself from the grasp of two red-faced policemen as the white-covered stretcher went by. "My baby!" she screamed. "Let me see my baby!"

The attendants moved impassively past her and out the door. David could see the crowd of reporters outside, pressing against the door as it opened and closed. He started down the staircase, hearing the old woman begin to scream again.

She had pulled herself partly free of one of the policemen and with one hand she held onto the railing of the staircase. "You murdered my son, you bitch!" The high-pitched voice seemed to fill the whole house. "You killed him because you found out he was coming back to me!" The old woman had her other hand free now. She seemed to be trying to pull herself up the stairs.

"Get that crazy old woman out of here!" David turned, startled at the harsh voice that came from the top of the stairway behind him.

Ilene stood there, a wild, angry look on her face. "Get her out!" she hissed harshly. "The doctor's having enough trouble with Rina as it is, without her having to listen to that crazy old bitch!"

David caught Richards' eye and nodded to him. Instantly, Richards walked over to one of the policemen and whispered to him. All pretense of politeness gone, the two policemen got a new grip on the old woman and, one of them covering her mouth with his hand, they half dragged, half carried her out of the room. A moment later, a side door slammed and there was silence.

David glanced back up the staircase but Ilene had already disappeared. He walked over to Richards. "I told the boys to take her over to Colton's Sanitarium," the ex-policeman whispered.

David nodded approvingly. Dr. Colton would know what to do. The studio sent many of their stars out there to dry out. He'd also make sure that she didn't speak to anyone until he had calmed her down.

"Call the studio and have them send a couple of your men out here. I don't want any reporters getting in when the police leave."

"I already did," Richards replied, taking his arm. "Come on into the living room. I want you to meet Lieutenant Stanley."

Lieutenant Stanley was seated at the small, kidney-shaped telephone desk, a notebook open in front of him. He got up and shook hands with David. He was a thin, gray-faced, gray-haired man, and David thought he looked more like an accountant than a detective.

"This is a pretty terrible thing, Lieutenant," David said. "Have you figured out what happened yet?"

The lieutenant nodded. "I think we've about got it put together. There's no doubt about it—he killed himself, all right. One thing bothers me, though."

"What's that?"

"We backtracked on Dunbar's movements like we usually do," the detective said. "And he picked up a young man in a cocktail lounge just before he came here. He flashed quite a roll of bills in the bar and we didn't find any money in his room. He's also got a couple of bruises on his head and back that the coroner can't explain. We got a pretty good description of him from the bartender. We'll pick him up."

David looked at him. "But what good will that do?" he asked. "You're sure that Dunbar killed himself; what more could he tell you?"

"Some guys think nothing of picking up a homo and beating him up a little for kicks, then rolling him for his dough."

"So?"

"So Dunbar isn't the only homo in our district," the lieutenant replied. "We got a list of them a yard long down at the station. Most of 'em mind their own business and they're entitled to some protection."

David glanced at Richards. The chief of the studio guards looked at him with impassive eyes. David turned back to the policeman. "Thank you very much for talking to me, Lieutenant," he said. "I'm very much impressed with the efficient manner in which you handled this."

He started out of the room, leaving Richards and the policeman alone. He could hear Richards' heavy whisper as he walked out the door.

"Look, Stan," the big ex-cop was saying. "If this hits the papers, there's goin' to be a mess an' the studio stands a chance of bein' hurt real bad an' it's bad enough just with the suicide."

David went through the door and crossed the foyer to the staircase. Bringing the old sergeant had been the smartest thing he could have done. He was sure now that there wouldn't be reference to any other man in the newspapers. He went up the stairs and into the small sitting room that led to Rina's bedroom. Ilene was slumped exhaustedly in a chair. She looked up as he entered. "How is she?"

"Out like a light," she answered in a tired voice. "The doctor gave her a shot big enough to knock out a horse."

"You could stand a drink." He walked over to the small liquor cabinet and opened it. "Me, too," he added. "Scotch all right?"

She didn't answer and he filled two glasses with Haig & Haig pinch bottle. He gave her one and sat down opposite her. A faint flush of color crept up into her face as the whisky hit her stomach. "It was terrible," she said.

He didn't answer.

She drank again from the glass. "Rina had a luncheon appointment so we got home from the studio about four o'clock. We came upstairs to dress about four thirty, and Rina said she thought she heard the water running in Claude's bathroom. The servants had the day off so she asked me to check. She must have sensed that something was wrong when I didn't come right back. She came into the bedroom while I was still phoning the police. I tried to keep her from seeing what had happened but she was already at the bathroom door when I turned around."

She put her glass down and hunted blindly for a cigarette. David lit one and handed it to her. She took it and placed it between her lips, the smoke curling up around her face. "She was standing there, staring down at him, staring down at that horrible mess of blood, and she was saying over and over to herself, 'I killed him, I killed him! I killed him like I killed everyone who ever loved me.' Then she began to scream." Ilene put her hands up over her ears.

David looked down at his glass. It was empty. Silently he got up and refilled it. Sitting down again, he looked into the amber liquid reflectively. "You know," he said, "what I can't understand is why she ever married him."

"That's just the trouble," she said angrily. "None of you ever tried to understand her. All she ever meant to any of you was a ticket at the box office, money in the bank. None of you cared what she was really like. I'll tell you why she married him. Because she was sorry for him, because she wanted to make a man of him. That's why she married him. And that's why she's lying there in her bedroom, crying even though she's asleep. She's crying because she failed."

The telephone rang. It rang again. David looked at her. "I'll get it," he said.

"Hello."

"Who is this?"

"David Woolf," he said automatically.

"Jonas Cord," the voice replied.

"Mr. Cord," David said. "I'm with Norman—"

"I know," Cord interrupted. "I remember you. You're the young man who does all the trouble-shooting for Bernie. I just heard over the radio about the accident. How's Rina?"

"She's asleep right now. The doctor knocked her out."

There was a long, empty silence on the line and David thought they might have been cut off. Then Cord's voice came back on the line. "Everything under control?"

"I think so," David said.

"Good. Keep it like that. If there's anything you need, let me know."

"I will."

"I won't forget what you're doing," Cord said.

There was a click and the line was dead. Slowly David put down the telephone. "That was Jonas Cord," he said.

Ilene didn't raise her face from her hands.

He turned and looked back at the telephone. It didn't make sense. From what he'd heard about Cord, he wasn't the kind of man who spent his time making sympathy calls. If anything, he was exactly the opposite.

Unconsciously he glanced at the closed door to Rina's bedroom. There had to be more to it than that, he thought.

It was four months before he saw Rina again. He looked up from the couch in his uncle's office as she swept into the room.

"Rina, darling!" Bernie Norman said, getting up from his desk and throwing his arms around her enthusiastically.

The producer stepped back and looked at her, walking around her as if she were a prize heifer in a cattle show. "Slimmer and more beautiful than ever."

Rina looked over. "Hello, David," she said quietly.

"Hello, Rina." He got to his feet. "How are you?"

"I'm fine," she answered. "Who wouldn't be after three months on a health farm?"

He laughed. "And your next picture will be another vacation," Norman interrupted.

Rina turned back to him, a faint smile coming over her face. "Go ahead, you old bastard," she said. "Con me into it."

Norman laughed happily. "For a minute, I was wondering if it was my old girl who was coming into the office, so nice she was!"

Rina laughed, too. "What's the vacation?" she asked.

"Africa!" Norman said triumphantly. "The greatest jungle script I read since *Trader Horn*."

"I knew it," Rina said, turning to David. "I knew the next thing he'd have me do would be a female Tarzan!"

After she was gone, David looked across the room at his uncle. "Rina seems quieter, more subdued, somehow."

Norman looked at him shrewdly. "So what?" he said. "Maybe she's growing up a *bissel* and settling down. It's about time." He got up from his desk and walked over to David. "Only six months we got to the stockholders' meeting next March."

"You still don't know who's selling us short?"

"No." Norman shook his head. "I tried everyplace. The brokers, the underwriters, the banks. They tried. Nobody knows. But every day, the stock goes down." He chewed on his unlit cigar. "I bought up every share I could but enough money I ain't got to stop it. All the cash I could beg or borrow is gone."

"Maybe the stock will go up when we announce Rina's new picture. Everyone knows she's a sure money-maker."

"I hope so," Norman said. "Everywhere we're losing money. Even the theaters." He walked back to his chair and slumped down into it. "That was the mistake I made. I should never have bought them. For them I had to float the stock, borrow all that money from the banks. Pictures I know; real estate, phooey! I should never have listened to those *chazairem* on Wall Street, ten years ago. Now I sold my company, the money I ain't got no more. And I don't even know who owns it!"

David got to his feet. "Well, there's no use in worrying about it. There's still six months till the meeting. And a lot can happen in six months."

"Yeah," Norman said discouragingly. "It can get worse!"

David closed the door of his office behind him. He sat down at his desk and ran down the list of enemies his uncle had made in the course of his life. It was a long list but there wasn't anyone who had the kind of money this operation required. Besides, most of them were in the picture business and they had done as much to his uncle as he had done to them. It was a kind of game among members of a club. They screamed and hollered a lot but none ever took it seriously enough to carry a grudge like this.

Suddenly, he remembered something—Rina. He glanced at the door, his hand going automatically to the telephone. He pulled his hand back sharply. There was no sense in making a fool of himself.

But he had a hunch. How right he was he wasn't to know until he had Ilene sign Rina into the hospital under a phony name six months later. She was just back from Africa after shooting *The Jungle Queen,* and suddenly took very sick. He hadn't wanted the press to find out until after the picture was released.

21

"JONAS CORD," NORMAN SAID BITTERLY. "JONAS Cord it was the whole time. Why didn't you tell me?"

David turned from the hotel window looking out over Central Park. "I didn't know. I was only guessing."

"Know, not know," the producer said, chewing on his dead cigar. "You should have told me, anyway."

"What good would it have done?" David asked. "I couldn't have proved it and even if I had, you didn't have the money to fight him."

Norman took the cigar out of his mouth and looked at it glumly. With an angry gesture, he threw it on the rug. "What did I ever do to him he should want to ruin me?" he asked angrily.

David didn't answer.

"Nothing! That's what I did. Only made money for him. More money that he should use to cut my throat with!" Bernie took a fresh cigar from his pocket and waved it in front of David's face. "That should be a lesson to you. Never do a favor for anybody, never make money for anybody, only yourself. Otherwise, you'll find a knife in your back made of your own silver!"

David looked at his uncle's angry purple face, remembering the scene that had taken place at the stockholders' meeting.

Norman had gone into it, feeling more confident than he had at any time during the past few months. The percentage of proxies that had been returned was about what they got every year. Only about twenty-five per cent of the stockholders ever bothered to send in their proxy forms. All they were interested in was when they'd begin receiving dividends again. But those proxies, plus the eight per cent of stock that Norman had in his own name, gave him a comfortable thirty-three per cent of the stock to vote.

The attendance at the meeting was the same as usual. A few retired businessmen and some women who wandered in off the street because they owned ten shares and it gave them something to do; those directors of the company who happened to be in town and the company officers from the New York office.

It was only after the formalities of the meeting were over and Norman was asking for nominations for the board of directors that he sensed there was something wrong. As he was speaking, Dan Pierce, the agent, and another man, whose face was familiar but whose name Norman couldn't remember, came into the room and sat down in the front row of the small auditorium.

A vice-president in charge of sales dutifully read off Norman's approved list of nominations for directorships. Another vice-president, in charge of theater operations, dutifully seconded the nominations. A third vice-president, in charge of foreign operations, then dutifully moved that the nominations be closed.

At that moment, Pierce got to his feet. "Mr. President," he said, "I have several more nominations to make for directors of the corporation."

"You got no right," Norman yelled from the podium.

"According to the bylaws of the company," Dan Pierce retorted, "any stockholder of record may nominate as many persons for directors as there are directors in the corporation!"

Norman turned to his vice-president and general counsel. "Is that true?"

The attorney nervously nodded. "You're fired, you dumb bastard, you!" Norman whispered.

He turned back to Pierce. "It's illegal!" he shouted. "A trick to upset the company."

The man seated alongside Pierce got to his feet. "Mr. Pierce's nominations are perfectly in order and I, personally, can attest to his legal right to make them."

It was then that Norman remembered the name—McAllister—Jonas Cord's attorney. He calmed down immediately. "I suppose you can prove you're stockholders?" he asked cannily.

McAllister smiled. "Of course."

"Let me see your proof. I got a right to demand that!"

"Of course you have," McAllister said. He walked up to the podium and handed up a stock certificate.

Norman looked down at it. It was a stock certificate for ten shares properly issued in the name of Daniel Pierce. "Is this all the stock you got?" he asked innocently.

McAllister smiled again. "It's all the proof I need," he said, evading the producer's attempt to find out just how much stock he represented. "May I proceed with the nominations?"

Norman nodded silently and Pierce got to his feet and presented six names for the nine-man board. Just enough to assure clear-cut control. Outside of his own and McAllister's, all the names were strange to Norman.

When the votes were ready to be counted, McAllister presented to the meeting proxies representing forty-one per cent of the company—twenty-six per cent in the name of Jonas Cord and fifteen held by various brokerage houses. All six of his nominees were elected.

Norman turned to his executives. He studied them silently for a moment, then withdrew six of his nominees, leaving only himself, David and the vice-president and treasurer on the board. The meeting over, he called for a directors' meeting at the company offices that afternoon, for the election of officers.

Silently he started out of the room, his usually ruddy face pale and white. Pierce stopped him at the door. "Bernie," Pierce said, "I'd like a minute with you before the directors' meeting."

Norman stared at him. "Traitors to their own kind I don't talk to," he said coldly. "Go talk to Hitler!" He stamped out of the room.

Dan Pierce turned to David. "David, make him listen to reason," he said. "Cord authorized me to offer three million bucks for the old man's shares. That's twice what they're worth. If he doesn't sell, Cord says he'll put the company in receivership and all the shares will be good for then is wallpaper."

"I'll see what I can do," David said, hurrying after his uncle.

Now Norman was yelling again, pacing up and down the room and threatening a proxy fight. He'd show that crazy Cord that Bernie Norman was no fool, that he hadn't built a business up from nothing with his bare hands without having something in his *kopf*.

"Wait a minute!" David said sharply. He had taken more than enough nonsense from his uncle. It was time somebody taught the old man the facts of life. "You're talking about a proxy fight?" he shouted. "With what are you going to fight him? Spitballs instead of money? And if you fight, do you honestly believe that anybody will go along with you? For the last four years, this company has been steadily losing money. The biggest picture we had during that time was *The Renegade*—Cord's picture, not ours. And the biggest picture on the market today is *Devils in the Sky*—Cord's picture, too. The one you wouldn't distribute for him because there wasn't enough *koom-shaw* in it for you! Do you think anybody in his right mind is going to pick you over Cord?"

The producer stared at him. "To think," he cried out, "that from my own flesh and blood should come such words!"

"Come off it, Uncle Bernie," David said. "Family's got nothing to do with it. I'm just looking at the facts."

"Facts?" Norman shouted. "Facts is it you want? Well, look at them. Who was it went out and bought *Sunspots,* a picture that won almost every award? Who? Nobody but me."

"It also lost a million dollars."

"That's my fault?" his uncle replied bitterly. "I didn't tell them before I did it? No, prestige they wanted, and prestige they got."

"That's over the dam, Uncle Bernie," David said. "It has nothing to do with today. Nobody cares about that any more."

"I care about it," Norman retorted. "It's my blood they're spilling. I'm the sacrifice they're making to the Golem. But not yet am I dead. When I tell them about the pictures I'm making with Rina Marlowe, I'll get all the proxies I want."

David stared at his uncle for a moment, then went to the telephone. "Long distance, please," he said. "I want to place a call to the Colton Hospital, Santa Monica, California, room three-o-nine, please."

He glanced at his uncle, who was looking out the window. "Ilene? This is David. How is she?"

"Not good," Ilene said, her voice so low he could scarcely hear her.

"What does the doctor say?"

David heard her begin to sob into the telephone. "Hold on," he said. "This is no time to start breaking down."

"He said—she's dying. That it's a miracle she's lasted this long. He doesn't know what's keeping her alive."

There was a click and the phone went dead in his hand. David turned to his uncle. "Rina won't make another picture for you or anybody else," he said. "She's dying."

The producer stared at him, his face going white. He sank back into a chair. "My God! Then what will happen to the company? She was the one chance we had to stay alive. Without her, the bottom will drop out of the stock, we're finished." He wiped at his face with a handkerchief. "Now even Cord won't bother with us."

David stared at his uncle. "What do you mean?"

"Shmuck!" Norman snapped. "Don't you see it yet? Do I got to draw for you diagrams?"

"See?" David asked, bewildered. "See what?"

"That Cord really don't give a damn about the company," the old man said. "That all he wants is the girl."

"The girl?"

"Sure," Norman said. "Rina Marlowe. Remember that meeting I had with him in the toilet at the Waldorf? Remember I told you what he said? How he wouldn't tell me the courvehs' names because I stole the Marlowe girl from under his nose?"

The light came on suddenly inside David's head. Why hadn't he thought of it? It tied up with the phone call from Cord the night Dunbar killed himself. He looked at his uncle with a new respect. "What are we going to do?"

"Do?" the old man said. "Do? We're going to keep our mouths shut and go down to that meeting. My heart may be breaking but if he offered three million for my stock, he'll go to five!"

The dream didn't slip away this time when Rina opened her eyes. If anything, it seemed more real than it had ever been. She lay very still for a moment, looking up at the clear plastic tent covering her head and chest. She turned her head slowly.

Ilene was sitting in the chair, watching her. She wished she could tell Ilene not to worry, there really wasn't anything to be afraid of. She had gone through this so many times before in the dream. "Ilene!" she whispered.

Ilene started and got up out of her chair. Rina smiled up at her. "It's really me, Ilene," she whispered. "I'm not out of my head."

"Rina!" She felt Ilene's hand take her own under the sheet. "Rina!"

"Don't cry, Ilene," she whispered. She turned her head to try and see the calendar on the wall but it was too far away. "What day is it?"

"It's Friday."

"The thirteenth?" Rina tried to smile. She saw the smile come to Ilene's face, despite the tears that were rolling down her cheeks. "Call Jonas," Rina said weakly. "I want to see him."

She closed her eyes for a moment and opened them when Ilene came back to the bed. "Did you get him?"

Ilene shook her head. "His office says he's in New York, but they don't know where to reach him."

"You get him, wherever he is!" Rina smiled. "You can't fool me any more," she said. "I've played this scene too many times. You call him. I won't die until he gets here." A faint, ironic smile came over her face. "Anyway, nobody dies out here on the weekend. The weekend columns have already gone to press."

JONAS—1935

Book Five

1

I PULLED THE STICK BACK INTO MY BELLY WITH A little left rudder. At the same time, I opened the throttle and the CA-4 leaped upward into the sky in a half loop, like an arrow shot from a bow. I felt the G force hold me flat against my seat and bubble the blood racing in my arms. I leveled her off at the top of the loop and when I checked the panel, we were doing three hundred, racing out over the Atlantic with Long Island already far behind us.

I reached forward and tapped the shoulder of the Army flier seated in front of me. "How about that, Colonel?" I shouted over the roar of the twin engines and the shriek of the wind against the plastic bubble over our heads.

I saw him bob his head in answer to my question but he didn't turn around. I knew what he was doing. He was checking out the panel in front of him. Lieutenant Colonel Forrester was one of the real fly boys. He went all the way back to Eddie Rickenbacker and the old Hat in the Ring squadron. Not at all like the old General we'd left on the ground back at Roosevelt Field, that the Army had sent out to check over our plane.

The General flew an armchair back in Purchasing and Procurement in Washington. The closest he ever came to an airplane was when he sat on the trial board at Billy Mitchell's court-martial. But he was the guy who had the O.K. We were lucky that at least he had one Air Corps officer on his staff.

I had tabbed him the minute he came walking into the hangar, with Morrissey, talking up a storm, trotting beside him. There were two aides right behind him—a full colonel and a captain. None of them wore the Air Corps wings on their blouse.

He stood there in the entrance of the hangar, staring in at the CA-4. I could see the frown of disapproval come across his face. "It's ugly," he said. "It looks like a toad."

His voice carried clear across the hangar to where I was, in the cockpit, giving her a final check. I climbed out onto the wing and dropped to the hangar floor in my bare feet. I started toward him. What the hell did he know about streamline and design? His head probably was as square as the desk he sat behind.

"Mr. Cord!" I heard the hissed whisper behind me. I turned around. It was the mechanic. There was a peculiar grin on his face. He had heard the General's remark, too.

"What d'yuh want?"

"I was jus' gettin' ready to roll her out," he said quickly. "An' I didn't want to squash yer shoes."

I stared at him for a moment, then I grinned. "Thanks," I said, walking back and stepping into them. By the time I reached Morrissey and the General, I was cooled off.

Morrissey had a copy of the plans and specs in his hand and was going over them for the benefit of the General. "The Cord Aircraft Four is a revolutionary concept in a two-man fighter-bomber, which has a flight range of better than two thousand miles. It cruises at two forty, with a max of three sixty. It can carry ten machine guns, two cannon, and mounts one thousand pounds of bombs under its wings and in a special bay in its belly."

I looked back at the plane as Morrissey kept on talking. It sure as hell was a revolutionary design. It looked like a big black panther squatting there on the hangar floor with its long nose jutting out in front of the swept-back wings and the plastic bubble over the cockpit shining like a giant cat's eye in the dim light.

"Very interesting," I heard the General say. "Now, I have just one more question."

"What's that, sir?" Morrissey asked.

The General chuckled, looking at his aides. They permitted a faint smile to come to their lips. I could see the old fart was going to get off one of his favorite jokes. "We Army men look over about three hundred of these so-called revolutionary planes every year. Will it fly?"

I couldn't keep quiet any longer. The million bucks it had cost me to get this far with the CA-4 gave me a right to shoot off my mouth. "She'll fly the ass off anything you got in your Army, General," I said. "And any other plane in the world, including the new fighters that Willi Messerschmitt is building."

The General turned toward me, a surprised look on his face. I saw his eyes go down over my grease-spattered white coveralls.

Morrissey spoke up quickly. "General Gaddis, Jonas Cord."

Before the General could speak, a voice came from the doorway behind him. "How do you know what Willi Messerschmitt is building?"

I looked up as the speaker came into view. The General had evidently brought a third aide with him. The silver wings shone on his blouse, matching the silver oak leaves on his shoulders. He was about forty, slim and with a flier's mustache. He wore just two ribbons on his blouse—the *Croix de guerre* of France and the Distinguished Flying Cross.

"He told me," I said curtly.

There was a curious look on the lieutenant colonel's face. "How is Willi?"

The General's voice cut in before I could answer. "We came out here to look over an airplane," he said in a clipped voice, "not to exchange information about mutual friends."

It was my turn to be surprised. I flashed a quick look at the lieutenant colonel but a curtain had dropped over his face. I could see, though, that there was no love lost between the two.

"Yes, sir," he said quickly. He turned and looked at the plane. "How do you think she looks, Forrester?"

Forrester cleared his throat. "Interesting, sir," he said. He turned toward me. "Variable-pitch propellers?"

I nodded. He had good eyes to see that in this dim light.

"Unusual concept," he said, "setting the wings where they are and sweeping them back. Should give her about four times the usual lift area."

"They do," I said. Thank God for at least one man who knew what it was all about.

"I asked how you thought she looks, Forrester?" the General repeated testily.

The curtain dropped down over Forrester's face again as he turned. "Very unusual, sir. Different."

The General nodded. "That's what I thought. Ugly. Like a toad sitting there."

I'd had about enough of his bullshit. "Does the General judge planes the same way he'd judge dames in a beauty contest?"

"Of course not!" the General snapped. "But there are certain conventions of design that are recognized as standard. For example, the new Curtiss fighter we looked at the other day. There's a plane that looks like a plane, not like a bomb with wings attached."

"That baby over there carries twice as much armor, plus a thousand pounds of bombs, seven hundred and fifty miles farther, five thousand feet higher and eighty miles an hour faster than the Curtiss fighter you're talking about!" I retorted.

"Curtiss builds good planes," the General said stiffly.

I stared at him. There wasn't any use in arguing. It was like talking to a stone wall. "I'm not saying they don't, General," I said. "Curtiss has been building good airplanes for many years. But I'm saying this one is better than anything around."

General Gaddis turned to Morrissey. "We're ready to see a demonstration of your plane," he said stiffly. "That is, if your pilot is through arguing."

Morrissey shot a nervous look at me. Apparently the General hadn't even caught my name. I nodded at him and turned back to the hangar.

"Roll her out!" I called to the mechanics, who were standing there waiting.

Morrissey, General Gaddis and his aides walked out. When I got outside I saw that Morrissey and the others had formed a group around the General but Forrester stood a little to one side, talking to a young woman. I shot a quick look at her. She was stuff, all right—wild eyes and sensuous mouth.

I followed the plane out onto the runway. Hearing footsteps

behind me, I turned around. It was Morrissey. "You shouldn't have teed off on the General like that."

I grinned at him. "Probably did the old bastard good. He's got enough yes men around him to be a movie producer."

"All the same, it's tough selling him as it is. I found out Curtiss is bidding their planes in at a hundred and fifty thousand each and you know the best we can do is two twenty-five."

"So what?" I said. "It's the difference between chicken shit and chicken salad. You can't buy a Cadillac for the same price as a Ford?"

He stared at me for a moment, then he shrugged his shoulders. "It's your money, Jonas."

I watched him walk back to the General. He might be a great aeronautical engineer, but he was too anxious ever to become a good salesman. I turned to the mechanic. "Ready?"

"Ready when you are, Mr. Cord."

"O.K.," I said, starting to climb up to the cockpit. I felt a hand tugging at my leg. I looked down.

"Mind if I come along for the ride?" It was the lieutenant colonel.

"Not at all," I said. "Hop in."

"Thanks. By the way, I didn't get your name."

"Jonas Cord," I said.

"Roger Forrester," he answered, holding out his hand.

I should have guessed it the minute I heard his name, but I didn't tie it up until now. Roger Forrester—one of the original aces of the Lafayette Escadrille. Twenty-two German planes to his credit. He'd been one of my heroes when I was a kid.

"I've heard about you," I said.

His smile changed into a grin. "I've heard quite a bit about you."

We both laughed and I felt better. I pulled on his hand and he came up on the wing beside me. He looked into the cockpit, then back at me.

"No parachute?"

"Never use 'em," I said. "Make me nervous. Psychological. Indicates a lack of confidence."

He laughed.

"I can get one for you if you like."

He laughed again. "To hell with it."

About thirty miles out over the ocean, I put her through all the tricks in the book and then some only the CA-4 could do, and he didn't bat an eyelash.

For a clincher, I took her all the way up in a vertical climb until, at fourteen thousand feet, she hung in the sky like a fly dancing on the tip of a needle. Then I let her fall off on a dead stick into a tailspin that whipped the air-speed indicator up close to the five hundred mark. When we got down to about fifteen hundred feet, I took both hands off the stick and tapped him on the shoulder.

His head whipped around so fast it almost fell off his neck. I laughed. "She's all yours, Colonel!" I shouted.

We were down to twelve hundred feet by the time he turned around; eight hundred feet by the time he had the spin under control; six hundred feet before he had her in a straight dive; and four hundred feet before he could pull back on the stick.

I felt her shudder and tremble under me and a shrill scream came from her wings, like a dame getting her cherry copped. The G pinned me back in my seat, choking the air back into my throat and forcing the big bubbles right up into my eyes. Suddenly, the pressure lifted. We were less than twenty-five feet off the water when we started to climb.

Forrester looked back at me. "I haven't been this scared since I soloed back in fifteen," he yelled, grinning. "How did you know she wouldn't lose her wings in a dive like that?"

"Who knew?" I retorted. "But this was as good a time as any to find out!"

He laughed. I saw his hand reach forward and knock on the instrument panel. "What a plane. Like you said, she sure does fly!"

"Don't tell me. Tell that old coot back there."

A shadow fell across his face. "I'll try. But I don't know if I can do much good. It's all yours," he said, raising his hands. "You take her back in now."

I could see Morrissey and the soldiers standing on the field, watching us through field glasses as we came in. I put her into a wide turn and tapped Forrester on the shoulder. He looked back at me. "Ten bucks says I can take the General's hat off on the first pass."

He hesitated a moment, then grinned. "You're on!"

I came down at the field from about a thousand feet and leveled off about fifteen feet over the runway. I could see the startled expression on their faces as we rushed toward them, then I pulled back the stick. We went over their heads, into an almost vertical climb, catching them full blast in the prop wash.

I looked back just in time to see the captain running after the General's hat. I tapped Forrester's shoulder again. He turned to look back. He was laughing so hard there were tears in his eyes.

She set down as lightly as a pigeon coming home to its roost. I slid back the plastic canopy and we climbed down. I glanced at Forrester's face as we walked over to the group. All the laughter was gone from it now and the wary mask was back on.

The General had his hat on his head again. "Well, Forrester," he said stiffly. "What do you think?"

Forrester looked into his commanding officer's face. "Without a doubt, sir, this is the best fighter in the air today," he said in a flat, emotionless voice. "I'd suggest, sir, that you have a test group make an immediate check to substantiate my opinion."

"Hmm," the General said coldly. "You would, eh?"

"I would, sir," Forrester said quietly.

"There are other factors to be considered, Forrester. Do you have any idea of what these planes might cost?"

"No, sir," Forrester answered. "My only responsibility is to evaluate the performance of the plane itself."

"My responsibilities go much further than that," the General said. "You must remember that we're operating under a strict budget."

"Yes, sir."

"Please bear it in mind," General Gaddis said testily. "If I went off half-cocked over every idea you Air Corps men had, there wouldn't be money enough left to keep the Army running for a month."

Forrester's face flushed. "Yes, sir."

I glanced at him, wondering why he stood there and took it. It didn't make sense. Not with the reputation he had. He could step out of the Army and knock down twenty times what he was making with any airline in the country. He had a name as good as Rickenbacker's any day.

The General turned to Morrissey. "Now, Mr. Morrissey," he said in an almost jovial voice. "Whom do we talk to about getting a few facts and figures on the cost of this airplane?"

"You can talk with Mr. Cord, sir."

"Fine!" boomed the General. "Let's go into the office and call him."

"You don't have to do that, General," I said quickly. "We can talk right here."

The General stared at me, then his lips broke into what he thought was an expansive smile. "No offense intended, son. I didn't connect the names."

"That's all right, General."

"Your father and I are old friends," he said. "Back during the last war, I bought a lot of the hard stuff from him and if it's all right with you, I'd like to talk this over with him. Purely for old times' sake, you understand. Besides, this can turn out to be a mighty big deal and I'm sure your daddy would like to get in on it himself."

I felt my face go white. I had all I could do to control myself. How long did you have to live in a man's shadow? My voice sounded flat and strained even to my own ears. "I'm sure he would, General. But I'm afraid you'll have to talk to me; you can't talk to him."

"Why not?" The voice was suddenly cold.

"My father's been dead for ten years," I said, turning my back on him and walking toward the hangar.

2

I WALKED THROUGH TO THE SMALL ROOM IN THE back that Morrissey used as an office. I shut the door behind me and crossing to his desk, took out the bottle of bourbon that was always there for me. Pouring a shot into a paper cup, I tossed the whisky down my throat. It burned like hell. I looked down at my hands. They were trembling.

There are some people who won't stay dead. It doesn't make any difference what you do to them. You can bury them in the ground, dump them into the ocean or cremate them. But the memory of them will still turn your guts into mush just as if they were still alive.

I remembered what my father said to me one morning down at the corral in back of the house. It was a little while after his marriage to Rina and I'd come down one morning to watch Nevada break a new bronc. It was along about five o'clock and the first morning sun was just raising its head over the desert.

The bronc was a mean one, a wiry, nasty little black bastard that, every time it threw Nevada, went after him with slashing hoofs and teeth. The last time it threw him, it even tried to roll on him. Nevada scrambled out of the way and just did make it over the fence.

He stood there leaning against the fence and breathing heavily while the Mex boys chased the bronc. Their shrill whoops and yells split the morning air. "He's a crazy one," Nevada said.

"What're you going to do with him?" I asked curiously. It wasn't often I saw Nevada take three falls in a row.

The Mexicans had the horse now and Nevada watched them lead it back. "Try him once more," he answered thoughtfully. "An' if that doesn't work, turn him loose."

My father's voice came from behind us. "That's just what he wants you to do."

Nevada and I turned. My father was already dressed as if he was going straight to the plant. He was wearing his black suit and the tie was neatly centered in the thickly starched white collar of his shirt. "Why don't you put a clamp on his muzzle so he can't snap at you?"

Nevada looked at him. "Ain't nobody can git near enough to that hoss without losin' an arm."

"Nonsense!" my father said tersely. He took a short lariat from the pegs on the fence and ducking between the bars, stepped out into the corral. I could see his hands working the rope into a small halter as he walked toward the horse.

The bronc stood there pawing the ground, its eyes watching my father balefully. The Mexicans tightened their grip on the lariats around the horse's neck. The bronc reared back as my father brought the loop up to catch it around the muzzle. At the same time, it lashed out with its forefeet. Father just got out of the way in time.

He stood there for a moment, staring into the horse's eyes, then reached up again. The bronc shook its head wildly and slashed savagely at my father's arm. Again the hoofs lashed out, just missing Father.

The bronc was really wild now, twisting and turning as if there were a rider on it. The Mexicans leaned on their lariats to hold it still. After a moment, it was quiet and Father walked back to it.

"You ornery son of a bitch," my father said quietly. The

bronc bared its teeth and snapped at him. Father seemed to move his arm just a fraction of an inch and the bronc's head flashed by his arm. "Let him go," my father yelled to the Mexicans.

The two boys looked at each other for a moment, then shrugging in that almost imperceptible manner they had to absolve themselves of responsibility, let up on their lariats.

Free of restraint, the bronc was motionless for a fraction of a second, bewildered. My father stood there in front of him, tall and broad in his black suit. Their eyes were about on a level. Then slowly my father started to bring his hand up again and the bronc exploded, its eyes flashing, its teeth bared, as it reared back and struck out with its hoofs. This time, my father stepped back and then darted as the bronc came down.

I saw my father's clenched fist hanging high in the air over his head for a flashing second. The bronc's four hoofs struck the ground and Father's fist came down like a hammer, just over the bronc's eyes. The thud of the blow echoed back against the side of the house like a small explosion. The bronc stood there for a moment, then sagged slowly to its knees, its front legs crumpling as if they had suddenly turned to rubber.

Quickly my father walked around to the side and slapped his open palm against the bronc's neck. The horse toppled over on its side. For a moment, it lay there, its sides heaving, then it raised its head and looked up at my father. The four of us—the Mexicans, Nevada and I—were silent as we stood there watching them.

The bronc's raised head threw a long morning shadow in the corral dirt that was dwarfed only by the shadow of my father as they stared into each other's eyes. Then the bronc seemed to heave a giant sigh and dropped its head back on the ground.

My father looked down at the bronc for a moment, then bent over and taking the reins near the bronc's mouth, pulled the horse to its feet. The bronc stood there, its legs trembling, its head hanging dejectedly. It didn't even raise its head as my father crossed in front of it and came back through the fence to us.

"You won't have any trouble with him now." My father hung the lariat back on the peg and started for the house. "Coming in for breakfast, Jonas?" he called without turning his head or breaking his stride.

Nevada was already back in the corral, walking toward the bronc. "Yes, sir," I said, starting after my father. I caught up to him on the back porch. We turned and watched Nevada mount the horse. The bronc bucked and sawed but it was easy to see his heart wasn't in it.

My father turned to me, unsmiling. "Some horses are like people. The only language they understand is a clout on the head."

"I didn't think you cared that much about the horses," I said. "You never come down to the corral."

"I don't," he said quickly. "It's you I care about. You've still got a lot to learn."

I laughed. "Fat lot I learned from your hitting a bronc on its head."

"You learned that Nevada couldn't ride that horse until I made it possible."

"So?"

My father turned. He was a big man, over six feet, but I was taller. "So," he said slowly, "no matter how big you get, you won't be big enough to wear my shoes until I let you."

I followed my father into the dining room. Rina's back was to me and her hair shone like silver as she raised her cheek for his morning kiss. There was a quiet triumph in my father's eyes as he straightened up afterward and looked at me. He didn't speak as he sat down in his chair. He didn't have to. I knew what he was thinking. He didn't have to hit me over the head.

"Joining us for breakfast, Jonas?" Rina asked politely.

I stared at her for a moment, then at my father. I could feel the sick knot tying up my guts. "No, thanks. I'm not hungry."

I turned and walked hurriedly back through the dining room door, almost colliding with Robair, who was just entering with a tray. By the time I got back to the corral, Nevada was walking the bronc up and down, breaking him to the meaning of the reins. Father had been right. The horse wasn't giving Nevada any trouble.

And here it was twelve years later and I could still hear his voice as it had echoed quietly on the back porch that morning.

"Let go, old man, let go!" I said angrily, my fist smashing down on the empty desk. The pain ran crazily up my arm into my shoulder.

"Mr. Cord!" I looked up in surprise. Morrissey was standing in the open doorway, his mouth partly open. It took an effort for me to bring myself back to the present.

"Don't stand there," I snapped. "Come in." He entered the office hesitantly, and a moment later, Forrester appeared in the doorway behind him. Silently they came into the office.

"Sit down and have a drink," I said, pushing the bottle of bourbon toward them.

"Don't mind if I do," Forrester said, picking up the bottle and a paper cup. He sloshed himself a good one. "Mud in your eye."

"Up the General's," I said. "By the way, where is the old boy?"

"On his way back to the city. He has a date with a toilet paper manufacturer."

I laughed. "At least, that's one thing he can test for himself."

Forrester laughed but Morrissey sat there glumly. I pushed the bottle toward him. "You on the wagon?"

He shook his head. "What are we going to do now?" he asked.

I stared at him for a moment, then picked up the bottle and refilled my paper cup. "I was just thinking about declaring war on the United States. That's one way we could show him how good our plane is."

Morrissey still didn't crack a smile. "The CA-4 is the best plane I ever designed."

"So what?" I asked. "What the hell, it didn't cost you anything. It was my dough. Besides, how much did you ever make out of building planes? It doesn't amount to one-twentieth of your annual royalties on that trick brassière you designed for Rina Marlowe."

It was true. But it had been McAllister who'd seen the commerical potential in the damn thing and applied for a patent in the name of Cord Aircraft. Morrissey had a standard employment contract, which provided that all his inventions and designs belonged to the company, but McAllister had been a sport about it. He'd given Morrissey a ten-per-cent interest in the royalties as a bonus and last year, Morrissey's share was in excess of a hundred thousand dollars. The market was getting bigger all the time. Tits weren't going out of fashion for a long time.

Morrissey didn't answer. But then, I hadn't expected him to. He was one of those guys who don't give a damn about money. All he lived for was his work.

I finished my drink and lit a cigarette. Silently I cursed myself. I should have known better than to let a chance remark about my father bug me like that. I could afford it but nobody likes to throw a million dollars down the drain.

"Maybe I can do something," Forrester said.

A ray of hope came into Morrissey's eyes. "Do you think you could?"

Forrester shrugged. "I don't know," he said slowly. "I said maybe."

I stared at him. "What do you mean?"

"It's the best plane I've seen," he said. "I wouldn't like to see us lose it because of the old man's stupidity."

"Thanks," I said. "We'd be grateful for anything you could do."

Forrester smiled. "You don't owe me anything. I'm one of those old-fashioned guys who wouldn't like to see us caught short if things suddenly started popping."

I nodded. "They'll start soon enough. Just as soon as Hitler thinks he's ready."

"When do you think that will be?"

"Three, maybe four years," I said. "When they have enough trained pilots and planes."

"Where'll he get them from? He hasn't got them now."

"He'll get them," I said. "The glider schools are turning out ten thousand pilots a month and before the summer is over, Messerschmitt will have his ME-109's on the production line."

"The general staff thinks he won't do much when he comes up against the Maginot line."

"He won't come up against it," I said. "He'll fly over it."

Forrester nodded. "All the more reason for me to try to get them to check out your plane." He looked at me quizzically. "You talk like you know."

"I know," I answered. "I was there less than nine months ago."

"Oh, yes," he said, "I remember. I saw something about it in the papers. There was some kind of a stink about it, wasn't there?"

I laughed. "There was. Certain people accused me of being a Nazi sympathizer."

"Because of the million dollars you turned over to the Reichsbank?"

I shot a quick glance at him. Forrester wasn't as simple as he pretended to be. "I guess so," I answered. "You see, I transferred the money just the day before Roosevelt slapped on his restriction."

"You knew the restriction was about to be placed, didn't you? You could have saved yourself the money by just waiting one day."

"I couldn't afford to wait," I said. "The money had to be in Germany, that was all there was to it."

"Why? Why did you send them the money when obviously you realize they're our potential enemy?"

"It was ransom for a Jew," I said.

"Some of my best friends are Jews," Forrester answered. "But I can't imagine shelling out a million dollars for one of them."

I stared at him for a moment, then refilled my paper cup. "This one was worth it."

His name was Otto Strassmer and he started out in life as a quality-control engineer in one of the many Bavarian china works. From ceramics he had turned to plastics and it was he who had invented the high-speed injection mold I'd bought and sold to a combine of American manufacturers. Our original deal had been on a royalty basis but after it had been in effect for several years Strassmer wanted to change it. That was in 1933, shortly after Hitler came to power.

He'd come into my hotel room in Berlin, where I'd been on my annual visit to Europe, and explained what he wanted. He was willing to relinquish all future share in royalties for a flat payment of one million dollars, to be held in escrow for him in the United States. This was agreeable to me, of course. His share of the royalties would amount to much more than that over the licensing period. But I didn't understand why. So I asked him.

He got up out of his chair and walked over to the window. "You ask me why, Herr Cord?" he asked in his peculiarly accented English. His hand pointed out the window. "That's why."

I walked over to the window and looked down. There in the street in front of the Adlon, a group of brown-shirted young men, scarcely more than boys, were tormenting an old frock-coated man. Twice while we were watching, they knocked the old man into the gutter. We could see him lying on the edge of the sidewalk, his head in the gutter, blood streaming from his nose. The boys stood there for a moment watching him, then walked away after kicking him several times contemptuously.

I turned to Strassmer questioningly.

"That was a Jew, Herr Cord," he said quietly.

"So what? Why didn't he call the police?"

Strassmer pointed across the street. Two policemen stood on the opposite corner. "They saw everything that happened."

"Why didn't they stop them?"

"They are under instructions not to," he answered. "Hitler claims that Jews have no right under German law."

"What has this got to do with you?"

"I am a Jew," he said simply.

I was silent for a moment. I took out a cigarette and lit it. "What do you want me to do with the money?"

"Keep it until you hear from me." He smiled. "My wife and daughter are already in America. I would be grateful if you'd let them know I'm all right."

"Why don't you join them?" I asked.

"Perhaps I will—in time. But I am German," he said. "And I still hope this madness will one day pass."

But Herr Strassmer's hopes were not to be realized. This I found out less than a year later, as I sat in the office of the Reichsmarschall. "The Jews of the world are doomed, as are the Jews of Germany," he said in his polite voice. "We of the New Order recognize this and welcome our friends and allies from across the sea who wish to join our crusade."

I was silent, waiting for him to speak again.

"We men of the air understand each other," he said.

I nodded. "Yes, Excellency."

"Good," he said, smiling. "Then we do not have to waste time." He threw some papers on the desk. "Under the new laws, the Reich has confiscated the properties of a certain Otto Strassmer. We understand there are certain monies due him which you are hereby instructed to pay over into the Reichsbank."

I didn't like the word "instructed." "I have been trying to get in touch with Herr Strassmer," I said.

Göring smiled again. "Strassmer had a severe breakdown and is presently confined to a hospital."

"I see," I said. I got to my feet.

"The Third Reich will not forget its friends," the Reichs-marschall said. He pressed a button on his desk.

A young German lieutenant appeared in the doorway. "Heil Hitler!" he said, his arm upraised in the Nazi salute.

"Heil Hitler!" Göring replied negligently. He turned to me. "Lieutenant Mueller will escort you to the Messerschmitt plant. I look forward to seeing you again at dinner, Herr Cord."

The Messerschmitt plant opened my eyes. There was nothing like it building airplanes in the United States. The only things comparable were the automobile production lines in Detroit. And when I saw some of the sketches of the ME-109 that adorned Messerschmitt's office, I didn't have to look twice. It was all over but the shouting unless we got up off our collective asses.

That night at dinner, the Reichsmarschall got me in a corner. "What did you think of our factory?"

"I'm impressed," I said.

He nodded, pleased. "It is modeled after your own plant in California," he said. "But much larger, of course."

"Of course," I agreed, wondering how they got in there. Then I realized it was no secret. Up to now, we'd never got any government work; all we'd built were commercial airlines.

He laughed pleasantly, then turned to move away. A moment later, he came back to me. "By the way," he whispered. "The Führer was very pleased about your co-operation. When may I inform him that we will receive the money?"

I stared at him. "On the day Herr Strassmer walks into my office in New York."

He stared back in surprise. "The Führer won't like this," he said. "I told him you were our friend."

"I'm also Herr Strassmer's friend."

He stared at me for another moment. "Now I don't know what to tell the Führer. He will be very disappointed when he learns we shall not receive the money."

"In that case," I said, "why disappoint him? One Jew more or less can't matter to Germany."

He nodded slowly. "Perhaps that is the best way."

Exactly a month later, the little German engineer walked into my office in New York.

"What are you going to do now?" I asked.

"First, I'm going to join my family in Colorado and rest for a while," he said. "Then I must look for work. I'm no longer a rich man."

I smiled at him. "Come to work for me. I'll consider the million dollars an advance against your royalties."

When he left the office, I gave Morrissey the O.K. to go ahead on the CA-4. If my hunch was right, there wasn't enough time left for any of us. But it was another story to make the U.S. Army believe that.

I looked across the desk at Forrester.

"I'll get back to town and make a few calls to Washington. I still have a few friends down there," he said. "I'll stop by and talk to the General. Maybe I can persuade him to listen."

"Good," I said. I looked at my watch. It was almost twelve thirty. The stockholders' meeting ought to be over by now. McAllister and Pierce should be back in the hotel with Norman tucked safely away in their back pockets.

"I have a one-o'clock appointment at the Waldorf," I said. "Can I drop you off?"

"Thanks," Forrester said gratefully. "I have a luncheon date that I'd hate to miss."

He came into the Waldorf with me and cut off toward Peacock Alley as I walked over to the elevators. As I stood there waiting, I saw a woman rise to meet him. It was the same one I had seen him with out at the field. I wondered vaguely why she hadn't waited for him out there.

Idly I watched Rico, the maître d', lead them around the corner to a hidden table. I walked over to the entrance and stood there until he came back.

"Ah, Monsieur Cord." He smiled. "Dining alone?"

"Not dining, Rico," I said, pressing a bill into his ever ready hand. "A question. The lady with Colonel Forrester—who is she?"

Rico smiled knowingly. He kissed his fingers. "Ah, most *charmante*," he said. "She is Madame Gaddis, the wife of the General."

I looked around the lobby as I walked back to the elevators. The General should be somewhere around. From what I had seen of his attitude toward Forrester, I figured there had to be more than just Army and airplanes between them.

I spotted him as he crossed the lobby to the men's room next to the nearest bank of elevators. He was scowling and his face was flushed. He looked like a man who needed more relief than he could find where he was going.

I waited until the door swung shut behind him before I walked over to the elevators. For the first time since I'd landed the CA-4 at Roosevelt Field, I began to feel better. Everything was falling into place now.

I wasn't worried any more. The only problem that remained was how many planes the Army would buy.

3

WHAT I WANTED MOST WAS TO GRAB A SHOWER and take a nap. I hadn't got to sleep until five o'clock that morning. I dropped my clothes on a chair and walked into the stall shower, turning on the needle spray. I could feel the tightness leave my muscles under the soothing warmth. The telephone rang several times while I was in the shower. I let it ring.

When I came out, I picked up the phone and told the operator I didn't want any calls put through until four o'clock.

"But Mr. McAllister told me to call him the moment you come in," she wailed. "He said it was very important."

"You can get him for me at four o'clock," I said. I put down the phone, dropped on the bed and went to sleep like a baby.

The ring of the telephone woke me. I looked at my wrist watch as I reached for the receiver. It was exactly four o'clock.

It was Mac. "I've been trying to get you all afternoon," he said. "Where the hell have you been?"

"Sleeping."

"Sleeping!" he shouted. "We have a board meeting over at the Norman offices. We're due there right now."

"You never told me."

"How in hell could I, when you wouldn't answer your phone?"

"Get General Gaddis for me," I told the operator. "I think he's registered here."

I lit a cigarette while I waited. The receiver crackled in my ear. "General Gaddis speaking."

"General, Jonas Cord here," I said. "I'm in my apartment. Thirty-one fifteen in the Towers. I'd like to talk with you."

The General's voice was cold. "We have nothing to discuss. You're an unconscionably rude young man—"

"It's not my manners I want to discuss, General," I interrupted. "It's your wife."

I heard him sputter through the telephone. "My wife? What's she got to do with our business?"

"A great deal, I believe, General," I said. "We both know whom she met in Peacock Alley today at one o'clock. I can't believe that the War Department would look favorably at a personal animosity being the basis for rejecting the CA-4."

There was a silence over the telephone.

"By the way, General," I asked, "what do you drink?"

"Scotch," he answered automatically.

"Good, I'll have a bottle here, waiting for you. Shall we say in about fifteen minutes?"

I hung up before he could answer and called room service. While I was waiting for an answer, a knock came at the outer door. "Come in," I yelled.

From the bed, I saw Mac and Dan Pierce enter. When they came into the bedroom, Mac's face wore its usual worried look but Dan's was wreathed in smiles. He was on the verge of getting everything he ever wanted.

Room service finally came on. In the background, I could hear the clatter of dishes and suddenly I was hungry. I hadn't eaten since breakfast. I ordered three steak sandwiches, a bottle of milk, a pot of black coffee, a bottle of Scotch, two bottles of bourbon and a double order of French fries. I put down the telephone and looked up at them. "Well, how'd it go?"

"Bernie squealed like a stuck pig." Pierce grinned. "But we had him by the short hairs and he knew it."

"What about his stock?"

"I don't know, Jonas," Mac said. "He wouldn't talk to Dan."

"I spoke to Dave Woolf, though," Dan said quickly. "I told him to get the old man in a selling mood or we'd throw the company into bankruptcy."

"You got the Section Seven Twenty-two ready?" I asked Mac. He knew what I was talking about—a petition to appoint a receiver in bankruptcy.

"In my brief case. Before the meeting this morning, I had a

brief discussion with our attorneys here. They feel they could swing a favorable appointment as receiver."

I stared at him. "You don't sound happy about it."

"I'm not," he said. "Norman's a crafty old man. I don't think you'll bluff him that easily. He knows you stand to lose as much as anyone if you bankrupt the company."

"He's a real greedy old bastard, too. And he won't take the chance of losing what he's got just for the satisfaction of keeping me company."

"I hope you're right."

"We'll find out soon enough." I turned to Dan. "Have you been able to reach Rina yet?"

He shook his head. "I've tried all over. No luck. There's no answer at her home. The studio doesn't know where she is. I even had a contact try Louella but she doesn't know."

"Keep trying," I said. "We've got to find her. I want her to read that script."

"I do, too," Dan said. "She's the only thing holding us up, now I've got the De Mille thing squared away with Paramount."

"Paramount O.K. it?"

"This morning," he said. "I've got the wire from Zukor in my pocket."

"Good," I said. This would be the biggest picture ever made and right up De Mille's alley. We were going to shoot it in a new process called Technicolor and it would cost over six million bucks. It was the story of Mary Magdalene and we were going to call it *The Sinner.*

"Aren't you getting a little ahead of yourselves?" McAllister asked. "What if she doesn't want to do it?"

"She'll do it," I said. "What the hell do you think I want the Norman company for? Their contract with her is the only asset they've got."

"But her contract gives her script approval."

"She'll approve it," I said. She had to. I had the damn thing written especially for her.

When room service came, I swung my feet over the side of the bed and had the waiter set the table right up in front of me. I hadn't realized how hungry I was. I'd already eaten one of the steak sandwiches and drunk half the bottle of milk before the waiter got out the door.

I was in the middle of my second sandwich when the General showed. Dan brought him into the bedroom and I introduced them, then asked them to excuse us.

"Sit down, General," I said when the door closed. "And pour yourself a drink. The bottle of Scotch is on the table."

"No, thanks," the General said tightly, still standing.

I shrugged my shoulders and picked up the third sandwich. I came right to the point. "What's it worth to you if I get Forrester to leave the Army?"

"What makes you think I want that?"

I swallowed a mouthful of sandwich. "Let's not horse around, General. I'm a big boy now and I got eyes. All I want is a fair test for the CA-4. From there on out, it's up to you. There are no other strings attached."

"What makes you think I won't give your plane a fair test now?"

I smiled at him. "And build Forrester up even more in your wife's eyes?"

I could see the tightness leave him. For a moment, I almost felt sorry for him. The brigadier's star on his shoulder meant nothing. He was just another old man trying to hold a young dame. I felt like telling him to stop knocking himself out. If it wasn't Forrester, it would be some other guy.

"I think I'll take that drink now."

"Help yourself," I said.

He opened the bottle and poured himself a straight shot. He drank it and sank into the chair opposite me. "My wife's not a bad girl, Mr. Cord," he said half apologetically. "It's just that she's young—and impressionable."

He wasn't fooling me. I wondered whether he was fooling himself. "I understand, General," I said.

"You know how it is with young girls," he continued. "They see only the glamour, the excitement in a uniform. A man like Forrester—well, it's easy enough to understand. The silver wings on his blouse, the D.F.C. and *Croix de guerre.*"

I nodded silently as I poured myself a cup of black coffee.

"I suppose that was the kind of soldier she thought I was when we were married," he said reflectively. "But it wasn't long before she found out I was nothing but a kind of glorified purchasing agent."

He refilled his glass and looked at me. "Today's Army is a complex machine, Mr. Cord. For every man in the front line, there have to be five or six men behind the lines just to keep him supplied. I always took pride in myself because I took care to see that that man got the best."

"I'm sure of that, General," I said, putting down my coffee cup.

He got to his feet and looked down at me. Maybe it was my imagination, but as he spoke, he seemed to grow taller and straighter. "That was why I came up to talk with you, Mr. Cord," he said with quiet dignity. "Not because you chose to bring my wife into an extraneous matter but to tell you that a test group will be at Roosevelt Field tomorrow morning to check out your airplane. I requested it this morning as soon as I got back into the city. I phoned your Mr. Morrissey but I guess he couldn't reach you."

I looked up at him with surprise. A feeling of shame began to run through me. I should have had brains enough to call Morrissey on my own before I shot off my big mouth.

A faint smile flitted across the General's face. "So you see, Mr. Cord," he said, "you don't have to make any deals with Forrester on my account. If your plane checks out, the Army will buy it."

The door closed behind him and I reached for a cigarette. I leaned back against the headboard of the bed and dragged the smoke deep into my lungs.

The telephone operator at the Chatham found Forrester in the bar. "Jonas Cord," I said. "I'm in the Waldorf Towers down the street. I'd like to talk with you."

"I'd like to talk with you, too," he said. "They're testing your plane in the morning."

"I know. That's what I want to talk to you about."

He was in my apartment in less than ten minutes. His face was flushed and he looked as if he'd spent the whole afternoon wrapping himself around a bottle. "Looks like the old man saw the light," he said.

"That what you really think?" I asked, as he poured himself a drink.

"You can say what you like about him, but Gaddis is a good soldier. He does his job."

"Pour a drink for me," I said.

He picked up another glass and held it toward me. I took it. "I think it's about time you quit playing soldier."

He stared at me. "What have you got in mind?"

"I think that Cord Aircraft is going to be doing a lot of business with the Army from now on," I said. "And I need someone who knows the ropes—the men, what they want in a plane. Make friends for us, contacts. You know what I mean."

"I know what you mean," he said. "Like not seeing Virginia Gaddis any more because it wouldn't look good for the company."

"Something like that," I said quietly.

He threw his drink down his throat. "I don't know whether I'd be any good at it. I've been in the Air Corps ever since I was a kid."

"You never know until you try it," I said. "Besides, you'll do the Air Corps more good out of it than in. There'll be nobody to stop you if you want to try out some of your ideas."

He looked at me. "Speaking of ideas," he asked, "whose was this—yours or Gaddis's?"

"Mine," I said. "I had my mind made up this morning after our little talk in Morrissey's office. And it had nothing to do with whether or not they took the CA-4."

He grinned suddenly. "My mind was made up this morning, too," he said. "I was going to take the job if you offered it to me."

"Where would you like to start?" I asked.

"At the top," he said promptly. "The Army respects nothing but the top man."

"Good enough," I said. It made sense. "You're the new president of Cord Aircraft. How much do you want?"

"You let me pick the job," he said. "I'll let you name the salary."

"Twenty-five thousand a year and expenses."

He whistled. "You don't have to go that high. That's four times what I'm getting now."

"Just remember that when you come asking for a raise," I said.

We both laughed and drank to it. "There's a few changes on the plane I wanted to talk to you about before the test tomorrow," he said.

Just then, McAllister came into the bedroom. "It's almost six o'clock, Jonas," he said. "How long do you think we can keep them waiting? Dan just spoke to David Woolf. He says Norman is threatening to walk out."

"I'll be with you as soon as I get my pants on." The telephone rang while I was buttoning my shirt. "Get it for me, will you?"

"What about the changes?" Forrester asked, while Mac was picking up the phone.

"Get out to the field and work them out with Morrissey."

"It's Los Angeles," McAllister said, covering the mouthpiece with his hand. "We haven't much time."

I looked at him for a moment. "Tell them I just left for a meeting. That they can reach me at the Norman offices in about two hours."

4

IT WAS JUST STARTING TO TURN COOL AND THE girls were coming out of their apartments along Park Avenue, dressed in their summer clothes, their fur stoles draped casually over their shoulders.

Over on Sixth Avenue, the girls were coming out, too. But these girls weren't getting into cabs; they were hurrying toward the subways and disappearing into those gaping maws, glad to be done with their day's work.

New York had a curious twisted form of vitality that belied the general air of depression that hung over the country. Building was going on here despite the moans and groans of Wall Street—office buildings and expensive apartments. If all the money was supposed to be gone, how come so many expensive whores were still living in the best places? It wasn't gone. It had just gone into hiding, burrowing into the ground like a mole, only to emerge when risks were less and profits greater.

On Sixth Avenue, the signs hung dejectedly in front of the employment agencies. The blackboards with their white chalk job listings were already beginning to look tired, and the two-dollar chippies were already beginning their dark sky patrol.

One of them, standing on the fringe of the crowd, turned to look at me as I came by. Her eyes were large and tired and weary and wise. I caught her whisper from almost motionless lips. "You'll be the first today, honey. How about starting the day right?"

I grinned at her and she took it for a sign of encouragement. She came toward me. "Just a deuce," she whispered quickly, "and I'll teach you things you never learned in school."

I stopped, still smiling. "I'll bet you would."

Mac and Dan had walked a few steps farther on. Mac turned back to me, an annoyed look on his face. The woman flashed a quick glance at them, then back at me. "Tell your friends I'll make a special price for all of you. Five bucks."

I dug into my pocket and came up with a dollar, which I pressed into her hand. "Some other time. But I don't think my teachers would approve."

She looked down at the dollar. A glint of humor came into her dark, tired eyes. "It's guys like you spoil a girl and make it tough for her to go to work."

She ducked into a cafeteria across the street as we turned into the lobby of the new RCA Building in Rockefeller Center.

I was still smiling when we walked into the board room. Norman sat at the head of the long table, David Woolf on his right and a man whom I had met at the studio—Ernest Hawley, the treasurer—on his left. Down the table sat our nominees, the two brokerage men, a banker and an accountant.

Dan and Mac took seats on opposite sides of the table, leaving the seat at the end open for me. I started to sit down.

Bernie got to his feet. "Just a minute, Cord," he said. "This meeting is for directors only." He glowered at me. "Before I'd sit at the same table with you, I'd leave myself."

I pulled a package of cigarettes from my pocket and lit one. "Then leave," I said quietly. "You won't have anything to do around here after this meeting anyway."

"Gentlemen, gentlemen," McAllister said quickly. "This is no way to conduct an important meeting. We have many grave problems concerning the future of this company to consider. We'll settle none of them in an atmosphere of distrust."

"Distrust!" Bernie yelled. "You expect me to trust him? After the way he stole my company from me behind my own back!"

"The stock was for sale on the open market and I bought it."

"At what price?" he shouted. "First he forces down the market, then he buys up the stock. Below value he gets it. He don't care how bad he makes the company look while he's doing it. Then he comes to me and expects me to sell my stock at the same depressed price he paid the others."

I smiled to myself. The trading was on. The old man figured the best way to get what he wanted was by attacking me. Already, the propriety of my presence at the meeting had been forgotten. "The price I offered was twice what I paid on the open market."

"You made the market."

"I wasn't running the company," I retorted. "You were—and for the last six years, running it at a loss."

He strode around the table. "And you could do better?"

"If I didn't think so, I wouldn't be putting up better than seven million dollars."

His eyes stared into mine angrily for a moment, then he walked back to his chair and sat down. He picked up a pencil and tapped it on the table in front of him. "The regular meeting of the board of directors of the Norman Picture Company, Incorporated, is hereby called to order," he said in a quieter tone of voice. He looked over at his nephew. "David, you will act as secretary until we appoint a new one."

The old man continued. "A quorum is present, and also present by invitation is Mr. Jonas Cord. Make a note of that, David. Mr. Cord is present by invitation of certain of the directors but over the objection of the President."

He stared at me, waiting for me to react to his statement. I sat there impassively.

"We will now proceed to the first order of business, which is the election of officers of the company for the coming year."

I nodded to McAllister. "Mr. President," he said, "may I suggest that we postpone the election of officers until after you and Mr. Cord have completed discussions regarding the sale of your stock?"

"What makes you think I'm interested in selling my stock?" Bernie asked. "My faith in the future of this company remains as strong as ever. I've made plans to insure the successful operation of this company and if you fellows think you can stop me, I'll throw you into a proxy fight like you never saw before."

Even McAllister had to smile at that. What would he fight with? We were voting forty-one per cent of the stock already. "If the President's concern for the future of this company were as sincere as ours," McAllister said politely, "surely he would see the damage that could be done by starting a proxy fight he couldn't possibly win."

A look of cunning came over Bernie's face. "I'm not such a fool as you think," he said. "I've been busy all afternoon. I got

pledges from enough stockholders to give me control if I fight.
I should live so long as to give up my own company—the company that I built with the sweat of my brow—to Cord so he can
donate more money to his friends the Nazis." He slammed his
fist dramatically down on the table. "No, not even if he gave me
seven million dollars for my stock alone."

I got to my feet, tight-lipped and angry. "I'd like to ask Mr.
Norman what he would do with the seven million dollars if I
did give it to him. Would he donate it to the Jewish Relief
Fund?"

"It's no business of Mr. Cord's what I do with my money,"
he shouted down the table at me. "I'm not a rich man like he is.
All I got is a few shares of my own company."

I smiled. "Mr. Norman, would you like me to read to the
board a list of your liquid assets and holdings, both in your
name and your wife's?"

Bernie looked confused. "List?" he asked. "What list?"

I looked at McAllister. He handed me a sheet of paper from
his brief case. I began to read from it. "Deposits in the name of
May Norman: Security National Bank, Boston—one million,
four hundred thousand; Bank of Manhattan Company, New
York—two million, one hundred thousand; Pioneer National
Trust Company, Los Angeles—seven hundred thousand;
Lehman Brothers, New York—three million, one hundred and
fifty thousand; plus other minor accounts throughout the country amounting to six or seven hundred thousand more. In addition to that, Mrs. Norman owns one thousand acres of prime
real estate in Westwood, near Beverly Hills, conservatively val-
ued at two thousand dollars an acre."

Bernie stared at me. "Where did you get that list?"

"Never mind where I got it."

The old man turned to his nephew. "See, David," he said in a
loud voice, "see what a good wife can save from her house
money."

If he wasn't such a thief, I'd have laughed. But a look at his
nephew's face showed that the boy hadn't known about those
particular assets. Something told me David was in for further
disillusionment.

The old man turned back to me. "So my wife put away a few
dollars. That gives you the right to rob me?"

"During the past six years, while your company was losing

about eleven million dollars, it seems strange to me that your wife should be depositing about a million dollars a year in her various accounts."

Bernie's face was flushed. "My wife is very clever with her investments," he said. "I don't spend my time looking over her shoulder."

"Maybe you should," I said. "You'd find out she has deals with practically every major supplier of equipment and services to the Norman Company. You can't tell me you're not aware that she takes a salesman's commission of from five to fifteen per cent on the gross purchases made by this company."

He sank back into his chair. "So what's wrong with that? It's perfectly normal business practice. She's our salesman on such sales, so why shouldn't she collect a commission?"

I'd had enough of his crap. "All right, Mr. Norman," I said. "Let's stop fooling around. I offered you a better than fair price for your stock. Do you want to sell it or don't you?"

"Not for three and a half million dollars, no. Five and I might listen."

"You're in no position to bargain, Mr. Norman," I said. "If you don't accept my offer, I'll put this company into receivership. Then we'll see if a Federal referee finds anything criminal in your wife's so-called legitimate transactions. You seem to have forgotten that what you do with the company is a Federal matter, since you sold stock on the open market. It's a little different than when you owned it all yourself. You might even wind up in jail."

"You wouldn't dare."

"No?" I said. I held out my hand. McAllister gave me the Section 722 papers. I threw them over to Bernie. "It's up to you. If you don't sell, these papers will be in court tomorrow morning."

He looked down at the papers, then back at me. There was a cold hatred in his eyes. "Why do you do this to me?" he cried. "Is it because you hate Jews so much, when all I tried to do was help you?"

That did it. I went around the table, pulled him out of his chair and backed him up against the wall. "Look, you little Jew bastard," I shouted. "I've had enough of your bullshit. Every time you offered to help me, you picked my pocket. What's bugging you now is I won't let you do it again."

"Nazi!" he spat at me.

Slowly I let him down and turned to McAllister. "File the papers," I said. "And also bring a criminal suit against Norman and his wife for stealing from the company."

I started for the door.

"Just a minute!" Bernie's voice stopped me. There was a peculiar smile on his face. "There's no need for you to go away mad just because I got a little excited."

I stared at him.

"Come back," he said, sitting down at the table again. "We can settle this whole matter between us in a few minutes. Like gentlemen."

I stood near the window, watching Bernie sign the stock transfers. There was something incongruous about the way he sat there, the pen scratching across the paper as he signed away his life's work. You don't have to like a guy to feel sorry for him. And in a way that was just how I felt.

He was a selfish, despicable old man. He had no sense of decency, no honor or ethics, he'd sacrifice anyone on the altar of his power, but as the pen moved across each certificate, I had the feeling his life's blood was running out of the golden nib along with the ink.

I turned and looked out the window, thirty stories down into the street. Down there the people were tiny, they had little dreams, minute plans. The next day was Saturday. Their day off. Maybe they'd go to the beach, or the park. If they had the money, perhaps they'd take a drive out into the country. They'd sit on the grass next to their wives and watch the kids having themselves a time feeling the fresh, cool earth under their feet. They were lucky.

They didn't live in a jungle that measured their worth by their ability to live with the wolves. They weren't born to a father who couldn't love his son unless he was cast in his own image. They weren't surrounded by people whose only thought was to align themselves with the source of wealth. When they loved, it was because of how they felt, not because of how much they might benefit.

I felt a sour taste come up into my mouth. That was the way it might be down there but I really didn't know. And I wasn't particularly anxious to find out. I liked it up here.

It was like being in the sky with no one around to tell you what you could do or couldn't do. In my world, you made up your own rules. And everybody had to live by them whether they liked it or not. As long as you were on top. I meant to stay on top a long time. Long enough so that when people spoke my name, they knew whose name they spoke. Mine, not my father's.

I turned from the window and walked back to the table. I picked up the certificates and looked at them. They were signed correctly. Bernard B. Norman.

Bernie looked up at me. He attempted a smile. It wasn't very successful. "Years ago, when Bernie Normanovitz opened his first nickelodeon on Fourth Street on the East Side, nobody thought he'd someday sell his company for three and a half million dollars."

Suddenly, I didn't care any more. I no longer felt sorry for him. He had raped and looted a company of more than fifteen million dollars and his only excuse was that he had happened to start it.

"I imagine you'll want this, too," he said, reaching into his inside jacket pocket and taking out a folded sheet of paper.

I took it from him and opened it. It was his letter of resignation as president and chairman of the board. I looked at him in surprise.

"Now, is there anything else I can do for you?"

"No," I said.

"You're wrong, Mr. Cord," he said softly. He crossed to the telephone on the table in the corner. "Operator, this is Mr. Norman. You can put that call for Mr. Cord through now."

He held the phone toward me. "For you," he said expressionlessly. I took the telephone and heard the operator's voice. "I have Mr. Cord on the line now, Los Angeles."

There was a click, then another, as the call went through on the other end. I saw Bernie look at me shrewdly, then walk toward the door. He turned and looked at his nephew. "Coming, David?"

Woolf started to get out of his chair.

"You," I said, covering the mouthpiece with my hand. "Stay."

David looked at Bernie, then shook his head slightly and sank back into his chair. The old man shrugged his shoulders. "Why should I expect any more from my own flesh and blood?" he said. The door closed behind him.

A woman's voice came on in my ear. There was something vaguely familiar about it. "Jonas Cord?"

"Speaking. Who's this?"

"Ilene Gaillard. I've been trying to locate you all afternoon. Rina—Rina—" Her voice broke.

I felt an ominous chill tighten around my heart. "Yes, Miss Gaillard," I asked, "what about Rina?"

"She's dying, Mr. Cord," she sobbed into the telephone. "And she wants to see you."

"Dying?" I repeated. I couldn't believe it. Not Rina. She was indestructible.

"Yes, Mr. Cord. Encephalitis. And you'd better hurry. The doctors don't know how long she can last. She's at the Colton Sanitarium in Santa Monica. Can I tell her you're coming?"

"Tell her I'm on my way!" I said, putting down the phone.

I turned to look at David Woolf. He was watching me with a strange expression on his face. "You knew," I said.

He nodded, getting to his feet. "I knew."

"Why didn't you tell me?"

"How could I?" he asked. "My uncle was afraid if you found out, you wouldn't want his stock."

A strange silence came into the room as I picked up the telephone again. I gave the operator Morrissey's number at Roosevelt Field.

"Do you want me to leave now?" Woolf asked.

I shook my head. I had been neatly suckered into buying a worthless company, shorn like a baby lamb, but I had no right to complain. I'd known all the rules.

But now even that didn't matter. Nothing mattered. The only thing that did was Rina. I swore impatiently, waiting for Morrissey to pick up the phone.

The only chance I had of getting to Rina in time was to fly out there in the CA-4.

5

THE BRIGHTLY LIT HANGAR WAS A FRENZY OF ACtivity. The welders were up on the wings, their masks down, their torches burning with a hot blue flame as they fused the reserve fuel tanks to the wings. The pile of junk beside the plane was growing as the mechanics stripped her of everything that added weight and yet was not absolutely essential to flight.

I checked my watch as Morrissey came toward me. It was almost twelve o'clock. That made it near nine in California. "How long now?" I asked.

"Not too long." He looked down at the sheet of paper in his hand. "With everything stripped off her, we're still fourteen hundred pounds over lift capacity."

The Midwest was completely locked in by storms, according to our weather checks. If I wanted to get through, I'd have to fly south around them. Morrissey had figured we'd need forty-three per cent more fuel just for the flight itself and at least seven per cent more for a safety margin.

"Why don't you hold off until morning?" Morrissey asked. "Maybe the weather will lift and you can go straight through."

"No."

"For Christ's sake," he snapped. "You'll never even get her off the ground. If you're that anxious to get yourself killed, why don't you use a gun!"

I turned and looked over at the pile of junk beside the plane. "How much does the radio weigh?"

"Five hundred and ten pounds," he answered quickly. Then he stared at me. "You can't dump that! How the hell will you know where you are or what the weather is like up ahead?"

"Same way I did before they put radios in planes. Dump it!"

He started to walk back to the plane, shaking his head. I had another idea. "The oxygen-pressure system for the cockpit?"

"Six hundred and seventy pounds, including the tanks."

"Dump that, too," I said. "I'll fly low."

"You'll need oxygen to get over the Rockies."

"Put a portable tank in the cockpit next to me."

I went into the office and called Buzz Dalton at the Inter-Continental office in Los Angeles. He'd already left so they transferred the call to his home. "Buzz, this is Jonas."

"I was wondering when I'd hear from you."

"I want you to do me a favor."

"Sure," he said quickly. "What?"

"I'm flying out to the Coast tonight," I said. "And I want you to have weather signals up for me at every ICA hangar across the country."

"What's the matter with your radio?"

"I'm taking the CA-4 out nonstop. And I can't drag the weight."

He whistled. "You'll never make it, buddy boy."

"I'll make it," I said. "Use the searchlight blinkers at night, paint the rooftops during the day."

"Will do," he said. "What's your flight pattern?"

"I haven't decided the pattern yet. Just have all the fields covered."

"Will do," he said. "Good luck."

I put down the telephone. That's what I liked about Buzz. He was dependable. He didn't waste time with foolish questions like why, when or where. He did as he was told. The only thing he cared about was the airline. That was why ICA was rapidly becoming the largest commercial airline in the country.

I took the bottle of bourbon out of the desk and took a long pull off it. Then I went over to the couch and stretched out. My legs hung over the edge but I didn't care. I could grab a little rest while the mechanics were finishing up. I closed my eyes.

I sensed Morrissey standing near me and opened my eyes. "Ready?" I asked, looking up at him.

He nodded.

I swung my feet down from the couch and sat up. I looked out at the hangar. It was empty. "Where is she?"

"Outside," he said. "I'm having her warmed up."

"Good," I said. I looked at my watch. It was a few minutes past three. He followed me into the john. "You're tired," he said, watching while I splashed cold water on my face. "Do you really think you should go?"

"I have to."

"I put six roast-beef sandwiches and two quart Thermos bottles of black coffee in the plane for you."

"Thanks," I said, starting out.

His hand stopped me. He held out a small white bottle. "I called my doctor," he said, "and he brought these out for you."

"What are they?"

"A new pill. Benzedrine. Take one if you get sleepy. It'll wake you up. But be careful with them. Don't take too many or you'll go through the roof."

We started out for the plane. "Don't open your reserve fuel tanks until you're down to a quarter tank. The gravity feed won't pull if she registers more than that and it might even lock."

"How will I know if the reserve tanks are working?" I asked.

He looked at me. "You won't until you run out of gas. And if she locks, the air pressure will keep your gauge at a quarter even if the tank is dry."

I shot a quick look at him but didn't speak. We kept on walking. I climbed up on the wing and turned toward the cockpit. A hand pulled at my trouser leg. I turned around.

Forrester was looking up at me with a shocked look on his face. "What are you doing with the plane?"

"Going to California."

"But what about the tests tomorrow?" he shouted. "I even got Steve Randall out here tonight to look at her."

"Sorry," I said. "Call it off."

"But the General," he yelled. "How'll I explain to him? He'll blow his stack!"

I climbed into the cockpit and looked down at him. "That's not my headache any more, it's yours."

"But what if something happens to the plane?"

I grinned suddenly. I'd been right in my hunch about him. He'd make a first-rate executive. There wasn't an ounce of concern about me, only for the plane. "Then build another one," I shouted. "You're president of the company."

I waved my hand, and releasing the brakes, began to taxi slowly out on the runway. I turned her into the wind and held her there while I revved up the motor. I pulled the canopy shut and when the tachometer reached twenty-eight, I let go of the brakes.

We raced down the runway. I didn't even try to lift her until my ground speed reached a hundred and forty. We were almost out of runway before she began to chew off a piece of sky. After that, she lifted easily.

I leveled off at four thousand feet and headed due south. I looked over my shoulder. The North Star was right in the middle of my back, flickering brightly in the clear, dark sky. It was hard to believe that less than a thousand miles from here the skies were locked in.

I was over Pittsburgh when I remembered something Nevada had taught me when I was a kid. We were trailing a big cat and he pointed up at the North Star. "The Indians have a saying that when the North Star flickers like that," he said, "a storm is moving south."

I looked up again. The North Star was flickering exactly as it had that night. I remembered another Indian saying that Nevada taught me. The quickest way west is into the wind.

My mind was made up. If the Indians were right, by the time I hit the Midwest, the storm would be south of me. I banked the plane into the wind and when I looked up from the compass, the North Star was dancing brightly off my right shoulder.

My back ached, everything ached—my shoulders, my arms and legs—and my eyelids weighed a ton. I felt them begin to close and reached for the coffee Thermos. It was empty. I looked at my watch. Twelve hours since I had left Roosevelt Field. I stuck my hand into my pocket and took out the box of pills Morrissey had given me. I put one in my mouth and swallowed it.

For a few minutes, I felt nothing, then I began to feel better. I took a deep breath and scanned the horizon. The way I figured, I shouldn't be too far from the Rockies. Twenty-five minutes later, they came into view.

I checked the fuel gauge. It held steady on one quarter. I had opened the reserve tanks. The fringe of the storm I'd passed through in the Midwest had cost me more than an hour's supply of gasoline and I'd need a break from the wind to get through.

I turned the throttle and listened to the engines. Their roar sounded full and heavy as the richer mixture poured into their veins. I leaned back on the stick and began to climb toward the mountains. I still felt a little tired so I popped another pill into my mouth.

At twelve thousand feet, I began to feel chilly. I slipped the huarachos back on my feet and reached for the oxygen tube. Almost immediately, I felt as if the plane had just jumped three thousand feet. I looked at the altimeter. It read only twelve four hundred.

I sucked again on the tube. A burst of power came roaring through my body and I placed my hands on the dashboard. To hell with the gasoline! I could lift this baby over the Rockies with my bare hands. It was only a question of will power. Like the fakirs in India said when they confounded you with their tricks of levitation—it was only a question of mind over matter. It was all in the mind.

Rina! I almost shouted aloud. I stared at the altimeter. The needle had dropped to ninety-five hundred feet and was still dropping. I stared over the plane at the mountain creeping up at me. I put my hand on the stick and pulled back. It seemed like forever until the mountain began to fall beneath me again.

I lifted my hands to wipe the sweat from my brow. My cheeks were wet with tears. The strange feeling of power was gone now and my head began to ache. Morrissey had warned me about the pills and the oxygen had helped a little, too. I touched the throttle and carefully regulated the mixture as it went into the motors.

I still had almost four hundred miles to go and I didn't want to run out of gas.

6

I PUT DOWN AT BURBANK AT TWO O'CLOCK. I HAD been in the air almost fifteen hours. I taxied over to the Cord Aircraft hangars, cut the engines and began to climb down. The engines were still roaring in my ears.

I stepped to the ground and a mob surrounded me. I recognized some of them, reporters. "I'm sorry, men," I said, pushing my way through them toward the hangar. "I'm still motor deaf. I can't hear what you're saying."

Buzz was there, too, a big grin on his face. He grabbed my hand and pumped it. His lips were moving but I missed the first part of what he said, then suddenly my hearing was back.

". . . set a new east-to-west coast-to-coast record."

Right now that didn't matter. "Do you have a car waiting for me?"

"Over at the front gate," Buzz said.

One of the reporters pushed forward. "Mr. Cord," he shouted at me. "Is it true you made this flight to see Rina Marlowe before she dies?"

He needed a bath after the look I gave him. I didn't answer.

"Is it true that you bought out Norman Pictures just to get control of her contract?"

I made it into the limousine but they were still popping questions at me. The car began to roll. A motorcycle cop cut in front of us and opened up his siren. We picked up speed as the traffic in front of us melted away.

"I'm sorry about Rina, Jonas," Buzz said. "I didn't know she was your father's wife."

I looked at him. "Where'd you find out?"

"It's in the papers," he said. "The Norman studio had it in their press release, together with the story about your flying out here to see her."

I shut my lips tight. That was the picture business for you. They were like ghouls hovering around a grave.

"I've got a container of coffee and a sandwich here if you want it."

I reached for the coffee. The black stuff was hot and I could feel it reach down inside me. I turned and looked out the window. My back began to throb and ache again.

I wondered if I could wait until we got to the hospital before I went to the bathroom.

The Colton Sanitarium is more like a hotel than a hospital. It's set back high in the Pacific Palisades, overlooking the ocean. In order to reach it, you come off the Coast Highway onto a narrow winding road and there's a guard standing at the iron gate. You get past him only after showing the proper credentials.

Dr. Colton is no California quack. He's just a shrewd man who's recognized the need for a truly private hospital. Movie stars go there for everything from having a baby to taking the cure, plastic surgery to nervous breakdowns. And once inside the iron gate, they can breathe safely and relax, for no reporter has ever been known to get inside. They can feel certain that no matter what they've gone there for, the only word that will ever reach the outside world will be theirs.

The gateman was expecting us, for he began to open the gate the minute he spotted the motorcycle cop. Reporters shouted at us and photographers tried to take pictures. One of them even clung to the running board until we got inside the gate. Then a second guard suddenly appeared and lifted the man off bodily.

I turned to Buzz. "They never give up, do they?"

Buzz's face was serious. "From now on, you'd better get used to it, Jonas. Everything you do will be news."

I stared at him. "Nuts," I said. "That's only for today. Tomorrow it'll be somebody else."

Buzz shook his head. "You haven't seen the papers or listened to the radio today. You're a national figure. Something about what you were doing caught the public imagination. Radio stations gave your flight progress every half hour. Tomorrow the *Examiner* begins running your life story. Nothing like you has swept the country since Lindbergh."

"What makes you say that?"

He smiled. "Today's *Examiner* trucks. They've got billboards with your picture. '*Read the life story of Hollywood's man of mystery*—Jonas Cord. By Adela Rogers St. Johns.'"

I stared at him. I guess I would have to get used to it. St. Johns was Hearst's top syndicated sob sister. That meant the old man up at San Simeon had put the finger of approval on me. From now on, I would be living in a fish bowl.

The car stopped and a doorman appeared. "If you'll kindly step this way, Mr. Cord," he said respectfully.

I followed him up the steps into the hospital. The white-uniformed nurse behind the desk smiled at me. She indicated a black, leather-bound register. "If you please, Mr. Cord," she said. "It's a rule of the hospital that all visitors have to sign in."

I signed the register quickly as she pressed a button underneath the counter. A moment later, another nurse appeared at the desk. "If you'll come with me, Mr. Cord," she said politely, "I'll take you to Miss Marlowe's suite."

I followed her to a small bank of elevators at the rear of the lobby. She pressed the button and looked up at the indicator. A frown of annoyance crossed her face. "I'm sorry to inconvenience you, Mr. Cord, but we'll have to wait a few minutes. Both elevators are up at the operating room."

A hospital was a hospital no matter how hard you tried to make it look like a hotel. I looked around the lobby until I located what I was looking for. It was a door marked discreetly GENTLEMEN.

I pulled a cigarette from my pocket as the elevator doors closed behind us. Inside, it smelled like every other hospital. Alcohol, disinfectant, formaldehyde. Sickness and death. I struck a match and held it to my cigarette, hoping the nurse wouldn't notice my suddenly trembling fingers.

The elevator stopped and the door rolled open. We stepped out into a clean hospital corridor. I dragged deeply on the cigarette as I followed the nurse. She stopped in front of a door. "I'm afraid you'll have to put out that cigarette, Mr. Cord."

I looked up at a small orange sign:

NO SMOKING ALLOWED
OXYGEN IN USE INSIDE!

I took another drag and put it out in a receptacle next to the door. I stood there, suddenly afraid to go inside. The nurse reached around me and opened the door. "You may go in now, Mr. Cord."

The door swung open, revealing a small anteroom. Another nurse was seated in an armchair, reading a magazine. She looked up at me. "Come in, Mr. Cord," she said in a falsely cheerful tone. "We've been expecting you."

I crossed the threshold slowly. I heard the door close behind me and the footsteps of my escort disappearing. There was another door opposite the entrance. The nurse crossed to it. "Miss Marlowe's in here," she said.

I stood in the doorway. At first, I couldn't see her. Ilene Gaillard, a doctor and another nurse were standing next to the bed, their backs toward me. Then, as if activated by some signal, they all turned at once. I walked toward the bed. The nurse moved away and Ilene and the doctor separated slightly to make room for me. Then I saw her.

A clear plastic tent was suspended over her head and shoulders and she seemed to be sleeping. All but her face was completely covered with a heavy white bandage, which hid all her shining white-blond hair. Her eyes were closed and I could see a faint blue tinge under the flesh of the lids. The skin was drawn tightly across her high cheekbones, leaving a hollow around her sunken cheeks, so that you had the feeling that the flesh beneath had disappeared. Her wide mouth, usually so warm and vivid, was pale and drawn back slightly from her even white teeth.

I stood there silently for a moment. I couldn't see her breathe. I looked at the doctor. He shook his head. "She's alive, Mr. Cord," he whispered, "but just barely."

"May I speak to her?"

"You can try, Mr. Cord. But don't be disappointed if she doesn't answer. She's been like this for the last ten hours. And if she should answer, Mr. Cord, she may not recognize you."

I turned back to her. "Rina," I said quietly. "It's me, Jonas."

She lay there quietly, not moving. I put my hand under the plastic tent and found hers. I pressed it. It felt cool and soft. Suddenly everything came to a wild stop inside me. Her hand was cool. She was already dead. She was dead.

I sank to my knees beside the bed. I pushed the plastic aside and leaned over her. "Please, Rina!" I begged wildly. "It's me, Jonas. Please, don't die!"

I felt a slight pressure from her hand. I looked down at her, the tears streaming down my cheeks. The movement of her hand grew a little stronger. Then her eyes opened slowly and she was looking up into my face.

At first, her eyes were vague and far away. Then they cleared and her lips curved into a semblance of a smile. "Jonas," she whispered. "I knew you'd come."

"All you ever had to do was whistle."

Her lips pursed but no sound came out. "I never could learn to whistle," she whispered.

The doctor's voice came from behind me. "You'd better get some rest now, Miss Marlowe."

Rina's eyes went past my shoulder to him. "No," she whispered. "Please. I haven't much time left. Let me speak to Jonas."

I turned to look at the doctor. "All right," he said. "But just for a moment."

I heard the door click behind me, then I looked down at Rina. Her hand lifted slightly and stroked my cheek. I caught her fingers and pressed them to my lips.

"I had to see you, Jonas."

"Why did you wait so long, Rina?"

"That's why I had to see you," she whispered. "To explain."

"What good are explanations now?"

"Please try to understand, Jonas. I loved you from the moment I first saw you. But I was afraid. I've been a jinx to everyone who ever loved me. My mother and my brother died because they loved me. My father died of a broken heart in prison."

"That wasn't your fault."

"I pushed Margaret down the stairs and killed her. I killed my baby even before it was born, stole Nevada's career from him, and Claude committed suicide because of what I was doing to him."

"Those things just happened. You weren't to blame."

"I was!" she insisted hoarsely. "Look what I did to you, to your marriage. I should never have come to your hotel that night."

"That was my fault. I made you."

"Nobody made me," she whispered. "I came because I wanted to. When she came, I knew how wrong I was."

"Why?" I asked bitterly. "Just because she had a belly way out to here? It wasn't even my child."

"What difference does that make? What if she did sleep with someone else before she met you? You must have known it when you married her. If it didn't matter then, why should it have mattered just because she was going to have his child?"

"It did matter," I insisted. "All she was interested in was my money. What about the half-million-dollar settlement she got when the marriage was annulled?"

"That's not true," she whispered. "She loved you. I could tell from the hurt I saw in her eyes. And if the money was so important to her, why did she give it all to her father?"

"I didn't know that."

"There's a lot you don't know," Rina whispered. "But I haven't time to tell you. Only this. I ruined your marriage. It's my fault that poor child is growing up without your name. And I want to make it up to her somehow."

She closed her eyes for a moment. "There may not be much left in my estate," she whispered. "I've never been much good with money, but I've left it all to her and appointed you my executor. Promise me you'll see that she gets it."

I looked down at her. "I promise."

She smiled slowly. "Thank you, Jonas. I always could count on you."

"Now try to rest a little."

"What for?" she whispered. "So I can live another few days in the mad, crazy world that's running around in my head? No, Jonas. It hurts too much. I want to die. But don't let me die here, locked up in this plastic tent. Take me out on the terrace. Let me look at the sky once more."

I stared at her. "The doctor—"

"Please, Jonas."

I looked down at her and she smiled. I smiled back and pushed the oxygen tent aside. I scooped her up in my arms and she was as light as a feather.

"It feels good to be in your arms again, Jonas," she whispered.

I kissed her on the forehead and stepped out into the sunlight. "I'd almost forgotten how green a tree can be," she whispered. "Back in Boston, there's the greenest oak tree you ever saw in your life. Please take me back there, Jonas."

"I will."

"And don't let them make a circus out of it," she whispered. "They can do that in this business."

"I know," I said.

"There's room for me, Jonas," she whispered. "Next to my father."

Her hand fell from my chest and a new kind of weight came into her body. I looked down at her. Her face was hidden against my shoulder. I turned and looked out at the tree that had reminded her of home. But I couldn't see it for my tears.

When I turned around, Ilene and the doctor were in the room. Silently I carried Rina back to the bed and gently laid her down on it. I straightened up and looked at them.

I tried to speak but for a moment, I couldn't. And when I could, my voice was hoarse with my grief. "She wanted to die in the sunlight," I said.

7

I LOOKED AT THE MINISTER, WHOSE LIPS WERE moving silently as he read from the tiny black-bound Bible in his hands. He looked up for a moment, then closed the Bible and started slowly down the walk. A moment later, the others began to follow him and soon Ilene and I were the only ones left at the grave.

She stood there opposite me, skinny and silent, in her black dress and hat, the tiny veil hiding her eyes. "It's over," she said in a tired voice.

I nodded and looked down at the grave marker. Rina Marlowe. Now it was nothing but a name. "I hope everything was the way she wanted it."

"I'm sure it was."

We fell silent then with the awkwardness of two people at a cemetery whose only link now lay in a grave. I took a deep breath. It was time to go. "Can I give you a lift back to the hotel?"

She shook her head. "I'd like to stay here a little while longer, Mr. Cord."

"Will you be all right?"

I caught a glimpse of her eyes beneath the veil. "I'll be all right, Mr. Cord," she said. "Nothing more can happen to me."

"I'll see that a car waits for you. Good-by, Miss Gaillard."

"Good-by, Mr. Cord," she answered formally. "And—and thank you."

I turned and walked down the path to the cemetery road. The morbid and curious were still there behind the police lines, on the far side of the street. A faint sound rose up from them as I came out the cemetery gate. I'd done the best I could but somehow there are always crowds of people.

The chauffeur opened the door of the limousine and I got in. He closed it and ran around to the driver's seat. The car began to move. "Where to, Mr. Cord?" he asked cheerfully. "Back to the hotel?"

I turned and looked out the rear window. We were atop a

small rise and I could see Ilene inside the cemetery. She sat beside the grave, a pitiful, shrunken figure in black, with her face hidden by her two hands. Then we went around a bend and she was gone from my sight.

"Back to the hotel, Mr. Cord?" the chauffeur repeated.

I straightened up and reached for a cigarette. "No," I said, lighting it. "To the airport."

I drew the smoke deep inside my lungs and let it burn there. Suddenly, all I wanted to do was get away. Boston and death, Rina and dreams. I had too many memories as it was.

The roaring filled my ears and I began to climb up the long black ladder out of the darkness over my head. The higher I climbed, the louder the noise got. I opened my eyes.

Outside the window, the Third Avenue El rattled by. I could see the people pressed together inside and on the narrow open platforms. Then the train had passed and a strange silence came into the room. I let my eyes wander.

It was a small, dark room, its white paper already beginning to turn brown on its walls. Near the window was a small table, on the wall over it a crucifix. I was in an old brass bed. Slowly I swung my feet to the floor and sat up. My head felt as if it were going to fall off.

"So, you're awake now, are you?"

I started to turn my head but the woman came around in front of me. There was something vaguely familiar about her face but I couldn't remember where I'd seen her before. I put my hand up and rubbed my cheek. My beard was as rough as sandpaper.

"How long have I been here?" I asked.

She laughed shortly. "Almost a week," she answered. "I was beginnin' to think there was no end to your thirst."

"I was drinking?"

"That you were," she said.

I followed her eyes to the floor. There were three cartons filled with empty whisky bottles. I rubbed the back of my neck. No wonder my head hurt. "How did I happen to get here?" I asked.

"You don't remember?"

I shook my head.

"You came up to me in front of the store on Sixth Avenue and took me by the arm, sayin' you was ready for the lesson now. You were already loaded then. Then we went into the White Rose Bar for a couple of drinks and it was there you got into a fight with the barkeep. So I brought you home for safekeepin'."

I rubbed my eyes. I was beginning to remember now. I had come from the airport and was walking up Sixth Avenue toward the Norman offices when I felt I needed a drink. After that, it was fuzzy. I remembered vaguely searching in front of a radio store for some whore who had promised to teach me some things I had never learned in school.

"Were you the one?" I asked.

She laughed. "No, I wasn't. But in the condition you were in, I didn't think it would make any difference. It wasn't a woman you were looking for, it was a sorrow you were drownin'."

I got to my feet. I was in my shorts. I looked up at her questioningly. "I took your clothes downstairs to the cleaner when you quit drinkin' yesterday. I'll go down now and get them while you're cleanin' up."

"The bathroom?"

She pointed to a door. "There isn't a shower but there's enough hot water for a tub. And there's a razor on the shelf over the sink."

The clothes were waiting for me when I came out of the bathroom. "Your money is on the dresser," she said, as I finished buttoning my shirt and put on my jacket. I walked over to the dresser and picked it up.

"You'll find it all there except what I took for the whisky."

Holding the bills in my hand, I looked at her. "Why did you bring me here?"

She shrugged her shoulders. "The Irish make lousy whores," she said. "We get sentimental over drunkards."

I looked down at the roll of bills in my hand. There was about two hundred dollars there. I took a five-dollar bill and stuck it in my pocket; the rest I put back on the bureau.

She took the money silently and followed me to the door.

"She's dead, you know," she said. "And all the whisky in the world won't be bringin' her back to life."

We stared at each other for a moment, then she closed the

door and I went down the dark staircase and out into the street. I walked into a drugstore on the corner of Third Avenue and Eighty-second Street and called McAllister.

"Where in hell have you been?" he asked.

"Drunk," I said. "Did you get the copy of Rina's will?"

"Yes, I got it. We've been searching the whole town for you. Do you realize what's happening over at the picture company? They're running around there like chickens with their heads cut off."

"Where is the will?"

"On the foyer table of your apartment, where you told me to leave it. If we don't have a meeting about the picture company pretty soon, you won't have to worry about your investment. There won't be any."

"O.K., set one up," I said, hanging up before he had a chance to answer.

I got out, paid the cabby and began to walk along the sidewalk in front of the houses. Children were playing on the grass and curious eyes followed me. Most of the doors were open, so I couldn't read the house numbers.

"Who you lookin' for, mister?" one of the kids called.

"Winthrop," I said. "Monica Winthrop."

"She's got a little girl?" the kid asked. "About five?"

"I think so," I said.

"Fourth house down."

I thanked the kid and started down the street. At the entrance of the fourth house, I looked at the name plate under the bell. Winthrop. There was no answer. I pressed the bell again.

"She's not home from work yet," a man called over to me from the next house. "She stops at the nursery school to pick up the kid first."

"About when does she get home?"

"Any minute now," he said.

I looked at my watch. It was a quarter to seven. The sun was starting to go down and with it went some of the heat of the day. I sat down on the steps and lit a cigarette. My mouth tasted awful and I could feel the beginnings of a headache.

The cigarette was almost finished when Monica turned the corner and started up the walk, a little girl skipping along in front of her.

I got to my feet as the child stopped and looked up at me. Her nose crinkled and her dark eyes squinted. "Mommy," she piped in a high-pitched voice, "there's a man standing on our steps."

I looked at Monica. For a moment, we just stood there staring at one another. She looked the same and yet changed somehow. Maybe it was the way she wore her hair. Or the simple business suit. But most of all, it was her eyes. There was a calm self-assurance in them that hadn't been there before. Her hand reached out and she drew the child to her. "It's all right, Jo-Ann," she said, picking the child up. "He's a friend of Mommy's."

The child smiled. "Hello, man."

"Hello," I said. I looked at Monica. "Hello, Monica."

"Hello, Jonas," she said stiffly. "How are you?"

"O.K. I want to see you."

"About what?" she asked. "I thought everything was settled."

"It's not about us," I said quickly. "It's about the kid."

She held the child closely to her in a sudden gesture. Something like fright came into her eyes. "What about Jo-Ann?"

"There's nothing to worry about," I said.

"Maybe we'd better go inside."

I stepped aside while she opened the door, and followed her into a small living room. She put the child down. "Go into your room and play with your dolls, Jo-Ann."

The child laughed happily and ran off. Monica turned back to me. "You look tired," she said. "Were you waiting long?"

I shook my head. "Not long."

"Sit down," she said quietly. "I'll make some coffee."

"Don't bother. I won't keep you long."

"That's all right," she said quickly. "I don't mind. It isn't often we have visitors."

She went into the kitchen and I sank into a chair. I looked around the room. Somehow, I couldn't get used to the idea that this was where she lived. It looked as if it was furnished from Gimbels basement. Not that it wasn't good. It was just that everything was neat and practical and cheap. And Monica used to be more the Grosfeld House type.

She came back into the room, carrying a steaming cup of black coffee, and put it down on the table next to me. "Two sugars, right?"

"Right."

Quickly she put two lumps of sugar into the coffee and stirred it. I sipped it and began to feel better. "That's good coffee," I said.

"It's G. Washington."

"What's that?"

"The working girl's friend," she said. "Instant coffee. It's really not too bad when you get used to it."

"What will they think of next?"

"Can I get you a couple of aspirins?" she asked. "You look as if you have a headache."

"How do you know?"

She smiled. "We were married for a while once, remember? You get a kind of wrinkle on your forehead when you have a headache."

"Two, then, please," I said. "Thanks."

She sat down opposite me after I'd taken them. Her eyes watched me steadily. "Surprised to see me in a place like this?"

"A little," I said. "I didn't know until just a little while ago that you hadn't kept any of the money I gave you. Why?"

"I didn't want it," she said simply. "And my father did. So I gave it to him. He wanted it for his business."

"What did you want?"

She hesitated a moment before she answered. "What I have now. Jo-Ann. And to be left alone. I kept just enough money to come East and have the baby. Then when she was old enough, I went out and got a job." She smiled. "I know it won't seem like much to you but I'm an executive secretary and I make seventy dollars a week."

I was silent for a moment while I finished the rest of the coffee. "How's Amos?" I asked.

She shrugged her shoulders. "I don't know. I haven't heard from him in four years. How did you find out where I was living?"

"From Rina," I said.

She didn't say anything for a moment. Then she took a deep breath. "I'm sorry, Jonas." I could see sympathy deep in her eyes. "You may not believe me but I'm truly sorry. I read about it in the papers. It was a terrible thing. To have so much and go like that."

"Rina had no surviving relatives," I said. "That's why I'm here."

A puzzled look came over her face. "I don't understand."

"She left her entire estate in trust for your daughter," I said quickly. "I don't know exactly how much, maybe thirty, forty thousand after taxes and debts. She appointed me executor and made me promise to see that the child got it."

She was suddenly pale and the tears came into her eyes. "Why did she do it? She didn't owe me anything."

"She said she blamed herself for what happened to us."

"What happened to us was your fault and mine," she said vehemently. She stopped suddenly and looked at me. "It's foolish to get excited about it at this late date. It's over and done with."

I looked at her for a moment, then got to my feet. "That's right, Monica," I said. "It's over and done with." I started for the door. "If you'll get in touch with McAllister, he'll have all the papers ready for you."

She looked up into my face. "Why don't you stay and let me fix you supper," she said politely. "You look tired."

There was no point in telling her that what she saw was the beginning of a hangover. "No, thanks," I said, equally polite. "I have to get back. I have some business appointments."

A wry, almost bitter look came over her face. "Oh, I almost forgot," she said. "Your business."

"That's right," I said.

"I suppose I should be thankful you took the time to come out." Before I could answer, she turned and called to the child. "Jo-Ann, come out here and say good-by to the nice man."

The little girl came into the room, clutching a small doll. She smiled up at me. "This is my dolly."

I smiled down at her. "It's a nice dolly."

"Say good-by, Jo-Ann."

Jo-Ann held out her hand to me. "Good-by, man," she said seriously. "Come an' see us again. Sometime. Soon."

I took her hand. "I will, Jo-Ann," I said. "Good-by."

Jo-Ann smiled and pulled her hand back quickly, then ran out of the room again.

I straightened up. "Good-by, Monica," I said. "If there's anything you need, give me a call."

"I'll be all right, Jonas," she said, holding out her hand. I took it. She smiled tentatively. "Thank you, Jonas," she said. "And I'm sure if Jo-Ann could understand, she'd thank you, too."

I smiled back. "She's a nice little girl."

"Good-by, Jonas." She took her hand from mine and stood in the open doorway while I went down the walk.

"Jonas," she called after me.

I turned. "Yes, Monica?"

She hesitated a moment, then laughed. "Nothing, Jonas," she said. "Don't work too hard."

I laughed. "I'll try not to."

She closed the door quickly and I continued on down the sidewalk. Forest Hills, Queens, a hell of a place to live. I had to walk six blocks before I could get a cab.

"But what are we going to do about the company?" Woolf asked.

I looked across the table at him, then picked up the bottle of bourbon and refilled my glass. I went to the window and looked out over New York.

"What about *The Sinner?*" Dan asked. "We'll have to decide what to do about that. I'm already talking to Metro about getting Jean Harlow."

I turned on him savagely. "I don't want Harlow," I snapped. "That was Rina's picture."

"But my God, Jonas," Dan exclaimed. "You can't junk that script. It'll cost you half a million by the time you get through paying off De Mille."

"I don't care what it costs!" I snarled. "I'm junking it!"

A silence came over the room and I turned back to the window. Over to my left, the lights of Broadway climbed up into the sky; on my right, I could see the East River. On the other side of that river was Forest Hills. I grimaced and swallowed my drink quickly. Monica had been right about one thing. I was working too hard.

I had too many people on my back, too many businesses. Cord Explosives; Cord Plastics; Cord Aircraft; Inter-Continental Airlines. And now I owned a motion-picture company I didn't even want.

"Well, Jonas," McAllister said quietly. "What are you going to do?"

I walked back to the table and refilled my glass. My mind was made up. I knew just what I was going to do from now on. Only what I wanted to. Let them earn their keep and show me how good they really were.

I stared at Dan Pierce. "You're always talking about how you could make better pictures than anyone in the business," I said. "O.K. You're in charge of production."

Before he had a chance to answer, I turned to Woolf. "You're worried about what's going to happen to the company. Now you can really worry about it. You're in charge of everything else—sales, theaters, administration."

I turned and walked back to the window.

"That's fine, Jonas," McAllister said. "But you haven't told us who the officers will be."

"You're chairman of the board, Mac," I said. "Dan, president. David, executive vice-president." I took a swallow from my glass. "Any more questions?"

They looked at each other, then Mac turned back to me. "While you were away, David had a study made. The company needs about three million dollars of revolving credit to get through this year if we're to maintain the current level of production."

"You'll get a million dollars," I said. "You'll have to make do with that."

"But, Jonas," Dan protested. "How do you expect me to make the kind of pictures I want to make if you won't let us have the money?"

"If you can't do it," I snarled, "then get the hell out and I'll get someone who can."

I could see Dan's face whiten. He closed his lips grimly and didn't answer. I looked from him to the others. "The same thing goes for all of you. From now on, I'm through playing wet nurse to the world. Any man that doesn't deliver can get out. From now on, nobody bothers me about anything. If I want you, I'll get in touch with you. If you have anything to report, put it in writing and send it to my office. That's all, gentlemen. Good night."

As the door closed behind them, I could feel the hard, angry knot tightening in my gut. I looked out the window. Forest Hills. I wondered what kind of schools they had out there that a kid like Jo-Ann could go to.

I swallowed the rest of my drink. It didn't untie the knot; it only pulled it tighter. Suddenly I wanted a woman.

I picked up the phone and called Jose, the headwaiter down at the Rio Club. "Yes, Mr. Cord."

"Jose," I said. "That singer with the rumba band. The one with the big—"

"Eyes," he interrupted, laughing quietly. "Yes, Mr. Cord. I know. She'll be at your place in half an hour."

I put down the telephone and walked back to the table.

I took the bottle to the window with me while I filled my glass. I'd learned something tonight.

People would pay any price for what they really wanted. Monica would live in Queens so she could keep her daughter. Dan would swallow my insults so he could make pictures. Woolf would do anything to prove he could run the company better than his uncle Bernie. And Mac kept on paying the price for the security I'd given him.

When you got down to it, people all had their price. The currency might differ. It could be money, power, glory, sex. Anything. All you needed to know was what they wanted.

A knock came on the door. "Come in," I called.

She came into the room, her dark eyes bright, her long black hair falling down her back almost to her hips, the black gown cut way down in front showing white almost to her navel. She smiled at me. "Hello, Mr. Cord," she said, without the accent she used in the café. "How nice of you to ask me up."

"Take off your dress and have a drink," I said.

"I'm not that kind of girl," she snapped, turning and starting for the door.

"I've got five hundred dollars that says you are."

She turned back to me, a smile on her lips, her fingers already busy with the zipper at the back of her dress. I turned and looked out the window while she undressed.

There weren't as many lights in Queens as there were in Manhattan. And what few lights there were weren't as bright. Suddenly, I was angry and I yanked the cord releasing the Venetian blind. It came down the window with a crash and shut out the city. I turned back to the girl.

She was staring at me with wide eyes. All she had on was a pair of skin-tight black sheer panties, and her hands were crossed over her bosom, hiding only the nipples of her large breasts. "What did you do that for?" she said. "No one out there can see in here."

"I'm tired of looking at Queens," I said and started across the room toward her.

The Story of
DAVID WOOLF

Book Six

1

DAVID WOOLF WALKED INTO THE HOTEL ROOM and threw himself down on the bed fully clothed, staring up at the dark ceiling. The night felt as if it were a thousand years old, even though he knew it was only a little past one o'clock. He was tired and yet he wasn't tired; he was elated and yet, somehow, depressed; triumphant and yet there was the faint bitter taste of intangible defeat stirring within him.

This was the beginning of opportunity, the first faint dawn of his secret ambitions, hopes and dreams. Then why this baffling mixture of emotions? It had never been like this before. He'd always known exactly what he wanted. It had been very simple. A straight line reaching from himself to the ultimate.

It must be Cord, he thought. It had to be Cord. There could be no other reason. He wondered if Cord affected the others in the same way. He still felt the shock that had gone through him when he entered the suite and saw him for the first time since the night Cord had left the board meeting to fly to the Coast.

Fifteen days had passed, two weeks during which panic had set in and the company had begun to disintegrate before his eyes. The whispering of the employees in the New York office still echoed in his ears, the furtive, frightened, worried glances cast as he passed them in the corridor. And there had been nothing he could do about it, nothing he could tell them. It was as if the corporation lay suspended in shock, awaiting the transfusion that would send new vitality coursing through its veins.

And now, at last, Cord sat there, a half-empty bottle of bourbon in front of him, a tortured, hollow shell of the man they had seen just a few short weeks ago. He was thinner and exhaustion had etched its weary lines deeply into his cheeks. But it was only when you looked into his eyes that you realized it wasn't a physical change that had taken place. The man himself had changed.

At first, David couldn't put his finger on it. Then, for a brief moment, the veil lifted and suddenly he understood. He sensed the man's unique aloneness. It was as if he were a visitor from another world. The rest of them had become alien to him, almost like children, whose simple desires he had long ago outgrown. He would tolerate them so long as he found a use for them, but once that purpose was served he would withdraw again into that world in which he existed alone.

The three of them had been silent as they came down in the elevator after leaving Cord's suite. It wasn't until they stepped out into the lobby and mingled with the crowd that was coming in for the midnight show on the Starlight Roof that McAllister spoke. "I think we'd better find a quiet spot and have a little talk."

"The Men's Bar downstairs. If it's still open," Pierce suggested.

It was and when the waiter brought their drinks, McAllister lifted his glass. "Good luck," they echoed, then drank and placed their glasses back on the table.

McAllister looked from one to the other before he spoke. "Well, from here on in, it's up to us. I wish I could be more direct in my contribution," he said in his somewhat stilted, formal manner. "But I'm an attorney and know almost nothing about motion pictures. What I can do, though, is to explain the reorganization plan for the company that Jonas approved before the deal was actually consummated."

It wasn't until then that David had got any idea of how

farseeing Jonas had been—retiring the old common stock in exchange for new shares, the issuance of preferred stock to meet certain outstanding debts of the corporation and debentures constituting a mortgage lien on all the real properties of the company, including the studio and theaters, in exchange for his putting up a million dollars' working capital.

The next item McAllister covered was their compensation. David and Dan Pierce would be offered seven-year employment contracts with a salary starting at sixty-five thousand dollars and increasing thirteen thousand dollars each year until the expiration of the agreement. In addition, each would be reimbursed completely for his expenses and bonused, if there were profits, to the amount of two and one half per cent, which could be taken either in stock or in cash.

"That's about it," McAllister said. "Any questions?"

"It sounds good," Dan Pierce said. "But what guarantee have we got that Jonas will keep us in business once the million dollars is gone? None at all. But he's completely covered by his stock and debentures."

"You're right," McAllister agreed. "You have no guarantee, but then, neither has he any guarantee about what his stock will be worth if your operation of the company should prove unsuccessful. As I see it, it's up to you two to make it work."

"But if the study David made is correct," Dan continued, "we won't be halfway through our first picture before we'll be unable to meet our weekly payroll. I don't know what got into Jonas. You can't make million-dollar pictures without money."

"Who says we have to make million-dollar pictures?" David asked quietly.

Suddenly, the whole pattern was very clear. Now he was beginning to understand what Jonas had done. At first, he had felt a disappointment at not being put in charge of the studio. He would have liked the title of President on his door. But Cord had cut through the whole business like a knife through butter. In reality, the studio was only a factory turning out the product of the company. Administration, sales and theaters were under his control and that was where the money came from. Money always dictated studio policy and he controlled the money.

"For a million bucks, we can turn out ten pictures. And be taking in revenue from the first before the fifth goes into production."

"Not me," Dan said quickly. "I haven't come this far in the business just to make quickies. That's for Republic or Monogram."

"Columbia, Warners and RKO aren't too proud," David said, a new hardness coming into his voice.

"Let them if they want to," Dan snapped. "I've got a reputation to maintain."

"Don't give me that crap," David exploded. "The only thing this business respects is success. And they don't care how you get it so long as it adds up at the box office. The whole industry knows you maneuvered Cord into buying the company so you could become a producer. You won't have any reputation left if you walk out."

"Who said anything about walking out?"

David relaxed in his chair. A new feeling of power came over him. Now he understood why his Uncle Bernie had found it so difficult to let go. He shrugged his shoulders. "You heard what Cord said. If you won't do it, somebody else will."

Pierce stared at him for a moment, then looked at McAllister. The attorney's face was impassive. "That's all very well for you to say," Pierce grumbled. "But while I'm out there getting my brains kicked in, what're you going to be doing?"

"Seeing to it that we survive long enough for you to get your production program working," David answered.

"How?" McAllister asked, an interested look coming over his face.

"Tomorrow I'm laying off forty per cent of personnel throughout the company."

"That's pretty drastic," McAllister said. "Will you be able to function under those conditions?"

David watched the attorney's face. This was another kind of test. "We'll be able to function," he said quietly.

"That's no way to make friends," Pierce injected.

"I couldn't care less," David replied caustically. "I'm not trying to win a popularity contest. And that will be only the beginning. I don't care who gets hurt—the company is going to survive."

For a moment, the attorney stared at him. Then David saw a frosty glimmer of a smile lurking deep in his eyes. McAllister turned to Dan. "What do you think?"

Dan was smiling. "I think we'll make it. Why do you think Jonas wanted him to stick around?"

McAllister reached into his brief case. "There's your contract," he said to David. "Jonas wants you to sign it tonight."

David stared at the lawyer. "What about Dan?"

McAllister smiled. "Dan signed his the day of the board meeting."

For a moment, David felt anger climbing up inside him. The whole thing had been an act. They had put him through the wringer just to see what would happen. Then he drew in his breath. What difference did it make? He reached for the fountain pen the attorney held out toward him.

This was only the beginning. They were still outsiders and it would be a long time before they knew as much about the company as he did. And by that time, it wouldn't matter any more.

Once he signed the contract, he was in charge.

The connecting door between his room and his uncle's opened and light spilled through into the darkness. "Are you in there, David?"

He sat up on the bed and swung his feet to the floor. He reached out and turned on the lamp next to the bed. "Yes, Uncle Bernie."

Norman came into the room. "*Nu?*" he said. "You saw him?"

David nodded, reaching for a cigarette. "I saw him." He lit the cigarette. "He looks terrible. Rina's death must have hit him pretty hard."

The old man laughed. "Sorry for him I can't feel," he said bitterly. "Not after what he's done to me." He took a cigar from his pocket and stuck it into his mouth unlit. "He offered you a job, no?"

David nodded.

"What job?"

"Executive vice-president."

His uncle raised his eyebrows. "That so?" he asked interestedly. "Who's president?"

"Dan Pierce. He's going to make the pictures. I'm to run everything else—administration, sales and theaters."

The cigar bobbed up and down excitedly in the old man's mouth. A broad smile came over his face. "My boy, I'm proud of you." He clapped his hand on David's shoulder. "I always said someday you'd amount to something."

David looked at his uncle in surprise. This wasn't the reaction he had expected. An accusation of betrayal would have been more like it. "You are?"

"Of course I am," Bernie said enthusiastically. "What else did I expect of my own sister's son?"

David stared up at him. "I thought—"

"Thought?" the old man said, still smiling. "What difference does it make what you thought? Bygones is bygones. Now we can really put our heads together. I'll show you ways to make money you never dreamed about."

"Make money?"

"Sure," Bernie replied, lowering his voice to a confidential tone. "A *goyishe kopf* is always a *goyishe kopf*. With you in charge, who will know what's going on? Tomorrow, I'll let all the suppliers know the old deal is still on. Only now you get twenty-five per cent of the kickback."

"Twenty-five per cent?"

"What's the matter?" Bernie asked shrewdly. "Twenty-five per cent isn't enough for you?"

David didn't answer.

"So your Uncle Bernie ain't a *chazer.* All right. Fifty, then."

David ground out his cigarette in the ash tray. He got to his feet and walked silently to the window. He looked down into the park across the street.

"What's the matter?" his uncle said behind him. "Fifty-fifty ain't fair? You owe me something. If it wasn't for me, you'd never have got this job."

David felt his bitterness rise up into his throat. He turned and looked at the old man. "I owe you something?" he said angrily. "Something for all those years you kept me hustling my tail off for a lousy three fifty a week? Every time I asked you for more money you cried about how much the company was losing. And all the time, you were siphoning off a million bucks a year into your own pocket."

"That was different," the old man said. "You don't understand."

David laughed. "I understand all right, Uncle Bernie. What I understand is that you've got fifteen million dollars free and clear. If you live to be a thousand, you couldn't spend all you've got. And still you want more."

"So what's wrong with that?" Bernie demanded. "I worked for it. I'm entitled to it. You want I should let go everything just because some *shlemiel* screwed me out of my own business?"

"Yes."

"You take the side of that—that Nazi against your own flesh and blood?" the old man shrieked at him, his face flushing angrily.

David stared at the old man. "I don't have to take sides, Uncle Bernie," he said quietly. "You yourself have admitted it's not your company any more."

"But you're running the company."

"That's right." David nodded. "I'm running the company. Not you."

"Then you're keeping everything for yourself?" the old man said accusingly.

David turned his back on his uncle, without speaking. For a moment, there was silence, then his uncle's voice. "You're even worse than him," Bernie said bitterly. "At least, he wasn't stealing from his own flesh and blood."

"Leave me alone, Uncle Bernie," David said without turning around. "I'm tired. I want to get some sleep."

He heard the old man's footsteps cross the room and the door slam angrily behind him. He leaned his head wearily against the side of the window. So that was why the old man hadn't gone back to California right after the meeting. He felt a lump come into his throat. He didn't know why but suddenly he felt like crying.

The faint sound of a clanging bell came floating up to him from the street. He moved his head slightly, looking out of the window. The clanging grew louder as an ambulance turned west on to Fifty-ninth from Fifth Avenue. He turned and walked slowly from the window back into the room, the clanging growing fainter in his ears. All his life it had been like that, somehow.

When he rode up front on the junk wagon, with his father sitting next to him on the hard wooden seat, it had seemed that was the only sound he'd ever heard. The clanging of a bell.

2

THE COWBELLS SUSPENDED ACROSS THE WAGON behind him clanged lazily as the weary horse inched along through the pushcarts that lined both sides of Rivington Street. The oppressive summer heat beat down on his head. He let the reins lay idle in his fingers. There wasn't much you could do to guide the horse. It would pick its own way through the crowded street, moving automatically each time a space opened up.

"Aiyee caash clothes!" His father's singsong call penetrated the sounds of the market street, lifting its message high to the windows of the tenements, naked, blind eyes staring out unseeing into the hungry world.

"Aiyee caash clothes!"

He looked down from the wagon to where his father was striding along the crowded sidewalk, his beard waving wildly as his eyes searched the windows for signs of business. There was a certain dignity about the old man—the broad-brimmed black beaver hat that had come from the old country; the long black coat that flapped around his ankles; the shirt with its heavily starched but slightly wilted wing collar; and the tie with the big knot resting just below his prominent Adam's apple. The face was pale and cool, not even a faint sign of perspiration dampened the brow, while David's was dripping with sweat. It seemed almost as if the heavy black clothing provided insulation against the heat.

"Hey, Mister Junkman!"

His father moved out into the gutter to get a better look. But it was David who saw her first—an old woman waving from the fifth-floor window. "It's Mrs. Saperstein, Pop."

"You think I can't see?" his father asked, grumbling. "Yoo-hoo, Mrs. Saperstein!"

"Is that you, Mr. Woolf?" the woman called down.

"Yes," the old man shouted. "What you got?"

"Come up, I'll show to you."

"I don't want winter clothes," the old man shouted. "Who's to buy?"

"Who said about winter clothes? Come up, you'll see!"

"Tie the horse over there," his father said, pointing to an open space between two pushcarts. "Then come to carry down the stuff."

David nodded as his father crossed the street and disappeared into the entrance of a house. He nudged the horse over and tied it to a fire hydrant. Then he slipped a feed bag over its weary muzzle and started after his father.

He felt his way up through the dark, unlit hallway and staircase and stopped outside the door. He knocked. The door opened immediately. Mrs. Saperstein stood there, her long gray hair folded in coils on top of her head. "Come in, come in."

David came into the kitchen and saw his father sitting at the table. In front of him was a plate filled with cookies. "A *gluz tay*, David?" the old woman asked, going to the stove.

"No, thanks, Mrs. Saperstein," he answered politely.

She took a small red can from the shelf over the stove, then carefully measured two teaspoonfuls of tea into the boiling water. The tea leaves immediately burst open and spun around madly on the surface. When she finally poured the tea into a glass through a strainer and set it in front of his father, it was almost as black as coffee.

His father picked up a lump of sugar from the bowl and placed it between his lips, then sipped the tea. After he swallowed the first scalding mouthful, he opened his mouth and said, "Ah!"

"Good, isn't it?" Mrs. Saperstein was smiling. "That's real tea. Swee-Touch-Nee. Like in the old country. Not like the *chazerai* they try to sell you here."

His father nodded and lifted the glass again. When he put it back on the table, it was empty and the polite formalities were over. Now it was time to attend to business. "*Nu*, Mrs. Saperstein?"

But Mrs. Saperstein wasn't quite ready to talk business yet. She looked over at David. "Such a nice boy, your David," she said conversationally. "He reminds me of my Howard at his age." She picked up the plate of cookies and held it toward him. "Take one," she urged. "I baked myself."

David took a cooky and put it in his mouth. It was hard and dry and crumbled into little pieces. "Take another," she urged. "You look thin, you should eat."

David shook his head.

"Mrs. Saperstein," his father said. "I'm a busy man, it's late. You got something for me?"

The old woman nodded. *"Kim shayn."*

They followed her through the narrow railroad flat. Inside one room, on the bed, were a number of men's suits, some dresses, shirts, one overcoat and, in paper bags, several pairs of shoes.

David's father walked over and picked up some of the clothing. "Winter clothing," he said accusingly. "For this I came up four flights of stairs?"

"Like new, Mr. Woolf," the old woman said. "My son Howard and his wife. Only one season. They were going to give to the Salvation Army but I made them send to me."

David's father didn't answer. He was sorting out the clothing rapidly.

"My son Howard lives in the Bronx," she said proudly. "In a new house on Grand Concourse. A doctor."

"Two dollars for the *ganse gesheft*," his father announced.

"Mr. Woolf," she exclaimed. "At least twenty dollars this is worth."

He shrugged. "The only reason I'm buying is to give to HIAS. Better the Salvation Army don't get."

David listened to their bargaining with only half a mind. HIAS was the abbreviation that stood for Hebrew Immigrant Aid Society. His father's statement didn't impress him one bit. He knew the clothing would never find its way there. Instead, after it was carefully brushed and cleaned by his mother, it would turn up in the windows of the secondhand clothing stores along the lower Bowery and East Broadway.

"Ten dollars," Mrs. Saperstein was saying. The pretense was gone now; she was bargaining in earnest. "Less I wouldn't take. Otherwise, it wouldn't pay my son Howard to bring it down. It costs him gas from the Bronx."

"Five dollars. Not one penny more."

"Six," the old woman said, looking at him shrewdly. "At least, the gasoline money he should get."

"The subways are still running," David's father said. "I should pay because your son is a big shot with an automobile?"

"Five fifty," the old woman said.

David's father looked at her. Then he shrugged his shoulders and reached under his long black coat. He took out a purse, tied to his belt by a long black shoestring, and opened it. "Five fifty," he sighed. "But as heaven is watching, I'm losing money."

He gestured to David and began counting the money out into the old woman's hand. David rolled all the clothing into the overcoat and tied it by the sleeves. He hefted the clothing onto his shoulder and started down the stairs. He tossed the bundle of clothing up into the cart and moved around to the front of the wagon. He lifted the feed bag from the horse, and untying the reins from the hydrant, climbed on the wagon.

"Hey, Davy!"

He looked down at the sidewalk. A tall boy stood there looking up at him and smiling. "I been lookin' for yuh all day."

"We been in Brooklyn," David answered. "My father will be here in a minute."

"I'll make it quick, then. Shocky'll cut yuh in for ten bucks if yuh bring the horse an' wagon tonight. We got to move a load uptown."

"But it's Friday night."

"That's why. The streets down here will be empty. There won't be nobody to wonder what we're doin' out at night. An' the cops won't bother us when they see the junky's license on the wagon."

"I'll try," David said. "What time, Needlenose?"

"Nine o'clock back of Shocky's garage. Here comes your ol' man. See yuh later."

"Who were you talking to?" his father asked.

"One of the fellers, Pop."

"Isidore Schwartz?"

"Yeah, it was Needlenose."

"Keep away from him, David," his father said harshly. "Him we don't need. A bum. A nogoodnik. Like all those other bums that hang around Shocky's garage. They steal everything they can get their hands on."

David nodded.

"Take the horse to the stable. I'm going to the *shul*. Tell Mama by seven o'clock she should have supper ready."

Esther Woolf stood in front of the *Shabbas nacht lichten*, the prayer shawl covering her head. The candles flickered into yellow flame as she held the long wooden match to them. Carefully she blew out the match and put it down in a plate on the small buffet table. She waited until the flame ripened into a bright white glow, then began to pray.

First, she prayed for her son, her *shaine Duvidele*, who came so late in life, almost when she and her husband, Chaim, had given up hope of being blessed. Then she prayed that Jehovah would give her husband, Chaim, a greater will to succeed, at the same time begging the Lord's forgiveness because it was the Lord's work at the *shul* that kept her husband from his own. Then, as always, she took upon herself the sin for having turned Chaim away from his chosen work.

He had been a Talmudical student when they'd first met in the old country. She remembered him as he was then, young and thin and pale, with the first soft curl of his dark beard shining with a red-gold glint. His eyes had been dark and luminous as he sat at the table in her father's house, dipping the small piece of cake into the wine, more than holding his own with the old rabbi and the elders.

But when they'd been married, Chaim had gone to work in her father's business. Then the pogroms began and the faces of Jews became thin and haunted. They left their homes only under the cover of night, hurrying about like little animals of the forest. Or they sat huddled in the cellars of their houses, the doors and windows barred and locked, like chickens trying to hide in the pen when they sense the approach of the *shochet*.

Until that night when she could stand it no longer. She rose screaming from the pallet at her husband's side, the letter from her brother Bernard, in America, still fresh in her mind. "Are we to live like rabbits in a trap, waiting for the Cossacks to come?" she cried. "Is it into this dark world that my husband expects I should bring forth a child? Even Jehovah could not plant his seed in a cellar."

"Hush!" Chaim's voice was a harsh whisper. "The name of the Lord shall not be taken in vain. Pray that He does not turn His face from us."

She laughed bitterly. "Already He has forsaken us. He, too, is fleeing before the Cossacks."

"Quiet, woman!" Chaim's voice was an outraged roar.

She looked at the other pallets in the damp cellar. In the dim light, she could barely see the pale, frightened faces of her parents. Just then there was a thunder of horses' hoofs outside the house and the sound of a gun butt against the locked door.

Quickly, her father was on his feet. "Quick, *kinder*," he whispered. "The storm cellar door at the back of the house. Through the fields, they won't see you leaving that way."

Chaim reached for Esther's hand and pulled her to the storm door. Suddenly, he stopped, aware that her parents were not following them. "Come," he whispered. "Hurry! There is no time."

Her father stood quietly in the dark, his arm around his wife's shoulder. "We are not going," he said. "Better someone be here for them to find or they will begin searching the fields."

The din over their heads grew louder as the gun butts began to break through the door. Chaim walked back to her father. "Then we all stay and face them," he said calmly, picking a heavy stave up from the floor. "They will learn a Jew does not die so easily."

"Go," her father said quietly. "We gave our daughter in marriage. It is her safety that should be your first concern, not ours. Your bravery is nothing but stupidity. How else have Jews survived these thousand years except by running?"

"But—" Chaim protested.

"Go," the old man hissed. "Go quickly. We are old, our lives are finished. You are young, your children should have their chance."

A few months later, they were in America. But it was to be almost twenty years before the Lord God Jehovah relented and let her have a child.

Last, she prayed for her brother Bernard, who was a *macher* now and had a business in a faraway place called California, where it was summer all year round. She prayed that he was safe and well and that he wasn't troubled by the Indians, like she saw in the movies when she used the pass he'd sent her.

Her prayers finished, she went back into the kitchen. The soup was bubbling on the stove, its rich, heavy chicken aroma almost visible in the air. She picked up a spoon and bent over the pot. Carefully she skimmed the heavy fat globules from the surface and put them in a jar. Later, when the fat was cold and had congealed, it could be spread on bread or mixed with chopped dry meats to give them flavor. While she was bent like this over the stove, she heard the front door open.

From the footsteps, she knew who it was. "That you, Duvidele?"

"Yes, Mama."

Her task finished, she put down the spoon and turned around slowly. As always, her heart leaped with pride as she saw her son, so straight and tall, standing there.

"Papa went to *shul*," David said. "He'll be home at seven o'clock."

She smiled at him. "Good," she said. "So wash your hands and clean up. Supper is ready."

3

WHEN DAVID TURNED THE HORSE INTO THE LIT-
tle alley that led to the back of Shocky's garage, Needlenose came hurrying up. "Is that you, David?"

"Who did yuh think it would be?" David retorted sarcastically.

"Geez, we didn't know whether you'd show up or not. It's almost ten o'clock."

"I couldn't sneak out until my old man went to sleep," David said, stopping the wagon at the side of the garage.

A moment later, Shocky came out, his bald head shining in the dim light. He was of medium height, with a heavy barrel chest and long tapering arms that reached almost to his knees. "You took long enough gettin' here," he grumbled.

"I'm here, ain't I?"

Shocky didn't answer. He turned to Needlenose. "Start loading the cans," he said. "He can help you."

David climbed down from the wagon and followed Shocky into the garage. The long row of metal cans gleamed dully in the light from the single electric bulb hanging high in the ceiling. David stopped and whistled. "There must be forty cans there."

"So he can count," Shocky said.

"That's four hundred pounds. I don't think Old Bessie can haul that much."

Shocky looked at him. "You hauled that much last time."

"No, I didn't," David said. "It was only thirty cans. And even then, there were times I thought Old Bessie was goin' to croak on me. Suppose she did? There I'd be with a dead horse and two hundred gallons of alky in the wagon. It's bad enough if my old man ever finds out."

"Just this once," Shocky said. "I promised Gennuario."

"Why don't you use one of your trucks?"

"I can't do that," Shocky replied. "That's just what the Feds are lookin' for. They won't be lookin' for a junk wagon."

"The most I'll take is twenty-five cans."

Shocky stared at him. "I'll make it twenty bucks this one time," he said. "You got me in a bind."

David was silent. Twenty dollars was more than his father netted in a whole week, sometimes. And that was going out with the wagon six days a week. Rain or shine, summer heat or bitter winter cold, every day except Saturday, which his father spent in *shul*.

"Twenty-five bucks," Shocky said.

"O.K. I'll take a chance."

"Start loadin', then." Shocky picked up a can with each of his long arms.

David sat alone on the wagon seat as Old Bessie slowly plodded her way uptown. He pulled up at a corner to let a truck go by. A policeman slowly sauntered over. "What're ye doin' out tonight, Davy?"

Furtively David cast a look at the back of the wagon. The cans of alcohol lay hidden under the tarpaulin, covered with rags. "I heard they're payin' a good price for rag over at the mill," he answered. "I thought I'd clean out the wagon."

"Where's your father?"

"It's Friday night."

"Oh," the policeman answered. He looked up at David shrewdly. "Does he know ye're out?"

David shook his head silently.

The policeman laughed. "You kids are all alike."

"I better get goin' before the old man misses me," David said. He clucked to the horse and Old Bessie began to move. The policeman called after him and David stopped and looked back.

"Tell your father to keep an eye peeled for some clothes for a nine-year-old boy," he called. "My Michael is outgrowin' the last already."

"I will, Mr. Doyle," David said and flicked the reins lightly. Shocky and Needlenose were already there when David pulled up against the loading platform. Gennuario stood on the platform watching as they began to unload.

The detectives appeared suddenly out of the darkness with drawn guns. "O.K., hold it!"

David froze, a can of alcohol still in his arms. For a moment, he thought of dropping the can and running but Old Bessie and the wagon were still there. How would he explain that to his father?

"Put the can down, boy," one of the detectives said.

Slowly David put down the can and turned to face them. "O.K., against the wall."

"Yuh shouldn't 'a' tried it, Joe," a detective said to Gennuario when he arrived.

Gennuario smiled. David looked at him. He didn't seem in the least disturbed by what had happened. "Come inside, Lieutenant," he said easily. "We can straighten this out, I'm sure."

The lieutenant followed Gennuario into the building and it seemed to David that they were gone forever. But ten minutes later, they came out, both smiling.

"All right, you guys," the lieutenant said. "It seems we made a big mistake. Mr. Gennuario explained everything. Let's go." As quickly as they had come, the detectives disappeared. David stood staring after them with an open mouth.

Needlenose sat silently on the wagon beside David as they turned into the stable. "I tol' yuh everything was fixed," he said when they came out in the street.

David looked at him. Fixed or not, this was as close as he wanted. Even the twenty-five dollars in his pocket wasn't worth it. "I'm through," he said to Needlenose. "No more."

Needlenose laughed. "Yuh scared?"

"Damn right I'm scared. There must be an easier way to make a living."

"If yuh find one," Needlenose said, "let me know." He laughed. "Shocky's got a couple of Chinee girls over at his flat. He says we can screw 'em tonight if we want."

David didn't answer.

"Sing Loo will be there," Needlenose said. "You know, the pretty little one, the dancer who shaves her pussy."

David hesitated, feeling the quick surge of excitement leap through him.

It was one o'clock by the big clock in the window of Goldfarb's Delicatessen when he turned the corner of his street. A police car was parked in front of the door. There was a group of people surging around, peering curiously into the hallway.

A sudden fear ran through David. Something had gone wrong. The police had come to arrest him. For a moment, he felt like running in the opposite direction. But a compulsion drew him toward the house. "What happened?" he asked a man standing on the edge of the crowd.

"I dunno," the man answered. He peered at him curiously. "I heard one of the cops say somebody was dying up there."

Suddenly, frantically, David pushed his way through the crowd into the house. As he ran up the staircase toward the apartment on the third floor, he heard the scream.

His mother was standing in the doorway, struggling in the arms of two policemen. "Chaim, Chaim!"

David felt his heart constrict. "Mama," he called. "What happened?"

His mother looked at him with unseeing eyes. "A doctor I call for, policemen I get," she said, then turned her face down the hallway toward the toilets. "Chaim, Chaim!" She screamed again.

David turned and followed her gaze. The door to one of the toilets stood open. His father sat there on the seat, leaning crazily against the wall, his eyes and mouth open, moisture trickling down into his gray beard.

"Chaim!" his mother screamed accusingly. "It was gas you told me you got. You didn't tell me you were coming out here to die."

4

"SO IT'S MY FAULT HIS FATHER DIES BEFORE HE can finish school?" Uncle Bernie said angrily. "Let him get a job and go nights if he wants to go so bad."

David sat on the edge of his chair and looked at his mother.

He didn't speak. "It's not charity I'm asking, Bernie," she said. "David wants a job. That's all I'm asking you for."

Norman turned and looked down at his nephew suspiciously. "Maybe a job you'd like in my company as a vice-president, hah?"

David got to his feet angrily. "I'm going out, Ma," he said. "Everything they said about him is true."

"Say about me?" his uncle shouted. "What do they say about me?"

David looked at him. "Down at the *shul* when I went to say *Yiskor* for Papa, they told me about you. They said you didn't come to the funeral because you were afraid somebody might ask you for a few pennies."

"From California I should come in one day?" Norman shouted. "Wings I ain't got."

He started for the door. "Wait a minute, David," his mother said quietly. She turned to her brother. "When you needed five hundred dollars before the war for your business, who did you get it from?"

She waited a moment before answering herself. "From your poor *schnorrer* of a brother-in-law, Chaim, the junkman. He gave you the money and you gave him a piece of paper. The piece of paper I still got but did we ever see the money?"

"Paper?" Bernie said. "What paper?"

"I still got it," she said. "In the box Chaim put it in that night, the night he gave you the money."

"Let me see." Bernie's eyes followed her as she left the room. He was beginning to remember now. It was a certificate promising his brother-in-law five per cent of the Norman Company stock when he bought out the old Diamond Film Company. He had forgotten all about it. But a smart lawyer could make it worth a lot of money.

His sister came back into the room and handed him a sheet of paper. It was faded and yellow but the date on it was still bright and clear. September 7, 1912. That was fourteen years ago. How time had flown.

He looked at his sister. "It's against my policy to hire relatives," he said. "It looks bad for the business."

"So who's to know he's your nephew?" Esther said. "Besides, who will do more for you than your own flesh and blood?"

He stared at her for a moment, then got to his feet. "All right, I'll do it. It's against my better judgment but maybe you're right. Blood is thicker than water. Over on Forty-third Street, near the river, we got a warehouse. They'll put him to work."

"Thank you, Uncle Bernie," David said gratefully.

"Mind you, not one word about being my nephew. One word I hear and you're finished."

"I won't say anything, Uncle Bernie."

Norman started for the door. But before he went out, he turned, the paper in his hand. He folded it and put it into his pocket. "This I'm taking with me," he said to his sister. "When I get back to my office, they'll send you a check for the five hundred dollars with interest for the fourteen years. At three per cent."

A worried look came over his sister's face. "Are you sure you can afford it, Bernie?" she asked quickly. "There is no hurry. We'll manage if David is working."

"Afford it, shmafford it," Norman said magnanimously. "Let nobody say that Bernie Norman doesn't keep his word."

It was a dirty gray factory building down near the Hudson River, which had fallen into disuse and been converted into lofts. There were two large freight elevators in the back and three small passenger elevators near the front entrance, scarcely large enough to handle the crowd of workers that surged in at eight o'clock each morning and out at six o'clock each night.

The building was shared by five tenants. The ground floor housed an automobile-parts company; the second, a commercial cosmetic manufacturer; the third, the pressing plant for a small record company; the fourth, the factory of the Henri France Company, the world's largest manufacturer of popular-priced contraceptives and prophylactics. The fifth and sixth floors belonged to Norman Pictures.

David arrived early. He got off the elevator on the sixth floor and walked slowly down the wide aisle between rows of steel and wooden shelves. At the end, near the back windows, were several desks, placed back to back.

"Hello," David called. "Anybody here?" His voice echoed eerily through the cavernous empty floor. There was a clock over one of the desks. It said seven thirty.

The freight-elevator door clanged open and a white-haired man stuck his head out and peered down the aisle at David. "I thought I heard somebody calling," he said.

David walked up to him. "I'm supposed to see the foreman about a job."

"Oh, are you the one?"

David was confused. "What d'yuh mean?"

"The new boy," the elevator operator replied. "Old man Norman's nephew."

David didn't answer. He was too surprised. The elevator operator got ready to swing shut the doors. "Nobody's here yet. They don't get in till eight o'clock."

The steel doors closed and the elevator moved creakingly down out of sight. David turned from the elevator thoughtfully. Uncle Bernie had told him not to say anything. He hadn't. But they already knew. He wondered if his uncle knew that they knew. He started back toward the desks.

He stopped suddenly in front of a large poster. The lettering was in bright red— *Vilma Banky and Rod LaRocque*. The picture portrayed Miss Banky lying on a sofa, her dress well up above her knees. Behind her stood Mr. LaRoque, darkly handsome in the current Valentino fashion, staring down at her with a look of smoldering passion.

David studied the poster. A final touch had been added by someone in the warehouse. A milky-white condom hung by a thumbtack from the front of the male star's trousers. Next to it, in neat black lettering, were the words: *Compliments of Henri France*.

David grinned and began to walk up the aisle. He looked into the steel bins. Posters, lobby cards, displays were stacked there, each representing a different motion picture. David looked them over. It was amazing how much each looked like the next one. Apparently, the only thing the artist did was to change the names of the players and the title of the picture.

He heard the passenger elevator stop, then the sound of footsteps echoed down the aisle. He turned and waited.

A tall, thin man with sandy-red hair and a worried look on his face turned the corner near the packing tables. He stopped and looked at David silently.

"I'm David Woolf. I'm supposed to see the foreman about a job here."

"I'm the foreman," the man said. He turned away and walked over to one of the desks. "My name is Wagner. Jack Wagner."

David held out his hand. "I'm pleased to meet you, Mr. Wagner."

The man looked at the outstretched hand. His handshake was soft and indecisive. "You're Norman's nephew," he said accusingly.

Suddenly, David realized the man was nervous, more nervous even than he was himself. He wondered why. It didn't make sense that the man should be upset because of his relationship to Uncle Bernie. But he wasn't going to talk about it, even though it seemed everyone knew.

"Nobody is supposed to know that but me," Wagner said. "Sit down here." He pointed to a chair near the desk, then took out a sheet of paper and pushed it over to David. "Fill out this personnel application. Where it asks for the name of any relatives working for the company, leave that one blank."

"Yes, sir."

Wagner got up from behind the desk and walked away. David began to fill out the form. Behind him, he heard the passenger-elevator doors open and close. Several men walked by. They glanced at him furtively as they walked over to their packing tables and began to get out equipment. David turned back to the form.

At eight o'clock, a bell rang and a faint hum of activity began to permeate the building. The day had begun.

When Wagner came back, David held out the application. Wagner looked it over carelessly. "Good," he said vaguely, and dropping it back on his desk, walked away again.

David watched him as he talked to the man at the first packing table. They turned their backs and David was sure they were discussing him. He began to feel nervous and lit a cigarette. Wagner looked over at him and the worried look on his face deepened.

"You can't smoke in here," he called to David. "Can't you read the signs?"

"Oh, I'm sorry," David answered, looking around for an ash tray. There wasn't any. Suddenly, he was aware that work had stopped and everyone was looking at him. He felt the nervous perspiration breaking out on his forehead.

"You can smoke in the can," Wagner called, pointing to the back of the warehouse. David walked down the aisle to the back, until he found the men's room. Suddenly he felt a need to relieve himself and stepped up to a urinal.

The door behind him opened and he sensed a man standing beside him. *"Khop tsech tu,"* he said.

David stared at him. The man grinned back, exposing a mouth filled with gold teeth. "You're Chaim Woolf's boy," he said in Yiddish.

David nodded.

"I'm the Sheriff. Yitzchak Margolis. From the Prushnitzer Society, the same as your father."

No wonder the word had got around so quickly. "You work here?" David asked curiously.

"Of course. You think I come this far uptown just to piss?" He lowered his voice to a confidential whisper. "I think it's very smart of your uncle to put you in here."

"Smart?"

The Sheriff nodded his bald head. "Smart," he repeated in the same stage whisper. "Now they got something to worry about. Too long they been getting way with murder. All you got to do is look at the tickets."

"Tickets?" David asked.

"Yeah, the shipping tickets. I pack three times in a day what it takes any of them a week. Me, I don't have to worry. But the loafers, let them worry about their jobs."

For the first time, David began to understand. The men were afraid of him, afraid for their jobs. "But they don't have to worry," he burst out. "I'm not going to take their jobs."

"You're not?" Margolis asked, a puzzled look in his eyes.

"No. I'm here because I need the job myself."

A disappointed look came over the Sheriff's face. Suddenly a shrewd look came into his eyes. "Smart," he said. "A smart boy. Of course you won't take away anybody's job. I'll tell 'em."

He started out. At the door, he stopped and looked back at David. "You remind me of your uncle," he said. "The old fart never lets his left hand know what his right hand is doing."

The door closed behind him and David flipped his cigarette into the urinal. He was half way down the aisle when he met Wagner.

"You know how to work a fork lift?"

"The kind they use to lift bales?"

The foreman nodded. "That's the kind I mean."

"Sure," David answered.

The anxious look left Wagner's eyes for a moment. "Good," he said. "There's a shipment of five hundred thousand heralds downstairs on the platform. Bring it up."

5

THE ELEVATOR JARRED TO A STOP AT THE GROUND floor and the heavy doors opened on the busy loading platform. Several trucks were backed up to the platform and men were scurrying back and forth, loading and unloading. Along the back wall of the platform were stacks of cartons and materials.

David turned to the elevator operator. "Which is the stuff I'm supposed to bring up?"

The man shrugged his shoulders. "Ask the platform boss. I jus' run the elevator."

"Which is the platform boss?"

The elevator operator pointed at a heavy-set man in an undershirt. Thick black hair spilled out from his chest and sprouted furiously from his forearms. His features were coarse and heavy and his skin had the red flush of a heavy drinker. David walked over to him.

"What d'yuh want?" he asked.

"Mr. Wagner sent me to pick up the heralds."

The platform boss squinted at him. "Wagner, huh? Where's Sam?"

David stared at him. "Sam?"

"Sam the receiving clerk, yuh dope."

"How the hell do I know?" David asked. He was beginning to get angry.

The platform boss looked over his head at the elevator operator. "They didn't can Sam to give this jerk a job, did they?" he yelled.

"Naw. I seen him workin' upstairs at one of the packing tables."

The platform boss turned back to David. "Over there." He pointed. "Against the wall."

The heralds were stacked on wooden racks in bundles of a thousand. There were four racks, one hundred and twenty-five bundles on each. David rolled the fork lift over to one and set the two prongs under it. He threw his weight back against the handles, but his one hundred and thirty pounds wasn't enough to raise the rack off the floor.

David turned around. The platform boss was grinning. "Can't you give me a lift with this?"

The man laughed. "I got my own work to do," he said derisively. "Tell ol' man Norman he hired a boy to do a man's job."

David was suddenly aware of the silence that had come over the platform. He looked around. The elevator operator had a peculiar smirk on his face; even the truck drivers were grinning. Angrily he felt the red flush creep up into his face. They were all in on it. They were waiting for the boss's nephew to fall flat on his face. He pulled a cigarette absently from his pocket and started to light it.

"No smoking on the platform," the boss said. "Down in the street if yuh want to smoke."

David looked at him a moment, then silently walked down the ramp to the street. He heard a burst of laughter behind him. The platform boss's voice carried. "I guess we showed the little Jew bastard where to get off!"

He walked around the side of the building and lit his cigarette. He wondered if they were all in on it. Even the foreman upstairs, Wagner, hadn't been exactly happy to see him He must have given him the job knowing he didn't have the weight to swing a fork lift.

He looked across the street. There was a garage directly opposite and it gave him an idea.

Fifty cents to the mechanic and he came back, pushing the big hydraulic jack the garage used for trucks. Silence came over the platform again as he jockeyed the jack under the wooden rack. Quickly he pumped the handle and the rack lifted into the air.

In less than five minutes, David had the four racks loaded on the elevator. "O.K.," he said to the operator. "Let's take her up." He was smiling as the doors clanged shut on the scowling face of the platform boss.

The men looked up from their packing tables as the elevator

door swung open. "Wait a minute," he said to the elevator operator. "I'll go ask Wagner where he wants these."

He walked down the aisle to the foreman's empty desk. He turned and saw the men watching from their tables. "Where's Wagner?"

They looked at each other awkwardly for a moment. Finally, the Sheriff answered him. "He's in the can, sneaking a smoke."

David thanked him and walked down the back aisle to the washroom. The foreman was talking to another man, a cigarette in his hand. David came up behind him. "Mr. Wagner?"

Wagner jumped. He turned around, a strange expression on his face. "What's the matter, David?" he asked angrily. "Can't you get those heralds up?"

David stared at him. The foreman was in on it, all right. They were all in on it. He laughed bitterly to himself. And Uncle Bernie had said it was going to be a secret.

"Well," the foreman said irritably, "if you can't do it, let me know."

"They're up here now. I just want to know where to put them."

"You got them up here already?" Wagner said. His voice lost the faint note of sureness it had contained a moment before.

"Yes, sir."

Wagner threw his cigarette in the urinal. "Good," he said, a faintly puzzled look on his face. "They go over on Aisle Five. I'll show you which bins."

It was almost ten thirty by the time David had the racks empty and the bins filled. He pushed the last package of heralds into place and straightened up. He felt the sweat streaming through his shirt and looked down at himself. The clean white shirt that his mother had made him wear was grimy with dust. He wiped his forehead on his sleeve and walked down to the foreman's desk. "What do you want me to do next?"

"Were there five hundred bundles?" the foreman asked.

David nodded.

The foreman pushed a sheet of paper toward him. "Initial the receipt slip, then."

David looked over the paper as he picked up a pencil. It was the bill for the heralds: "500 M Heralds @ $1.00 per M—

$500.00." Expensive paper, he thought, as he scribbled his initials across the bottom.

The telephone on the desk rang and the foreman picked it up. "Warehouse."

David could hear a voice crackling at the other end, though he could not distinguish the words. Wagner was nodding his head. "Yes, Mr. Bond. They just came in."

Wagner looked over at David. "Get me a sample of one of those heralds," he said, shielding the phone with his hand.

David nodded and ran down the aisle. He pulled a herald from one of the bundles and brought it back to the foreman. Wagner snatched it from his hand and looked at it. "No, Mr. Bond. It's only one color."

The voice on the other end of the telephone rose to a shriek. Wagner began to look uncomfortable, and shortly afterward, put the receiver down slowly. "That was Mr. Bond in purchasing."

David nodded. He didn't speak.

Wagner cleared his throat uncomfortably. "Those heralds we just got. It was supposed to be a two-color job."

David looked down at the black-and-white handbill. He couldn't see what they were so excited about. After all, they were only throw-aways. What difference did it make whether it was one color or two?

"Mr. Bond says to junk 'em."

David looked at him in surprise. "Junk 'em?"

Wagner nodded and got to his feet. "Get them out of the bins and downstairs again." he said. "We'll need the space. The new ones will be here this afternoon."

David shrugged. This was a screwy business, when something could be junked even before it was paid for. But it was none of his concern. "I'll get right on it."

It was twelve thirty when he came out on the loading platform, pushing the first rack of heralds. The platform boss yelled. "Hey, where yuh goin' with that?"

"It's junk."

The platform boss walked over and looked into the elevator. "Junk, eh?" he asked. "All of it?"

David nodded. "Where shall I put it?"

"You ain't puttin' it no place," the boss said. "Beat it right back upstairs an' tell Wagner to shell out five bucks if he expects me to get rid of his junk."

Again David could feel his anger rising slowly.

Wagner was at his desk when David got back upstairs. "The platform boss wants five bucks to get rid of that junk."

"Oh, sure," Wagner said. "I forgot." He took a tin box out of his desk and opened it. He held out a five-dollar bill.

David stared down at it. "You mean you really got to give to him?" he asked in disbelief.

Wagner nodded.

"But that's good newspaper stock," David said. "My father would haul that away all day long. It's worth a dime a hundredweight. That batch would bring fifty bucks at any junk yard."

"We haven't the time to bother with it. Here, give him the five bucks and forget about it."

David stared at him. Nothing in this business made any sense to him. They junked five hundred dollars' worth of paper before they'd paid for it, then didn't even want to salvage fifty bucks out of it. They'd rather pay five bucks more just to get rid of it.

His uncle couldn't be as smart as they said he was if he ran his business like this. He must be lucky. If it wasn't luck, then his father would have been a millionaire. He took a deep breath. "Do I get an hour for lunch, Mr. Wagner?"

The foreman nodded. "Sure. We all do."

"Is it all right if I start my lunch hour now?"

"You can start right after you take care of the heralds."

"If it's all right with you," David said, "I'll get rid of them on my lunch hour."

"It's O.K. with me, but you don't have to. You get a full hour off for lunch."

David looked at the telephone. "May I make a call?"

Wagner nodded and David called Needlenose at Shocky's garage. "How quick can you get here with a truck?" he asked, quickly explaining the deal.

"Twenty minutes, Davy," Needlenose said. There was a moment's silence, then Needlenose came on again. "Shocky says he'll only blast yuh ten bucks for the truck."

"Tell him it's a deal," David said quickly. "And bring along a pair of dusters. We might have a little trouble."

"Gotcha, Davy," Needlenose said.

"O.K., I'll be out in front."

Wagner looked at him anxiously as he put down the telephone. "I don't want any trouble," he said nervously.

David stared at him. If they were all so afraid of him they wouldn't let him do his job, he might as well give them something to be afraid of. "You'll know what trouble is, Mr. Wagner, if Uncle Bernie ever finds out you've been spending five dollars to lose fifty."

The foreman's face suddenly went pale. A faint beading of perspiration came out on his forehead. "I don't make the rules," he said quickly. "I just do what purchasing tells me."

"Then you've got nothing to worry about."

Wagner put the five-dollar bill back in the tin box, then put the box back in his desk and locked the drawer. He got to his feet. "I think I'll go to lunch," he said.

David sat down in the foreman's chair and lit a cigarette, ignoring the no-smoking sign. The men at the packing tables were watching him. He stared back at them silently. After a few minutes, they began to leave, one or two at a time, apparently on their way to lunch. Soon the only one left was the Sheriff.

The old man looked up from the package he was tying. "You take my word for it," he said. "It ain't worth you getting killed over. That Tony downstairs, he's a Cossack. You tell your uncle to give you a different job."

"How can I do that, pop?" David asked. "It was tough enough talking him into this one. If I come cryin' to him now, I might as well quit."

The old man walked over toward him. "You know where they went?" he asked in a shrill voice. "All of them? They didn't go to lunch. They're downstairs in the street. They're waiting to see Tony kill you."

David dragged on his cigarette thoughtfully.

"How come five bucks is that important?"

"From every tenant in the building he gets a little payoff. He can't afford to let you off the hook. Then he loses everybody."

"Then he's a *shmuck*," David said, suddenly angry. "All I wanted to do was my job. Nothing would have happened; he could still have gone on collecting his little graft."

David got to his feet and threw the cigarette on the floor. He ground it out under his heel. There was a bitter taste in his mouth. The whole thing was stupid. And he was no smarter than the rest; he let himself fall right into the trap they'd prepared for him. He couldn't back down now even if he wanted to. Neither could he afford to lose the fight downstairs. If he did, his uncle sure as hell would hear about it. And that would be the end of the job.

Needlenose was waiting for him downstairs.

"Where's the truck?" David asked.

"Across the street. I brought the dusters. Which ones do you want—plain or spiked?"

"Spiked."

Needlenose's hand came out of his pocket and David took the heavy set of brass knuckles. He looked down at them. The round, pointed spikes shone wickedly in the light. He slipped them into his pocket.

"How do we handle the guy?" Needlenose asked. "Chinee style?"

It was a common trick in Chinatown. A man in front, a man behind. The victim went for the man in front of him and got clipped from the rear. Nine times out of ten, he never knew what hit him. David shook his head. "No," he said. "I gotta take care of this one myself if it's going to do any good."

"The guy'll kill yuh," Needlenose said. "He's got fifty pounds on yuh."

"If I get into trouble, you come and get me out."

"If you get into trouble," Needlenose said dryly, "it'll be too late to do anything except bury yuh."

David looked at him, then grinned. "In that case, send the bill to my Uncle Bernie. It was all his idea. Let's go."

6

THEY WERE WAITING, ALL RIGHT. THE SHERIFF had been right. The whole building knew what was going to happen. Even some girls from the cosmetic company and Henri France.

It was hot and David felt the perspiration coming through his clothing. The platform had been a clatter of sound— people talking, pretending to eat their sandwiches or packed lunches. Now the pretense was gone, conversations and lunches forgotten.

The wave of silence rolled over him and he felt their curious, almost detached stares. Casually he looked over the crowd. He recognized several of the men from the packing tables upstairs. They averted their eyes when he passed by.

Suddenly, he was sick inside. This was madness. He was no hero. What purpose would it serve? What was so big about this lousy job that he had to get himself killed over it? Then he saw the platform boss and he forgot it all. There was no turning back.

It was the jungle all over again—the streets down on the East Side, the junk yards along the river, and now a warehouse on Forty-third Street. Each had its little king who had to be ever ready to fight to keep his little kingdom—because someone was always waiting to take it away from him.

A great realization came to David and with it a surge of strength and power. The world was like this; even his uncle, sitting way up on top there was a king in his own way. He wondered how many nights Uncle Bernie stayed awake worrying about the threats to his empire.

Kings had to live with fear—more than other people. They had more to lose. And the knowledge was always there, buried deep inside them, that one day it would be over. For kings were human, after all, and their strength would lessen and their minds would not think as quickly. And kings must die and their heirs inherit. It would be that way with the platform boss and it would be that way with his Uncle Bernie. Someday, all this would be his, for he was young.

"Get the truck," he said, out of the corner of his mouth.

Needlenose walked down the ramp and across the street to where the truck was parked. David turned and pushed the big jack over to the nearest wooden rack. He pumped the handle and the rack lifted off the floor. He came to the edge of the loading platform just as Needlenose backed the truck to a stop.

Needlenose came down from behind the wheel. "Want a hand, Davy?"

"I'll manage," David said. He pushed the loaded jack onto the open platform of the truck and pulled the release. The wooden platform sank to the truck floor. He sneaked a look at the platform boss as he went back for the next rack of heralds. The man hadn't moved.

A faint hope began to stir inside David. Maybe he'd been

wrong, maybe they'd all been wrong. He rolled the last rack onto the truck and pulled the release. There wasn't going to be a fight after all.

He heard a faint sigh come from the people on the platform as he turned the jack around to wheel it off the truck. He looked up. The platform boss was standing there, blocking the end of the truck. Stolidly David pushed the jack toward him. As he neared the platform boss, he put his foot on the front of the jack and stared at David silently. David looked down at his foot. The thick-soled, heavy-toed work boot rested squarely on the front of the jack.

David looked up at the man and tried to push the jack up onto the loading platform. The platform boss's foot moved quickly. The handle of the jack was torn from David's grasp and the jack itself skidded to the side, the front half completely off the truck. Its wheels spun in the narrow space between the loading platform and the truck. The nervous sigh came again from the crowd.

The platform boss spoke in a flat voice. "It'll cost yuh five bucks to get off that truck, Jew boy," he said. "If yuh ain't got it, jus' stay there!"

David slipped his hand into his pocket. The metal was icy cold against his fingers as he slipped the brass knuckles over his hand. "I got something for you," he said quietly, as he walked toward the man, his hand still in his pocket.

"Now you're getting smart, Jew boy," the boss said, his eyes turning away from David toward the crowd. It was at that moment David hit him. He felt the shock of pain run up his arm as the duster tore into the man's face. A half scream of pain came from his throat as the metal spikes tore his cheek open like an overripe melon.

He turned, swinging wildly at David, the blow catching him on the side of the head, slamming him back against the side of the truck. David could feel his forehead beginning to swell. It had to be a quick fight or the man would kill him. He shook his head to clear it and looked up to see the platform boss coming at him again. He braced his feet against the side of the truck and using the added leverage this gave him, lashed out at the man's face.

The blow never reached its target. The platform boss caught

it on his raised arm but it spun him backward toward the edge of the platform. Again David lashed out at him. He sidestepped the blow but stumbled and fell from the platform to the ground.

David leaned over the big hydraulic jack and looked down at him. He was getting to his hands and knees. He turned his face up to David, the blood running down his cheeks, his lips drawn savagely back across his teeth. "I'll kill yuh for this, yuh Jew bastard!"

David stared down at him. The man was up on one knee. "You wanted it like this, mister," David said as he reached for the handle of the jack.

The platform boss screamed once as the heavy jack came down on him. Then he lay quietly, face on the ground, the jack straddling his back like a primeval monster.

Slowly David straightened up, his chest heaving. He stared at the crowd. Already they were beginning to melt away, their faces white and frightened. Needlenose climbed up on the truck. He looked down at the platform boss. "Yuh think yuh croaked him?"

David shrugged. He slipped the brass knuckles into his friend's pocket. "You better get the truck out of here."

Needlenose nodded and climbed behind the wheel as David stepped across onto the loading platform. The truck pulled out into the street just as Wagner came up with a policeman. The policeman looked at David. "What happened?"

"There's been an accident," David answered.

The policeman looked down at the platform boss. "Call an ambulance," he said quickly. "Somebody help me get this thing off him."

David turned and went up in the freight elevator. He heard the clanging of the ambulance while he was in the bathroom, washing up. The door behind him opened and he turned around.

The Sheriff was standing there, a towel in his hand. "I thought you could use this."

"Thanks." David took the towel and soaked it in hot water, then held it to his face. The heat felt soothing. He closed his eyes. The sound of the ambulance grew fainter. "You all right?" the old man asked.

"I'm O.K.," David answered.

He heard the old man's footsteps. The door closed behind him and David took the towel from his face. He stared at himself in the mirror. Except for a slight lump on his temple, he looked all right. He rinsed his face with cold water and dried it. Leaving the towel hanging over the edge of the sink, he walked out.

A girl was standing near the staircase, wearing the blue smock with Henri France lettered on the pocket. He stopped and looked at her. She looked vaguely familiar. She must have been one of the girls he had seen downstairs.

She smiled at him boldly, revealing not too pretty teeth. "Is it true you're old man Norman's nephew?"

He nodded.

"Freddie Jones, who runs your still lab, says I ought to be in pictures. He had me pose for him."

"Yeah?"

"I got them here," she said. "Want to see 'em?"

"Sure."

She smiled and took some photographs out of her pocket. He took the pictures and looked at them. This Freddie, whoever he was, knew how to take pictures. She looked much better without a smile. And without her clothes.

"Like 'em?"

"Yeah."

"You can keep 'em," she said.

"Thanks."

"If you get a chance, show 'em to your uncle sometime," she said quickly. "Lots of girls get started in pictures that way."

He nodded.

"I seen what happened downstairs. It was sure time that Tony got his lumps."

"You didn't like him?"

"Nobody liked him," she said. "But they were all afraid of him. The cop asked me what happened. I told him it was an accident. The jack fell on him."

He looked into her eyes. They were hard and shining.

"You're nice," she said. "I like you." She took something out of her pocket and gave it to him. It looked like a small tin of aspirin but the lettering read: *Henri France De Luxe*.

"You don't have to worry about those," she said. "They're the best we make. You can read a newspaper through 'em. I inspected and rolled them myself."

"Thanks."

"Got to get back to work," she said. She walked back to the stairway. "See yuh."

"See yuh." He looked down at the small tin in his hand and opened it. She was right. You could read right through them. There was a slip of paper in the bottom. Written on it in black pencil was the name Betty and a telephone number.

Wagner was sitting at his desk when David walked by. "You were pretty lucky," he said. "The doctor said that all Tony has is a concussion and a couple of broken ribs. He'll need twelve stitches in his cheek, though."

"He was lucky," David said. "It was an accident."

The supervisor's gaze fell before his. "The garage across the street wants ten bucks to fix the jack."

"I'll give it to them tomorrow."

"You don't have to," Wagner said quickly. "I already did."

"Thanks."

The foreman looked up from his desk. His eyes met David's squarely. "I wish we could pretend this morning never happened," he said in a low voice. "I'd like to start all over again."

David stared at him for a moment. Then he smiled and held out his hand. "My name is David Woolf," he said. "I'm supposed to see the foreman about a job."

The foreman looked at David's hand and got to his feet. "I'm Jack Wagner, the foreman," he said, and his grip was firm. "Let me introduce you to the boys."

When David turned toward the packaging tables, all the men were grinning at him. Suddenly, they weren't strangers any more. They were friends.

7

BERNARD NORMAN WALKED INTO HIS NEW YORK office. It was ten o'clock in the morning and his eyes were bright and shining, his cheeks pink from the winter air, after his brisk walk down from the hotel.

"Good morning, Mr. Norman," his secretary said. "Have a nice trip?"

He smiled back at her as he walked on into his private office and opened the window. He stood there breathing in the cold fresh air. Ah, this was *geshmach*. Not like the day-in, day-out sameness of California.

Norman went over to his desk and took a large cigar from the humidor. He lit it slowly, relishing the heavy aromatic Havana fragrance. Even the cigars tasted better in New York. Maybe, if he had time, he'd run down to Ratner's on Delancey Street and have blintzes for lunch.

He sat down and began to go over the reports lying on his desk. He nodded to himself with satisfaction. The billings from the exchanges were up over last year. He turned to the New Yorker theater reports. The Norman Theater, his première house on Broadway, had picked up since they started having stage shows along with the picture. It was holding its own with Loew's State and the Palace. He leafed through the next few reports, then stopped and studied the report from the Park Theater. An average gross of forty-two hundred dollars a week over the past two months. It must be a mistake. The Park had never grossed more than three thousand tops. It was nothing but a third-run house on the wrong side of Fourteenth Street.

Norman looked further down the report and his eyes came to rest on an item labeled Employee Bonuses. They were averaging three hundred a week. He reached for the telephone. Somebody must be crazy. He'd never O.K.'d bonuses like that. The whole report must be wrong.

"Yes, Mr. Norman?" his secretary's voice came through.

"Tell Ernie to get his ass in here," Norman said. "Right away." He put down the telephone. Ernie Hawley was his treasurer. He'd be able to straighten this out.

Hawley came in, his eyes shadowed by his thick glasses. "How are you, Bernie?" he asked. "Have a good trip?"

Norman tapped the report on his desk. "What's with this on the Park Theater?" he said. "Can't you bastards get anything right?"

Hawley looked confused. "The Park? Let's see it."

Norman gave him the report, then leaned back in his chair, savagely puffing at his cigar. Hawley looked up. "I can't see anything wrong with this."

"You can't?" Norman said sarcastically. "You think I don't know the Park never grossed more than three thousand a week since it was built? I'm not a dope altogether."

"The gross on the report is correct, Bernie. Our auditors check it every week."

Bernie scowled at him. "What about those employee bonuses? Twenty-four hundred dollars in the last two months! You think I'm crazy? I never O.K.'d anything like that."

"Sure you did, Bernie," Hawley replied. "That's the twenty-five-per cent manager's bonus we set up to help us over the slump after Christmas."

"But we set the top gross for the theaters as a quota," Norman snapped. "We figured out it would cost us next to nothing. What figure did we use for the Park?"

"Three thousand."

Bernie looked down at the report. "It's a trick," he said. "Taubman's been stealing us blind. If he wasn't, how come all of a sudden he's grossing forty-two hundred?"

"Taubman isn't managing the theater now. He's been out with appendicitis since right after Christmas."

"His signature's on the report."

"That's just a rubber stamp. All the managers have them."

"So who's managing the theater?" Norman asked. "Who's the wise guy beating us out of three hundred a week?"

Hawley looked uncomfortable. "We were in a spot, Bernie. Taubman caught us at a bad time; we didn't have anybody else to send in."

"So stop beating around the bush and tell me already," Norman snapped.

"Your nephew, David Woolf," the treasurer said reluctantly.

Norman clapped his hand to his head dramatically. "Oy! I might have known."

"There wasn't anything else we could do." Hawley reached for a cigarette nervously. "But the kid did a good job, Bernie. He made tie-ins with all the neighborhood stores, pulled in some give-aways and he swamps the neighborhood with heralds twice a week. He even started what he calls family night, for Monday and Tuesday, the slow nights. A whole family gets in for seventy-five cents. And it's working. His candy and popcorn sales are four times what they were."

"So what's the extra business costing us?"

Again the treasurer looked uncomfortable. "It added a little to operating expenses but we figure it's worth it."

"So?" Norman said. "Exactly how much?"

Hawley picked up the report. He cleared his throat. "Somewhere between eight and eight fifty a week."

"Somewhere between eight and eight fifty a week," Bernie repeated sarcastically. He got to his feet and glared at the treasurer. "A bunch of *shmucks* I got working for me," he shouted suddenly. "The whole increase does nothing for us. But for him it's fine. Three hundred a week extra he puts in his pocket."

He turned and stormed over to the window and looked out. The cold air came in through the open frame. Angrily he slammed down the window. The weather was miserable here, not warm and sunny like it was in California.

"I wouldn't say that," Hawley said. "When you figure the over-all, including the concession sales, we're netting a hundred and fifty a week more."

Norman turned around. "Nine hundred a week of our money he spends to make himself three hundred. We should maybe give him a vote of thanks that he lets us keep the hundred and fifty?" His voice rose to a shrill shriek. "Or maybe it's because he ain't yet figured out a way to beat us out of that!"

He stamped back to his desk angrily. "I don't know what it is, but every time I come to New York, I got to find *tsoris!*" He threw the cigar into the wastebasket and took a new one from the humidor. He put it between his lips and began to chew it.

"A year and a half ago, I come to New York and what do I find? He's working by the warehouse a little over a year and already he's making more on it than we do. A thousand a year he's making selling junked heralds, two thousand selling dirty pictures he's printing by the hundreds on our photo paper in our own still laboratory. A concession he's developed in all our offices around the country selling condoms wholesale. It's a lucky thing I stopped him, or we all would have wound up in jail."

"But you got to admit, Bernie, the warehouse never ran more smoothly," Hawley said. "That rotating perpetual inventory saved us a fortune in reorders."

"Hah," Norman exclaimed. "You think he thought about us

when he did it? Don't be a fool! Seventeen dollars a week his salary was and every day he drives to work in a twenty-three-hundred-dollar Buick."

Bernie struck a match and held it to his cigar, puffing rapidly until it was lit. Then he blew out a gust of smoke and threw the match into the ash tray. "So I put him into the Norman as an assistant manager. Everything will be quiet now, I think. I can sleep in peace, I think. What trouble can he make for me in a big house like that?

"Trouble, hah!" He laughed bitterly. "Six months later, when I come back, I find he's turned the theater into a whorehouse and bookie joint! All the vaudeville acts in the country suddenly want to play the Norman. And why shouldn't they? Does Loew's State or the Palace have the prettiest usherettes on Broadway, ready to hump from ten o'clock in the morning until one o'clock at night? Does Loew's or the Palace have an assistant manager who'll take your bet on any track in the country, you shouldn't ever have to leave your dressing room?"

"But Gallagher and Shean, Weber and Fields, and all the other big acts played the house, didn't they?" Hawley asked. "And they're still playing it. It made the theater for us."

"It's a lucky thing I got him out of there and sent him to the Hopkins in Brooklyn before the vice squad got wise," Norman said. "Now I don't have a worry, I think. He can stay there as assistant manager the rest of his life. What can he do to us in Brooklyn, I think. I go back to the Coast, my mind at ease. I can forget about him."

Suddenly, he got to his feet again. "So six months later, I come back and what do I find? He's making a monkey out of the whole company. He's taking home more money than a vice-president."

Hawley looked at him. "Maybe that's what you ought to do."

"What?"

"Make him a vice-president," Hawley said.

"But—but he's only a kid," Norman said.

"He was twenty-one last month. He's the type boy I'd like on our side."

"No," Norman said, sinking back into his chair. He looked at the treasurer thoughtfully. "How much is he getting now?"

"Thirty-five a week," Hawley answered quickly.

Norman nodded. "Take him out of there, transfer him to the

publicity department at the studio," he said. "He won't get into any trouble out there. I'll keep an eye on him myself."

Hawley nodded and got to his feet. "I'll take care of it right away, Bernie."

Bernie watched the treasurer leave the office, then reached for the telephone. He would call his sister and tell her not to worry. He would pay their moving expenses to California. Then he remembered. She had no telephone and they'd have to call her from the candy store downstairs. He put the telephone back on the desk. He'd take a run up to see her after he got through with his blintzes and sour cream at lunch. She never went anywhere. She was always home.

He felt a strange pride. That nephew of his was a bright boy, even if he had crazy ideas. With a little guidance from himself, something the boy never got from his own father, who could know what might happen? The boy might go far.

He smiled to himself as he picked up the report. His sister had been right.

Blood was thicker than water.

8

HARRY RICHARDS, CHIEF OF THE STUDIO POLICE, was in the booth when Nevada drove into the main gate of the studio. He came out of the booth, his hand outstretched. "Mr. Smith. It's great to see you again."

Nevada returned his smile, pleased by the man's obvious warmth. He shook his hand. "Good to see you again, Harry."

"It's been a long time," Richards said.

"Yeah." Nevada smiled. "Seven years." The last time he'd been at the studio was just after *The Renegade* had been released, in 1930. "I've got an appointment with Dan Pierce."

"He's expecting you," Richards said. "He's in Norman's old office."

Nevada nodded. He shifted into gear and Richards stepped back from the car. "I hope everything works out, Mr. Smith. It would be like old times having you back."

Nevada smiled and turned the car down the road to the executive building. One thing, at least, hadn't changed around the studio. There were no secrets. Everybody knew what was going on. They obviously knew more than he did. All he knew was what he'd read in Dan's telegram.

He'd come in from the range and found it lying on the table in the entranceway. He picked it up and ripped it open quickly.

HAVE IMPORTANT PICTURE DEAL FOR YOU. WOULD APPRE-
CIATE YOU CONTACT ME RIGHT AWAY.

DAN PIERCE.

Martha came into the hall while he was reading it. She had an apron on over her dress, having just come from the kitchen. "Lunch is about ready," she said.

He handed her the telegram. "Dan Pierce has a picture deal for me."

"They must be in trouble," she said quietly. "Why else would they call you after all these years?"

He shrugged his shoulders, pretending a casualness he didn't feel. "It doesn't have to be that," he said. "Jonas ain't like Bernie Norman. Maybe things have changed since he took over the studio."

"I hope so," she said. Her voice took on a little spirit. "I just don't want them using you again." She turned and went back into the kitchen.

He stared after her for a moment. That was what he liked about her. She was solid and dependable. She was for him and nobody else, not even herself. Somehow, he had known it would be like that when they were married two years ago. Charlie Dobbs's widow was the kind of woman he should have married a long time ago.

He followed her into the kitchen. "I've got to go up to Los Angeles, to see the bank about the thousand acres I'm buying from Murchison," he said. "It wouldn't do any harm to drop by and see what Dan has on his mind."

"No, it wouldn't," she said, putting the coffeepot on the table.

He straddled a chair and filled his cup. "Tell yuh what," he said suddenly. "We'll drive up there. We'll stay at the Ambassador an' have ourselves a high old time."

She turned to look at him. There was a sparkling excitement hidden deep in his eyes. It was then she knew he'd go back if there was anything for him. It wasn't that they needed the money. Nevada was a rich man now by any standards. Everything was paying off—the Wild-West show, which still used his name; the dude ranch in Reno in which he and her late husband had been partners; and the cattle ranch here in Texas, where they were living.

No, it wasn't the money. He'd turned down an offer of a million dollars' down payment against royalties for the mineral rights to the north quarter. Oil had been found on the land adjoining it. But he wanted to keep the range the way it was, didn't want oil derricks lousing up his land.

It was the excitement, the recognition that came when he walked down the street. The kids clamoring and shouting after him. But they had other heroes now. That was what he missed. That—and Jonas.

In the end, it was probably Jonas. Jonas was the son he'd never had. Everything else was a substitute—even herself. For a moment, she felt sorry for him.

"How about it?" he asked, looking up at her.

A feeling of tenderness welled up inside her. It had always been like that. Even years ago, when they'd been very young and he'd come up from Texas to the ranch in Reno where she and Charlie had settled. Weary and beaten and hiding from the law, he'd had a haunted, lonely look in his eyes. Even then she'd felt the essential goodness in him.

She smiled. "I think that would be real nice," she said, almost shyly.

"It's a rat race," Dan said. "We don't make pictures any more. We're a factory. We have to grind out a quota of film each month."

Nevada slid back in his chair and smiled. "It seems to agree with you, Dan. You don't look none the worse for it."

"The responsibilities are killin' me. But it's a job."

Nevada looked at him shrewdly. Pierce had put on weight. "But it beats the hell out of workin' for a livin', don't it?"

Dan held up his hands. "I knew there'd be no point in looking for sympathy from you, Nevada." They both laughed and

Dan looked down at his desk. When he looked up again, his face was serious. "I suppose you're wondering why I sent you that telegram?"

Nevada nodded. "That's why I'm here."

"I appreciate your coming," Pierce said. "When this deal came up, you were the first one I thought about."

"Thanks," Nevada said dryly. "What's the hitch?"

Dan's eyes grew round and large and pretended hurt. "Nevada, baby," he protested. "Is that the way to talk to an old friend? I used to be your agent. Who got you your first job in pictures?"

Nevada smiled. "Who sold my show down the river when he found he could get more money for the Buffalo Bill show?"

Pierce dismissed it with a wave of his hand. "That was a long time ago, Nevada. I'm surprised you even brought it up."

"Only to keep the record straight, Dan," Nevada said. "Now, what's on your mind?"

"You know how pictures are being sold nowadays?" Pierce asked, then went on without waiting for Nevada to answer. "We sell a whole year in advance. So many A pictures, so many B's, so many action-adventures, so many mystery-horrors and so many Westerns. Maybe ten per cent of the program is filmed when the sale's made, the rest as we go along. That's what I meant by rat race. We're lucky if we can keep ahead of our contracts."

"Why don't you accumulate a backlog for release?" Nevada asked. "That ought to solve your problem."

Dan smiled. "It would but we haven't the cash reserve. We're always waiting for the buck to come in from the current release so we can produce the next one. It's a vicious cycle."

"I still haven't heard your proposition," Nevada said.

"I'm going to lay it right on the line. I feel I can speak frankly to you."

Nevada nodded.

"Jonas has us on a short budget," Dan said. "I'm not complaining; maybe Jonas is right. At least, we didn't lose any money last year and it's the first time in almost five years we broke even. Now, this year, the sales department thinks they can sell fourteen Westerns."

"Sounds fine," Nevada said.

"We haven't got the money to make them. But the bank will lend us the money if you'll star in them."

"You know?" Nevada asked.

Pierce nodded. "I spoke to Moroni myself. He thought it was a great idea."

"How much will they advance you?" Nevada asked.

"Forty thousand a picture."

Nevada laughed. "For the entire negative cost?"

Dan nodded.

Nevada got to his feet. "Thanks, pal."

"Hold on a minute, Nevada," Dan said. "Wait until I finish. You didn't think I'd get you up here unless I thought you could make a buck, did you?"

Nevada sank back into his seat silently.

"I know how you feel about quickies," Dan said. "But believe me, these will be different. We still have the sets we used for *The Renegade*, out on the back lot. Dress them up a little and they'll be good as new. I'll use my top production staff. You can have your choice of any director and cameraman on the lot. That goes for writers and producers, too. I think too much of you, baby, to louse you up."

"That's fine," Nevada said. "But what am I supposed to work for? Spit and tobacco?"

"I think I've got a good deal for you. I had our accountants look into it and figure out a way you can keep some money instead of paying it all out in these damn taxes Roosevelt is slapping on us."

Nevada stared at him. "This better be good."

"We'll salary you ten grand a picture," Dan said. "That breaks down to five grand a week, because each picture will only take two weeks to shoot. You defer your salary until first profits and we'll give you the picture outright after seven years. You'll own the entire thing—negative and prints—lock, stock and barrel. Then, if you want, we'll buy it back from you. That'll give you a capital gain."

Nevada's face was impassive. "You sound just like Bernie Norman," he said. "It must be the office."

Pierce smiled. "The difference is that Norman was out to screw you. I'm not. I just want to keep this factory running."

"What would we use for stories?"

"I didn't want to look into that until after I'd talked to you," Dan said quickly. "You know I always had a high regard for your story sense."

Nevada smiled. He knew from Pierce's answer that he hadn't even thought about stories yet. "The important thing would be to hang the series on a character people can believe in."

"Exactly how I felt about it," Dan exclaimed. "I was thinking maybe we'd have you playing yourself. Each time, you'd get into another adventure. You know, full of the old stunts, tricks and shoot-outs."

Nevada shook his head. "Uh-uh. I can't buy that. It always seems phony. Gene Autry and Roy Rogers do that at Republic. Besides, I don't think anybody else would believe it. Not with this white hair of mine."

Pierce looked at him. "We could always dye it black."

Nevada smiled. "No, thanks," he said. "I kinda got used to it."

"We'll come up with it," Dan said. "Even if we have to pick up something from Zane Grey or Clarence Mulford. Just you say the word and we're off."

Nevada got to his feet. "Let me think about it a little," he said. "I'll talk it over with Martha and let you know."

"I heard you got married again," Dan said. "My belated congratulations."

Nevada started for the door. Halfway there, he paused and looked back. "By the way," he asked, "how's Jonas?"

For the first time since they had met, Pierce seemed to hesitate. "All right, I guess."

"You guess?" Nevada asked. "Why? Haven't you seen him?"

"Not since New York, about two years ago," Pierce answered. "When we took over the company."

"And you haven't seen him since?" Nevada asked incredulously. "Doesn't he ever come to the studio?"

Dan looked down at his desk. He seemed almost embarrassed. "Nobody sees him much any more. Once in a while, if we're lucky, he'll talk to us on the telephone. Sometimes he comes here. But it's always late at night, when there's nobody around. We know he's been here by the messages he leaves."

"But what if something important comes up?"

"We call McAllister, who lets Jonas know we want to talk to him. Sometimes he calls us back. Most of the time, he just tells Mac how he wants it handled."

Suddenly, Nevada had the feeling that Jonas needed him. He looked across the room at Dan. "Well, I can't make up my mind about this until I talk to Jonas."

"But I just got through telling you, nobody sees him."

"You want me to do the pictures?" Nevada asked.

Pierce stared at him. "He may not even be in this country. We might not hear from him for a month."

Nevada opened the door. "I can wait," he said.

9

"ARE YOU STAYING FOR SUPPER, DUVIDELE?"

"I can't, Mama," David said. "I just came by to see how you were."

"How am I? I'm the way I always am. My arthritis is bothering me. Not too much, not too little. Like always."

"You should get out in the sun more often. For all the sun you get, you might as well be living back in New York."

"A son I got," Mrs. Woolf said, "even if I never see him. Even if he stays in a hotel. Once every three months, maybe, he comes. I suppose I should be glad he comes at all."

"Cut it out, Mama. You know how busy I am."

"Your Uncle Bernie found time to come home every night," his mother said.

"Times were different then, Mama," he said lamely. He couldn't tell her that her brother had been known all over Hollywood as the matinee man. Besides, Aunt May would have killed him if he stayed out. She kept a closer guard on him than the government kept on Fort Knox.

"One week you're here already and this is only the second time you've been to see me. And not even once for supper!"

"I'll make it for supper soon, Mama. I promise."

She fixed him with a piercing glance. "Thursday night," she said suddenly.

He looked at her in surprise. "Thursday night? Why Thursday night, all of a sudden?"

A mysterious smile came over her face. "I got someone I want you should meet," she said. "Someone very nice."

"Aw, Mama," he groaned. "Not another girl?"

"So what's wrong with meeting a nice girl?" his mother asked in hurt innocence. "She's a very nice girl, David, believe me. Money her family's got. A college girl, too."

"But, Mama, I don't want to meet any girls. I haven't the time."

"Time you haven't got?" his mother demanded. "Already thirty years old. It's time you should get married. To a nice girl. From a nice family. Not to spend your whole life running around in night clubs with those *shiksas*."

"That's business, Mama. I have to go out with them."

"Everything he wants to do he tells me is business," she said rhetorically. "When he doesn't want to do, that's business, too. So tell me, are you coming to dinner or not?"

He stared at his mother for a moment, then shrugged his shoulders resignedly. "All right, Mama. I'll come. But don't forget, I'll have to leave early. I've got a lot of work to do."

She smiled in satisfaction. "Good," she said. "So don't be late. By seven o'clock. Sharp."

There was a message to call Dan Pierce waiting for him when he got back to the hotel. "What is it, Dan?" he asked, when he got him on the telephone.

"Do you know where Jonas is?"

David laughed. "That name sounds familiar."

"Quit kidding," Dan said. "This is serious. The only way we'll get Nevada to make those Westerns is if Jonas talks to him."

"You really mean he'll go for the deal?" David asked. He hadn't really believed that Nevada would. He didn't need the money and everybody knew how he felt about quickies.

"He'll go," Dan said, "after he talks to Jonas."

"I'd like to talk to him myself," David said. "The government is starting that antitrust business again."

"I know," Dan said. "I got the unions on my neck. I don't know how long I can keep them in line. You can't cry poverty to them; they saw the last annual reports. They know we're breaking even now and should show a profit next year."

"I think we better talk to Mac. We'll lay it on the line. I think two years without a meeting is long enough."

But McAllister didn't know where Jonas was, either. As David put down the telephone, a faint feeling of frustration ran through him. It was like working in a vacuum. Everywhere you turned, there was nothing. All you did was try and make deals. Deals. Piled one on top of the other like a pyramid that had no end. You traded with Fox, Loew's, RKO, Paramount, Warner. You played their theaters, they played yours. All you could do was stand on one foot, then on the other.

He wondered why Jonas took that attitude toward them. He wasn't like that with his other interests. Cord Aircraft was rapidly becoming one of the giants of the industry. InterContinental Airlines was already the largest commercial line in the country. And Cord Explosives and Cord Plastics were successfully competing against Du Pont.

But when it came to the picture company, they were just keeping alive. Sooner or later, Jonas would have to face up to it. Either he wanted to stay in this business or he'd have to get out. You had to keep pushing forward. That was the dynamics of action in the picture business. If you stopped pushing, you were dead.

And David had done all the pushing he could on his own. He'd proved that the company could be kept alive. But if they were ever going to make it for real, they'd have to come up with something really big. Deals or pictures—he didn't care which.

Actually, he preferred deals. They were safer and much less risky than big-budget pictures. Disney, Goldwyn and Bonner were all looking for new distribution outlets. And they all came up with big pictures, which grossed big and, best of all, were completely financed by themselves. He was still waiting for replies to the feelers he'd put out to Goldwyn and Disney. He'd already had one meeting with Maurice Bonner. But the approval for any such deal had to come from Jonas. It could come from no one else.

Bonner wanted the same kind of setup that Hal Wallis had at Warner's, or Zanuck had over at Twentieth Century-Fox—over-all executive supervision of the program, personal production of his own four major projects each year, stock and options in the company.

It was a stiff price to pay but that was what you paid if you wanted the best. Skouras hadn't hesitated when he wanted Zanuck. One man like that could add twenty million to your gross. It was the difference between existing and reaching for the brass ring.

But meanwhile, where was Jonas? Jonas held the one key that could unlock the golden door.

"There's a Mr. Irving Schwartz calling," his secretary said on the intercom.

David frowned. "What does he want? I don't know any Irving Schwartz."

"He says he knows you, Mr. Woolf. He told me to say Needlenose."

"Needlenose!" David exclaimed. He laughed. "Why didn't he say so the first time? Put him on."

The switch clicked as the girl transferred the call. "Needlenose!" David said. "How the hell are you?"

Needlenose laughed softly. "O.K. And you, Davy?"

"Fine. I've been working like a dog, though."

"I know," Needlenose said. "I been hearin' lots of good things about you. Makes a guy feel good when he sees one of his friends from the old neighborhood make it big."

"Not so big. It's still nothing but a job." This was beginning to sound like a touch. He figured rapidly how much old friends were worth. Fifty or a hundred?

"It's an important job, though."

"Enough about me," David said, eager to change the subject. "What about you? What are you doing out here?"

"I'm doin' O.K. I'm livin' out here now. I got a house up in Coldwater Canyon."

David almost whistled. His old friend was doing all right. Houses up there started at seventy-five grand. At least it wasn't a touch. "That's great," he said. "But it's a hell of a long way from Rivington Street."

"It sure is. I'd like to see you, Davy boy."

"I'd like to see you, too," David said. "But I'm so goddamned tied up here."

Needlenose's voice was still quiet, but insistent. "I know you are, Davy," he said. "If I didn't think it was important, I wouldn't bother you."

David thought for a moment. Now that it wasn't a touch, what could it be that was so important? "Tell you what," he said. "Why don't you come out to the studio? We can have lunch here, then I'll show you around."

"That's no good, Davy. We got to meet someplace where nobody'd see us."

"What about your house, then?"

"No good," Needlenose replied. "I don't trust the servants. No restaurants, either. Someone might snoop us out."

"Can't we talk on the telephone?"

Needlenose laughed. "I don't trust telephones much, either."

"Wait a minute," David said, remembering suddenly. "I'm having dinner at my mother's tonight. Come and eat with us. She's at the Park Apartments in Westwood."

"That sounds O.K. She still make those *knaidlach* in soup swimming with chicken fat?"

David laughed. "Sure. The matzo balls hit your stomach like a ton of bricks. You'll think you never left home."

"O.K.," Needlenose said. "What time?"

"Seven o'clock."

"I'll be there."

David put down the telephone, still curious about what Needlenose wanted. He didn't have long to wonder, for Dan came into his office, his face flushed and excited, his heavy jowls glistening with sweat. "You just get a call from a guy named Schwartz?"

"Yeah," David said, surprised.

"You going to see him?"

"Tonight."

"Thank God!" Dan said, sinking into a chair in front of the desk. He took out a handkerchief and mopped at his face.

David looked at him curiously. "What's so important about my seeing a guy I grew up with?"

Dan stared at him. "Don't you know who he is?"

"Sure," David said. "He lived in the house next to me on Rivington Street. We went to school together."

Dan laughed shortly. "Your friend from the East Side has come a long way. They sent him out here six months ago when Bioff and Brown got into trouble. He's union officially, but he's also top man for the Syndicate on the West Coast."

David stared at him, speechless.

"I hope you can get to him," Dan added. "Because, God

knows, I tried and I couldn't. If you don't, we'll be out of business in a week. We're going to have the biggest, goddamnedest strike you ever saw. They'll close down everything. Studio, theaters, the whole works."

10

DAVID LOOKED AT THE DINING-ROOM TABLE AS HE followed his mother into the kitchen. Places were set for five people. "You didn't tell me you were having a lot of company for dinner."

His mother, who was peering into a pot on the stove, didn't turn around. "A nice girl should come to supper for the first time with a young man without her parents?"

David suppressed a groan. It was going to be even worse than he'd suspected. "By the way, Mama," he said. "You better set another place at the table. I invited an old friend to have dinner with us."

His mother fixed him with a piercing glance. "Tonight, you invited?"

"I had to, Mama," he said. "Business."

The doorbell rang. He looked at his watch. It was seven o'clock. "I'll get it, Mama," he said quickly. It was probably Needlenose.

He opened the door on a short, worried-looking man in his early sixties with iron-gray hair. A woman of about the same age and a young girl were standing beside him. The worried look disappeared when the man smiled. He held out his hand. "You must be David. I'm Otto Strassmer."

David shook his hand. "How do you do, Mr. Strassmer."

"My wife, Frieda, and my daughter, Rosa," Mr. Strassmer said.

David smiled at them. Mrs. Strassmer nodded nervously and said something in German, which was followed by the girl's pleasant, "How do you do?"

There was something in her voice that made David suddenly look at her. She was not tall, perhaps five four, and from what he could see, she was slim. Her dark hair, cropped in close ringlets to her head, framed a broad brow over deep-set gray eyes that were almost hidden behind long lashes. There was a faint defiance in the curve of her mouth and the set of her chin. An instant realization came to David. The girl no more cared for this meeting than he did.

"Who is it, David?" His mother called from the kitchen.

"I beg your pardon," he said quickly. "Won't you come in?" He stepped aside to let them enter. "It's the Strassmers, Mama."

"Take them into the living room," his mother called. "There's schnapps on the table."

David closed the door behind him. "May I take your coat?" he asked the girl.

She nodded and slipped it off. She was wearing a simple man-tailored blouse and a skirt that was gathered at her tiny waist by a wide leather belt. He was surprised. He was experienced enough to know that the pert thrust of her breasts against the silk of the blouse was not fashioned by any brassière.

Her mother said something in German. Rosa looked at him. "Mother says you and Papa go in and have your drink," she said. "We'll go into the kitchen and see if we can help."

David looked at her. Again that voice. An accent and yet not an accent. At least, it wasn't an accent like her father's. The women turned and started toward the kitchen. He looked at Mr. Strassmer. The little man smiled and followed him into the living room.

David found a bottle of whisky on the coffee table, surrounded by shot glasses. A pint bottle of Old Overholt. David suppressed a grimace. It was the traditional whisky that appeared at all ceremonies—births, *bar mizvahs*, weddings, deaths. A strong blend of straight rye whiskies that burned your throat on the way down and flooded your nose unpleasantly with the smell of alcohol. He should have had enough brains to bring a bottle of Scotch. He was sure it was Old Overholt that had kept the Jews from ever acquiring a taste for whisky.

It was apparent that Mr. Strassmer didn't share his feelings. He picked up the bottle and looked at it. He turned to David, smiling. "Ah, *Gut* schnapps."

David smiled and took the bottle from his hand. "Straight or with water?" he asked, breaking the seal. That was another thing that was traditional. The bottle was always sealed. Once it was opened and not finished, it was never brought out for company again. He wondered what happened to all the open, half-empty bottles. They must be languishing in some dark closet awaiting the day of liberation.

"Straight," Mr. Strassmer said, a faintly horrified note in his voice.

David filled a shot glass and handed it to him. "I'll have to get a little water," he apologized.

Just then Rosa came in, carrying a pitcher of water and some tumblers. "I thought you might need this." She smiled, setting them on the coffee table.

"Thank you."

She smiled and went out again as David mixed himself a drink, liberally diluting it with water. He turned to Mr. Strassmer. The little German held up his glass. "*L'chaim.*"

"*L'chaim,*" David repeated.

Mr. Strassmer swallowed his drink in one head-tilted-back gesture. He coughed politely and turned to David, his eyes watering. "*Ach, gut.*"

David nodded and sipped at his own. It tasted terrible, even with water. "Another?" he asked politely.

Otto Strassmer smiled. David refilled his glass and the little man turned and sat down on the couch. "So you're David," he said. "I've heard a great deal about you."

David smiled back and nodded. This was the kind of evening it would be. By the time it was over, his face would ache from all this polite smiling.

"Yes," Mr. Strassmer continued. "I have heard a great deal about you. For a long time, I've wanted to meet you. We both work for the same man, you know."

"The same man?"

"Yes." Mr. Strassmer nodded. "Jonas Cord. You work for him in the movie business. I work for him in the plastics business. We met your mother at *shul* last year when we went there for the High Holy Day services." Mr. Strassmer smiled. "We got to talking and found that my wife, Frieda, was a second cousin to your father. Both families came originally from Silesia."

He swallowed the whisky in his glass. Again he coughed, and looked up at David through teary eyes. "A small world, isn't it?"

"A small world," David agreed.

His mother's voice came from behind him. "So, *nu,* it's time to sit down to supper already and where's this friend?"

"He should be here any minute, Mama."

"Seven o'clock you told him?" his mother asked suspiciously. David nodded.

"So why isn't he here? Don't he know when it's time to eat, you should eat or everything gets spoiled?"

Just then the doorbell rang and David heaved a sigh of relief. "Here he is now, Mama," he said, starting for the door.

The tall, good-looking young man who stood in the doorway was nothing like the thin, intense, dark-eyed boy he remembered. In place of the sharp, beaklike proboscis that had earned him his nickname was a fine, almost aquiline nose that contrasted handsomely with his wide mouth and lantern-like jaw. He smiled when he saw David's startled expression. "I went to a face factory and had it fixed. It wouldn't look good I should walk around Beverly Hills with an East Side nose." He held out his hand. "It's good to see you, Davy."

David took his hand. The grip was firm and warm. "Come on in," he said. "Mama's ready to bust. Dinner's ready."

They went into the living room. Mr. Strassmer got to his feet and his mother looked at Needlenose suspiciously. David glanced around quickly. Rosa was not in the room. "Mama," he said. "You remember Irving Schwartz?"

"Hello, Mrs. Woolf."

"Yitzchak Schwartz," she said. "Sure I remember. What happened to your nose?"

"Mama," David protested.

Needlenose smiled. "That's all right, David. I had it fixed, Mrs. Woolf."

"A *mishegass*. With such a small nose, it's a wonder you can breathe. You got a job, Yitzchak?" she demanded belligerently. "Or are you still hanging around with the bums by Shocky's garage?"

"Mama!" David said quickly. "Irving lives out here now."

"So it's Irving now." His mother's voice was angry. "Fixing his nose is not enough. His name, too, he's got to fix. What's wrong with the name your parents gave you—Isidore—hah?"

Needlenose began to laugh. He looked at David. "I see what you mean," he said. "Nothing's changed. Nothing's wrong with it, Mrs. Woolf. Irving's easier to spell."

"You'd finish school like my son, David," she retorted, "it shouldn't be so hard to spell."

"Come on, Mrs. Woolf. David promised me *knaidlach*. I couldn't wait; all day I was so hungry thinking about it."

Mrs. Woolf stared at him suspiciously. "You be a good boy, now," she said, somewhat mollified, "and every Friday you come for *knaidlach*."

"I will, Mrs. Woolf."

"All right," she said. "So now I'll go see if the soup is hot."

Rosa came into the room just as David was about to introduce Needlenose to the Strassmers. She stopped in the doorway, a look of surprise on her face. Then she smiled and came into the room. "Why, Mr. Schwartz," she said. "How nice to see you."

Irving looked up. He held out his hand. "Hey, Doc," he said. "I didn't know you knew my friend David."

She took his hand. "We just met this evening."

Irving looked at David. "Doc Strassmer did my nose retread. She's really great, David. Did you know she did that job on Linda Davis last year?"

David looked at Rosa curiously. No one had ever said anything about her being a doctor. And the Linda Davis operation had been a big one. The actress's face had been cut to ribbons in an automobile accident, yet when she went before the cameras a year later, there wasn't the slightest visible trace of disfigurement.

He was suddenly aware that Mr. and Mrs. Strassmer were staring at him nervously. He smiled at Rosa. "Doctor, you're just the one I wanted to talk to. What do you think I ought to do about the terribly empty feeling I suddenly got in my stomach?"

She looked at him gratefully. The nervousness was gone from her eyes now and they glinted mischievously. "I think a few of your mother's *knaidlach* might fix that."

"*Knaidlach?* Who said something about my *knaidlach?*" his mother said from the doorway. She bustled into the room importantly. "So everybody sit down," she said. "The soup's on the table and already it's getting cold."

11

WHEN THEY HAD FINISHED DINNER, ROSA LOOKED
at her watch. "You'll have to excuse me for a little while," she
said. "I have to run over to the hospital to see a patient."

David looked at her. "I'll drive you over, if you like."

She smiled. "You don't have to do that. I have my own car."

"It's no bother," David said politely. "At least, let me keep
you company."

Irving got to his feet. "I have to be going, too," he said. He
turned to Mrs. Woolf. "Thank you for a delicious dinner. It
made me homesick."

David's mother smiled. "So be a good boy, Yitzchak," she
said, "and you can come again."

Rosa smiled at David's mother. "We won't be long."

"Go," Mrs. Woolf said. "Don't you children rush." She
glanced beamingly at Rosa's parents. "We older ones have a lot
to talk about."

"I'm sorry, Irving," David said as they came out of the apartment house. "We didn't have much of a chance to talk. Maybe
we can make it tomorrow?"

"We can talk right now," Irving said quietly. "I'm sure we
can trust Rosa. Can't we, Doc?"

Rosa made a gesture. "I can wait in the car," she said quickly.

David stopped her. "No, that's all right." He turned back to
Irving. "I must have seemed stupid when you called yesterday.
But Dan Pierce mostly handles our labor relations."

"That's O.K., Davy," Irving said. "I figured something like
that."

"Dan tells me we're looking down the throat of a strike. I
suppose you know we can't afford one. It'll bust us."

"I know," Irving answered. "And I'm trying to help. But I'm
in a spot unless we can work out some kind of a deal."

"What kind of a spot can you be in? Nobody's pressing you
to go out on strike. Your members are just getting over the effects of the depression layoffs."

"Yeah." Irving nodded. "They don't want to strike but the commies are moving in. And they're stirring up a lot of trouble about how the picture companies are keeping all the gravy for themselves. A lot of people are listening. They hear about the high salaries stars and executives get and it looks good to them. Why shouldn't they get a little of it? And the commies keep them stirred up."

"What about Bioff and Brown?"

"They were pigs," Irving said contemptuously. "One side wasn't enough for them. They were trying to take it from both. That's why we dumped them."

"You dumped them?" David asked skeptically. "I thought they got caught."

Irving stared at him. "Where do you think the government got its documentation to build a case? They didn't find it layin' around in the street."

"It seems to me you're trying to use us to put out a fire your own people started," David said. "You're using the commies as an excuse."

Irving smiled. "Maybe we are, a little. But the communists are very active in the guilds. And the entire industry just signed new agreements with the Screen Directors Guild and Screen Writers Guild calling for the biggest increase they ever got. The commies are taking all the credit. Now they're starting to move in on the craft unions. And you know how the crafts are. They'll figure that if the commies can do it for the guilds, they can do it for them. The craft-union elections are coming up soon. The commies are putting up a big fight and if we don't come up with something soon, we're going to be on the outside looking in. If that happens, you'll find they're a lot harder to deal with than we were."

David looked at him. "What you're suggesting, then, is for us to decide who we want to deal with—you or the communists. How do the members feel about it? Haven't they got anything to say?"

Irving's voice was matter-of-fact. "Most of them are jerks," he said contemptuously. "All they care about is their pay envelope and who promises them the most." He took out a package of cigarettes. "Right now, the commies are beginning to look real good to them."

David was silent while his friend lit a cigarette. The gold

lighter glowed briefly, then went back into Irving's pocket. His jacket opened slightly and David saw the black butt of a gun in a shoulder holster.

Gold lighters and guns. And two kids from the East Side of New York standing in a warm spring night under the California stars talking about money and power and communism. He wondered what Irving got out of it but he knew better than to ask. There were some things that were none of his business.

"What do you want me to do?" he asked.

Irving flicked the cigarette into the gutter. "The commies are asking an increase of twenty-five cents an hour and a thirty-five-hour week. We'll settle for five cents an hour now, another nickel next year and a thirty-seven-and-a-half-hour work week." He looked into David's eyes. "Dan Pierce says he hasn't the authority to do anything about it. He says he can't get to Cord. I been waiting three months. I can't wait any longer. You sit on your can, the strike is on. You lose and we lose. Only you lose more. Your whole company goes down the drain. We'll still get lots of action other places. The only real winners are the commies."

David hesitated. He had no more authority than Dan to make this kind of deal. Still, there wasn't time to wait for Jonas. Whether Jonas liked it or not, he'd have to back him up.

He drew in his breath. "It's a deal."

Irving's white teeth flashed in a grin. He punched David lightly on the shoulder. "Good boy," he said. "I didn't think I'd have any trouble making you see the light. The negotiating committee has a meeting with Pierce tomorrow morning. We'll let them make the announcement."

He turned to Rosa. "Sorry to bust in on your party like this, Doc," he said. "But it was good seeing you again."

"That's all right, Mr. Schwartz."

They watched Irving walk over to the curb and get into his car, a Cadillac convertible. He started the motor and looked up at them. "Hey, you two. Yuh know what?"

"What?" David asked.

Irving grinned. "Like your Mama would say, you make a nice-looking couple."

They watched him turn the corner, then David looked at Rosa. It seemed to him that her face was slightly flushed. He took her arm. "My car is across the street."

She was silent almost the whole way to the hospital. "Something bothering you, Doc?" he asked.

"Now you're doing it," she said. "Everybody calls me Doc. I liked it better when you called me Rosa."

He smiled. "What's on your mind, Rosa?"

She looked down at the dashboard of the car. "We came all the way to America to get away from them."

"Them?" David asked.

"The same as in Germany," she said tersely. "The Nazis. The gangsters. They're the same, really. They both say the same things. Take us or you'll get the communists. And we'll be easier to get along with, you can deal with us." She looked up at him. "But what do you say when you find they've taken everything away from you? That was the gimmick they used to take over Germany. To save it from the communists."

"You're intimating my friend Irving Schwartz is a Nazi?"

She stared at him. "No, your friend is not a Nazi," she said seriously. "But the same insanity for power motivates him. Your friend is a very dangerous man. He carries a gun, did you know that?"

David nodded. "I saw it."

"I wonder what he would have done if you'd refused him," she said softly.

"Nothing. Needlenose wouldn't harm me."

Again her gray eyes flashed at him. "No, not with a gun," she said quickly. "Against you, he has other weapons. Economic weapons that could bankrupt your business. But a man does not carry a gun if he does not intend to use it, sooner or later."

David stopped the car in front of the hospital. "What do you think I should have done? Refuse to make a deal with Irving and let everything I've worked for all these years go to pot? Ruin every lousy investor who has put his faith and money in the company? Put our employees out on the streets looking for jobs? Is that what I should have done? Is it my fault that my employees haven't brains enough to choose decent representatives and see to it that they have an honest union?" Without realizing it, his voice had risen in anger.

Suddenly, she leaned over and put her hand on his where it rested on the wheel. Her hand was warm and firm. "No, of course it's not your fault," she said quickly. "You did what you thought was right."

A doorman came down the long steps and opened the car door. "Good evening, Dr. Strassmer."

"Good evening, Porter," she said. She straightened up and looked at David. "Would you like to come in and see where I work?"

"I don't want to get in your way. I don't mind waiting here if you'd rather."

She smiled and pressed his hand suddenly. "Please come," she said. "It would make me feel happier. Then, at least, I'd know you weren't angry at me for putting my—how do you say it— two cents into your business."

He laughed, and still holding his hand, she got out of the car and led him up the steps to the hospital.

He stood in the doorway and watched as she gently lifted the bandage from the child's face. She held out her hand silently and the nurse took a swab from a bottle and handed it to her. "This may hurt a little, Mary," she said. "But you won't move or talk, will you?"

The girl shook her head.

"All right, then," Rosa said. "Now we'll be still, very still." Her voice murmured, low and soothing, as her hand quickly traced the edge of the girl's lips with the swab. David saw the child's eyes fill with sudden tears. For a moment, he thought she was going to move her head but she didn't.

"That's fine," Rosa said softly as the nurse took the swab from her hand. "You're a brave girl." The nurse efficiently replaced the bandage across the girl's mouth. "Tomorrow morning, we'll take off the bandage and you'll be able to go home."

The girl reached for a pad and pencil on the table next to her bed. She scribbled quickly for a moment, then handed it to Rosa. She looked down at the paper and smiled. "Tomorrow morning, after the bandage comes off."

David saw the sudden smile that leaped into the child's eyes. Rosa turned to him as they walked down the corridor. "We can go back to your mother's now."

"That was a pretty little girl," he said as they waited for the elevator.

"Yes."

"What was the matter with her?"

She looked at him. "Harelip," she said. "The child was born

with it." A note of quiet pride came into her voice. "Now she'll be just like anyone else. No one will stare at her or laugh when she talks."

The door opened and they stepped into the elevator. David pressed the button and the door closed. He noticed the note the girl had given Rosa still in her hand. He took it from her. It was in a childish scrawl. "When will I be able to talk?"

He looked at Rosa. "It must make you feel good."

She nodded. "Plastic surgery isn't all nose jobs, or double-chin corrections for movie stars. The important part is helping people so they can live normal lives. Like Mary up there. You've no idea how a deformity like that can affect a child's life."

A new respect for her grew in him as they crossed the lobby toward the front door. The doorman touched his cap. "I'll get your car, sir."

As he ran down the steps and crossed over to the parking lot, a big limousine came to a stop in front of them. David glanced at it casually, then turned toward Rosa. He pulled a package of cigarettes from his pocket. "Cigarette, Rosa?"

He heard the limousine door open behind him as Rosa took the cigarette. He put one in his own mouth and held a light for her. "You wanted to see me, David?"

David spun around, almost dropping his lighter. He saw the white blur of a shirt, then a head and shoulders appeared in the open doorway of the limousine. It was Jonas Cord. David stared at him silently.

Involuntarily David glanced at Rosa. There was a strange look in her eyes. He thought she might be frightened and his hand reached out for her.

Jonas' voice was a quiet chuckle behind him. "It's all right, David," he said. "You can bring Rosa with you."

12

ROSA SANK BACK ONTO THE SEAT IN THE CORNER of the limousine. She glanced at David sitting next to her, then at Jonas. It was dark inside the car and occasionally the light from an overhead street lamp would flicker across Jonas' face as he sat facing them on the jump seat, his long legs stretched across the tonneau.

"How is your father, Rosa?"

"He is fine, Mr. Cord. He speaks of you often."

She sensed rather than saw his smile. "Give him my best when you see him."

"I will do that, Mr. Cord," she said.

The big automobile picked up speed as they came out on the Coast Highway. Rosa glanced out of the window. They were going north toward Santa Barbara, away from Los Angeles.

"McAllister said you wanted to see me, David."

She felt David stir on the seat beside her. He leaned forward. "We've gone about as far as we can on our own, Jonas. If we're to go any further, we'll need your O.K."

Jonas' voice was emotionless. "Why go any further?" he asked. "I'm satisfied with the way things are. You've eliminated your operating losses and from now on, you should be in the black."

"We won't stay in the black for long. The unions are demanding increases or they'll strike. That will absorb any profits."

"Let them," Jonas said, his voice still emotionless. "You don't have to give it to them."

"I already did," David answered.

Rosa could almost hear the moment's silence. She looked from one to the other, though she couldn't see their faces.

"You did?" Jonas said quietly, but an undercurrent of coldness had come into his voice. "I thought union negotiations were Dan's province."

David's voice was steady. There was a cautious note in it but it was the caution used by a man seeking his way through unknown territory, not that of fear. "It was, until tonight," he said. "Until it affected the welfare of the company. Then it became my business."

"Why couldn't Dan settle it?"

"Because you never replied to his messages," David said quietly. "He felt he couldn't make a deal without your approval."

"And you felt differently?"

"Yes."

Jonas' voice grew colder. "What makes you think you don't need my approval any more than he does?"

She heard a click as David flicked his lighter and held the

flame to his cigarette. Light danced across his face for a moment, then went out. The cigarette glowed in the dark. "Because I assumed that if you'd wanted me to bankrupt the company, you'd have told me so two years ago."

Jonas ignored the answer. "What else did you want to see me about?"

"The government's starting that antitrust business again," David said. "They want us to separate the theaters from the studio. I sent you all the pertinent data some time ago. We'll have to give them an answer."

Jonas sounded uninterested. "I've already told Mac what to do about that. We'll be able to stall until after the war, when we ought to get a good price for the theaters. There's always an inflation in real estate after a war."

"What if we don't have a war?"

"We'll have a war," Jonas said flatly. "Sometime within the next few years, Hitler is going to find himself in a bind. He'll have to expand or bust the whole phony prosperity he's brought to Germany."

Rosa felt a knot in her stomach. It was one thing to feel that it was inevitable because you always kept hoping you were wrong. But to put it as simply and concisely as Jonas . . . Sans emotion; one plus one equals two. War. And then there would be no place left to go. Germany would rule the world. Even her father said that the Fatherland was so far ahead of the rest of the world that it would take them a century to catch up.

She stared at David. How could Americans know so little? Did they honestly believe that they could escape this war unscathed? How could he sit there talking business as if nothing were going to happen? He was a Jew. Didn't he, too, feel the shadow of Hitler falling across him?

She heard David chuckle. "Then we're in the same boat," he said. She stared at him in shocked surprise as he went on talking. "What we've done by virtue of enforced economies is to build a false economy for ourselves. One in which we count as profit the savings produced by eliminating the waste from our own body. But we haven't created any new sources of real profit."

"And that's why you've been talking to Bonner?"

She felt David start in surprise. For the first time that evening, his voice wasn't assured. "Yes," he answered.

"I suppose you felt it was quite within your authority to initiate such discussions without prior consultations with me?" Jonas' voice was still quiet.

"As far back as a year ago, I sent you a note asking your permission to talk to Zanuck. I never received a reply and Zanuck signed with Fox."

"If I'd wanted you to talk to him, I'd have let you know," Jonas said sharply. "What makes you think Dan can't do what Bonner can?"

David hesitated. He ground his cigarette out in the ash tray on the arm rest beside him. "Two things," he said cautiously. "I'm not knocking Dan. He's proved himself an extremely able administrator and studio executive. He has developed a program that keeps the factory working at maximum efficiency, but one of the things he lacks is the creative conceit of men like Bonner and Zanuck. The ability to seize an idea and personally turn it into a great motion picture."

He stared at Jonas in the dark. They passed a street lamp, which revealed Jonas for a moment, his eyes hooded, his face impassive. "Lack of creative conceit is the difference between a real producer and a studio executive, which Dan really is. The creative conceit to make him believe he can make pictures better than anyone else and the ability to make others believe it, too. To my mind, you showed more of it in the two pictures you made than Dan has in the fifty-odd pictures he's produced in the last two years."

"And what's the second?" Jonas asked, ignoring the implied flattery of David's words. Rosa smiled to herself as she realized that he'd accepted the remark as fact.

"The second is money," David replied. "Assuming Dan could develop this quality, it would take money to find out. Five million dollars, to make two or three big pictures. Money which you don't want to invest. Bonner brings his own financing. He'll make four pictures a year, and our own investment is minimal, only the overhead on each. Between distribution fees and profit-sharing, we can't get hurt, no matter what happens. And his supervision of the rest of the program can do nothing but help us."

"You've thought about what this would do to Dan?" Jonas asked.

David took a deep breath. "Dan is your responsibility, not

mine. My responsibility is to the company." He hesitated a moment. "There'd still be a lot Dan could do."

"Not the way you want it," Jonas said flatly. "No business can run with two heads."

David was silent.

Jonas' words cut sharply through the dark like a knife. "All right, make your deal with Bonner," he said. "But it'll be up to you to get rid of Dan."

He turned in the jump seat. "You can take us back to Mr. Woolf's car now, Robair."

"Yes, Mr. Cord."

Jonas turned back to them. "I saw Nevada earlier," he said. "He'll make that series for us."

"Good. We'll begin checking story properties right away."

"You don't have to," Jonas said. "We settled that already. I suggested to him we pick up the character Max Sand from *The Renegade* and take it from there."

"How can we? At the end of the picture, he rode off into the hills to die."

Jonas smiled. "We'll presume he didn't. Suppose he lived, took another name and got religion. And that he spends the rest of his life helping people who have no one else to turn to. He uses his gun only as a last resort. Nevada liked it."

David stared at Jonas. Why shouldn't Nevada like it? It captured the imagination immediately. There wasn't a Western star in the business who wouldn't jump at the chance of making a series like that. That was what he'd meant by creative conceit. Jonas really had it.

The car came to a stop in front of the hospital. Jonas leaned over and opened the door. "You get off here," he said quietly.

The meeting was over.

They stood in front of his car and watched the big black limousine disappear down the driveway. David opened the door and Rosa looked up at him. "It's been a big night, hasn't it?" she asked softly.

He nodded. "A very big night."

"You don't have to take me back. I can get a cab here. I'll understand."

He looked down at her, his face serious, then he smiled. "What do you say we go someplace for a drink?"

She hesitated a moment. "I have a cottage at Malibu," she said. "It's not far from here. We could go there if you'd like."

They were at the cottage in fifteen minutes. "Don't be upset at how the place looks," she said, putting the key into the lock. "I haven't had time lately to straighten up."

She flicked on the light and he followed her into a large living room that was very sparsely furnished. A couch, several occasional chairs, two small tables with lamps. At one end was a fireplace, at the other a solid glass wall facing the ocean. In front of it was an easel holding a half-finished oil painting. A smock and palette lay on the floor.

"What do you drink?" she asked.

"Scotch, if you have it."

"I have it. Sit down while I get ice and glasses."

He waited until she went into another room, then crossed to the easel. He looked at the painting. It was a sunset over the Pacific, with wild red, yellow and orange hues over the almost black water. He heard ice clink in a glass behind him and turned. She held out a drink to him.

"Yours?" he asked, taking the glass from her.

She nodded. "I'm not really good at it. I play the piano the same way. But it's my way of relaxing, of working off my frustrations over my incapabilities. It's my way of compensating for not being a genius."

"Not many people are," he said. "But from what I've heard, you're a pretty good doctor."

She looked at him. "I suppose I am. But I'm not good enough. What you said tonight was very revealing. And very true."

"What was that?"

"About creative conceit, the ability to do what no other man can do. A great doctor or surgeon must have it, too." She shrugged her shoulders. "I'm a very good workman. Nothing more."

"You might be judging yourself unfairly."

"No, I'm not," she replied quickly. "I've studied under doctors who were geniuses and I've seen enough others to know what I'm talking about. My father, in his own way, is a genius. He can do things with plastics and ceramics that no other man in the world can. Sigmund Freud, who is a friend of my father's, Picasso, whom I met in France, George Bernard Shaw, who lectured at my college in England—they are all geniuses. And they all have that one quality in common. The creative conceit that enables them to do things that no other man before them could do." She shook her head. "No, I know better. I'm no genius."

He looked at her. "I'm not, either."

David turned toward the ocean as she came and stood beside him. "I've known some geniuses, too," he said. "Uncle Bernie, who started Norman Pictures, was a genius. He did everything it now takes ten men to do. And Jonas Cord is a genius, too, in a way. But I'm not sure yet in what area. There are so many things he can do, it's a pity."

"I know what you mean. My father said almost the same thing about him."

He looked down at her. "It's sad, isn't it?" he said. "Two ordinary nongeniuses, standing here looking out at the Pacific Ocean."

A glint of laughter came into her eyes. "And such a big ocean, too."

"The biggest," he said solemnly. "Or so some genius said. The biggest in the world." He held up his glass. "Let's drink to that."

They drank and he turned again to the ocean. "It's warm, almost warm enough to swim."

"I don't think the ocean would object if two just ordinary people went for a swim."

He looked at her and smiled slowly. "Could we?"

She laughed. "Of course. You'll find swimming trunks in the locker in the utility room."

David came out of the water and collapsed on the blanket. He rolled over on his side and watched her running up the beach toward him. He held his breath. She was so much a woman that he had almost forgotten she was also a doctor.

She dropped beside him and reaching for a towel, threw it across her shoulders. "I didn't think the water would be so cold."

He laughed. "It's wonderful." He reached for a cigarette. "When I was a kid, we used to go swimming off the docks in the East River. It was never like this." He lit the cigarette and passed it to her.

"Feel better now?" she asked.

He nodded. "It's just what the doctor ordered." He laughed. "All the knots came untied."

"Good," she said. She dragged on the cigarette and passed it back to him.

"You know, Rosa," he said, almost shyly, "when my mother asked me to dinner to meet you, I didn't want to come."

"I know," she said. "I felt the same way. I was sure you'd be a real slob."

She came down into his arms, her mouth tasting of ocean salt. His hand found her breast inside her bathing suit. He felt a shiver run through her as the nipple grew into his palm, then her fingers were on his thigh, capturing his manhood.

Slowly he reached up and slipped the suit from her shoulders and drew it down over her body. He could hear her breath whistling in her chest as he pressed his face against her breasts. Her arms locked around his head, closing out the night. Suddenly, her fingers were frantic, leading him to her, her voice harsh and insistent. "Don't be so gentle, David. I'm a woman!"

13

ROSA CAME INTO THE COTTAGE AND WENT DIRECTLY into the bedroom. She glanced at the clock on the night table. It was time for the six-o'clock news. She turned on the radio and the announcer's voice filled the room as she began to undress:

Today the pride of the German army, Rommel, the "Desert Fox," got his first real taste of what it felt like to eat desert sand as, in the midst of a whirling, blinding sandstorm, Montgomery began to push him back toward Tobruk. Obviously inadequately prepared for the massive onslaught, the Italians, supporting Rommel's flanks, were surrendering en masse. With his flanks thus exposed, Rommel had no choice but to begin to fall back to the sea. In London today, Prime Minister Winston Churchill said—

She flicked off the radio. War news. Nothing but war news. Today she didn't want to hear it. She turned and looked at her naked body in the mirror over the dresser.

She pressed her hand to her stomach. It felt strong and somehow full to her. She turned sideways and studied herself. She was still flat and straight. But in a little while, she would begin to get round and full. She smiled to herself as she remembered the surprise she had heard in Dr. Mayer's voice. "Why, Doctor, you're pregnant!" There had been a look of amazement in his eyes.

She had laughed. "That's what I thought, Doctor."

"Well," he sputtered. "Well!"

"Don't be so shocked, Doctor," she said, almost dryly. "These things are known to happen to many women."

Then she was surprised by the sudden feeling of pride and happiness that swept through her. She had never thought she would feel like this. The thought of having a child had always frightened her. Not a physical kind of fear but rather that pregnancy might keep her from her work, interfere with her life.

But it turned out to be not like that at all. She was proud and happy and excited. This was something only she could do. There had never been a man, in all medical history, who had given birth to a child.

She threw a robe around her shoulders and went into the bathroom, turning on the tub water. Almost languidly she sprinkled the bath salts into it. The fragrance came up and tickled her nostrils. She sneezed. *"Gesundheit!"* she said aloud to herself and pressed her hands to her stomach.

She laughed aloud. The baby wasn't even shaped inside her yet and already she was talking to it. She looked at her face in the bathroom mirror. Her skin was clear and pink and her eyes were sparkling. She smiled again. For the first time in her life, she was glad she was a woman.

Carefully she stepped into the tub and sank into the warm water. She would not soak too long. She wanted to be at the telephone at seven o'clock when David called from New York. She wanted to hear the happiness in his voice when she told him.

David looked down at the blue, leather-bound book of accounts. Six million dollars' profit this year. Almost two million last year. If nothing else, the figures proved how right had been the deal he made with Bonner three years ago.

True, Bonner made almost as much for himself. But he had a right to it. Almost all that profit had come from his own big pictures, those he had produced and financed himself. If only

David had been able to persuade Jonas to come up with the financing when Bonner offered it to them. If he had, the profit this year would have been ten million dollars.

Only one thing troubled David. During the past year, Cord had been gradually liquidating part of his stock as the market rose. He'd already recovered his original investment and the twenty-three per cent of the stock he still owned was free and clear. Ordinarily, in a company this size, that meant control. But someone was buying. It was the story of Uncle Bernie all over again. Only this time, Jonas was on the wrong side of the fence.

One day, a broker named Sheffield had come to see David. He was rumored to be the head of a powerful syndicate and their holdings in the company were considerable. David had looked at him questioningly, as he sat down.

"For almost a year now, we've been trying to arrange a meeting with Mr. Cord to discuss our mutual problems," Sheffield said. "But no one seems to know where he is or how he can be reached. We've never even received an answer to our letters."

"Mr. Cord is a busy man."

"I know," Sheffield said quickly. "I've had dealings with him before. The least I can say is that he's erratic." He drew a gold cigarette case from his pocket and opened it. Carefully he took out a cigarette and placed it between his lips. He lit the cigarette and as carefully put the case back in his pocket. He blew a cloud of smoke toward David. "Our patience is at an end," he said. "We have a considerable investment in this company, an investment that will tolerate neither a dilettante operation nor an obvious neglect of profit opportunities."

"It seems to me the investors have very little to complain about," David said. "Especially in view of the profits this year."

"I commend your loyalty, Mr. Woolf," Sheffield said. He smiled. "But we both know better. My group of investors was willing to advance the financing needed for certain pictures which might have doubled our profit. Mr. Cord was not. We are willing to work out an equitable stock and profit-sharing plan for certain key executives. Mr. Cord is not. And definitely we are not interested in burdening the company with certain expenses, like those at the Boulevard Park Hotel."

David had been wondering how long it would take him to get around to that. It was an open secret in the industry. Cord's harem, they called it.

It had begun two years ago, when Jonas tried to get a suite in the hotel for a girl and was refused. Using the picture company as a subterfuge, he then rented several floors of the staid establishment on the fringe of Beverly Hills. On the day the lease was signed, he had the studio move in all the girls on the contract-players' list.

There had almost been a riot as thirty girls swarmed into as many apartments under the shocked eyes of the hotel management. The newspapers had a field day, pointing out that none of the girls made as much in a year as each apartment would have ordinarily cost in a month.

That had been two years ago but the lease ran for fifteen years. Admittedly, it cost the company a great deal of money. The hotel would have been only too willing to cancel the lease but Jonas would have no part of it. Gradually most of the girls moved out. Now most of the apartments were empty, except when Jonas came across a girl he thought had possibilities.

David leaned back in his chair. "I don't have to point out, of course, that Mr. Cord receives no remuneration or expenses from the company."

Sheffield smiled. "We would have no objections if Mr. Cord rendered any service to the company. But the truth is that he is not at all active. He has not attended a single board meeting since his association with the company began."

"Mr. Cord bought the controlling interest in the company," David pointed out. "Therefore, his association with it is not in the ordinary category of employees."

"I'm quite aware of that," Sheffield said. "But are you quite sure control of the company still remains in his hands? We now have as much and perhaps more stock than he has. We feel we're entitled to a voice in management."

"I'll be glad to relay your suggestion to Mr. Cord."

"That won't be necessary," Sheffield said. "We are certain, because of his refusal to reply to our requests for a meeting, that he is not interested."

"In that case, why did you come to me?" David asked. Now the preliminaries were over; they were getting down to the heart of things.

Sheffield leaned forward. "We feel that the success of this company is directly attributed to you and your policies. We have the highest regard for your ability and would like to see you take your proper place in the company as chief executive officer." He ground out his cigarette in the ash tray before him. "With proper authority and compensation, of course."

David stared at him. The world on a silver platter. "That's very gratifying," he said cautiously. "What if I were to ask you to leave things as they are? What if I were to persuade Mr. Cord to adopt some of your suggestions? Would that be satisfactory to you?"

Sheffield shook his head. "With all due respect to your sincerity—no. You see, we're firmly convinced that Cord is detrimental to the progress of this company."

"Then you'd launch a proxy fight if I didn't go along with you?"

"I doubt that it would be necessary," Sheffield said. "I have already mentioned that we own a considerable amount of the stock outstanding. Certain brokers have pledged us an additional five per cent." He took a paper from his pocket and handed it to David. "And here is a commitment from Mr. Bonner to sell us all of the stock in his possession on December fifteenth, the day of the annual meeting, next week. Mr. Bonner's ten per cent of the stock brings our total to thirty-eight per cent. With or without the five per cent you own, we have more than sufficient stock to take control of the company. Even with proxies, Mr. Cord would not be able to vote more than thirty per cent of the stock."

David picked up the sheet of paper and looked at it. It was a firm commitment, all right. And it was Bonner's signature. He pushed the paper back to Sheffield silently. Suddenly, he remembered the old Norman warehouse, where he had first gone to work. The king must die. But now it was no mere platform boss, it was Jonas. Until this moment, he had never let himself think about it. Jonas had seemed invulnerable.

But all that had changed. Jonas was slipping. And what Sheffield was saying in effect was, string along with us and we'll make you king. David took a deep breath. Why shouldn't it be he? It was something he had felt ever since that first day in the warehouse.

Rosa put the newspaper down on the bed and reached for a cigarette. She looked at the clock. It was after eight. That made it after eleven o'clock in New York. David should have called by now. Usually, if he expected to be out late, he would let her know.

Could something have happened to him? Could he be lying hurt in the streets of New York, three thousand miles away, and she'd never know until it was too late?

She picked up the telephone and called him at his hotel in New York. She heard the rapid relay of the telephone across the country, then the phone ringing in his suite. It rang for a long time.

"Hello," he said. His voice was low and cautious.

"David, are you all right?"

"I'm fine," he said.

"I was worried. Why didn't you call?"

"I'm in the middle of a meeting."

"Oh. Are you alone? Are you in the bedroom?"

"Yes," he answered, in the same low, cautious voice. "I'm in the bedroom."

"Are you sitting on the bed?"

"Yes."

"I'm lying on the bed." She waited for him to ask the usual question. This time he didn't, so she told him, anyway. "I have nothing on," she whispered. A sudden warmth rose up in her. "Oh, David, I miss you so. I wish you were here beside me."

She heard the faint sound of a striking match. "I'll be out there by the end of the week."

"I can't wait, David. Can you?"

"No," he said, still cautiously.

"Stretch out on the bed for a moment, David," she whispered. "I want you to feel me as I feel you."

"Rosa—"

"Oh, David," she whispered, interrupting. "I can see you now. Hard and strong. I can feel you pouring life into me." She closed her eyes against the flush of heat spreading upward from her loins. She could hear his breathing in the telephone. "David," she whispered. "I cannot wait."

"Rosa!" His voice was harsh. "I—"

Her voice was warm and languid. "Freud would have a wonderful time with me," she whispered. "Are you angry with me, David, for being so greedy?"

"No," he said.

She took a deep breath. "I'm glad," she said. "I have wonderful news to tell you, darling."

"Can it wait until tomorrow, Rosa?" he said quickly. "I'm in the middle of an important meeting."

She hesitated in stunned silence.

He took it for acquiescence. "That's a good girl, darling," he said. "Bye now."

There was a click and he was off the line before she could answer. She stared at the telephone in bewilderment for a moment, then put it down slowly.

She reached for the cigarette still smoldering in the ash tray. The acrid smoke burned in her throat. Angrily she ground it out. She turned her face into the pillow and lay there silently.

I shouldn't have called him, she thought. He said he was busy. She got up from the bed and went into the bathroom. She looked at herself in the mirror.

You ought to be able to understand, she told herself. There have been times you've been too busy to come to the telephone when he called. You, of all people.

Almost surprised, she saw the tears well up into her eyes and begin to run down her cheeks. Then they overwhelmed her and she sank to her knees, her face against the cold porcelain bathtub. She covered her face with her hands.

Was this what it meant to be a woman?

14

MAURICE BONNER SAT UP IN THE BED AND watched the girl walk over to a chair and sit down. He studied her appreciatively. The girl was naked. And beautiful. The strong, full breasts resting on the finely boned rib cage. The flat, hard stomach swelling abruptly into the surprising rise of her pubis, then tapering gently into the thighs of her long, slim legs.

He watched the muscles of her back suddenly come into play as she turned to pick up a pack of cigarettes from the table. He nodded to himself. She was beautiful, all right. Perhaps not in the ordinary sense of the word but beautiful as a whore had any right to be. And never was.

"Christ, you're ugly," the girl said, looking at him.

He grinned, exposing the crooked, uneven teeth in his long horse face. What she said was nothing new. He was not unaware of it himself; he could see it in his mirror. He threw back the sheet and got out of bed.

"Here, cover yourself," the girl said, flinging a towel at him. "You look like an ape with your cock hanging down like that." He caught the towel deftly and wrapped it around his waist. "Was it any good?" he asked curiously, taking a cigarette from the package.

She didn't answer.

"Was it worth it?"

"I guess it was," she said unemotionally.

He went back to the bed and sat down on the edge. "Is that all it is to you?" he asked. "Just another John?"

She stared at him. "You're supposed to be a pretty hep guy. You want the truth?"

He smiled again. "The truth, of course."

"You're all the same to me," she said, meeting his gaze steadily. "You might as well be goosing me with a Coca-Cola bottle for all the difference it makes."

"Don't you feel anything, ever?"

"Sure," she answered. "I'm human. But not with the customers. I can't afford it. They pay for perfection." She ground out the cigarette in the tray. "When I feel I got to get my kicks, I take a week off and go out to one of those dude ranches that cater to married women on holiday. There's always some cowpoke out there who thinks he's making it big for me. And he is, because I don't have to give him the best. But the Johns pay. You're entitled."

"But aren't you cheating the Johns?"

She smiled at him. "Do you feel cheated?"

"No," he said. Then he added quickly, "I don't know. I didn't know you were acting."

"I wasn't acting," she said, taking another cigarette. "I was working. That's my job."

He didn't speak.

She lit the cigarette and gestured toward him. "Look," she said. "You eat a good dinner. Afterwards, you say to your friends, that was a great steak. The greatest. You don't mind talking about it. You even tell your friends where you had it so they can get themselves one. Right?"

He nodded.

"It's like that with me," she said. "You got a friend. This time it's Irv Schwartz. You're playing gin and he looks at you and says, 'I had a great piece last night. The greatest. Jennie Denton. Give her a blast.' So you come over and put your money on the table. You climb up, you climb down. You get filled with air like a balloon and float around the world. I'll bet it's a long time since you popped three times in as many hours. Do you still feel cheated?"

He laughed, suddenly feeling young and strong. She was right. He hadn't felt like this in a long time, maybe twenty years. He felt the warmth return to his loins. He got up, letting the towel fall to the floor.

She laughed. "You're younger than I thought. Look, it's midnight."

"So?" He stared at her.

"The deal was two bills till midnight," she said. "You're all paid up. It's three bills from here till morning. But that includes breakfast."

He laughed. "You're worse than MCA. O.K., it's a deal."

She smiled and got to her feet. "Come on."

He followed her into a large bathroom with a giant square marble tub sunken into the floor. There was a rubbing table against the wall under the window. She gestured to it. "Get up there."

He sat on the edge of the table and watched her open the medicine cabinet. She took down a safety razor, a tube of shaving cream and a brush. She filled a tumbler with water and soaked a washcloth under the tap. These she placed on the edge of the sink near the table. "Lie down," she said, dipping the brush into the tumbler and working up a lather with the cream.

"What are you going to do?"

"What does it look like?" she asked. "I'm going to shave you."

"I shaved this evening."

She laughed. "Not your face, stupid." She reached out a hand and pressed him back onto the table. "I want to see what you look like underneath all that fur."

"But—"

"Lie still," she said fiercely, already beginning to brush the lather on his chest. "I won't cut you. I used to do this all the time when I worked in the hospital."

The lather was oddly soothing. "You worked in a hospital?"

She nodded. "I graduated from nursing school when I was twenty," she said. "Cum laude, too."

"Why'd you leave it?"

He scarcely felt the razor moving over his body. She turned to rinse it under the tap. "Sixty-five a month, eighteen hours a day," she said, turning back to him. She began to lather the other side of his chest. "And too many jokers thinking it was free."

He laughed as the razor glided across his stomach. "That tickles."

She rinsed the razor again. "Turn over," she said. "I want to do your back and shoulders."

He rolled over on his stomach and rested his face on his arms. The faint menthol smell of the lather came up into his nostrils. He felt the razor moving quickly over him. He closed his eyes.

She tapped him on the shoulders and he opened his eyes. She reached into the cabinet and took out a bar of soap. Breaking off the wrapping, she handed it to him. "Now take a hot shower and scrub yourself clean."

The water shot down at him in a needle spray, filling the stall with steam and the scent of jasmine from the soap. He could feel his skin beginning to tingle and glow. When he came out, his face was ruddy and smiling.

She held a large bath sheet toward him. "Dry yourself and get back on the table."

He toweled himself quickly and stretched out. She took a small hand vibrator from the cabinet and plugged it into the socket. She began to massage him slowly. The buzzing sound of the vibrator seemed to stretch and loosen the muscles in his body. "This is better than a Turkish bath," he said.

"This is a Turkish bath," she said dryly, then switched off the vibrator and threw the towel over him. "Now, you just lie there for a few minutes."

He watched as she leaned over the marble tub and turned on the water. She tested it carefully until it was just the temperature she wanted, then let it run. When the water had risen about four inches up the side of the tub, she turned it off. "O.K.," she said. "Get up."

He sat up, the towel falling behind him. "You know," she said, "you don't look half bad with all that hair off." She kicked the bathroom door closed, revealing a full-length mirror on the back.

He looked into the mirror and a smile broke over his lips. She was right. Suddenly, he looked twenty years younger. His body was clean and white under all that hair. He even felt slimmer.

She smiled at him in the mirror. "Enough narcissism," she said. "Get into the tub."

He sat down in the water. It was just slightly warmer than body temperature. "Stretch out. I'll be right back."

He leaned back in the tub and in a moment, she came back into the bathroom. In one hand she carried a magnum bottle of champagne, in the other a small vial. She put the champagne on the floor, opened the vial and let a few drops from it fall into the water. The heavy scent of jasmine immediately filled the room. She put the vial back on the basin and picked up the champagne bottle.

Expertly she ripped the foil and sprung the wire from around the cork. The cork popped and the champagne flowed over her fingers. "You forgot the glasses," he said, watching her.

"Don't be silly. Only fools drink this stuff. This is for the tub. It's better than bubble bath." She began to empty the bottle into the water around him.

The wine fizzed and tickled his skin with a refreshing sensation. She put the empty bottle on the floor and took a cigarette box from the cabinet. Opening it, she took out a cigarette and lit it. He smelled the dull, acrid pungency of marijuana.

She dragged once on the cigarette and held it toward him. "Here," she said. "Two puffs. No more."

He shook his head. "No, thanks. I don't go for that stuff."

"Don't give me a hard time," she said. "I only want to slow you down a little."

He took the cigarette from her hand and gingerly put it between his lips. He drew on it. The smoke went down deep inside him. There was no need for him to blow it out. His body had soaked it up like a sponge.

He looked down at himself in wonder. Suddenly he felt so buoyant. His body was so clean and strong. He looked up at her as she stepped into the tub. He dragged on the cigarette again. He could feel himself floating lightly in the water.

"That's enough." She took the cigarette from his lips and tossed it into the bowl.

"This is crazy," he said, smiling, as she stretched out in the water beside him.

"It had better be," she said, lowering her head to his chest, where he lay covered with a shallow layer of water. He gave a start of surprise as he felt her teeth scrape lightly across his breast. She raised her head, smiling as she looked at him. "It had better be," she repeated. "That bottle of champagne cost me twenty bucks."

He never knew exactly when the idea came to him. It was probably while he was asleep. But it didn't matter. It was there when he came down to breakfast that morning. And he had the confidence that came with the success of many such ideas in the past.

She looked up from the dining-room table when she heard the sound of his feet on the staircase. "Good morning, Mr. Bonner. Hungry?"

He returned her smile with appreciation. "Starved," he said, surprising himself. It had been a long time since he'd felt like eating a good breakfast. Juice and coffee was his usual routine.

He saw her foot move as she pressed a button on the floor under the table. A chime echoed from the kitchen in the back of the house. "Drink your juice," she said. "Your breakfast will be out in a minute."

He sat down opposite her and lifted the large glass of tomato juice out of the ice in which it had been resting. "Cheers."

He looked at her with approval. In the clear light of morning, there wasn't a trace of a line on her face. Her eyes were clear and dark and there was only a light touch of color on her lips. Her pale-brown hair was secured neatly behind her head in a pony tail. Her arms were tan against her white, short-sleeved sport blouse, which was tucked neatly, almost primly, into a casually tailored, gored skirt.

The door behind her opened and a heavy-set Mexican woman waddled in carrying a large tray, the contents of which she transferred to the huge Lazy Susan in the center of the table. Then she deftly removed the empty glass from in front of him and replaced it with a large dinner plate. *"Café, un momento,"* she said quickly and vanished.

"Help yourself, Mr. Bonner," Jennie said. "You'll find ham, bacon, steak, kippers and kidneys on the plates with the green covers. There are fried eggs, scrambled eggs and French fries under the yellow covers."

He spun the Lazy Susan until he found the ham and served himself. As he filled his plate, the Mexican woman came back with a pot of coffee and hot rolls and toast. He looked down at his plate. The ham was just the way he liked it.

Jennie was helping herself to a generous portion of steak. "You set a hell of a fine table," he said as the Mexican woman filled his coffee cup.

Jennie smiled at him. "There's nothing cheap in this house."

The Mexican servant walked over and filled Jennie's cup, then waddled back into the kitchen. "You look like you're playing tennis this morning," he said.

She nodded. "That's exactly what I'm doing. I play for two hours every morning."

"Where do you play?"

"Bel Air. I have a standing date with Frankie Gardner."

He raised an eyebrow. Frankie Gardner was one of the top tennis pros in the country. He was expensive—at least twenty-five dollars an hour. "Is he one of your customers?" he asked curiously.

"I don't play with my customers. It's bad for business. I buy his time like anybody else."

"Why?"

"I like the exercise," she said. "It helps me keep in shape. You know by now that sometimes I put in some pretty long hours."

"I see what you mean. Have you ever thought about doing anything else?"

"What do you mean?" she asked. "I told you I studied nursing."

"I don't mean that. How come you never tried the movies?"

She laughed merrily. "I'm a native Californian, Mr. Bonner. I've seen what happens to the kids that come out here. Better-looking than I ever was. They wind up as car hops, hustling hamburgers, or five-dollar whores working the Strip. I know better."

"I mean it," he said earnestly. "Do you know who I am?"

"Of course, Mr. Bonner. I read the papers. You're one of the biggest producers in Hollywood."

"So maybe I know what I'm talking about, eh?"

"Maybe you do." She smiled. "But I know myself and I'm no actress."

"That wasn't what you said last night."

"That's something else," she said. "That's my business. Besides, you see the way I live. It would be a long time before I could earn a grand a week in pictures."

"How do you know? We've had a script around for five years that we haven't been able to find a lead for. It was written for Rina Marlowe. I think you could do it."

"You're crazy!" She laughed. "Rina Marlowe was one of the most beautiful women on the screen. I couldn't hold a candle to her."

He was suddenly serious. "There are things about you that remind me of her."

"Could be," she said. "I hear she was pretty wild."

"That, too," he said, leaning toward her. "But that isn't what I'm talking about. Come down to the studio tomorrow and I'll set up a screen test. If it doesn't work, we forget about it. If it does—well, there's just one man's approval I need and you're good for two grand a week."

"Two grand?" She stared at him. "You're joking."

He shook his head. "I don't joke about money."

"Neither do I," she said seriously. "Who is this man whose approval you'd need?"

"Jonas Cord."

"We might as well forget about it," she said. "From all I heard around town from some of the girls, he's a real nut."

15

IRVING FOLLOWED DAVID INTO THE LIVING ROOM as Rosa began to clear the dishes. "I never saw her looking so good," he said, stretching out in a chair in front of the fire.

David nodded absently. "Yeah."

Irving looked at him. "You got something on your mind, Davy?"

"The usual things," David said evasively.

"That ain't the way I hear it."

Something in his voice made David tense. "What do you hear?"

"The word is out they're giving your boy the squeeze," Irving said in a low voice.

"What else do you hear?"

"The new crowd wants to make you top dog if you throw in with them," Irving said. "They're also saying that Bonner has sold out to them already."

David was silent. He couldn't believe that Jonas didn't know about what was happening. But it was possible.

"You ain't talking, Davy," Irving said quietly. "You didn't bring me out here for nothing."

"How did you find out?"

Irving shrugged his shoulders. "We got stock," he said casually. "Some of the boys called up and told me that their brokers were contacted. They want to know what we should do."

"How much stock?"

"Oh, eighty, ninety thousand shares around the country. We figured it would be a good deal the way you were running things."

"Have you—" David corrected himself. "Have the boys made up their minds yet which way they're going?" That stock could be important. It was over three per cent of the two and a half million shares outstanding.

"No, we're pretty conservative," Irving said. "We like to go where the money is. And they been making it sound real pretty. Complete financing, doubling the profits, maybe even splitting the stock in a couple of years."

David nodded. He reached for a cigarette thoughtfully. It hung in his lips unlit. Why hadn't Jonas replied to his messages? Three times he'd tried to locate him and each time there had been no reply. Surely he must know by now. The last place he checked had sent word that Jonas was out of the country. If that was true, the whole thing would be a *fait accompli* by the time he returned.

"What are you going to do, Davy?" Irving asked softly.

"I don't know," he said. "I don't know what to do."

"You can't ride the fence much longer, chum," Irving said. "There's no way on earth to live with the loser."

"I know." David nodded. He finally struck a match and held

it to his cigarette. "But it's like this. I know Cord doesn't pay much attention to us, maybe sometimes he even holds us back a little. But I also know he can make a picture, he's got a real feel for this business. That's why he bought in. It's not just all cold ass like it is with Sheffield and the others. Plain banker-and-broker arithmetic and to hell with everything except the profit-and-loss statement and balance sheet."

"But the bankers and brokers hold all the cards," Irving said. "Only a fool bucks the house."

"Yeah," David said almost savagely, grinding out his cigarette.

Irving was silent for a moment, then he smiled. "Tell you what, Davy. I'll get all our proxies together and deliver 'em to you. When you decide what's best, vote 'em for us."

David stared at him. "You'd do that?"

Irving laughed. "The way I see it, I got no choice. Didn't you haul that alky for us from Shocky's garage?"

"Here comes the coffee," Rosa announced, carrying in a tray.

"Jesus!" Irving exclaimed. "Lookit that choc'late layer cake."

Rost laughed in a pleased voice. "I baked it myself."

Irving leaned back against the couch. "Oh, Doctor!" he said, looking at Rosa and rolling his eyes.

"Another piece?"

"I had three already. Another and you'll have to do a plastic job on my stomach to get me back in shape."

"Better have some more coffee, then," she said, refilling his cup. She began to gather up the cake plates.

"I meant to ask you, Davy," Irving said. "You ever hear of a broad named Jennie Denton?"

"Jennie Denton?" David shook his head. "No."

"I forgot," Irving said, glancing up at Rosa. "You been out of circulation."

"What about her?" Rosa asked. "I knew a Jennie Denton."

"You did? Where did you know her, Doc?"

"At the hospital. Four years ago there was a nurse there by that name."

"About five six, dark eyes, long, light-brown hair, good figure and an interesting way of walking?"

Rosa laughed. "Sexy, you mean?"

Irving nodded. "Yeah, that's what I mean."

"Sounds like the same girl," Rosa said.

"What about her?" David asked.

"Well, Jennie is probably the most expensive hooker in L.A. She has her own six-room house in the hills and you want to see her, it's by appointment only and you go there. She won't walk into a hotel room. She's got a real exclusive list and you want a date, you got to wait maybe two, three weeks. She only works a five-day week."

"If you're recommending her to my husband," Rosa interrupted, smiling, "you'd better stop right there."

Irving smiled. "Well, it seems one night, earlier this week, Maurice Bonner went there and she gave him the full treatment. So, nothing will do the next day but he has Jennie down to the studio for a screen test. He shoots her in color, some scenes from some old script he's got laying around. While he's at it, he decides to make it real good. He dresses her in a white silk sheet. It's supposed to be a baptism scene and when she comes up out of the water in the big tank on Stage Twelve, you can see everything she's got. In two days, that test becomes the biggest picture on the home circuit. Bonner's got more requests for it than Selznick's got for *Gone With the Wind!*"

There was only one script David remembered that had a baptism scene. "You wouldn't remember the name of the script?" he asked. "Was it *The Sinner?*"

"Could be."

"If it was, that's the script Cord had written especially for Rina Marlowe before she died."

"I don't care who it was written for." Irving smiled. "You gotta see that test. You'll flip. I sat through it twice. And so did everybody else in the projection room."

"I'll look at it tomorrow," David said.

"I'd like to see it, too."

David looked at Rosa. He smiled. It was the first time she'd ever expressed any interest in a picture. "Come down to the studio at ten o'clock," he said. "We'll both look at it."

"If I didn't have an important meeting," Irving said, "I'd be down there myself."

David tied the sash of his pajamas and sat down in the chair near the window, looking out at the ocean.

He could hear the water running in the bathroom basin and the faint sound of Rosa's voice, humming as she rinsed her face. He sighed. At least, she could be happy in her work. A doctor didn't have to survive a war of nerves in order to practice medicine.

The door clicked open behind him and he turned around. She looked at him, a musing expression on her face, as she stood in the doorway.

"You had something to tell me?" He smiled. "Go ahead."

"No, David," she replied, her eyes warm. "It's a wife's duty to listen when her lord and master speaks."

"I don't feel much like a lord and master."

"Is anything wrong, David?"

"I don't know," he said and began to tell her the story, beginning with his meeting with Sheffield the night she had called. She walked over to him and put her arms around his head, drawing him to her bosom. "Poor David," she whispered sympathetically. "So many problems."

He turned his face up to her. "I'll have to make a decision soon," he said. "What do you think I ought to do?"

She looked down at him, her gray eyes glowing. She felt strong and capable, as if her roots were deep into the earth. "Whatever decision you make, David," she said, "I feel sure will be the right one for us."

"For us?"

She smiled slowly. This new-found strength, too, was what it meant to be a woman. Her voice was low and happy.

"We're going to have a baby," she said.

16

THE BRIGHT SUNLIGHT HURT THEIR EYES AFTER the dark of the screening room. They walked along silently toward David's office, in one of the executive cottages.

"What are you thinking, David?" she asked quietly. "That test make you sorry you're married?"

He looked at her and laughed. He opened the door to his cottage and they went past his secretary into his private office. David walked around behind his desk and sat down.

She seated herself in a leather chair in front of his desk. The thoughtful expression was still on his face. She took out a cigarette and lit it.

"What did you think of the test?" he asked.

She smiled. "Now I understand why she's driving all the men crazy," she answered. "The way that sheet clung to her when she came out of the water was the most suggestive thing I ever saw."

"Forget that scene. If it weren't in the test, what would you think of her?"

She dragged on the cigarette and the smile left her face. "I thought she was wonderful. She almost tore my heart out in that scene where all you saw was Jesus' feet walking, the bottom of the Cross dragging along as she crawled in the dirt after Him, trying to kiss His feet. I found myself crying with her." She was silent for a moment. "Were those real tears or make-up?"

David stared at her. "They were real tears," he said. "They don't use make-up tears in tests."

He felt his excitement begin to hammer inside him. In her own way, Rosa had given him the answer. He hadn't felt like this since he'd first seen Rina Marlowe on the screen. They'd all been too blinded by the baptismal scene to see it.

He pulled a buck slip from the holder on his desk and began to write on it. Rosa watched him for a moment, then walked around the desk and looked down curiously over his shoulder. He had already finished his scribbling and was reaching for the telephone.

JONAS—

I THINK IT'S ABOUT TIME WE GOT BACK INTO THE PIC-
TURE BUSINESS. LET ME HEAR FROM YOU.

DAVID

"Get me McAllister, in Reno," David said into the telephone. He looked up at Rosa and smiled. She smiled back and returned to her chair.

"Hello, Mac," David said, his voice firm and forceful. "Two questions you can answer for me."

A feeling of pride began to run through her. She was glad she'd come down to the studio. This was a facet of her husband she had never known before.

"First," David said into the telephone, "can I sign an actress to a contract with Cord Explosives? I have specific reasons for not wanting to sign her with us. Important reasons." David relaxed slightly.

"Good. Next question. I have some film I want Jonas to see right away. Can you get it to him?"

He waited a moment. "Can't ask for anything more than that. I'll have the film at your L.A. office in two hours. Thanks, Mac. Good-by."

He pressed down the bar on the telephone and raised it again. "Miss Wilson, get me Jess Lee in printing and developing, then come right in here."

He held onto the telephone and reached for a cigarette. He put it in his mouth. She leaned across the desk with a match. He drew in on the cigarette and smiled at her.

"Jess," he said, as the door opened and his secretary came in. "I'm shooting down a buck slip to you. I want you to photograph it on the title card and splice it onto the end of the Jennie Denton test, right away."

David covered the mouthpiece with his hand. "Take that buck slip down to Jess Lee yourself," he said to the secretary, indicating the paper on his desk. She picked it up silently and walked out.

"I know it's a wild test, Jess," he said into the phone. "Make up one print with my buck slip and shoot it right over to Mr. McAllister's secretary at Cord Aircraft. It's got to be there by noon."

"You've made up your mind?"

He nodded. "I'm playing a long shot," he said. "If I'm wrong, it won't matter which of them wins. I lose."

Rosa smiled. "There comes a time like that in every operation. You're the surgeon, you hold the knife and the patient is open before you. According to the book, there are many things you can do, many ways you can go. But you have only one way to go—the right way. So you make the decision. Your way. No matter what the pressures are, no matter what the books say. You have to go your own way." She looked at him, still smiling. "Is that what you're doing, David?" she asked gently. "Going your own way?"

He looked at her, marveling at her insight and knowledge. "Yes," he said unhesitantly. "I'm going my own way."

He had never thought of it quite like that. She was right, though. He was on his own now.

Jennie was sitting at her desk in the living room, writing checks for the monthly bills, when the door chime rang. She heard the Mexican woman waddle past her on the way to answer it. She frowned, looking down at the desk.

She'd been a fool, she thought bitterly, letting herself be talked into that screen test. She should have known the John was only shooting his mouth off. Now they were laughing their heads off all over Hollywood. At least four other Johns had called her up, sarcastically congratulating her on her screen test. They'd all seen it.

She had known she wasn't an actress. Why the hell had she fallen for the gag? Just like every stage-struck kid that came out here. But she thought she was too wise. She'd never fall into a trap like that. Then she'd gone for it, just like all the others.

She should have known the moment she stood in front of the cameras that it wasn't for her. But she'd read the script. Mary Magdalene. At first, she'd almost died laughing. No wonder Bonner had thought of her. It was type-casting of a high order.

Then something of the story had got to her. She'd felt moved and shaken. She'd lost herself in the part and there were times when she cried while the cameras were on her. And that was something she hadn't done since she was a little girl. No wonder they were laughing. She'd have laughed herself if it had been anyone else. The whore crying for the whore. She never should have listened. The week had gone by and there hadn't been even a word from Bonner.

The heavy footsteps of the Mexican woman sounded behind her. She looked around. The servant's beady eyes were inscrutable. *"Señor Woolf está aquí."*

Woolf. She knew no one by that name. Maybe he was the new man from the cops. They'd told her a new man was coming around to pick up the pay-off.

"De las películas," the servant added quickly.

"Oh." She nodded. *"Tráigale aquí."* She turned back to her desk as the servant moved away. Quickly Jennie made a neat pile of the bills and put them in a drawer. She turned in her chair just as the Mexican returned with a young man.

She looked coldly at him, rising from her chair. "Bonner sent you?"

"No," he said. "As a matter of fact, Bonner doesn't even know I'm here."

"Oh." She knew now why he had come. "You saw the test?"

He nodded.

Her voice grew even colder. "Then you might as well go," she said. "I see no one except by appointment."

A faint smile tugged at his lips. She grew even angrier. "And you can tell Bonner for me that he'd better stop showing that test around town or he'll regret it."

He laughed, then his face grew serious. "I've already done that, Miss Denton."

"You have?" She felt her anger dissipating. "A thing like that could ruin my business."

"I think you're out of that business," he said quietly.

She stared at him, her eyes large. "What do you mean?"

"I'm afraid you don't understand," he said, taking a card from his pocket and handing it to her. She looked down at it. It was an expensive engraved card. David Woolf, it read simply, and down in one corner, the words: Executive Vice-President. Below that was the name of the motion-picture company Bonner was connected with. Now she remembered who he was. She'd read about him in the papers. The bright young man. Cord's boy wonder. She looked up at him.

The faint smile was playing around his lips again. "Would you like to play Mary Magdalene?"

Suddenly, she was nervous. "I don't know," she said hesitantly. "I thought—it was all a kind of joke to Bonner."

"Perhaps it was," David Woolf said quickly. "I don't know what he thought. But it's no joke to me. I think you can be a great star." He was silent for a moment. "And my wife does, too."

She looked at him questioningly.

"Rosa Strassmer. She knew you at the hospital four years ago."

A light came into her eyes. "You mean Dr. Strassmer? The one who performed the skin graft on Linda Davis' face?"

He nodded again, smiling.

"I was chief nurse in surgery that day," she said. "She was great."

"Thank you. Now, would you like to play Mary Magdalene?"

Suddenly, she wanted to more than anything else in the world. "Yes."

"I hoped that would be your answer," he said, taking a folded sheet of paper from his inside pocket. "How much did Bonner say he would pay you?"

"Two thousand a week."

He already had the pen in his hand and was writing on the sheet of paper. "Wait a minute, Mr. Woolf," she said quickly. "I know Bonner only meant it as a gag. You don't have to pay me that much."

"Perhaps he did. But I don't. He said two thousand, that's what you'll get." He finished writing and handed the contract to her. "You'd better read that carefully."

She looked down at the printed form. The only thing written on it was her name and the salary figure. "Do I have to?"

David nodded. "I think you should," he said. "Contracts are easy to sign but not that easy to get out of."

Jennie sank back into the chair and began to read the contract. "I notice it's with Cord Explosives."

"That's standard practice with us. Cord owns the company."

"Oh." She finished reading and reached for a pen. Quickly she signed her name and handed the contract back to him. "Now what do we do?" she asked, smiling.

He put the contract into his pocket. "The first thing we do is change your name."

"What's the matter with it?"

"Too many people will recognize it," he said. "It might prove embarrassing later."

Jennie thought for a moment, then laughed. "I don't give a damn," she said. "Do you?"

David shook his head. "Not if you don't."

She laughed again. Let the Johns eat their hearts out over what they were missing.

He looked around the room. "Do you own or rent this?" he asked.

"Rent."

"Good," he said. "Close down and go away for a while. Out on the desert. Palm Springs, maybe. Don't let anyone know where you are except me."

"O.K.," she said. "What do I do then?"

"You wait," he said. "You wait until we discover you!"

17

"SORRY, DAVID," PIERCE SAID, GETTING TO HIS FEET. He was smiling but his eyes were cold. "I can't help you out."

"Why not?"

"Because I sold the stock a year ago."

"To Sheffield?" David asked.

The agent nodded.

"Why didn't you get in touch with Jonas?"

"Because I didn't want to," Pierce snapped. "He's used me enough. I was good enough for him during the rough years. To do the dirty work and keep the factory going. But the minute things were good enough to make the big ones, he brings in Bonner."

"You used him, too. He went into the hole for millions because you wanted a studio to play with. You're a rich man because of him. And you knew by the time Bonner came that you were an agent, not a producer. The whole industry knew it."

"Only because he never gave me a chance." Dan grinned mirthlessly. "Now it's his turn to sweat a little. I'm waiting to see how he likes it." He walked angrily to the door but by the time he turned back to David, his anger seemed to have disappeared. "Keep in touch, David. There's an outside chance I could spring Tracy and Gable from Metro on loan if you came up with the right property."

David nodded as the agent walked out. He looked down at his desk. Business as usual, he thought bitterly. Pierce would think nothing of setting up a deal like that and handing the company a million-dollar profit. That was his business. It had nothing to do with Jonas Cord personally. But the sale of his stock in the company was another matter.

He picked up the telephone on his desk wearily. "Yes, Mr. Woolf."

"Call Bonner's office and find out if I can see him right away."

"In your office or his?" his secretary asked.

He smiled at himself. Ordinarily, protocol dictated that Bonner come to him. But it was amazing how sensitive the studio grapevine was. By now, everyone was aware that something was up, and even his secretary wasn't completely sure of his position. This was her way of probing.

"My office, of course," he said testily, putting down the telephone.

Bonner came into his office about three-quarters of an hour later. It wasn't too bad, considering their relative importance. Not too long to appear rude, not too quickly to appear subservient. He crossed the room to David's desk and sat down. "Sorry to disturb you, Maurice," David said politely.

"That's quite all right, David," Bonner answered, equally polite. "I managed to finish the morning production meeting."

"Good. Then you have a little time?"

Bonner looked at his watch. "I do have a story conference due about now."

David smiled. "Writers are used to waiting."

Bonner looked at David curiously. Unconsciously, his hand crept inside his jacket and he scratched his shirt. David noticed and grinned. "Got a rash?"

"You heard the story?" Bonner asked.

David nodded.

Bonner grinned, scratching himself overtly now. "It's driving me nuts. It was worth it, though. You got to try Jennie sometime. That girl can make your old fiddle twang like a Stradivarius."

"I'll bet. I saw the test."

Bonner looked at him. "I meant to ask you. Why did you pull all the prints?"

"I had to," David said. "*The Sinner* isn't our property. It belongs to Cord personally. And you know how he is. I wasn't looking for any trouble."

Bonner stared at him silently. There wasn't any point in beating around the bush, David decided. "Sheffield showed me your commitment to sell him your stock."

Bonner nodded. He wasn't scratching now. "I figured he would."

"Why?" David asked. "If you wanted to sell, why didn't you talk to Cord?"

Bonner was silent for a moment. "What would be the point? I never even met the man. If he wasn't polite enough to look me up just once in the three years I've been working for him, I see no reason to start running after him now. Besides, my contract is up next month and nobody has come around to talk about renewing it. I didn't even hear from McAllister." He began scratching again.

David lit a cigarette. "Why didn't you come to me?" he asked softly. "I brought you over here."

Bonner didn't meet his gaze. "Sure, David, I should have. But everybody knows you can't do anything without Cord's O.K. By the time you could have got to him, my contract would have run out. I'd have looked like a damn fool to the whole industry."

David dragged the smoke deep into his lungs. They were all alike—so shrewd, so ruthless, so capable in many ways, and still, so like children with all their foolish pride.

Bonner took his silence as resignation. "Sheffield told me he'd take care of us," he said quickly. "He wants us both, David. You know that. He said he'll set up a new deal the minute he takes over. He'll finance the pictures, give us a new profit-sharing plan and some real stock options."

"Do you have that in writing?"

Bonner shook his head. "Of course not," he said. "He can't sign me to a contract before he's taken over. But his word is good. He's a big man. He's not a goof ball like Cord who runs hot and cold."

"Did Cord ever break his word to you?"

Bonner shook his head. "No. He never had a chance to. I had a contract. And now that it's almost over, I'm not going to give him a chance."

"You're like my uncle." David sighed. "He listened to men like Sheffield and ended up in stocks and bonds instead of pictures. So he lost his company. Now you're doing the same thing. He can't give you a contract because he doesn't control the company, yet you give him a signed agreement making it possible for him to take over." David got to his feet, his voice angry. "Well, what are you going to do, you damn fool, when he tells you, after he's got control, that he can't keep his promise?"

"But he needs us to run the business. Who's going to make the pictures for him if I don't?"

"That's what my Uncle Bernie thought, too," David said sarcastically. "But the business ran without him. And it will run without us. Sheffield can always get someone to run the studio for him. Schary at MGM is waiting for a job like this to open up. Matty Fox at Universal would take to it like a duck takes to water. It wouldn't be half as tough for him here as it is over there."

David sat down abruptly. "Do you still think he can't run the company without us?"

Bonner stared at him, his face white. "But what can I do, David? I signed the agreement. Sheffield can sue the ass off me if I renege."

David put out his cigarette slowly. "If I remember your agreement," he said, "you agreed to sell him all the stock you owned on December fifteenth?"

"That's right."

"What if you only happened to own one share of stock on that day?" David asked softly. "If you sell him that one share, you've kept your word."

"But that's next week. Who could you get to buy the stock before then?"

"Jonas Cord."

"But what if you can't reach him in time? Then I'm out four million dollars. If I sell that stock on the open market, it'll knock the price way down."

"I'll see to it you get your money." David leaned across his desk. "And, Maurice," he added softly. "You can start writing your own contract, right now."

"Four million bucks!" Irving screamed. "Where the hell do you think I can lay my hands on that kind of money?"

David stared at his friend. "Come on, Needlenose. This is *tuchlas*."

"And what if Cord says he don't want the stock?" Irving asked in a quieter voice. "What do I do with it then? Use it for toilet paper?" He chewed on his cigar. "You're supposed to be my friend. I go wrong on a deal like this, I'm nobody's friend. The late Yitzchak Schwartz, they'll call me."

"It isn't as bad as that."

"Don't tell me how bad it is," Irving said angrily. "From jobs like mine you don't get fired."

David looked at him for a moment. "I'm sorry, Irving, I have no right to ask you to take a chance like this." He turned and started for the door.

His friend's voice stopped him. "Hey, wait a minute! Where d'you think you're going?"

David stared at him.

"Did I say I definitely wouldn't do it for you?" Irving said.

Aunt May's ample bosom quivered indignantly. "Like a father your Uncle Bernie was to you," she said in her shrill, rasping voice. "Were you like a son to him? Did you appreciate what he done for you? No. Not once did you say to your Uncle Bernie, while he was alive, even a thank you." She took a handkerchief from the front of her dress and began to dab at her eyes, the twelve-carat diamond on her pinkie ring flashing iridescently like a spotlight. "It's by the grace of God your poor *tante* isn't spending the rest of her days in the poorhouse."

David leaned back in the stiff chair uncomfortably. He felt the chill of the night in the big, barren room of the large house. He shivered slightly. But he didn't know whether it was the cold or the way this house always affected him. "Do you want me to start a fire for you, *Tante?*"

"You're cold, Duvidele?" his Aunt May asked.

He shrugged his shoulders. "I thought you might be chilly."

"Chilly?" she repeated. "Your poor old *tante* is used to being chilly. It's only by watching my pennies I can afford to live in this house."

He looked at his watch. "It's getting late, *Tante*. And I have to get going. Are you going to give me the proxies?"

The old woman looked at him. "Why should I?" she asked. "I should give proxies to help that *momser*, that no-good, who stole his company from your uncle?"

"Nobody stole the company. Uncle Bernie would have lost it anyway. He was lucky to find a man like Cord to let him off so easy."

"Lucky he was?" Her voice was shrill again. "Out of all the shares he had, only twenty-five thousand I got left. What happened to the rest of them? Tell me. What happened, hah?"

"Uncle Bernie got three and a half million dollars for them."

"So what?" she demanded. "They were worth three times that."

"They were worth *bupkas*," he said, losing his temper. "Uncle Bernie was stealing the company blind and you know it. The stock wasn't worth the paper it was printed on."

"Now you're calling your uncle a thief." She rose to her feet majestically. "Out!" she screamed, pointing at the door. "Out from my house!"

He stared at her for a moment, then started for the door. Suddenly he stopped, remembering. Once his uncle had chased him out of his office, using almost the same words. But he'd got what he wanted. And his aunt was greedier than Bernie had ever been. He turned around.

"True, it's only twenty-five thousand shares," he said. "Only a lousy one per cent of the stock. But now it's worth something. At least, you got somebody in the family looking out for your interests. But give your proxies to Sheffield and see what happens. He's the kind that got Uncle Bernie into Wall Street in the first place. If you do, I won't be there to watch your interests. Your stock won't be worth *bupkas* again."

She stared at him for a moment. "Is that true?"

He could see the calculating machine in her head spinning. "Every last word of it."

She took a deep breath. "So come," she said. "I'll sign for you the proxies." She turned and waddled to a cabinet. "Your uncle, *olev a'sholem*, always said I should listen to you when I wanted advice. That David, he said, has a good head on his shoulders."

He watched her take some papers from the cabinet. She walked over to a desk, picked up a pen and signed them. He took them and put them in his jacket pocket. "Thanks, Aunt May."

She smiled up at him. He was surprised when she reached out her hand and patted his arm almost timidly. "Your uncle and me, we were never blessed with children," she said in a tremulous voice. "He really thought of you like his own son." She blinked her eyes rapidly. "You don't know how proud he was, even after he retired from the company, when he read about you in the trade papers."

He felt a knot of pity for the lonely old woman gather in his throat. "I know, Aunt May."

She tried to smile. "And such a pretty wife you got," she said. "Don't be a stranger. Why don't you sometime bring her here to have tea with me?"

He put his arms around the old woman suddenly and kissed her cheek. "I will, Aunt May," he said. "Soon."

Rosa was waiting in his office when he got back to the studio. "When Miss Wilson called and told me you'd be late, I thought it would be nice if I came down and we had dinner out."

"Good," he said, kissing her cheek.

"Well?"

He sat down heavily behind his desk. "Aunt May gave me her proxies."

"That means you've got nineteen per cent to vote."

He looked at her. "It won't do much good if Jonas doesn't back me up. Irving told me he'd have to sell the stock to Sheffield if Cord wouldn't pick it up."

She got to her feet. "Well, you've done all you could," she said in a practical voice. "Now let's go to dinner."

His secretary came in just as David got to his feet. "There's a cablegram from London, Mr. Woolf."

He took the envelope and opened it.

SET PRODUCTION DATE SINNER MARCH I.
CORD.

Just as he was about to hand it to Rosa, the door opened and his secretary came in again. "Another cablegram, Mr. Woolf."

Quickly he ripped it open. His eyes skimmed through it and he felt a sudden relief surge through him.

MCALLISTER READY WHATEVER CASH NEEDED SPIKE SHEFFIELD. GIVE IT TO HIM GOOD.

Like the first cablegram, it was signed CORD. He passed them both to Rosa. She read them and looked up at him with shining eyes. "We did it!" he said excitedly. He had started to pick her up in his arms when the door opened again.

"Yes, Miss Wilson?" he said in an annoyed voice.

The girl stood hesitantly in the doorway. "I'm sorry to disturb you, Mr. Woolf," she said, "but another cablegram just arrived."

"Well, don't stand there. Give it to me." He looked at Rosa. "This one is for both of us," he said, handing it to her. "You open it."

She looked down at the envelope, then back at David. A smile came over her face.

He looked down at the cable in her hand.

MAZEL TOV! HOPE IT WILL BE TWINS!

This one was signed JONAS.

JONAS—1940

Book Seven

1

"THIS IS DAMN STUPID!" FORRESTER MUTTERED as he lifted the CAB-200 into the air behind the formation of Spitfires.

"What's stupid?" I asked, looking down behind me from the copilot's seat, to see London dropping back into the early-morning haze. There were several fires still burning from last night's raid. "They didn't buy our plane but they'll buy all the B-17's we can turn out. What the hell, we both know they have to standardize."

"I'm not talking about that," Roger grumbled.

"Engines one and two, check," Morrissey called from behind us. "Engines three and four, check. You can cut the fuel now."

"Check." Roger turned down the mixture. "That's what I'm talking about," he said, motioning toward Morrissey, who was acting as flight engineer. "It's stupid—all of us on the same plane. What if it went down? Who'd be left to run the company?"

I grinned at him. "You worry too much."

He returned my smile without humor. "That's what you pay me for. The president of the company has to worry. Especially the way we're growing. We grossed over thirty-five million last year; this year we'll go over a hundred million with war orders. We'll have to start bringing up personnel who can take over in case something happens to us."

I reached for a cigarette. "What's going to happen to us?" I asked, lighting it. I looked at him through the cloud of smoke. "Unless you got a little jealous of the R.A.F. back there and are thinking about going back into the service."

He reached out and took the cigarette from my mouth and put it between his lips. "You know better than that, Jonas. I couldn't keep up with those kids. They'd fly rings around me. If I have to be an armchair pilot, I'd rather do it here, where at least I'm on your general staff."

There was something in what he said. The war was pushing us into an expansion that neither of us had ever dreamed of. And we weren't even in it yet.

"We'll have to get someone to run the Canadian plant."

I nodded silently. He'd been right—it was a hell of a wise move. We'd fabricate the parts in our plants in the States and ship them to Canada, where they'd go on the production line. As they rolled off, the R.C.A.F. would fly them to England. If it worked, we could knock about three weeks off the production time for each plane.

The idea also had some fiscal advantages. The British and Canadian governments were willing to finance the building of the plant and we'd save two ways. The factory would cost less because we would have no interest charges and the tax on net income could be taken in Canada, where the depreciation allowance was four times that allowed by Uncle Sam. And His Majesty's boys were happy, too, because living in the sterling bloc, they'd have fewer American dollars to pay out.

"O.K., I agree. But none of the boys working for us has the experience to take on a big job like that except Morrissey. And we can't spare him. You got anybody in mind?"

"Sure," he said, shooting a curious look at me. "But you aren't going to like it."

I stared at him. "Try me and see."

"Amos Winthrop."

"No!"

"He's the only man around who can handle it," he said. "And he won't be available for long. The way things are going, somebody's going to snap him up."

"Let them! He's a prick and a lush. Besides, he's bombed out on everything he ever did."

"He knows aircraft production," Forrester said stubbornly. He glanced at me again. "I heard what happened between you two but that's got nothing to do with this."

I didn't answer. Up ahead of us, I saw the Spitfire formation leader waggle his wings. It was the signal to break radio silence. Forrester leaned forward and flipped the switch. "Yes, Captain?"

"This is where we leave you, old boy."

I looked down. The gray waters of the Atlantic stared back at me. We were a hundred miles off the coast of the British Isles.

"O.K., Captain," Forrester said. "Thank you."

"Safe home, chaps. And don't forget to send us the big ones. We'll be needing them next summer to pay Jerry back a little."

Forrester laughed in his mike. The British had just taken the shellacking of their lives and here they were worried about getting their licks in. "You'll have them, Captain."

"Righto. Radio out."

He waggled the wings of his Spitfire again and the formation peeled away in a wide, sweeping circle back toward their coast. Then there was silence and we were alone over the Atlantic on our way home.

I pulled out of my safety belt and stood up. "If it's O.K. with you, I'm going back and grab a little snooze."

Roger nodded. I opened the compartment door. "You just think about what I said," he called after me.

"If you're talking about Amos Winthrop, forget it."

Morrissey was sitting dejectedly in the engineer's bucket seat. He looked up when I came in. "I don't understand it," he said sadly.

I sat down on the edge of the bunk. "It's easy enough to figure out. The B-17 flies with a five-man crew against our nine. That means they can put almost twice as many planes in the air. Round trip to Germany at the most is two thousand miles, so they don't need a five-thousand-mile range. Besides, the operational costs are just a little more than half ours."

"But this plane can go ten thousand feet higher and two hundred miles an hour faster," Morrissey said. "And it carries almost twice the pay load of bombs."

"The trouble with you, Morrissey, is you're ahead of the times. They're not ready for planes like this one yet."

I saw the stricken look come over his face. For a moment, I felt sorry for him. And what I'd said was true. For my money, he was the greatest aircraft engineer in the world. "Forget it. Don't worry, they'll catch up to you yet. Someday, they'll be flying planes like this by the thousands."

"Not in this war," he said resignedly. He picked up a Thermos from a cardboard carton. "I think I'll take some coffee up to Roger."

He went forward into the pilot's compartment and I stretched out on the bunk. The drone of the four big engines buzzed in my ears. I closed my eyes. Three weeks in England and I don't think I had a good night's rest the whole time. Between the bombs and the girls. The bombs and the girls. The bombs. The girls. I slept.

The shrill shriek of the falling bomb rose to its orgiastic climax as it fell nearby. All conversation at the dinner table hung suspended for a moment.

"I'm worried about my daughter, Mr. Cord," the slim, gray-haired woman on my right said.

I looked at her, then glanced at Morrissey, seated opposite me. His face was white and strained. I turned back to the woman. The bomb had landed practically next door and she was worried about her daughter, safe in America. Maybe she should be. She was Monica's mother.

"I haven't seen Monica since she was nine years old," Mrs. Holme continued nervously. "That was almost twenty years ago. I think of her often."

You didn't think of her often enough, I thought to myself. I used to think it was different with mothers. But they were no different than fathers. They thought of themselves first. At least that was one thing I'd had in common with Monica. Our parents never gave a damn about us. My mother died and hers had run away with another man.

She looked up at me from the deep violet eyes under the long black lashes and I could see the beauty she'd passed on to her daughter. "Do you think you might see her when you return to the States, Mr. Cord?"

"I doubt it, Mrs. Holme," I said. "Monica lives in New York now. I live in Nevada."

She was silent for a moment, then again came the piercing look from her eyes. "You don't like me very much, do you, Mr. Cord?"

"I hadn't really thought about it, Mrs. Holme," I said quickly. "I'm sorry if I give that impression."

She smiled. "It wasn't anything you said. It was just that I could sense a shrinking in you when I told you who I was." She played nervously with her spoon. "I expect Amos told you all about me—about how I ran off with someone else, leaving him with a child to raise alone?"

"Winthrop and I were never that close. We never discussed you."

"You must believe me, Mr. Cord," she whispered, a sudden intensity in her voice. "I didn't abandon my daughter. I want her to know that, to understand it."

Nothing ever changed. It was still more important for parents to be understood than to understand.

"Amos Winthrop was a woman-chaser and a cheat," she said quietly, without bitterness. "The ten years of our marriage were a hell. On our honeymoon, I discovered him with other women. And finally, when I fell in love with a decent, honest man, he blackmailed me into giving up my daughter under the threat of exposure and the ruination of that man's career in His Majesty's service."

I looked at her. That made sense. Amos was a cute one with tricks like that. I knew. "Did you ever write Monica and tell her that?"

"How does one write something like that to one's own daughter?"

I didn't answer.

"About ten years ago, I heard from Amos that he was sending her over to stay with me. I thought then that when she got to know me, I'd explain and she'd understand." She nodded slightly. "I read in the papers of your marriage and she never came."

The butler came and took away the empty plates. Another servant placed demitasse cups before us. When he went away, I spoke. "Just what is it you would like me to do, Mrs. Holme?"

Her eyes studied my face for a moment. I saw the slight hint of moisture in them. Her voice was steady, though. "If you should happen to speak with her, Mr. Cord," she said, "let her know that I asked for her, that I think of her and that I'd appreciate hearing from her."

I nodded slowly. "I'll do that, Mrs. Holme."

The butler began to pour coffee as the dull thud of bombs rolled into the heavily draped room like a muffled sound of thunder in peacetime London.

The roar of the four big motors came back into my ears as I opened my eyes. Morrissey was in the bucket seat, his head tilted uncomfortably to one side as he dozed. He opened his eyes as I sat up. "How long was I sleeping?" I asked.

"About four hours."

"I better give Roger some relief," I said, getting to my feet.

Forrester looked up as I came into the compartment. "You must have been tired. For a while, you were snoring so loud back there I was beginning to think we had five motors instead of four."

I sank into the copilot's seat. "I thought I'd give you a little relief. Where are we?"

"About here," he said, his finger pointing to the map on the holder between us. I looked down. We were about a thousand miles out over the ocean.

"We're slow."

He nodded. "We ran into heavy head winds."

I reached for the wheel and pulled it back to me until it locked in. "O.K.," I said. "I got her."

He released his wheel, got to his feet and stretched. "I think I'll try to get a nap."

"Fine," I said, looking out through the windshield. It was beginning to rain.

"Sure you can keep your eyes open for a few hours?"

"I'll manage."

He laughed. "Either you're a better man than I am, Gunga

Din, or I'm getting old. For a while, back there, I thought you were going to fuck every woman in England."

I looked up at him, grinning. "With the way those bombs were coming down, I thought I better make the most of it."

He laughed again and left the compartment. I turned back to the controls. Apparently, I wasn't the only one who felt that way. The girls must have felt it, too. There'd been something desperate in the way they insisted you accept their favors.

It was beginning to snow now, heavy, swirling flakes against the windshield. I switched the de-icers on and watched the snowflakes turn to water against the Plexiglas. The air speed was two hundred and slowing. That meant the head winds were picking up speed. I decided to see if we could climb up over it.

I moved the wheel back and the big plane began to lift slowly. We came through the clouds at thirteen thousand feet into bright sunlight. I locked in the gyrocompensator and felt the plane level off.

It was a clear and smooth flight all the rest of the way home.

2

ROBAIR WAS STANDING IN THE OPEN DOORWAY when I came out of the elevator. Though it was four o'clock in the morning, he looked as fresh and wide-eyed as if he'd just awakened. His dark face gleamed in a welcoming smile over his white shirt and faultlessly tailored butler's jacket. "Good morning, Mr. Cord. Have a good flight?"

"Fine, thank you, Robair."

He closed the door behind him. "Mr. McAllister's in the living room. Been waiting since eight o'clock last night."

"I'll talk to him," I said, starting through the foyer.

"I'll fix some steak sandwiches and coffee, Mr. Cord."

I stopped and looked back at the tall Negro. He never seemed to age. His hair was still black and thick, his frame giant-sized and powerful. "Hey, Robair, you know something? I missed you."

He smiled again. There was nothing subservient or false about his smile. It was the smile of a friend. "I missed you, too, Mr. Cord."

I turned and walked into the living room. Robair was more than just a friend. In a way, he was my guardian angel. I don't know how I would have held together after Rina died if it hadn't been for Robair.

By the time I'd got back to Reno from New York, I was a wreck. There was nothing I wanted to do. Just drink and forget. I'd had enough of people.

My father rode my shoulders like a desert Indian on a pony. It had been his woman I had wanted. It had been his woman who had died. Why did I cry? Why was I so empty?

Then one morning, I awakened in the dirt of the yard, back of Nevada's room in the bunkhouse, to find Robair bending over me. I vaguely remembered having leaned my back against the wall of the bunkhouse while I finished a bottle of bourbon. That had been last night. I turned my head slowly. The empty bottle lay beside me.

I placed my hands in the dirt and braced myself. My head hurt and my mouth was dry and when I tried to get to my feet, I found I didn't have the strength.

I felt Robair's arm slip around behind me and lift me to my feet. We started to walk across the hard-packed earth. "Thank you," I said, leaning against him gratefully. "I'll be all right once I get a drink."

His voice had been so soft that at first I thought I hadn't heard him. "No more whisky, Mr. Cord."

I stared up into his face. "What did you say?"

His large eyes were impassive. "No more whisky, Mr. Cord," he repeated. "I reckon it's time you stopped."

The anger pulled up in me and gave me strength. I shoved myself away from him. "Just who in hell do you think you are?" I shouted. "If I want a drink, I'll take a drink!"

He shook his head. "No more whisky. You're not a little boy no more. You can't run an' hide your head in the whisky bottle ever' time a little bad comes your way."

I stared at him, speechless for a moment, as the shock and anger ran through me in ice-cold waves. Then I found my voice. "You're fired!" I screamed. "No black son of a bitch is going to own me!"

I turned and started for the house. I felt his hand on my shoulder and turned. There was a look of sadness on his face. "I'm sorry, Mr. Cord," he said.

"There's no use in apologizing, Robair."

"I'm not apologizing for what I said, Mr. Cord," he replied in a low voice. Then I saw his giant, hamlike fist racing toward me. I tried to move away but nothing in my body seemed to work the way it should and I plunged into the dark again.

This time when I woke up, I was in bed, covered with clean sheets. There was a fire going in the fireplace and I felt very weak. I turned my head. Robair was sitting in a chair next to the bed. There was a small tureen of hot soup on the table next to him. "I got some hot soup here for you," he said, his eyes meeting mine levelly.

"Why'd you bring me up here?"

"The mountain air'll do you good."

"I won't stay," I said, pushing myself up. I'd had enough of this cabin when I was here the last time. On my honeymoon.

Robair's big hand pushed me back against the pillow. "You'll stay," he said quietly. He picked up the tureen and dipped a spoon into it, then held the spoon of soup out to me. "Eat."

There was such a note of authority in his quiet voice that involuntarily I opened my mouth before I thought. The hot soup scalded its way down. Then I pushed his hand away. "I don't want any."

I stared into his dark eyes for a moment, then I felt rise up inside me a hurt and a loneliness that I had never felt before. Suddenly, I began to cry.

He put down the tureen. "Go ahead an' weep, Mr. Cord. Cry yourself out. But you'll find tears won't drown you any more than whisky."

He was sitting on the porch in the late-afternoon sun when I finally came out. It was green all around, bushes and trees all the way down the side of the mountain, until it ran into the red and yellow sands of the desert. He got to his feet when I opened the door.

I walked over to the railing and looked down. We were a long way from people. I turned and looked back at him. "What's for dinner, Robair?" I asked.

He shrugged his shoulders. "To tell the truth, Mr. Cord, I was kind of waitin' on how you felt."

"There's a brook near here that has the biggest trout you ever saw."

He smiled. "A mess o' trout sounds fine, Mr. Cord."

It was almost two years before we came down from the mountain. Game was plentiful and once a week, Robair would drive down for supplies. I grew lean and dark from the sun and the bloat of the cities disappeared as the muscles tightened and hardened in my body.

We developed a routine and it was amazing how well the business got along without me. It merely proved the old axiom: once you reached a certain size, it was pretty difficult to stop growing. All the companies were doing fine except the picture company. It was undercapitalized but it didn't matter that much to me any more.

Three times a week, I spoke to McAllister on the telephone. That was generally sufficient to take care of most problems. Once a month, Mac would come driving up the winding road to the cabin, his brief case filled with papers for me to sign or reports for me to study.

Mac was a remarkably thorough man. There was very little that escaped his observant eye. In some mysterious way, everything of importance that was going on in any of the companies found its way into his reports. There were many things I knew I should attend to personally but somehow, everything seemed a long way off and very unimportant.

We'd been there almost a year and a half when we had our first outside visitor. I'd been out hunting and was coming back up the trail, with a brace of quail swinging from my hand, when I saw a strange car parked in front of the cabin. It was a Chevy with California license plates.

I walked around and looked at the registration on the steering column: Rosa Strassmer, M.D., 1104 Coast Highway, Malibu, Cal. I turned and walked into the cabin. There was a young woman seated on the couch, smoking a cigarette. She had dark hair, gray eyes and a determined jaw.

When she stood up, I saw she was wearing a faded pair of Levi's that somehow accentuated the slim, feminine curve of her hips. "Mr. Cord?" she asked, holding her hand out to me, a curious, faint accent in her voice. "I'm Rosa Strassmer, Otto Strassmer's daughter."

I took her hand, staring at her for a moment. Her grip was firm. I tried to keep the faint tinge of annoyance from showing in my voice. "How did you know where to find me?"

She took out an envelope and gave it to me. "Mr. McAllister asked me to drop this off when he heard I was driving through here on my vacation."

I opened the envelope and looked at the paper inside. It was nothing that couldn't have waited until his next visit. I dropped it on the table. Robair came into the room just then. He looked at me curiously as he took the brace of quail and my gun and went back into the kitchen.

"I hope I haven't disturbed you, Mr. Cord," she said quickly.

I looked at her. Whatever it was I felt, it wasn't her fault. It was Mac's not too subtle reminder that I couldn't stay on the mountain forever. "No," I answered. "You must forgive my surprise. We don't get many visitors up here."

She smiled suddenly. When she smiled, her face took on a strange bright beauty. "And I can understand why you don't ask people to come, Mr. Cord," she said. "More than two people would crowd a paradise like this."

I didn't answer.

She hesitated a moment, then started for the door. "I must be going now," she said awkwardly. "I'm glad to have met you. I've heard so much about you from my father."

"Dr. Strassmer!"

She turned toward me in surprise. "Yes, Mr. Cord?"

"I'll have to ask you to forgive me again," I said quickly. "Living up here as I have, I seem to have forgotten my manners. How is your father?"

"He's well and happy, Mr. Cord, thanks to you. He never gets tired of telling me how you blackmailed Göring into letting him out of Germany. He thinks you're a very brave man."

I smiled. "It's your father who is brave, doctor. What I did was very little."

"To Mother and me, it was a great deal," she said. She hesitated again. "Now I really must be going."

"Stay for dinner," I said. "Robair has a way of stuffing quail with wild rice that I think you'd enjoy."

Her eyes searched mine for a moment. "I will," she answered. "Under one condition—that you call me Rosa, not doctor."

"Agreed. Now sit down again and I'll get Robair to bring you something to drink."

But Robair was already in the doorway with a pitcher of Martinis. It was too late for her to leave when we were through with dinner, so Robair fixed up the tiny guest room for her. She went to bed and I sat in the living room for a while and then went to my room.

For the first time in a long while, I could not fall asleep. I stared up at the shadows dancing on the ceiling. There was a sound at the door and I sat up in the bed.

She stood there silently in the doorway for a moment, then came into the room. She stopped at the side of my bed and looked down at me. "Don't be frightened, lonely man," she whispered in a soft voice. "I want nothing more from you than this night."

"But, Rosa—"

She pressed a silencing finger to my lips and came down into the bed, all warmth and all woman, all compassion and all understanding. She cradled my head against her breast almost as a mother would a child. "Now I understand why McAllister sent me here."

I cupped my hands beneath her firm young breasts. "Rosa, you're beautiful," I whispered.

I heard her laugh softly. "I know I'm not beautiful, but I am happy that you should say so."

She lay her head back against the pillow and looked up at me, her eyes soft and warm. *"Kommen sie, liebchen,"* she said gently, reaching for me with her arms. "You brought my father back to his world, let me try to bring you back to yours."

In the morning, after breakfast, when she had gone, I walked back into the living room thoughtfully. Robair looked at me from the table, where he was clearing away the dishes. We didn't speak. We didn't have to. In that moment, we both understood that it was only a matter of time before we would leave the mountain.

The world was not that far away any more.

★ ★ ★

McAllister was asleep on the couch when I entered the living room. I walked over to him and touched his shoulder. He opened his eyes and looked up at me. "Hello, Jonas," he said, sitting up and rubbing his eyes. He took a cigarette and lit it. A moment later, the sleep was gone from his eyes. "I waited for you because Sheffield is pressing for a meeting," he said.

I dropped into the chair opposite him. "Did David pick up the stock?"

"Yes."

"Does Sheffield know it yet?"

"I don't think so," he said. "From the way he's talking, my guess is he still thinks he's got it in the bag." He ground the cigarette out in the ash tray. "Sheffield said that if you'd meet with him before the meeting, he'd be inclined to give you some consideration for your stock."

I laughed. "That's very kind of him, isn't it?" I kicked off my shoes. "Tell him to go to hell."

"Just a minute, Jonas," Mac said quickly. "I think you'd better meet with him, anyway. He can make a lot of trouble. After all, he'll be voting about thirty per cent of the stock."

"Let him," I snapped. "If he wants a fight, I'll curl his hair."

"Meet him, anyway," Mac urged. "You've got too many things coming up to get involved in a fight right now."

He was right, as usual. I couldn't be in six places at one time. Besides, if I wanted to make *The Sinner*, I didn't want a stupid minority-stockholder's suit holding up production.

"O.K. Call him and tell him to come over right now."

"Right now?" Mac asked. "My God! It's four o'clock in the morning."

"So what? He's the one who wanted a meeting."

Mac went over to the telephone.

"And when you get through talking to him," I said, "call Moroni on the Coast and find out if the bank will let me have the money to buy in Sheffield's stock if I give them a first mortgage on the theaters."

There was no sense in using any more of my own money than I had to.

3

I WATCHED SHEFFIELD LIFT THE COFFEE CUP TO HIS lips. His hair was a little grayer, a little thinner, but the rimless eyeglasses still shone rapaciously over his long, thin nose. Still, he accepted defeat much more graciously than I would have, if the shoe had been on the other foot.

"Where did I go wrong, Jonas?" he asked casually, his voice as detached as that of a doctor with a clinic patient. "I certainly was willing to pay enough."

I slumped down in my chair. "You had the right idea. The thing was that you were using the wrong currency."

"I don't understand."

"Movie people are different. Sure, they like money just like everybody else. But there's something they want even more."

"Power?"

I shook my head. "Only partly. What they want more than anything else is to make pictures. Not just movies but pictures that will gain them recognition. They want to regard themselves as artists. Well insulated by money, of course, but artists, just the same."

"Then because you've made motion pictures, they accepted your promises rather than mine?"

"I guess that's about it." I smiled. "When I produce a picture, they feel I'm sharing the same risks they are. I'm not risking money. Everything I am goes on the line. My reputation, my ability, my creative conceit."

"Creative conceit?"

"It's a term I got from David Woolf. He used it to rate certain producers. Those who had it made great pictures. Those who didn't, made pictures. In short, they preferred me because I was willing to be judged on their own terms."

"I see," Sheffield said thoughtfully. "I won't make the same mistake again."

"I'm sure you won't." I felt a suspicion growing in me. This was too easy. He was being too nice about it. He was a fighter. And fighters die hard.

Besides, his whole approach had been inconsistent with his usual way of doing business. Sheffield was a financial man. He dealt with business people about finances. Yet, in this case, he'd gone directly to the picture people. Ordinarily, he'd have contacted me right off the bat and we'd have battled it out. We'd each have compromised a little and been satisfied.

There could be only one answer. Something that had happened in England when I was there began suddenly to make sense. I'd come out of the projection room of our office in London, where I had gone to see the Jennie Denton test, with our British sales manager.

The telephone had rung when we walked into his office. He picked it up and spoke into it a few minutes, then put it down. He looked up at me.

"That was the circuit-buyer for the Engel theater chain," he said. "They are frantic for product now. Their studios were lost completely in the first raid and they had never made a deal for American product, as have the other companies."

"What are they going to do?" I asked, still thinking about the test. For the first time since Rina had died, I began to feel the excitement that came only from making a motion picture again. I only half listened to his answer.

"I don't know," he replied. "They have four hundred theaters and if they can't get additional product in six months, they'll have to close half of them."

"Too bad," I said. I couldn't care less. Engel, like Korda, had come to England from Middle Europe and gone into the picture business. But while Korda had concentrated on production, Engel had gone in for theaters. He came into production only as an answer to his problem of supply. Rank, British Lion, Gaumont and Associated among them managed to control all the product, both British and American. Still, there was no reason to mourn for him. I had heard that his investments in the States were worth in excess of twenty million dollars.

I'd forgotten about the conversation until now. It all fitted together neatly. It would have been a very neat trick if Engel could have stolen the company right out from under my nose. And it was just the kind of deal his Middle-European mind would have dreamed up.

I looked at Sheffield. "What does Engel plan to do with the stock now?" I asked casually.

"I don't know." Then he looked at me. "No wonder," he said softly. "Now I know why we couldn't get anywhere. You knew all along."

I didn't answer. I could see the look of surprise on Mac's face behind him but I pretended I hadn't.

"And I was beginning to believe that stuff you were handing me about picture people standing together," Sheffield said.

I smiled. "Now that the deal fell through, I suppose Engel has no choice but to close those theaters. He can't get product anywhere else."

Sheffield was silent, his eyes wary. "All right, Jonas," he said. "What's on your mind?"

"How would Mr. Engel like to buy the Norman Film Distributors of England, Ltd.? That would assure him access to our product and he might not have to close those theaters."

"How much would it cost him?" Sheffield asked.

"How many shares of stock does he own?"

"About six hundred thousand."

"That's what it would cost him," I said.

"That's five million dollars! British Norman only nets about three hundred thousand a year. At that rate, it would take him almost twenty years to get his money back."

"It all depends on your point of view. Closing two hundred theaters would mean a loss to him of over a million pounds a year."

He stared at me for a moment and then got to his feet. "May I use your phone for a call to London? In spite of the time difference, I just might still catch Mr. Engel before he leaves the office."

"Help yourself," I said. As he walked to the telephone, I looked down at my watch. It was nine o'clock and I knew I had him. Because no one, not even Georges Engel, left his office at two o'clock in the afternoon. Not in merry old England, where the offices were open until six o'clock and the clerks still sat at their old-fashioned desks on their high stools. Engel was probably waiting at the telephone right now for Sheffield's call.

By noon it was all arranged. Mr. Engel and his attorneys would be in New York the next week to sign the agreement. There was only one thing wrong with it: I would have to remain in New York. I reached for the telephone.

"Who're you calling?" Mac asked.

"David Woolf. He's the executive officer of the company. He might as well be here to sign the papers."

"Put down the telephone," Mac said wearily. "He's in New York. I brought him along with me."

"Oh," I said. I walked over to the window and looked down. New York in midmorning. I could sense the tension in the traffic coming up Park Avenue. I was beginning to feel restless already.

I turned back to McAllister. "Well, get him up here. I'm starting a big picture in two months. I'd like to know what's being done about it."

"David brought Bonner along to go over the production details with you."

I stared at him. They'd thought of everything. I threw myself into a chair. The doorbell rang and Robair went to open it. Forrester and Morrissey came in. I looked up at them as they crossed the room.

"I thought you were supposed to leave for California this morning, Morrissey," I said coldly. "How the hell are we ever going to get that new production line started?"

"I don't know if we can, Jonas," he said quickly.

"What the hell do you mean?" I shouted. "You said we could do it. You were there when we signed that contract."

"Take it easy, Jonas," Forrester said quietly. "We have a problem."

"What kind of problem?"

"The U.S. Army just ordered five CA-200's. They want the first delivery by June and we're in a bind. We can't make them B-17's on the same production line. You're going to have to decide which comes first."

I stared at him. "You make the decision. You're president of the company."

"You own the goddamn company," he shouted back. "Which contract do you want to honor?"

"Both of them. We're not in the business of turning away money."

"Then we'll have to get the Canadian plant in operation right away. We could handle prefabrication if the B-17's were put together up there."

"Then do it," I said.

"O.K. Get me Amos Winthrop to run it."

"I told you before—no Winthrop."

"No Winthrop, no Canadian plant. I'm not going to send a lot of men to their death in planes put together by amateurs just because you're too damn stubborn to listen to reason."

"Still the fly-boy hero?" I sneered. "What's it to you who puts the planes together? You're not flying them."

He crossed the room and stood over my chair, looking down at me. I could see his fists clench. "While you were out whoring around London, trying to screw everything in sight, I was out at the airfields watching those poor bastards come in weary and beat from trying to keep the Jerry bombs off your fucking back. Right then and there, I made up my mind that if we were lucky enough to get that contract, I'd personally see to it that every plane we shipped over was the kind of plane I wouldn't be afraid to take up myself."

"Hear, hear!" I said sarcastically.

"When did you decide you'd be satisfied to put your name on a plane that was second best? When the money got big enough?"

I stared at him for a moment. He was right. My father said the same thing in another way once. We'd been walking through the plant back in Nevada and Jake Platt, the plant supervisor, came up to him with a report on a poor batch of powder. He suggested blending it in with a large order so the loss would be absorbed.

My father towered over him in rage. "And who would absorb the loss of my reputation?" he shouted. "It's my name that's on every can of that powder. Burn it!"

"All right, Roger," I said slowly. "You get Winthrop."

He looked into my eyes for a moment. When he spoke, his voice was quieter. "You'll have to find him for us. I'm sending Morrissey up to Canada to get the new plant started. I'll go out to the Coast and start production."

"Where is he?"

"I don't know," he answered. "Last I heard, he was in New York, but when I checked around this morning, nobody seemed to know where he is. He seems to have dropped out of sight."

4

I SLUMPED BACK INTO A CORNER OF THE BIG LIM-
ousine as we came off the Queensboro Bridge. Already, I regretted my decision to come out here. There was something
about Queens that depressed me. I looked out the window
while Robair expertly threaded the big car through the traffic.
Suddenly, I was annoyed with Monica for living out here.

I recognized the group of houses as the car rolled to a stop.
They hadn't changed, except that the lawn was dull and brown
with winter now, where it had been bright summer-green the
last time.

"Wait here," I said to Robair. I went up the three steps and
pressed the doorbell. A chill wind whistled between the buildings and I pulled my light topcoat around me. I shifted the
package uncomfortably under my arm.

The door opened and a small girl stood there, looking up at
me. Her eyes were dark violet and serious. "Jo-Ann?" I asked
tentatively.

She nodded silently.

I stared at her for a moment. Leave it to children to remind
you of the passing of time. They have a way of growing that
ticks off your years more accurately than a clock. The last time
I had seen her, she was little more than a baby. "I'm Jonas
Cord," I said. "Is your mother home?"

"Come in," she said in a small, clear voice. I followed her
into the living room. She turned to face me. "Sit down.
Mummy's dressing. She said she wouldn't be long."

I sat down and she sat in a chair opposite me. She stared at me
with wide, serious eyes but didn't speak. I began to feel uncomfortable under her candid scrutiny and lit a cigarette. Her eyes
followed my hand as I searched for an ash tray for my match.
"It's over there," she said, pointing to a table on my right.

"Thanks."

"You're welcome," she said politely. Then she was silent
again, her eyes watching my face. I dragged on the cigarette and

after a moment's silence, spoke to her. "Do you remember me, Jo-Ann?"

Her eyes dropped and she was suddenly shy, her hands smoothing the hem of her dress across her knees in a typically feminine gesture. "Yes."

I smiled. "The last time I saw you, you were just so big," I said, holding my hand out just about level with my knee.

"I know," she whispered, not looking at me. "You were standing on the steps waiting for us to come home."

I took the package out from under my arm. "I brought you a present," I said. "A doll."

She took the package from me and sat down on the floor to open it. Her eyes were smiling now. She lifted out the doll and looked at me. "It's very pretty."

"I hoped you'd like it," I said.

"I do. Very much." Her eyes grew solemn again. "Thank you," she said.

A moment later, Monica came into the room. Jo-Ann leaped to her feet and ran to her. "Mummy! Look what Mr. Cord brought me!"

"It was very thoughtful of you, Jonas," Monica said.

I struggled to my feet. We stood looking at each other. There was an almost regal quality of self-possession about her. Her dark hair fell almost to her bare shoulders over a black cocktail dress.

Then the doorbell rang. It was the baby sitter and Jo-Ann was so busy showing her the new doll, she didn't even have time to say good-by when we left.

Robair was standing at the car door when we came out. "Robair!" Monica put out her hand. "It's nice to see you again."

"It's nice to see you again, Miss Monica," he said as he bowed over her hand.

I looked out at the cruddy Queens scenery as the car rolled back to Manhattan. "What do you want to live out here for?" I asked.

She reached for a cigarette and waited while I held the match for her. "Jo-Ann can play outside when the weather is good and I don't have to worry about her being hurt in the city streets. And I can afford it. It's much more reasonable than the city."

"From what I hear, you're doing all right. If you want to live in the suburbs, why don't you move up to Westchester? It's nicer up there."

"It's still too expensive," she said. "I don't make that kind of money. I'm only the office manager at the magazine. I'm not an editor yet."

"You look like an editor."

She smiled. "I don't know whether you mean that as a compliment or not. But at *Style*, we try to look the way our readers think we should."

I stared at her for a moment. *Style* was one of the most successful new fashion magazines aimed at the young matron. "How come you're not an editor yet?"

She laughed. "I'm one step away. Mr. Hardin's an old-fashioned businessman. He believes that every editor should put in some time on the practical side. That way, they learn something about the business problems involved in getting out a magazine. He's already hinted that the next editorial opening is mine."

I knew old Hardin. He was a magazine publisher from way back. He paid off in promises, not in dollars. "How long has he been promising?"

"Three years," she said. "But I think it will happen soon. He's planning a new movie magazine. A slick. Something on the order of the old *Photoplay*. We'd have been on the presses, only the finances are holding it up."

"What would you do on it?"

"Feature editor," she said. "You know, arrange stories about the stars, that sort of thing."

I glanced at her. "Wouldn't you have to be out in Hollywood for that?"

She nodded. "I suppose so. But Hardin hasn't got the money yet so I'll cross that bridge when I come to it."

Monica put her coffee cup down and smiled at me. "It's been a perfectly lovely dinner, Jonas, and you've been a charming host. Now tell me why."

"Does there have to be a reason?"

She shook her head. "There doesn't have to be," she said. "But I know you. When you're charming, you want something."

I waited until the waiter finished holding a match for her cigarette. "I just got back from England," I said quietly. "I ran into your mother over there."

A kind of veil dropped over her eyes. "You did?"

I nodded. "She seems very nice."

"I imagine she would be, from what I can remember of her," Monica said, a slight edge of bitterness in her voice.

"You must have a very good memory. Weren't you about Jo-Ann's age?"

The violet eyes were hard. "Some things you don't forget," she said. "Like your mother telling you how much she loves you, then disappearing one day and never coming back."

"Maybe she couldn't help it. Maybe she had a good reason."

"What reason?" she asked scornfully. "I couldn't leave Jo-Ann like that."

"Perhaps if you wrote to your mother, she could tell you."

"What could she tell me?" she said coldly. "That she fell in love with another man and ran away with him? I can understand that. What I can't understand is why she didn't take me with her. The only reason I can see is that I didn't matter."

"You may not know your mother, but you do know your father. You know how he can hate when he feels someone has crossed him."

Her eyes looked into mine. "Someone like you?"

I nodded. "Someone like me," I said. "That night, when you both came up to the hotel in Los Angeles—was he thinking about you or was he thinking about how much he wanted to get even with me?"

She was silent for a moment, then her eyes softened. "Was it like that with my mother, too?"

I nodded again. "Something like that," I said quietly.

She looked down at the tablecloth silently. When she looked up at me, her eyes were clear once more. "Thank you for telling me, Jonas. Somehow, I feel better now."

"Good." The waiter came by and refilled our coffee cups. "By the way," I said, "seen anything of your father lately?"

She shook her head with a wry smile. "About two years ago, he came out to dinner and borrowed a thousand dollars. That's the last I saw of him."

"Do you have any idea where he might be?"

"Why?"

"I've got a good job for him up in Canada, but he seems to have dropped out of sight."

A strange look came into her eyes. "You mean you'd give him a job after what he did to you?"

"I haven't much choice," I said reluctantly. "I don't especially like the idea but there's a war on. I need a man like him."

"I had a letter from him about a year ago. He said something about taking over as manager of the Teterboro Airport."

"Thanks," I said. "I'll look out there."

Her hand suddenly came across the table and pressed mine. I looked at her in surprise. She smiled. "You know, Jonas, I have the strangest feeling you're going to make a much better friend than husband."

5

MCALLISTER WAS WAITING FOR ME IN THE HOTEL when I got back the next afternoon. "You find him?" he asked.

I shook my head. "He only stayed out there long enough to pass a bum check for five hundred bucks on some poor jerk."

"That's pretty far down the ladder for him. Any idea where he went next?"

"No," I said. I threw my topcoat across a chair and sat down. "For all I know, he's in jail in some hick town we never heard of. Bum check—Jesus!"

"What do you want me to do?" Mac asked.

"Nothing," I said. "But I promised Roger I'd try to find him. We better put an agency on the job. If they can't turn him up, at least Roger will know I tried. You call Hardin?"

Mac looked at me curiously. "Yes. He'll be here any minute now. Why do you want to see him?"

"We might go into the publishing business."

"What for?" Mac asked. "You don't even read the papers."

I laughed. "I hear he's thinking of putting out a movie magazine. I'm making a picture. The best way I know to grab space is to own a magazine. I figure if I help him out with the movie magazine, he'll give us a plug in his others. That adds up to twelve million copies a month."

Mac didn't say anything. The doorbell rang and Robair went to open it. It was S. J. Hardin, right on time. He came into the room, his hand outstretched. "Jonas, my boy," he wheezed in his perennially hoarse voice. "It's good to see you."

We shook hands. "You know my attorney, Mr. McAllister?" I said.

S. J. gave him the glad eye. "It's a real pleasure, sir," he said, pumping Mac's hand enthusiastically. He turned back to me. "I was surprised to get your message. What's on your mind, boy?"

I looked at him. "I hear you're thinking about putting out a movie magazine."

"I have been thinking about it," he admitted.

"I also hear that you're a little short of cash to get it started."

He spread his hands expressively. "You know the publishing business, boy," he said. "We're always short of cash."

I smiled. To hear him, one would think he didn't have a pot to piss in. But S. J. had plenty, no matter how much he cried. The way he raided his own company made old Bernie Norman look like a Boy Scout.

"I'm about to make my first movie in eight years."

"Congratulations, Jonas," he boomed. "That's the best news I've heard in years. The movies can use a man like you. Remind me to tell my broker to pick up some Norman stock."

"I will, S. J."

"And you can be sure my magazines will give you a big play," he continued. "We know what makes good copy."

"That's what I wanted to talk to you about, S. J. I think it's a shame your chain has no movie magazine in it."

He fixed me with a shrewd glance. "I feel the same way, Jonas."

"How much would it take to get one on the stands?" I asked.

"Oh, two, maybe three hundred thousand. You've got to make sure of a year's run. It takes that long for a magazine to catch on."

"A magazine like that depends on the kind of editor you have, doesn't it? The right kind of editor and you got it made."

"That's entirely correct, boy," he said heartily. "And I have the finest group of editors in the business. I see you know the publishing business, Jonas. I'm always interested in a fresh point of view. That's what makes the news."

"Who's going to be your feature editor?"

"Why, Jonas," he said in wide-eyed innocence. "I thought you knew. The little lady you had dinner with last night, of course."

I started to laugh. I couldn't help it. The old bastard was smarter than I figured. He even had spies planted in "21."

After he left, I turned to McAllister. "I don't really have to stay here to sign those Engel papers, do I?"

He looked at me sharply. "I don't suppose so. Why?"

"I want to go to the Coast," I said. "Here I'm about to make a picture. What am I doing in New York, getting nothing done?"

"David and Bonner are here. They've been waiting for a call from you."

"Get David on the phone for me." A moment later, he handed me the telephone. "Hello, David. How's Rosa?"

"She's fine, Jonas, and very happy."

"Good," I said. "I just wanted to tell you what a great job I thought you did on that stock bit. Look, I don't feel right hanging around New York while I'm trying to get *The Sinner* ready. I'm going to shove off for the Coast."

"But, Jonas. I brought Bonner into New York."

"That's fine," I said. "But you get him back to the studio and tell him I'll see him there. That's the only place to handle a picture."

"O.K., Jonas," he said, a faint disappointment in his voice. "You flying out?"

"Yeah. I think I can make the ICA two-o'clock flight. That way, I'll be in California tomorrow morning."

"Give Rosa a call, will you, Jonas? She'd be pleased to hear from you."

"I will, David," I said. "By the way, how do I get in touch with that Jennie Denton? I think I ought at least to meet the girl who's going to play the lead in *The Sinner*."

"She's in Palm Springs, at the Tropical Flower Hotel, registered under the name of Judy Belden."

"Thanks, David," I said. "Good-by."

"Have a safe trip, Jonas."

It was 11:30 A.M., California time, the next day, when I parked my convertible in the driveway of the Tropical Flower Hotel in Palm Springs. I checked at the desk and walked down to Cottage No. 5. When I knocked on the door, there was no answer. But the door was unlocked, so I walked in. "Miss Denton?" I called.

There was no answer. Then I heard the shower running in the bathroom. I walked through and opened the bathroom door. I could see the outline of her body against the opaque shower curtain. She was singing in a low, husky voice.

I closed the bathroom door behind me and sat down on the can. I lit a cigarette while I watched her through the shower curtain. I didn't have to wait long.

She turned off the water and I could hear her sniff at the cigarette smoke. Her voice, from behind the curtain, was calm. "If that's one of the bellboys waiting out there, he'd better go before I come out," she said, "or I report him to the desk."

I didn't answer.

She stuck her head through the shower curtain, groping for a towel. I reached over and put one in her hand. Through the curtain, I could see her wrap it around herself, then the curtain slid back and she stared at me. Her eyes were dark gray and unafraid. "The bellboys in this hotel are the worst," she said. "They walk in on you at the oddest times."

"You could try locking your door."

She stepped out of the tub. "What for? They all have pass keys."

I got to my feet. "Jennie Denton?"

"It's Judy Belden on the register." A questioning look came over her face. "You the law?"

I shook my head. "No. I'm Jonas Cord."

She looked up at me, a slow smile spreading over her face. "Well, hey! I've been waiting to meet you."

I smiled back at her. "What for?"

She came very close to me and reached up to put her arms around my neck. She drew my face down and the towel slipped from her body to the floor as she stretched up to her tiptoes and kissed me. Then she leaned her head back and looked up at me with mischievous, laughing eyes.

"Boss," she whispered, "ain't it about time you signed my contract?"

6

IT WAS THE SAME BUNGALOW OFFICE I'D USED TEN years ago, when we were making *The Renegade*. Nothing had changed except the secretaries. "Good morning, Mr. Cord," they trilled in unison as I came in.

I said good morning and walked through to my office. Bonner was pacing up and down nervously. Dan Pierce was seated on the long couch underneath the window. I looked at him for a moment, then without speaking, walked behind my desk and sat down.

"I asked Pierce to come over and help convince you," Bonner said. "You can't make a picture costing this much without a name."

"Dan couldn't convince me to go to the can if I had the runs."

"Wait a minute, Jonas," Dan said quickly. "I know how you feel. But believe me, I'm only looking out for your good."

I turned to him. "Like you did when you sold your stock to Sheffield without checking with me?"

"The stock was mine," he said hotly. "I didn't have to check with anybody. Besides, who could get in touch with you? Everybody knew that you didn't give a damn about the company, that you were unloading part of your own stock."

I reached for a cigarette. After a moment, I nodded. "You're right, Dan," I said. "The stock was yours; you didn't owe me anything. You did your job and I paid you for it—in full, for the five years your contract still had to run." I leaned back in the chair and dragged on the cigarette. "I just made a mistake. You were a good agent when I met you. I should have left well enough alone."

"I'm trying to keep you from making another mistake, Jonas. When the script of *The Sinner* was written, it was a vehicle for a big star—Rina Marlowe. She was the biggest there was. You can't just take a girl with no experience, and who nobody's heard of, and put her in a picture without stars to support her. They'll laugh you out of the theater."

I looked up quizzically. "What do you think I ought to do, then?"

I could see the quick look of confidence come into his eyes. "Get a couple of big names," he said. "Use the girl if you want but back her up. Bogart. Tracy. Colman. Gable. Flynn. Any one of them insures it for you."

"I suppose you can get them for me?"

He missed the sarcasm. "I think I could help," he said cautiously.

"Well, bless your little bleeding, ten-per-centing heart. That's very kind of you." I got to my feet. "Get out, Dan. Get out before I throw you out. And don't ever come back on this lot while I'm on it."

He stared at me, his face turning white. "You can't talk to me like that," he blustered. "I'm not one of your flunkies who you can buy and sell."

"I bought you and I sold you," I said coldly. "You're the same guy you were when you tried to dump Nevada's show for Buffalo Bill's. You'd sell your own mother if there was anything in it for you. But you're not selling me any more. I'm not buying."

I pressed the buzzer on my desk and one of the secretaries came in. "Yes, Mr. Cord?' she asked from the open doorway.

"Mr. Pierce was just leaving—"

Dan's face was livid with rage. "You'll regret this, Jonas."

The door slammed behind him and I turned to Bonner. "I'm sorry, Jonas," he stammered. "I—didn't know—"

"That's O.K.," I said easily. "You didn't know."

"But the way the picture is shaping up now, it's going over three million dollars. I'd feel better if we had some stars in it."

I shook my head. "Stars are great, I'm not fighting them. But not this time. We're doing a story based on the Bible. When somebody looks up at that screen at John or Peter, I want them to see John or Peter, not Gable, Tracy or Bogart. Besides, the girl is the important thing."

"But nobody ever heard of the girl."

"So what?" I asked. "What have we got a publicity department for? By the time this picture comes out, there won't be a man, woman or child in the world who won't know her name. You thought enough of her to make the test, didn't you? And all you knew about her was that she was a girl you met at a party."

A curiously embarrassed look came over Bonner's face.

"That was different. It was almost a gag. I never thought anybody would take it seriously."

"David saw the test and took it seriously. So did I."

"But a test isn't a whole picture. Maybe she can't sustain—"

I cut him short. "She'll sustain," I said. "And you know it. You knew it when you asked her to make the test."

He looked at me with his ugly horse face. Nervously his hand scratched at himself. "She—she told you about the party?" he asked hesitantly.

I nodded. "She told me how you'd watched her all evening, how you came over and asked her to take the test." I laughed. "You guys beat me. You find a Lana Turner at a soda fountain. You find Jennie at a dinner party. How do you do it?"

A puzzled look came into his eyes. He started to say something but the telephone on my desk rang. I picked it up. It was one of the secretaries. "Miss Denton is finished in Hairdressing. Do you want her to come down?"

"Yes." I put down the phone and turned back to Bonner. "I sent Jennie up to Hairdressing. I had an idea I wanted to try out."

The door opened and Jennie came in. She moved slowly, almost hesitantly, to the center of the office. She stopped in front of my desk. She spun slowly, her long hair no longer a pale brown but a sparkling champagne. It swirled down around her neck and shoulders, spilling a translucent radiance around her tanned face.

Bonner's voice was an eerie whisper. "My God!"

I looked at him. There was a strange look on his face. His lips moved silently, his eyes were fixed on her. "It's as if—as if she was standing here."

"That's right," I said slowly. I looked back up at Jennie. I began to feel a pressure in my heart. Rina.

"I want Ilene Gaillard to dress her," I said softly, to Bonner.

"I don't know," he said. "She's retired. She's moved back East. Boston, I think."

I remembered the forlorn, white-haired figure kneeling by Rina's grave. "Send her a picture of Jennie. She'll come."

Bonner walked over to the desk and stood next to Jennie, looking down at me. "By the way, I heard from Austin Gilbert. He likes the script. He's coming over to see the test this afternoon. If he likes the girl, he'll do the picture."

"Good," I said. That was the way it was with big directors.

The two hundred grand you paid them meant nothing; they could get that on any picture. The important thing was the script. And the players.

Bonner walked to the door and stood there a moment, looking back at Jennie. "So long," he said finally.

"Good-by, Mr. Bonner," Jennie said politely.

I nodded as he went out the door.

"Can I sit down now?" Jennie asked.

"Help yourself."

She sat down and watched silently as I ran through the papers on my desk. The preliminary budget. Set-construction estimates. Bonner was right—this was going to cost money.

"Do I have to look like her?" Jennie asked softly.

I glanced up. "What?"

"Do I have to look like her?"

"Why do you ask?"

She shook her head. "I don't know. I just feel funny, that's all. Like it's not me, any more. Like I'm a ghost."

I didn't answer.

"Is that all you saw in the test—Rina Marlowe?"

"She was the biggest thing ever to hit the screen."

"I know," she said slowly. "But I'm not her. I could never be."

I stared at her. "For two thousand dollars a week," I said, "you'll be whatever I tell you to be."

She didn't answer. Just looked at me. Her eyes were masked and somber and I couldn't tell what she was thinking. "You remember that," I said quietly. "A thousand girls like you come to Hollywood every year. I could take my pick of any of them. If you don't like it, go back to what you were doing before Bonner saw you at that party."

A kind of caution came into her eyes. It wouldn't hurt to have her a little afraid of me. She was entirely too cocky. "Bonner told you about me?"

"Not a word. He didn't have to. You told me all I needed to know. Girls like you are always looking for a producer to impress. Well, you were lucky—you got one. Don't louse it up."

She let her breath out slowly. The cautious look had gone out of her eyes. Suddenly, she smiled. "O.K., massa, anything you say."

I walked around the desk, and pulled her up into my arms. Her mouth was soft and warm and when I looked down, her eyes were closed. And then the damn telephone rang. I reached around behind her and picked it up. It was McAllister, calling from New York.

"That agency located Winthrop for you," he said.

"Good. Get in touch with him and tell him to get his ass out here."

"Their man says he won't come."

"Then call Monica and have her talk to him. He'll listen to her."

"I did," Mac said quickly. "But she's already left for California, on the Twentieth Century, this noon. If you want him, you'd better do it yourself."

"I'm too busy to come running back to New York."

"You don't have to. Amos is in Chicago. The agency office out there will tell you how to locate him."

"Chicago? Well, I guess I'll have to go after him." I put down the telephone and looked at Jennie.

"The weekend's coming up," she said softly. "I'm not doing anything. Chicago's a great town."

"You'll come?" I asked.

She nodded. "We'll fly, won't we?"

"All the way," I said.

7

JENNIE LOOKED AT ME. "THIS IS THE WAY TO travel," she said. "A whole plane to ourselves."

I looked around the empty cabin of the ICA that Buzz had put on special flight for me when I had called. I checked my watch. It was almost nine o'clock. I moved it forward two hours to Chicago time. I felt the slight change of pressure in my ears. We were starting to come down.

"It must be great to own an airline," Jennie said, smiling.

"It comes in handy when you have to get someplace in a hurry."

"I don't get you."

"What don't you get, girl?"

"You," Jennie said. "You baffle me. Most guys I understand. They got their eye on the ball and they're always for making points. But you, you're different. You already got everything."

"Not everything."

She nodded at the lights of Chicago below us. "By that, I suppose you mean you don't own what's down there."

"That's right. I don't want much though, I'm satisfied just owning what's in here."

Her eyes grew cloudy. "What happens if we go boom?"

I snapped my fingers. "What the hell! Easy come, easy go."

"Just like that?"

"Just like that."

She glanced out of the window for a moment, then turned back to me. "I guess you do own me in a kind of way."

"I wasn't talking about you," I said. "I was talking about this plane."

"I know, but all the same, it's true. You do own everybody who works for you, even if you don't feel you do. Money does that."

"Money does lots of things for me," I said.

"Why don't you let it buy you a pair of shoes?"

I looked down at my stockinged feet. "Don't worry," I said. "I got shoes. They're somewhere on this plane."

She laughed, then became serious again. "Money can buy you time. It also lets you make people over, into what you want them to be."

I raised an eyebrow. "I didn't know you were a philosopher as well as an actress."

"You don't know that I'm an actress—yet."

"You better be," I said. "Otherwise, I'm going to look awful foolish."

Again, her eyes were serious. "You wouldn't like that, would you?"

"Nobody likes it," I said. "I'm no different than anybody else."

"Then why do you do it, Jonas? You don't need to. You don't need the money. What do you want to make pictures for?"

I leaned my head back against the seat. "Maybe because I want them to remember me for something else besides gunpowder, airplanes and plastic dishes."

"They'll remember you longer for that than a movie."

"Will they?" I turned my head to look at her. "How do you remember a man? Because of the thrill he gave you? Or because he built the tallest building in the world?"

"You remember all those things," she said softly. "If those were the things he did."

"You *are* a philosopher. I didn't think you understood men so well."

She laughed. "I've been a woman all my life. And men are the first thing a girl tries to understand."

I felt the wheels touch and we were on the ground. Unconsciously I felt myself leaning forward against the wheel to keep her from bucking. Then I relaxed. Habit was a funny thing. You landed every plane, whether you were at the controls or not.

Jennie shivered and pulled her thin coat around her as the first cold blast of air came through the open door. There was snow on the ground as we walked across the landing strip to the terminal.

A chauffeur stopped me, his hand touching his cap respectfully. "Your car's right outside, Mr. Cord."

Jennie was still shivering as we got into the car. "I forgot how cold winter can be," she said.

In forty-five minutes, we were at the Drake Hotel. The assistant manager greeted us at the door. "Good to see you again, Mr. Cord. Your apartment is all ready. Your office called from the Coast." He snapped his fingers and an elevator appeared by magic. We sped up with him in solitary splendor.

"I took the liberty of ordering a hot supper for you, Mr. Cord."

"Thank you, Carter," I said. "That was thoughtful of you."

Carter held open the apartment door. A small table was set up in the dining alcove and there were fresh, gleaming bottles on the bar.

"If you'll just call down when you're ready, Mr. Cord, we'll send it right up."

"Give us a few minutes to wash up, Carter," I said.

"Very good, sir."

I glanced at Jennie, who was still shivering from the cold. "Carter!"

"Yes, Mr. Cord?"

"Miss Denton obviously wasn't prepared for the cold. Do you think we could manage to get her a warm coat?"

Carter allowed himself a brief glance at Jennie. "I believe it could be arranged, sir. Mink, of course?"

"Of course," I said.

"Very good, sir. I'll have a selection up here shortly for mademoiselle."

"Thank you, Carter."

He bowed and the door closed behind him. Jennie turned to me, her eyes wide. "That does it! I thought nothing could impress me any more but that does. Do you know what time it is?"

I looked at my watch. "Ten after twelve."

"Nobody, but nobody, can go shopping for mink coats after midnight."

"We're not going shopping. They're being sent up here."

She stared at me for a moment, then nodded. "Oh, I see," she said. "That makes a difference?"

"Of course."

"Tell me. What makes you so big around here?"

"I pay my rent."

"You mean you keep this apartment all the time?"

"Of course," I said. "I never know when I might be in Chicago."

"When were you here last?"

I rubbed my cheek. "About a year and a half ago."

The telephone rang. I picked it up, then held it out to Jennie. A look of surprise came over her face. "For me?" she said. "But nobody knows I'm here."

I went into the bathroom and closed the door. When I came out, a few minutes later, she was sitting on the side of the bed, a dazed look on her face. "It was the furrier," she said. "He wanted to know which I preferred—light or dark mink. Also, what size."

"What size did you tell him?"

"Ten."

I shook my head. "I would have thought you took a twelve. Nobody ever buys a mink coat size ten. It hardly pays."

"Like I said, you're crazy," she said. Then she threw herself into my arms and hugged me. "But you're crazy nice."

I laughed aloud. Mink will do it every time.

8

THE MAN FROM THE DETECTIVE AGENCY ARRIVED while we were eating supper. His name was Sam Vitale and if he thought it was odd that Jennie was eating in a full, almost black mink coat, his weary, wise eyes evinced no surprise.

"It's cold in Chicago," Jennie explained.

"Yes, ma'am," he answered politely.

"Did you have any trouble finding him?" I asked.

"Not too much. All we had to do was check the credit agencies. He left a trail of bad checks. It was just a matter of time. When we narrowed it down to around Chicago, we checked Social Security. They may change their names but they generally don't fool with their Social Security. He's going under the name of Amos Jordan."

"Where is he working?" I asked curiously.

"In a Cicero garage, as a mechanic. He makes enough to keep him in booze. He's hitting the bottle pretty hard."

"Where does he live?"

"In a rooming house, but he only goes there to sleep. He spends most of his spare time in a clip joint called La Paree. You know the kind of joint. Continuous entertainment. There's always a stripper working on the stage, while the other girls take turns hustling the suckers for drinks."

Amos hadn't changed, I thought. He still went where the girls were. I pushed back my coffee cup. "O.K., let's go get him."

"I'm ready," Jennie said.

Vitale looked at her. "Maybe you'd better stay here, ma'am. It's a pretty rough place."

"What?" Jennie said quickly. "And miss the chance of breaking in my new mink coat?"

La Paree was one of about twenty similar clubs on a street that looked like every other Strip Street clear across the country. Its windows were covered with posters of half-naked girls— Maybellene, Charlene, Darlene and the inevitable Rosie Tookus. All were dancing tonight.

The doorman wore an ear-to-ear grin as the big limousine rolled to a stop. He opened the door with a flourish. "Welcome, folks. They come from all over the world to La Paree."

They certainly did. The doorman rushed into the club, where a small man in a dark suit materialized before us. A hat-check girl, in a pair of tights, took our coats. Jennie shook her head and kept her coat on as we followed him down the dark, narrow smoke-filled room to a tiny table right in front of the stage.

A stripper was working just over our heads. The drums were taking a slow beat and she was grinding away, almost down to the bare essentials.

"Two bottles of your best champagne," I said. This wasn't the place to order whisky. Not unless you had a zinc-lined stomach.

At the word champagne, the stripper paused in her routine, right in the middle of a bump, and looked down. I saw her appraising eyes flick over me as she put on her most seductive smile.

Then Jennie let her coat fall back on the seat and took off her turban. Her long blond hair caught all the flashes of light from the spot as it tumbled down around her shoulders. As quickly as it had appeared, the stripper's smile vanished.

I looked at Jennie. She smiled back at me. "You gotta fight fire with fire," she said.

I laughed. A white-shirted waiter came up with two bottles of champagne in a bucket. Quickly he put three glasses down on the table and opened the first bottle. The cork popped and the champagne spilled down over the sides of the bottle. He filled all three glasses without waiting for me to taste the wine and hurried off.

It was still warm but it was a good champagne. I looked at the bottle. Heidsieck, 1937. Even if the label was a phony, it wasn't half bad. Then I noticed a white chit beside me on the table. Eighty dollars.

"If you'd come in a cab," Vitale said, "it only would have cost you twenty bucks a bottle."

"How much if we'd walked?"

He grinned. "Fifteen."

"Cheers," I said, lifting my glass.

No sooner had we put down our glasses than the waiter was

refilling them. He moved quickly, slopping some over the edge of the glasses, then started to upend the bottle into the ice bucket.

I stopped him with my hand. "Not so fast, friend. If I don't squawk at the tariff, the least you can do is let us finish the bottle."

He stared at me, then nodded. He put the bottle into the bucket right side up and disappeared. There was a roll of drums and the stripper went off, to a desultory clatter of half-hearted applause.

"He's over there, down at the end of the bar," Vitale said.

I turned to look. There still wasn't much light. All I could see was a figure hunched over the bar, a glass cupped in his hands.

"I might as well go get him."

"Think you'll need any help?" Vitale asked.

"No. You stay here with Miss Denton."

The lights went down again and another stripper came on. As I walked toward the bar, a girl brushed against me in the dark. "Looking for someone, big boy?" she whispered. It was the stripper who had just come down off the stage.

I ignored her and walked down the bar to Amos. He didn't look up as I climbed onto the empty stool alongside him. "A bottle of Budweiser," I said to the bartender. The bottle was in front of me and my dollar gone before I was fully settled on the stool.

I turned to look at Amos, who was watching the stage, and a feeling of shock ran through me. He was old. Incredibly old and gray. His hair was thin and his skin hung around his cheeks and jowls the way a skinny old man's flesh hangs.

He lifted his drink to his lips. I could see his hand shaking and the grayish-red blotches on the back of it. I tried to think. He couldn't be that old. The most he could be was his middle fifties. Then I saw his eyes and I knew the answer.

He was beat and there was nothing left for him but yesterdays. The dreams were gone because he'd failed all the challenges and the dry rot of time had set in. There was nowhere left for him to go but down. And down and down, until he was dead.

"Hello, Amos," I said quietly.

He put his drink down and turned his head slowly. He looked at me through bloodshot, watery eyes. "Go away," he whispered in a hoarse, whisky-soaked voice. "That's my girl dancing up there."

I glanced up at the stage. She was a redhead who'd seen better years. They were a good combination, the two of them. They'd both fought the good fight—badly—and lost.

I waited until the music crashed to its finale before I spoke again. "I got a proposition for you, Amos."

He turned toward me. "I told your messenger I wasn't interested."

For a moment, I was ready to get down off that stool and walk off. Out into the fresh, cold night and away from the stench of stale beer and sickness and decay. But I didn't. It wasn't only the promise I'd made Forrester. It was also that he'd been Monica's father.

The bartender came up and I ordered us both a round. He picked up the five and left.

"I told Monica about the job. She was very happy about it."

He turned and looked at me again. "Monica always was a damn fool," he said hoarsely, and laughed. "You know, she didn't want to divorce you. She was crazy mad, but afterward she didn't want to divorce you. She said she loved you."

I didn't answer and he laughed again. "But I straightened her out," he continued. "I told her you were just like me, that neither of us could ever resist the smell of cunt."

"That's over and done with," I said. "A long time ago."

He slammed the glass down on the bar with a trembling hand. "It's not over!" he shouted. "You think I can forget how you screwed me out of my own company? You think I can forget how you beat me out of every contract, wouldn't let me get started again?" He laughed craftily. "I'm no fool. You think I didn't know you had men following me all over the country?"

I stared at him. He was sick. Much sicker than I had thought.

"And now you come with a phony proposition, huh?" He smiled slyly. "Think I'm not wise to you? Think I don't know you're tryin' to get me out of the way because you know if they ever get a look at my plans, you're through?"

He slid off the stool and came at me with wildly surging fists. "Through, Jonas!" he screamed. "Through! Do you hear me?"

I swung around on the stool and caught at his hands. His wrists were thin and all fragile old bone. I held his arms and suddenly he slumped against me, his head on my chest.

I looked down at him and saw that his eyes were filled with weak old tears of rage at his helplessness. "I'm so tired, Jonas," he whispered. "Please don't chase me any more. I'm sorry. I'm so tired I can't run any—"

Then he slipped from my grasp and slid down to the floor. The redhead, who had come up behind him, screamed and the music stopped, suddenly. There was a press of people around us as I started to get down from the stool. I felt myself pushed back against the bar violently and I stared into the face of a big man in a black suit. "What's goin' on here?"

"Let him go, Joe." Vitale's voice came from behind and the bouncer turned his head around. "Oh, it's you, Sam." The pressure against my chest relaxed.

I looked down at Amos. Jennie was already kneeling beside him, loosening his shirt collar and slipping down his tie. I bent over. "He pass out?"

Jennie looked up at me. "I think it's more than that," she said. "He feels like he's burning up with fever. I think we'd better get him home."

"O.K.," I said. I took out a roll and threw a hundred-dollar bill down on the bar. "That's for my table." I looked up and saw the redhead staring at me, a mascara track of tears streaming down her cheeks. I peeled off another hundred and pressed it into her hand. "Go dry your tears."

Then I bent down and picking Amos up in my arms, started for the door. I was surprised at how light he was. Vitale got our coats from the hat-check girl and followed me outside.

"He lives just a couple of blocks away," he said as I put Amos into the car.

It was a dirty gray rooming house and two cats stood on open garbage cans in front of the door, glaring at us with their baleful yellow night eyes. I looked up at the building from the car window. This was no place for a man to be sick in.

The chauffeur jumped out and ran around to open the back door. I reached out and pulled the door shut. "Go back to the Drake, driver," I said.

I turned and looked down at Amos, stretched out on the back seat. Just because he was sick didn't make me feel any different about him. But I couldn't get over the feeling that if things had turned out a little differently, it might have been my own father lying there.

9

THE DOCTOR CAME OUT, SHAKING HIS HEAD. JENnie was right behind him. "He'll be all right when he wakes up in the morning. Somebody fed him a slug of sodium amytal."

"What?"

"Knockout drops," Jennie said. "A Mickey."

I smiled. My hunch was right. Vitale had left nothing to chance. I wanted Amos, he saw to it that I got him.

"He's very run down," the doctor added. "Too much whisky and too little food. He has some fever but he'll be all right with a little care."

"Thank you, doctor," I said, getting up.

"You're welcome, Mr. Cord. I'll stop by in the morning to have another look at him. Meanwhile, Miss Denton, give him one of those pills every hour."

"I'll do that, doctor."

The doctor nodded and left.

I looked at Jennie. "Wait a minute. You don't have to sit up all night taking care of that slob."

"I don't mind," she said. "It won't be the first time I sat up with a patient."

"A patient?"

"Of course." She looked at me quizzically. "Didn't I ever tell you I graduated from nursing school?"

I shook my head.

"St. Mary's College of Nursing, in San Francisco," she said. "Nineteen thirty-five. I worked as a nurse for a year. Then I quit."

"Why'd you quit?"

"I got tired of it," she said, her eyes masking over.

I knew better than to push. It was her own business, anyway. "Want a drink?" I asked, going over to the bar.

She shook her head. "No, thanks. Look, there's no sense in both of us staying up all night. Why don't you go to bed and get some rest?"

I looked at her questioningly.

"I'll be O.K. I can catch up on my sleep in the morning."
She came over and kissed me on the cheek. "Good night, Jonas.
And thank you. I think you're a very nice man."

I laughed. "You didn't think I'd let you walk around Chicago
in a light coat like that?"

"For the coat, too. But not only for the coat," she said
quickly. "I heard what he said about you. And still you brought
him here."

"What else could I do? I couldn't just leave him lying there."

"No, of course not," she said, her eyes wide. "Now go to bed."

I turned and walked into the bedroom. It was a dark and
crazy night. In my dreams, Amos and my father were chasing
me around a room, each trying to make me do what he was
shouting at me. But I couldn't understand them—they were
speaking a kind of gibberish. Then Jennie, or maybe Rina,
came into the room dressed in a white uniform and the two of
them began running after her. I tried to stop them and finally, I
managed to get her out of the room and shut the door. I turned
and took her in my arms but it turned out to be Monica and she
was crying. Then somebody slammed me back against the wall
and I stared into the face of the bouncer at La Paree. He began
to shine a flashlight in my eyes and the light grew brighter and
brighter and brighter.

I opened my eyes and blinked them. The sunlight was pouring in the window and it was eight o'clock in the morning.

Jennie was sitting in the living room with a pot of coffee and
some toast in front of her. "Good morning. Have some coffee?"

I nodded, then walked over to Amos' room and looked in.
He was lying on his back, sleeping like a baby. I closed his door,
walked over to the couch and sat down beside her. "You must
be tired," I said, picking up my coffee cup.

"A little. But after a while, you don't feel it any more. You
just keep on going." She looked at me. "He talked quite a bit
about you."

"Yeah? Nothing good, I hope?"

"He blames himself for breaking up your marriage."

"All of us had a little to do with it," I said. "It was no more
his fault than it was mine—or hers."

"Or Rina Marlowe's?"

"Most of all, not Rina's," I said quickly. I reached for a cigarette. "Mainly, it was because Monica and I were too young. We never should have got married in the first place."

She picked up her coffee cup and yawned. "Maybe you better get some rest now," I said.

"I thought I'd stay up until the doctor came."

"Go on to bed. I'll wake you when he comes."

"O.K.," she said. She got up and started for the bedroom. Then she turned and walked back, picking up her mink coat from the chair.

"You won't need it," I said. "I left the bed nice and warm."

She nuzzled her face against the fur. "Sounds nice."

She went inside, closing the door behind her. I filled my coffee cup again and picked up the telephone. Suddenly, I was hungry. I told room service to send up a double order of ham and eggs and a fresh pot of coffee.

Amos came out while I was eating breakfast. He had a blanket wrapped around him like a toga. He shuffled over to the table and looked down at me. "Who stole my clothes?"

In the daylight, he didn't look as bad as he had the night before. "I threw them out," I said. "Sit down and have some breakfast."

He remained standing. He didn't speak. After a moment, he looked around the apartment. "Where's the girl?"

"Sleeping," I said. "She was up all night, taking care of you."

He thought about that. "I passed out?" It was more a statement than a question. I didn't answer.

"I thought so," he said, nodding. Then he groaned. He raised his hand to his forehead, almost losing his blanket. "Somebody slipped me a Mickey," he said accusingly.

"Try some food. It's supposed to have vitamins."

"I need a drink," he said.

"Help yourself. The bar's over there."

He shuffled over to the bar and poured himself a shot. He drank it swiftly, throwing it down his throat. "Ah," he said. He took another quick one. Some color flooded back into his gray face.

He shuffled back to the table, the bottle of whisky still in his hand, and slumped into the chair opposite me. "How'd you find me?"

"It was easy. All we had to do was follow the trail of rubber checks."

"Oh," he said. He poured another drink but left this one

standing on the table in front of him. Suddenly, his eyes filled with tears. "It wouldn't be so bad if it was anyone but you."

I didn't answer; just kept on eating.

"You don't know what it is to get old. You lose your touch."

"You didn't lose it," I said. "You threw it away."

He picked up the whisky glass.

"If you're not interested in my proposition," I said, "just go ahead and drink that drink."

He stared at me silently for a moment. Then he looked at the small, amber-filled glass in his hand. His hand trembled slightly and some of the whisky spilled on the tablecloth. "What makes you such a do-gooder all of a sudden?"

"I'm not," I said. I reached for my coffee cup and smiled at him. "I haven't changed at all. I still think you're the world's champion prick. If it was up to me, I wouldn't touch you with a ten-foot pole. But Forrester wants you to run our Canadian factory. The damn fool doesn't know you like I do. He still thinks you're the greatest."

"Roger Forrester, huh?" he asked. Slowly the whisky glass came down to the table. "He tested the Liberty Five I designed right after the war. He said it was the greatest plane he ever flew."

I stared at him silently. That was more than twenty years ago and there had been many great planes since then. But Amos remembered the Liberty Five. It was the plane that set him up in business.

A hint of the Amos Winthrop I had known came into his face. "What's my end of the deal?" he asked shrewdly.

I shrugged my shoulders. "That's between you and Roger," I said.

"Good." A kind of dignity came over him as he got to his feet. "If I had to deal with you, I wouldn't be interested, at any price."

He stalked back to his bedroom door. He turned and glared at me. "What do I do about clothes?"

"There's a men's shop downstairs. Call them and have them send up what you want."

The door closed behind him and I reached for a cigarette. I could hear the faint murmur of his voice on the telephone. Leaning back in the chair, I let the smoke drift idly out through my nose.

When the clothing arrived, I had them leave it in his bedroom. Then the buzzer sounded again and I cursed to myself as I went to the door. I was beginning to feel like a bloody butler. I opened the door. "Hello, Mr. Cord."

It was a child's voice. I looked down in surprise. Jo-Ann was standing next to Monica, clutching the doll I had given her in one hand and her mother's coat in the other.

"McAllister sent me a telegram, on the train," Monica explained. "He said you'd probably be here. Did you find Amos?"

I stared at her dumbly. Mac must be losing his marbles. He must have known there was a three-hour layover in Chicago and that Monica would show up here. What if I didn't want to see her?

"Did you find Amos?" Monica repeated.

"Yes, I found him."

"Oh, goody," Jo-Ann suddenly exclaimed, spotting the breakfast table. "I'm hungry." She ran past me and climbing up on a chair, picked up a piece of toast. I stared after her in surprise.

Monica looked up at me apologetically. "I'm sorry, Jonas," she said. "You know how children are."

"You said we'd have breakfast with Mr. Cord, Mommy."

Monica blushed. "Jo-Ann!"

"It's all right," I said. "Won't you come in?"

She came into the room and I closed the door. "I'll order some breakfast for you," I said, going to the telephone.

Monica smiled. "Just coffee for me," she said, taking off her coat.

"Is the doctor here yet, Jonas?"

Monica stared.

I stared.

Jennie stood in the open doorway, her long blond hair spilling down over the dark mink coat, which she held wrapped around her like a robe. Her bare neck and legs made it obvious she wore nothing beneath it.

The smile had gone from Monica's face. Her eyes were cold as she turned to me. "I beg your pardon, Jonas," she said stiffly. "I should have known from experience to call before I came up."

She crossed the room and took the child's hand. "Come on, Jo-Ann."

They were almost to the door before I found my voice. "Wait a minute, Monica," I said harshly.

Amos' voice cut me off. "Ah, just in time, child," he said calmly. "We can leave together."

I turned to look at him. The sick, dirty old man we had found in the bar last night had disappeared. It was the Amos of old who stood there, dressed neatly in a gray, pin-striped, double-breasted suit, with a dark chesterfield thrown casually over his arm. He was every inch the senior executive, the man in charge.

There was a faintly malicious smile on his lips as he crossed the room and turned, his hand on the door. "My children and I do not wish to impose—" He paused and bowed slightly in the direction of Jennie. Angrily I started toward the door. I opened it and heard the elevator doors open and close, then there was silence in the hall.

"I'm sorry, Jonas," Jennie said. "I didn't mean to louse things up for you."

I looked at her. Her eyes were large with sympathy. "You didn't do anything," I said. "Things were loused up a long time ago."

I went to the bar and poured myself a drink. All the good feeling had gone. This was the last time I'd ever play the good Samaritan. I swallowed the drink and turned back to Jennie. "Did you ever get laid in a mink coat?" I asked angrily.

There was sadness and understanding on her face. "No."

I poured myself another drink and swallowed it. We stood there, looking at each other silently across the room for a moment. Finally, I spoke. "Well?"

Her eyes still on mine, she nodded slowly. Then she raised her arms and held them out toward me, the coat falling open, away from her naked body. When she spoke, there was a note in her voice as if she'd always known that this was the way it was going to be. "Come to mother, baby," she whispered gently.

1

JENNIE WALKED THROUGH THE CURTAINED DOOR-
way into the camera and the director shouted, "Cut! Wrap it
up!" And it was over.

She stood there for a moment, dazed, blinking her eyes for a
moment as the powerful kliegs dimmed. Then the oppressive
August heat came down on her and she felt faint. She reached
out a hand to steady herself. As if from a distance, she heard the
giant sound stage turn into bedlam. It seemed that everybody
was laughing and talking at once.

Someone pressed a glass of water into her hands. She drank it
quickly, gratefully. Suddenly, she began to shiver, feeling a chill,
and the dresser quickly threw a robe over her shoulders, covering the diaphanous costume. "Thank you," she whispered.

"You're welcome, Miss Denton," the dresser said. He looked
at her peculiarly for a moment. "You feeling all right?"

"I'm fine," Jennie said. She felt cold perspiration breaking out on her forehead. The dresser gestured and the make-up man hurried up. He swabbed at her face quickly with a moist sponge. The faint aroma of witch hazel came up in her nostrils and she began to feel better.

"Miss Denton," the make-up man said, "you'd better lie down for a while. You're exhausted."

Docilely she let him lead her back to the small portable dressing room. She looked back over her shoulder as she went in. The bottles were out and the whisky flowing. Everyone was gathered around the director, shouting congratulations, supplying him with the adoration they felt necessary to insure their employment on his next picture. Already, they seemed to have forgotten her.

She closed the door behind her and stretched out on the cot. She closed her eyes wearily. The three months the picture was supposed to take had stretched out into five. Five months of day-and-night shooting, of exhaustion, of getting up at five o'clock in the morning and falling into bed like a stone at midnight, and sometimes later. Five months, until all the meaning that had been in the script was lost in a maze of retakes, rewrites and plain confusion.

She began to shiver again and pulled the light wool blanket up over her and lay there trembling. She closed her eyes. She turned on her side, drawing her knees up and hugging herself. Slowly the heat from her body condensed around her and she began to feel better.

When she opened her eyes, Ilene Gaillard was seated on a chair opposite. She hadn't even heard her come into the small room. "Hello," Jennie said, sitting up. "Was I asleep long?"

Ilene smiled. "About an hour. You needed it."

"I feel so silly," Jennie said. "I usually don't go off like that. But I felt so weak."

"You've been under a terrible strain. But you have nothing to worry about. When this picture comes out, you're going to be a big star—one of the biggest."

"I hope so," Jennie said humbly. She looked at Ilene. "When I think of all those people, how hard they worked and how much they put into the picture. I couldn't bear it if I turned out to be a disappointment to them."

"You won't. From what I saw of the rushes, you were great."

Ilene got to her feet and looked down at Jennie. "I think you could use a hot drink."

Jennie smiled when she saw Ilene take down the can of co-coa. "Chocolate?"

"Why not?" Ilene said. "It will give you more energy than tea. Besides, you don't have to worry about your diet any more. The picture is finished."

"Thank God for that," Jennie said, standing up. "One more lunch of cottage cheese and I was ready to throw up." She crossed the tiny room to the closet. "I might as well get out of this."

Ilene nodded. She watched as Jennie slipped out of the costume—the sheer, flowing silk harem pantaloons, the diaphanous gauze blouse and gold-beaded blue velvet jacket that had been her costume in the last scene. She scanned the girl's figure appreciatively, her designer's eyes pleased with what she saw.

She was glad now that Jonas had sent for her. She had not felt that way at first. She hadn't wanted to come back to Hollywood, back to the gossip, the jockeying for importance, the petty jealousies. But most of all, she hadn't wanted to come back to the memories.

But as she'd studied the photograph, something about the girl had drawn her back. She could understand what Jonas had seen in her. There was something of Rina about her but she also had a quality that was peculiarly her own.

It wasn't until she'd studied the photograph a long while that she realized what it was. It was the strangely ascetic translucence that shone from the photograph despite its purely sensuous appeal. The eyes in the picture looked out at you with the clear innocence of a child, behind their worldly knowledge. It was the face of a girl who had kept her soul untouched, no matter what she had experienced.

Jennie fastened her brassière and pulled the thick black sweater down until it met the top of her baggy slacks. She sat down and took the cup of steaming chocolate from Ilene. "Suddenly, I'm empty," she said, sipping at it. "I'm all used up."

Ilene smiled and tasted her own cup of chocolate. "Everyone feels like that when a picture is finished."

"I feel that I could never make another movie," Jennie continued thoughtfully. "That another part wouldn't make any sense to me at all. Somehow, it's like all of me went into this picture and I've nothing left at all."

Ilene smiled again. "That will disappear the moment they put the next script into your hands."

"Do you think so?" Jennie asked. "Is that what happens?"

Ilene nodded. "Every time."

A blast of noise came through the thin walls. Jennie smiled. "They're having themselves a ball out there."

"Cord ordered a table of food sent down from the commissary. He's got two men tending bar." Ilene finished her chocolate and put the cup down. She got to her feet and looked down at the girl. "I really came in to say good-by."

Jennie looked up at her questioningly. "You're leaving?"

Ilene nodded. "I'm going back East on the train tonight."

"Oh," Jennie said. She put down her cup and stood up. She held her hand out to Ilene. "Thank you for everything you've done. I've learned a great deal from you."

Ilene took her hand. "I didn't want to come back but I'm glad now that I did."

They shook hands formally. "I hope we'll work together again," Jennie said.

Ilene started for the door. She looked back at Jennie. "I'm sure that we will," she said. "If you want me, write. I'd be glad to come."

In a moment, the door opened again and Al Petrocelli, the publicity manager, stuck his head in. A blast of music came from behind him. "Come on," he said. "The party's going great guns. Cord sent over an orchestra."

She put down her cigarette. "Just a minute," she said, turning to the mirror and straightening her hair.

He stared at her. "You're not coming like that?" he asked incredulously.

"Why not? The picture's finished."

He came into the room and closed the door behind him. "But, Jennie baby, try to understand. *Life* magazine is covering the party. How would it look to their readers if the star of the biggest picture we've made in ten years was wearing a loose black sweater and pants? We've got to give 'em more to look at than that."

"I'm not getting into that costume again," Jennie said stubbornly.

"Please, baby. I promised them some cheesecake."

"If that's what they want, give them the photo file."

"Now is no time to make with the temperament," Al said. "Look, you've been a good girl up to now. Just this once, please."

"It's O.K., Al." Bonner's voice came from behind him. "If Jennie doesn't want to change, she doesn't have to." He smiled his pleasantly ugly smile as he came into the tiny dressing room. "As a matter of fact," he said, "I think it might be a welcome change for *Life's* readers."

Al looked at him. "O.K. if you say so, Mr. Bonner," he said.

Bonner turned to her, smiling. "Well, you did it."

She didn't answer, just looked at him.

"I've been thinking about you," he said, his eyes on her face. "You're going to be a big star."

She didn't say anything.

"*The Sinner* is going to be a tough picture to follow."

"I hadn't thought about it," she said.

"Of course. You haven't and neither has Jonas." Bonner laughed. "But why should you? That's not your job. It's mine. All Jonas does is what he feels like doing. If he wants to make a picture, he makes a picture. But it might be another eight years before he feels like it again."

"So?" she said, meeting his eyes levelly.

He shrugged his shoulders. "It's up to me to keep you working. If you go that long between pictures, they'll forget all about you." He reached into his jacket for a package of cigarettes. "Is that Mexican woman still working for you?"

"Yes."

"Still living in the same place?"

"Of course."

"I thought I might drop by one evening next week," he said. "I've got some scripts we might go over."

She was silent.

"Jonas is going away," he said. "To Canada, on a business trip." He smiled. "You know, I think it's fortunate he hasn't heard any of the stories about you, don't you?"

She let her breath out slowly. "Yes."

"I thought maybe Wednesday night."

"You'd better call first," she said through stiff lips.

"Of course, I forgot. Nothing has changed, has it?"

She looked up at him. "No," she said dully. Then she walked past him to the door. A great weariness came into her. Nothing had changed. Things turned out the way they always did for her. Nothing ever changed but the currency.

2

SHE AWOKE TO THE SIGHT OF WHITE LINEN FLOAT-ing in the wind on the clothesline outside the window. The rich aroma of corned beef and cabbage, wafting into her room on the heavy summer breeze from the kitchen next door, told her it was Sunday. It was always like that on Sundays, only when you were a little girl it had been more fun.

On Sundays, when she'd returned from church with her mother, her father would be awake and smiling, his mustache neatly trimmed and waxed, his face smooth and smelling of bay rum. He tossed her into the air and caught her as she came down, hugging her close to him and growling, "How is my little Jennie Bear this morning? Is she sweet and filled with God's holiness fresh from the fount in the back of the church?"

He laughed and she laughed and sometimes even her mother laughed, saying, "Now, Thomas Denton, is that the proper way for a father to talk to his own daughter, sowing in her the seeds of his own disobedience to God's will?"

Her father and mother were both young and filled with laughter and happiness and God's own good sunshine that shone down on San Francisco Bay. And after the big dinner, he dressed himself carefully in his good blue suit and took her by the hand and they went out of the house to seek adventure.

They first met adventure on the cable car that ran past their door. Holding her in his arms, her father leaped aboard the moving car, and waving his blue-and-white conductor's pass, which entitled him to ride free on any of the company's cars, pushed forward to the front of the car, next to the motorman. There he held her face up to the rushing wind until the breath caught in her throat and she thought she'd burst with the joy of the fresh, sweet wind in her lungs.

"This is my daughter, my Jennie Bear," he shouted to all who would listen, holding her proudly so that all who cared to look could see.

And the passengers, who up to now had been engrossed in their own private thoughts, smiled at her, sharing somehow in the joy that glowed like a beacon in her round and shining face. Then they went to the park, or sometimes to the wharf, where they ate hot shrimp or crabs, swimming in garlic, and her father drank beer, great foaming glasses of it, bought from the bootlegger who operated quite openly near the stands. But only to wash away the smell of the garlic, of course. Or sometimes, they went out to the zoo and he bought her a bag of peanuts to feed the elephant or the monkeys in their cages. And they returned in the evening, and she was tired and sometimes asleep in her father's arms. And the next day was Monday and she couldn't wait until it would be Sunday again.

No, nothing passed as quickly as the Sundays of your childhood. And then she went to school, frightened at first of the sisters, who were stern and forbidding in their black habits. Her small round face was serious above her white middy blouse and navy-blue guimpe. But they taught you the catechism and you made your confirmation and lost your fear as bit by bit you accepted them as your teachers, leading you into a richer Christian life, and the happy Sundays of your childhood fled deeper and deeper into the dim recesses of your mind, until you hardly remembered them any more.

Jennie lay quietly on her sixteen-year-old bed, her ears sharpening to the sounds of the Sunday morning. For a moment, there was only silence, then she heard her mother's shrill voice. "Mr. Denton, for the last time, it's time to get up and go to Mass."

Her father's voice was husky, the words indistinguishable. She could see him in her mind's eyes, lying unshaven and bloated with Saturday-night beer in his long woolen underwear, on the soft, wide bed, burying his face in the big pillow. She heard her mother again. "But I promised Father Hadley ye'd come this Sunday for sure. If ye have no concern for your own soul, at least have some for your wife's and daughter's."

She heard no reply, then the door slammed as her mother retreated to the kitchen. Jennie swung her bare feet onto the floor, searching for her slippers. She found them and stood up, the long white cotton nightgown trailing down to her ankles as she crossed the room.

She came out into the kitchen on her way to the bathroom and her mother turned from the stove. "Ye can wear the new blue bonnet I made for ye to Mass, Jennie darlin'."

"Yes, Mother," she said.

She brushed her teeth carefully, remembering what Sister Philomena had told the class in Hygiene. Circular strokes with the brush, reaching up onto the gums, then down, would remove all the food particles that might cause decay. She examined her teeth carefully in the mirror. She had nice teeth. Clean and white and even.

She liked being clean. Not like many of the girls at Mercy High School, who came from the same poor neighborhood and bathed only once a week, on Saturdays. She took a bath every night—even if she had to heat the water in the kitchen of the old tenement in which they lived.

She looked at her face out of her clear gray eyes and tried to imagine herself in the white cap and uniform of a nurse. She'd have to make up her mind soon. Graduation was next month and it wasn't every student who could get a scholarship to St. Mary's College of Nursing.

The sisters liked her and she'd always received high marks throughout her attendance at Mercy. Besides, Father Hadley had written Mother M. Ernest, commending her for her devout attendance and service to the church, not like so many of the young ladies today, who spent more time in front of a mirror over their make-up than on their knees in church in front of their God. Father Hadley had expressed the hope that the Good Mother would find a way to reward this poor deserving child for her devotion.

The scholarship to St. Mary's was given each year to the one student whose record for religious and scholastic achievements was deemed the most worthy by a committee headed by the Archbishop. This year, it was to be hers, if she decided to become a nurse. This morning, after church, she'd have to present herself to Mother M. Ernest, at the Sister House, to give her answer.

"It is God's mercy you'll be dispensing," Sister Cyril had said, after informing her of the committee's choice. "But you will have to make the decision. It may be that attending the sick and helpless is not your true vocation."

Sister Cyril had looked up at the girl standing quietly in front of her desk. Already, Jennie was tall and slim, with the full body of a woman, and yet there was a quiet innocence in the calm gray eyes that looked back at her. Jennie did not speak. Sister Cyril smiled at her. "You have a week to make up your mind," she said gently. "Go to the Sister House next Sunday after Mass. Mother Mary Ernest will be there to receive your answer."

Her father had cursed angrily when he heard of the scholarship. "What kind of life is that for a child? Cleaning out the bedpans of dirty old men? The next thing you know, they'll talk her into becoming a nun."

He turned violently to her mother. "It's all your doing," he shouted. "You and those priests you listen to. What's so holy about taking a child with the juices of life just beginning to bubble inside of her and locking her away behind the walls of a convent?"

Her mother's face was white. "It's blasphemy you're speaking, Thomas Denton," she said coldly. "If only once you'd come and speak to the good Father Hadley, ye'd learn how wrong ye are. And if our daughter should become a religious, it's the proudest mother in Christendom I'd be. What is wrong in giving your only child as a bride to Christ?"

"Aye," her father said heavily. "But who'll be to blame when the child grows up and finds you've stolen from her the pleasures of being a woman?"

He turned to Jennie and looked down at her. "Jennie Bear," he said softly, "it's not that I object to your becoming a nurse if you want to. It's that I want you to do and be whatever you want to be. Your mother and I, we don't matter. Even what the church wants doesn't matter. It's what you want that does." He sighed. "Do you understand, child?"

Jennie nodded. "I understand, Papa."

"Ye'll not be satisfied till ye see your daughter a whore," her mother suddenly screamed at him.

He turned swiftly. "I'd rather see her a whore of her own free choice," he snapped, "than driven to sainthood."

He looked down at Jennie, his voice soft again. "Do you want to become a nurse, Jennie Bear?"

She looked up at him with her clear gray eyes. "I think so, Papa."

"If it's what you want, Jennie Bear," he said quietly, "then I'll be content with it."

Her mother looked at him, a quiet triumph in her eyes. "When will ye learn ye cannot fight the Lord, Thomas Denton?"

He started to answer, then shut his lips tightly and strode from the apartment.

Sister Cyril knocked at the heavy oaken door of the study. "Come in," called a strong, clear voice. She opened the door and gestured to Jennie.

Jennie walked into the room hesitantly, Sister Cyril behind her. "This is Jennie Denton, Reverend Mother."

The middle-aged woman in the black garb of the Sisterhood looked up from her desk. There was a half-finished cup of tea by her hand. She studied the girl with curiously bright, questioning eyes. After a moment, she smiled, revealing white, even teeth. "So you're Jennie Denton," she said, holding out her hand.

Jennie curtsied quickly and kissed the ring on the finger of the Reverend Mother. "Yes, Reverend Mother." She straightened up and stood in front of the desk stiffly.

Mother M. Ernest smiled again, a hint of merriment coming into her eyes. "You can relax, child," she said. "I'm not going to eat you."

Jennie smiled awkwardly.

The Reverend Mother raised a questioning eyebrow. "Perhaps you'd like a cup of tea?" she asked. "A cup of tea always makes me feel better."

"That would be very nice," Jennie said stiffly.

The Reverend Mother looked up and nodded at Sister Cyril. "I'll get it, Reverend Mother," the nun said quickly.

"And another cup for me, please?" Mother M. Ernest turned back to Jennie. "I do love a good cup of tea." She smiled. "And they do have that here. None of those weak tea balls they use in the hospitals; real tea, brewed in a pot the way tea should be. Won't you sit down, child?"

The last came so fast that Jennie wasn't quite sure she'd heard it. "What, ma'am?" she stammered.

"Won't you sit down, child? You don't have to be nervous with me. I want to be your friend."

"Yes, ma'am," Jennie said and sat down, even more nervous than before.

The Reverend Mother looked at her for a few moments. "So you've decided to become a nurse, have you?"

"Yes, Reverend Mother."

Now the Reverend Mother's curiously bright eyes were upon her. "Why?" she asked suddenly.

"Why?" Jennie was surprised at the question. Her eyes fell before the Reverend Mother's gaze. "Why?" She looked up again, her eyes meeting the Reverend Mother's. "I don't know. I guess I never really thought about it."

"How old are you, child?" the Reverend Mother asked.

"I'll be seventeen next month, the week before graduation."

"It was always your ambition to be a nurse and help the sick, ever since you were a little child, wasn't it?"

Jennie shook her head. "No," she answered candidly. "I never thought about it much until now."

"Becoming a nurse is very hard work. You'll have very little time to yourself at St. Mary's. You'll work and study all day; at night, you'll live at the school. You'll have only one day off each month to visit your family." The Reverend Mother turned the handle of her cup delicately so that it pointed away from her. "Your boy friend might not like that."

"But I haven't got a boy friend," Jennie said.

"But you came to the junior and senior proms with Michael Halloran," the Reverend Mother said. "And you play tennis with him every Saturday. Isn't he your boy friend?"

Jennie laughed. "No, Reverend Mother. He's not my boy friend, not that way." She laughed again, this time to herself, as she thought of the lanky, gangling youth whose only romantic thoughts were about his backhand. "He's just the best tennis player around, that's all." Then she added, "And someday I'm going to beat him."

"You were captain of the girl's tennis team last year?"

Jennie nodded.

"You won't have time to play tennis at St. Mary's," the Reverend Mother said.

Jennie didn't answer.

"Is there anything you'd rather be than a nurse?"

Jennie thought for a moment. Then she looked up at the

Reverend Mother. "I'd like to beat Helen Wills for the U.S. tennis championship."

The Reverend Mother began to laugh. She was still laughing when Sister Cyril came in with the tea. She looked across the desk at the girl. "You'll do," she said. "And I have a feeling you'll make a very good nurse, too."

3

TOM DENTON KNEW THERE WAS SOMETHING wrong the moment he came up to the window for his pay envelope. Usually, the paymaster was ready with a wisecrack, like did he want him to hold the envelope for his wife so that the Saturday-night beer parlors wouldn't get it? But there was no wisecrack this time, no friendly raillery, which had been a part of their weekly meeting for almost fifteen years. Instead, the paymaster pushed the envelope under the slotted steel bars quickly, his eyes averted and downcast.

Tom stared at him for a moment. He glanced quickly at some of the faces on the line behind him. They knew, too. He could see it from the way they were looking at him. An odd feeling of shame came over him. This couldn't be happening to him. Not after fifteen years. His eyes fell and he walked away from the window, the envelope in his hand.

Nobody had to tell him times were bad. This was 1931 and the evidence was all around him. The families on relief, the bread lines, the endless gray, tired faces of the men who boarded his car every morning.

He was almost out of the barn now. Suddenly, he couldn't wait any longer and he ducked into a dark corner to open the pay envelope. He tore at it with trembling fingers. The first thing that came to his hand was the dreaded green slip.

He stared at it unbelievingly. It must be a mistake. They couldn't mean him. He wasn't a one-year or two-year man, not even a five-year man. He had seniority. Fifteen years. They weren't laying off fifteen-year men. Not yet.

But they were. He squinted at the paper in the dim light. Laid off. What a bitter irony. That was the reason given for all the pay cuts—to prevent layoffs. Even the union had told them that.

He shoved the envelope into his pocket, trying to fight the sudden sick feeling of fear that crawled around in his stomach. What was he to do now? All he knew was the cars. He'd forgotten all about everything else he'd ever done. The only other thing he remembered was working as a hod-carrier when he was young.

He came out of the dark barn, blinking his eyes at the daylight. A group of men were standing there on the sidewalk, their worn blue uniforms purplish in the light. One of them called to him. "You got it, too, Denton?"

Tom looked at him. He nodded. "Yes."

"We did, too," another said. "They're letting out the senior men because we're getting a higher rate. All the new men are being kept on."

"Have you been to the union yet?" Tom asked.

"We've been there and back. The hall is closed. The watchman there says come back on Monday."

"Anybody call Riordan?"

"His home phone don't answer."

"Somebody must know where Riordan is," Tom said. "Let's go to the hall and make the watchman let us in. After all, what do we pay dues for if we can't meet there?"

"That's a good idea, Tom. We can't just let them replace us with fifty-five-centers, no matter what they say."

They began to walk to the union hall, about two blocks from the car barn. Tom strode along silently. In a way, he still couldn't believe it. Ten cents an hour couldn't mean that much to the company. Why, he'd have taken even another cut if they'd asked him. It wasn't right, the way they were doing it. They had to find Riordan. He'd know the answers. He was the union man.

The union hall was dark when they got there and they banged on the door until the old night watchman opened it. "I tol' you fellers Riordan ain't here," he said in an aged, irritated voice.

"Where is Riordan?"

"I don't know," the watchman answered, starting to close the door. "You fellers go home."

Tom put his foot in the door and pushed. The old man went flying backward, stumbling, almost falling. The men surged into the building behind Tom.

"You fellers stay outa here," the old man cried in his querulous voice.

They ignored him and pushed their way into the meeting hall, which was a large room at the end of the corridor. By now, the crowd had swelled to close to thirty men. Once they were in, they stood there uncertainly, not knowing what to do next. They milled around, looking at each other. "Let's go into Riordan's office," Tom suggested. "Maybe we can find out where he is in there."

Riordan's office was a glass-enclosed partition at the end of the meeting hall. They pushed down there but only a few of them were able to squeeze into the tiny cubbyhole. Tom looked down at the organizer's desk. There was a calendar, a green blotter and some pencils on it. He pulled open a drawer, then, one after another, all of them. The only thing he could find were more pencils, and dues blanks and receipts.

The watchman appeared at the back of the hall. "If you fellers don't get outa here," he shouted, "I'm gonna call the cops."

"Go take a shit, old man," a blue-coated conductor shouted back at him.

"Yeah," shouted another. "This is our union. We pay the dues and the rent. We can stay here if we want."

The watchman disappeared back into the corridor. Some of the men looked at Tom. "What do we do now?"

"Maybe we better come back Monday," one of them suggested. "We'll see what Riordan has to say then."

"No," Tom said sharply. "By Monday, nobody will be able to do nothing. We got to get this settled today."

"How?" the man asked.

Tom stood there for a moment, thinking. "The union's the only chance we got. We got to make the union do something for us."

"How can we if Riordan ain't here?"

"Riordan isn't the union," Tom said. "We are. If we can't find him, we got to do it without him." He turned to one of the men. "Patrick, you're on the executive board. What does Riordan usually do in a case like this?"

Patrick took off his cap and scratched at his gray hair. "I dunno," he said thoughtfully. "But I reckon the first thing he'd do would be to call a meetin'."

"O.K." Tom nodded. "You take a bunch of the men back to the barns and tell the day shift to come down here to a meeting right away."

The men moved around excitedly and after a few minutes, several of them left to go back to the car barns. The others stood around, waiting. "If we're to have a meetin'," someone said, "we gotta have an agenda. They don't have no meetin's without they have an agenda."

"The agenda is, can the company lay us off like this," Tom said. They nodded agreement. "We got rights."

"This meetin' business is givin' me a awful thirst," another man said. "All this talkin' has dried out me throat somethin' terrible."

"Let's send out for a barrel of beer," a voice yelled from the back.

There was real enthusiasm in the shout of agreement and a collection was quickly taken up. Two men were dispatched on the errand and when they returned, the keg was mounted on a table at the back of the room.

"Now," said one of them, waving his beer glass in front of him, "now we can get down to business!"

The meeting hall was a bedlam of noise and confusion as more than a hundred men milled around, talking and shouting. The first keg of beer had run out long ago. Two new ones rested on the table, pouring forth their refreshment.

Tom pounded on the table with the gavel he'd found in Riordan's desk. "The meeting will now come to order!" he shouted, for the fifth time in as many minutes. He kept pounding on the table until he caught the attention of a few men down at the front.

"Quiet!" one of them bellowed. "Le's hear what good ol' Tom has to say."

The noise subsided to a murmur, then all the men were watching him. Tom waited until it was as quiet as he thought it would get, then he cleared his throat nervously. "We called this meetin' because today the company laid off fifty men an' we couldn't find Riordan to tell us why." He fumbled with the gavel for a moment. "The union, which is supposed to give us protection on our jobs, has now got to act, even if we don't know where Riordan is. The men that were laid off today had seniority an' there's no reason why the company shouldn't take them back."

A roar burst from the crowd.

"While you fellers was drinkin' beer," Tom said, "I looked up the rules in the bylaws printed in my union book, an' it says that a meetin' is entitled to call for a strike vote if more than twenty-five members is present. There's more than twenty-five members here an' I say we should vote a strike by Monday, unless the company takes us back right away."

"Strike! Strike!"

"We've all been faithful employees of the company for many years an' always gave them an honest count an' they got no right to kick us out like that."

"Y-aay!"

"Don't let the nickels stick to your fingers, Tom," a man in the back shouted. "There may be a spotter in the crowd."

There was laughter.

"If there is a spotter," Tom said grimly, "let him go back to the company an' tell 'em what we're doin' here. We'll show 'em they can't push us around."

There was a burst of applause.

Tom waved his hand. "Now we'll vote on a strike," he said. "All in favor say aye."

The men were suddenly quiet. They looked at each other nervously. The door at the back of the hall had opened and Riordan was standing in it. "What's all this loose talk about a strike, men?"

They turned in surprise and stared at him. The ruddy-faced, heavy-set union organizer started down through the meeting hall. A buzz came up as they saw him. It was almost a sigh of relief. Riordan was here. He'd tell them what to do. He'd straighten everything out.

"Hello, Tom," Riordan said, walking around the table. He held out his hand. Tom shook hands with him. It was the first time he'd done so.

"We came down here because we thought the union should be doin' somethin' for us."

Riordan gave him a shrewd look. "Of course, Tom," he said soothingly. "And it's the right thing ye did, too."

Tom sighed in relief. For a moment, he had thought Riordan

would be angry at the way they'd come in and taken over the hall. He watched as Riordan turned toward the men and held up his hand. A silence came over the hall.

"Men," Riordan said in his deep voice, "the reason you couldn't find me was I beat it up to the company office the minute I learned about the layoffs. There was no time to call a meeting but I want you to know that the union was right on the job."

A cheer went up from the men. They looked at each other embarrassedly.

"And I want to express my appreciation to Brother Tom Denton here for his prompt action in bringing you all down here to the union hall. It shows that Tom Denton, like every one of you, knows that the union is his friend."

Tom blushed as the men cheered again. Riordan turned back to the crowd. "I've been working all afternoon, fighting with the management, and finally I got them to back down a little."

A loud cheer shook the ceiling.

Riordan raised his hand, smiling. "Don't cheer yet, boys. Like I say, I only got them to back down a little bit, but it's a start. They promised to have more meetings with me next month."

"Are they takin' us back?" Tom asked.

Riordan looked at him, then turned back to the men. "The management agreed to take back ten of the men who were laid off this week. They also agreed to take back ten more men next month."

A strange silence came over the room. The men eyed each other nervously. "But more than fifty of us were laid off," Tom said loudly. "What's ten men out of that many?"

"It's a start, Tom," he said. "You can't do it all at once."

"Why not?" Tom demanded hotly. "They laid us all off at once."

"That's different," Riordan said. "The company has the right to lay off if business is bad."

"We know that. What we're sore about is the way they did it. They paid no attention to the seniority they agreed to in the union agreement. They laid off all the sixty-five-cent men and kept the fifty-five-centers."

"I know," Riordan said. A harsh edge had come into his voice. "But their taking back ten men is a start. It's better than having all fifty of ye out on the street." He turned back to the men. "Ten of you will go back to work. Maybe next month, ten more will go back. That's better than nothing. The company doesn't care if you go on strike. They claim they'll save money by not running."

"I say we take it," one of the men shouted. "Ten of us workin' is better than none workin', like Riordan says."

"No," Tom said angrily, getting to his feet. "The company should take us all back. Each of us has as much right to work as the next one. If all us sixty-five-cent men would accept a cut to fifty-five cents, the company could keep us all on."

Riordan laughed hoarsely. "You hear that, men?" he shouted. "Would you like to take another pay cut?"

There was a murmur from the crowd. They shifted uneasily. "I'd rather take a pay cut than have us all laid off," Tom said.

Riordan glared at him. There was no friendliness in his eyes now. He had been angry ever since he got a call from the company personnel manager, advising him he'd better get down to the union hall. The call had caught him at a very embarrassing time. He got out of bed, cursing as he struggled into his clothing. "What is it, honey?"

"Some jerky conductor has taken over the hall and is talking strike to the boys."

"But he can't do that," his paramour answered in a shocked voice. "You promised the company they'd have no trouble."

"They won't," he said harshly. "Nobody can make Riordan break his word!"

By the time he'd driven down to the union hall, he'd simmered down. But now he was getting angry again. He had a hard enough job explaining to his wife where he was spending his Saturday nights, without having it loused up by a bunch of stupid trolley men.

He turned back to the crowd. "I propose we settle this here and now," he shouted. "You have a choice. Ten men go back to work or you strike."

"Wait a minute," Tom protested.

"The men already turned your proposal down," Riordan snapped. He raised his right hand. "All in favor of returning to work raise your right hand."

About ninety men raised their hands.

"Nays?"

There were only a few raised hands besides Tom's.

"The ayes have it. Now you men go home to your wives. I'll let you know on Monday which of you go back to work."

Slowly the men began to file out of the room. Tom looked at Riordan but the man didn't meet his eyes. Instead, he went back into his little glass cubbyhole and picked up the telephone.

Tom walked wearily toward the door. Some of the men looked at him, then quickly hurried by, as if they were ashamed to meet his gaze. At the doorway, he turned and looked back. Riordan was still using the telephone.

The night was clear and bright and a warm breeze came in from the bay. He walked along thoughtfully. He wasn't going to be one of the lucky ten who were going to be taken back. He was sure of that. He'd seen the anger in Riordan's eyes. He turned the corner and walked to the car stop on the next block. Idly he wondered if his pass was still good now that he was laid off.

Two men came past him on the darkened street. One of them stopped. "Got a match?"

"Sure," Tom said. He fumbled in his pocket. He might not have a job but matches he still had. He struck the match. The sudden hardening in the man's eyes and the sound of footsteps behind him were a warning that came too late. There was a sharp blow to the back of his head and he stumbled to his knees.

He reached out, grabbing the man in front of him around the legs. The man swore under his breath and kicked upward with his knee, catching Tom in the groin.

Tom grunted from the pain as he went over backward, his head striking the sidewalk. As if from a long way off, he felt the men kicking at him as he lay there. He rolled over toward the edge of the sidewalk and into the gutter.

He felt a hand reach into his pocket and take out his pay envelope. Feebly he tried to grab the hand. "No," he pleaded. "Please, no, that's my pay, it's all I got!"

The man laughed harshly. He aimed a final kick at the side of Tom's head.

Tom saw the heavy boot coming but he couldn't duck away from it. Then the lights exploded in his face and he rolled over, face down, in a puddle of water in the gutter. He came to slowly, painfully, to the sound of water against his face. He moved his head wearily. A gentle rain had begun to fall.

His body ached as he pushed himself up on his hands and slowly got to his feet. He swayed dizzily for a moment and reached out to the street lamp to steady himself. The lamp flickered and then went out. It was almost morning. The sick gray light of the day spilled down around him.

He saw his blue conductor's cap lying in the gutter, not far from where he stood. Slowly he knelt and picked it up. He brushed it off against his coat and walked toward the corner. There was a mirror in the corner of the drugstore window. He paused in front of it and looked at himself.

His uniform was torn and shredded, his tie askew, the shirt buttons ripped away. He put his hand up to his face in touching wonder. His nose was puffed and swollen, and one eye had already turned purple. With the tip of his tongue, he could feel the jagged edges of broken teeth.

He stared for a moment, numb with shock, then he began to understand what had happened to him. Riordan had done it. He was sure of that. That's why Riordan had been on the telephone when he'd left the union hall.

Suddenly, he realized he'd never be able to go back to work for the cable-car company. Riordan would see to that, too. He stood there looking at himself and the tears began to run down his cheeks. Everything had gone wrong. Everything. Now he had no job and no money. And worst of all, he'd have to tell Ellen.

She'd never believe he hadn't been out on a drunk, and the ironic thing was that he hadn't so much as taken one glass of beer.

4

"ARE YE GOIN' TO BE SITTIN' THERE ALL DAY reading the newspapers, studyin' what kind of a job would suit your highness best?" Ellen Denton asked caustically.

Her face was grim as she wrapped Jennie's lunch in a piece of wax paper. Tom didn't speak, looking down at the paper again as Jennie came into the room. "Good morning, Mom," she said brightly. "Morning, Daddy."

"Good morning, Jennie Bear," he said, smiling at her. "How's my Winnie Winkle this morning?"

"Just fine, Daddy." It was a private joke between them. He'd called her that when she got a job as a typist in the insurance company last month. It had been just five weeks after he'd lost his job on the cable cars and two weeks after she graduated from Mercy High School.

"You're the Winnie Winkle," he'd said. "But I'll get something in a few weeks. Then you'll be able to go to St. Mary's, like you planned."

"Ye have too much lipstick on, Jennie," her mother said. "Best take some of it off."

Tom looked at his daughter. She didn't have that much lipstick on. It was much less than most of the girls wore whom he used to see every morning on the cable car.

"Oh, Mother." Jennie protested. "I'm working in an office now, not going to school. I have to look decent."

"Decent ye should look, not painted."

"Aw, Ellen, leave the girl alone," Tom said slowly.

Ellen glared angrily at him. "When you're bringin' home some of the money to feed your family, then ye can talk."

Tom stared at her, his face setting grimly. He could feel the color draining from it. Jennie smiled sympathetically at him and that made it even worse. He never expected Jennie to be pitying him. He tightened his lips against a flood of angry words.

"Golly, I'm going to be late," Jennie said, jumping to her feet. She snatched at the paper bag on the table and started for the door. " 'By, Mom," she said over her shoulder. " 'By, Daddy. Good luck today."

Tom could hear her footsteps running down the stairs. He looked down at the paper again. "Could I have another cup of coffee?"

"No, one cup is all ye get. How much coffee d'ye think we can afford on the child's eleven dollars a week?"

"But you have the coffee right there. It's already made."

"It's for warming again tomorrow mornin'," she said.

He folded the paper carefully, got up and walked into the bathroom. He turned on the tap and let the water run as he took down his shaving brush and razor. He held his hand under the tap. The water was still cold. "Ellen, there's no hot water for my shave."

"Use the cold, then," she called. "Unless ye have a quarter for the gas meter. I'm savin' the gas we have left for the child's bath."

He looked at himself in the mirror. His face had healed from the beating, but his nose was a little crooked now and there were broken edges on his two front teeth. He put down the brush and walked into the kitchen.

Ellen's back was still toward him. He put his hands on her shoulders and turned her around. "Ellen, Ellen," he said gently. "What's happened to us?"

She stared up into his face for a moment, then reached up and pushed his hands from her shoulders. "Don't touch me, Thomas Denton. Don't touch me."

His voice was resigned. "Why, Ellen, why? It's not my fault what happened. It was God's will."

"God's will?" She laughed shrilly. "You're the one to be talkin' of God's will. Him that hasn't been in the church for more years than I can remember. If ye thought more of your Saviour than you did of your Saturday-night beer, He'd have shown ye some of His mercy."

He took a deep breath and let it out slowly. Then he turned, went back into the bathroom and began to shave with the cold water. She hadn't always been like this—sharp-tongued and acid-touched. And fanatical about the church and the priests. Once, she'd been Ellen Fitzgerald, with laughing eyes and dancing feet, and he remembered her at the Irish Ballroom on Day Street the time he first met her.

She was the prettiest girl on the floor that night, with her dark-brown hair and blue eyes and tiny feet. That was in 1912 and they were married the next year. A year after that, Jennie had been born.

He was a motorman with the car line even then, and when he came back from the war, they moved into this apartment. A year later, a son was born.

Poor tiny little Tommy. The world was not long for him and when he was two years old, they laid him to rest in Calvary Cemetery. Jennie was eight then and barely understood what had happened to her brother, but Ellen found her solace in the quiet of the church, and every day she took her daughter there with her. At first, he didn't pay much attention. Ellen's overattachment to her church was only natural; it would wear off soon enough.

But it didn't. He found that out one night, when he reached for her in the bed and found her cold and unresponsive. He felt for her breast inside the heavy cotton nightgown but she turned her back to him. "You've not made your confession in months. I'll not have ye planting another child in me."

He tried to make a joke of it. "Who wants to make a baby? All I want is a bit of lovin'."

"That's even worse, then," she said, her voice muffled by the pillow. "It's sinful and I'll share no part of that sin."

"Is that what the priests have been dunning into your ears? To deny your husband?"

She didn't answer. He gripped her shoulder and forced her to turn toward him. "Is that it?" he asked fiercely.

"The priests have told me nothing. What I do is of me own doing. I know the Book enough to know right from wrong. And stop your shouting. You'll be waking Jennie in the next room."

"I'll stop shouting," he said angrily, as the heat of her shoulder came warm into his hands and the fever rose up in him and he took her by force. The spasm shook him and he subsided into a heavy-breathing quiet atop her, his eyes staring into hers.

She looked up at him quietly, not moving, passive as she had been all through his assault upon her. A last shiver drained his vitals. Then she spoke. Her voice was calm and distant and detached, as if he weren't there at all. "Are ye all through spending your filth in me?"

He felt a cold sickness rising in his stomach. He stared at her for a moment more, then rolled off her onto his side of the bed. "I'm all through," he said tonelessly.

She got out of the bed and knelt beside the tiny crèche she had placed beneath the crucifix. He could sense her face turning toward him in the darkness. "I shall pray to the Virgin Mother that your seed has found no home in me," she whispered harshly.

He closed his eyes and turned his back. This was what they'd done to her, spoiled everything between them. A bitterness began to gall him.

He never set foot in a church again.

5

IT WAS QUIET HERE IN THE NAVE OF THE CHURCH. Ellen Denton, on her knees before the holy statuary, her head bowed and her beads threaded through her clasped fingers, was at peace. There was no prayer on her lips, no disturbing thoughts in her mind—only a calm, delicious emptiness. It permeated her whole being and closed off the world, beyond the comforting walls.

The sins of omission, which plagued her hours while she was outside these walls, were but faint distant echoes. Little Tommy lay quiet in his grave, no reproach on his tiny rosebud lips, for her neglect during his illness. No memories rose to torture her of her white, naked body, writhing in passion and pleasure, while her son lay dying in the same room.

It had seemed just a tiny cold, a cold such as children have so often and awaken free from in the morning. How was she to know that while she lay there, whispering her delight into her husband's ear, a minute piece of phlegm had lodged in her son's throat, shutting off the air from his lungs? So that, when she got up to adjust his covers, as she usually did before she closed her eyes for the night, she found him strangely cold and already blue. How was she to know that this was to be her punishment for her own sins?

Father Hadley had tried to comfort her in her grief. "Do not blame yourself, my child. The Lord giveth, the Lord taketh away. His will be done."

But she'd known better. The memory of her joy in her sin was still too strong within her, though she sought to free her soul of its burden by a thousand visits to the confessional. But all the soothing words of the priests brought no solace to her soul. Her guilt was her own and only she, herself, could expunge it. But here, in the quiet peace of the nave, beneath the silent, sorrowing Virgin, there was calmness and emptiness and oblivion.

★ ★ ★

Johnny Burke was bored. He took a last drag on the butt and spun it out into the gutter. The pimply-faced boy next to him said, "Let's go over and see if Tessie is busy."

"Tessie is always busy. Besides, I hear she give a feller a dose. I ain't takin' any chances." Johnny took out another cigarette and lit it, his eyes nervously looking up the street. "Just for once, I'd like to get me a dame that nobody else has banged."

"How yuh goin' do that, Johnny?"

"There are ways, Andy," Johnny said mysteriously. "There are ways."

Andy looked at him interestedly. "You talk like yuh know."

Johnny nodded. He tapped his pocket. "I got a little somethin' in here that'll make any girl put out."

"Yeah, Johnny?" Andy asked quickly. "What?"

Johnny lowered his voice carefully. "Mosca cantharides."

"What's that?"

"Spanish fly, yuh dope," Johnny said. "I stole some when Doc asked me to watch the store while he went upstairs."

"Gee," Andy said, impressed. "Will it work on any girl?"

Johnny nodded. "Sure. If yuh can slip it into her drink. Just a little an' she's as hot as a biscuit right out of the oven."

The druggist stuck his head out of the doorway. "Johnny, watch the store for me, will you? I want to run upstairs a minute."

"O.K., Doc."

They watched him turn into the entrance next door, then went into the drugstore. Johnny walked behind the counter and leaned carelessly against the cash register.

"How about a Coke, Johnny?"

"Uh-uh," Johnny said. "No handouts while I'm watchin' the store for Doc." Idly Johnny opened and closed some drawers under the counter. "Hey, Andy," he called. "Want to see where Doc keeps all the rubbers?"

"Sure," Andy said. He walked around behind the counter.

"May I have a Coke, please?"

The girl's voice came from the soda fountain. Both boys looked up guiltily. Quickly Johnny snapped the drawer shut. "Sure, Jennie."

"Where's Doc?"

"He went upstairs for a minute."

"She saw us," Andy whispered. "She knows what we were lookin' at."

Johnny looked at Jennie as he walked over to the soda fountain. Maybe she did. There was a peculiar smile on her face. He pressed the plunger on the Coke-sirup pump and watched the dark fluid squirt into the glass. "Yuh hear from the Champ yet, Jennie?"

She shook her head. "We were supposed to go to the movies tonight but he didn't get back from Berkeley. I hope nothing went wrong with his scholarship."

Johnny smiled. "What could go wrong with it?" he said. "He already took the state finals."

Andy came up behind him. "Will it work on her?" he whispered. Johnny knew what he meant. He looked up suddenly. All at once it seemed to him that he'd never really seen Jennie. She was one of the cherries and usually he paid no attention to them. She had left her Coke and was over looking at the magazines. He liked the way the thin summer dress clung to her. He never knew she had such big ones. No wonder Mike Halloran kept her on the leash. Suddenly, he put his hand in his pocket and took out the little piece of paper and emptied the pinch of powder into her glass.

Jennie took a magazine from the rack and went back to the fountain. Johnny looked down at her glass. Some traces of powder were still floating on top. He took it and put in another squirt of sirup, then held the glass under the soda spigot while he stirred vigorously. He put the drink down in front of her and looked up at the clock. "Kind of late for you to be out, isn't it?"

"It's Saturday night," Jennie answered. "It was so hot in the apartment, I thought I'd come down for some air." She put a nickel on the counter and took a straw from the glass container.

Johnny anxiously watched her sip the drink. "Is it all right?"

"A little sweet, maybe."

"I'll put a little more soda in it," Johnny said quickly. "How's that?"

She sipped at it. "Fine now. Thanks."

He picked up the nickel, went back to the cash register and rang it up. "I saw what you did," Andy whispered.

"Shut up."

Jennie was turning the pages of the magazine slowly as she

sipped her drink. Her glass was half empty when the druggist came back into the store. "Everything O.K., Johnny?"

"O.K., Doc."

"Thanks, Johnny. Want a Coke?"

"No, thanks, Doc. See you tomorrow."

"What did you go an' do that for?" Andy asked, when they came out onto the street. "Now we won't never know if it worked."

"We'll know," Johnny said, turning to look through the window.

Jennie had finished her drink and was climbing down from the stool. She put the magazine back on the rack and started for the door. Johnny moved over to intercept her.

"Going home, Jennie?"

She stopped and smiled at him. "I thought I'd go down to the park. Maybe there's a cool breeze coming in from the bay."

"Mind if we come along?" Johnny asked. "We're not doin' anything."

She wondered what made Johnny ask to walk with her all of a sudden. He'd never seemed interested in her before.

It was almost ten o'clock when Tom Denton came out of the saloon across from the car barn. He was drunk. Sad, weeping, unhappy drunk. He stared across the street at the car barn. Old Two-twelve was in there. His old car. But she wasn't his car any more. She'd never be his car any more. She was somebody else's car now.

The tears began to roll down his cheeks. He was a failure. No car, no job, not even a wife to come home to. Right now she was probably sitting in a corner of the church, praying.

Didn't she understand a man had to have more than a prayer when he got into bed? If he had a couple of dollars in his pocket, he knew where he'd go. The girls at Maggie's knew how to treat a man. He fished in his pocket for some coins. Carefully he counted them. Thirty-five cents. He thought about going back into the saloon. He had enough for one more drink. But then he'd have to ask Ellen for pocket money on Monday.

He felt the effects of the liquor beginning to wear off. Angrily he put the change back in his pocket. Drinking wasn't any fun when you had to worry about every nickel you spent. Almost sober now, he began to walk home slowly.

He was sitting at the kitchen table in the dark when Ellen came home half an hour later. He looked up wearily as she turned on the light. "I didn't expect ye home so early," she said. "What happened? Did they run out of whisky?"

He didn't answer.

She walked out of the kitchen into the narrow hallway. He heard her open Jennie's door, then close it. A moment later, she came back into the kitchen. "Where's Jennie?"

"I don't know. She's probably out with Mike."

"Mike is still in Berkeley. Jennie was here when I left for church. She said she was going to bed early."

"It's warm," he said. "She probably went out for a breath of air."

"I don't like her being out alone like that."

"Now, don't start on her, Ellen," he said. "She's a big girl now."

She took a kettle down from the shelf and filled it with water. She placed it on the stove and lit the gas under it. "Would ye like a cup of tea?"

He looked up in surprise. It had been a long time since Ellen asked him to share an evening cup of tea. He nodded gratefully.

She took the cups from the cupboard and placed them on the table. Then she sat down opposite him to wait for the water to boil. There was a worried expression on her face.

"Don't worry," he said, suddenly feeling sorry for her. "Jennie'll be home any minute now."

She looked up, and in a rare moment of insight, saw what she was doing to him and to herself. She felt the tears coming into her eyes and placed her hand over his. "I'm sorry, Tom. I don't know what's the matter with me. Half the time, I imagine things that never happen."

"I know, Ellen," he said gently. "I know."

It was then that the policeman came to the door and told them that Jennie had been found in the park, raped and beaten. And from the look on Ellen's face, Tom knew that they were lost forever.

6

THE THREE OF THEM CAME OUT OF THE CHURCH into the bright sunlight. They felt almost immediately the curious watching eyes. Tom felt the sudden shrinking in his daughter and noticed the flush of shame creeping up into her face, still puffed from the beating of almost two weeks ago. Her eyes looked down at the steps as they began to walk down toward the sidewalk.

"Hold your head up, Jennie Bear," he whispered. "It's their sons should bear the shame, not you."

Jennie lifted her head and smiled at him gratefully. "And you, too, Ellen Denton," he added. "Stop lookin' down at the ground."

In a way, Ellen felt a sort of triumph. Her husband had finally returned to the church. She thought of how it had been early that morning. She'd been all dressed and ready to leave for church when she called Jennie. She opened the door of Jennie's room. Her daughter was sitting in a chair, staring out the window. "You're not dressed yet, Jennie," she said in a shocked voice. "It's time we were leaving for Mass."

"I'm not going, Mama," Jennie said tonelessly.

"But you've not been to church since ye came home from the hospital. You've scarcely been out of the house."

"I've been out, Mama." She turned toward her mother and the dark circles under her eyes looked even darker in the light. "And everybody stared at me and whispered as I went by. I can't stand it. I won't go to church and be a freak for everybody to stare at."

"You're denying the Savior!" Ellen said heatedly. "How do ye expect forgiveness for your sins if you don't attend church?"

"What sins does the child need forgiveness for?" Her husband's voice came from behind her. She whirled around, her temper immediately rising.

"It's enough we have one traitor to the church in this house," she said. "We don't need another." She turned to Jennie. "Get dressed. You're coming with me if I have to drag ye."

"I'm not going, Mama," Jennie said. "I can't."

Ellen took a threatening step toward her daughter. She raised her hand. Suddenly, she felt her wrist caught in a grip of steel and she turned to look up into the face of her husband. His usually soft blue eyes were cold and hard. "Leave the child be! Have you gone completely mad?"

She looked up at him for a moment and then the flashing anger dissolved within her, leaving her spent and weak. The tears started in her eyes. "Father Hadley asked me to bring her. He said he'd offer up a prayer for her comfort."

He felt the release of her anger and let go of her wrist. Her arm fell limply at her side. He turned to his daughter. "Is that the reason you won't go to church, Jennie Bear?" he asked gently. "Because they stare at you?"

She nodded silently.

"Would you go if I were to come with you?" he asked suddenly.

Jennie looked into his eyes and saw the love there. After a moment, she nodded. "Yes, Daddy."

"All right, then. Get dressed. I'll be shaved in a minute." He turned and left the room quickly. Ellen stared after him, almost too surprised to realize what had happened.

There had been a buzz of surprise as they walked down the aisle to their pew. Tom could see heads twisting as they gaped, and a shudder ran through him at all the cruelty that was inherent in all human beings. His hand tightened on his daughter's and he smiled as he knelt toward the altar and crossed himself before taking his seat.

But as bad as it had been when they came in, it was that much worse when they came out. The curious had had time to gather on the steps in the bright morning sunshine. It was like running a gantlet of idiots.

"It's over now," he said softly as they turned the corner.

They crossed the street, walking toward the drugstore on the next corner. A group of boys were lounging about the store window, dressed in their Sunday best. The boys fell silent as they approached, staring at them with their wise, street-corner eyes. Tom stared back angrily at them and their eyes fell before his. They walked by and turned the corner to their house.

From around the corner behind him, Tom could hear the sudden explosion of their whispered conversation. Then one boy snickered and another boy laughed and the merriment had a sick, dirty sound to it that tore at his heart. Abruptly he let go of Jennie's arm and walked back around the corner. They looked at him in surprise, the laughter frozen on their lips.

"What's the joke, boys?" he asked, his anger making his face white and cold. "Tell it to me so I may laugh with you."

They stared at him silently, shamefaced. They looked down at their feet, they shuffled awkwardly, glancing at each other with secret looks filled with a meaning that Tom remembered from his own youth. It was as if they'd been surprised looking at dirty pictures.

A shame for what he'd been at their age came over him and a sick weariness replaced the anger. "Get off this corner," he said softly. "And if ever I hear of any of you laughing or making any remarks about me or any member of my family, I'll come down here and tear the lot of you apart with my bare hands!"

The tallest of the boys took a step toward him. His eyes were sly and insolent. He was slightly taller than Tom and he looked down at him with a faint, contemptuous smile. "It's a free country. We can stand here if we like."

The resentment in Tom suddenly exploded. He seized the boy by his jacket lapels and forced him to his knees. "Free, is it?" he shouted, his veins purple on his forehead. "Free for you to stand here and choose who you'll rape tonight?" He raised an open hand to slap the boy across the face.

The boy cringed, the insolence gone from his face. "What yuh pickin' on us for, Mr. Denton? We aren't the ones fucked Jennie."

The words seemed to freeze the blood in Tom's veins. He stood there, his hand still upraised, staring down at the boy. Fucked Jennie. They could say that about his own daughter and there was nothing he could do that could change the fact of it. Slowly he let his hand fall to his side, then with a violent gesture, he flung the boy away from him.

Tom glared at them, looking from one to another. They were only boys, he told himself. He couldn't hate all boys because of what two had done. The boy was right. They weren't the guilty ones.

A sense of failure came over him. If anyone was guilty, he was the guiltiest of all. If he'd been a man and kept his job, all this might never have happened. "Get off this corner," he said. "If any of you ever see me coming this way again, you'd better be on the other side of the street."

They looked at him and then at each other and it almost seemed now as if they were pitying him. Suddenly, as if a secret message had been passed mysteriously between them, they began to disperse in ones and twos.

A moment later, he was alone on the corner. He stood there for a moment to quiet the sudden trembling that came over him, then he, too, turned and walked around the corner to where his wife and daughter were waiting for him. "It's over now," he said for the second time that morning, as he took Jennie's arm and started for the house again. But this time, he knew, even as he said it, that it wasn't over—that it would never be over as long as he was alive to remember.

The cool September breeze held the first hint of autumn. Jennie looked out the cable-car window toward her stop. Her father was standing there under the street lamp, waiting for her as he did each night now. The car stopped and she stepped down.

"Hello, Daddy."

"Hi, Jennie Bear."

She fell into step beside him as they turned the corner toward home. "Any luck today?"

He shook his head. "I don't understand it. There just are no jobs."

"Maybe there'll be one tomorrow."

"I hope so," he said. "Maybe after the election, things will look up. Roosevelt says the government has to take the lead in providing work, that big business has fallen down on its responsibilities. He makes more sense for the working man than Hoover and the Republicans." He looked at her. "How did it go today?"

"All right," she said. But there still was an uncomfortable feeling in the office. Many of the company agents had taken to stopping at her desk on their way in and out of the office. Sometimes they just chatted, but some of them had tried to date her. Maybe if things had been different, she'd have gone out with them. But when she looked up from her desk into their eyes, she knew what they were thinking. She'd refuse politely and some of them would stammer or even blush, for they knew somehow that she knew.

"You don't have to meet me every night, Daddy," she said suddenly. "I'm not afraid to come home alone."

"I know you're not. I've known it from that first day I came to meet you. But I want to do it. It's the one time of the whole day that I feel I've really got something to do."

Jennie didn't answer and they walked along silently for a moment. "Do you want me to stop?"

"Not if you want to meet me, Daddy."

They were at the steps of the house now and she started up. Her father placed a hand on her arm. "Let's not go up just yet, Jennie Bear. Let's sit here and talk a minute."

She looked down at him. His face was serious. "What is it, Daddy?"

"I didn't tell your mother. I went to see Father Hadley today."

"Yes?"

"He won't come down to court to testify to your character. He told me it's against the rules of the church. And the same goes for the sisters at the school."

"Oh," she said. The sick feeling came up inside her again. The lawyer had been right. He'd come to see them a month ago, a little man with the eyes of a weasel.

He'd sat down in the kitchen and looked across the table at them. "Mr. Burke and Mr. Tanner asked me to see you," he said. "I think you know how much they regret this, er—" He had glanced at her quickly and then away. "—this incident and they would like to make amends if they can."

Her father's face had flushed angrily. "In the first place, Mr. O'Connor," he had said quickly. "That incident you are referring to was not an incident. Those two boys ra—"

The lawyer held up his hand interrupting. "We know what they did," he said. "But surely, Mr. Denton, what purpose would their trial serve except to call even greater attention to your daughter and remind her of what already must be a painful experience. And what if the boys should be adjudged not guilty?"

Her father laughed. "Not guilty? I was at the station when the police brought them in. I heard them sniveling and crying then how sorry they were that they did it."

"What they said then, Mr. Denton," the attorney had said, "is unimportant. It's what they say in court that counts. And they will say that your daughter led them on, that she asked them to go to the park with her."

"They will have to prove that," Tom said grimly.

"It will be harder for you to disprove it," the lawyer said. "There's two of them and only the word of your daughter. And they will have as many character witnesses for them as you will have to have for your daughter."

"It's beginning to sound as if my daughter were on trial, not them!" Tom burst out.

"Exactly," the lawyer nodded. "That is the way it is in these cases. The accuser stands to lose more than the accused."

"My daughter's reputation speaks for itself," Tom said. "Father Hadley of St. Paul's and the sisters at Mercy High School will tell you of my Jennie."

The lawyer had smiled mysteriously. "I doubt it, Mr. Denton," he said quietly. "I doubt it very much." He glanced at Jennie again, then back at Tom. "I am authorized by my clients to offer you a thousand dollars if your daughter will drop the charges against the boys."

"I think you might as well go, Mr. O'Connor," her father had said, getting to his feet. "You cannot buy what's already been stolen."

The attorney rose also. He took a card from his pocket and placed it on the table and walked to the door. "You can reach me at my office any time before the trial begins if you should change your mind."

"What do we do now, Daddy?" she asked, back in the present again.

"Father Hadley said they'd told your mother the same thing three weeks ago."

She stared at her father. "Then she knew all along and never told us?"

He nodded. A chill ran through her. There was something wrong with a God who would let a mother expose her own child to shame and ridicule just to save her own conscience.

"Father Hadley also said the scholarship to St. Mary's is still open if you want it, Jennie."

Suddenly, she began to laugh. They refused to give her a good name, yet were willing to give her charity. She couldn't reconcile the two attitudes. Was one merely to compensate for the other?

Tom looked up at her in surprise. "What are you laughing at, Jennie?"

Her laughter died and she looked at him, unsmiling. "Nothing, Daddy," she said. "I think you might as well give that lawyer a call."

"Then you'll take the thousand dollars?"

She nodded. "And the scholarship to St. Mary's, too. That way, you'll be able to live while I'm away."

"I won't accept your money."

"Yes, you will, Daddy," she said softly. "At least, until you find a job and get back on your feet again."

He felt the tears rush into his eyes and suddenly he pulled her to him. "Do you love me, Jennie Bear? Do you love your poor miserable failure of a father?"

"You know I do, Daddy," she said quickly, her head against his chest. And they clung to each other, crying, there on the steps in the quiet, cool autumn twilight.

7

THE ONLY SOUND FOR A MOMENT WAS THE SLIGHT hissing that came from the fluorescent lamps over the surgical area. Dr. Grant's hands were quick and sure as he deftly lifted the perfectly normal appendix from the heavy-set, wealthy woman lying on the operating table. His deep, masculine voice rumbled in the silence. "That will do it," he said, sighing in satisfaction. "You can close her up now, Dr. Lobb."

He turned away from the table and one of the nurses quickly wiped the perspiration from his face as the surgical resident began to clamp the edges of the incision together.

Jennie glanced up at Sister M. Christopher. If the senior nurse was aware that the appendix had not been infected, her dark eyes, visible over the face mask, gave no indication.

"Suture," Dr. Lobb grunted, holding out his hand. Automatically Jennie gave it to him. Then she didn't have time to look up for a few minutes. She was too busy. But she was aware that Sister Christopher was watching her. It didn't make her nervous, as it had at first. But that was almost three years ago. Next month was graduation.

Sister Christopher watched Jennie with approbation. This girl was one of the bright spots in her class. Perhaps one girl in a hundred had a vocation for surgery the way Jennie had. There were so many things needed and Jennie had them all. The sight of blood didn't upset her, not even the first time she'd experienced it. And Jennie was deft and sure in her actions. Quickly she'd developed an affinity between herself and the instruments, then between herself and the surgeons. Without the affinity, which permitted an unspoken form of communication between the doctor and the nurse, surgery could be dangerously delayed while instruments were fumbled back and forth.

The final important factor was strength. No one ever quite realized how important it was for a surgical nurse to be strong. To be able to stand for hours beside the quiet white table, even though your feet hurt and your thighs and back ached from that peculiar, slightly-leaning-forward position. To be able to feed the doctor that strength and reassure him with it, so that the chain of healing formed one unbroken line. And the strength to be stoic when the chain was broken and the now forever silent patient was wheeled away; to stand there quietly and begin to scrub up again, sure that the chain would rebuild itself when a new patient was wheeled in.

Dr. Lobb looked up and nodded. "Dressing." He held his white-gloved hand out over the neatly stitched incision.

Jennie was ready with the gauze packing as he lifted his hand. Immediately, she covered the incision, while with her other hand, she lifted the strips of adhesive tape from the clip board at the side of the table. She pressed the tape down firmly with her fingers, checking the bandage for smoothness and support, then lifted both hands to signify she had finished.

Sister Christopher nodded and the patient was quickly wrapped and transferred to another table by the assistants. There was a click as the fluorescents went out. The morning operating-room schedule at St. Mary's had been completed.

"That's the fourth good appendix he's taken out this month," Jennie whispered above the gush of water into the basin. "Why does he do it?"

The young resident laughed. "At two hundred and fifty dollars a crack, you don't fight the patients."

"But he doesn't have to," she whispered. "He's a great surgeon. He has scarcely enough time for all he has to do."

"Sure," Dr. Lobb whispered back. "But even great surgeons

have to eat. Most of the trick cases are either for free or tough collections. So who's to blame if once in a while, he lifts a harmless appendix from some rich old hypochondriac? There's no risk in it. The doctor can pay his bills and the patient can brag about his operation."

He straightened up, reaching for a towel. "Oh-oh," he said warningly. "Here comes the great man himself."

Jennie took a towel from the rack and began to dry her hands. The doctor's voice came from behind her. "Miss Denton?"

She turned around, looking at him. "Yes, Dr. Grant?"

"I understand you're graduating next month."

"I hope so."

"I don't think you have anything to worry about," he said. "I was just talking to Sister Christopher. She thinks a great deal of you. And so do I."

"Thank you."

"Have you made any plans yet for after graduation?"

"Not really," Jennie answered. "I'm going to take the state exam and get my name on the lists for one of the big hospitals."

"All hospitals are pretty well staffed."

Jennie knew what he really meant. They weren't well staffed, at all. Actually, they were all understaffed because there was no money to pay for the staff they needed. Especially those in the operating room. They were the best paid of all. "I know," she said.

He hesitated a moment. "Are you doing anything right now?"

"I was just going down to the cafeteria for lunch."

"I'd like to talk to you. Sister Christopher said it would be all right if you left the hospital for lunch. How about the Steak 'n' Sauce?"

"That sounds fine," Jennie said.

"Good." He smiled. "I'll meet you down at my car. It's the black Packard."

"I know," she said quickly. All the nurses knew the car. It was always parked just opposite their dormitory. Outside of Dr. Gedeon's black Cadillac, it was the most expensive car at the hospital.

"See you in fifteen minutes, then."

Jennie walked out into the corridor and pressed the button for the elevator. The door opened and she stepped in. Dr. Lobb rushed in right after her.

"The Steak 'n' Sauce!"

"I wonder what he wants?" Jennie asked.

His grin grew broader. "I know what he wants," he said lewdly. "But I didn't have any luck getting it at the Greasy Spoon."

She returned his grin. "His luck won't be any better at the Steak 'n' Sauce."

"I don't know." He laughed. "One of these days, you're goin' to give it up to somebody. There's no sense feeding it to the worms."

"That will never happen," she said. Too late for that, she thought. But it didn't matter now. It was forgotten and no one here had heard about it. "I still wonder what he wants?"

"Maybe he wants you to work for him. Ever think of that?"

"I thought about it," she admitted. "But it doesn't make sense. Why me? He can have his pick of the best around."

Dr. Lobb grinned but his eyes were serious. "You are the best around, honey. It's about time you realized that."

The elevator door opened and they stepped out into the basement corridor, where the employees' cafeteria was. Jennie looked down at her white uniform. "I'd better get out of this and into a dress."

"I'd be just as happy if you just got out of that." He laughed. "You don't have to put on a dress for me."

She looked up at him, smiling. Someday, this young man was going to be one of the really good ones. "Maybe I'll surprise you sometime."

"Surprise me by bringing back a steak sandwich," he called after her. "I've about given up on the other."

Doctor Grant held a package of cigarettes out toward her. She took one and he held a match. His eyes met hers over the flickering flame. "I suppose you're wondering why I asked you to lunch?"

She nodded. "I was curious, to say the least."

He smiled. "I'm sorry if I provoked your curiosity. But I really meant it when I said I like to forget about my practice during lunch. But I guess now it's time to get down to business."

She didn't answer.

"During the past year, Miss Denton, I've had an excellent opportunity to observe your work in surgery. From the very first,

I was aware of your aptitude and I have always appreciated, as a surgeon, the extremely competent manner in which you render assistance."

"Thank you, Dr. Grant."

"As you may know, Miss Denton, I have a rather extensive and busy practice. There are many physicians who refer their patients to me for surgery. Much of this practice is of a minor nature and under proper conditions, can be attended to in my office. It relieves the patient of a considerable part of the economic burden."

Jennie nodded silently.

"This morning, I learned from Miss Janney, who's been associated with me for many years, that she's getting married and plans to move to Southern California." He drew on his cigarette. "When I came to the hospital today, I took the liberty of speaking to Sister Christopher about you. She agrees that you'd make an excellent replacement for Miss Janney."

"You mean you want me to work for you?"

He smiled. "In my roundabout manner, that is what I was about to ask. Are you interested?"

"Of course. What girl wouldn't be?"

"It's not an easy job, you know," he said. "I have a few beds in my clinic and very often, we'll have to work late. Occasionally, I even keep a patient overnight. At such times, you'd have to remain on duty."

"Dr. Grant," Jennie said, smiling. "I've put in two eight-hour shifts a day with only four hours' sleep between, for the last week. Working for you will seem like a picnic."

He smiled and reaching across the table, patted her hand reassuringly. Jennie smiled back at him. He wasn't so bad, after all, even if he did take out a few perfectly healthy appendixes. He was only the surgeon. He couldn't be responsible for the faulty diagnosis of every physician who sent him a patient.

But that was before she went to work for him and found out that healthy appendixes weren't the only things he removed. He also had a very busy practice in unborn babies up to ten weeks after conception. As a matter of fact, he was probably the busiest abortionist in California.

But by the time she was aware of that, it didn't matter, because she was in love with him. Nor did it matter that he was already married and had three children.

8

THE TELEPHONE RANG JUST AS SHE WAS ABOUT TO leave the tiny two-room apartment over the clinic. She went back and picked it up. "Dr. Grant's office," she said. It was an extension of the telephone in the office downstairs.

"Jennie?" came the whisper.

"Yes."

"Will you be there for a while?"

"I was just leaving to see my folks. I haven't seen them for three weeks. This is the third Sunday in a row—"

His voice interrupted her. "I'll see to it you have time off during the week. Please, Jennie, I've got to see you."

She hesitated a moment and he sensed her faltering over the telephone. "Please, Jennie! I'll go crazy if I don't see you."

She looked across at the clock. It was already after seven o'clock. By the time she got across town, it would almost be time for her father to go to bed. He had a WPA job and had to be at work very early.

"Oh, all right," she said quietly.

Some of the tension left his voice. "Good, Jennie. I'll be there in twenty minutes. I love you."

"I love you," she said and heard the click as he put down the phone. She replaced the receiver and slowly took off her coat. Carefully she put it back in the closet, walked over to the couch and sat down. She lit a cigarette thoughtfully.

Who would have thought when she came to work here, three months ago, that he'd fall in love with her? And she with him. But then, how could she help herself? Especially when she knew what it was like for him at home. Married to a spoiled rich young woman who constantly threw up to him that it was her money that had enabled him to open his office, that it was her father's influence that had established him in the community. Married to a woman who bore him three children not out of love for him but out of an insane desire to keep him forever bound to her.

No wonder he'd found refuge in his work and spent almost

every waking moment at his practice. Now she understood what drove him. And those girls and young women who came for his surgery? And he'd explained why he did it, she understood that, too.

She saw the inner kindness in his sensitive face as he spoke. "What am I to do, Jennie?" he'd asked. "Turn them away and let them ruin their lives because of one foolish mistake? Or let them fall into the hands of some quack who'll make them sick forever or perhaps even kill them, all because of some outworn religious code? Religious laws like that have hung on until gradually they've become dogma, just like the Jewish nonsense about kosher meat. Even our civil laws permit abortion under certain circumstances. Someday, it will be open and aboveboard, as it is in many countries throughout the world—Cuba, Denmark, Sweden, many others."

He'd turned his deep-set brown eyes toward her. "I took an oath when I became a doctor, that I would strive to do my best for my patients, to help them in every way I could, physically and psychologically. That oath is more important than anything else to me. When some poor, frightened child comes to me for help, I can't play God and refuse her."

It made sense to her. There were many things about the church she did not understand. She knew how they'd acted in her own case and the bitterness still rankled deep within her. If her goodness had been so important, why wouldn't they come forward to support her good name? All they really sought was power over her, not responsibility for her.

So, gradually she'd come to recognize the women who came to him for help and feel a compassion for them. The young matron who couldn't afford to leave her job because already she and her husband had more children than they could support; the frightened young girls, some still in school or just out; the middle-aged women just approaching the change of life, with their families already grown; even the call girls, who lived casually from day to day, yet came into the office with a haunting fear buried deep beneath their bright, brittle laughter. She had the capacity to feel sorry for them, even as he had. And from there, it was only one step to falling in love with him.

It happened after she'd been there about a month. She was upstairs in the apartment and heard a noise in the office below It was about eight o'clock at night. At first, she was confused thinking that this was an office night. But then she realized it was Tuesday, and the doctor had office hours only on Monday, Wednesday and Friday evenings. She turned down the flame under the coffeepot and reaching for her robe, went down to investigate.

When she opened the door to his private office and looked in, he was seated behind his desk, his face gray and tired-looking. "I beg your pardon, Doctor. I didn't know it was you. I heard a noise——"

He smiled wearily. "That's all right, Miss Denton."

"Good night, Doctor," she said, starting to close the door.

"Just a minute, Miss Denton," he said suddenly.

She opened the door and looked at him. "Yes, Doctor?"

He smiled again. "We've been so busy, I haven't had time to ask. Are you happy here?"

She nodded. "Yes, Doctor. Very."

"I'm glad."

"You ought to be getting home, Doctor. You look exhausted."

"Home?" he asked, a wry smile coming to his lips. "This is my home, Miss Denton. I just sleep in that other place."

"I—I don't understand, Doctor."

"Of course you don't," he said gently. "I wouldn't expect you to. You're much too young and beautiful to worry about the likes of me." He got to his feet. "Go back upstairs now, Miss Denton. I'll try to be very quiet and not disturb you."

The light from the lamp on his desk shining up onto his face made him look even more handsome than usual. She stood in the doorway, staring at him. She felt her heart pumping strangely within her. "But I do worry about you, Doctor. You work too hard."

"I'll be all right," he said in a toneless voice. He turned to look at her and their eyes locked and held. It seemed as if she were spinning into a swirling vortex deep in his gentle brown eyes. She felt a trembling in her legs and placed her hand on the doorjamb quickly, to support herself. No words came to her lips; she stared at him, speechless.

"Is anything wrong, Miss Denton?"

It took a desperate effort for her to shake her head. "No," she whispered, forcing her eyes to turn away. "No." Suddenly, she and ran toward the stairway.

wasn't even aware that he had come after her until he

caught her in the doorway of her apartment. The warmth of his hand touching her shoulder came through the thin robe. "Are you afraid of me, Jennie?" he asked harshly.

She looked up into his face and saw the anguish in his eyes. A curious weakness came over her and she would have fallen if he had not been holding her. "No," she whispered.

"Then what is it?"

She looked down, not speaking, the warmth from his hand beginning to radiate into a fire inside her. "Tell me!" he urged, shaking her.

She looked up at him, the tears coming into her eyes. "I can't."

"You can, Jennie, you can," he said insistently. "I know what you feel. You feel the same things I feel. I can't sleep without dreaming of you, without feeling you close to me."

"No. Please! It's not right."

His strong surgeon's hand held her chin. "I love you, Jennie," he said. "I love you."

She stared up into his eyes, seeing his face coming closer and closer, then his mouth pressed down on hers. She closed her eyes for a moment, feeling the fire envelop her. Abruptly she tore her face away. She backed into the apartment. He stepped in after her, kicking the door shut with his foot. "You love me," he said. "Say it!"

Her eyes were wide as she stared up at him. "No," she whispered.

He stepped forward again, his strong fingers digging deep into her shoulders. "Say it!" he commanded harshly.

She felt the weakness as his touch flowed through her again. She couldn't turn her face from his eyes. "I love you," she said.

He pressed his mouth to hers again and kissed her. She felt his hands inside her robe, his fingers on her back unfastening her brassière, her breasts rising from their restraint, the nipples leaping joyfully into his hands. A shiver of ecstasy raced through her and she almost fell. "Please don't," she whispered, her lips moving under his. "It's wrong."

He picked her up in his arms and carried her across the room to the bed. He placed her on it gently and knelt beside her. "When a man and a woman are in love," he whispered, "nothing they do in the privacy of their own home is ever wrong. And this is our home."

He pressed his lips down on her mouth again.

★ ★ ★

Tom looked across the table at the kitchen clock. It was a few minutes past ten. He folded his newspaper. "I guess she won't be coming now," he said, "so I might as well be turning in." He got to his feet. "The boys down at the Alliance tell me I'll be making supervisor any day now, so I better get my sleep. It won't do for me to be showing up late to work."

Ellen sniffed contemptuously. "If ye keep listenin' to them communists down at the Workers' Alliance, you'll be lucky even to hold your job with the WPA."

"They're in pretty good, you can't deny that. It was them that got me onto full time instead of half time and you know it. It's them that's for the working man."

"Communists are heathens," she said. "Father Hadley told me they're against the church because they don't believe in God. He says they're only playing up to the workin' man until they get in power, like in Russia. Then they'll close the churches and make slaves out of us all."

"What if they are?" he asked. "I don't see Father Hadley getting me a job or paying our bills. No, it was the Alliance that put me to work and saw to it I earned enough to pay rent and buy food. I don't care what Father Hadley calls them, as long as they do good for me."

She smiled bitterly. "A fine family I have. A husband who's a communist and a daughter who never has the time to come home."

"Maybe she's busy," Tom said lamely. "You know it's a responsible position she's got. Didn't the sister at St. Mary's say, when she graduated, that she was very lucky to be working for such an important doctor?"

"Yes, but she still should come home once in a while. I'm willin' to bet she hasn't been to Mass since she left St. Mary's."

"How do you know?" Tom asked angrily. "St. Paul's ain't the only church in San Francisco."

"I know," she said. "I feel it. She doesn't want to come see us. She's makin' so much money now, she's ashamed of us."

"And what has she got to be proud of? With you preaching religion at her all the time and the boys on the street still sniggering and laughing behind her back when she walks by? Do you think that's something to make a young girl want to come home?"

Ellen ignored him. "It's not right that a girl should stay away like this," she said stubbornly. "We both know what goes on up there on the hill, with everybody sleepin' with each other's wives and the drink. I read the papers, too, ye know."

"Jennie's a good girl. She wouldn't do a thing like that."

"I'm not too sure. Sometimes a taste of temptation is like a spoonful of honey. Just enough to sweeten your tongue but not enough to fill your whole mouth. And we both know she's tasted temptation."

"You still don't believe her, do you?" he asked bitterly. "You'd rather take the word of those two hoodlums than your own daughter."

"Then why didn't she go into court? If there wasn't just a little truth in what they said, she wouldn't have been afraid. But no, she takes the thousand dollars and lets herself be labeled a whore."

"You know as well as I why she didn't," Tom answered. "And you can thank your church for it. They'd not even come into court to say she was a good girl. No, they were afraid the boys' parents might not like it and cut off their weekly contributions."

"The church sent her to college. And they found her this job. They did their duty."

"Then what are you complaining about?"

She sat there quietly for a moment, listening to him drop his shoes angrily to the floor as he undressed in the bedroom. Then she got out of the chair and felt the hot-water heater. A hot bath would soothe her aches and pains a little; all this damp fall weather was bringing out her arthritis. She took a match and kneeled down beside the heater. Striking the match, she turned the pet cock. The flame caught for a moment, then died out in a tiny yellow circle. She looked up at the meter. They were out of gas. The red flag was up. She got to her feet and walked over to her pocketbook. She opened the small change purse and searched through it. She had no quarters, only nickels and dimes. For a moment, she thought of asking Tom for a quarter, then shrugged her shoulders. She'd had enough of his blasphemous tongue. She'd do without her bath. She could take it in the morning, when she came back from Mass. She went into the bathroom and used the last of the hot water to wash her face. Tom was standing in the kitchen when she came out, his chest bare above his trousers. She swept by him silently and closed the bedroom door behind her.

Tom went into the bathroom and washed up noisily. Suddenly, the water went cold. He swore and dried himself quickly, then fished in his pocket for a quarter. He reached up and put the quarter into the meter, then watched the red on the dial disappear. He nodded, satisfied.

In the morning, he'd turn on the heater and in a few minutes, he'd have enough hot water for his shave. He went into the bedroom, leaving the door open behind him, unaware of the slight hiss coming from under the heater.

He draped his pants on the chair and sat down on the bed. After a moment, he stretched out with a sigh. His shoulder touched Ellen and he felt her turn away.

Ah, the hell with her, he thought, turning on his side, his back to her. Maybe the commies were right with their ideas of free love. At least a man wouldn't have to put up with a woman like her.

His eyes began to feel heavy. He could hear the soft, even sounds of her breath. She was asleep already. He smiled to himself in the dark. With free love, he'd have his pick of women. She'd act different then, all right. His eyelids drooped and closed and he joined his wife in slumber. And death.

Jennie sat up in the bed, clutching the sheet to her naked body and staring with wide, frightened eyes at the woman who stood in the doorway. On the other side of the bed, Bob was already hurriedly buttoning his shirt.

"Did you think he'd leave me for you?" she screamed at Jennie. "Did you think you were the first? Hasn't he told you how many times I've caught him like this?" Her voice grew contemptuous. "Or do you think he's really in love with you?"

Jennie didn't answer.

"Tell her, Robert," his wife said angrily. "Tell her you wanted to make love to me tonight and when I refused, you came running over here. Tell her."

Jennie stared at him. His face was white and he didn't look in her direction. He grabbed his coat from the chair and walked over to his wife. "You're all upset. Let me take you home."

Home. Jennie felt a sick feeling in her stomach. This was home—his and hers. He had said so. It was here they had loved, here they had been together. But he was talking about someplace else. Another place.

"I'm always upset, aren't I, Robert? Every time you promise it will never happen again. But I know better, don't I? All right," she said suddenly, her voice hard and cold. "We'll go. But not until you tell her."

"Please, dear," he said quickly. "Another time. Not now."

"Now, Robert," she said coldly. "Now—or the whole world will know about Dr. Grant, the quack, the abortionist, the great lover."

He turned and looked back at Jennie on the bed. "You'll have to leave, Miss Denton," he said huskily. "You see, I don't love you," he said in a strained voice. "I love my wife."

And almost at the same moment that the door closed behind him, there was an explosion in an old tenement on the other side of the city. After the firemen pulled the charred bodies from the fire, they gave their verdict. The victims had been fortunate. They were already dead before the fire started.

9

CHARLES STANDHURST WAS EIGHTY-ONE YEARS old when he met Jennie Denton. It was eight o'clock of a spring morning in 1936 and he was in the operating room of the Colton Sanitarium at Santa Monica. He was the patient just being placed on the operating table and she was acting as Chief Nurse in Surgery.

He felt them place his legs over the stirrups and quickly arrange a sheet so that even if he moved his head, he could not see his lower half. When they had finished, he saw her come from somewhere behind him and walk down to the foot of the table. She lifted up the sheet.

He felt a moment's embarrassment at the impersonal manner in which she scrutinized his private parts. After five wives, countless mistresses and more than forty children that he was sure about, only eight of whom were the result of his marriages, it seemed strange to him that anyone could look at him in such a detached manner. So much life had sprung from that fountain.

She let the covering fall around him again and looked up. A glint of humor flickered in her intelligent gray eyes and he knew that she understood.

She came around to the side of the table and reached for his pulse. He looked up at her as she studied her watch. "Where's Dr. Colton?"

"He'll be along in a minute. He's washing up."

She let go of his wrist and said something to someone behind him. He rolled his eyes back and caught a glimpse of another nurse. Feeling the prick of a needle in his arm, he turned his head back quickly. Already, she was taking the small hypodermic out of his arm. "Hey, you're fast," he said.

"That's my job."

"I am, too."

Again that smile in her gray eyes. "I know. I read the papers."

Just then, Dr. Colton came in. "Hello, Mr. Standhurst," he said in his jovial manner. "Did we pass any water today?"

"Maybe you did, Doc, but you know damn well I didn't," Standhurst said dryly. "Or they'd never have got me back in this slaughterhouse."

Dr. Colton laughed. "Well, you've got nothing to worry about. We'll have those kidney stones out in a jiffy."

"All the same, Doc, I'm glad we've got a specialist doing it. If I left it up to you, God knows what you'd cut out."

His sarcasm didn't disturb Dr. Colton. They'd known each other for too long. It was Charles Standhurst who'd advanced him most of the money to start this hospital. He laughed again.

The surgeon came in and stood beside Dr. Colton. "Ready, Mr. Standhurst?"

"Ready as I'll ever be. Just leave something for the girls, eh, Doc?"

The surgeon nodded and Standhurst felt a prick in his other arm. He turned his head and saw Jennie standing there. "Gray eyes," he said to her. His second wife had had gray eyes. Or was it his third? He didn't remember. "I suppose you wouldn't take your mask off so that I could see the rest of your face?"

Again he saw the glint of humor. "I don't think the doctors would approve," she said. "But after the operation, I'll come visit you. Will that do?"

"Fine. I've got a feeling you're beautiful."

He didn't see the anesthetist behind him nod. Jennie leaned over his face. "Now, Mr. Standhurst," she said, "count down from ten with me. Ten, nine, eight—"

"Seven, six, four, five, two, nine." His lips were moving slowly and everything seemed so comfortable and far away. "Ten, eight, one, three . . . six . . . four . . . one . . . two. . . ." His voice faded away.

The anesthetist looked up at the surgeon. "He's under," he said.

They all saw it at the same time, looking down into the cavity the surgeon had cut into his body—the mass of brackish gray covering almost the entire side of one kidney and threading its way in thin, radiating lines across the other. Without raising his head, the surgeon dropped the two pieces of matter he'd snipped away onto the slides that Jennie held under his hand. She gave the slides to a nurse standing behind her without turning around. "Pathology," she whispered.

The nurse left quickly and Jennie, with the same deft motion, picked up two hemostats. The assisting surgeon took them from her hand and tied off two veins as the surgeon's knife exposed them.

"Aren't you going to wait for the biopsy?" Dr. Colton asked from his position next to the surgeon. The surgeon didn't look up. His fingers were busy probing at the mass. "Not unless you want me to, Doctor." He held out his hand and Jennie placed a fine curette in it. He was working quickly now, preparing to remove the infected kidney.

Colton hesitated. "Charles Standhurst isn't just an ordinary man." Everyone around the operating table knew that. At one time or another, the old man quietly lying there could have been almost anything he'd wanted. Governor, senator, anything. With more than twenty major newspapers stretched across the nation and a fortune founded from oil and gold, he'd never really wanted anything more than to be himself. He was second only to Hearst in the state's pride for its home-grown tycoons.

The surgeon, a comparatively young man who'd rapidly become one of the foremost GU men in the world and had been flown out from New York especially for this job, began to lift out the kidney. The nurse behind Jennie tapped her on the shoulder. Jennie took the slip of paper from her and held it out for him to see. She could see the typed words plainly.

Carcinoma. Metastasis. Malignant.

The surgeon sighed softly, and glanced up at Dr. Colton. "Well, he's an ordinary enough man now."

Mr. Standhurst was awake the next morning when the surgeon came into his hospital room. If he paid any attention to the teletype clicking away in the corner, it wasn't apparent. He walked over to the side of the bed and looked down. "I came in to say good-by, Mr. Standhurst. I'm leaving for New York this morning."

The old man looked up and grinned. "Hey, Doc," he said. "Anybody ever tell you that your old man was a tailor?"

"My father was a tailor, Mr. Standhurst."

"I know," Standhurst said quickly. "He still has the store on Stanton Street. I know many things about you. You were president of the Save Sacco-Vanzetti Society at City College when you graduated in twenty-seven, a registered member of the Young Socialists during your first year at P. and S., and the first surgeon ever to become an F.A.C.S. in his first year of practice. You're still a registered Socialist in New York and you'll probably vote for Norman Thomas for President."

The surgeon smiled. "You know a great deal about me."

"Of course I do. You don't think I'd let just anybody cut me up, do you?"

"I should think you'd have worried just a little knowing what you do about me," the doctor said. "You know what we Socialists think of you."

The old man started to laugh, then grimaced in pain. "Hell! The way I figure it, you're a doctor first and a Socialist second." He looked up shrewdly. "You know, Doc, if you voted the straight Republican ticket, I could make you a millionaire in less than three years."

The doctor laughed and shook his head. "No, thanks. I'd worry too much."

"How come you don't ask me how I feel, Doc? Colton's been in here four times already and each time he asked me."

The doctor shrugged his shoulders. "Why should I? I know how you feel. You hurt."

"I hurt like hell, Doc," Standhurst said. "Colton said those stones you took out of me were big as baseballs."

"They were pretty big, all right."

"He also said I'd be wearing this bag you hooked into me until the kidney healed and took over again."

"You'll be wearing it quite a while."

The old man stared at him. "You know, you're both full of shit," he said calmly. "I'll wear this in my grave. And that isn't too far off, either."

"I wouldn't say that."

"I know you wouldn't," Standhurst said. "That's why I'm saying it. Look, Doc. I'm eighty-one years old. And at eighty-one, if a man lives that long, he gets to be a good smeller of death—for anyone, including himself. You learn to see it, in the face or eyes. So don't bullshit me. How long have I got?"

The doctor looked into the old man's eyes and saw that he wasn't afraid. If anything, there was a look of lively curiosity reflected there. He made up his mind quickly. Colton was all wrong in the way he was handling it. This was a man. He deserved the truth. "Three months, if you're lucky, Mr. Standhurst. Six, if you're not."

The old man didn't blink an eyelash. "Cancer?"

The surgeon nodded. "Malignant and metastatic," he answered. "I removed one complete kidney and almost half of the other. That's why you have that waste bag."

"Will it be painful?"

"Very. But we can control it with morphine."

"To hell with that," the old man said. "Dying is about the only thing in life I haven't experienced. It's something I don't want to miss."

The teletype began to clatter suddenly and the old man glanced over at it, then back at the doctor. "How will I know when it's close, Doc?"

"Watch the urine in that bag," the doctor said. "The redder it gets, the nearer it is. That means the kidney is passing clear blood instead of urine, because the cancer will have choked off the kidney completely."

The look in the old man's eyes was bright and intelligent. "That means I'll probably die of uremic poisoning."

"Possibly. If nothing else goes wrong."

Standhurst laughed. "Hell, Doc," he said, "I could have done that twenty years ago if I'd just kept on drinking."

The surgeon laughed. "But look at all the fun you'd have missed."

The old man smiled up at him. "You Socialists will probably declare a national holiday."

"I don't know, Mr. Standhurst." The doctor returned his smile. "Who would we have to complain about then?"

"I'm not worried," the old man said. "Hearst and Patterson will still be around."

The doctor held out his hand. "Well, I've got to be going, Mr. Standhurst."

Standhurst took his hand. "Good-by, Doc. And thanks."

The surgeon's dark eyes were serious. "Good-by, Mr. Standhurst," he said. "I'm sorry." He started for the door. The old man's voice turned him around.

"Will you do me a favor, Doc?"

"Anything I can, Mr. Standhurst."

"That nurse up in the operating room," Standhurst said. "The one with the gray eyes and the tits."

The surgeon knew whom he meant. "Miss Denton?"

"If that's her name," the old man said.

The surgeon nodded.

"She said if I wanted to see her without her mask, she'd come down. Would you leave word with Colton on your way out that I'd like her to join me for lunch?"

The surgeon laughed. "Will do, Mr. Standhurst."

10

JENNIE PICKED UP THE BOTTLE OF CHAMPAGNE and poured it into the tall glass filled with ice cubes. The wine bubbled up with a fine frothy head, then settled back slowly as she filled it to the brim. She put the glass straw into the glass and handed it to Standhurst. "Here's your ginger ale, Charlie."

He grinned at her mischievously. "If you're looking for

something to bring up the gas," he said, "champagne beats ginger ale any time." He sipped at it appreciatively. "Ah," he said and burped. "Have some, maybe it will make you feel sexy."

"What good would it do you if I did?" Jennie retorted.

"I'd feel good just remembering what I'd have done if it were twenty years ago."

"Better make it forty, to be safe."

"No." He shook his head. "Twenty was the best. Maybe it's because I appreciated it more then, knowing it wasn't going to last very long."

The teletype in the corner of the library began to chatter. Jennie got up out of the chair and walked over to it. When it stopped, she tore the message off and came back to him. "They just nominated Roosevelt for a second term." She handed him the yellow sheet.

"I expected that," he said. "Now they'll never get the son of a bitch out of there. But why should I worry? I won't be around."

The telephone began to ring almost as he finished speaking. It was the direct wire from his Los Angeles paper. She picked it up off the desk and brought it over to him. "Standhurst," he said into it.

She could hear a faint buzz on the other end of the wire. His face was expressionless as he listened. "Hell, no! There's time enough to editorialize after he's made his acceptance speech. At least, then we'll have an idea of what promises he's going to break. No editorials until tomorrow. That goes for all the papers. Put it on the teletype."

He put down the telephone and looked at her. Immediately, the teletype began to clatter again. She walked over and looked down at it. Green letters began to appear on the yellow paper.

FROM CHARLES STANDHURST TO ALL PAPERS: IMPORTANT. ABSOLUTELY NO EDITORIALS RE NOMINATION ROOSEVELT UNTIL ACCEPTANCE SPEECH IS MADE AND EVALUATED. REPEAT. ABSOLUTELY NO EDITORIALS RE NOMINATION ROOSE—

She walked away from the teletype while it was still chattering. "That's your orders, boss."

"Good. Now turn the damn thing off so we can talk."

She went over and flipped the switch, then came back and sat down opposite him. She took a cigarette and lit it as he sipped the champagne through the straw reflectively. "What are your plans when this job is over?"

"I haven't thought much about it."

"You better start," he said. "It won't be long now."

She smiled at him. "Anxious to get rid of me?"

"Don't be silly," he said. "The only reason I've stayed alive this long is because I didn't want to leave you."

Something in his voice made her look searchingly at him. "You know, Charlie, I believe you really mean that."

"Of course I do," he snapped.

Suddenly touched, she came over to the side of his chair and kissed his cheek. "Hey, Nurse Denton," he said. "I think you're breaking down. I'll get you in the sack yet."

"You got me a long time ago, Charlie. The only trouble is, we didn't meet soon enough."

When she thought about it, that was true. The very first time she'd come down to have lunch with him in the hospital, the day after the operation, she'd liked him. She knew he was dying and after a moment, she knew that he knew it. But it didn't stop him from playing the gallant. None of that bland, tasteless hospital food for him, even if he couldn't eat.

Instead, the food was rushed by motorcar from Romanoff's with a police escort out in front and the siren blaring all the way. And along with the food came a maître d' and two waiters to serve it.

He sat up in his bed, sipping champagne and watching her eat. He liked the way she ate. Picky eaters were usually selfish lovers. They gave you nothing, demanding the same sort of un-attainable satisfaction in bed that they demanded from the table. He made up his mind instantly, as he always did. "I'm going to be sick for a while," he said. "I'm going to need a nurse. How would you like the job?"

She'd looked up from her coffee, her gray eyes quizzical. "There are nurses who specialize in home care, Mr. Standhurst. They'd probably be better at it than I am."

"I asked you."

"I have a job at Los Angeles General," she said. "A good job. Then sometimes I get special calls to help out here, like this one. It's the kind of work I'm good at."

"How much do you make?"

"Eighty-five a month, room and board."

"I'll pay you a thousand a week, room and board," he said.

"But that's ridiculous!"

"Is it?" he asked, watching her steadily. "I can afford it. When the doctor left here this morning, he told me I've only got three months to go. I always expect to pay a little bit more when I can't offer a steady job."

She looked down as the waiter refilled her coffee cup. "You'll be here for about three weeks," she said. "That will give me time to give notice. When do you want me to start?"

"Right now. And don't worry about the notice. I already told Colton and Los Angeles General that you were coming to work for me."

She stared at him for a moment, then put down her cup and got to her feet. She gestured to the maître d' and immediately the waiters began to wheel the table out. "Hey, what's the idea?" Standhurst asked.

Jennie didn't answer as she walked to the foot of the table and picked up the chart. She studied it for a moment and then came over and took the glass of champagne out of his hand. "If I'm working for you now," she said, "it's time you got some rest."

Time never passes as quickly as when it's running out, he thought. Somehow, everything seems sharper, clearer to the mind, even decisions are arrived at more easily. Perhaps it was because the responsibility for them couldn't come home to roost. No one can win an argument with a grave.

He felt the pain race through him like a knife. He didn't flinch but from her face, he knew that she knew. A strange kind of communication had grown between them. Words weren't necessary. There were times he thought she felt the pain, too.

"Maybe you'd better go to bed," she said.

"Not just yet. I want to talk to you."

"O.K.," she said. "Go ahead."

"You're not going back to the hospital, are you?"

"I don't know. I haven't really thought about it."

"You'll never be happy in a job like that again. I've spoiled you. There's nothing like a lot of money."

She laughed. "You're so right, Charlie. I've been thinking about that. Nothing's going to seem right ever again."

He studied her thoughtfully. "I could leave you something in my will, or even marry you. But my children would probably make a federal case out of it and say you influenced me. All you'd get is a lot of grief."

She met his gaze. "Thanks for thinking about it, anyway, Charlie."

"You need to make a lot of money," he said. "Why did you decide to be a nurse? You always wanted to be one?"

"No." She shrugged her shoulders. "What I really wanted to be was another Helen Wills. But I got a scholarship to St. Mary's, so I went."

"Even being a tennis bum takes money."

"I know. Anyway, it's too late now. I'd be satisfied if I could just make enough to hire the best pro around and play two hours every day."

"See!" he said triumphantly. "That's a hundred bucks a day, right there."

"Yeah. I'll probably end up back at the hospital."

"You don't have to."

"What do you mean?" she asked, looking at him. "That's all I ever trained for."

"You started training for something else long before you studied nursing. Becoming a woman."

"Well, I couldn't have trained so well, then," she said wryly. "The first time I ever acted like a woman, I got my head knocked off."

"You mean Dr. Grant in Frisco?"

"How do you know about that?"

"Mostly a guess," he said. "But the paper automatically checks up on everyone who comes near me. Grant's got that reputation and the fact that you worked for him and left in such a hurry led me to that surmise. What happened? His wife catch you?"

She nodded slowly. "It was horrible."

"It always is when you're emotionally involved," he said. "It's happened to me more than once." He refilled his glass with champagne. "The trick is not to become emotionally involved."

"How do you do that?"

"By making it pay," he said.

"What you're saying, then, in effect, is that I should become a whore?" she said in a shocked voice.

He smiled. "That's only the Catholic in you that's talking. In the back of your mind, even you have to admit that it makes sense."

"But a whore?" she said, her voice still shocked.

"Not a whore, a courtesan or its modern equivalent, the call girl. In ancient civilizations, being a courtesan was a highly respected profession. Statesmen and philosophers alike sought their favors. And it isn't only the money that made it attractive. It's a way of life that's most complete. Luxurious and satisfying."

She began to laugh. "You're nothing but a dirty old man, Charlie. When do you bring out the French postcards?"

He laughed with her. "Why shouldn't I be? I was a dirty young man, too. But I was never stupid. You have all the equipment necessary to become a great courtesan. The body, the mind—even your nurse's training won't be wasted. True sex demands a greater intellectualism than simple animal rutting."

"Now I know it's time for you to go to bed." She laughed. "Next thing I know, you'll be suggesting I go to a school to learn all about it."

"That's an idea." He chuckled. "They're always after me to endow one college or another. Why didn't I think of it? The Standhurst College of Sex. Otherwise known as the Old Fucking School." He began to laugh heartily, then suddenly he grimaced in pain. His face whitened and beads of perspiration broke out on his forehead. He hunched over in his wheel chair.

In a moment, she was at his side, pushing up the sleeve of his robe, exposing his arm. Quickly she shot the syrette of morphine into his vein. His bony fingers gripped her arm, trying to push it away, as he stared at her with agony-laden eyes.

"For Christ's sake, Charlie," she said angrily. "Give yourself a break. Stop fighting it!" His grip relaxed for a moment and she emptied another syrette into him. She looked into his eyes and saw him fighting the comfort the drug would bring him. She took his fragile, thin hand and raised it swiftly to her lips.

He smiled as the drug began to cloud his eyes. "Poor little Jennie," he said softly. "Any other time and I'd have made you my queen!" His fingers brushed her cheek gently. "But I won't forget what we were talking about. I'm not going to let you go to waste just because I'm not going to be around to enjoy it!"

11

THREE DAYS LATER THEY WERE HAVING LUNCH ON the terrace when she saw the gray Rolls-Royce come to a stop in the driveway. A smartly dressed chauffeur opened the door and a woman stepped out. A few minutes later, the butler appeared on the terrace. "A Mrs. Schwartz to see you, Mr. Standhurst."

Standhurst smiled. "Set another place, Judson, and ask Mrs. Schwartz if she'll join us."

The butler bowed. "Yes, Mr. Standhurst."

A moment later, a woman came through the doorway. "Charlie!" she said, unmistakable pleasure in her voice. She held her hands out toward him as she walked. "How good to see you."

"Aida." Standhurst kissed her hand. "Forgive my not getting up." He looked into her face. "You're as beautiful as ever."

"You haven't changed a bit, Charlie. You can still keep a straight face and lie like hell."

Standhurst laughed. "Aida, this is Jennie Denton."

"How do you do?" Jennie said. She saw a woman, perhaps in her middle or late fifties, quietly and expensively dressed. The woman turned, her smile warm and friendly, but Jennie suddenly had the feeling that there was little about her that the woman didn't take in.

She turned back to Standhurst. "Is this the girl you spoke to me about on the phone?"

Standhurst nodded.

The woman turned back to Jennie. This time, her eyes were openly appraising. She smiled suddenly. "You may have lost your balls, Charlie," she said in a conversational tone of voice, "but you certainly haven't lost your taste."

Jennie's mouth hung open as she stared at them. Standhurst began to laugh and the butler reappeared at the doorway, carrying a chair. He held it for Mrs. Schwartz as she sat down at the table.

"A sherry flip for Mrs. Schwartz, Judson." The butler bowed

and disappeared. Standhurst turned to Jennie. "I suppose you're wondering what this is all about?"

Jennie nodded, still unable to speak.

"Twenty-five years ago, Aida Schwartz ran the best cat house west of the Everleigh sisters in Chicago."

Mrs. Schwartz reached over and patted his hand. "Charlie remembers everything," she said to Jennie. "He even remembered that I never drink anything but a sherry flip." She looked down at his glass on the table. "And I suppose you still drink champagne in a tall glass over ice?"

He nodded. "Old habits, like old friends, Aida, are hard to give up."

The butler placed a drink in front of her. She raised the glass daintily to her lips and sipped. She looked at the butler and smiled. "Thank you."

"Thank you, madam."

She raised her eyebrows in good-humored surprise. "This is very good," she said. "You don't know how hard it is to get a decent cocktail, even in the most expensive restaurants. It seems that ladies drink nothing but Martinis nowadays." She shuddered politely. "Horrible. In my time, no lady would dream of even tasting anything like that."

Standhurst looked at Jennie. "Aida would never let any of her girls drink anything but sherry."

"Whisky befuddles the brain," Aida said primly. "And my girls weren't being paid for drinking."

The old man chuckled reminiscently. "They certainly weren't. Aida, do you remember before the war when I used to come down to your house for a prostate massage?"

"I do, indeed." She smiled.

He looked across the table at Jennie. "I'd developed a bit of trouble and the doctor recommended prostate massage three times a month. The first time I went to his office. After that, I made up my mind that if I had to have massage, I'd at least enjoy it. So, three evenings a week, I showed up at Aida's for my treatment."

"What he didn't tell you," Aida added, "was that the treatments got him terribly aroused. And my girls were trained never to disappoint a guest. When Charlie went back to see the doctor two weeks later and explained, the doctor was horribly upset."

Standhurst was still laughing. "The doctor said he'd bring Aida up before the authorities on charges of practicing medicine without a license."

Mrs. Schwartz reached over and patted Standhurst's hand fondly. "And do you remember Ed Barry?"

"I certainly do." He chuckled and looked at Jennie. "Ed Barry was one of those hard-shelled Southern Baptists who look down the end of their nose at everything and immediately label it sin. Well, this was election eve and Ed was running for governor on a reform ticket. I managed to get him drinking in the excitement of it all and by midnight, he was weeping drunk. So without telling him where I was taking him, we went down to Aida's. He never forgot it."

Standhurst laughed, wiping the tears from his eyes. "Poor old Ed, he never knew what hit him. He lost the election but he never seemed to mind it. On the day Aida closed down her place, after we got into the war, he was downstairs in the bar, weeping as if the world had come to an end."

"Those were the good old days," Aida said. "We'll never see them again."

"Why did you close down?" Jennie asked curiously.

"There were several reasons," Aida said seriously, turning to Jennie. "After and during the war, there was too much free competition. It seemed as if every girl was determined to give it away. And it simply became too difficult to find girls who were interested and dedicated enough in their work to measure up to the high standards I wanted to maintain. All they were interested in was being whores. Since I didn't need the money, I closed up."

"Aida's a very wealthy woman. She put all her money into real estate and apartment houses, here and in most of the big cities around the country." Standhurst looked over at her. "Just about what are you worth right now, Aida?"

She shrugged her shoulders. "About six million dollars, give or take a little," she said casually. "Thanks to you and a few good friends like you."

Standhurst grinned. "Now are you still determined to go back to the hospital?"

Jennie didn't answer.

"Well, Jennie?" he asked.

Jennie stared at him, then at Aida. They were watching her

intently. She started to speak but no words came to her lips.

Mrs. Schwartz reached over suddenly and patted her hand reassuringly. "Give her a little time to think it over, Charlie," she said gently. "It's a decision a girl has to make for herself."

There was a curiously fond look in Standhurst's eyes as he smiled at Jennie. "She'll have to make up her mind pretty soon," he said softly. "There isn't that much time left."

He didn't know it then, but there were exactly two days.

He turned his head to watch her as she came into his room two mornings later. "I think I'll stay in bed today, Jennie," he said in a low voice. Drawing the drapes back from the windows, she looked at him in the light that spilled across the bed. His face was white and the skin parchment-thin over the bones. He kept his eyes partly closed, as if the light hurt them.

She crossed to the side of the bed and looked down. "Do you want me to call the doctor, Charlie?"

"What could he do?" he asked, a faint line of perspiration appearing on his forehead. She picked up a small towel from the bedside table and wiped his face. Then she pulled down the blanket and lifted his old-fashioned nightshirt. Quickly she replaced the waste pouch and saw his eyes dart to the pouch as she covered him. She picked up the waste bag and went into the bathroom.

"Pretty bad?" he asked, his eyes on her face, when she returned.

"Pretty bad."

"I know," he whispered. "I looked before you came in. It was as black as the hubs of hell."

She slipped an arm behind him and held him up as she straightened his pillow. She let him sink back gently. "I don't know. Some mornings I've seen it worse."

"Don't kid me." He closed his eyes for a moment, then opened them. "I got a hunch today's the day," he whispered, his eyes on her face.

"You'll feel better after I get some orange juice into you."

"The hell with that," he whispered vehemently. "Who ever heard of going to hell on orange juice? Get me some champagne!"

Silently she put down the orange juice and picked up a tall glass. She filled it with cubes from the Thermos bucket and poured the champagne over it. Putting the glass straw into the glass, she held it for him.

"I can still hold my own drink," he said.

The teletype in the corner of the room began to chatter. She walked over to look at it. "What is it?"

"Some speech Landon made at a Republican dinner last night."

"Turn it off," he said testily.

He held out the glass to her and she took it and put it back on the table. The telephone began to ring. She picked it up. "It's the feature editor in L.A.," she said. "He's returning the call you made to him yesterday."

"Tell him I want Dick Tracy for the paper out here." She nodded and repeated the message into the telephone and hung up. She turned back and saw his face was covered with perspiration again.

"Your son Charles made me promise to call him if I thought it was necessary."

"Don't," he snapped. "Who needs him here to gloat over me? The son of a bitch has been waiting around for years for me to kick off. He wants to get his hands on the papers." He chuckled soundlessly. "I'll bet the damn fool has the papers come out for Roosevelt the day after the funeral."

A spasm of pain shot through him and he sat up suddenly, almost bolt upright, in the bed. "Oh, Jesus!" he said, clutching at his belly. Instantly, her arm was around his shoulders, supporting him, while with her other hand, she reached for a syrette of morphine. "Not yet, Jennie, please."

She looked at him for a moment, then put the syrette back on the table. "All right," she said. "Tell me when."

He sank back against the pillow and she wiped his face again. He closed his eyes and lay quietly for a moment. Then he opened them and there was a look of terror in them she had never seen before. "I feel like I'm choking!" he said, sitting up, his hand over his mouth.

Quickly, without turning around, she reached for the drain pan on the table behind her and held it under his mouth. He coughed and heaved and brought up a black brackish bile. She put down the pan and wiped his mouth and chin and let him sink to the pillow again.

He looked up at her through tear-filled eyes, trying to smile.

"Christ," he whispered hoarsely. "That tasted like my own piss!"

She didn't answer and he closed his eyes wearily. She could see him shiver under the onslaught of the pain. After a few minutes, he spoke without opening his eyes. "You know, Jennie," he whispered, "I thought the sweetest agony I'd ever know was coming. But going's got it beat a million miles."

He opened his eyes and looked at her. The terror was gone from them and a deep, wise calm had taken its place. He smiled slowly. "All right, Jennie," he whispered, looking into her eyes. "Now!"

Her eyes still fastened to his, she reached behind her for a syrette. Automatically she found the sunken vein and squeezed the syrette dry. She picked up another. He smiled again as he saw it in her hand. "Thanks, Jennie," he whispered.

She bent forward and kissed the pale, damp forehead. "Goodby, Charlie."

He leaned back against the pillow and closed his eyes as she plunged the second syrette into his arm. Soon there were six empty syrettes lying on the cover of the bed beside him. She sat there very quietly, her fingers on his pulse, as the beat grew fainter and fainter. At last, it stopped completely. She stared down at him for a moment, then pressed down the lids over his eyes and drew the cover over his face.

She got to her feet, putting the syrettes into her uniform pocket as she wearily crossed the room and picked up the telephone.

The butler met her in the hallway as she was going to her room. He had an envelope in his hand. "Mr. Standhurst asked me to give this to you, Miss Denton. He gave it to me before you came on duty this morning."

"Thank you, Judson." She closed the door behind her and tore open the envelope as she crossed the room. Enclosed were five thousand-dollar bills and a small note in his scratchy handwriting.

DEAR JENNIE,

By now you must understand the reason I wanted you to stay with me. One thing I could never understand is that false mercy so many proclaim while prolonging the agony of approaching death.

Enclosed find your severance pay. You may use it as you

will—to provide for a rainy day while you continue to waste your life in the generally unrewarding care of others; or, if you've half the intelligence I give you credit for and are half the woman I think, you'll use it as tuition to Aida's school, which for the sake of a better name I shall call Standhurst College, and go on from there to a more luxurious manner of living.

With gratitude and affection, I remain,

Sincerely,

C. STANDHURST

Still holding the note in her hand, she went to the closet and took down her valise. She placed it on the bed and slowly began to pack. Less than an hour later, she left the cab and hurried up the steps into the church, adjusting the scarf she wore around her throat over her head. She genuflected at the back of the church and hurried down the aisle to the altar, turning left toward the statue of the Virgin.

She knelt and clasped her hands as she bowed her head for a moment. Then she turned and took a candle from the rack and held a burning taper to it before placing it among the other candles beneath the statue. Again she bowed her head and knelt for a moment, then turned and hurried back up the aisle. At the door, she dipped her fingers into the Holy Fount and blessed herself, then opened her purse and pressed a bill into the slot of the collection box.

That night, the rector had a very pleasant surprise. There, in the collection box, amidst all the silver and copper coins, was a neatly folded thousand-dollar bill.

The gray Rolls-Royce was parked in the driveway of the old house on Dalehurst Avenue in Westwood as Jennie pulled up in a cab. She got out and paid the driver, then went to the door and put her valise down as she pressed the bell.

From somewhere in the house, a chime sounded. A moment later, the door opened and a maid said, "This way, please, miss."

Aida was seated on the couch, a tray of tea and cookies on the table before her. "You can put the valise with the others, Mary."

"Yes'm," the maid said.

Jennie turned and saw the maid put her valise next to some others standing by the door. She turned back to Aida. A newspaper was open on the couch beside her, the big, black headlines staring up.

STANDHURST DEAD!

Aida got up and took her hand, gently pulling her down to the couch. "Sit down, my dear," she said softly. "I've been expecting you. We have plenty of time for a cup of tea before we go to the train."

"To the train?"

"Of course, my dear," Aida said. "We're going to Chicago. It's the only place in the United States for a girl to start her career."

12

THE BIG TWENTY-FOUR SHEET FROM THE BILL-board hung over the makeshift stage at the Army camp. It was an enlargement of the famous color photograph from the cover of *Life* magazine. Looking up at it, Jennie remembered the photographer perching precariously on the top rung of the ladder near the ceiling, aiming his camera down toward her on the bed.

From that angle, her legs had been too long and had gone out of the frame, so he'd turned her around and placed her feet up on the white satin tufted headboard. Then the flash bulb had gone off, blinding her for a moment as they always did, and history had been made.

She'd been wearing a decorously cut black lace nightgown, which covered her completely from throat to ankles. Yet it had clung so revealingly, the soft tones of her flesh glowing in contrast to the black lace, that it left nothing to the imagination—the swollen nipples, irritated by the material across her jutting breasts, the soft curve of her stomach, and the sharply rising pubis, which couldn't be hidden because of the position of her legs. Her long blond hair spilled downward over the edge of the bed and the blinding light of the flash bulb had thrown a sensual invitation into her eyes as she smiled at the invisible onlooker, upside down, from the lower-left-hand corner.

Life had published the photograph with but one word emblazoned in white block letters beneath it:

DENTON

That had been almost a year ago, in October of 1941, about the time *The Sinner* was having its world première in New York. She remembered the surprise she'd felt, walking through the lobby of the Waldorf, with Jonas at her side, coming onto rows of photographs of herself hanging across the newsstand magazine racks.

"Look," she'd said, stopping in wonder. Jonas smiled at her in that particular way which, she knew by now, meant he was particularly pleased with something. He'd crossed to the newsstand and throwing a coin down picked up the magazine from the rack. He handed it to her as they went into the elevator.

She opened the magazine on the way up. The headline loomed over the text: *Spirituality in Sex.*

Jonas Cord, a wealthy young man, who makes airplanes, explosives, plastics and money (see *Life*, Oct. '39) and, when the spirit moves him, occasionally makes a motion picture (*The Renegade*, 1930, *Devils in the Sky*, 1932), has come up with a highly personalized version, in the De Mille tradition, of the story of Mary Magdalene. He calls it, with his customary frankness, *The Sinner.*

Without a doubt, the single most important factor contributing to the impact of this motion picture is the impressive performance of the young woman Mr. Cord selected to play the title role, Jennie Denton.

Miss Denton, without prior experience in motion pictures or at acting, has a most newsworthy effect upon audiences. With all the overtly sexual awareness that the motions of her body (37-21-36) seem to suggest, the viewer is at the same time aware of the deeply spiritual quality that always emanates from her. Perhaps this stems from her eyes, which are wide-set and gray and deep with a knowledge and wisdom of pain and love and death, far beyond her years. In some strange manner, she appears to project the paradoxical contrasts of our times—the self-seeking aggressions of man's search for physical satisfaction and his desire for spiritual values greater than himself.

The elevator door opened and she felt Jonas' hand on her arm. She closed the magazine and they walked out of the elevator. "My God, do they really believe that?"

He smiled. "I guess they do. That's one magazine you can't buy for advertising. I told you you were going to be a star," he said as they walked into his apartment.

She was to leave for the Coast immediately after the première to begin another picture. She saw the script lying on the table in front of the couch. Jonas walked over and picked it up, and riffled the pages. "I don't like it."

"I don't like it, either. But Maurice says it will make a mint."

"I don't care," he said. "I just don't like the idea of you being in it." He crossed to the telephone. "Get me Mr. Bonner at the Sherry-Netherland."

"Maurice, this is Jonas," he said curtly, a moment later. "Cancel *Stareyes*. I don't want Denton in it."

She heard Bonner's excited protest all the way across the room. "I don't care," Jonas said. "Get someone else to play it. . . . Who? . . . Hayworth, Sheridan. Anyone you want. And from now on, Denton isn't to be scheduled for any picture until I approve the script."

He put down the telephone and turned to her. He was smiling. "You hear that?"

She smiled back at him. "Yes, boss."

The photograph had been an instant success. Everywhere you went, it stared out at you—from walls, from display counters, from calendars and from posters. And she, too, had gone on to fame. She was a star and when she returned to the Coast, she found that Jonas had approved a new contract for her.

But a year had gone by, including the bombs at Pearl Harbor, and still she had made no other picture. Not that it mattered. *The Sinner* was in its second year at the big Norman Theater in New York and was still playing limited-first-run engagements wherever it opened. It was proving to be the biggest-grossing picture the company had ever made.

Her routine became rigid and unvarying. Between publicity appearances at each première, as the picture opened across the country, she remained on the Coast. Each morning, she'd go to the studio. There her day would be filled—dramatic lessons in the morning; luncheon, generally with some interviewer; voice, singing and dancing lessons in the afternoon. Her evenings were generally spent alone, unless Jonas happened to be in town. Then she was with him every night.

Occasionally, she'd have dinner with David and Rosa Woolf. She liked Rosa and their happy little baby, who just now was learning how to walk and bore the impressive name of Henry Bernard, after David's father and uncle. But most of the time she spent alone in her small house with the Mexican woman. The word was out. She was Jonas' girl. And Jonas' girl she remained.

It was only when she was with him that she did not feel the loneliness and lack of purpose that was looming larger and larger inside. She began to grow restless. It was time for her to go to work. She read scripts avidly and several times, when she thought she'd found one she might like to do, she got in touch with Jonas. As always, he'd promise to read it and then call her several days later to say he didn't think it was right for her. There was always a reason.

Once, in exasperation, she'd asked him why he kept her on the payroll if he had nothing for her to do. For a moment, he'd been silent. When he spoke, his voice was cold and final. "You're not an actress," he said. "You're a star. And stars can only shine when everything else is right."

A few days later, Al Petrocelli, the publicity man, came to her dressing room at the studio. "Bob Hope's doing a show for the boys at Camp Pendleton. He wants you on it."

She turned on the couch on which she was sitting and put down the script she'd been reading. "I can do it?" she asked, looking at him.

They both knew what she meant. "Bonner talked to Cord. They both agreed the exposure would be good for you. Di Santis will be in charge of whipping up an act for you."

"Good," she said, getting to her feet. "It will be great having something to do again."

And now, after six weeks of extensive rehearsal of a small introductory speech and one song, which had been carefully polished, phrased and orchestrated to show her low, husky voice to its greatest advantage, she stood in the wings of the makeshift stage, waiting to go on. She shivered in the cool night air despite the mink coat wrapped around her.

She peeked out from behind the wings at the audience. A roar of laughter rolled toward her from the rows upon rows of soldiers, stretching into the night as far as the eye could see. Hope had just delivered one of his famous off-color, serviceman-only kind of jokes that could never have got on the air during his coast-to-coast broadcasts. She pulled her head back, still shivering. "Nervous, eh?" Al asked. "Never worked before an audience before? Don't worry, it'll soon pass."

A sudden memory of Aida and the routine she'd made her perform before a small but select group of wealthy men in New Orleans flashed through her mind. "Oh, I've worked in front of an audience before." Then when she saw the look of surprise on his face, "When I was in college," she added dryly. She turned back to watch Bob Hope. Somehow, the memory made her feel better.

Al turned to the soldier standing next to him. "Now, you know what you got to do, Sergeant?"

"I got it down perfect, Mr. Petrocelli."

"Good," Al said. He glanced out at the stage. Hope was nearing the end of his routine. Al turned back to the soldier, a twenty-dollar bill appearing magically in his hand. "She'll be going on any minute," he said. "Now, you get down there in the front near the stage. And don't forget. Speak up loud and clear."

"Yes, Mr. Petrocelli," the soldier said, the twenty disappearing into his pocket.

"There'll be another after the show if everything goes right."

"For another twenty, Mr. Petrocelli," the soldier said, "you don't have to worry. They'll hear me clear to Alaska."

Al nodded worriedly and turned toward the stage as the soldier went out and around the wings. Hope was just beginning Jennie's introduction. "And now, men," he said into the microphone, "for the high spot of the evening—" He paused for a moment, holding up his hands to still the starting applause. "The reason we're all here. Even the entire officer's club." He waited until the laughter died away. "Girl-watching!"

"Now, men," he continued, "when I first told the War Department who was coming here tonight, they said, 'Oh, no, Mr.

Hope. We just haven't enough seat belts for that many chairs.' But I reassured them. I told them you soldiers knew how to handle any situation." There was laughter again but this time, there was an expectancy in its sound. Hope held up his hands. "And so, fellers, I give you—"

The lights suddenly dimmed and a baby spot picked up Jennie's head as she peeked out past the curtain. "Fasten your seat belts, men!" Hope shouted. "Jennie Denton!"

And the stage went to black except for the spotlight on Jennie. A roar burst from the audience as she cautiously and tentatively, in the manner in which she had thoroughly rehearsed, walked out on the stage, covered completely by the full mink coat.

The noise washed over her and she felt its vibrations in the wooden floor beneath her feet as she came to a stop in front of the microphone. She stood there quietly, looking at them, her blond page-boy haircut catching and reflecting the gleaming light. The soldiers whistled and screamed and stomped.

After a few minutes had passed, during which the noise showed no signs of abatement, she leaned toward the microphone. "If you men will give me just a minute," she said in a low voice, letting her coat slip from one shoulder, "I'll take my coat off."

If possible, the noise grew even louder as she slowly and deliberately took off the coat. She let it fall to the stage behind her and stood there, revealed in a white, diamond-sequined, skin-tight evening gown. She leaned toward the microphone again and one shoulder strap slipped from her shoulder. Quickly she caught at it. "This is most embarrassing. I've never been with so many men before."

They roared enthusiastically.

"Now I don't know what to do," she said in a soft voice.

"Don't do nothin', baby," came a stentorian roar from down front, near the stage, "Jus' stand there!"

Again, pandemonium broke loose as she smiled and peered in the direction of the voice. She waited until the sound died down slightly. "I have a little song I'd like to sing for you," she said. "Would you like that?"

"Yes!" The sound came back from a thousand throats.

"O.K.," she said and moved closer to the microphone, clutching again at her falling strap. "Now, if you'll just pretend you're at home, listening to the radio, if you'll close your eyes—"

"Close our eyes?" the stentorian voice roared again. "Baby, we may be in the Army but we're not crazy!"

She smiled helplessly at the roar of laughter as the music slowly came up. Slowly the spot narrowed to just her face as silence came down on the audience. The music was the studio arranger at his best. An old torch song but done in beguine rhythm with the piano, the winds and the violins playing the melody against the rhythm of the drums and the big bass.

She came in right on cue, her eyes half closed against the spotlight, her lower lip shining. "I wanna be loved by you," she sang huskily. "And nobody else but you.

"I wanna be loved by you.

"A-low-oh-ohne."

The roar that came rolling out from the audience all but drowned out her voice and for a moment she was frightened by all the repressed sexuality she heard in it.

13

MAURICE BONNER WALKED INTO THE HOLLYWOOD Brown Derby, the thick blue-paper-bound script under his arm. The headwaiter bowed. "Good afternoon, Mr. Bonner. Mr. Pierce is already here."

They walked down to a booth in the rear of the restaurant. Don looked up from a copy of the *Hollywood Reporter.* He put down the paper next to his drink. "Hello, Maurice."

Bonner dropped into the seat opposite him. "Hello," he said. He looked over at the trade paper. "See the write-up our girl got?"

Dan nodded.

"That wasn't the half of it," Bonner said. "Al Petrocelli told me he never saw anything like it. They wouldn't let her get off the stage and then when it was over, they almost tore her clothes off while she was getting to the car. Hope called me first thing this morning and said he wants her any time she's available."

"More proof that I'm right," Pierce said. "I think she's bigger now than Marlowe ever was." He shot a shrewd glance at Bonner. "Still going up there one night a week?"

Bonner smiled. There were no secrets in this town. "No. After *The Sinner* opened in New York, Cord tore up her old contract and gave her a new one."

"I don't get it."

"It's simple," Bonner said. "The morning she got the contract, she came into my office. She borrowed my pen and signed it, then looked up at me and said, 'Now I don't have to fuck for nobody. Even you!' And she picks up the contract and walks out."

Pierce laughed. "I don't believe her. Once a cunt, always a cunt. She's got an angle."

"She has. Jonas Cord. I got a hunch she's going to marry him."

"That would serve the son of a bitch right," Pierce said harshly. "He still doesn't know she was a whore?"

"He doesn't know."

"Just shows you. No matter how smart you think you are, there's always some bint that's smarter." Pierce laughed. "How's Jonas doing?"

"Making nothing but money," Bonner said. "But you know Jonas. He still isn't happy."

"Why not?"

"He tried to get into the Air Corps and they wouldn't take him. They refused to give him a commission, saying he was too important to the war effort. So he leaves Washington in a huff and flies to New York and enlists as a private, the *schmuck*."

"But he still ain't in the Army," Pierce said.

"Of course not. He flunked the physical—perforated eardrums or something stupid like that. So they classify him 4-F and the next week, they take Roger Forrester back as a brigadier general."

"I hear David's going up for his physical soon," Pierce said.

"Any day now, the jerk. He could easily get a deferment. Married, with a baby; especially now the industry's got an essential rating. But he won't ask for it." He looked across the table at Pierce. "Even Nevada's taking his Wild-West show out on the road to work for free on the War Bond drives."

"It just proves that there are still some people around who think the world is flat," Dan said. He signaled the waiter for another round of drinks. "All those guys. I practically started them in the business. Today they all got it made and where am I? Still trying to make a deal."

Bonner looked at him. He didn't feel sorry for Pierce. Dan was still one of the most successful agents in Hollywood. "Yeah," he said sarcastically. "My heart bleeds for you. I already heard the story of your life, Dan. That isn't why I came to lunch."

Dan was a sharp enough agent to know he was in danger of losing his audience. He turned off the complaints and lowered his voice to a confidential tone. "You read the script?"

Bonner picked the script up from the seat beside him and placed it on the table. "I read it."

"Great, isn't it?" Pierce asked, the selling enthusiasm beginning to creep into his voice.

"It's good." Bonner nodded his head pedantically. "Needs a lot of work, though."

"What script doesn't?" Pierce asked with a smile. He leaned forward. "Now, the way I see it, this script needs a strong producer like you. Wanger, over at Universal, is nuts about it. So is Zimbalist, over at Metro. But I can't see it for them. They just ain't got the feel and showmanship you got."

"Let's skip the bullshit, Dan. We both know the script is good only if we can get a certain girl to play in it. And we both know who that is."

"Denton," Pierce said quickly. "That's my thinking, too. That's why I brought it to you. She's under contract to your studio."

"But Jonas has the final say on what pictures she makes. And he's turned thumbs down on some pretty good ones."

"What's he trying to do?" Pierce asked. "Hide her away in a closet and keep her for himself? You can't do that to a star. Sooner or later, she busts out."

Bonner shrugged. "You know Jonas. Nobody asks why."

"Maybe he'll like the script."

"Even if he did," Bonner said, "once he sees you're the agent, the whole deal goes out the window."

"What if the girl puts the pressure on and says she's got to do it?"

Bonner shrugged. "Your guess is as good as mine. But I'm

not going to give it to her. I'm not getting into trouble over any script. No matter how good it is, there's always another."

Pierce stared at him, his fleshy lips tightening grimly. "I got an idea we can make her see it our way," he said. "I got my hands on—"

Bonner stopped him. "Don't tell me. If it happens, let it come as a pleasant surprise. I don't want to know anything about it."

Pierce stared at him for a moment, then relaxed back into his seat. He picked up the menu. "O.K., Maurice," he said, smiling. "What you going to eat?"

The mail was on the small desk in the living room when Jennie got back from the studio. She walked over to the desk and sat down. "We'll have dinner about eight thirty," she said. "I want to take a bath and rest up first."

"*Sí, señorita,*" Maria answered and waddled away.

Jennie looked at the mail. There were two envelopes, one large manila one, which from experience she guessed contained a script, and a letter. She opened the letter first. The letterhead across the top read: *St. Mary's College of Nursing.* Her eyes flicked down the page. It was in Sister M. Christopher's precise script.

DEAR JENNIE,

This is just a short note to express the appreciation of the students and the staff of St. Mary's College for the special screening of your picture which you were kind enough to arrange for us.

The Reverend Mother and the sisters, including myself, were all most impressed by the moving expression of the faith and love for our Saviour, Jesus Christ, that you brought to your interpretation of what must have been a most exacting and difficult portrayal. It is unfortunate indeed that the makers of the motion picture thought it necessary to include certain scenes which we felt could very easily have been omitted without impairment to the story of the Magdalen. But on the whole, we were extremely pleased that in these troubled times, so noble a demonstration of the Redeeming Grace to be found in the Love of Our Lord is available for all to see.

Now I must close for I am soon due in Surgery. Since the war, all of us in the school, and in the hospital, are working double shifts due to the shortages of help. But with Our Lord's Grace, we shall redouble our poor efforts to extend His Mercy.

The Reverend Mother extends to you Her Most Gracious blessing and prays that you may continue to find success and happiness in your new career.

Sincerely yours in J. C.,
SISTER M. CHRISTOPHER

A vision of the sister's austere, observant face flashed through her mind, together with a twinge of nostalgia for the years she had spent at the college. Somehow, it seemed such a long time ago. It was as if she were a completely different person from the wide-eyed, nervous grl who first appeared in the Reverend Mother's office.

She remembered the quiet hours of study and the long hours of training and the exhausting hours of sheer drudgery in the hospital. There had been times when she'd cry out of sheer frustration at her inability to learn all that was taught her. It was during those moments that the mask of austerity would disappear from the sister's face and she would place her hand comfortingly on the girl's shoulder. "Work hard and pray hard, Jennie," she'd say gently, "and you will learn. You have the true gift of healing within you."

And she would feel comforted and her strength would be renewed as she saw how unsparingly the sister gave of herself to all, both patients and students. It seemed that no matter what hour of the day or night Jennie was on duty, Sister Christopher was always nearby.

Jennie reached for a cigarette. All of them must be working terribly hard if the sister mentioned it in a letter. Sister Christopher was never given to make much of her own efforts. A feeling of uselessness swept through Jennie as she thought of the comparatively easy life she led. She looked down at her strong, lean hands. She did so little with them now. The knowledge that was in them seemed to tingle in her fingertips. There must be something she could do to help the sisters.

There was. She reached for the telephone at the same time she had the idea and dialed quickly. "Rosa? This is Jennie."

"How are you, Jennie? David told me how you almost broke up the United States Army with the Hope show."

Jennie laughed. "The poor kids have been away from women too long."

"Don't hand me that. The trade papers said you were great."

"Don't tell me David's got you reading them?"

"Sure thing," Rosa said. "Isn't that what every wife in the business does? It's the only way they can keep track of what their husbands are doing."

"How's little Bernie?"

"Why don't you come over for dinner one night and see for yourself? It's been a long time."

"I will. Soon."

"Do you want to talk to David?"

"If he's there," Jennie said politely.

"Good-by, dear," Rosa said, "and dinner real soon? Here's David."

"How's the pride and joy of the Norman lot?"

"Fine. I'm sorry to disturb you at home, David, but I had a little problem I thought you could advise me on."

His voice became serious. "Shoot."

She cleared her throat. "I went to St. Mary's College of Nursing on a scholarship and I was wondering if I could arrange with the studio to take something out of my pay check each week and send it to them the way they do with the Motion Picture Relief Fund. It would be sort of paying them back a little for all they did for me."

"That's easy." David laughed, a kind of relief in his voice. "Just send a note to my office tomorrow morning telling me how much you want taken off and we'll do the rest. Anything else?"

"No, that's all."

"Good. Now, you come to dinner like Rosa said."

"I will, David. Good-by."

She put down the telephone and looked at the letter again. She began to feel better. At least, even if she couldn't be there herself to help, her money would do some good. She put down the letter and picking up the manila envelope, ripped it open. She had been right. It was a script, a long one.

Curiously she read the title on the blue cover. *Aphrodite; a screenplay based on a novel by Pierre Louÿs.* She opened the script to the first page and a note fell out. It was brief and to the point.

DEAR MISS DENTON:

It has been a long time since you made a motion picture and I believe you were wise to wait for the proper script with which to follow up your tremendous success in *The Sinner*.

Aphrodite, I believe, is that script. It is the one property I have seen that has the scope and the quality to add luster to your career. I shall be most interested in your reaction.

Sincerely,
DAN PIERCE

She folded the letter and put it back in the script. That Dan Pierce was a cutie. He knew better than to submit the script to the studio in the usual manner. She picked up the script and started upstairs to her room. She would read it in bed after dinner.

14

DEAR MR. PIERCE:

Thank you for sending me the enclosed script of *Aphrodite*, which I am returning. It is a most interesting screenplay. However, it is not one that I should particularly care to do.

JENNIE DENTON

She wondered whether she had been right in so summarily dismissing the script. She had mixed feelings about it. At night, in bed, reading it for the first time, she could not put it down. There was a fascination about the story that brought to her mind Standhurst's description of the courtesan who helped rule the world. The screenplay seemed to capture the sensual imagery and poetry of the original work and yet bring it all within the limitations and confines of the Motion Picture Code. Yet, the more she read, the less enthusiastic she became.

There was not one single line or scene that could be found

objectionable. On the surface. Yet, beneath the surface, there was an acute awareness of the erotic byplay that would subtly work on an audience's subconscious. By the time she reached the end of the screenplay, she felt this was the writer's only purpose.

She fell asleep, oddly disturbed, and awoke still disturbed. At the studio, the next morning, she'd sent to the library for a copy of the original novel, then spent all of that day and part of the next reading it. After that, she again read the screenplay. It was not until then that she realized how boldly the beauty and purpose of the story had been distorted.

Still, there was no doubt in her mind that it could be made into a great motion picture. And even less doubt that the actress who played Aphrodite would become the most talked about and important actress of that season. The Aphrodite of the script was truly the goddess and woman who was all things to all men.

But that was not enough. For, nowhere in the screenplay could she find the soul of Aphrodite, the one moment of spiritual love and contemplation that would lift her out of herself and make her one truly with the gods. She was beautiful and warm and clever and loving and even moral, according to her own concept. But she was a whore, no better than any since time immemorial, no better than any Jennie had known, no better than Jennie herself had been. And something inside Jennie was appalled by what she had read. For, in another time and another place, she saw herself—what she had been and what she still remained.

She put the envelope on the dressing table and pressed the button for a messenger just as the telephone rang. She picked it up. It was not until she heard his voice that she knew how much she'd missed him. "Jonas! Where are you? When did you get in?"

"I'm at the plant in Burbank. I want to see you."

"Oh, Jonas, I want to see you, too. It will seem like such a long day."

"Why wait until tonight? Can't you come over here for lunch?"

"You know I can."

"One o'clock?"

"I'll be there," she said, putting down the telephone.

"You can leave it here, John," Jonas said. "We'll help ourselves."

"Yes, Mr. Cord." The porter looked at Jennie, then back at Jonas. "Would it," he began hesitantly, "would it be all right if I troubled Miss Denton for her autograph?"

Jonas laughed. "Ask her."

The porter looked inquiringly at Jennie. She smiled and nodded. He took a pencil and paper from his pocket and quickly she scrawled her name on it. "Thank you, Miss Denton."

Jennie laughed as the door closed behind him. "Signing my autograph always makes me feel like a queen." She looked around the office. "This is nice."

"It's not mine," Jonas said, pouring coffee into two cups. "It's Forrester's. I'm just using it while he's away."

"Oh," she said curiously. "Where is yours?"

"I don't have any, except the one that used to be my father's in the old plant in Nevada. I'm never in any one place long enough to really need one." He pulled a chair around near her and sat down. He drank his coffee and looked at her quietly.

She could feel an embarrassed blush creeping over her face. "Do I look all right? Is my make-up smeared or something?"

He shook his head and smiled. "No. You look fine."

She sipped at her coffee and an awkward silence came between them. "What have you been doing?" she asked.

"Thinking, mostly. About us," he answered, looking at her steadily. "You. Me. This last time I was away from you, for the first time in my life I was lonely. Nothing was right. I wanted to see no other girls. Only you."

Her heart seemed to swell, choking her. She felt, somehow, that if she tried to move, she would faint. Jonas put his hand in his pocket and came out with a small box, which he handed to her. She stared down at it dumbly. The small gold letters stared up at her. *Van Cleef & Arpels.*

Her fingers trembled as she opened it. The beautifully cut heart-shaped diamond suddenly released its radiance. "I want to marry you," he said softly.

She felt the hot, grateful tears push their way into her eyes as she looked at him. Her lips trembled but she could not speak.

It was the headline and lead story in Louella's column the next day. The telephone had been ringing in her dressing room all morning, until finally she'd asked the switchboard to screen all her calls. The operator's voice had a new respect in it. As Jennie started to put the telephone down the operator said, "Miss Denton?"

"Yes."

"The girls on the switchboard all wish you the best of luck."

Jennie felt a sudden happy rush of warmth go through her. "Why, thank you."

Later in the afternoon, Rosa called. "I'm so happy for both of you."

"I'm in a daze," Jennie laughed, looking down at the diamond sparkling on her finger.

"You know that dinner invitation?"

"Yes."

"David and I were just thinking. How would you like to make it an engagement party? At Romanoff's with all the trimmings."

"I don't know." Jennie hesitated. "I'd better check with Jonas."

Rosa laughed. "Jonas? Who's he? Only the groom. Nobody ever asks the groom what he wants. It doesn't have to be a big party, if you don't want one."

"All right." Jennie laughed. "You've twisted my arm."

"And you'll have a chance to show off your engagement ring. I hear it's a real smasher."

Jennie held out her hand and the diamond winked at her. "It's very nice," she said.

"Bernie is yelling for his dinner. I'll call you at home tonight and we'll make the arrangements."

"Thanks, Rosa. 'By."

There was a strange car parked in the driveway when she got home from the studio that night. She drove into the garage and entered the house through the back door. If it was another reporter, she didn't want to see him. The Mexican woman was in the kitchen. "A Señor Pierce is in the living room, señorita."

What could he want, she wondered. Perhaps he hadn't received the script yet and had dropped by for it. Pierce was seated in a deep chair, a copy of the script open on his lap. He got to his feet and nodded. "Miss Denton."

"Mr. Pierce. Did you get the script? I sent it out several days ago."

He smiled. "I got it. But I thought perhaps we might discuss it further. I'm hoping I can talk you into changing your mind."

She shook her head. "I don't think so."

"Before we talk about it," he said quickly, "may I offer my congratulations on your engagement?"

"Thank you. But now I must ask you to excuse me. I do have an appointment."

"I'll only take a few minutes of your time." He bent over and picked up a small carrying case that had been lying on the floor behind the chair.

"But, really, Mr. Pierce—"

"I'll only be a few minutes." There was a peculiar sureness in his voice. It was as if he knew she would not dare to refuse him. He pressed a button and the top of the carrying case popped open. "Do you know what this is, Miss Denton?" he asked.

She didn't answer. She was beginning to get angry. If this was his idea of a joke, she wasn't going to like it. "It's an eight-millimeter projector," he said in a conversational tone, as he snapped on a lens. "The kind ordinarily used for the showing of home movies."

"Very interesting. But I hardly see what it has to do with me."

"You will," he promised, looking up. His eyes were cold. He turned, looking for an electrical outlet. He found one against the wall behind the chair and swiftly plugged the cord from the projector into it.

"I think that white wall across from you will do very well for a screen, don't you?" He turned the projector toward it and flicked a switch. "I took the liberty of putting on the reel of film before I came here."

The whir of film sounded and Jennie turned to watch the picture being thrown against the wall. The scene showed two naked girls on a couch, their arms around each other, their faces hidden. A warning bell echoed in her mind. There was something curiously familiar about the scene.

"I got this film from a friend of mine in New Orleans." Pierce's voice came casually from behind her as a man walked into the scene. He, too, was nude and one of the girls turned toward him, facing directly into the camera.

Unconsciously Jennie let out a gasp. The girl was herself.

Then she remembered. It had been that time in New Orleans. She turned to stare at Dan Pierce, her face white.

"You were photogenic even then. You should have made sure there was no camera."

"There wasn't any," she gasped. "Aida would never have permitted it." She stared at him silently, her mouth and throat suddenly dry.

He pressed a switch and as the film stopped, the light faded. "I can see you're not very interested in home movies."

"What do you want?" she asked.

"You." He began to close up the machine. "But not in the usual sense," he added quickly. "I want you to play Aphrodite."

"And if I don't choose to?"

"You're lovely, you're a star, you're engaged," he said casually. "You might not be any of the three if this film should happen to fall into the wrong hands. Together with a summary of your professional activities." His cold eyes flashed at her. "No man, even one as crazy as Jonas Cord, wants to marry the town whore."

"I'm under contract to Norman. My contract doesn't allow me to make any outside pictures."

"I know," Dan said calmly. "But I'm sure Cord would authorize the purchase of this script if you asked him. Bonner will make the picture."

"What if he won't? Jonas has pretty definite ideas about pictures."

A faint smile came to his lips. "Then, make him change them."

She drew in her breath slowly. "And if I do?"

"Why, then you get the film, of course."

"The negative, too?"

He nodded.

"How do I know that there are no dupes?"

His eyebrows went up approvingly. "I see you've learned," he said. "I paid five thousand dollars for that little can of film. And I wouldn't have done that if I hadn't been sure there were no other copies. Besides, why kill the goose? We may want to do business together again sometime."

He packed up the projector. "I'll leave the script with you."

She didn't answer.

He turned, his hand on the door, and looked back. "I told you I'd only be a few minutes," he said.

15

DAN PIERCE GOT TO HIS FEET, RAPPING HIS CUP with a tiny spoon. He surveyed the table owlishly. He was drunk, happy drunk, as much on success as on the Scotch whisky he had so generously imbibed.

He nodded his head as they all looked up at him. "Dan Pierce doesn't forget who his friends are. He does things righ'. I brought the engaged couple each a presen'." He turned, snapping his fingers.

"Yes, Mr. Pierce," the maître d' said quickly. He gestured and a waiter came up with two packages, looked down at the tag on each and deposited the large gold-wrapped box in front of Jonas, the smaller silver-wrapped package by Jennie.

"Thank you, Dan," Jonas said.

"Open it up, Jonas," Dan said drunkenly. "I wan' ev'ybody to see the presents."

Jennie felt a strange foreboding. "We'll open them later, Dan."

"No," he said insistently. "Now."

She looked around the table. They were all watching curiously. She looked at Jonas. He shrugged his shoulders and smiled at her. She started to open her gift. It was wrapped so tight, she reached for a knife to cut it just as Jonas finished taking the wrapping from his. "Hey," Jonas said, laughing, as he held it up for all to see. "A magnum of champagne!"

Her present was in a small but beautifully inlaid mahogany case. She opened it and stared down, feeling the color drain from her face. Jonas took the case from her hands and held it up for everyone to see. "It's a set of English razors." he said and grinned at Dan. "The waiter must have got the labels mixed. Thanks again, Dan."

Abruptly Pierce sat down. He was smiling.

Jennie felt them all watching her. She raised her head and looked around the table. It was as if she knew what they were thinking. Of the twelve other couples seated around the large table, she had known five of the men before she'd made the test. Irving Schwartz, Bonner, three others, who were top-ranking executives with other companies. The other seven men all knew. Some of their wives, too. She could see it in their eyes. In only two of the men could she see any sympathy. David and Nevada Smith.

David she could understand. But she did not understand why Nevada should feel sorry for her. He scarcely knew her. He had always seemed so quiet, even shy, when they met at the studio. But now there was a wild sort of anger deep in his black Indian eyes as he looked from her to Dan Pierce.

Thirteen men, she thought, and all but one of them knew her for what she'd been. And the thirteenth was the unlucky one. He was going to marry her. She felt a light touch on her arm. Rosa's voice broke the silence that threatened to engulf her. "I think it's about time we went to the little girl's room."

Jennie nodded dumbly and followed her from the table silently. She could feel the eyes of other diners following her. Without even returning their glances, she recognized several other men she had known and saw their wise, knowing smiles. She began to feel sick. Rosa drew the curtain in front of the small alcove in the corner as Jennie sank silently onto the couch. Rosa lit a cigarette and handed it to her.

Jennie looked up at her, the cigarette in her fingers already forgotten. The tears started to come into her eyes. "Why?" she asked in a hurt, bewildered voice. "I don't understand. What did I ever do to him?"

She began to cry silently as Rosa sat down beside her and drew her head down to her shoulder.

Dan Pierce chuckled to himself as he threaded his way to his car through the dark and deserted parking lot. Wait until he told the story in the locker room at Hillcrest tomorrow morning. The men would laugh their heads off. None of them really liked Jonas, anyway.

True, they tolerated him. But they didn't accept him. There was a difference. They all respected Jonas' success but they wouldn't lift a finger to help him. Not like they would for Dan Pierce if he needed their help, which he didn't. He was one of them, he'd grown up in the business with them. They had their rules. They stuck together.

Wait until he told them how the broad looked. Like she was ready to sink through the floor, while all the time, Jonas stood there like a *shmuck*, smiling and thinking how nice everybody was. It would break them up.

A dark figure suddenly appeared out of the shadows in front of him. He peered anxiously through the darkness as it silently came closer. "Oh, it's you, Nevada. I didn' know who it was."

Nevada stood there silently.

Dan laughed aloud as he remembered. "Wasn' that a bitch, though?" He chortled, reaching out a hand toward Nevada to steady himself. "I thought she'd bust when she opened the case and saw the razors. An' Jonas, the jerk, he don' even know what he's gettin' into—"

Dan's voice suddenly choked off in a grunt of pain as Nevada sank his fist into his belly. He fell back against a car, clutching at it to hold himself up. He stared at Nevada. "Wha' you go an' do that for?" he asked in a hurt voice. "We're ol' buddies."

He saw Nevada's hand coming toward his face and tried to duck. He wasn't quick enough and felt the pain explode in his eyes. Again the hammer tore into his belly. He bent over, retching, and another blow on the side of his face sent him sprawling into his own vomit. He looked up at Nevada with frightened eyes.

It was not until then that Nevada spoke, and an icy fear came up and clutched at Dan's heart. "I should've done this a long time ago," Nevada said, looking down at him. "I oughta kill you. But you ain't worth goin' to the gas chamber for."

He turned his back contemptuously and walked away. Dan waited until the sound of the high-heeled boots faded away. Then he put his face down on his hands against the cold concrete. "It was only a joke," he cried drunkenly. "It was only a joke."

Jonas followed Jennie into the darkened house. "You're tired," he said gently, looking down at her white face. "It's been a big night. Go on up to bed. I'll see you tomorrow."

"No," she said flatly. She knew what she had to do. She turned and walked into the living room, switching on the light. He followed her curiously.

She turned, slipping the ring from her finger, and held it out to him. He looked at it, then at her. "Why?" he asked. "Is it because of anything I did tonight?"

She shook her head. "No," she said quickly. "It has nothing to do with you at all. Just take the ring, please."

"I'm entitled to know why, Jennie."

"I don't love you," she said. "Is that reason enough?"

"Not now it isn't."

"Then I have a better reason," she said tightly. "Before I made that screen test, I was the highest-priced whore in Hollywood."

He stared at her for a moment. "I don't believe you," he said slowly. "You couldn't have fooled me."

"You're a fool," she said sharply. "If you don't believe me, ask Bonner or any of the other four men at the table who laid me. Or any of a dozen other men I saw in the restaurant tonight."

"I still don't believe you," he said in a low voice.

She laughed. "Then ask Bonner why Pierce gave me that present. There wasn't any mix-up, he meant the razors for me. The story was all over Hollywood, the morning after Bonner left here. How I shaved all the hair off his body, then blew him in a bathtub filled with champagne."

He began to look sick.

"And why do you think I asked you to let me do *Aphrodite?*" she continued. "Not because I thought it was any good. It was to pay Pierce off for this." She walked quickly to the desk and took out two small reels of film. She spun one out at him, the film unwinding from the reel like a roll of confetti. "My first starring role," she said sarcastically. "A pornographic picture."

She took a cigarette from the box on the desk and lit it. She turned back to him. Her voice was quieter now. "Or maybe you're the kind of man who enjoys being married to that kind of woman, so that every time you meet another man, you can wonder. Did he or didn't he? When, where and how?"

He took a step toward her. "That's over now. It doesn't matter."

"It doesn't? Just because I was a fool for a moment, you don't have to be. How much of tonight do you think you'd have been able to take if you'd known what you know now?"

"But I love you!"

"You even kid yourself about that. You don't love me. You never have. You're in love with a memory. The memory of a girl who preferred your father to you. The first chance you had, you tried to make me over in her image. Even in bed—the things you wanted me to do. Did you really think I was so naïve I didn't know those were the things she did to you?"

The ring was still in her hand. She put it on the table in front of him. "Here," she said.

He stared down at the ring. The diamond seemed to shoot angry sparks at him. He looked up at her, his face lined and drawn. "Keep it," he said curtly and walked out.

She stood there until she heard his car pull out of the driveway. Then she turned out the light and walked upstairs, leaving the ring on the table and the film, like confetti after a party, on the floor.

She lay wide-eyed on her bed staring up into the night. If she could only cry she would feel better. But she was empty inside, eaten away by her sins. There was nothing left for her to give anyone. She had used up her ration of love.

Once, long ago, she had loved and been loved. But Tom Denton was dead, lost forever, beyond recall.

She cried out into the darkness, "Daddy, help me! Please! I don't know what to do."

If she could only go back and begin again. Back to the familiar Sunday smell of corned beef and cabbage, to the gentle sound of a whispered morning Mass in her ears, to the sisters and the hospital, to the inner satisfaction of being a part of God's work.

Then her father's voice came whispering to her out of the gray light of the morning, "Do you really want to go, Jennie Bear?"

She lay very still for a moment thinking, remembering. Was that time forever gone? If she were to withhold from confession that part of her life which no longer seemed to belong to her it need not be. They would not know. It was her one real transgression. The rest of her life they already knew about.

To do so would be a sin. A sin of omission. It would invalidate any future confession that she might make. But she had so much to give and without giving it she was denying not only herself but others who would have need of her help. Which was the greater sin? For a moment she was frightened, then decided that this was a matter between her and her Maker. The decision was hers, and she alone could be held responsible, both now and at any future time.

Suddenly she made her mind up and she was no longer afraid.

"Yes, Daddy," she whispered.

His soft voice came echoing back on the wind. "Then get dressed, Jennie, and I'll go with you."

16

IT WAS ALMOST TWO YEARS FROM THE NIGHT OF the party before Rosa heard from Jennie again. It was almost six months from the time she received the dreaded impersonal message from the War Department that David had been killed at the Anzio beachhead in May of 1944.

No more dreams, no more big deals, no more struggles and plans to build a giant monument of incorporation that would span the earth, linked by thin and gossamer strands of celluloid. They had come to a final stop for him, just as they had for a thousand others, in the crashing, thundering fire of an early Italian morning.

The dreams had stopped for her, too. The whisper of love in the night, the creaking of the floor beneath the footsteps on the other side of the bed, the excitement and warmth of shared confidences and plans for tomorrow.

For once, Rosa was grateful for her work. It used her mind and taxed her energy and consumed her with the day-to-day responsibilities. In time, the hurt was pushed back into the corner recesses of her mind, to be felt only when she was alone.

Then, bit by bit, the understanding came to her, as it always must to the survivors, that only a part of the dreams had been buried with him. His son was growing and one day, as she saw him running across the green lawn in the front of their home, she heard the birds begin to sing again. She looked up at the blue sky, at the white sun above her head, and knew that once again she was a living, breathing human being with the full, rich blood of life in her body. And the guilt that had been in her, because she had remained while he had gone, disappeared.

It all happened that day after she read Jennie's letter. It was addressed to her in a small, feminine script that she did not recognize. At first, she thought it another solicitation when she saw the imprimatur on the letterhead.

✝

Sisters of Mercy
Burlingame, California

October 10, 1944

DEAR ROSA,

It is with some trepidation and yet with the knowledge that you will respect my confidence that I take my pen in hand to write. I do not seek to reopen wounds which by this time have already partly healed but it is only a few days ago that I learned of your loss and wanted to extend to you and little Bernie my sympathy and prayers.

David was a fine man and a genuinely kind human being. All of us who knew him will miss him. I mention him in my prayers each day and I am comforted by the words of Our Lord and Saviour: "I am the resurrection and the life; he who believes in me, even if he die, shall live; and whoever lives and believes in me shall never die."

Sincerely yours in J. C.
SISTER M. THOMAS
(JENNIE DENTON)

It was then, when Rosa went outside to call her son in from his play, that she heard the birds singing. The next weekend, she drove to Burlingame to visit Jennie.

There were tiny white puff balls of clouds in the blue sky as Rosa turned her car into the wide driveway that led to the Mother House. It was a Saturday afternoon and there were many automobiles parked there already. She pulled into an open space some distance from the sprawling building.

She sat in the car and lit a cigarette. She felt a doubt creeping through her. Perhaps she shouldn't have come. Jennie might not want to see her, wouldn't want to be reminded of that world she'd left behind. It was pure impulse that she had followed in driving here and she couldn't blame Jennie if she refused to see her.

She remembered the morning after the engagement party. When Jennie hadn't shown up at the studio, no one had thought very much about it. And David, who been trying to reach Jonas at the plant in Burbank, told her that he couldn't locate him, either.

When the next day and the day after that had passed and there was still no word from Jennie, the studio really began to worry. Jonas had finally been located in Canada at the new factory and David called him there. His voice had been very curt over the telephone as he told David that the last time he'd seen Jennie was when he left her home the night of the party.

David immediately called Rosa and suggested she run out to Jennie's house. When she got there, the Mexican servant came to the door. "Is Miss Denton in?"

"Señorita, she not in."

"Do you know where she is?" Rosa asked. "It's very important that I get in touch with her."

The servant shook her head. "The señorita go away. She not say where."

Deliberately Rosa walked past her into the house. There were packed boxes all along the hallway. On the side of one was stenciled *Bekins, Moving & Storage*. The servant saw the surprise on her face. "The señorita tell me to close the house and go away, too."

Rosa didn't wait until she got home, but called David from the first pay telephone she came to. He said he'd try to speak to Jonas again.

"Did you reach Jonas?" she asked, as soon as he came in the door that evening.

"Yes. He told me to close down *Aphrodite* and have Pierce thrown off the lot. When I said we might wind up with a lawsuit, he told me to tell Dan that if he wanted to start anything, Jonas would spend his last dollar to break him."

"But what about Jennie?"

"If she doesn't show up by the end of the week, Jonas told me to have her put on the suspended list and stop her salary."

"And their engagement?"

"Jonas didn't say, but I guess that's over, too. When I asked him if we should prepare a statement for the press, he told me to tell them nothing and hung up."

"Poor Jennie. I wonder where she is?"

Now Rosa knew. She got out of the car and started to walk slowly toward the Mother House.

* * *

Sister M. Thomas sat quietly in her small room, reading her Bible. A soft knock came at the door. She got to her feet, the Bible still in her hand, and opened it. The light from the window in the hall outside her room turned her white novice's veil a soft silver. "Yes, sister?"

"There's a visitor to see you, sister. A Mrs. David Woolf. She's in the visitors' room downstairs."

Sister Thomas hesitated a moment, then spoke. Her voice was calm and quiet. "Thank you, sister. Please tell Mrs. Woolf that I shall be down in a few minutes."

The nun bowed her head and started down the corridor as Sister Thomas closed the door. For a moment, she leaned her back against it, weak and breathless. She had not expected Rosa to come. She drew herself up and crossed the small room to kneel before the crucifix on the bare wall near her bed. She clasped her hands in prayer. It was as if it were only yesterday that she had come here, that she was still the frightened girl who had spent all her life trying to hide from herself her love for God.

She remembered the kind voice of the Mother Superior as she had knelt before her, weeping, her head in the soft material across the Mother Superior's lap. She felt once again the gentle touch of the stroking fingers on her head.

"Do not weep, my child. And do not fear. The path that leads to Our Lord may be most grievous and difficult but Jesus Christ, Our Saviour, refuses none who truly seeks Him."

"But, Reverend Mother, I have sinned."

"Who among us is without sin?" the Reverend Mother said softly. "If you take your sins to Him who takes all sins to Himself to share, and convince Him with your penitence, He will grant you His holy forgiveness and you will be welcome in His house."

She looked up at the Reverend Mother through her tears. "Then, I may stay?"

The Mother Superior smiled down at her. "Of course you may stay, my child."

Rosa rose from the chair as Sister Thomas came into the visitors' room. "Jennie?" she said tentatively. "Sister Thomas, I mean."

"Rosa, how good it is to see you."

Rosa looked at her. The wide-set gray eyes and lovely face belonged to Jennie, but the calm serenity that glowed beneath the novice's white veil came from Sister Thomas. Suddenly, she knew that the face she was looking at was the same face she had once seen on the screen, enlarged a thousand times and filled with the same love as when the Magdalen had stretched forth her hand to touch the hem of her Saviour's gown.

"Jennie!" she said, smiling. "Suddenly, I'm so happy that I just want to hug you."

Sister Thomas held out her arms.

Later, they strolled the quiet paths around the grounds in the afternoon sunlight and when they came to the top of a hill, they paused there, looking down into the green valley below them.

"His beauty is everywhere," Sister Thomas said softly, turning to her friend, "I have found my place in His house."

Rosa looked at her. "How long do you remain in the novitiate?"

"Two years. Until next May."

"And what do you do then?" Rosa questioned.

"If I prove worthy of His grace, I take the black veil and go forth in the path of the Founding Mother, to bring His mercy to all who may need it."

She looked into Rosa's eyes and once again Rosa saw the deep-lying pool of serenity within them. "And I am more fortunate than most," Sister Thomas added humbly. "He has already trained me in His work. My years in the hospital will help me wherever I may be sent, for it is in this area I can best serve."

JONAS—1945

Book Nine

1

OUTSIDE, THE WHITE-HOT MID-JULY SUN BEAT down on the Nevada air strip, but here in the General's office, the overworked air-conditioner whirred and kept the temperature down to an even eighty degrees. I looked at Morrissey, then across the table to the General and his staff.

"That's the story, gentlemen," I said. "The CA-JET X.P. should reach six hundred easier than the British De Havilland-Rolls jet did the five-o-six point five they're bragging about." I smiled at them and got to my feet. "And now, if you'll step outside, gentlemen, I'll show you."

"I have no doubt about that, Mr. Cord," the General said smoothly. "If there'd been any doubts in our minds, you never would have got the contract."

"Then what are we waiting for? Let's go."

"Just a moment, Mr. Cord," the General said quickly. "We can't allow you to demonstrate the jet."

I stared at him. "Why not?"

"You haven't been cleared for jet aircraft," he said. He looked down at a sheet of paper on his desk. "Your medical report indicates a fractional lag in your reflexes. Perfectly normal, of course, considering your age, but you'll understand why we can't let you fly her."

"That's a lot of crap, General. Who the hell do you think flew her down here to deliver her to you?"

"You had a perfect right to—then," the General replied. "It was your plane. But the moment she touched that field outside, according to the contract, she became the property of the Army. And we can't afford the risk of allowing you to take her up."

I slammed my fist into my hand angrily. Rules, nothing but rules. That was the trouble with these damn contracts. Yesterday, I could have flown her up to Alaska and back and they couldn't have stopped me. Or for that matter, even catch me. The CA-JET X.P. was two hundred odd miles an hour faster than any of the conventional aircraft the Army had in the air. Someday, I'd have to take the time to read those contracts.

The General smiled and came around the table toward me. "I know just how you feel, Mr. Cord," he said. "When the medics told me I was too old for combat flying and put me behind a desk, I wasn't any older than you are right now. And I didn't like it any more than you do. Nobody likes being told he is growing older."

What the hell was he talking about? I was only forty-one. That isn't old. I could still fly rings around most of those damp-eared kids walking around on the field outside with gold and silver bars and oak leaves on their shoulders. I looked at the General.

He must have read the surprise in my eyes, for he smiled again. "That was only a year ago. I'm forty-three now." He offered me a cigarette and I took it silently. "Lieutenant Colonel Shaw will take her up. He's on the field right now, waiting for us."

Again, he read the question in my eyes. "Don't worry about it," he said quickly. "Shaw's completely familiar with the plane. He spent the last three weeks at your plant in Burbank checking her out."

I glanced at Morrissey but he was carefully looking somewhere else at the time. He'd been in on it, too. I'd make him weat for that one. I turned back to the General. "O.K., General. Let's go outside and watch that baby fly."

Baby was the right word and not only for the plane. Lieutnant Colonel Shaw couldn't have been more than twenty ears old. I watched him take her up but somehow I couldn't and there squinting up at the sky, watching him put her rough her paces. It was like going to a lot of trouble to set ourself up with a virgin and then when you had everything armed up and ready, you opened the bedroom door and found nother guy copping the cherry right under your nose.

"Is there anywhere around here I could get a cup of coffee?"

"There's a commissary down near the main gate," one of the oldiers said.

"Thanks."

"You're welcome," he said automatically, never taking his yes from the plane in the sky, while I walked away.

The commissary wasn't air-conditioned but they kept it dark nd it wasn't too bad, even if the ice cubes in the iced coffee had nelted before I got the glass back to my seat. I stared morosely ut of the window in front of my table. Too young or too old. hat was the story of my life. I was fourteen when the last one nded, in 1918, and almost over the age limit when we got into nis one. Some people never had any luck. I always thought that ar came to every generation but I was neither one nor the ther. I had the bad fortune to be born in between.

A medium-size Army bus pulled up in front of the commisry. Men started to pile out and I watched them because there as nothing else to look at. They weren't soldiers; they were vilians, and not young ones, either. Most of them carried their cket over their arm and a brief case in their free hand and ere were some with gray in their hair and many with no hair all. One thing about them caught my eye. None of them vere smiling, not even when they spoke to one another in the nall groups they immediately formed on the sidewalk in front f the bus.

Why should they smile, I asked myself bitterly. They had othing to smile about. They were all dodoes like me. I took ut a cigarette and struck a match. The breeze from the circuiting fan blew it out. I struck another, turning away from the n and shielding the cigarette in my cupped hands.

"Herr Cord! This is indeed a surprise! What are you doir here?"

I looked up at Herr Strassmer. "I just delivered a new plane I said, holding out my hand. "But what are you doing out her I thought you were in New York."

He shook my hand in that peculiarly European way of hi The smile left his eyes. "We, too, made a delivery. And now w go back."

"You were with that group outside?"

He nodded. He looked out through the window at them ar a troubled look came into his eyes. "Yes," he said slowly. "W all came together in one plane but we are going back on sep rate flights. Three years we worked together but now the job finished. Soon I go back to California."

"I hope so," I laughed. "We sure could use you in the pla but I'm afraid it'll be some time yet. The war in Europe may l over but if Tarawa and Okinawa are any indication, we're goo for at least six months to a year before Japan quits."

He didn't answer.

I looked up and suddenly I remembered. These Europea were very touchy about manners. "Excuse me, Herr Strassmer I said quickly. "Won't you join me in some coffee?"

"I have not the time." There was a curiously hesitant look i his eyes. "Do you have an office here as you do everywher else?"

"Sure," I said, looking up at him. I'd passed the door marke *Men* on my way over. "It's in the back of this building."

"I will meet you there in five minutes," he said and hurried ou

Through the window, I watched him join one of the group and begin to talk with them. I wondered if the old boy was go ing crackers. You couldn't tell, but maybe he had been workin too hard and thought he was back in Nazi Germany. There ce tainly wasn't any reason for him to be so secretive about bein seen talking to me. After all, we were on the same side.

I ground my cigarette into an ash tray and sauntered out. H never even glanced up as I walked past his group on my way the john. He came into the room a moment after I had got ther His eyes darted nervously toward the booths. "Are we alone?"

"I think so," I said, looking at him. I wondered what you di to get a doctor around here if there were any signs of his crack ing up.

He walked over to the booths, opened the doors and looked. Satisfied, he turned back to me. His face was tense and pale and there were small beads of perspiration across his forehead. I thought I'd begun to recognize the symptoms. Too much of this Nevada sun is murder if you're not used to it. His first words convinced me I was right.

"Herr Cord," he whispered hoarsely. "The war will not be over in six months."

"Of course not," I said soothingly. From what I had heard, the first thing to do was agree with them, try to calm them down. I wished I could remember the second thing. I turned to the sink. "Here, let me get you a glass of—"

"It will be over next month!"

What I thought must have been written on my face, for my mouth hung open in surprise. "No, I'm not crazy, Herr Cord," Strassmer said quickly. "To no one else but you would I say this. It is the only way I can repay you for saving my life. I know how important this could be to your business."

"But—but how—"

"I cannot tell you more," he interrupted. "Just believe me. By next month. Japan will be *verfallen!*" He turned and almost ran out the door.

I stared after him for a moment, then went over to the sink and washed my face in cold water. I felt I must be even crazier than he was, because I was beginning to believe him. But why? It just didn't make any sense. Sure, we were pushing the Nips back, but they still held Malaya, Hong Kong and the Dutch East Indies. And with their kamikaze philosophy, it would take a miracle to end the war in a month.

I was still thinking about it when Morrissey and I got on the train. "You know who I ran into back there?" I asked. I didn't give him a chance to answer. "Otto Strassmer."

There seemed to be a kind of relief in his smile. I guess he'd been expecting to catch hell for not telling me about that Air Corps test pilot. "He's a nice little guy," Morrissey said. "How is he?"

"Seemed all right to me," I said. "He was on his way back to New York." I looked out the window at the flat Nevada desert. "By the way, did you ever hear exactly what it was he was working on?"

"Not exactly."

I looked at him. "What was it you did hear?"

"I didn't hear it from him," Morrissey said. "I got it from a friend of mine down at the Engineers' Club, who worked on it for a little while. But he didn't know very much about it, either. All he knew was that it was called the Manhattan Project and that it had something to do with Professor Einstein."

I could feel my brows knit in puzzlement. "What could Strassmer do for a man like Einstein?"

He smiled again. "After all, Strassmer did invent a plastic beer can that was stronger than metal."

"So?" I asked.

"So maybe the Professor got Otto to invent a plastic container to store his atoms in," Morrissey said, laughing.

I felt a wild excitement racing inside me. A container for atoms, energy in a bottle, ready to explode when you popped the cork. The little man hadn't been crazy. He knew what he was talking about. I'd been the crazy one.

It would take a miracle, I'd thought. Well, Strassmer and his friends had come into the desert and made one and now they were going home, their job done. What it was or how they did it I couldn't guess and didn't care.

But deep inside me, I was sure that it had happened.

The miracle that would end the war.

2

I GOT OFF THE TRAIN AT RENO, WHILE MORRISSEY went on to Los Angeles. There was no time to call Robair at the ranch, so I took a taxi to the factory. We barreled through the steel-wire gate, under the big sign that read **CORD EXPLOSIVES,** now more than a mile from the main plant.

The factory had expanded tremendously since the war. For that matter, so had all our companies. It seemed that no matter what we did, there never was enough space.

I got out and paid the cabby and as he pulled away, I looked up at the familiar old building. It was worn now, and looked dingy and obsolete compared with the new additions, but its roof was gleaming white and shining in the sun. Somehow, I could never bring myself to move out of it when the other executives had moved their offices into the new administration building. I dropped my cigarette on the walk and ground it into dust beneath my heel, then went into the building.

The smell was the same as it always was and the whispers that rose from the lips of the men and women working there were the same as I always heard when I passed by. "*El hijo.*" The son. It had been twenty years and most of them hadn't even been there when my father died and still they called me that. Even the young ones, some of them less than half my age.

The office was the same, too. The heavy, oversized desk and leather-covered furniture now showed the cracks and wear of time. There was no secretary in the outer office and I was not surprised. There was no reason for one to be there. They hadn't expected me.

I walked around behind the desk and pressed the switch down on the squawk box that put me right through to McAllister's office in the new building, a quarter of a mile away. The surprise echoed in his voice as it came through the box. "Jonas! Where did you come from?"

"The Air Corps," I said. "We just delivered the CA-JET X.P."

"Good. Did they like it?"

"I guess they did," I answered. "They wouldn't trust me to take it up." I leaned over and opened the door of the cabinet below the telephone table, taking out the bottle of bourbon that was there. I put the bottle on the desk in front of me. "How do we stand on war-contract cancellations in case the war ends tomorrow?"

"For the explosive company?" Mac asked.

"For all the companies," I said. I knew he kept copies of every contract we ever made down here because he considered this his home office.

"It'll take a little time. I'll put someone on it right away."

"Like about an hour?"

He hesitated. When he spoke, a curious note came into his voice. "All right, if it's that important."

"It's that important."

"Do you know something?"

"No," I said truthfully. I really didn't know. I was only guessing. "I just want it."

There was silence for a moment, then he spoke again. "I just got the blueprints from Engineering on converting the radar and small-parts division of Aircraft to the proposed electronics company. Shall I bring them over?"

"Do that," I said, flipping up the switch. Taking a glass from the tray next to the Thermos jug, I filled it half full with bourbon. I looked across the room to the wall where the portrait of my father looked down on me. I held the glass up to him.

"It's been a long time, Pop," I said and poured the whisky down my throat.

I took my hands from the blueprints on the desk and snapped and rolled them up tight, like a coil spring. I looked at McAllister. "They look all right to me, Mac."

He nodded. "I'll mark them approved and shoot them on to Purchasing to have them requisition the materials on standby orders, to be delivered when the war ends." He looked at the bottle of bourbon on the desk. "You're not very hospitable. How about a drink?"

I looked at him in surprise. Mac wasn't much for drinking. Especially during working hours. I pushed the bottle and a glass toward him. "Help yourself."

He poured a small shot and swallowed it neat. He cleared his throat. I looked at him. "There's one other postwar plan I wanted to talk to you about," he said awkwardly.

"Go ahead."

"Myself," he said hesitantly. "I'm not a young man any more. I want to retire."

"Retire?" I couldn't believe my ears. "What for? What in hell would you do?"

Mac flushed embarrassedly. "I've worked pretty hard all my life," he said. "I've got two sons and a daughter and five grandchildren, three of whom I've never seen. The wife and I would like to spend a little time with them, get to know them before it's too late."

I laughed. "You sound like you expect to kick off any minute. You're a young man yet."

"I'm sixty-three. I've been with you twenty years."

I stared at him. Twenty years. Where had they gone? The Army doctors had been right. I wasn't a kid any more, either. "We'll miss you around here," I said sincerely. "I don't know how we'll manage without you." I meant it, too. Mac was the one man I felt I could always depend on, whenever I had need for him.

"You'll manage all right. We've got over forty attorneys working for us now and each is a specialist in his own field. You're not just one man any more, you're a big company. You have to have a big legal machine to take care of you."

"So what?" I said. "You can't call up a machine in the middle of the night when you're in trouble."

"This machine you can. It's equipped for all emergencies."

"But what will you do? You can't tell me you'll be happy just lying around playing grandpa. You'll have to have something to occupy your mind."

"I've thought about that," he said, a serious look coming over his face. "I've been playing around so long with corporate and tax laws that I've almost forgotten about the most important part of all. The laws that have to do with human beings." He reached for the bottle again and poured himself another small drink. It wasn't easy for him to sit there and tell me what he was thinking.

"I thought I'd hang my shingle outside my house in some small town. Just putter around with whatever happened to come in the door. I'm tired of always talking in terms of millions of dollars. For once, I'd like to help some poor bastard who really needs it."

I stared at him. Work with a man for twenty years and still you don't know him. This was a side to McAllister that I'd never even suspected existed.

"Of course, we'll abrogate all of the contracts and agreements between us," he said.

I looked at him. I knew he didn't need the money. But then, neither did I. "Why in hell should we? Just show up at the board of directors' meeting every few months so at least I can see you once in a while."

"Then you—you agree?"

I nodded. "Sure, let's give it a spin when the war is over."

The sheets of white paper grew into a stack as he skimmed through the summary of each of the contracts. At last, Mac was finished and he looked up at me. "We have ample protective-cancellation clauses in all the contracts except one," he said. "That one is based on delivery before the end of the war."

"Which one is that?"

"That flying boat we're building for the Navy in San Diego."

I knew what he was talking about. *The Centurion*. It was to be the biggest airplane ever built, designed to carry a full company of one hundred and fifty men, in addition to the twelve-man crew, two light amphibious tanks and enough mortar, light artillery, weapons, ammunition and supplies for an entire company. It had been my idea that a plane like that would prove useful in landing raiding parties behind the lines out in the small Pacific islands.

"How come we made a contract like that?"

"You wanted it," he said. "Remember?"

I remembered. The Navy had been skeptical that the big plane could even get into the air, so I'd pressured them into making a deal predicated on a fully tested plane before the war ended. That was over seven months ago.

Almost immediately, we'd run into trouble. Stress tests proved that conventional metals would make the plane too heavy for the engines to lift into the air. We lost two months there, until the engineers came up with a Fiberglas compound that was less than one tenth the weight of metal and four times as strong. Then we had to construct special machinery to work the new material. I even brought Amos Winthrop down from Canada to sit in on the project. The old bastard had done a fantastic job up there and had a way of bulling a job through when no one else was able to.

The old leopard hadn't changed any of his spots, either. He had me by the shorts and he knew it. He held me up for a vice-presidency in Cord Aircraft before he'd come down.

"How much are we in for up to now?" I asked.

Mac looked down at the sheet. "Sixteen million, eight hundred seventy-six thousand, five hundred ninety-four dollars and thirty-one cents, as of June thirtieth."

"We're in trouble," I said, reaching for the telephone. The operator came on. "Get me Amos Winthrop in San Diego. And while I'm waiting to talk to him, call Mr. Dalton at the Inter-Continental Airlines office in Los Angeles and ask him to send down a special charter for me."

"What's the trouble?" Mac asked, watching me.

"Seventeen million dollars. We're going to blow it if we don't get that plane into the air right away."

Then Amos came on the phone. "How soon do you expect to get *The Centurion* into the sky?" I asked.

"We're coming along pretty good now. Just the finishing touches. I figure we ought to be able to lift her sometime in September or early October."

"What's missing?"

"The usual stuff. Mountings, fittings, polishing, tightening. You know."

I knew. The small but important part that took longer than anything else. But nothing really essential, nothing that would keep the plane from flying. "Get her ready," I said. "I'm taking her up tomorrow."

"Are you crazy? We've never even had gasoline in her tanks."

"Then fill her up."

"But the hull hasn't been water-tested yet," he shouted. "How do you know she won't go right to the bottom of San Diego Bay when you send her down the runway?"

"Then test it. You've got twenty-four hours to make sure she floats. I'll be up there tonight, if you need a hand."

This was no cost-plus, money-guaranteed project, where the government picked up the tab, win, lose or draw. This was my money and I didn't like the idea of losing it.

For seventeen million dollars, *The Centurion* would fly if I had to lift her out of the water with my bare hands.

3

I HAD ROBAIR TAKE ME OUT TO THE RANCH, where I took a hot shower and changed my clothes before I got on the plane to San Diego. I was just leaving the house when the telephone rang.

"It's for you, Mr. Jonas," Robair said. "Mr. McAllister."

I took the phone from his hand. "Yes, Mac?"

"Sorry to bother you, Jonas, but this is important."

"Shoot."

"Bonner just called from the studio," he said. "He's leaving at the end of the month to go over to Paramount. He's got a deal with them to make nothing but blockbusters."

"Offer him more money."

"I did. He doesn't want it. He wants out."

"What does his contract say?"

"It's over the end of this month," he said. "We can't hold him if he wants to go."

"To hell with him, then. If he wants to go, let him."

"We're in a hole," Mac said seriously. "We'll have to find someone to run the studio. You can't operate a motion-picture company without someone to make pictures."

That was nothing I didn't know. It was too bad that David Woolf wasn't coming back. I could depend on him. He felt the same way about movies that I did about airplanes. But he'd caught it at Anzio.

"I want to make San Diego tonight," I said. "Let me think about it and we'll kick it around in your office in L.A. the day after tomorrow." I had bigger worries on my mind just now. One *Centurion* cost almost as much as a whole year's production at the studio.

We landed at the San Diego Airport about one o'clock in the morning. I took a taxi right from there to the little shipyard we had rented near the Naval base. I could see the lights blazing from it ten blocks away. I smiled to myself. Leave it to Amos to get things done. He had a night crew working like mad, even if he had to break the blackout regulations to get it done.

I walked around the big old boat shed that we were using for a hangar just in time to hear someone yell, "Clear the runway!"

And then *The Centurion* came out of the hangar, tail first, looking for all the world like an ugly giant condor flying backward. Like a greased pig, it shot down the runway toward the water. A great roar came from the hangar and I was almost knocked over by a gang of men, who came running out after the plane. Before I knew it, they'd passed me and were down at the water's edge. I saw Amos in the crowd and he was yelling as much as any of them.

There was a great splash as *The Centurion* hit the water, a moment's groaning silence as the tail dipped backward, almost covering the three big rudders, and then a triumphant yell as she straightened herself out and floated easily on the bay. She began to turn, drifting away from the dock, and I heard the whir of the big winches as they spun the tie lines, drawing her back in.

The men were still yelling when I got to Amos. "What the

hell do you think you're doing?" I shouted, trying to make myself heard over the noise.

"What you told me to do—water-test her."

"You damn fool! You might've sunk her. Why didn't you get a pressure tank?"

"There wasn't time. The earliest I could've got one was three days. You said you were taking her up tomorrow."

The winches had hauled the plane partly back on the runway, with her prow out of the water. "Wait here a minute," Amos said, "I gotta get the men to work. They're all on triple time."

He went down the dock to where a workman had already placed a ladder against the side of the giant plane. Scrambling up like a man half his age, Amos opened the door just behind the cabin and disappeared into the plane. A moment later, I heard the whir of a motor from somewhere inside her and the giant boarding flap came down, opening a gaping maw in her prow that was big enough to drive a truck through. Amos appeared at the top of the ramp inside the plane. "O.K., men. You know what we gotta do. Shake the lead out. We ain't paying triple time for conversation."

He came back up the dock toward me and we walked back into his office. There was a bottle of whisky on his desk. He took two paper cups from the wall container and began to pour whisky into them. "You mean it about taking her up tomorrow?"

I nodded.

He shook his head. "I wouldn't," he said. "Just because she floats don't mean she'll fly. There's still too many things we're not sure of. Even if she does get up, there's no guarantee she'll stay up. She might even fall apart in the sky."

"That'll be rough," I said. "But, I'm taking her up, anyway."

He shrugged his shoulders. "You're the boss," he said, handing me one of the paper cups. He raised his to his lips. "Here's luck."

By two o'clock the next afternoon, we still weren't ready. The number-two starboard engine spit oil like a gusher every time we started it up and we couldn't find the leak. I stood on the dock, staring up at her. "We'll have to pull her off," Amos said, "and get her up to the shop."

I looked at him. "How long will that take?"

"Two, three hours. If we're lucky and find what's wrong right away. Maybe we better put off taking her up until tomorrow."

I looked at my watch. "What for? We'll still have three and a half hours of daylight at five o'clock." I started back toward his office. "I'm going back to your office and grab a snooze on the couch. Call me as soon as she's ready."

But I might as well have tried to sleep in a boiler factory, for all the shouting and cursing and hammering and riveting. Then the telephone rang and I got up to answer it. "Hello, Dad?" It was Monica's voice.

"No, this is Jonas. I'll get him for you."

"Thanks."

Laying the telephone down on the desk, I went to the door and called Amos. I went back to the couch and stretched out as he picked up the phone. He shot a peculiar look at me when he heard her voice. "Yes, I'm a little busy." He was silent for a little while, listening to her. When he spoke again, he was smiling. "That's wonderful. When are you leaving? . . . Then I'll fly to New York when this job is finished. We'll have a celebration. Give my love to Jo-Ann."

He put down the telephone and came over to me. "That was Monica," he said, looking down at me.

"I know."

"She's leaving for New York this afternoon. S. J. Hardin just made her managing editor of *Style* and wants her back there right away."

"That's nice," I said.

"She's taking Jo-Ann back with her. You haven't seen the kid for a long time now, have you?"

"Not since the time you walked the two of them out of my apartment at the Drake in Chicago, five years ago."

"You oughta see her. The kid's turning into a real beauty."

I stared up at him. Now I'd seen everything—Amos Winthrop playing proud grandpa. "Man, you've really changed, haven't you?"

"Sooner or later, a man has to wise up," Amos said, flushing embarrassedly. "You find out you did a lot of fool things to hurt the people you love and if you're not a prick altogether, you try to make up for them."

"I heard about that, too," I said sarcastically. I wasn't in the mood for any lectures from the old bastard, no matter how much he'd reformed. "They tell me that generally happens when you can't get it up any more."

A trace of the old Amos came into his face. He was angry, I could see it. "I got a mind to tell you a couple of things."

"Like what, Amos?"

"Ready to remount the engine, Mr. Winthrop," a man called from the doorway.

"I'll be there in a minute." Amos turned back to me. "You remind me of this after we get back from the test flight."

I grinned, watching him walk out the door. At least, he hadn't gone so holy-holy that I couldn't get his goat. I sat up and started looking under the couch for my shoes.

When I got outside, the engine was turning over, sweet and smooth. "She seems O.K. to me now," Amos said, turning to me.

I looked at my watch. It was four thirty. "Then, let's go. What're we waiting for?"

He put a hand on my arm. "Sure I can't make you change your mind?"

I shook my head. Seventeen million dollars was a lot of argument. He raised his hands to his mouth, making a megaphone of them. "Everybody off the ship except the flight crew."

Almost immediately, there was a silence in the yard as the engine shut off. A few minutes later, the last of them came down the boarding flap. A man stuck his head out of the small window in the pilot's cabin. "Everybody off except the crew, Mr. Winthrop."

Amos and I walked up the flap into the plane, then up the small ladder from the cargo deck to the passenger cabin and on forward into the flight cabin. Three young men were there. They looked at me curiously. They were still wearing the hard hats from the shipyard.

"This is your crew, Mr. Cord," Amos said formally. "On the right, Joe Cates, radioman. In the middle, Steve Jablonski, flight engineer starboard engines, one, three and five. On the left, Barry Gold, flight engineer port engines, two, four and six. You don't have to worry about them. They're all Navy veterans and know their work."

We shook hands all around and I turned back to Amos. "Where's the copilot and navigator?"

"Right here," Amos said.

"Where?"

"Me."

"What the hell—"

He grinned at me. "You got anybody knows this baby better? Besides, I been sleeping every night with her for more than half a year. Who's got a better right to get a piece of her first ride?"

I stared at him for a moment. Then I gave in. I knew exactly how he felt. I felt the same way myself yesterday, when they wouldn't let me fly the jet.

I climbed up into the pilot's seat. "Take your stations, men."

"Aye, aye, sir."

I grinned to myself. They were Navy men, all right. I picked up the check list on the clip board. "Boarding ramp up," I said, reading.

A motor began to whine beneath me. A moment later, a red light flashed on the panel in front of me and the motor cut off. "Boarding ramp up, sir."

"Start engines one and two," I said, reaching forward and flicking down the switches that would let the flight engineers turn them over. The big engines coughed and belched black smoke. The propellers began to turn sluggishly, then the engines caught and the propellers settled into a smooth whine.

"Starboard engine one turning over, sir."

"Port engine two turning over, sir."

The next one on the check list was a new one for me. I smiled to myself. This wasn't an airplane, it was really a Navy ship with wings. "Cast off," I said.

From the seat to my right, Amos reached up and tripped the lever that released the tow lines. Another red light flashed on the panel before me and I could feel *The Centurion* slide back into the water. There was a slight backward dip as she settled in with a slight rocking motion. The faint sound of water slapping against her hull came up from beneath us. I leaned forward and turned the wheel. Slowly the big plane came about and started to move out toward the open bay. I looked over at Amos. He grinned at me.

I grinned back. So far, so good. At least we were seaborne.

4

A WAVE BROKE ACROSS THE PROW OF THE PLANE, throwing salt spray up on the window in front of me, as I came to the last item on the check list. There had been almost a hundred of them and it seemed like hours since we'd started. I looked down at my watch. It was only sixteen minutes since we'd left the dock. I looked out the windows. The six big engines were turning over smoothly, the propellers flashing with sun and spray. I felt a touch on my shoulder and looked back.

The radioman stood behind me, an inflatable Mae West in one hand and a parachute pack hanging from the other. "Emergency dress, sir."

I looked at him. He was already wearing his; so were the other two men. "Put it behind my seat."

I looked across at Amos. He already had the vest on and was tightening the cross belt of the parachute. He sank back into his seat with an uncomfortable grunt. He looked at me. "You ought to put it on."

"I've got a superstition about 'em," I said. "If you don't wear 'em, you'll never need 'em." He didn't answer, shrugging his shoulders as the radioman went back to his seat and fastened his seat belt. I looked around the cabin. "Secure in flight stations?"

They all answered at once. "Aye, aye, sir!"

I reached forward and flipped the switch on the panel and all the lights turned from red to green. From now on, they'd only go back to red if we were in trouble. I turned the plane toward the open sea. "O.K., men. Here we go!"

I opened the throttle slowly. The big plane lurched, its prow digging into the waves then slowly lifting as the six propellers started to chew up the air. Now we started to ride high, like a speedboat in the summer races. I looked at the panel. The airspeed indicator stood at ninety.

Amos' voice came over to me. "Calculated lift velocity, this flight, one ten."

I nodded without looking at him and kept opening the throttle. The needle went to one hundred, then one ten. The waves were beating against the bottom of the hull like a riveting hammer. I brought the needle up to one fifteen, then I started to ease back on the stick.

For a moment, nothing happened and I increased our speed to one twenty. Suddenly, *The Centurion* seemed to tremble, then jump from the water. Free of the restraining drag, she seemed to leap into the air. The needle jumped to one sixty and the controls moved easily in my hands. I looked out the window. The water was two hundred feet beneath us. We were airborne.

"Hot damn!" one of the men behind me muttered.

Amos squirmed around in his seat. "O.K., fellers," he said, sticking out his hand. "Pay me!" He looked over at me and grinned. "Each of these guys bet me a buck we'd never get off the water."

I flashed a grin at him and kept the ship in a slow climb until we reached six thousand feet. Then I turned her west and aimed her right at the setting sun.

"She handles like a baby carriage." Amos chortled gleefully from his seat.

I looked up at him from behind the radioman, where I had been standing as he explained the new automatic signaling recorder. All you had to do was give your message once, then turn on the automatic and the wire recorder would repeat it over and over again until the power gave out.

The sun had turned Amos' white hair back to the flaming red of his youth. I looked down at my watch. It was six fifteen and we were about two hundred miles out over the Pacific. "Better turn her around and take her back, Amos," I said. "I don't want it to be dark the first time we put her down."

"The term in the Navy, captain, is 'Put her about'." The radioman grinned at me.

"O.K., sailor," I said. I turned to Amos. "Put her about."

"Aye, aye, sir."

We went into a gentle banking turn as I bent over the radioman's shoulder again. Suddenly, the plane lurched and I almost fell over him. I grabbed at his shoulder as the starboard engineer yelled, "Number five's gone bad again."

I pushed myself toward my seat as I looked out the window. The engine was shooting oil like a geyser. "Kill it!" I shouted, strapping myself into my seat.

The cords on Amos' neck stood out like steel wire as he ought the wheel on the suddenly bucking plane. I grabbed at y wheel and together we held her steady. Slowly she eased off our grip.

"Number five dead, sir," the engineer called.

I glanced out at it. The propeller turned slowly with the ind force but the oil had stopped pouring from the engine. I oked at Amos. His face was white and perspiration was drip-ing from it, but he managed a smile. "We can make it back on ve engines without any trouble."

"Yeah." We could make it back on three engines, according the figures. But I wouldn't like to try it. I looked at the panel. he red light was on for the number-five engine. While I was atching, a red light began to flicker on and off at number four. What the hell?"

It began to sputter and cough even as I turned to look at it. Check number four!" I yelled. I turned back to the panel. The d light was on for the number-four fuel line.

"Number-four fuel line clogged!"

"Blow it out with the vacuum!"

"Aye, aye, sir!" I heard the click as he turned on the vacuum ump. Another red light jumped on in front of me. "Vacuum ump out of commission, sir!"

"Kill number four!" I said. There was no advantage in leav-ig the line open in the hopes that it would clear itself. Clogged ıel lines have a tendency to turn into fires. And we still had ur engines left.

"Number four dead, sir!"

I heaved a sigh of relief after ten minutes had gone by and here was nothing new to worry about. "I think we'll be O.K. ow," I said.

I should have kept my big fat mouth shut. No sooner had I poken than the number-one engine started to choke and sput-r and the instrument panel in front of me began to light up ke a Christmas tree. The number-six engine began to choke.

"Main fuel pump out!"

I threw a glance at the altimeter. We were at five thousand nd dropping. "Radio emergency and prepare to abandon hip!" I shouted.

I heard the radioman's voice. "Mayday! Mayday! Cord Air-raft Experimental. Going down Pacific. Position approx one

two five miles due west San Diego. I repeat, position appro
one two five miles due west San Diego. Mayday! Mayday!"

I heard a loud click and the message began over again. I felt
hand on my shoulder. I looked around quickly. It was the r.
dioman. There was a faint surprise in the back of my mind un
til I remembered the recorder was now broadcasting the call f
help. "We'll stay if you want us, sir," he said tensely.

"This isn't for God and country, sailor! This is for money. G
goin'!"

I looked over at Amos, who was still in his seat. "You, to
Amos!"

He didn't answer. Just pulled off his safety belt and got ou
of his seat. I heard the cabin door behind me open as the
went through to the emergency door in the passenger con
partment.

The altimeter read thirty-eight hundred and I killed the on
and six engines. Maybe I could set her down on the water if th
two remaining engines could hold out on the fuel that woul
be diverted from the others. We were at thirty-four hundre
when the red light for the emergency door flashed on as
opened. I cast a quick look back out the window. Three para
chutes opened, one after the other, in rapid succession. I looke
at the board. Twenty-eight hundred.

I heard a noise behind me and looked around. It was Amo
getting back into his seat. "I told you to get out!" I yelled.

He reached for the wheel. "The kids are off and safe. I figur
between the two of us, we got a chance to put her down on to
of the water."

"Suppose we don't?" I yelled angrily.

"We won't be missing much. We ain't got as much time t
lose as they have. Besides, this baby cost a lot of dough!"

"So what?" I yelled. "It's not your money!"

There was a curiously disapproving look on his face. "Mone
isn't the only thing put into this plane. I built her!"

We were at nine hundred feet when number three began t
conk out. We threw our weight against the wheel to compen
sate for the starboard drag. At two hundred feet, the number
three engine went out and we heeled over to the starboar
"Cut the engines!" Amos yelled. "We're going to crash!"

I flipped the switch just as the starboard wing bit into the wa
ter. It snapped off clean as a matchstick and the plane slamme

into the water like a pile driver. I felt the seat belt tear into my guts until I almost screamed with the pressure, then suddenly it eased off. My eyes cleared and I looked out. We were drifting on top of the water uneasily, one wing pointing to the sky. Water was already trickling into the cabin under our feet.

"Let's get the hell out of here," Amos yelled, moving toward the cabin door, which had snapped shut. He turned the knob and pushed. Then he threw himself against it. The door didn't move. "It's jammed!" he yelled, turning to me.

I stared at him and then jumped for the pilot's emergency hatch over our heads. I pulled the hatch lock with one hand and pushed at the hatch with the other. Nothing happened. I looked up and saw why. The frame had buckled, locking it in. Nothing short of dynamite would open it.

Amos didn't wait for me to tell him. He pulled a wrench from the emergency tool kit and smashed at the glass until there was only a jagged frame left in the big port. He dropped the wrench, picked up the Mae West and threw it at me. I slipped into it quickly, making sure the automatic valve was set so it would work the minute I hit the water.

"O.K.," he said. "Out you go!"

I grinned at him. "Traditions of the sea, Amos. Captain's last off the ship. After you, Alphonse."

"You crazy, man?" he shouted. "I couldn't get out that port if they cut me in half."

"You ain't that big," I said. "We're going to give it a try."

Suddenly, he smiled. I should have known better than to trust Amos when he smiled like that. That peculiarly wolfish smile came over him only when he was going to do you dirty. "All right, Gaston. You're the captain."

"That's better," I said, bracing myself and making a sling step with my hands to boost him up to the port. "I knew you'd learn someday who's boss."

But he never did. And I never even saw what he hit me with. I sailed into Dream Street with a full load on. I was out but I wasn't all the way out. I knew what was going on but there was nothing I could do about it. My arms and legs and head, even my body—they all belonged to someone else.

I felt Amos push me toward the port, then there was a burning sensation, like a cat raking her claws across your face. But I was through the narrow port and falling. Falling about a thousand miles and a thousand hours and I was still looking for the rip cord on my parachute when I crashed in a heap on the wing.

I pulled myself to my feet and tried to climb back the cabin wall to the port. "Come on out of there, you no-good, dirty son of a bitch!" I yelled. I was crying. "Come on outa there and I'll kill you!"

Then the plane lurched and a broken piece of something came flying up from the wing and hit me in the side, knocking me clear out into the water. I heard the soft hiss of compressed air as the Mae West began to wrap her legs around me. I put my head down on those big soft pillows she had and went to sleep.

5

In Nevada, where I was born and raised, there is mostly sand and rocks and a few small mountains. But there are no oceans. There are streams and lakes, and swimming pools at every country club and hotel, but they're all filled with fresh, sweet water that bubbles in your mouth like wine, if you should happen to drink it instead of bathe in it.

I've been in a couple of oceans in my time. In the Atlantic, off Miami Beach and Atlantic City, in the Pacific, off Malibu, and in the blue waters of the Mediterranean, off the Riviera. I've even been in the warm waters of the Gulf Stream, off the white, sandy beach of Bermuda, chasing a naked girl whose only ambition was to do it like a fish. I never did get to find out the secret of how the porpoises made it, because somehow, in the salt water, everything eluded me. I never did like salt water. It clings too heavily to your skin, burns your nose, irritates your eyes. And if you happen to get a mouthful, it tastes like yesterday's leftover mouthwash.

So what was I doing here?

Hot damn, little man, all the stars are out and laughing at you. This'll teach you some respect for the oceans. You don't like salt water, eh? Well, how do you like a million, billion, trillion gallons of it? A gazillion gallons?

"Aah, the hell with you," I said and went back to sleep.

* * *

I came trotting around the corner of the bunkhouse as fast as my eight-year-old legs could carry me, dragging the heavy cartridge belt and holstered gun in the sand behind me.

I heard my father's voice. "Hey, boy! What have you got there?"

I turned to face him, trying to hide the belt and gun behind me. "Nothin'," I said, not looking up at him.

"Nothing?" my father repeated after me. "Then, let me see."

He reached around behind me and tugged the belt out of my grip. As he raised it, the gun and a folded piece of paper fell from the holster. He bent down and picked them up. "Where'd you get this?"

"From the wall in the bunkhouse near Nevada's bed," I said. "I had to climb up."

My father put the gun back in the holster. It was a black gun, a smooth, black gun with the initials M. S. on its black butt. Even I was old enough to know that somebody had made a mistake on Nevada's initials.

My father started to put the folded piece of paper back into the holster but he dropped it and it fluttered open. I could see it was a picture of Nevada, with some numbers above it and printing below. My father stared at it for a moment, then refolded the paper and shoved it into the holster.

"You put this back where you got it," he said angrily. I could tell he was mad. "Don't you ever let me catch you taking what doesn't belong to you again or I'll whomp you good."

"Ain't no need to whomp 'im, Mr. Cord." Nevada's voice came from behind us. "It's my fault for leavin' it out where the boy could get to it." We turned around. He was standing there, his Indian face dark and expressionless, holding out his hand. "If you'll jus' give it to me, I'll put it back."

Silently my father handed him the gun and they stood there looking at each other. Neither of them spoke a word. I stared up at them, bewildered. Both seemed to be searching each other's eyes. At last, Nevada spoke. "I'll draw my time if you want, Mr. Cord."

I knew what that meant. Nevada was going away. Immediately, I set up a howl. "No," I screamed. "I won't do it again. I promise."

My father looked down at me for a moment, then back at Nevada. A faint smile came into his eyes. "Children and animals, they really know what they want, what's best for them."

"They do say that."

"You better put that away where nobody'll ever find it."

The faint smile was in Nevada's eyes now. "Yes, Mr. Cord. I sure will."

My father looked down at me and his smile vanished. "You hear me, boy? Touch what isn't yours and you'll get whomped good."

"Yes, Father," I answered, loud and strong. "I hear you."

I got a mouthful of salt water and I coughed and choked and sputtered and spit it out. I opened my eyes. The stars were still blinking at me but over in the east, the sky was starting to turn pale. I thought I heard the sound of a motor in the distance but it was probably only an echo ringing in my ears.

There was a pain in my side and down my leg, like I'd gone to sleep on it. When I moved, it shot up to my head and made me dizzy. The stars began to spin around and I got tired just watching them, so I went back to sleep.

The sun on the desert is big and strong and rides the sky so close to your head that sometimes you feel like if you reached up to touch it, you'd burn your fingers. And when it's hot like that, you pick your way carefully around the rocks, because under them, in the shade, sleeping away the heat of the day, are the rattlers, coiled and sluggish, with the unhappy heat in their chilled blood. They're quick to anger, quick to attack, with their vicious spittle, if by accident you threaten their peace. People are like that, too.

Each of us has his own particular secret rock, under which we hide, and woe to you if you should happen to stumble across it. Because then we're like the rattlers on the desert, lashing out blindly at whoever happens to come by.

"But I love you," I said and even as I said them, I knew the hollowness of my words.

And she must have known, too, for in her scathing self-denunciation, she was accusing me with the sins of all the men she'd known. And not unjustly, for they were also my sins.

"But I love you," I repeated and as I said it, I knew she recognized the weakness in my words. They turned empty and hollow in my mouth. If I had been honest, even unto my secret

self, this is what I would have said: "I want you. I want you to
be what I want you to be. A reflection of the image of my
dreams, the mirror of my secret desires, the face that I desire to
show the world, the brocade with which I embroider my glory.
If you are all these things, I will grace you with my presence and
my house. But these are not for what you are, but for me and
what I want you to be."

And I did little but stand there, mumbling empty platitudes,
while the words that spilled from her mouth were merely my
own poison, which she turned into herself. For unknowing, she
had stumbled across my secret rock.

I stood there in the unaccustomed heat and blazing brightness of the sun, secretly ashamed of the cool chill of the blood
that ran through my veins and set me apart from the others of
this earth. And unprotesting, I let her use my venom to destroy
herself.

And when the poison had done its work, leaving her with
nothing but the small, frightened, unshriven soul of her beginnings, I turned away.

With the lack of mercy peculiar to my kind, I turned my
back. I ran from her fears, from her need of comfort and reassurance, from her unspoken pleading for mercy and love and
understanding. I fled the hot sun, back to the safety of my secret rock.

But now there was no longer comfort in its secret shade, for
the light continued to seep through, and there was no longer
comfort in the cool detached flowing of my blood. And the
rock seemed to be growing smaller and smaller while the sun
was growing larger and larger. I tried to make myself tinier, to
find shelter beneath the rock's shrinking surface, but there was
no escape. Soon there would be no secret rock for me. The sun
was growing brighter and brighter. Brighter and brighter.

I opened my eyes.

There was a tiny pinpoint of light shining straight into them.
I blinked and the penetrating pinpoint moved to one side. I
could see beyond it now. I was lying on a table in a white room
and beside me was a man in a white gown and a white skullcap.
The light came from the reflection in a small, round mirror that
he wore over his eye as he looked down at me. I could see on
his face the tiny black hairs that the razor had missed. His lips
were grim and tight.

"My God!" The voice came from behind him. "His face is a mess. There must be a hundred pieces of glass in it."

My eyes flickered up and saw the second man as the first turned toward him. "Shut up, you fool! Can't you see he's awake?"

I began to raise my head but a light, quick hand was on my shoulder, pressing me back, and then her face was there.

Her face, looking down at me with a mercy and compassion that mine had never shown.

"Jennie!"

Her hand pressed against my shoulder. She looked up at someone over my head. "Call Dr. Rosa Strassmer at Los Angeles General or the Colton Sanitarium in Santa Monica. Tell her Jonas Cord has been in a bad accident and to come right away."

"Yes, Sister Thomas." It was a young girl's voice and it came from behind me. I heard footsteps moving away.

The pain was coming back into my side and leg again and I gritted my teeth. I could feel it forcing the tears into my eyes. I closed them for a moment, then opened them and looked up at her. "Jennie!" I whispered. "Jennie, I'm sorry!"

"It's all right, Jonas," she whispered back. Her hands went under the sheet that covered me. I felt a sharp sting in my arm. "Don't talk. Everything's all right now."

I smiled gratefully and went back to sleep, wondering vaguely why Jennie was wearing that funny white veil over her beautiful hair.

6

FROM OUTSIDE MY WINDOWS, FROM THE STREETS, bright now with the morning sun, still came the sounds of celebration. Even this usually staid and quiet part of Hillcrest Drive skirting Mercy Hospital was filled with happy noises and throngs of people. From the Naval Station across the city of San Diego came the occasional triumphant blast of a ship's horn. It had been like this all through the night, starting early the evening before, when the news came. Japan had surrendered. The war was over.

I knew now what Otto Strassmer had been trying to tell me.

I knew now of the miracle in the desert. From the newspapers and from the radio beside my bed. They had all told the story of the tiny container of atoms that had brought mankind to the gates of heaven. Or hell. I shifted in my bed to find another position of comfort, as the pulleys that suspended my leg in traction squeaked, adding their mouselike sound to the others.

I had been lucky, one of the nurses told me. Lucky. My right leg had been broken in three places, my right hip in another, and several ribs had been crushed. Yet I still looked out at the world, from behind the layer of thick bandages which covered all of my face, except the slits for my eyes, nose and mouth. But I'd been lucky. At least I was still alive.

Not like Amos, who still sat in the cabin of *The Centurion* as it rested on the edge of a shelf of sand, some four hundred odd feet beneath the surface of the Pacific Ocean. Poor Amos. The three crewmen had been found unscathed and I was still alive, by the grace of God and the poor fishermen who found me floating in the water and brought me to shore, while Amos sat silent in his watery tomb, still at the controls of the plane he had built and would not let me fly alone.

I remembered the accountant's voice over the telephone from Los Angeles as he spoke consolingly. "Don't worry, Mr. Cord. We can write it all off against taxes on profits. When you apply the gross amount to the normal tax of forty per cent and the excess-profits tax of ninety per cent, the net loss to us comes to under two million—"

I had slammed down the phone, cutting him off. It was all well and good. But how do you charge off on a balance sheet the life of a man who was killed by your greed? Is there an allowable deduction for death on the income-tax returns? It was I who had killed Amos and no matter how many expenses I deducted from my own soul, I could not bring him back.

The door opened and I looked up. Rosa came into the room, followed by an intern and a nurse wheeling a small cart. She came over to the left side of my bed and stood there, smiling down at me. "Hello, Jonas."

"Hello, Rosa," I mumbled through the bandages. "Is it time to change them again? I didn't expect you until the day after tomorrow."

"The war is over."

"Yes," I said. "I know."

"And when I got up this morning, it was such a beautiful morning, I decided to fly down here and take off your bandages."

I peered up at her. "I see," I said. "I always wondered where doctors got their logic."

"That isn't doctor's logic, that's woman's logic. I have the advantage of having been a woman long before I became a doctor."

I laughed. "I'm grateful for the logic, whichever one of you it belongs to. It will be nice to have the bandages off, even for a little while."

She was still smiling, though her eyes were serious. "This time, they're coming off for good, Jonas."

I stared at her as she picked up a scissors from the cart. I reached up and stayed her hand. Suddenly, I was afraid to have her remove the bandages. I felt safe having them wrapped about my face like a cocoon, shielding me from the prying eyes of the world. "Is it soon enough? Will it be all right?"

She sensed my feeling. "Your face will be sore for a while yet," she said, snipping away at the cocoon. "It will be even sorer as the flesh and muscles take up their work again. But that will pass. We can't spend forever hiding behind a mask, can we?"

That was the doctor talking, not the woman. I looked up at her face as she snipped and unwound, snipped and uncovered, until all the bandage was gone and I felt as naked as a newborn baby, with a strange coolness on my cheeks. I tried to see myself reflected in her eyes but they were calm and expressionless, impersonal and professionally detached. I felt her fingers press against my cheek, the flesh under my chin, smooth the hair back from my temples. "Close your eyes."

I closed them. I felt her fingers touch the lids lightly. "Open."

I opened them. Her face was still quiet and unrevealing. "Smile," she said. "Like this." She made with a wide, humorless grin that was a slapstick parody of her usual warm smile.

I grinned. I grinned until the tiny pains that came to my cheeks began to burn like hell. And still I grinned.

"O.K.," she said, suddenly smiling now. Really smiling. "You can stop now."

I stopped and stared up at her. "How is it, Doc?" I tried to keep it light. "Pretty horrible?"

"It's not bad," she said noncommittally. "You were never a

raving beauty, you know." She picked up a mirror from the cart. "Here. See for yourself."

I didn't look at the mirror. I didn't want to see myself just yet. "Can I have a cigarette first, Doc?"

Silently she put the mirror back on the cart and took a package of cigarettes from her coat pocket. She sat down on the edge of my bed, put one in her mouth, lit it, then passed it to me. I could taste the faint sweetness of her lipstick as I drew the smoke into me.

"You were cut pretty badly when Winthrop pushed you through that port. But fortunately—"

"You knew about that?" I asked, interrupting. "About Amos, I mean. How did you find out?"

"From you. While you were under the anesthetic. We kept getting the story in fragments, along with the fragments of glass we were picking out of your face. Fortunately, none of your important facial muscles were severely damaged. It was largely a matter of surface lesions. We were able to make the necessary skin grafts quickly. And successfully, I might add."

I held out my hand. "I'll take the mirror now, Doc."

She took my cigarette and handed me the mirror. I raised it and when I looked into it, I felt a chill go through me.

"Doc," I said hoarsely. "I look exactly like my father!"

She took the mirror from my hand and I looked up at her. She was smiling. "Do you, Jonas? But that's the way you've always looked."

Later that morning, Robair brought me the papers. They were filled with the story of Japan's capitulation. I glanced at them carelessly and tossed them aside. "Can I get you something else to read, Mr. Jonas?"

"No," I said. "No, thanks. I just don't feel much like reading."

"All right, Mr. Jonas. Maybe you'd like to sleep some." He moved toward the door.

"Robair."

"Yes, Mr. Jonas?"

"Did I—" I hesitated, my fingers automatically touching my cheek. "Did I always look like this?"

His white teeth flashed in a smile. "Yes, Mr. Jonas."

"Like my father?"

"Like his spittin' image."

I was silent. Strange how all your life you tried not to be like someone, only to learn that you'd been stamped indelibly by the blood that ran in your veins.

"Is there anything else, Mr. Jonas?"

I looked up at Robair and shook my head. "I'll try to sleep now."

I leaned back against the pillow and closed my eyes. I heard the door close and gradually the noise from the street faded to the periphery of my consciousness. I slept. It seemed to me I'd been sleeping a great deal lately. As if I was trying to catch up on all the sleep I'd denied myself for the past few hundred years. But I could not have slept long before I became aware that someone was in the room.

I opened my eyes. Jennie was standing next to my bed, looking down at me. When she saw my eyes open, she smiled. "Hello, Jonas."

"I was sleeping," I said, like a child just waking from a nap. "I was dreaming something foolish. I was dreaming I was hundreds of years old."

"It was a happy dream, then. I'm glad. Happy dreams will help you get well faster."

I raised myself up on one elbow and the pulleys squeaked as I reached for the cigarettes on the table next to the bed. Quickly she fluffed the pillows and moved them in behind me to support my back. I dragged on the cigarette. The smoke drove the sleep from my brain.

"In another few weeks, they'll have the cast off your leg and you can go home."

"I hope so, Jennie," I said.

Suddenly, I realized she wasn't wearing her hospital white. "This is the first time I've seen you in a black veil, Jennie. Is it something special?"

"No, Jonas. This is what I always wear, except when I'm on duty in the hospital."

"Then this is your day off?"

"There are no days off in the service of Our Saviour," she said simply. "No, Jonas, I've come to say good-by."

"Good-by? But I don't understand. You said it would be a few weeks before I—"

"I'm going away, Jonas."

I stared up at her stupidly. "Going away?"

"Yes, Jonas," she said quietly. "I've only been here at Mercy Hospital until I could get transportation to the Philippines. We're rebuilding a hospital there that was destroyed in the war. Now I am free to leave, by plane."

"But you can't, Jennie," I said. "You can't leave the people you know, the language you speak. You'll be a stranger there, you'll be alone."

Her fingers touched the crucifix hanging from the black leather cincture beneath her garment. A quiet look of calm deepened in her gray eyes. "I am never alone," she said simply. "He is always with me."

"You don't have to, Jennie," I said. I took the pamphlet that I'd found on the table by my bed and opened it. "You've only made a temporary profession. You can resign any time you want. There's still a three-year probationary period before you take your final vows. You don't belong here, Jennie. It's only because you were hurt and angry. You're much too young and beautiful to hide your life away behind a black veil."

She still did not answer.

"Don't you understand what I'm saying, Jennie? I want you to come back where you belong."

She closed her eyes slowly and when she opened them, they were misted with tears. But when she spoke, her voice was steady with the sureness of her knowledge and faith. "It's you who don't understand, Jonas," she said. "I have no place to which I desire to return, for it is here, in His house, that I belong."

I started to speak but she raised her hand gently. "You think I came to Him out of hurt and anger? You're wrong," she said quietly. "One does not run from life to God, one runs to God for life. All my years I sought Him, without knowing what I was seeking. The love I found out there was a mere mockery of what I knew love could be; the charity I gave was but the smallest fraction of the charity in me to give; the mercy I showed was nothing compared with His mercy within me. Here, in His house and in His work, I have found a greater love than any I have ever known. Through His love, I have found security and contentment and happiness, in accordance with His divine will."

She paused for a moment, looking down at the crucifix in her fingers. When she looked up again, her eyes were clear and untroubled. "Is there anything in this world, Jonas, that can offer more than God?"

I didn't answer.

Slowly she held out her left hand toward me. I looked down and saw the heavy silver ring on her third finger. "He has invited me into His house," she said softly, "and I have taken His ring to wear so that I may dwell in His glory forever."

I took her hand and pressed my lips to the ring. I felt her fingers brush my hair lightly, then she moved to the foot of my bed, where she turned to look at me. "I shall think of you often, my friend," she said gently. "And I shall pray for you."

I was silent as I ground my cigarette out. There was a beauty in Jennie's eyes that had never been there before. "Thank you, Sister," I said quietly.

Without another word, she turned and went out the door. I stared down at the foot of the bed where she had stood, but now even the ghost of her was gone.

I turned my face into the pillow and cried.

7

I LEFT THE HOSPITAL EARLY IN SEPTEMBER. I WAS sitting in the wheel chair, watching Robair pack the last of my things into the valise, when the door opened. "Hi, Junior."

"Nevada! What are you doing way down here?"

"Came to carry you home."

I laughed. Funny how you can go along for years hardly thinking about someone, then all of a sudden be so glad to see him. "You didn't have to do that," I said. "Robair could have managed all right."

"I asked him to come up, Mr. Jonas. I figured it would be like old times. It gets mighty lonely out there at the ranch with nothing to do."

"An' I figured I could use a vacation," Nevada said. "The war's over an' the show's closed down for the winter. And there's nothin' Martha likes better than to do a little invalidin'. She's down there now, gittin' things ready for us."

I looked at the two of them and grinned. "It's a put-up job, huh?"

"That's right," Nevada said. He came over behind the wheel chair. "Ready?"

Robair closed the valise and snapped it shut. "All set, Mr. Nevada."

"Let's go, then," Nevada said, and started the wheel chair through the door.

"We have to stop off at Burbank," I said, looking back at him. "Mac has a flock of papers for me to sign." I might be laid up, but business went on.

Buzz Dalton had an ICA charter waiting for us at the San Diego airport. We were at Burbank by two o'clock that afternoon. McAllister got up and came around his desk when they wheeled me into his office. "You know, this is the first time I can remember seeing you sit down."

I laughed. "Make the most of it. The doctors say I'll be moving around as good as new in a couple of weeks."

"Well, meanwhile, I'm going to take advantage of it. Push him around behind the desk, fellows. I've got the pen ready."

It was almost four o'clock when I'd signed the last of a stack of documents. I looked up wearily. "So what else is new?"

Mac looked at me. He walked over to a table against the wall. "This is," he said, and took the cover off something that looked like a radio with a window in it.

"What is it?"

"It's the first product of the Cord Electronics Company," he said proudly. "We knocked it out in the converted radar division. It's a television set."

"Television?" I asked.

"Pictures broadcast through the air like radio," he said. "It's picked up on that screen, like home movies."

"Oh, that's the thing that Dumont was kicking around before the war. It doesn't work."

"Does now," Mac said. "It's the next big thing. All the radio and electronics companies are going into it. RCA, Columbia, Emerson, IT&T, GE, Philco. All of them. Want to see how it works?"

"Sure."

He walked over and picked up the phone. "Get me the lab." He covered the mouthpiece. "I'll have them put something on," he said.

A moment later, he went over to the set and turned a knob. A light flashed behind the window, then settled into a series of circles and lines. Gradually, letters came into view.

CORD ELECTRONICS PRESENTS—

Suddenly, the card was replaced by a picture, a Western scene with a man riding a horse toward the camera. The camera dollied in real close on the face and I saw it was Nevada. I recognized the scene, too. It was the chase scene from *The Renegade*. For five minutes, we watched the scene in silence.

"Well, I'll be damned," Nevada said, when it was over.

I looked across at Robair. There was an expression of rapt wonder on his face. He looked at me. "There's what I call a miracle, Mr. Jonas," he said softly. "Now I can watch a movie in my own home without goin' to sit in no nigger heaven."

"So that's why they all want to buy my old pictures," Nevada said.

I looked up at him. "What do you mean?"

"You know those ninety-odd pictures we made and I own now?"

I nodded.

"People been after me to sell 'em. Offered me good money for 'em, too. Five thousand dollars each."

I stared at him. "One thing I learned in the picture business," I said. "Never sell outright what you can get a percentage on."

"You mean rent it to 'em like I do to a theater?"

"That's right," I said. "I know those broadcasting companies. If they'll buy it for five, they plan to make fifty out of it."

"I'm no good at big deals like that," Nevada said. "Would you be willin' to handle it for me, Mac?"

"I don't know, Nevada. I'm no agent."

"Go ahead and do it, Mac," I said. "Remember what you told me about making a point where it counts?"

He smiled suddenly. "O.K., Nevada."

Suddenly, I was tired. I slumped back in my chair. Robair was at my side instantly. "You all right, Mr. Jonas?"

"I'm just tired," I said.

"Maybe you better stay at the apartment tonight. We can go on out to the ranch in the morning."

I looked at Robair. The idea of getting into a bed was very appealing. My ass was sore from the wheel chair.

"I'll order a car," Mac said, picking up the phone. "You can drop me at the studio on your way into town. I've got some work to finish up there."

My mind kept working all the time we rode toward the stu-
o. When the car stopped at the gates, suddenly everything was
ear to me.

"We'll have to do something about a replacement for Bonner,"
ac said, getting out. "It isn't good business having a lawyer run
studio. I don't know anything about motion pictures."

I stared at him thoughtfully. He was right, of course. But
en, who did? Only David, and he was gone. I didn't care any
ore. There were no pictures left in me, no one I wanted to
ace up there on the screen for all the world to see. And back
the office I'd just left, there was a little box with a picture
indow and soon it would be in every home. Rich or poor.
hat little box was really going to chew up film, like the the-
ers had never been able to. But I still didn't care.

Even when I was a kid, when I was through with a toy, I was
rough with it. And I'd never go back to it. "Sell the theaters,"
whispered to Mac.

"What?" he shouted, as if he couldn't believe his ears.
They're the only end of this business that's making any
oney."

"Sell the theaters," I repeated. "In ten years, no one will want
come to them, anyway. At least, not the way they have up to
ow. Not when they can see movies right in their own home."

Mac stared at me. "And what do you want me to do about
e studio?" he asked, a tinge of sarcasm coming into his voice.
Sell that, too?"

"Yes," I said quietly. "But not now. Ten years from now,
aybe. When the people who are making pictures for that little
ox are squeezed and hungry for space. Sell it then."

"What will we do with it in the meantime? Let it rot while
e pay taxes on it?"

"No," I said. "Turn it into a rental studio like the old Gold-
yn lot. If we break even or lose a little, I won't complain."

He stared at me. "You really mean it?"

"I mean it," I said, looking away from him up at the roof over
e stages. For the first time, I really saw it. It was black and ugly
ith tar. "Mac, see that roof?"

He turned and looked, squinting against the setting sun.

"Before you do anything else," I said softly, "have them paint
white."

I pulled my head back into the car. Nevada looked at me

strangely. His voice was almost sad. "Nothing's changed, has it Junior?"

"No," I said wearily. "Nothing's changed."

8

I SAT ON THE PORCH, SQUINTING OUT INTO THE afternoon sun. Nevada came out of the house behind me and dropped into a chair. He pulled a plug out of his pocket and biting off a hunk, put the plug back. Then from his other pocket, he took a piece of wood and a penknife and began to whittle.

I looked at him. He was wearing a pair of faded blue levis. A sweat-stained old buckskin shirt, that had seen better days, clung to his deep chest and broad shoulders and he had a red-and-white kerchief tied around his neck to catch the perspiration. Except for his white hair, he looked as I always remembered him when I was a boy, his hands quick and brown and strong.

He looked up at me out of his light eyes. "Two lost arts," he said.

"What?"

"Chewin' an' whittlin'," he said.

I didn't answer.

He looked down at the piece of wood in his hands. "Many's the evenin' I spent on the porch with your pa, chewin' an' whittlin'."

"Yeah?"

He turned and let fly a stream of tobacco juice over the porch rail into the dust below. He turned back to me. "I recall one night," he said. "Your pa an' me, we were settin' here, just like now. It'd been a real bitcheroo of a day. One of them scorchers that make your balls feel like they're drownin' in their own sweat. Suddenly he looks up at me an' says, 'Nevada, anything should happen to me, you look after my boy, hear? Jonas is a good boy. Sometimes his ass gets too much for his britches but he's a good boy an' he's got the makin's in him to be a better man than his daddy, someday. I love that boy, Nevada. He's all I got.'"

"He never told me that," I said, looking at Nevada. "Not ever. Not once!"

Nevada's eyes flashed up at me. "Men like your daddy ain't given much to talkin' about things like that."

I laughed. "He not only didn't talk it," I said. "He never showed it. He was always chewing on my ass for one thing or another."

Nevada's eyes bore straight into mine. "He was always there whenever you were in trouble. He might have hollered but he never turned you down."

"He married my girl away from me," I said bitterly.

"Maybe it was for your own good. Maybe it was because he knew she never really was for you."

I let that one go. "Why are you telling me this now?" I asked.

I couldn't read those Indian eyes of his. "Because your father asked me once to look after you. I made one mistake already. I seen how smart you was in business, I figured you to be growed up. But you wasn't. An' I wouldn' like to fail a man like your father twice."

We sat there in silence for a few minutes, then Martha came out with my tea. She told Nevada to spit out the chaw and stop dirtying up the porch. He looked at me almost shyly, got up and went down to get rid of the chaw behind the bushes.

We heard a car turn up our road as he came back to the porch. "I wonder who that is?" Martha asked.

"Maybe it's the doctor," I said. Old Doc Hanley was supposed to come out and check me over once a week.

By that time, the car was in the driveway and I knew who it was. I got to my feet, leaning on my cane, as Monica and Jo-Ann approached us. "Hello," I called.

They'd come back to California to close up their apartment, Monica explained, and since she wanted to talk to me about Amos, they'd stopped off in Reno on their way back to New York. Their train wasn't due to leave until seven o'clock.

I saw Martha glance meaningfully at Nevada when she heard that. Nevada got to his feet and looked at Jo-Ann. "I've got a gentle bay horse out in the corral that's just dyin' for some young lady like you to ride her."

Jo-Ann looked up at him worshipfully. You could tell she'd been to the movies from the way she looked at him. He was a real live hero. "I don't know," she said doubtfully. "I've never really ridden a horse before."

"I can teach you. It's easy, easier than fallin' off a log."

"But she's not dressed for riding," Monica said.

She wasn't. Not in that pretty flowered dress that made her look so much like her mother. Martha spoke up quickly. "I got a pair of dungarees that shrunk down to half my size. They'll fit her."

I don't know whose dungarees they were but one thing was for sure. They'd never been Martha's. Not the way they clung to Jo-Ann's fourteen-year-old hips, tight and flat with just the suggestion of the curves to come. Jo-Ann's dark hair was pulled back straight from her head in a pony tail and there was something curiously familiar about the way she looked. I couldn't quite figure out what it was.

I watched her run out the door after Nevada and turned to Monica. She was smiling at me. I returned her smile. "She's growing up," I said. "She's going to be a pretty girl."

"One day they're children, the next they're young ladies. They grow up too fast."

I nodded. We were alone now and an awkward silence came down between us. I reached for a cigarette and looked at her. "I want to tell you about Amos."

It was near six o'clock when I finished telling her about what happened. There were no tears in her eyes, though her face was sad and thoughtful. "I can't cry for him, Jonas," she said, looking at me. "Because I've already cried too many times because of him. Do you understand?"

I nodded.

"He did so many things that were wrong all his life. I'm glad that at last he did one thing right."

"He did a very brave thing. I always thought he hated me."

"He did," she said quickly. "He saw in you everything that he wasn't. Quick, successful, rich. He hated your guts. I guess at the end he realized how foolish that was and how much harm he'd already done you, so he tried to make it right."

I looked at her. "What wrong did he do me? There was nothing but business between us."

She gave me a peculiar look. "You can't see it yet?"

"No."

"Then I guess you never will," she said and walked out onto the porch.

We could hear Jo-Ann's shout of laughter as she rode the big bay around the corral. She was doing pretty good for a beginner. I looked down at Monica. "She takes to it like she was born to the saddle."

"Why shouldn't she?" Monica replied. "They say such things are inherited."

"I didn't know you rode."

She looked up at me, her eyes hurt and angry. "I'm not her only parent," she snapped coldly.

I stared at her. This was the only time she'd ever mentioned anything about Jo-Ann's father to me. It was sort of late to be angry about it now.

I heard the chug of Doc Hanley's old car turning into the driveway. He stopped near the corral and getting out of the car, walked over to the fence. He never could drive past a horse.

"That's Doc Hanley. He's supposed to check me out."

"Then I won't keep you," Monica said coolly. "I'll say good-by here."

She went down the steps and started walking toward the corral. I stared after her bewilderedly. I never could figure her out when she got into those crazy moods. "I'll have Robair drive you to the station," I called after her.

"Thanks!" She flung it back over her shoulder without turning around. I saw her stop and talk to the doctor, then I turned and walked back into the house. I went into the room that my father used as his study and sank down on the couch. Monica always did have a quick temper. You'd think by now she'd have learned to control it. I started to smile, thinking of how straight her back was and how sassy she'd looked walking away from me, her nose in the air. She still looked pretty good for a woman her age. I was forty-one, which meant she was thirty-four. And nothing on her jiggled that shouldn't.

The trouble with Doc Hanley is that he's a talker. He talks you deaf, dumb and blind but you don't have much choice. Since the war started, it's been him or nothing. All the young docs were in the service.

It was six thirty by the time he'd finished his examination

and begun to close up his instrument case. "You're doin' all right," he said. "But I don't hold with them newfangled notions of getting you out as soon as you kin move. If it'd been up to me, now, I'd have kept you in the hospital another month."

Nevada leaned against the study wall, smiling as I climbed into my britches. I looked at him and shrugged. I turned to the doctor. "How long now before I can really begin to do some walking?"

Doc Hanley peered at me over the edges of his bifocals. "You kin start walkin' right now."

"But I thought you didn't agree with those city doctors," I said. "I thought you wanted me to rest some more."

"I don't agree with them," he said. "But since you're out, an' there ain't nothin' that can be done about that, you might as well git to movin' about. There ain't no sense in you jist layin' aroun'."

He snapped his case shut, straightened up and walked to the door. He turned and looked back at me. "That's a right pert gal you got there, your daughter."

I stared at him. "My daughter?"

"That's right," he said. "With her hair tied back like that, I never seen a gal who took so after her father. Why, she's the spittin' image of you when you was a boy."

I couldn't speak, only stare. Had the idiot gone off his rocker? Everybody knew Jo-Ann wasn't my daughter.

Doc laughed suddenly and slapped his hand on his thigh. "I'll never forget the time her mother came down to my office," he said. "She was your wife then, of course. I never seen such a big belly. I figured, no wonder you got married so sudden like. You'd been doin' your plantin' early."

He looked up at me, still smiling. "That was before I examined her, you understand," he said quickly. "You could have knocked me over with a feather when the examination showed her only six weeks gone. It was just one of those peculiar things where she carried real high. She was so nervous an' upset just about then that she blew up with gas like a balloon. I even went back to the papers an' checked your weddin' date just to make sure. An' dang my britches if it weren't a fact you'd knocked her up at most two weeks after you were married. But there's one thing I got to say for yuh, boy." He turned back at the door. "When you ram 'em, you ram 'em good. Right up the ol' gazizzis, where it sticks!" And still laughing lewdly, he walked out.

I felt the tight, sick knot ball up inside me. I sat down on the couch. All these years. All these years and I had been wrong. Suddenly, I knew what Amos had been going to tell me after we returned from the flight. He'd seen how crazy I'd been that night and turned my own hate against me. And there was little Monica could have done about it.

What a combination, Amos and me. But at least, he'd seen the light by himself. No one had to hit him over the head with it. And he'd tried to make up for it. But I—I never even turned my head to seek the truth. I'd been content to go along blaming the world for my own stupidity. And I was the one who'd been at war with my father because I thought he didn't love me. That was the biggest joke of all.

Now I could even face the truth in that. It never had been his love that I'd doubted. It had been my own. For deep inside of me, I'd always known that I could never love him as much as he loved me. I looked up at Nevada. He was still leaning against the wall, but he wasn't smiling now. "You saw it, too?"

"Sure." He nodded. "Everybody saw it—but you."

I closed my eyes. Now I could see it. It was like that morning in the hospital when I looked into the mirror and saw my father's face. That was what I'd seen in Jo-Ann when I thought she looked so familiar this afternoon. Her father's face. My own.

"What shall I do, Nevada?" I groaned.

"What do yuh want to do, son?"

"I want them back."

"Sure that's what you want?"

I nodded.

"Then get 'em back," he said. He looked at his watch. "There's still fifteen minutes before the train pulls out."

"But how? We'd never get there in time!"

He gestured to the desk. "There's the phone."

I looked at him wildly, then hobbled to the phone. I called the stationmaster's office at Reno and had them page her. While I was waiting for her to come on, I looked at Nevada. Suddenly, I was frightened, and when I'd been little, I'd always turned to Nevada when I was frightened. "What if she won't come back?"

"She'll come back," he said confidently. He smiled. "She's still in love with you. That's something else everybody knew but you."

Then she was on the phone, her voice worried and anxious. "Jonas, are you all right? Is there anything wrong?"

For a moment, I couldn't speak, then I found my voice. "Monica," I said. "Don't go!"

"But I have to, Jonas. I have to be on the job by the end of the week."

"Screw the job, I need you!"

The line was silent, and for a moment, I thought she'd hung up. "Monica, are you there?"

I heard her breathe in the receiver. "I'm still here, Jonas."

"I've been wrong all the time. I didn't know about Jo-Ann. Believe me." Again the silence.

"Please, Monica!"

Now she was crying. I could hear her whispered voice in my ear. "Oh, Jonas, I've never stopped loving you."

I looked up at Nevada. He smiled and went out, closing the door behind him.

I heard her sniffle, then her voice suddenly cleared and filled with the warm sound of love. "When Jo-Ann was a little girl she always wanted a baby brother."

"Hurry home," I said, "I'll do my best."

She laughed and there was a click as the line went dead in my hands. I didn't put the phone down because I felt that as long as I held it, she was close to me. I looked down at the photograph of my father on the desk.

"Well, old man," I said, asking his approval for the first time in my life, "did I do right?"